BRAIN SHIPS

Baen Books by Anne McCaffrey

The Planet Pirate Series:
Sassinak (with Elizabeth Moon)
The Death of Sleep (with Jody Lynn Nye)
Generation Warriors (with Elizabeth Moon)
Also available in a one-volume book:
The Planet Pirates

The "Brainship" Series:
The Ship Who Searched (with Mercedes Lackey)
Partnership (with Margaret Ball)
(available in one volume as *Brain Ships*)
The City Who Fought (with S.M. Stirling)
The Ship Who Won (with Jody Lynn Nye)
The Ship Errant
by Jody Lynn Nye
The Ship Avenged
by S.M. Stirling

Baen Books by Mercedes Lackey

BARDIC VOICES
The Lark & the Wren
The Robin & the Kestrel
The Eagle & the
Nightingales
The Free Bards
(omnibus)
Four & Twenty Blackbirds
Bardic Choices:
A Cast of Corbies
(with Josepha Sherman)

The Fire Rose
Fiddler Fair
Werehunter
Wing Commander:
Freedom Flight
(with Ellen Guon)
Lammas Night
(ed. by Josepha Sherman)

URBAN FANTASIES
Bedlam's Bard
(omnibus with Ellen Guon)
Beyond World's End
(with Rosemary Edghill)
Spirits White as Lightning
(with Rosemary Edghill)
Mad Maudlin (with Rosemary Edghill)

The SERRAted Edge:
Chrome Circle (with Larry Dixon)
The Chrome Borne
(omnibus with Larry Dixon)
The Otherworld
(omnibus with Mark Shepherd
& Holly Lisle)

THE BARD'S TALE NOVELS
Castle of Deception
(with Josepha Sherman)
Fortress of Frost & Fire
(with Ru Emerson)
Prison of Souls
(with Mark Shepherd)

BRAIN SHIPS

Anne McCaffrey

Mercedes Lackey

Margaret Ball

Copyright © 2003 by Bill Fawcett & Associates. *The Ship Who Searched* © 1992 by Bill Fawcett & Associates; *PartnerShip* © 1992 by Bill Fawcett & Associates.

A Baen Books Original

Baen Publishing Enterprises
P.O. Box 1403
Riverdale, NY 10471
www.baen.com

ISBN: 0-7434-7166-0

Cover art by Tom Kidd

First printing in this format, November 2003

Distributed by Simon & Schuster
1230 Avenue of the Americas
New York, NY 10020

Production by Windhaven Press, Auburn, NH
Printed in the United States of America

10 9 8 7 6 5 4 3 2 1

CONTENTS

THE SHIP WHO SEARCHED

Anne McCaffrey & Mercedes Lackey

CHAPTER ONE

The ruby light on the com unit was blinking when Hypatia Cade emerged from beneath the tutor's hood, with quadratic equations dancing before her seven-year-old eyes. Not the steady blink that meant a recorded message, nor the triple-beat that meant Mum or Dad had left her a note, but the double blink with a pause between each pair that meant there was someone Upstairs, waiting for her to open the channel.

Someone Upstairs meant an unscheduled ship—Tia knew very well when all the scheduled visits were; they were on the family calendar and were the first things reported by the AI when they all had breakfast. That made it Important for her to answer, quickly, and not take the time to suit up and run to the dig for Mum or Dad. It must not have been an emergency, though, or the AI would have interrupted her lesson.

She rubbed her eyes to rid them of the dancing variables, and pushed her stool over to the com-console so she could reach all the touch-pads when she stood on it. She would never have been able to reach things sitting in a chair, of course. With brisk efficiency that someone three times her age might have envied, she cleared the board, warmed up the relay, and opened the line.

"Exploratory Team Cee-One-Two-One," she enunciated carefully, for the microphone was old, and often lost anything not spoken clearly. "Exploratory Team Cee-One-Two-One, receiving. Come in, please. Over."

She counted out the four-second lag to orbit and back, nervously. *One-hypotenuse, Two-hypotenuse, Three-hypotenuse, Four-hypotenuse.* Who could it be? They didn't get unscheduled ships very often, and it meant bad news as often as not. Planet pirates, plague, or slavers. Trouble with some of the colony-planets. Or worse—artifact thieves in the area. A tiny dig like this one was all too vulnerable to a hit-and-run raid. Of course, digs on the Salomon-Kildaire Entities rarely yielded anything a collector would lust after, but would thieves know that? Tia had her orders if raiders came and she was alone—to duck down the hidden escape tunnel that would blow the dome; to run to the dark little hidey away from the dig that was the first thing Mum and Dad put in once the dome was up. . . .

"This is courier TM Three-Seventy. Tia, dearest, is that you? Don't worry, love, we have a non-urgent message run and you're on the way, so we brought you your packets early. Over." The rich, contralto voice was a bit flattened by the poor speaker, but still welcome and familiar. Tia jumped up and down a bit on her stool in excitement.

"Moira! Yes, yes, it's me! But—" She frowned a little. The last time Moira had been here, her designation had been CM, not TM. "Moira, what happened to Charlie?" Her seven-year-old voice took on the half-scolding tones of someone much older. "Moira, did you scare away *another* brawn? Shame on you! Remember what they told you when you kicked Ari out your airlock! Uh—over."

Four seconds; an eternity. "I didn't scare him away, darling," Moira replied, though Tia thought she sounded just a little guilty. "He decided to get married, raise a brood of his own, and settle down as a dirtsider. Don't worry, this will be the last one, I'm sure of it. Tomas and I get along famously. Over."

"That's what you said about Charlie," Tia reminded her darkly. "And about Ari, and Lilian, and Jules, and—"

She was still reciting names when Moira interrupted her. "Turn on the landing beacon, Tia, please. We can talk when I'm not burning fuel in orbital adjustments." Her voice turned a little bit sly. "Besides, I brought you a birthday present. That's why I couldn't miss stopping here. Over."

As if a birthday present was going to distract her from the litany of Moira's failed attempts to settle on a brawn!

Well—maybe just a little.

She turned on the beacon, then feeling a little smug, activated the rest of the landing sequence, bringing up the pad lights and guidance monitors, then hooking in the AI and letting it know it needed to talk to Moira's navigational system. She hadn't known how to do all *that*, the last time Moira was here. Moira'd had to set down with no help at all.

She leaned forward for the benefit of the mike. "All clear and ready to engage landing sequence, Moira. Uh—what did you bring me? Over."

"Oh, you bright little penny!" Moira exclaimed, her voice brimming with delight. "You've got the whole system up! You *have* been learning things since I was here last! Thank you, dear—and you'll find out what I brought when I get down there. Over and out."

Oh well, she had tried. She jumped down from her stool, letting the AI that ran the house and external systems take over the job of bringing the brainship in. Or rather, giving the brainship the information she needed to bring *herself* in; Moira never handed over her helm to anyone if she had a choice in the matter. That was part of the problem she'd had with keeping brawns. She didn't trust them at the helm, and let them know that. Ari, in particular, had been less than amused with her attitude and had actually tried to disable her helm controls to prove *he* could pilot as well as she.

Now, the next decision: should she suit up and fetch Mum and Dad? It was no use trying to get them on the com; they probably had their suit-speakers off. Even though they weren't *supposed* to do that. And this wasn't an emergency; they would be decidedly annoyed if she buzzed in on them, and they found out it was just an unscheduled social call from a courier ship, even if it was Moira. They might be more than annoyed if they were in the middle of something important, like documenting a find or running an age-assay, and she joggled their elbows.

Moira didn't say it was important. She wouldn't have talked about errant brawns and birthday presents if what she carried was really, really earth-shaking.

Tia glanced at the clock; it wasn't more than a half hour until lunch break. If there was one thing that Pota Andropolous-Cade

(Doctor of Science in Bio-Forensics, Doctor of Xenology, Doctor of Archeology), and her husband Braddon Maartens-Cade (Doctor of Science in Geology, Doctor of Physics in Cosmology, Associate Degree in Archeology, and licensed Astrogator) had in common—besides daughter Hypatia and their enduring, if absent-minded love for each other—it was punctuality. At precisely oh-seven-hundred every "morning," no matter where they were, the Cades had breakfast together. At precisely twelve-hundred, they arrived at the dome for lunch together. The AI saw that Hypatia had a snack at sixteen-hundred. And at precisely nineteen-hundred, the Cades returned from the dig for dinner together.

So in thirty minutes, *precisely*, Pota and Braddon would be here. Moira couldn't possibly land in less than twenty minutes. The visitor—or visitors; there was no telling if there was someone on board besides the brawn, the yet-unmet Tomas—would not have long to wait.

She trotted around the living room of the dome; picking up her books and puzzles, straightening the pillows on the sofa, turning on lights and the holoscape of waving blue trees by a green lagoon on Mycon, where her parents had met. She told the kitchen to start coffee, overriding the lunch program to instruct it to make selection V-1, a setup program Braddon had logged for her for munchies for visitors. She decided on music on her own; the *Arkenstone Suite*, a lively synthesizer piece she thought matched the holo-mural.

There wasn't much else to do, so she sat down and waited—something she had learned how to do very early. She thought she did it very well, actually. There had certainly been enough of it in her life. The lot of an archeologists' child was full of waiting, usually alone, and required her to be mostly self-sufficient.

She had never had playmates or been around very many children of her own age. Usually Mum and Dad were alone on a dig, for they specialized in Class One Evaluation sites; when they weren't, it was usually on a Class Two dig, Exploratory. Never a Class Three Excavation dig, with hundreds of people and their families. It wasn't often that the other scientists her parents' age on a Class Two dig had children younger than their teens. And even those were usually away somewhere at school.

She knew that other people thought that the Cades were eccentric for bringing their daughter with them on every dig—especially so young a child. Most parents with a remote job to do left their offspring with relatives or sent them to boarding schools. Tia listened to the adults around her, who usually spoke as if she couldn't understand what they were talking about. She learned a great deal that way; probably more even than her Mum and Dad suspected.

One of the things she overheard—quite frequently, in fact—was that she seemed like something of an afterthought. Or perhaps an "accident"—she'd overheard that before, too.

She knew very well what was meant by the "afterthought or accident" comment. The last time someone had said *that*, she'd decided that she'd heard it often enough.

It had been at a reception, following the reading of several scientific papers. She'd marched straight up to the lady in question and had informed her solemnly that she, Tia, had been planned very *carefully*, thank you. That Braddon and Pota had determined that their careers would be secure just about when Pota's biological clock had the last few seconds on it, and *that* was when they would have one, singular, female child. Herself. Hypatia. Planned from the beginning. From the leave-time to give birth to the way she had been brought on each assignment; from the pressure-bubble glove-box that had served as her cradle until she could crawl, to the pressure-tent that became a crib, to the kind of AI that would best perform the dual functions of tutor and guardian.

The lady in question, red-faced, hadn't known what to say. Her escort had tried to laugh it away, telling her that the "child" was just parroting what she'd overheard and couldn't possibly understand any of it.

Whereupon Tia, well-versed in the ethnological habits—including courtship and mating—of four separate sapient species, including *homo sap.*, had proceeded to prove that he was wrong.

Then, while the escort was still spluttering, she had turned back to the original offender and informed her, with earnest sincerity, that *she* had better think about having *her* children soon, too, since it was obvious that *she* couldn't have much more time before menopause.

Tia had, quite literally, silenced that section of the room. When reproached later for her behavior by the host of the party, Tia had been completely unrepentant. "She was being rude and nasty," Tia had said. When the host protested that the remark hadn't been meant for her, Tia had replied, "Then she shouldn't have said it so loudly that everyone else laughed. And besides," she had continued with inexorable logic, "being rude *about* someone is worse than being rude *to* them."

Braddon, summoned to deal with his erring daughter, had shrugged casually and said only, "I warned you. And you didn't believe me."

Though exactly what it was Dad had warned Doctor Julius about, Tia never discovered.

The remarks about being "unplanned" or an "accident" stopped, at least in her presence—but people still seemed concerned that she was "too precocious," and that she had no one of her own age to socialize with.

But the fact was that Tia simply didn't care that she had no other children to play with. She had the best lessons in the known universe, via the database; she had the AI to talk to. She had plenty of things to play with and lots of freedom to do what she wanted once lessons were done. And most of all, she had Mum and Dad, who spent *hours* more with her than most people spent with their children. She knew that, because both the statistics in the books she had read on child-care and the Socrates, the AI that traveled with them everywhere, told her so. They were never boring, and they always talked to her as if she was grown up. If she didn't understand something, all she had to do was tell them and they would backtrack and explain until she did. When they weren't doing something that meant they needed all their concentration, they encouraged her to come out to the digs with them when her lessons were over. She hadn't ever heard of too many children who got to be with their parents at work.

If anything, sometimes Mum and Dad explained a little *too* much. She distinctly remembered the time that she started asking "Why?" to everything. Socrates told her that "Why?" was a stage all children went through—mostly to get attention. But Pota and Braddon had taken her literally. . . .

The AI told her not long ago that her "Why?" period might have been the shortest on record—because Mum and Dad answered every "Why?" in detail. *And* made sure she understood, so that she wouldn't ask that particular "Why?" again.

After a month, "Why?" wasn't fun anymore, and she went on to other things.

She really didn't miss other children at all. Most of the time when she'd encountered them, it had been with the wary feeling of an anthropologist approaching a new and potentially danger-ous species. The feeling seemed to be mutual. And so far, other children had proven to be rather boring creatures. Their interests and their worlds were very narrow, their vocabulary a fraction of Tia's. Most of them hadn't the faintest idea of how to play chess, for instance.

Mum had a story she told at parties about how Tia, at the age of two, had stunned an overly effusive professorial spouse into absolute silence. There had been a chess set, a lovely antique, up on one of the tables just out of Tia's reach. She had stared long-ingly at it for nearly half an hour before the lady noticed what she was looking at.

Tia remembered that incident quite well, too. The lady had picked up an intricately carved knight and waggled it at her. "See the horsie?" she had gushed. "Isn't it a pretty horsie?"

Tia's sense of fitness had been outraged—and that wasn't all. Her intelligence had been insulted, and she was *very* well aware of it.

She had stood up, very straight, and looked the lady right in the eye. "Is *not* a horsie," she had announced, coldly and clearly. "Is a *knight*. It moves like the letter L. And Mum says it is piece most often sacri—sacer—sacra—"

Mum had come up by then, as she grew red-faced, trying to remember how to say the word she wanted. "Sacrificed?" Mum had asked, helpfully. "It means 'given up.'"

Beaming with gratitude, Tia had nodded. "Most often *given up* after the pawn." Then she glared at the lady. "Which is *not* a little man!"

The lady had retired to a corner and did not emerge while Tia and her parents were there, although her Mum's superior had then taken down the set and challenged Tia to a game. He had won, of course, but she had at least shown she really knew how to play. He had been impressed and intrigued, and had taken her out on the porch to point out various species of birds at the feeders there.

She couldn't help but think that she affected grownups in only two ways. They were either delighted by her, or scandalized by her. Moira was among the "delighted" sort, though most of her brawns hadn't been. Charlie had, though, which was why she had thought that he just might be the one to stay with the brainship. He actually seemed to enjoy the fact that she could beat him at chess.

She sighed. Probably this new brawn would be of the other sort.

Not that it really mattered how she affected adults. She didn't see that many of them, and then it was never for very long. Though it was important to impress Mum's and Dad's superiors in a positive sense. She at least knew that much now.

"Your visitor is at the airlock," said the AI, breaking in on her thoughts. "His name is Tomas. While he is cycling, Moira would like you to have me turn on the ground-based radio link so that she can join the conversation."

"Go ahead, Socrates," she told the AI. That was the problem with AIs; if they didn't already have instructions, you had to tell them to do something before they would, where a shellperson would just do it if it made sense.

"Tomas has your birthday present," Moira said, a moment later. "I hope you like it."

"You mean, you hope I like *him*," she replied shrewdly. "You hope I don't scare him."

"Let's say I use you as a kind of litmus test, all right?" Moira admitted. "And, darling—Charlie really *did* fall in love with a ground-pounder. Even I could see he wanted to be with her more than he wanted space." She sighed. "It was really awfully romantic; you don't see old-style love at first sight anymore. Michiko is such a charming little thing—I really can't blame him. And it's partly your fault, dear. He was so taken with you that all he could talk about was how he wanted children just like you. Well, anyway, she persuaded Admin to find him a ground job, and they traded me Tomas for him, with no fine, because it wasn't my fault this time."

"It's going to take you *forever* to buy out those fines for bouncing brawns," Tia began, when the inner airlock door cycled, and a pressure-suited person came through, holding a box and his helmet.

Tia frowned at seeing the helmet; he'd taken it off in the lock, once the pressure was equalized. That wasn't a good idea, because locks had been known to blow, especially old ones like the Class One digs had. So already he was one in the minus column as far as Tia was concerned. But he had a nice face, with kind eyes, and that wasn't so bad; a round, tanned face, with curly black hair and bright brown eyes, and a wide mouth that didn't have those tense lines at the corners that Ari'd had. So that was one in the plus column. He came out even so far.

"Hello, Tomas," she said, neutrally. "You shouldn't take your helmet off in the lock, you know—you should wait until the interior door cycles."

"She's right, Tomas," Moira piped up from the com console. "These Class One digs always get the last pick of equipment. All of it is old, and some of it isn't reliable. Door seals blow all the time."

"It blew last month, when I came in," Tia added helpfully. "It took Mum hours to install the new seal, and she's not altogether happy with it." Tomas' eyes were wide with surprise, and he was clearly taken aback. He had probably intended to ask her where her parents were. He had not expected to be greeted by a lecture on pressure-suit safety.

"Oh," was all he could say. "Ah, thank you. I will remember that in the future."

"You're welcome," she replied. "Mum and Dad are at the dig; I'm sorry they weren't here to meet you."

"I ought to make proper introductions," Moira said from the console. "Tomas, this is Hypatia Cade. Her mother is Doctor Pota Andropolous-Cade and her father is Doctor Braddon Maartens-Cade. Tia, this is Tomas Delacorte-Ibanez."

"I'm very pleased to meet you, Tomas," she replied with careful formality. "Mum and Dad will be here in—" she glanced at her wrist-chrono "—ten minutes. In the meantime, there is fresh coffee, and may I offer you anything to eat?"

Once again, he was taken aback. "Coffee, please," he replied after a moment. "If you would be so kind."

She fetched it from the kitchen; by the time she returned with the cup balanced in one hand and the refreshments in the other, he had removed his suit. She had to admit that he did look very handsome in the skintight ship-suit he wore beneath it. But then, all of Moira's brawns had been good-looking. That was part of the problem; she tended to pick brawns on the basis of looks first and personality second.

He accepted the coffee and food from her gravely, and a little warily, for all the world as if he had decided to treat her as some kind of new, unknown sentient. She tried not to giggle.

"That is a very unusual name that you were given," he said, after an awkward pause. "Hypatia, is it?"

"Yes," she said, "I was named for the first and only female librarian of the Great Library at Alexandria on Terra. She was also the last librarian there."

His eyes showed some recognition of the names at least. So he wasn't completely ignorant of history, the way Julio had been. "Ah. That would have been when the Romans burned it, in the time of Cleopatra—" he began. She interrupted him with a shake of her head.

"No, the library wasn't destroyed then, not at all, not even close. It persisted as a famous library into the day of Constantine," she continued, warming to her favorite story, reciting it exactly as Pota had told it to her, as it was written in the history database. "It was when Hypatia was the librarian that a pack of unwashed Christian fanatics stormed it—led by some people who called themselves prophets and holy men—intending to burn it to the ground because it contained 'pagan books, lies, and heresies.' When Hypatia tried to stop them, she was murdered, stoned to death, then trampled."

"Oh," Tomas said weakly, the wind taken quite out of his sails. He seemed to be searching for something to say, and evidently chose the first thing that sprang to mind. "Uh—why did you call them 'unwashed Christian fanatics?'"

"Because they *were*," she replied impatiently. "They were fanatics, and most of them were stylites and other hermits who made a point of not ever bathing because taking baths was Roman and pagan and not taking baths was Christian and mortifying the flesh." She sniffed. "I suppose it didn't matter to them that it was also giving them fleas and making them smell. I shan't even *mention* the disease!"

"I don't imagine that ever entered their minds," Tomas said carefully.

"Anyway, I think Hypatia was very brave, but she could have been a little smarter," Tia concluded. "I don't think I would have stood there to let them throw stones at me; I would have run away or locked the door or something."

Tomas smiled unexpectedly; he had a lovely smile, very white teeth in his darkly tanned face. "Well, maybe she didn't have much choice," he said. "I expect that by the time she realized she wasn't going to be able to stop those people, it was too late to get away."

Tia nodded, slowly, considering the ancient Alexandrian garments, how cumbersome they were and how difficult to run in. "I think you're right," she agreed. "I would hate to think that the librarian was stupid."

He laughed at that. "You mean you'd hate to think that the great lady you were named for was stupid," he teased. "And I don't blame you. It's much nicer to be named for someone who was brave and heroic on purpose than someone people *think* was a hero just because she was too dense to get out of the way of trouble!"

Tia had to laugh at that, and right then was when she decided that she was going to like Tomas. He hadn't quite known what to make of her at first, but he'd settled down nicely and was treating her quite like an intelligent sentient now.

Evidently Moira had decided the same thing, for when she spoke, her voice sounded much less anxious. "Tomas, aren't you forgetting? You brought Tia her late birthday present."

"I certainly did forget!" he exclaimed. "I do beg your pardon, Tia!"

He handed her the box he had brought, and she controlled herself very well, taking it from him politely, and not grabbing like a little child would have. "Thank you, Moira," she said to the com-console. "I don't mind that it's late—it's kind of like getting my birthday all over again this way."

"*You* are just too civilized for your own good, dear," Moira giggled. "Well, go ahead, open it!"

She did, carefully undoing the fastenings of the rather plain box and exposing bright-colored wrapping beneath. The wrapped package within was odd-shaped, lumpy—

She couldn't stand it any longer; she tore into the present just like any other child.

"Oh!" she exclaimed when she revealed her prize, for once caught without a word, holding him up to the light.

"Do you like it?" Moira asked anxiously. "I mean, I know you asked, but you grow so fast, I was afraid you'd have outgrown him by now—"

"I *love* him!" Tia exclaimed, hugging the bright blue bear suddenly, reveling in the soft fur against her cheek. "Oh Moira, I just *love* him!"

"Well, it was quite a trick to find him, let me tell you," Moira replied, her voice sounding very relieved, as Tomas grinned even wider. "You people move around so much—I had to find a teddy bear that would take repeated decontam procedures, one that would stand up to about anything quarantine could hand out. And it's hard to *find* bears at all, they seem to have gone right out of style. You don't mind that he's blue?"

"I like blue," she said happily.

"And you like him fuzzy? That was Tomas' idea."

"Thank you, Tomas," she told the brawn, who beamed. "He feels *wonderful*."

"I had a fuzzy dog when I was your age," he replied. "When Moira told me that you wanted a bear like the one she had before she went into her shell, I thought this fellow felt better than the smooth bears."

He leaned down confidentially, and for a moment Tia was afraid that he was going to be patronizing just because she'd gone so enthusiastic over the toy.

"I have to tell you the truth, Tia, I really enjoyed digging into all those toy shops," he whispered. "A lot of that stuff is wasted on children. I found some logic puzzles you just wouldn't believe and a set of magic tricks I couldn't resist, and I'm afraid I spent far too much money on spaceship models."

She giggled. "I won't tell if you don't," she replied, in a conspiratorial whisper.

"Pota and Braddon are in the airlock," Socrates interrupted. "Shall I order the kitchen to make lunch now?"

"So why exactly *are* you here?" Tomas asked, after all the initial topics of conversation had been exhausted, and the subject turned, inevitably, to Pota and Braddon's work. He gestured at the landscape beyond the viewport; spectacular mountains, many times taller than anything found on Terra or any other inhabited planet. This little ball of rock with a thin skin of dirt was much like the wilder parts of Mars before it had been terraformed, and had a sky so dark at midday that the sun shared the sky with the stars. "I wouldn't expect to find much of anything out there for an archeologist—it's the next thing to airless, after all. The scenery is amazing, but that's no reason to stay here—"

Braddon chuckled, the generous mouth in his lantern-jawed face widening in a smile, and Tia hid a grin. Whether or not Tomas knew it, he had just triggered her Dad's lecture mechanism. Fortunately, Braddon had a gift for lecturing. He was always a popular speaker whenever he could be tempted to go to conferences.

"No one expected to find anything on planets like this one, Tomas," Braddon replied, leaning back against the supporting cushions of the sofa and tucking his hands behind his head. "That's why the Salomon-Kildaire culture is so intriguing. James Salomon and Tory Kildaire discovered the first buildings on the fourth moon of Beta Orianis Three—and there have never been *any* verifiable artifacts uncovered in what you and I would call 'normal' conditions. Virtually every find has been on airless or near-airless bodies. Pota and I have excavated over a dozen sites, doing the Class One studies, and they're all like this one."

Tomas glanced out the viewport again. "Surely that implies that they were—"

"Space-going, yes," Pota supplied, nodding her head so that her gray-brown curls vibrated. "I don't think there's any doubt of it. Although we've never found any trace of whatever it was they used to move them from colony to colony—but that isn't the real mystery."

Braddon gestured agreement. "The real mystery is that they never seem to have set up anything *permanent*. They never seem to have spent more than a few decades in any one place. No one knows why they left, or why they came here in the first place."

Tomas laughed. "They seem to have hopped planets as often as you two," he said. "Perhaps they were simply doing what *you* are doing—excavating an earlier culture and following *it* across the stars."

Braddon exclaimed in mock horror. "Please!" he said. "Don't even think that!"

Pota only laughed. "If they had been, we'd have found signs of that," she told both of them, tapping Braddon's knee in playful admonition. "After all, as bleak as these places are, they preserve things wonderfully. If the EsKays had been archeologists, we'd have found the standard tools of the trade. We break and wear out brushes and digging tools all the time, and just leave them in our discard piles. They would have done the same. No matter how you try to alter it, there are only so many ways you can make a brush or a trowel—"

"There would be bad castings," Tia piped up. "You throw out bad castings all the time, Mum; if they were archeologists, we'd find a pile of bad castings somewhere."

"Bless me, Tia's right," Braddon nodded. "There you are, Tomas; irrefutable proof."

"Good enough for me," Tomas replied, good-naturedly.

"And if that idea was true, there also ought to be signs of the earlier culture, shouldn't there?" Moira asked. "And you've never found anything mixed in with the EsKay artifacts."

"Exactly so," Pota replied, and smiled. "And so, Tomas, you see how easily an archeologist's theories can be disposed of."

"Then I'm going to be thankful to be Moira's partner," Tomas said gracefully, "and leave all the theorizing to better heads than mine."

After a while, the talk turned to the doings of the Institute, and both professional and personal news of Pota and Braddon's friends and rivals. Tia glanced at the clock again; it was long past time when her parents would have gone back to the dig—they must have decided to take the rest of the day off.

But these weren't subjects that interested her, especially not when the talk went into politics, both of the Institute and the Central Worlds government. She took her bear, politely excused herself, and went back to her room.

She hadn't had a chance to really look him over when Tomas gave him to her. The last time Moira had come to visit, she'd told Tia some stories about what going into the shellperson program had been like, for unlike most shellpersons, she hadn't been popped into her shell until she'd been nearly four. Until that time, there had been some hope that there would have been a palliative for her particular congenital condition— premature aging that had caused her body to resemble a sixty-year-old woman at the age of three. But there was no cure, and at four, her family finally admitted it. Into the shell she went, and since there was *nothing* wrong with her very fine brain, she soon caught up and passed by many of her classmates that had been in their shells since birth.

But one of the toys she'd had—her very favorite, in fact—had been a stuffed teddy bear. She'd made up adventures for Ivan the Bearable, sending him in a troika across the windswept steppes of Novi Gagarin, and she'd told Tia some of those stories. That, and the *Zen of Pooh* book Moira brought her, had solidified a longing she hadn't anticipated.

For Tia had been entranced by the tales and by Pooh—and had wanted a bear like Moira's. A simple toy that did *nothing*, with no intel-chips; a toy that couldn't talk, or teach, or walk. Something that was just there to be hugged and cuddled; something to listen when she didn't want anything else to overhear....

Moira had promised. Moira didn't forget.

Tia closed the door to her room and paged the AI. "Socrates, would you open a link to Moira in here for me, please?" she asked. Moira would be perfectly capable of following the conversation in the other room and still talk to her in here, too.

"Tia, do you really like your present?" Moira asked anxiously, as soon as the link had been established.

"He's wonderful," Tia answered firmly. "I've even got a name for him. Theodore Edward Bear."

"Or Ted E. Bear for short?" Moira chuckled. "I like it. It fits him. He's such a solemn-faced little fellow. One would think he was a software executive. He looks like a bear with a great deal on his mind."

Tia studied Ted carefully. Moira was right; he was a sober little bear, with a very studious expression, as if he was listening very hard to whatever was being said. His bright blue coloration in no way contradicted the seriousness of his face, nor did the frivolous little red shirt he was wearing with the blue and yellow Courier Service circle-and-lightning-bolt on the front.

"Is there anything going on that I need to know, Moira?" she asked, giving over her careful examination of her new friend and hugging him to her chest instead.

"The results of your last batch of tests seems to have satisfied all the Psych people out there that you're a perfectly well-balanced and self-sufficient girl," Moira replied, knowing without Tia prompting her just what was on her mind. "So there's no more talk of making your parents send you to boarding school."

Tia sighed with relief; that had been a very real worry the last time Moira had been here. The ship had left with the results of a battery of tests and psych-profiles that had taken two days to complete.

"I have to tell you that I added to that," Moira said, slyly. "I told them what kind of a birthday present you had asked for from me."

"What did they say?" Tia asked, anxiously. Had they thought she was being immature—or worse yet, that it meant she harbored some kind of neurosis?

"Oh, it was funny. They were questioning me on open com, as if I was some kind of AI that wouldn't respond to anything that wasn't a direct question, so of course I could hear everything *they* said. There was silence for a moment, and then the worst of the lot finally blurted out, 'Good heavens, the child is *normal*,' as if he'd expected you to ask for a Singularity simulator or something." Moira chuckled.

"I know who it was, too," Tia said shrewdly. "It was Doctor Phelps-Pittman, wasn't it?"

"Dead on the target, wenchette," Moira replied, still chuckling. "I still don't think he's forgiven you for beating him in Battle Chess. By the way, what is your secret?"

"He moves the Queen too often," Tia said absently. "I think he likes to watch her hips wiggle when she walks. It's probably something Freudian."

A splutter of static was all that followed that pronouncement, as Moira lost control of the circuit briefly. "My, my," she replied, when she came back online. "You *are* a little terror. One might almost suspect you of having as much control as a shellperson!"

Tia took that in the spirit it was meant, as a compliment.

"I promise not to tell him *your* weakness," the ship continued, teasingly.

"What's that?" Tia was surprised; she hadn't known she had one.

"You hate to see the pawns sacrificed. I think you feel sorry for the little guys."

Tia digested this in silence for a moment, then nodded reluctant agreement. "I think you're right," she admitted. "It seems as if everybody can beat them up, and it doesn't seem fair."

"You don't have the problem with an ordinary holoboard game," Moira observed casually.

"That's because they're just little blobby pieces on a holoboard game," Tia explained. "In Battle Chess they're little pikemen. And they're cute." She giggled. "I really love it when Pawn takes Knight and he hits the Knight with the butt of his pike right in the—"

"And *that's* why you frighten old Phelps-Pittman," Moira said severely, though Tia could tell she didn't mean it. "He keeps thinking you're going to do the same to him."

"Well, I won't have to see old sour-face for another year and a half," she said comfortably. "Maybe I can figure out how to act like a *normal girl* by then."

"Maybe you can," Moira replied. "I wouldn't put even that past you. Now, how about a game of Battle Chess? Ted Bear can referee."

"Of course," she agreed. "You can use the practice. I'll even spot you a pawn."

"Oh come now! You haven't gotten *that* much better since I saw you last." At Tia's continued silence, the ship asked, tentatively, "Have you?"

Tia shrugged. "Check my record with Socrates," she suggested.

There was silence as Moira did just that. Then. "Oh, *decom* it," she said in mock disgust. "You really *are* exasperating. I should demand that you spot me two pawns."

"Not a chance," Tia replied, ordering the AI to set up the game, with a Battle Chess field in front of her. "You're taking advantage enough of a child as it is."

"Taking advantage of a child? Ha!" Moira said ironically. "You're not a child. I'm beginning to agree with Phelps-Pittman. You're an eighty-year-old midget in a little-girl costume."

"Oh, all right," Tia said, good-naturedly. "I won't give you another pawn, but I will let you have white."

"Good." Moira studied the analog of the board in her memory, as Tia studied the holoboard in front of her. "All right, unnatural child. Have at ye!"

Moira and Tomas couldn't stay long; by dinner the ship had lifted, and the pad was empty—and the Cade family was back on schedule.

Pota and Braddon spent the evening catching up with the message-packets Moira had brought them—mostly dispatches from friends at other digs, more scholarly papers in their various fields, and the latest in edicts from the Institute. Since Tia knew, thanks to Moira, that none of those edicts concerned *her*, she was free to watch one of the holos Moira had brought for her entertainment. All carefully screened by the teachers at the Institute, of course, who oversaw the education of every child that was on-site with its parents. But even the teachers didn't see anything wrong with history holos, provided they were properly educational and accurate. The fact that most of these holos had been intended for adult viewing didn't seem to bother them.

Perhaps it was just as well that the Psychs had no idea what she was watching. They would probably have gone into strong hysterics.

Moira had an uncanny ability to pick out the ones that had good scripts and actors—unlike whoever it was that picked out most of the holos for the Remote Educational Department.

This one, a four-part series on Alexander the Great, looked especially good, since it covered only the early parts of his life, before he became a great leader. Tia felt a certain kinship for anyone who'd been labeled "precocious"; and although she already knew that Alexander's childhood had been far from happy, she was looking forward to viewing this.

Having Ted beside her to whisper comments to made it even more fun.

At the end of the first part, even though she was fascinated, she virtuously told Socrates to shut everything down and went into the main room to say good-night to her Mum and Dad. The next courier wasn't due for a while, and she wanted to make her treats last as long as possible.

Both of them were so deep in their readers that she had to shake their elbows to get them to realize she was there, but once they came out of their preoccupied daze, they gave her big hugs and kisses, with no sign of annoyance at being interrupted.

"I have a really *good* Mum and Dad," she told Ted before drifting off to sleep. "I really, really do. Not like Alexander. . . ."

The next day, it was back to the usual schedule. Socrates woke her, and she got herself cleaned up and dressed, leaving Ted to reside on the carefully made bed until she returned. When she entered the main room, Pota and Braddon were already there, blinking sleepily over steaming cups of coffee.

"Hello, darling," Pota greeted her as she fetched her milk and cereal from the kitchen. "Did you enjoy Alexander?"

"We-ell, it was *interesting*," Tia said truthfully. "And I liked the actors and the story. The costumes and the horses were really stellar! But his mother and father were kind of—odd—weren't they?"

Braddon looked up from his coffee with his curly dark hair over one brown eye, and gave his daughter a wry grin. "They were certifiable crazy-cases by our standards, pumpkin," he replied. "But after all, there wasn't anyone around to apply those standards back then."

"And no Board of Mental Health to enforce them," Pota added, her thin, delicate face creasing with a puckish smile. "Remember, oh curious little chick, they were *not* the ones that had the most influence on Alexander. That was left to his tutors—Aristotle, of course, being the main one—and nurses. I think he succeeded in spite of his parents, personally, and not because of them."

Tia nodded sagely. "Can I come help at the dig today?" she asked eagerly. This was one of the best things about the fact that her parents had picked the EsKays to specialize in. With next to no atmosphere, there were no indigent life-forms to worry about. By the time Tia was five, she had pressure-suit protocol down pat, and there was no reason why she couldn't come to the digs, or even wander about within specified limits on her own. "The biggest sandbox in the universe," Braddon called it; so long as she stayed within eye- and earshot, neither of them minded having her about outside.

"Not today, dearest," Pota said apologetically. "We've found some glassware, and we're making holos. As soon as we're done with that, we'll make the castings, and after that you can come run errands for us." In the thin atmosphere and chill of the site, castings were tricky to make; one reason why Pota discarded so many. But no artifact could be moved without first making a good casting of it, as well as holos from all possible angles—too many times the artifacts crumbled to nothing, despite the most careful handling, once they were moved.

She sighed; holos and castings meant she couldn't even come near the site, lest the vibrations she made walking interfere. "All right," she agreed. "Can I go outside, though? As long as I stay close to the airlock?"

"Stay close to the lock and keep the emergency cart nearby, and I don't see any reason why you can't play outside," Pota said after a moment. Then she smiled. "And how is your dig coming?"

"You mean really, or for pretend?" she asked.

"Pretend, of course," said Braddon. "Pretend is always more fun than really. That's why *we* became archeologists in the first place— because we get to play pretend for months at a time until we have to be serious and write papers!"

He gave her a conspiratorial grin, and she giggled.

"We-ell," she said, and drew her face down into a frown *just* like Doctor Heinz Marius-Llewellyn, when he was about to put everyone to sleep. "I've found the village site of a race of flint-using primitives who were used as slave labor by the EsKays at *your* site."

"Have you!" Pota fell right in with the pretense, as Braddon nodded seriously. "Well that certainly explains why we haven't found any servos. They must have used slaves to do all their manual labor!"

"Yes. And the Flint People worshipped them as gods from the sky," Tia continued. "That was why they didn't revolt; all the slave labor was a form of worship. They'd go back to their village and then they'd try to make flint tools just like the things that the sky-gods used. They probably made pottery things, too, but I haven't found anything but shards."

"Well, pottery doesn't hold up well in conditions like this," Pota agreed. "It goes brittle very quickly under the extremes of surface temperature. What have you got so far?"

"A flint disruptor-pistol, a flint wrist-com, a flint flashlight, and some more things," she said solemnly. "I haven't found any arrow-heads or spear-points or things like that, but that's because there's nothing to hunt here. They were vegetarians, and they ate nothing but lichen."

Braddon made a face. "Awful. Worse than the food at the Institute cafeteria! No wonder they didn't survive—the food probably bored them to death!"

Pota rose and gathered up their plates and cups, stowing them neatly in the dishwasher. "Well, enjoy your lessons, pumpkin. We'll see you at lunch."

She smiled, hugged them both goodbye before they suited up, then went off to the schoolroom.

That afternoon, once lessons were done, she took down her own pressure-suit from the rack beside the airlock inner door. Her suit was designed a little differently from her parents', with accordion folds at wrists and elbows, ankles and knees, and at the waist, to allow for the growth-spurts of a child. This was a brand new suit, for she had been about to outgrow the last one just before they went out on this dig. She liked it a lot better than the old one;

the manufacturer of the last one had some kind of stupid idea that a child's suit should have cavorting flowers with smiling faces all over it. She had been ashamed to have anyone but her parents *see* her in the awful thing. She thought it made her look like a little clown.

It had come second-hand from a child on a Class Three dig— like most of the things that the Cades got. Evaluation digs simply didn't have that high a priority when it came to getting anything other than the bare essentials. But Tia'd had the bright idea when her birthday came around to ask her parents' superiors at the Institute for a new pressure-suit. And when it came out that she was imitating her parents, by creating her own little digsite, she had so tickled them that they actually sent her one. Brand new, good for three or four years at least, and the *only* difference between it and a grown-up suit was that hers had extra helmet lights and a com that couldn't be turned off, a locator-beacon that was always on, and bright fluorescent stripes on the helmet and down the arms and legs. A small price to pay for dignity.

The flowered suit had gone back to the Institute, to be endured by some other unfortunate child.

And the price to be paid for her relative freedom to roam was waiting in the airlock. A wagon, child-sized and modified from the pull-wagon many children had as toys—but this one had powered crawler-tracks and was loaded with an auxiliary power unit and air-pack and full face-mask. If her suit failed, she had been drilled in what to do so many times she could easily have saved herself when asleep. *One*, take a deep breath and pop the helmet. *Two*, pull the mask on, making sure the seals around her face were secure. *Three*, turn on the air and *Four*, plug into the APU, which would keep the suit heat up with the helmet off. Then walk—slowly, carefully, to the airlock, towing the wagon behind. There was no reason why she should suffer anything worse than a bit of frostbite.

It had never happened. That didn't mean it wouldn't. Tia had no intention of becoming a tragic tale in the newsbytes. Tragic tales were all very well in drama and history, but they were not what one wanted in real life.

So the wagon went with her, inconvenient as it was.

The filters in this suit were good ones; the last suit had always smelled a little musty, but the air in this one was fresh and clean.

She trotted over the uneven surface, towing the cart behind, kicking up little puffs of dust and sand. Everything out here was very sharp-edged and clear; red and yellow desert, reddish-purple mountains, dark blue sky. The sun, Sigma Marinara, hung right above her head, so all the shadows were tiny pools of dark black at the bases of things. She hadn't been out to her "site" for several weeks, not since the last time Mum and Dad had asked her to stay away. That had been right at the beginning, when they first got here and uncovered enough to prove it was an EsKay site. Since that time there had been a couple of sandstorms, and Tia was a bit apprehensive that her "dig" had gotten buried. Unlike her parents' dig, *she* did not have force-shields protecting her trench from storms.

But when she reached her site, she discovered to her amazement that *more* was uncovered than she had left. Instead of burying her dig in sand, the storm had scoured the area clean—

There were several likely-looking lumps at the farther end of the trench, all fused together into a bumpy whole. Wonderful! There would be hours of potential pretend here; freeing the lumps from the sandy matrix, cleaning them off, figuring out what the Flint People had been trying to copy. . . .

She took the tools her parents had discarded out of the wagon; the broken trowel that Braddon had mended for her, the worn brushes, the blunted probes, and set to work.

Several hours later, she sat back on her heels and looked at her first find, frowning. This wasn't a lump of flint after all. In fact, it seemed to be some kind of layered substance, with the layers fused together. Odd, it looked kind of wadded up. It certainly wasn't any kind of layered rock she'd ever seen before, and it didn't match any of the rocks she'd uncovered until now.

She chewed her lower lip in thought and stared at it, letting her mind just drift, to see if it could identify what kind of rock it was. It didn't look sedimentary.

Actually, it didn't look much like a rock at all. . . .

Not like a rock. What if it isn't a rock?

She blinked, and suddenly knew what it *did* look like. Layers of thin cloth or paper, wadded up, then discarded.

Finagle! Have I—

She gently—very gently—pried another lump off the outcropping, and carefully freed it of its gritty coating. And there was *no* doubt this time that what she had was the work of intelligent hands. Under the layer of half-fused sand and flaking, powdery dust, gleamed a spot of white porcelain, with the matte edge of a break showing why it had been discarded.

Oh, decom—I found the garbage dump!

Or, at least, she had found a little trash heap. That was *probably* it; likely there was just this lump of discards and no more. But anything the EsKays left behind was important, and it was equally important to stop digging *now*, mark the site in case another sandstorm came up and capriciously buried it as it had capriciously uncovered it, and bring some evidence to show Mum and Dad what she had found.

Except that she didn't have a holo-camera. Or anything to cast with.

Finally she gave up trying to think of what to do. There was only one thing for it. Bring her two finds inside and show them. The lump of fabric might not survive the touch of real air, but the porcelain thing surely would. Porcelain, unlike glass, was more resilient to the stresses of repeated temperature changes and was not likely to go to powder at the first touch of air.

She went back inside the dome and rummaged around for a bit before returning with a plastic food container for the artifacts, and a length of plastic pipe and the plastic tail from a kite-kit she'd never had a chance to use. Another well-meant but stupid gift from someone Dad worked with; someone who never once thought that on a Mars-type world there weren't very many opportunities to fly kites—

With the site marked as securely as she could manage, and the two artifacts sealed into the plastic tub, she returned to the dome again, waiting impatiently for her parents to get back.

She had hoped that the seal on the plastic tub would be good enough to keep the artifacts safely protected from the air of the dome. She knew as soon as the airlock pressurized, though, that her attempt to keep them safe had failed. Even before she pulled off her helmet, the external suit-mike picked up the *hiss* of air leaking into the container. And when she held the plastic tub up to the light, it was easy enough to see that one of the lumps had begun to disintegrate. She pried the lid off for a quick peek, and sneezed at the dust. The wadded lump was not going to look like much when her parents got home.

Decom it, she thought resentfully. *That's not fair!*

She put it down carefully on the countop; if she didn't jar it, there might still be enough left when Mum and Dad got back in that they would at least be able to tell what it *had* been.

She stripped out of her suit and sat down to wait. She tried to read a book, but she just couldn't get interested. Mum and Dad were going to be *so* surprised—and even better, now the Psychs at the Institute would have no reason to keep her away from the Class Two sites anymore—because *this* would surely prove that she knew what to do when she accidentally found something. The numbers on the clock moved with agonizing slowness, as she waited for the moment when they would finally return.

The sky outside the viewport couldn't get much darker, but the shadows lengthened, and the light faded. Soon now, soon—

Finally she heard them in the outer lock, and her heart began to beat faster. Suddenly she was no longer so certain that she had done the right thing. What if they were angry that she dissected the first two artifacts? What if she had done the wrong thing in moving them?

The "what ifs" piled up in her head as she waited for the lock to cycle.

Finally the inner door hissed, and Braddon and Pota came through, already pulling off their helmets and continuing a high-speed conversation that must have begun back at the dig.

"—but the matrix is all wrong for it to be a food preparation area—"

"—yes, yes," Pota replied impatiently, "but what about the integument—"

"Mum!" Tia said, running up to them and tugging at her mother's elbow. "I've found something!"

"Hello, pumpkin, that's very nice," her mother replied absently, hugging her, and going right on with her conversation. Her intense expression showed that she was thinking while she spoke, and her eyes never wandered from her husband's face—and as for Braddon, the rest of the world simply did not exist.

"*Mum!*" Tia persisted. "I've found an artifact!"

"In a moment, dear," Pota replied. "But what about—"

"*MUM!*" Tia shouted, disobeying *every* rule of not interrupt-ing grown-ups in desperation, knowing from all the signs that she would *never* get their attention otherwise. Conversations like *this* one could go on for hours. "*I've found an artifact!*"

Both her parents stopped their argument in mid-sentence and stared at her. Silence enveloped the room; an ominous silence. Tia gulped nervously.

"Tia," Braddon finally said, disapproval creeping into his voice. "Your mother and I are in the middle of a very important conversation. This is *not* the time for pretend."

"Dad, it's *not* pretend!" she said insistently, pointing to her plastic box. "It's not! I found an artifact, and there's more—"

Pota raised an eyebrow at her husband and shrugged. Braddon picked up the box, carelessly, and Tia winced as the first lump inside visibly disintegrated more.

"I am going to respect your intelligence and integrity enough to assume that you *think* you found an artifact," Braddon replied, prying the lid from the container. "But Tia, you know better than to—"

He glanced down inside—and his eyebrows arched upward in the greatest show of surprise that Tia had ever seen him make.

"I *told* you," Tia could not resist saying, triumphantly.

"—so they took the big lights out to the trench, and the extra field-generators," she told Ted E. Bear after she'd been put to bed for the night. "They were out there for *hours*, and they let me wait up to hear what it was. And it *was*, I *did* find a garbage dump! A big one, too! Mum made a special call to the Institute, 'cause this is the first really big EsKay dump anybody's ever found."

She hugged Ted closer, basking in the warmth of Pota's praise, a warmth that still lingered and made her feel happy right down to her toes. "You did everything *exactly* right with the equipment you had," Pota had told her. "I've had undergraduates that didn't do as well as you did, pumpkin! You remember what I told you, when you asked me about why I wanted to find garbage?"

"That we learn more from sentients' garbage than from anything other than their literature," she'd recited dutifully.

"Well," Pota had replied, sitting on the edge of her bed and touching her nose with one finger, playfully. "You, my curious little chick, have just upgraded this site from a Class One to a Class Three with four hours of work! That's more than Braddon and I have *ever* done!"

"Does that mean that we'll be leaving?" she'd asked in confusion.

"Eventually," Pota told her, a certain gloating glee in her voice. "But it takes time to put together a Class Three team, and *we* happen to be right here. Your father and I will be making gigabytes of important discoveries before the team gets here to replace us. And with that much already invested—they may *not* replace us!"

Tia had shaken her head, confused.

Pota had hugged her. "What I mean, pumpkin, is that there is a *very* good chance that we'll stay on here—as the dig supervisors! An instant promotion from Class One supervisor to Class Three supervisor! There'll be better equipment, a better dome to live in—you'll have some playmates—couriers will be by every week instead of every few months—not to mention the raises in pay and status! All the papers on this site will go out under *our* names! And all because *you* were my clever, bright, careful little girl, who knew what she saw and knew when to stop playing!"

"Mum and Dad are really, really happy," she told Ted, thinking about the glow of joy that had been on both their faces when they finished the expensive link to the nearest Institute supervisor. "I think we did a good thing. I think maybe you brought us luck, Ted." She yawned. "Except about the other kids coming. But we don't have to play with them if we don't want to, do we?"

Ted agreed silently, and she hugged him again. "I'd rather talk to you, anyway," she told him. "You never say anything dumb. Dad says that if you can't say something intelligent, you shouldn't say anything; and Mum says that people who know when to shut up are the smartest people of all, so I guess you must be pretty smart. Right?"

But she never got a chance to find out if Ted agreed with that statement, because at that point she fell right asleep.

Over the course of the next few days, it became evident that this was not just an ordinary garbage dump; this was one containing scientific or medical debris. That raised the status of the site from "important" to "priceless," and Pota and Braddon took to spending every waking moment either at the site or preserving and examining their finds, making copious notes, and any number of speculations. They hardly ever saw Tia anymore; they had changed their schedule so that they were awake long before she was and came in long after she went to bed.

Pota apologized—via a holo that she had left to play for Tia as soon as she came in to breakfast this morning.

"Pumpkin," her image said, while Tia sipped her juice. "I hope you can understand why we're doing this. The more we find out before the team gets sent out, the more we make ourselves essential to the dig, the better our chances for that promotion." Pota's image ran a hand through her hair; to Tia's critical eyes, she looked very tired, and a bit frazzled, but fairly satisfied. "It won't be more than a few weeks, I promise. Then things will go back to normal. Better than normal, in fact. I promise that we'll have a Family Day before the team gets here, all right? So start thinking what you'd like to do."

Well, *that* would be stellar! Tia knew exactly what she wanted to do—she wanted to go out to the mountains on the big sled, and she wanted to drive it herself on the way.

"So forgive us, all right? We don't love you any less, and we think about you all the time, and we miss you like anything." Pota blew a kiss toward the camera. "I know you can take care of yourself; in fact, we're counting on that. You're making a big difference to us. I want you to know that. Love you, baby."

Tia finished her juice as the holo flickered out, and a certain temptation raised its head. This could be a really unique opportunity to play hooky, just a little bit. Mum and Dad were not going to be checking the tutor to see how her lessons were going—and the Institute Psychs wouldn't care; they thought she was too advanced for her age anyway. She could even raid the library for the holos she wasn't precisely supposed to watch. . . .

"Oh, Finagle," she said, regretfully, after a moment. It might be fun—but it would be *guilty* fun. And besides, sooner or later Mum and Dad would find out what she'd done, and *ping!* there would go the Family Day and probably a lot of other privileges. She weighed the immediate pleasure of being lazy and watching forbidden holos against the future pleasure of being able to pilot the sled up the mountains, and the latter outranked the former. Piloting the sled was the closest *she* would get to piloting a ship, and she wouldn't be able to do that for years and years and years yet.

And if she fell on her nose *now*, right when Mum and Dad

trusted her most—they'd probably restrict her to the dome for ever and ever.

"Not worth it," she sighed, jumping down from her stool. She frowned as she noticed that the pins-and-needles feeling in her toes still hadn't gone away. It had been there when she woke up this morning. It had been there yesterday too, and the day before, but by breakfast it had worn off.

Well, it didn't bother her that much, and it wouldn't take her mind off her Latin lesson. Too bad, too.

"Boring language," she muttered. "*Ick, ack, ock!*"

Well, the sooner she got it over with, the better off she'd be, and she could go back to nice logical quadratics.

The pins-and-needles feeling hadn't worn off by afternoon, and although she felt all right, she decided that since Mum and Dad were trusting her to do everything right, she probably ought to talk to the AI about it

"Socrates, engage Medic Mode, please," she said, sitting down reluctantly in the tiny medic station. She *really* didn't like being in the medic-station; it smelled of disinfectant and felt like being in a too-small pressure suit. It was just about the size of a tiny lav, but something about it made it *feel* smaller. Maybe because it was dark inside. And of course, since it had been made for adults, the proportions were all wrong for her. In order to reach hand-plates she had to scoot to the edge of the seat, and in order to reach foot-plates she had to get right off the seat entirely. The screen in front of her lit up with the smiling holo of someone that was supposed to be a doctor. Privately, she doubted that the original had ever been any closer to medicine than wearing the jumpsuit. He just looked too—polished. *Too* trustworthy, *too* handsome, *too* competent. Any time there was anything official she had to interface with that seemed to scream *trust me* at her, she immediately distrusted it and went very wary. Probably the original for this holo had been an actor. Maybe he made adults feel calm, but he made her think about the Psychs and their too-hearty greetings, their nosy questions.

"Well, Tia," said the AI's voice—changed to that of the "doctor." "What brings you here?"

"My toes feel like they're asleep," she said dutifully. "They kind of tingle."

"Is that all?" the "doctor" asked, after a moment for the AI to access his library of symptoms. "Are they colder than normal? Put your hand on the hand-plate, and your foot on the foot-plate, Tia."

She obeyed, feeling very like a contortionist.

"Well, the circulation seems to be fine," the "doctor" said, after the AI had a chance to read temperature and blood pressure, both of which appeared in the upper right-hand corner of the screen. "Have you any other symptoms?"

"No," she replied. "Not really." The "doctor" froze for a moment, as the AI analyzed all the other readings it had taken from her during the past few days—what she'd eaten and how much, what she'd done, her sleep-patterns.

The "doctor" unfroze. "Sometimes when children start growing very fast, they get odd sensations in their bodies," the AI said. "A long time ago, those were called 'growing pains.' Now we know it's because sometimes different kinds of tissue grow at different rates. I think that's probably what your problem is, Tia, and I don't think you need to worry about it. I'll prescribe some vitamin supplements for you, and in a few days you should be just fine."

"Thank you," she said politely, and made her escape, relieved to have gotten off so lightly.

And in a few days, the pins-and-needles sensation *did* go away, and she thought no more about it. Thought no more, that is, until she went outside to her new "dig" and did something she hadn't done in a year—she fell down. Well, she didn't exactly fall; she *thought* she'd sidestepped a big rock, but she hadn't. She rammed her toes right into it and went heavily to her knees.

The suit was intact, she discovered to her relief—and she was quite ready to get up and keep going, until she realized that her foot didn't hurt.

And it should have, if she'd rammed it against the outcropping hard enough to throw her to the ground.

So instead of going on, she went back to the dome and peeled off suit and shoe and sock—and found her foot was completely numb, but black-and-blue where she had slammed it into the unyielding stone.

When she prodded it experimentally, she discovered that her whole foot was numb, from the toes back to the arch. She peeled off her other shoe and sock, and found that her left foot was as numb as her right.

"Decom it," she muttered. This surely meant another check-in with the medic.

Once again she climbed into the claustrophobic little closet at the back of the dome and called up the "doctor."

"Still got pins-and-needles, Tia?" he said cheerfully, as she wriggled on the hard seat.

"No," she replied, "But I've mashed my foot something awful. It's all black-and-blue."

"Put it on the foot-plate, and I'll scan it," the "doctor" replied. "I promise, it won't hurt a bit."

Of course it won't, it doesn't hurt now, she thought resentfully, but did as she was told.

"Well, no bones broken, but you certainly did bruise it!" the "doctor" said after a moment. Then he added archly, "What were you doing, kicking the tutor?"

"No," she muttered. She really *hated* it when the AI program made it get patronizing. "I stubbed it on a rock, outside."

"Does it hurt?" the "doctor" continued, oblivious to her resentment.

"No," she said shortly. "It's all numb."

"Well, if it does, I've authorized your bathroom to give you some pills," the "doctor" said with cloying cheer. "Just go right ahead and take them if you need them—you know how to get them."

The screen shut down before she had a chance to say anything else. *I guess it isn't anything to worry about,* she decided. *The AI would have said something otherwise. It'll probably go away.*

But it didn't go away, although the bruises healed. Before long she had other bruises, and the numbness of her feet extended to her ankles. But she told herself that the AI had said it would go away, eventually—and anyway, this wasn't so bad, at least when she mashed herself it didn't *hurt.*

She continued to play at her own little excavation, the new one—which she had decided was a grave-site. The primitives burned their dead though, and only buried the ashes with their flint-replicas of the sky-gods' wonderful things—hoping that the dearly departed would be reincarnated as sky-gods and return in wealth and triumph. . . .

It wasn't as much fun though, without Mum and Dad to talk to; and she was getting kind of tired of the way she kept tripping and falling over the uneven ground at the new "site." She hadn't damaged her new suit yet, but there were sharp rocks that could rip holes even in the tough suit fabric—and if her suit was torn, there would go the promised Family Day.

So, finally, she gave up on it and spent her afternoons inside.

A few nights later, Pota peeked in her room to see if she was still awake.

"I wanted you to know we were still flesh-and-blood and not holos, pumpkin," her mum said, sitting down on the side of her bed. "How are your excavations coming?"

Tia shook her head. "I kept tripping on things, and I didn't want to tear my suit," she explained. "I think that the Flint People must have put a curse on their grave-site. I don't think I should dig there anymore."

Pota chuckled, hugged her, and said, "That could very well be, dear. It never pays to underestimate the power of religion. When the others arrive we'll research their religion and take the curse off, all right?"

"Okay," she replied. She wondered for a moment if she should mention her feet—

But Pota kissed her and whisked out the door before she could make up her mind.

Nothing more happened for several days, and she got used to having numb feet. If she was careful to watch where she stepped, and careful never to go barefoot, there really wasn't anything to worry about. And the AI had *said* it was something that happened to other children.

Besides, now Mum and Dad were *really* finding important things. In a quick breakfast-holo, a tired but excited Braddon said that what they were uncovering now might mean a whole lot more than just a promotion. It might mean the establishment of a fieldwide reputation.

Just what that meant, exactly, Tia wasn't certain—but there was no doubt that it must be important or Braddon wouldn't have been so excited about it. So she decided that whatever was wrong with her could wait. It wouldn't be long now, and once Mum and Dad weren't involved in this day-and-night frenzy of activity, she could explain everything and they would see to it that the medics gave her the right shot or whatever it was that she needed.

The next morning when she woke up, her fingers were tingling.

Tia sighed and took her place inside the medic booth. This was getting very tiresome.

The AI ran her through the standard questions, which she answered as she had before. "So now you have that same tingling in your hands as you did in your feet, is that right?" the "doctor" asked.

"That's right," she said shortly.

"The same tingling that went away?" the "doctor" persisted.

"Yes," she replied. *Should I say something about how it doesn't tingle anymore, about how now it's numb?* But the AI was continuing.

"Tia, I can't really find anything wrong with you," it said. "Your circulation is fine, you don't have a fever, your appetite and weight are fine, you're sleeping right. But you *do* seem to have gotten very accident prone lately." The "doctor" took on a look of concern covering impatience. "Tia, I know that your parents are very busy right now, and they don't have time to talk to you or play with you. Is *that* what's really wrong? Are you angry with your parents for leaving you alone so much? Would you like to talk to a Counselor?"

"No!" she snapped. The idea! The *stupid* AI actually thought she was making this up to get attention!

"Well, you simply don't have any other symptoms," the "doctor" said, none too gently. "This hasn't got to the point where I'd have to insist that you talk to a Counselor, but really, without anything else to go on, I can't suggest anything else except that this is a phase you'll grow out of."

"This hasn't got to the point where I'd have to insist that you talk to a Counselor." Those were dangerous words. The AI's "Counselor" mode was only good for so much—and every single thing she said and did would be recorded the moment that she started "Counseling." Then all the Psychs back at the Institute would be sent the recordings via compressed-mode databurst—and they'd be all over them, looking for something wrong with her that needed Psyching. And if they found anything, anything at all, Mum and Dad would get orders from the Board of Mental Health that they couldn't ignore, and she'd be shipped back to a school on the next courier run.

Oh no. You don't catch me that easy.

"You're right," she said carefully. "But Mum and Dad trust me to tell you *everything* that's wrong, so I am."

"All right then." The "doctor's" face lost that stern look. "So long as you're just being conscientious. Keep taking those vitamin supplements, Tia, and everything will be fine."

But everything wasn't fine. Within days, the tingling had stopped, to be replaced by numbness. Just like her feet. She began having trouble holding things, and her lessons took twice as long now, since she couldn't touch-type anymore and had to watch where her fingers went.

She completely gave up on doing anything that required a lot of manual dexterity. Instead, she watched a lot of holos, even boring ones, and played a great deal of holo-chess. She read a lot too, from the screen, so that she could give one-key page-turning commands rather than trying to turn paper pages herself. The numbness stopped at her wrists, and for a few days she was so busy getting used to doing things without feeling her hands, that she didn't notice that the numbness in her legs had spread from her ankles to her knees. . . .

Now she was afraid to go to the AI "doctor" program, knowing that it would put her in for Counseling. She tried looking things up herself in the database, but knew that she was going to have to be very sneaky to avoid triggering flags in the AI. As the numbness stopped at the knees, then began to spread up her arms, she kept telling herself that it wouldn't, couldn't be much longer now. Soon Mum and Dad would be done, and they would know she wasn't making this up to get attention. Soon she would be able to tell them herself, and they'd make the stupid medic work right. Soon.

She woke up, as usual, to hands and feet that acted like wooden blocks at the ends of her limbs. She got a shower—easy enough, since the controls were pushbutton, then struggled into her clothing by wriggling and using teeth and fingers that didn't really want to move. She didn't bother too much with hair and teeth, it was just too hard. Shoving her feet into slippers, since she hadn't been able to tie her shoes for the past couple of days, she stumped out into the main room of the dome—

Only to find Pota and Braddon waiting there for her, smiling over their coffee.

"Surprise!" Pota said cheerfully. "We've done just about every-thing we can on our own, and we zipped the findings off to the Institute last night. *Now* things can get back to normal!"

"Oh *Mum!*" She couldn't help herself, she was so overwhelmed by relief and joy that she started to run across the room to fling herself into their arms—

Started to. Halfway there, she tripped, as usual, and went fly-ing through the air, crashing into the table and spilling the hot coffee all over her arms and legs.

They picked her up, as she babbled apologies about her clum-siness. She didn't even notice what the coffee had done to her, didn't even think about it until her parents' expressions of hor-ror alerted her to the fact that there were burns and blisters already rising on her lower arms.

"It doesn't hurt," she said, dazedly, without thinking, just say-ing the first thing that came into her mind. "It's okay, really, I've been kind of numb for a while so it doesn't hurt, honest—"

Pota and Braddon both froze. Something about their expres-sions startled her into silence.

"You don't feel anything?" Pota said, carefully. "No pain, nothing at all?"

She shook her head. "My hands and feet were tingling for a while, and then they stopped and went numb. I thought if I just waited you could take care of it when you weren't so busy—"

They wouldn't let her say anything else. Within moments they had established through careful prodding and tests with the end of a sharp probe that the numb area now ended at mid-thigh and mid-shoulder.

"How long has this been going on?" Braddon asked, while Pota flew to the AI console to call up the medical program the adults used.

"Oh, a few weeks," she said vaguely. "Socrates said it wasn't anything, that I'd grow out of it. *Then* he acted like I was mak-ing it up, and I didn't want him to get the Psychs on me. So I figured I would. . . ."

Pota returned at that moment, her mouth set in a grim line. "You are going straight to bed, pumpkin," she said, with what Tia could tell was forced lightness. "Socrates thinks you have pinched nerves; possibly a spinal defect that he can't scan for. So you are going to bed, and we are calling for a courier to come get you. All right?"

Braddon and Pota exchanged one of *those* looks, the kind Tia couldn't read, and Tia's heart sank. "Okay," she sighed with resignation. "I didn't mean to be such a bother, honest, I didn't—"

Braddon scooped her up in his arms and carried her off to her room. "Don't even *think* that you're being a bother," he said fiercely. "We love you, pumpkin. And we're going to see that you get better as quickly as we can."

He tucked her into bed, with Ted beside her, and called up a holo from the almost-forbidden collection. "Here," he said, kissing her tenderly. "Your Mum is going to be in here in a minute to put something on those burns. Then we're going to spend all our time making you the most disgustingly spoiled little brat in known space! What *you* have to do is lie there and think really hard about getting better. Is it a deal?"

"Sure, Dad," she replied, managing to find a grin for him somewhere. "It's a deal."

CHAPTER TWO

Because Tia was in no danger of dying—and because there was no craft available to come fetch her capable of Singularity Drive—the AI-drone that had been sent to take her to a Central Worlds hospital took two more weeks to arrive. Two more long, interminable weeks, during which the faces of her Mum and Dad grew drawn and frightened—and in which her condition not only did not improve, it deteriorated.

By the end of that two weeks, she was in much worse shape; she had not only lost all feeling in her limbs, she had lost use of them as well. The clumsiness that had begun when she had trouble with buttons and zippers had turned into paralysis. If she hadn't felt the need to keep her parents' spirits up, she'd have cried. She couldn't even hold Ted anymore.

She joked about it to her Mum, pretending that she had always wanted to be waited on hand and foot. She *had* to joke about it; although she was terrified, the look of fear in her parents' eyes drove her own terrors away. She was determined, absolutely determined, not to let them know how frightened she was. They were already scared enough—if she lost her courage, they might panic.

The time crawled by, as she watched holo after holo and played endless games of chess against Braddon, and kept telling herself that once she got to the hospital everything would be fine. Of course it would be fine. There wasn't anything that a Central

Worlds hospital couldn't cure. Everyone knew that! Only congenital defects couldn't be cured. But she had been fine, right up until the day this started. It was probably something stupid.

"Socrates says it has to be pinched nerves," Pota repeated, for the hundredth time, the day the ship was due. "Once they get you to the hospital, you'll have to be really brave, pumpkin. They're probably going to have to operate on you, and it's probably going to take several months before you're back to normal—"

She brushed Tia's hair and tied it in back in a neat tail, the way Tia liked it. "I won't be able to do any lessons, then, will I?" she asked, mostly to keep her mother's mind busy with something trivial. *Mum doesn't handle reality and real-time very well . . . Dad doesn't either.* "They're probably going to have me in a cast or something, and all dopey with pain-pills. I'm going to fall behind, aren't I?"

"Well," Pota said, with false cheer, "yes, I'm afraid so. But that will probably make the Psychs all very happy, you know, they think that you're too far ahead as it is. But just think—you'll have the whole library at the hospital to dig into any time you want it!"

That was enough even to divert her for a minute. The entire library at the hospital—magnitudes bigger than any library they could carry with them. All the holos she wanted to watch—and proper reading screens set up, instead of the jury-rig Dad had put together—

"They're here—" Braddon called from the outer room. Pota compressed her lips into a line again and lifted Tia out of the bed. And for the first time in weeks, Tia was bundled into her pressure-suit, put inside as if Pota was dressing a giant doll. Braddon came in to help in a moment, as she tried to cooperate as much as she could. She would be going outside again. This time, though, she probably wouldn't be coming back. Not to this dome, anyway.

"Wait!" she called, just before Pota sealed her in. "Wait, I want my bear!" And at the look of doubt her parents exchanged, she put on the most pleading expression she could manage. "Please?" She couldn't stand the idea that she'd be going off to a strange place with nothing familiar or warm in it. Even if she couldn't hold him, she could still talk to him and feel his fur against her cheek. "*Please?*"

"All right, pumpkin," Pota said, relenting. "I think there's just room for him in there with you." Fortunately Ted was very squashable, and Tia herself was slender. There *was* room for him in the body of the suit, and Tia took comfort in the feel of his warm little bulk against her waist.

She didn't have any time to think of anything else—for at that moment, two strangers dressed in the white pressure-suits of CenCom Medical came in. There was a strange hiss at the back of her air-pack, and the room went away.

She woke again in a strange white room, dressed in a white paper gown. The only spot of color in the whole place was Ted. *He* was propped beside her, in the crook of her arm, his head peeking out from beneath the white blanket

She blinked, trying to orient herself, and the cold hand of fear clamped down on her throat. Where was she? A hospital room, probably, but where were Mum and Dad? How did she get here so *fast*? What had those two strangers done to her?

And why wasn't she feeling better? Why couldn't she feel *anything*?

"She's awake," said a voice she didn't recognize. She turned her head, which was all she could move, to see someone in another white pressure-suit standing beside her, anonymous behind a dark faceplate. The red cross of Medical was on one shoulder, and there was a name-tag over the breast, but she couldn't read it from this angle. She couldn't even tell if the person in the suit was male or female, or even human or humanoid.

The faceplate bent over her; she would have shrunk away if she could, feeling scared in spite of herself—the plate was so blank, so impersonal. But then she realized that the person in the suit had bent down so that she could see the face inside, past the glare of lights on the plexi surface, and she relaxed a little.

"Hello, Hypatia," said the person—a lady, actually, a very nice lady from her face. Her voice sounded kind of tinny, coming through the suit speaker; a little like Moira's over the ancient com. The comparison made her feel a little calmer. At least the lady knew her name and pronounced it right.

"Hello," she said cautiously. "This is the hospital, isn't it? How come I don't remember the ship?"

"Well, Hypatia—may I call you Tia?" At Tia's nod, the lady continued. "Tia, our first thought was that you might have some kind of plague, even though your parents were all right. The doctor and medic we sent on the ship decided that it was better to be completely safe and keep you and your parents in isolation. The easiest way to do that was to put all three of you in cold sleep and keep you in your suits until we got you here. We didn't want to frighten you, so we asked your parents not to tell you what we were going to do."

Tia digested that. "All right," she said, trying to be agreeable, since there wasn't anything she could have done about it anyway. "It probably would have gotten really boring on the ship. There probably wasn't much to watch or read, and they would have gotten tired of playing chess with me."

The lady laughed. "Given that you would have beaten the pants off both of them, quite probably," she agreed, straightening up a little. Now that Tia knew there was a person behind the faceplate, it didn't seem quite so threatening. "Now, we're going to keep you in isolation for a while longer, while we see what it is that bit you. You'll be seeing a lot of me—I'm one of your two doctors. My name is Anna Jorgenson-Kepal, and you can call me Anna, or Doctor Anna if you like, but I don't think we need to be that formal. Your other doctor is Kennet Uhua-Sorg. You *won't* be seeing much of him until you're out of isolation, because he's a paraplegic and he's in a Moto-Chair. Can't fit one of *them* into a pressure-suit."

The holo-screen above the bed flickered into life, and the head and shoulders of a thin, ascetic-looking young man appeared there. "Call me Kenny, Tia," the young man said. "I absolutely refuse to be stuffy with you. I'm sorry I can't meet you in person, but it takes *forever* to decontam one of these fardling chairs, so Anna gets to be my hands."

"That's—your chair—it's kind of like a modified shell, isn't it?" she asked curiously, deciding that if they were going to bring the subject up, *she* wasn't going to be polite and avoid it. "I know a shellperson. Moira, she's a brainship."

"Dead on!" Kenny said cheerfully. "Medico on the half-shell, that's me! I just had a stupid accident when I was a tweenie, not like you, getting bit by alien bugs!"

She smiled tentatively. *I think I'm going to like him.* "Did anyone ever tell you that you look *just* like Amenemhat the Third?"

His large eyes widened even more. "Well, no—that is definitely a new one. I hope it's a compliment! One of my patients said I looked like Largo Delecron, the synthcom star, but I didn't know she thought Largo looked like a refugee from a slaver camp!"

"It is," she assured him hastily. "He's one of my favorite Pharaohs."

"I'll have to see if I can't cultivate the proper Pharaonic majesty, then," Kenny replied with a grin. "It might do me some good when I have to drum some sense into the heads of some of the Psychs around here! They've been trying to get at you ever since we admitted you."

If she could have shivered with apprehension, she would have. "I don't have to see them, do I?" she asked in a small voice. "They never stop asking stupid questions!"

"Absolutely not," Anna said firmly. "I have a double-doctorate; one of them is in headshrinking. I am *quite* capable of assessing you all by myself."

Tia's heart sank when Anna mentioned her degree in Psych—but it rose the moment she referred to Psych as "headshrinking." None of the Psychs who had plagued her life until now *ever* called their profession by something as frivolous as "headshrinking."

She patted Tia's shoulder. "Don't worry, Tia. It's my opinion that you are a very brave young lady—a little *too* responsible, but otherwise just fine. *They* spend too much time analyzing children and not enough time actually seeing them or paying attention to them." She smiled inside her helmet, and a curl of hair escaped down to dangle above her left eyebrow, making her look a lot more human.

"Listen, Tia, there's a little bit of fur missing from your bear, and a scrap of stuffing," Kenny said. "Anna says you wouldn't notice, but I thought we ought to tell you anyway. We checked him over for alien bugs and neurotoxins, and he's got a clean bill of health. When you come out of Coventry, we'll decontam him again to be sure, but we *know* he wasn't the problem, in case you were wondering."

She had wondered. . . . Moira wouldn't have done anything on purpose, of course, but it would have been horrible if her sickness had been due to Ted. Moira would have felt awful, not to mention how Tomas would feel.

"What's his name?" Anna asked, busying herself with something at the head of the bed. Tia couldn't turn her head far enough to see what it was.

"Theodore Edward Bear," she replied, surreptitiously rubbing her cheek against his soft fur. "Moira gave him to me, because she used to have a bear named Ivan the Bearable."

"Excellent name, Theodore. It suits him," Anna said. "You know, I think your Moira and I must be about the same age—there was a kind of fad for bears when I was little. I had a really nice bear in a flying suit called Amelia Bearhart." She chuckled. "I still have her, actually, but she mostly sits on the bureau in my guest room. She's gotten to be a very venerable matriarch in her old age."

But bears weren't really what she wanted to talk about. Now that she knew where she was, and that she was in isolation. "How long am I going to be in here?" she asked in a small voice.

Kenny turned very serious, and Anna stopped fiddling with things. Kenny sucked on his lower lip for a moment before actually replying, and the hum of the machinery in her room seemed very loud. "The Psychs were trying to tell us that we should try and cushion you, but—Tia, we think that you are a very unusual girl. We think you would rather know the complete truth. Is that the case?"

Would she? Or would she rather pretend—

But this wasn't like making up stories at a dig. If she pretended, things would only seem worse when they finally told her the truth, if it was bad.

"Ye-es," she told them both, slowly. "Please."

"We don't know," Anna told her. "I wish we did. We haven't found anything in your blood, and we're only just now trying to isolate things in your nervous system. But—well, we're assuming it's a bug that got you, a proto-virus, maybe, but we don't know, and that's the truth. Until we know, we won't know if we can fix you again."

Not when. If.

The possibility that she might *stay* like this for the rest of her life chilled her.

"Your parents are in isolation, too," Kenny said, hastily, "but they are one hundred percent fine. There's nothing wrong with them at all. So that makes things harder."

"I understand, I think," she said in a small, nervous-sounding voice. She took a deep breath. "Am I getting worse?"

Anna went very still. Kenny's face darkened, and he bit his lower lip.

"Well," he said quietly. "Yes. We're having to think about mobility, and maybe even life-support for you. Something considerably more than my chair. I wish I could tell you differently, Tia."

"That's all right," she said, trying to ease his distress. "I'd rather know."

Anna leaned down to whisper something through her suit-mike. "Tia, if you're afraid of crying, don't be. If I were in your position, I'd cry. And if you would like to be alone, tell us, all right?"

"Okay," she replied, faintly. "Uh, can I be alone for a while, please?"

"Sure." She stopped pretending to fuss with equipment and nodded shortly at the holo-screen. Kenny brought up one hand to wave at her, and the screen blinked out. Anna left through what Tia now realized was a decontam-airlock a moment later. Leaving her alone with the hissing, humming equipment, and Ted.

She swallowed a lump in her throat and thought very hard about what they'd told her.

She wasn't getting any better, she was getting worse. They didn't know what was wrong. That was on the negative side. On the plus side, there was nothing wrong with Mum and Dad, and they hadn't said to give up all hope.

Therefore, she should continue to assume that they *would* find a cure.

She cleared her throat. "Hello?" she said.

As she had thought, there was an AI monitoring the room.

"Hello," it replied, in the curiously accentless voice only an AI could produce. "What is your need?"

"I'd like to watch a holo. History," she said, after a moment of thought. "There's a holo about Queen Hatshepsut of Egypt. It's called *Phoenix of Ra*, I think. Have you got that?"

That had been on the forbidden list at home; Tia knew why. There had been some pretty steamy scenes with the Pharaoh and her architect in there. Tia was fascinated by the only female to declare herself Pharaoh, however, and had been decidedly annoyed when a little sex kept her from viewing this one.

"Yes, I have access to that," the AI said after a moment. "Would you like to view it now?"

So they hadn't put any restrictions on her viewing privileges!

"Yes," she replied; then, eager to strike while she had the chance, "And after that, I'd like to see the *Aten* trilogy, about Ahnkenaten and the heretics—that's *Aten Rising, Aten at Zenith, and Aten Descending.*"

Those had more than a few steamy scenes; she'd overheard her mother saying that some of the theories that had been dramatized fairly explicitly in the trilogy, while they made comprehensible some otherwise inexplicable findings, would get the holos banned in some cultures. And Braddon had chuckled and replied that the costumes alone—or lack of them—while completely accurate, would do the same. Still—Tia figured she could handle it. And if it was that bad, it would *certainly* help keep her mind off her own troubles!

"Very well," the AI said agreeably. "Shall I begin?"

"Yes," she told it, with another caress of her cheek on Ted's soft fur. "Please."

Pota and Braddon watched their daughter with frozen faces, faces that Tia was convinced covered a complete welter of emotions that they didn't want her to see. She took a deep breath, enunciated "Chair forward, five feet," and her Moto-Chair glided forward and stopped before it touched them.

"Well, now I can get around at least," she said, with what she hoped sounded like cheer. "I was getting awfully tired of the same four walls!"

Whatever it was that she had—and now she heard the words "proto-virus" and "dystrophic sclerosis" bandied about more often than not—the medics had decided it wasn't contagious. They'd let Pota and Braddon out of isolation, and they'd moved Tia to another room, one that had a door right onto the corridor. Not that it made much difference, except that Anna didn't have to use a decontam airlock and pressure-suit anymore. And now Kenny came to see her in person. But four white walls were still four white walls, and there wasn't much variation in rooms.

Still—she was afraid to ask for things to personalize the room. Afraid that if she made it more her own—she'd be stuck in it. Forever.

Her numbness and paralysis extended to most of her body now, except for her facial muscles. And there it stopped. Just as inexplicably as it had begun.

They'd put her in the quadriplegic version of the Moto-Chair;

just like Kenny's except that she controlled hers with a few commands and series of tongue-switches and eye movements. A command sent it forward, and the direction she looked would tell it where to go. And hers had mechanical "arms" that followed set patterns programmed in to respond to more commands. Any command had to be prefaced by "chair" or "arm." A clumsy system, but it was the best they could do without direct synaptic connections from the brainstem, like those of a shellperson.

Her brainstem was still intact, anyway. Whatever it was had gotten her spine, but not that.

Other than that, Mrs. Lincoln, she thought with bitter irony, *how was the play?*

"What do you think, pumpkin?" Braddon asked, his voice quivering only a little.

"Hey, this is stellar, Dad," she replied cheerfully. "It's just like piloting a ship! I think I'll challenge Doctor Kenny to a race!"

Pota swallowed very hard and managed a tremulous smile. "It won't be for too long," she said without conviction. "As soon as they find out what's set up housekeeping in there, they'll have you better in no time."

She bit her lip to keep from snapping back and dug up a fatuous grin from somewhere. The likelihood of finding a cure diminished more with every day, and she knew it. Neither Anna nor Kenny made any attempt to hide that from her.

But there was no point in making her parents unhappy. They already felt bad enough.

She tried out all the points of the chair for them, until not even they could stand it anymore. They left, making excuses and promising to come back—and they were succeeded immediately by a stream of interns and neurological specialists, each of whom had more variations on the same basic questions she had answered a thousand times, each of whom had his own pet theory about what was wrong.

"First my toes felt like they were asleep when I woke up one morning, but it wore off. Then it didn't wear off. Then instead of waking up with tingles, I woke up numb. No, sir, it never actually hurt. No, ma'am, it only went as far as my heel at first. Yes, sir, then after two days my fingers started. No ma'am, just the fingers not the whole hand. . . ."

Hours of it. But she knew that they weren't being nasty, they were trying to *help* her, and being able to help her depended on how cooperative she was.

But their questions didn't stop the questions of her own. So far it was just sensory nerves and voluntary muscles and nerves. What if it went to the involuntary ones, and she woke up unable to breathe? What then? What if she lost control of her facial muscles? Every little tingle made her break out in a sweat of panic, thinking it was going to happen. . . .

Nobody had answers for any questions. Not hers, and not theirs.

Finally, just before dinner, they went away. After about a half an hour, she mastered control of the arms enough to feed herself, saving herself the humiliation of having to call a nurse to do it. And the chair's own plumbing solved the humiliation of the natural result of eating and drinking. . . .

After supper, when the tray was taken away, she was left in the growing darkness of the room, quite alone. She would have slumped, if she could have. It was just as well that Pota and Braddon hadn't returned; having them there was a strain. It was harder to be brave in front of them than it was in front of strangers.

"Chair, turn seventy degrees right," she ordered. "Left arm, pick up bear."

With a soft whir, the chair obeyed her.

"Left arm, put bear—cancel. Left arm, bring bear to left of face." The arm moved a little. "Closer. Closer. Hold."

Now she cuddled Ted against her cheek, and she could pretend that it was her own arm holding him there.

With no one there to see, slow, hot tears formed in her eyes and trickled down her cheeks. She leaned her head to the left a little, so that they would soak into Ted's soft blue fur and not betray her.

"It's not fair," she whispered to Ted, who seemed to nod with sad agreement as she rubbed her cheek against him. "It's not fair. . . ."

I wanted to find the EsKay homeworld. I wanted to go out with Mum and Dad and be the one to find the homeworld. I wanted to write books. I wanted to stand up in front of people and make them laugh and get excited, and see how history and archeology aren't dead, they're just asleep. I wanted to do things they make holos out of. I wanted—I wanted—

I wanted to see things! I wanted to drive grav-sleds and swim in a real lagoon and feel a storm and—

—and I wanted—

Some of the scenes from the holos she'd been watching came back with force now, and memories of Pota and Braddon, when they thought she was engrossed in a book or a holo, giggling and cuddling like tweenies. . . .

I wanted to find out about boys. Boys and kisses and—

And now nobody's ever going to look at me and see me. All they're going to see is this big metal thing. That's all they see now. . . .

Even if a boy ever wanted to kiss me, he'd have to get past a half ton of machinery, and it would probably bleep an alarm.

The tears poured faster now, with the darkness of the room to hide them.

They wouldn't have put me in this thing if they thought I was going to get better. I'm never going to get better. I'm only going to get worse. I can't feel anything, I'm nothing but a head in a machine. And if I get worse, will I go deaf? Blind?

"Teddy, what's going to happen to me?" she sobbed. "Am I going to spend the rest of my life in a room?"

Ted didn't know, any more than she did.

"It's not fair, it's not fair, I never did anything," she wept, as Ted watched her tears with round, sad eyes, and soaked them up for her. "It's not fair. I wasn't finished. I hadn't even started yet. . . ."

Kenny grabbed a tissue with one hand and snapped off the camera-relay with the other. He scrubbed fiercely at his eyes and blew his nose with a combination of anger and grief. Anger, at his own impotence. Grief, for the vulnerable little girl alone in that cold, impersonal hospital room, a little girl who was doing her damnedest to put a brave face on everything.

In public. He was the only one to watch her in private, like this, when she thought there was no one to see that her whole pose of cheer was nothing more than a facade.

"I wasn't finished. I wasn't even started yet."

"Damn it," he swore, scrubbing at his eyes again and pounding the arm of his chair. "*Damn* it anyway!" What careless god had caused her to choose the very words *he* had used, fifteen years ago?

Fifteen years ago, when a stupid accident had left him paralyzed from the waist down and put an end—he thought—to his dreams for med school?

Fifteen years ago, when Doctor Harwat Kline-Bes was *his* doctor and had heard him weeping alone into his pillow?

He turned his chair and opened the viewport out into the stars, staring at them as they moved past in a panorama of perfect beauty that changed with the rotation of the station. He let the tears dry on his cheeks, let his mind empty.

Fifteen years ago, another neurologist had heard those stammered, heartbroken words, and had determined that they would *not* become a truth. He had taken a paraplegic young student, bullied the makers of an experimental Moto-Chair into giving the youngster one—then bullied the dean of the Meyasor State Medical College into admitting the boy. *Then* he had seen to it that once the boy graduated, he got an internship in this very hospital—a place where a neurologist in a Moto-Chair was no great curiosity, not with the sentients of a hundred worlds coming in as patients *and* doctors. . . .

A paraplegic, though. Not a quad. Not a child with a brilliant, flexible mind, trapped in an inert body.

Brilliant mind. Inert body. Brilliant—

An idea blinded him, it occurred so suddenly. He was *not* the only person watching Tia—there was one other. Someone who watched every patient here, every doctor, every nurse. . . . Someone he didn't consult too often, because Lars wasn't a medico, or a shrink—

But in this case, Lars' opinion was likely to be more accurate than anyone else's on this station. Including his own.

He thumbed a control. "Lars," he said shortly. "Got a minute, buddy?"

He had to wait for a moment. Lars was a busy guy—though hopefully at this hour there weren't too many demands on his conversational circuits. "Certainly, Kenny," Lars replied after a few seconds. "How can I help the neurological *wunderkind* of Central Worlds MedStation *Pride of Albion*? Hmm?" The voice was rich and ironic; Lars rather enjoyed teasing everyone onboard. He called it "therapeutic deflation of egos." He particularly liked deflating Kenny's—he had said more than once that everyone else was so afraid of being "unkind to the poor cripple" that they danced on eggs to avoid telling him when he was full of it.

"Can the sarcasm, Lars," Kenny replied. "I've got a serious problem that I want your opinion on."

"My opinion?" Lars sounded genuinely surprised. "This must be a personal opinion—I'm certainly not qualified to give you a medical one."

"Most definitely, a very personal opinion, one that you are the best suited to give. On Hypatia Cade."

"Ah." Kenny thought that Lars' tone softened considerably. "The little child in the Neuro unit, with the unchildlike taste in holos. She still thinks I'm the AI. I haven't dissuaded her."

"Good, I want her to be herself around you, for the gods of space know she won't be herself around the rest of us." He realized that his tone had gone savage and carefully regained control over himself before he continued. "You've got her records and you've watched the kid herself. I know she's old for it—but how would she do in the shell program?"

A long pause. Longer than Lars needed simply to access and analyze records. "Has her condition stabilized?" he asked, cautiously. "If it hasn't—if she goes brain-inert halfway into her schooling—it'd not only make problems for anyone else you'd want to bring in late, it'll traumatize the other shell-kids badly. They don't handle death well. I wouldn't be a party to frightening them, however inadvertently."

Kenny massaged his temple with the long, clever fingers that had worked so many surgical miracles for others and could do nothing for this little girl. "As far as we can tell anything about this—disease—yes, she's stable," he said finally. "Take a look in there and you'll see I ordered a shotgun approach while we were testing her. She's had a full course of every anti-viral neurological agent we've got a record of. *And* non-invasive things like a course of ultra—well, you can see it there. I think we killed it, whatever it was."

Too late to help her. Damn it.

"She's brilliant," Lars said cautiously. "She's flexible. She has the ability to multi-thread, to do several things at once. And she's had good, positive reactions to contact with shellpersons in the past."

"So?" Kenny asked, impatiently, as the stars passed by in their courses, indifferent to the fate of one little girl. "Your opinion."

"I think she can make the transition," Lars said, with more emphasis than Kenny had ever heard in his voice before. "I think she'll not only make the transition, she'll do *well*."

He let out the breath he'd been holding in a sigh.

"Physically, she is certainly no worse off than many in the shellperson program, including yours truly," Lars continued. "Frankly, Kenny, she's got so much potential it would be a crime to let her rot in a hospital room for the rest of her life."

The careful control Lars normally had over his voice was gone; there was passion in his words that Kenny had never heard him display until this moment. "Got to you, too, did she?" he said dryly.

"Yes," Lars said, biting off the word. "And I'm not ashamed of it. I don't mind telling you that she had me in—well, not tears, but certainly the equivalent."

"Good for you." He rubbed his hands together, warming cold fingers. "Because I'm going to need your connivance again."

"Going to pull another fast one, are you?" Lars asked with ironic amusement.

"Just a few strings. What good does being a stellar intellect do me, if I can't make use of the position?" he asked rhetorically. He shut the viewport and pivoted his chair to face his desk, keying on his terminal and linking it directly to Lars and a very personal database. One called "Favors." "All right, my friend, let's get to work. First, whose strings can you jerk? Then, who on the political side has influence in the program, of that set, who owes me the most, and of that subset, who's due here the soonest?"

A Sector Secretary-General did not grovel, nor did he gush, but to Kenny's immense satisfaction, when Quintan Waldheim-Querar y Chan came aboard the *Pride of Albion*, the very first thing he wanted, after all the official inspections and the like were over, was to meet with the brilliant neurologist whose work had saved his nephew from the same fate as Kenny himself. He already knew most of what there was to know about Kenny and his meteoric career.

And Quintan Waldheim-Querar y Chan was not the sort to avoid an uncomfortable topic.

"A little ironic, isn't it?" the Secretary-General said, after the firm handshake, with a glance at Kenny's Moto-Chair. He stood up and did *not* tug self-consciously at his conservative dark blue tunic.

Kenny did not smile, but he took a deep breath of satisfaction. *Doubly good. No more calls, we have a winner.*

"What, that my injury was virtually identical to Peregrine's?" he replied immediately. "Not ironic at all, sir. The fact that I found myself in this position was what prompted me to go into neurology in the first place. I won't try to claim that if I *hadn't* been injured, and *hadn't* worked so hard to find a remedy for the same injuries, someone else might not have come up with the same answer that I did. Medical research is a matter of building on what has come before, after all."

"But without your special interest, the solution might well have come too late to do Peregrine any good," the Secretary-General countered. "And it was not only your technique, it was your skill that pulled him through. There is no duplication of that—not in this sector, anyway. That's why I arranged for this visit. I wanted to thank you."

Kenny shrugged deprecatingly. This was the most perfect opening he'd ever seen in his life—and he had no intention of letting it get away from him. Not when he had the answer to Tia's prayers trapped in his office.

"I can't win them all, sir," he said flatly. "I'm not a god. Though there are times I wish most profoundly that I was, and right now is one of them."

The Great Man's expression sobered. The Secretary-General was not just a Great Man because he was an excellent administrator; he was one because he had a human side, and that human and humane side could be touched. "I take it you have a case that is troubling you?" Then, conscious of the fact that he Owed Kenny, he said the magic words. "Perhaps I can help?"

Kenny sighed, as if he were reluctant to continue the discussion. *Wouldn't do to seem too eager.* "Well—would you care to see some tape of the child?"

Child. Children were one of the Great Man's weaknesses. He had sponsored more child-oriented programs than any three of his predecessors combined. "Yes. If it would not be violating the child's privacy."

"Here—" Kenny flicked a switch, triggering the holo-record he already had keyed up. A record he and Anna had put together. Carefully edited, carefully selected, compiled from days of recordings with Lars' assistance and the psych-profile of the Great Man to guide them. "I promise I won't take more than fifteen minutes of your time."

The first seven and a half minutes of this recording were of Tia at her most attractive; being very brave and cheerful for the interns and her parents. "This is Hypatia Cade, the daughter of Pota Andropolous-Cade and Braddon Maartens-Cade," he explained, over the holo. Quickly he outlined her background and her pathetic little story, stressing her high intelligence, her flexibility, her responsibility. "The prognosis isn't very cheerful, I'm afraid," he said, watching his chrono carefully to time his speech with the end of that section of tape. "No matter what we do, she's doomed to spend the rest of her life in some institution or other. The only way she could be at all mobile would be through direct synaptic connections—well, we don't do that here—they can only link in that way at Lab Schools, the shellperson project—"

He stopped, as the holo flickered and darkened. Tia was alone.

The arm of her chair reached out and grasped the sad little blue bear, hidden until now by the tray table and a pillow. It brought the toy in close to her face, and she gently rubbed her cheek against its soft fur coat. The lightning-bolt of the Courier Service on its shirt stood out clearly in this shot . . . one reason why Kenny had chosen it.

"They've gone, Ted," she whispered to her bear. "Mum and Dad—they've gone back to the Institute. There's nobody left here but you, now."

A single bright tear formed in one corner of her eye and slowly rolled down her cheek, catching what little light there was in the room.

"What? Oh, no, it's not their fault, Ted—they had to. The Institute said so, I saw the dispatch. It said—it said since I w-w-wasn't going to get any b-b-b-better there was no p-p-p-point in—in—wasting v-v-valuable t-t-time—"

She sobbed once, and buried her face in the teddy bear's fur.

After a moment, her voice came again, muffled. "Anyway, it hurts them so m-much. And it's s-s-so hard to be b-brave for them. But if I cried, th-they'd only feel w-worse. I think m-maybe it's b-better this way, don't you? Easier. F-for every-b-b-b-body. . . ."

The holo flickered again; same time, nearly the same position, but a different day. This time she was crying openly, tears coursing down her cheeks as she sobbed into the bear's little shirt. "We've given her the complete run of the library and the holo collection," Kenny said, very softly. "Normally, they keep her relatively amused and stimulated—but just before we filmed this, she picked out an episode of *The Stellar Explorers*—and—well—her parents said she had planned to be a pilot, you see—"

She continued to cry, sobbing helplessly, the only understandable words being "—Teddy—I wanted—to go—I wanted to see the *stars*—"

The holo flickered out, as Kenny turned the lights in his office back up. He reached for a tissue and wiped his eyes without shame. "I'm afraid she affects me rather profoundly," he said, and smiled weakly. "So much for my professional detachment."

The Great Man blinked rapidly to clear his own eyes. "Why isn't something being done for that child?" he demanded, his voice hoarse.

"We've done all we can—here," Kenny said. "The only possibility of giving that poor child any kind of a life is to get her into the shellperson program. But the Psychs at the Laboratory Schools seem to think she's too old. They wouldn't even send someone to come evaluate her, even though the parents petitioned them and we added our own recommendations. . . ."

He let the sentence trail off significantly. The Secretary-General gave him a sharp look. "And you don't agree with them, I take it?"

Kenny shrugged. "It isn't just my opinion," he said smoothly. "It's the opinion of the staff Psych assigned to her, the shellperson running this station, and a brainship friend of hers in the Courier Service. The one," he added delicately, "who gave her that little bear."

Mentioning the bear sold the deal; Kenny could see it in the Great Man's expression. "We'll just see about that," the Secretary-General said. "The people you talked to don't have all the answers—and they *certainly* don't have the final say." He stood up and offered Kenny his hand again. "I won't promise anything—but don't be surprised if there's someone from the Laboratory Schools here to see her in the next few days. How soon can you have her ready for transfer, if they take her?"

"Within twelve hours, sir," Kenny replied, secretly congratulating himself for getting her parents to sign a writ-of-consent before they left. Of course, they thought it was for experimental procedures.

Then again, Pota and Braddon had been the ones who'd broached the idea of the shellperson program to the people at the Laboratory Schools and been turned down because of Tia's age.

"Twelve hours?" The Great Man raised an eyebrow. Kenny returned him look for look.

"Her parents are under contract to the Archeological Institute," he explained. "The Institute called them back out into the field, because their parental emergency leave was up. They weren't happy, but it was obey or be fired. Hard to find another job in that field that isn't with the Institute." He coughed. "Well, they trusted my work, and made me Tia's full guardian before they left."

"So you have right-of-disposition and guardianship. Very tidy." The Secretary-General's wry smile showed that he knew he had been maneuvered into this—and that he was not annoyed. "All right. There'll be someone from the schools here within the week. Unless there's something you haven't told me about the girl, he should finish his evaluation in two days. At the end of those two days . . ." One eyebrow raised significantly. "Well, it would be very convenient if he could take the new recruit back with him, wouldn't it?"

"Yes, sir," Kenny said happily. "It would indeed, sir."

If it hadn't been for Doctor Uhua-Sorg's reputation and the pleas of his former pupil, Lars Mendoza, Philip Gryphon bint Brogen would have been only too happy to tell the committee where to stick the Secretary-General's request. *And* what to do with it after they put it there. One did *not* pull strings to get an unsuitable candidate into the shell program! Maybe the Secretary-General thought he could get away with that kind of politicking with Academy admissions, but he was going to find out differently *here.*

Philip was not inclined to be coaxed and *would not* give in to bullying. So it was in a decidedly belligerent state of mind that he disembarked from his shuttle onto the docks of the *Pride of Albion.* Like every hospital station, this one affronted him with its sterile white walls and atmosphere of self-importance.

There was someone waiting—obviously for him—in the reception area. Someone in a Moto-Chair. A handsome young man with thick dark hair and a thin, ascetic face.

If they think they can soften me up by assigning me to someone they think I won't dare be rude to—he thought savagely, as the young man glided the Chair toward him. *Conniving beggars*—

"Professor Brogen?" said the ridiculously young, vulnerable-looking man, holding out his hand. "I'm Doctor Sorg."

"If you think I'm going to—" Brogen began, *not* reaching out to take it—then the name registered on him and he did a classic double-take. "*Doctor* Sorg? Doctor Uhua-Sorg?"

The young man nodded, just the barest trace of a smile showing on his lips.

"Doctor *Kennet* Uhua-Sorg?" Brogen asked, feeling as if he'd been set up, yet knowing he had set up himself for this particular fall.

"Yes indeed," the young man replied. "I take it that you weren't—ah—expecting me to meet you in person."

A chance for an out—not a graceful one, but an out—and Brogen took it. "Hardly," he replied brusquely. "The Chief of Neurosurgery and Neurological Research usually does not meet a simple professor on behalf of an ordinary child."

"Tia is far from ordinary, Professor," Doctor Sorg responded, never once losing that hint of smile. "Any more than you are a 'simple' professor. But, if you'll follow me, you'll find out about Tia for yourself."

Well, he's right about one thing, Brogen thought grudgingly, after an hour spent in Tia's company while hordes of interns and specialists pestered, poked and prodded her. *She's not ordinary. Any "ordinary" child would be having a screaming tantrum by now.* She was an extraordinarily attractive child as well as a patient one; her dark hair had been cropped short to keep it out of the way, but her thin, pixie-like face and big eyes made her look like the model for a Victorian fairy. A fairy trapped in a fist of metal . . . tormented and teased by a swarm of wasps.

"How much longer is this going to go on?" he asked Kennet Sorg in an irritated whisper.

Kennet raised one eyebrow. "That's for you to say," he replied. "You are here to evaluate her. If you want more time alone with her, you have only to say the word. This is her second session for the day, by the way," he added, and Brogen could have sworn there was a hint of—smugness?—in his voice. "She played host to another swarm this morning, between nine and noon."

Now Brogen was outraged, but on the child's behalf. Kennet Sorg must have read that in his expression, for he turned his chair towards the cluster of white-uniformed interns, cleared his throat, and got their instant attention.

"That will be all for today," he said quietly. "If you please, ladies and gentlemen, Professor Brogen would like to have some time with Tia alone."

There were looks of disappointment and some even of disgust cast Brogen's way, but he ignored them. The child, at least, looked relieved.

Before he could say anything to Kennet Sorg, he realized that the doctor had followed the others out the door, which was closing behind his chair, leaving Brogen alone with the child. He cleared his own throat awkwardly.

The little girl looked at him with a most peculiar expression in her eyes. Not fear, but wariness.

"You're not a Psych, are you?" she asked.

"Well—no," he said. "Not exactly. I'll probably ask some of the same questions, though."

She sighed, and closed her blue eyes for a moment. "I'm *very* tired of having my head shrunk," she replied forthrightly. "Very, *very* tired. And it isn't going to make any difference at all in the way I think, anyway. It isn't *fair*, but this—" she bobbed her chin at her chair "—isn't going to go away because it isn't fair. Right?"

"Sad, but true, my dear." He began to relax, and realized why. Kennet Sorg was right. This was no ordinary child; talking with her was not like talking to a child—but it *was* like talking to one of the kids in the shell program. "So—how about if we chat about something else entirely. Do you know any shellpersons?"

She gave him an odd look. "They must not have told you very much about me," she said. "Either that, or you didn't pay very much attention. One of my very best friends is a brainship—Moira Valentine-Maya. She gave me Theodore."

Theodore? Oh—right. The bear—He cast a quick glance over towards the bed—and there was the somber-looking little bear in a Courier Service shirt that he'd been told about.

"Did you ever think about what being in a shell must be like?" he asked, fishing for a way to explain the program to her without letting her know she was being evaluated.

"Of *course* I did!" she said, not bothering to hide her scorn. "I told Moira that I wanted to be just like her when I grew up, and she laughed at me and told me all about what the schools were like and everything—"

And then, before he could say anything, the unchildlike child proceeded to tell *him* about his own program. The brainship side, at any rate.

Pros and cons. From having to be able to multi-task, to the thrill of experiencing a singularity and warp-space firsthand. From being locked forever in a metal skin, to the loneliness of knowing that you were going to outlive all your partners but the last . . .

"I told her that I guessed I didn't want to go in when I figured out that you could never touch anybody again," she concluded, wearily. "I know you've got sensors to the skin and everything, but that was what I didn't like. Kind of funny, huh?"

"Why?" he asked without thinking.

"Because now—I can't touch anybody. And I won't ever again. So it's kind of funny. I can't touch anyone anymore, but I can't be a brainship either." The tired resignation in her voice galvanized him.

"I don't know why you couldn't," he said, aware that he had already made up his mind, and both aghast and amused at himself. "There's room in this year's class for another couple of new candidates; there's even room in the brainship category for one or two pupils."

She blinked at him, then blurted, "But they told me I was too old!"

He laughed. "My dear, *you* wouldn't be too old if you were your mother's age. You would have been a good shell-program candidate well past puberty." He still couldn't believe this child; responsible, articulate, flexible. . . . Lars and Kennet Sorg had been right. It made him wonder how many other children had been rejected out of hand, simply because of age—how many had been lost to a sterile existence in an institution, just because they had no one as persistent and as influential as Kennet Sorg to plead their cases.

Well, one thing at a time. Grab this one now. Put something in place to take care of the others later. "I'm going to have to go through the motions and file the paperwork—but Tia, if you want, you can consider yourself recruited this very instant."

"*Yes!*" she burst out. "Oh, yes! Yes, yes, yes! Oh, please, thank you, thank you so much—" Her cheeks were wet with tears, but the joy on her face was so intense that it was blinding. Professor Brogen blinked and swallowed a lump in his throat.

"The advantage of recruiting someone your age," he said, ignoring her tears and his tickling eyes, "is that you can make your career path decision right away. Shellpersons don't all go into brainships—for instance, you *could* opt for a career with the Institute; they've been asking to hire a shellperson to head their home-base research section for the last twenty years. You could do original research on the findings of others—even your parents' discoveries. You could become a Spaceport Administrator, or a Station Administrator. You could go into law, or virtually any branch of science. Even medicine. With the synaptic links we have, there is no career you cannot consider."

"But I want to be a brainship," she said firmly.

Brogen took a deep breath. While he agreed with her emotionally—well, there were some serious drawbacks. "Tia, a lot of what a brainship does is—well, being a truck driver or a cabby. Ferrying people or things from one place to another. It isn't very glamorous work. It *is* quite dangerous, both physically and psychologically. You would be very valuable, and yet totally unarmed, unless you went into the military branch, which I don't think you're suited for, frankly. You would be a target for thieves and malcontents. And there is one other thing; the *ship* is very expensive. In my not-so-humble opinion, brainship service is just one short step from indentured slavery. You are literally paying for the use and upkeep of that ship by mortgaging yourself. There is very little chance of buying your contract out in any reasonable length of time unless you do something truly spectacular or take on very dangerous duties. The former isn't likely to happen in ordinary service—and you won't be able to exchange boring service for whatever your fancy is."

Tia looked stubborn for a moment, then thoughtful. "All of that is true," she said, finally. "But—Professor, Dad always said I had his astrogator genes, and I was already getting into tensor physics, so I *have* the head for starflight. And it's what I want."

Brogen turned up his hands. "I can't argue with that. There's no arguing with preferences, is there?" In a way, he was rather pleased. As self-possessed as Tia was, she would do very well in brainship service. And as stable as she seemed to be, there was very little chance of her having psychological problems, unless something completely unforeseen came up.

She smiled shyly. "Besides, I talked this over with Moira—you know, giving her ideas on how she could get some extra credits to help with all her fines for bouncing her brawns? Since she was with Archeology and Exploration as a courier, there were lots of chances for her to see things that the surveyors might not, and I kind of told her what to look for. I kind of figured that with my background, it wouldn't be too hard to get assigned to A and E myself, and I could do the same things, only better. I could get a *lot* of credits that way. And once I owned my ship—well, I could do whatever I wanted."

Brogen couldn't help himself; he started to laugh. "You are quite the young schemer, did you know that?"

She grinned, looking truly happy for the first time since he had seen her. Now that he had seen the real thing, he recognized all her earlier "smiles" for the shams that they had been.

Leaving her here would have been a crime. A sin.

"Well, you can consider yourself recruited," he said comfortably. "I'll fill out the paperwork tonight, databurst it to the schools as soon as I finish, and there should be a confirmation waiting for us when we wake up. Think you can be ready to ship out in the morning?"

"Yes, sir," she said happily.

He rose and started to leave—then paused for a moment.

"You know," he said, "you were right. I really didn't pay too much attention to the file they gave me on you, since I was so certain that—well, never mind. But I am terribly curious about your name. Why on earth did your parents call you 'Hypatia'?"

Tia laughed out loud, a peal of infectious joy.

"I think, Professor Brogen," she said, "that you'd better sit back down!"

CHAPTER THREE

CenCom's softperson operator had a pleasant voice and an equally pleasant habit of *not* starting a call with a burst of static or an alert-beep. "XH One-Oh-Three-Three, you have an incoming transmission. Canned message beam."

Tia tore herself away from the latest papers on the Salomon-Kildaire Entities with a purely mental sigh of regret. Oh, she could take in a databurst *and* scan the papers at the same time, certainly, but she wanted to do more than simply scan the information. She wanted to absorb it, so that she could think about it later in detail. There were nuances to academic papers that simple scanning wouldn't reveal; places where you had to know the personality of the author in order to read between the lines. Places where what *wasn't* written were as important as what *was*.

"Go ahead, CenCom," she replied, wondering who on earth—or off it, for that matter—could be calling her.

Strange how we've been out of Terran subspace for so long, and yet we still use expressions like "how on earth" . . . there's probably a popular-science paper in that.

The central screen directly opposite the column she was housed in flickered for a moment, then filled with the image of a thin-faced man in an elaborate Moto-Chair. No—more than a Moto-Chair; this one was kind of a platform for something else. She saw what could only be an APU, and a short-beam broadcast unit of

61

some kind. It looked like his legs and waist were encased in the bottom half of space armor!

But there was no mistaking who was in the strange exoskeleton. Doctor Kenny.

"Tia, my darling girl, congratulations on your graduation!" Kenny said, eyes twinkling. "You should—given the vagaries of the CenCom postal system—have gotten your graduation present from Lars and Anna and me. I hope you liked it—them—"

The graduation present *had* arrived on time, and Tia had been enthralled. She loved instrumental music, synthcom in particular, but these recordings had special meaning for any shellperson, for they had been composed and played by David Weber-Tcherkasky, a shellperson himself, and they were not meant for the limited ears of softpeople. The composer had made use of every note of the aural spectrum, with super-complexes of overtones and counterpoint that left softpersons squinting in bewilderment. They weren't for everyone—not even for some shellpersons—but Tia didn't think she would ever get tired of listening to them. Every time she played them, she heard something new.

"—anyway, I remembered you saying in your last transmission how much you liked Lanz Manhem's synthcom recordings, and Lars kept telling me that Tcherkasky's work was to Manhem's what a symphony was to birdsong." Kenny shrugged and grinned. "We figured that it would help to while away the in-transit hours for you, anyway. Anna said the graduation was stellar—I'm sorry I couldn't be there, but you're looking at the reason why."

He made a face and gestured down at the lower half of his body. "Moto-Prosthetics decided in their infinite wisdom that since I had benefited from their expertise in the past, I *owed* them. They convinced the hospital Admin Head that I was the only possible person to test this contraption of theirs. This is *supposed* to be something that will let me stroll around a room—or more importantly, stand in an operating theater for as long as I need to. When it's working, that is." He shook his head. "Buggy as a new software system, let me tell you. Yesterday the fardling thing locked up on me, with one foot in the air. Wasn't *I* just a charming sight, posing in the middle of the hall like a dancer in a Greek frieze! Think I'm going to rely on my old Chair when I really *need* to do something, at least for a while."

Tia chuckled at the mental image of Kenny frozen in place and unable to move.

He shook his head and laughed. "Well, between this piece of—ah—hardware, and my patients, I had to send Anna as our official deputation. Hope you've forgiven Lars and me, sweetheart—"

A voice, warm and amused, interrupted Doctor Kenny. "There was just a wee problem with *my* getting leave, after all," Lars said, over the office speakers, as Kenny grinned. "And they simply wouldn't let me de-orbit the station and take it down to the schools for the graduation ceremony. *Very* inconsiderate of them, *I* say."

Tia had to laugh at that.

"That just means you'll have to come visit *me*. Now that you're one of the club, far-traveler, we'll have to exchange softie-jokes. How many softies *does* it take to change a lightbulb?"

Kenny made a rude noise. Although he looked tired, Tia noted that he seemed to be in very good spirits. There was only one thing that combination meant; he'd pulled off another miracle. "I resemble that remark," he said. "Anyway, Lars got your relay number, so you'll be hearing from us—probably more often than you want! We love you, lady! Big Zen hugs from both of us!"

The screen flickered and went blank; Tia sighed with contentment. Lars had been the one to come up with "Zen hugs"—"the hugs that you would get, if we were there, if we could hug you, but we aren't, and we can't"—and he and Kenny began using them in their weekly transmissions to Tia all through school. Before long her entire class began using the phrase, so pointedly apt for shellpeople, and now it was spreading across known space. Kenny had been amused, especially after one of his recovering patients got the phrase in a transmission from his stay-at-home, technophobic wife!

Well, the transmission put the cap on her day, that was certain. And the perfect climax to the beginning of her new life. Anna and her parents at the graduation ceremony, Professor Brogen handing out the special awards she'd gotten in Xenology, Diplomacy, and First Contact Studies, Moira showing up at the landing field the same day she was installed in her ship, still with Tomas, wonder of wonders. . . .

Having Moira there to figuratively hold her hand during the nasty process of partial anesthesia while the techs hooked her up in her column had been worth platinum.

She shuddered at the memory. Oh, they could *describe* the feelings (or rather, lack of them) to you, they could psych you up for experience, and you *thought* you were ready, but the moment of truth, when you lost everything but primitive com and the few sensors in the shell itself . . . was horrible. Something out of the worst of nightmares.

And she still remembered what it had been like to live with only softperson senses. She couldn't imagine what it was like for those who'd been popped into a shell at birth. It had brought back all the fear and feeling of helplessness of her time in the hospital.

It had been easier with Moira there. But if the transfer had been a journey through sensory-deprivation hell, waking up in the ship had been pure heaven.

No amount of simulator training conveyed what it *really* felt like, to have a living, breathing ship wrapped around you.

It was a moment that had given her back everything she had lost. Never mind that her "skin" was duralloy metal, her "legs" were engines, her "arms" the servos she used to maintain herself inside and out. That her "lungs" and "heart" were the life-support systems that would keep her brawn alive. That all of her senses were ship's sensors linked through brainstem relays. None of that mattered. She had a body again! That was a moment of ecstasy no one plugged into a shell at birth would ever understand. Moira did, though . . . and it had been wonderful to be able to share that moment of elation.

And Tomas understood, as only a brawn-partner of long-standing could. Tomas had arranged for Theodore Edward Bear to have his own little case built into the wall of the central cabin as *his* graduation present. "And decom anyone who doesn't understand," he said firmly, putting a newly cleaned Ted behind his plexi panel and closing the door. "A brawn is only a brawn, but a bear is a friend for life!"

So now the solemn little blue bear in his Courier Service shirt reigned as silent supervisor over the central cabin, and to perdition with whatever the brawns made of him. Well, let them think it was some kind of odd holo-art. Speaking of which, the next set of brawn-candidates was due shortly. *We'll see how they react to Ted.*

Tia returned to her papers, keeping a running statistical analysis and cross-tabulations on anything that seemed interesting. And there *were* things that seemed to be showing up, actually. Pockets of mineral depletions in the area around the EsKay sites; an astonishing similarity in the periodicity and seasonality of the planets and planetoids. Insofar as a Mars-type world could *have* seasons, that is. But the periodicity—identical to within an hour. Interesting. Had they been *that* dependent on natural sunlight? Come to think of it—yes, solar distances were very similar. And they were all Sol-type stars.

She turned her attention to her parents' latest papers, letting the EsKay discoveries stew in the back of her mind. Pota and Braddon were the Schliemanns of modern archeology, but it wasn't the EsKays that brought them fame, at least, not directly. After Tia's illness, they couldn't bring themselves to return to their old dig, or even the EsKay project—and for once, the Institute committees acted like something other than AIs with chips instead of hearts. Pota and Braddon were reassigned to a normal atmosphere water-world of high volcanic activity and thousands of tiny islands with a good population of nomadic sentients, something as utterly unlike the EsKay planets as possible. And it had been there that they made their discovery. Tracing the legends of the natives, of a king who first defied the gods and then challenged them, they replicated Schliemann's famous discovery of ancient Troy, uncovering an entire city buried by a volcanic eruption. Perfectly preserved for all time. For this world and these people, it was the equivalent of an Atlantis and Pompeii combined, for the city was of Bronze Age technology while the latter-day sentients were still struggling along with flint, obsidian, and shell, living in villages of no more than two hundred. While the natives of the present day were amphibious, leaning towards the aquatic side, *these* ancients were almost entirely creatures of dry land....

The discovery made Pota and Braddon's reputation; there was more than enough there to keep fifty archeologists busy for a hundred years. Ta'hianna became their life-project, and they rarely left the site anymore. They even established a permanent residence aboard a kind of glorified houseboat.

Tia enjoyed reading their papers—and the private speculations they had brought her, with some findings that weren't in the papers yet—but the Ta'hianna project simply didn't give her the thrill of mystery that the EsKays did.

And—there was one other thing. Years of analyzing every little nuance of those dreadful weeks had made her decide that what had happened to her could just as easily happen to some other unwitting archeologist. Or even—another child.

Only finding the homeworld of the EsKays would give the Institute and Central World's Medical the information they needed to prevent another tragedy like Tia's.

If Tia had anything at all to say about it, *that* would never happen again. The next person infected might not be so lucky. The next person, if an adult, or even a child unfortunate enough to be less flexible and less intelligent than she had been, would likely have no choice but to spend the remainder of a fairly miserable life in a Moto-Chair and a room. . . .

"XH One-Oh-Three-Three, your next set of brawn-candidates is ready," CenCom said, interrupting her brooding thoughts. "You *are* going to pick one of these, aren't you?" the operator added wearily.

"I don't know yet," she replied, levelly. "I haven't interviewed them." She had rejected the first set of six entirely. CenCom obviously thought she was being a prima donna. *She* simply thought she was being appropriately careful. After all, since she was officially assigned to A and E with special assignment to the Institute, she had gotten precisely what she expected—a ship *without* Singularity Drive. Those were top-of-the-line, expensive, and not the sort of thing that the Institute could afford to hire. So, like Moira, she would be spending a *lot* of time in transit. Unlike Moira, she did not intend to find herself bouncing brawns so often that her buy-out had doubled because of the fines.

Spending a lot of time in transit meant a lot of time with only her brawn for company. She wanted someone who was bright, first of all. At least as bright as Tomas and Charlie. She wanted someone who would be willing to add her little crusade to the standard agenda and give it equal weight with what they had officially been assigned. She rather thought she would like to have a male, although she hadn't rejected any of the brawns just because they were female.

Most of all, she wanted someone who would *like* her; someone who would be a real partner in every sense. Someone who would willingly spend time with her when he could be doing other things; a friend, like Kenny and Anna, Moira and Lars.

And someone with some personality. Two of the last batch—both females—had exhibited all the personality of a cube of tofu.

That might do for another ship, another brain that didn't want to be bothered with softpersons outside of duty, but she wanted someone she could *talk* to! After all, she had been a softperson once.

"Who's first?" she asked CenCom, lowering her lift so that he—or she—could come aboard without having to climb the stairs.

"That'll be Donning Chang y Narhan," CenCom replied after a moment. "Really high marks in the Academy."

She scanned the databurst as Donning crossed the tarmac to the launch pad; he'd gotten high marks all right, though not stellar. Much like her; in the top tenth of the class, but not the top one percent. *Very* handsome, if the holo was to be believed; wavy blond hair, bright blue eyes, sculptured face with holo-star looks—sculptured body, too. But Tia was wary of good looks by now. Two of the first lot had been gorgeous; one had been one of the blocks of tofu, with nothing between the ears but what the Academy had put there, and the other had only wanted to talk about himself.

Movement outside alerted her to Donning's arrival; to her annoyance, he operated the lift manually instead of letting her handle it.

To her further annoyance, he treated her like some kind of superior AI; he was obviously annoyed with having to go through an interview in the first place and wanted to be elsewhere.

"Donning Chang y Narhan, reporting," he said in a bored tone of voice. "As ordered." He proceeded to rattle off everything that had been in the short file, as if she couldn't access it herself. He did not sit down. He paid no attention to Ted.

"Have you any questions?" he asked, making it sound as if questions would only mean that she had not been paying attention.

"Only a few," she replied. "What is your favorite composer? Do you play chess?"

He answered her questions curtly, as if they were so completely irrelevant that he couldn't believe she was asking them.

She obliged him by suggesting that he could leave after only a handful of questions; he took it with bad grace and left in a hurry, an aroma of scorched ego in his wake.

"Garrison Lebrel," CenCom said, as Donning vacated the lift.

Well, Garrison was possible. Good academic marks, not as high as Donning's but not bad. Interest in archeology . . . she perked up when she saw *what* he was interested in. Nonhumans, especially presumed extinct space-going races, including the EsKays!

Garrison let her bring him in and proved to be talkative, if not precisely congenial. He was *very* intense.

"We'll be spending a lot of time in transit," he said. "I wasn't able to keep up with the current literature in archeology while I was in the Academy, and I planned to be doing a lot of reading."

Not exactly sociable. "Do you play chess?" she asked hopefully. He shook his head. "But I do play sennet. That's an ancient Egyptian game—I have a very interesting software version I could install; I doubt it would take you long to learn it, though it takes a lifetime to master."

The last was said a bit smugly. And there had been no offer from him to learn *her* game. Still, she did have access to far more computing power than he did; it wouldn't take her more than an hour to learn the game, if that.

"I see that your special interest is in extinct spacegoing races," she ventured. "I have a very strong background in the Salomon-Kildaire Entities."

He looked skeptical. "I think Doctor Russell Gaines-Barklen has probably dealt with them as fully as they need to be, although we'll probably have some chances to catch things survey teams miss. That's the benefit of being trained to look for specifics."

She finally sent him back with mixed feelings. He was arrogant, no doubt about it. But he was also competent. He shared her interests, but his pet theories differed wildly from hers. He was possible, if there were no other choices, but he wasn't what she was looking for.

"Chria Chance is up next," CenCom said when she reported she was ready for the next. "But you won't like her."

"Why, because she's got a name that's obviously assumed?" Neither CenCom nor the Academy cared what you called yourself, provided they knew the identity you had been born with and the record that went with it. Every so often someone wanted to adopt a pseudonym. Often it was to cover a famous High Family name—either because the bearer was a black sheep, or because (rarely) he or she didn't want special treatment. But sometimes a youngster got a notion into his or her head to take on a holostartype name.

"No," CenCom replied, not bothering to hide his amusement. "You won't like her because—well, you'll see."

Chria's records were good, about like Garrison's—with one odd note in the personality profile. *Nonconformist*, it said.

Well, there was nothing wrong with that. Pota and Braddon were certainly not conformists in any sense.

But the moment that Chria stepped into the central room, Tia knew that CenCom was right.

She wore her Academy uniform, all right—but it was a specially tailored one. Made entirely of leather; real leather, not synthetic. And she wore it entirely too well for Tia to feel comfortable around her. For the rest, she was rapier-thin, with a face like a clever fox and hair cut aggressively short. Tia already felt intimidated, and she hadn't even said anything yet!

Within a few minutes worth of questions, Chria shook her head. "You're a nice person, Tia," she said forthrightly, "and you and I would never partner well. I'd run right over you, and you'd sit there in your column, fuming and resentful, and you'd never say a word." She grinned with feral cheer. "I'm a carnivore, a hunter. I need someone who'll fight back! I enjoy a good fight!"

"You'd probably have us go chasing right after pirates," Tia said, a little resentful already. "If there were any in the neighborhood, you'd want us to look for them!"

"You bet I would," Chria responded without shame.

A few more minutes of exchange proved to Tia that Chria was right. It would never work. With a shade of regret, Tia bade her farewell. While she liked a good argument as well as the next person, she *didn't* like for arguments to turn into shouting matches, which was precisely what Chria enjoyed. She claimed it purged tensions.

Well, maybe it did. And maybe that was why her favorite form of music—to the exclusion of everything else—was opera. She was a fanatic, to put it simply, And Tia—well—wasn't.

But there was certainly a lot of emotion-purging and carrying on in those old operas. She had the feeling that Chria fancied herself as a kind of latter-day Valkyrie.

Hoy-yo to-ho.

She reported her rejection to CenCom, with the recommendation that *she* thought Chria Chance had the proper mental equipment to partner a ship in the Military Courier Service. "Between you, me, and the airwaves," CenCom replied, "that's my opinion, too. Bloodthirsty wench. Well, she'll get her chance. Military got your classmate Pol, and he's just as bloody-minded as she is. I'll see the recommendation goes in; meanwhile, next up is Harkonen Carl-Ulbright."

Carl was a disappointment. Average grades, and while he was congenial, Tia knew that *she* would run right over the top of *him*. He was shy, hardly ever ventured an opinion, and when he did, he could be induced to change it in an eye-blink. However—"Carl," she said, just before he went to the lift, making no effort to hide his discouragement. "My classmate Raul is the XR One-Oh-Two-Nine. I think you two would get along splendidly. I'm going to ask CenCom to set up your very next interview with him—he was just installed today and I *know* he hasn't got a brawn yet. Tell him I sent you."

That cheered up the young man considerably. He would be even more cheered when he learned that Raul had a Singularity Drive ship. And Tia would bet that his personality profile and Raul's matched to a hair. They'd make a great team, especially when their job included carrying VIP passengers. Neither of them would get in the way or resent it if the VIPs ignored them.

"I got all that, Tia," CenCom said as soon as the boy was gone. "Consider it logged. They ought to make you a Psych; a Counselor, at least. It was good of you to think of Raul; none of us could come up with a match for him, but we were trying to match him with females."

If she'd had hands, she would have thrown them up. "Become a Psych? Saints and agents of grace defend us!" she quipped. "I think *not*! Who's next?"

"Andrea Polo y de Gras," CenCom said. "You won't like her, either. She doesn't want you."

"With the Polo y de Gras name, I'm not surprised," Tia sighed. "Wants something with a little more zing to it than A and E, hmm? Would she be offended if I agreed with her before she bothered to come out here?"

"I doubt it," CenCom replied, "but let me check." A pause, and then he came back. "She's very pleased, actually. I think that she has something cooking with the Family, and the strings haven't had time to get pulled yet. Piff. High Families. I don't know *why* they send their children to Space Academy in the first place."

Tia felt moved to contradict him. "Because some of them do very well and become a credit to the Services," she replied, with just a hint of reproach.

"True, and I stand corrected. Well, your last brawn-candidate is the late Alexander Joli-Chanteu." The cheer in his voice told her that he was making a bad joke out of the situation.

"Late, hmm? That isn't going to earn *him* any gold stars in his Good-Bee Book," Tia said, a bit acidly. Her parents' fetish for punctuality had set a standard she expected those around her to match. *Especially* brawn-candidates.

Well, I can at least go over his records. She scanned them quickly and came up—confused. When Alexander was good, he was very, very, good. And when he was bad, he was abysmal. Often in the same subject. He would begin a class with the lowest marks possible, then suddenly catch fire, turn around, and pull a miraculous save at the end of the semester. *Erratic performances,* said his personality profile. Tia not only agreed, she thought that the evaluator was understating the case.

CenCom interrupted her confusion. "Whoop! He got right by me! Here he comes, Tia, ready or not!"

Alexander didn't bother with the lift, he ran up the stairs, arriving out of breath, with longish hair mussed and uniform rumpled.

That didn't earn him any points either, although it was better than Chria's leather.

He took a quick look around to orient himself, then turned immediately to face the central column where she was housed, a nicety that only Carl and Chria had observed. It didn't matter, really, and a lot of shellpersons didn't care, so long as the softpersons faced one set of "eyes" at least—but Tia felt, as Moira did, that it was more considerate of a brawn to face where you *were,* rather than empty cabin.

"Hypatia, dear lady, I am most humbly sorry to be late for this interview," he said, slowly catching his breath. "My *sensei* engaged me in a game of Go, and I completely lost all track of time."

He ran his blunt-fingered hand through his unruly dark hair and grinned ruefully, little smile-crinkles forming around his brown eyes. "And here I had a perfectly *wonderful* speech all memorized, about how fitting it is that the lady named for the last librarian at Alexandria and the brawn named for Alexander should become partners—and the run knocked it right out of my head!"

Well! He knows where my name came from! Or at least he had the courtesy and foresight to look it up. Hmm. She considered that for a moment, then put it in the "plus" column. He was not handsome, but he had a pleasant, blocky sort of face. He was short—well, so was the original Alexander, by both modern standards and those of his own time. She decided to put his general looks in the "plus" column too, along with his politeness. While she certainly wasn't going to choose her brawns on the basis of looks, it would be nice to have someone who provided a nice bit of landscape.

"Minus," of course, were for being late and very untidy when he finally did arrive.

"I think I can bring myself to forgive you," she said dryly. "Although I'm not certain just what exactly detained you."

"Ah—besides a hobby of ancient history, Terran history, that is, especially military history and strategy, I, ah—I cultivate certain kinds of martial arts." He ran his hand through his hair again, in what was plainly a nervous gesture. "Oriental martial arts. One soft form and one hard form. Tai Chi and Karate. I know most people don't think that's at all necessary, but, well, A and E Couriers *are* unarmed, and I don't like to think of myself as helpless. Anyway, my *sensei*—that's a martial arts Master—got me involved in a game of Go, and when you're playing against a Master there is *nothing* simple about *Go*." He bowed his head a moment and looked sheepish. "I lost all track of time, and they had to page me. I really am sorry about making you wait."

Tia wasn't quite sure what to make of that. "Sit down, will you?" she said absently, wondering why, with this fascination with things martial and military, he hadn't shown any interest in the Military Services. "Do you play chess as well?"

He nodded. "Chess, and Othello, and several computer games. And if you have any favorites that I don't know, I would be happy to learn them." He sat quietly, calmly, without any of Garrison's fidgeting. In fact, it was that very contrast with Garrison that made her decide resolutely *against* that young man. A few months of fidgeting, and she would be ready to trank him to keep him quiet.

"Why Terran history?" she asked, curiously. "That isn't the kind of fascination I'd expect to find in a—a space-jockey."

He grinned. It was a very engaging, lopsided grin. "What, haven't you interviewed my classmate Chria yet? Now there is someone with odd fascinations!" Behind the banter, Tia sensed a kind of affection, even though the tips of his ears went lightly red. "I started reading history because I was curious about *my* name, and got fascinated by Alexander's time period. One thing led to another, and the next thing *I* knew, every present I was getting was either a historical holotape or a bookdisk about history, and I was actually quite happy about the situation."

So he *did* know the origin of her name. "Then why military strategy?"

"Because all challenging games are games of strategy," he said. "I, ah—have a friend who's really a big games buff, my best friend when I was growing up, and I had to have some kind of edge on him. So I started studying strategy. *That* got me into *The Art of War* and that got me into Zen which got me into martial arts." He shrugged. "There you have it. One neat package. I think you'd really like Tai Chi, it's all about stress and energy flow and patterns, and it's a lot like Singularity mechanics and—"

"I'm sure," she interrupted, hauling him verbally back by the scruff of his neck. "But why didn't you opt for Military Service?"

"The same reason I studied martial arts—I don't like being helpless, but I don't want to *hurt* anyone," he replied, looking oddly distressed. "Both Tai Chi and Karate are about never using a bit more force than you need to, but Tai Chi is the essence of using greater force against itself, just like in *The Art of War*, and—"

Once again she had to haul him back to the question. He tended to go off on verbal tangents, she noticed. She continued to ask him questions, long after the time she had finished with the other brawns, and when she finally let him go, it was with a sense of dissatisfaction. He was the best choice so *far*, but although he was plainly both sensitive and intelligent, he showed no signs at all of any interest in *her* field. In fact, she had seen and heard nothing that would make her think he would be ready to help her in any way with her private quest.

As the sky darkened over the landing field, and the spaceport lights came on, glaring down on her smooth metal skin, she pondered all of her choices and couldn't come up with a clear winner. Alex was the best—but the rest were, for the most part, completely unsuitable. He was obviously absentminded, and his care for his person left a little to be desired. He wasn't exactly slovenly, but he did not wear his uniform with the air of distinction that Tia felt was required. In fact, on him it didn't look much like a uniform at all, more like a suit of comfortable, casual clothes. For the life of her, she couldn't imagine how he managed *that.*

His tendency to wander down conversational byways could be amusing in a social situation, but she could see where it could also be annoying to—oh—a Vegan, or someone like them. No telling what kind of trouble that could lead to, if they had to deal with AIs, who could be very literal-minded.

No, he wasn't perfect. In fact, he wasn't even close.

"XH One-Oh-Three-Three, you have an incoming transmission," CenCom broke in, disturbing her thoughts. "Hold onto your bustle, lady, it's the Wicked Witch of the West, and I think someone just dropped a house on her sister."

Whatever allusions the CenCom operator was making were lost on Tia, but the sharply impatient tone of her supervisor was not. "XH One-Oh-Three-Three, have you selected a brawn *yet?*" the woman asked, her voice making it sound as if Tia had been taking weeks to settle on a partner, rather than less than a day.

"Not yet, Supervisor," she replied, cautiously. "So far, to be honest, I don't think I've found anyone I can tolerate for truly long stretches of time."

That wasn't exactly the problem, but Beta Gerold y Caspian wouldn't understand the real problem. *She* might just as well be Vegan. She made very few allowances for the human vagaries of brawns and none at all for shellpersons.

"Hypatia, you're wasting time," Beta said crisply. "You're sitting here on the pad, doing nothing, taking up a launch-cradle, when you could already be out on courier-supply runs."

"I'm doing my best," Tia responded sharply. "But neither you nor I will be particularly happy if I toss my brawn out after the first run!"

"You've rejected six brawns that all *our* analysis showed were good matches for your personality," Beta countered. "All you'd have to do is compromise a little."

Six of those were matches for me? she thought, aghast. *Which ones? The tofu-personalities? The Valkyrie warrior? Spirits of space help me—Garrison? I thought I was nicer and—more interesting than that!*

But Beta was continuing, her voice taking on the tones of

a cross between a policeman and a professorial lecturer. "You know very well that it takes far too long between visits for these Class One digs. It leaves small parties alone for weeks and months at a time. Even when there's an emergency, our ships are so few and so scattered that it takes them days to reach people in trouble—and sometimes an *hour* can make all the difference, let alone a day! We needed you out there the *moment* you were commissioned!"

Tia winced inwardly.

She'd have suspected that Beta went straight for the sore spot deliberately, except that she knew that Beta did not have access to her records. So she didn't know Tia's background. The agency that oversaw the rights of shellpersons saw to that—to make it difficult for supervisors to use personal knowledge to manipulate the shellpersons under their control. In the old days, when supervisors had known everything about their shellpersons, they had sometimes deliberately created emotional dependencies in order to assure "loyalty" and fanatic service. It was far, far too easy to manipulate someone whose only contact to the real world was through sensors that could be disconnected.

Still, Beta was right. *If I'd had help earlier, I might not be here right now. I might be in college, getting my double-docs like Mum, thinking about what postgraduate work I wanted to do....*

"I'll tell you what," she temporized. "Let me look over the records and the interviews again and sleep on it. One of the things that the schools told us over and over was to *never* make a choice of brawns feeling rushed or forced." She hardened her voice just a little. "You don't want another Moira, do you?"

"All right," Beta said grudgingly. "But I have to warn you that the supply of brawns is not unlimited. There aren't many more for you to interview in this batch, and if I have to boot you out of here without one, I will. The Institute can't afford to have you sitting on the pad for another six months until the next class graduates."

Go out without a brawn? Alone? The idea had very little appeal. Very little at all. In fact, the idea of six months alone in deep space was frightening. She'd never had to do without *some* human interaction, even on the digs with Mum and Dad.

So while CenCom signed off, she reran her tapes of the interviews and re-scanned information on the twelve she had rejected.

And still could not come up with anyone she *knew,* without a shadow of a doubt, that she'd like to call "friend."

Someone was knocking—quietly—on the closed lift door. Tia, startled out of her brooding, activated the exterior sensors. Who could *that* be? It wasn't even dawn yet!

Her visitor's head jerked up and snapped around alertly to face the camera when he heard it swivel to center on him. The lights from the field were enough for her to "see" by, and she identified him immediately. "Hypatia, it's Alex," he whispered unnecessarily. "Can I talk to you?"

Since she *couldn't* reply to him without alerting the entire area to his clandestine and highly irregular visit, she lowered the lift for him, keeping it darkened. He slipped inside, and she brought him up.

"What are you *doing* here?" she demanded, once he was safely in her central cabin. "This is not appropriate behavior!"

"Hey," he said, "I'm unconventional. I like getting things done in unconventional ways. *The Art of War* says that the best way to win a war is never to do what they expect you to do—"

"I'm sure," she interrupted. "That may be all very well for someone in Military, but this is *not* a war, and I should be reporting you for this." Tia let a note of warning creep into her voice, wondering why she wasn't doing just that.

He ignored both the threat and the rebuke. "Your supervisor said you hadn't picked anyone yet," he said instead. "Why not?"

"Because I haven't," she retorted. "I don't like being rushed into things. Or pressured, either. Sit down."

He sat down rather abruptly, and his expression turned from challenging to wistful. "I didn't think you'd hold my being late against me," he said plaintively. "I thought we hit it off pretty well. When your supervisor said you'd spent more time with me than any of the other brawns, I thought for sure you'd choose me! What's wrong with me? There must be something! Maybe something I can change!"

"Well—I—" She was taken so aback by his bluntness, and caught unawares by his direct line of questioning, that she actually answered him. "I expect my brawns to be punctual—because they have to be precise, and not being punctual implies carelessness," she said. "I thought you looked sloppy, and I don't like sloppiness.

You seemed absentminded, and I had to keep bringing you back to the original subject when we were talking. Both of those imply wavering attention, and that's not good either. I'll be alone out there with my brawn, and I need someone I can depend on to do his job."

"You didn't see me at my best," he pointed out. "I was distracted, and I was thrown completely off-center by the fact that I had messed up by being late. But that isn't all, is it?"

"What do you mean by that?" she asked, cautiously.

"It wasn't just that I was—less than perfect. *You* have a secret . . . something you really want to do, that you haven't even told your supervisor." He eyed the column speculatively, and she found herself taken completely by surprise by the accuracy of his guess. "I don't match the profile of someone who might be interested in helping you with that secret. Right?"

His expression turned coaxing. "Come on, Hypatia, you can tell me," he said. "I won't tattle on you. And I might be able to help! You don't know that much about me, just what you got in an hour of talking and what's in the short-file!"

"I don't know what you're talking about," she said lamely.

"Oh, sure you do. Come on, every brainship wants to buy her contract out—no matter what they say. And every ship has a hobby-horse of her own, too. Barclay secretly wants to chase pirates all over known space like a holo-star, Leta wants to be the next big synthcom composer, even quiet old Jerry wants to buy himself a Singularity Drive *just* so he can set interstellar records for speed and distance!" He grinned. "So what's your little hidden secret?"

She only realized that she'd been manipulated when she found herself blurting out her plans for doing some amateur archeological sleuthing on the side, and both the fact that *she* wanted a bit of archeological glory for herself, and that she expected to eventually come up with something worth a fair number of credits toward her buy-out. She at least kept back the other wish; the one about finding the bug that had bitten her. By now, the three desires were equally strong, for reading of her parents' success had reawakened all the old dreams of following in Pota's footsteps, dealing with Beta had given her more than enough of being someone else's contract servant, and her studies of brainship chronicles had awakened a new fear—plague.

And what would happen if the bug that paralyzed *her* got loose on a planetarywide scale?

As she tried to cover herself, she inadvertently revealed that the plans were a secret held successfully not only from her CenCom supervisors but from everyone she'd ever worked with except Moira.

"It was because I thought that they'd take my determination as something else entirely," she confessed. "I thought they'd take it as a fixation, and a sign of instability."

All through her confession, Alex stayed ominously silent. When she finished, she suddenly realized that she had just put him in a position to blackmail her into taking him. All he had to do was threaten to reveal her fixation, and she'd be decommissioned and put with a Counselor for the next six months.

But instead of saying anything, he began laughing. Howling with laughter, in fact. She waited in confusion for him to settle down and tell her what was going on.

"You didn't look far enough into my records, lovely lady," he said, calming down and wiping his eyes. "Oh, my. Call up my file, why don't you. Not the Academy file; the one with my application for a scholarship in it."

Puzzled, she linked into the CenCom net and accessed Alex's public records. "Look under 'hobbies,'" he suggested.

And there it was. Hobbies and other interests.

Archeology and Xenology.

She looked further, without invitation, to his class records. She soon saw that in lower schools, besides every available history class, he had taken every archeological course he could cram into a school day.

She wished that she had hands so that she could rub her temples; as it was, she had to increase her nutrients a tad, to rid herself of a beginning headache.

"See?" he said. "I wouldn't mind my name on a paper or two myself. Provided, of course, that there aren't any curses attached to our findings! And—well, who *couldn't* use a pile of credits? I would very much like to retire from the Service with enough credit to buy myself—oh, a small planetoid."

"But—why didn't you apply to the university?" she asked. "Why didn't you go after your degree?"

"Money," he replied succinctly, leaning back in his seat and steepling his fingers over his chest. "Dinero. Cash. Filthy lucre. My family didn't have any—or rather, they had just enough that I didn't qualify for scholarships. Oh, I could have gotten a Bachelor's degree, but those are hardly worth bothering about in archeology. Heck, Hypatia, *you* know that! You know how long it takes to get *one* Doctorate, too—four years to a Bachelor's, two to a Master's, and *then* years and years *and years* of field work before you have enough material to do an original dissertation. And a working archeologist, one getting to go out on Class One digs or heading Class Two and Three, can't just have one degree, he has to have a double-doc or a quad-doc." He shook his head, sadly. "I've been an armchair hobbyist for as long as I've been a history buff, dear lady, but that was all that I could afford. Books and papers had to suffice for me."

"Then why the Academy?" she asked, sorely puzzled.

"Good question. Has a complicated answer." He licked his lips for a moment, thinking, then continued. "Say I got a Bachelor's in Archeology and History. I *could* have gotten a bottom-of-the-heap clerking job at the Institute with a Bachelor's—but if I did that, I might as well go clerk anywhere else, too. Clerking jobs are all the same wherever you go, only the jargon changes, never the job. But I could have done that, and gotten a work-study program to get a Master's. Then I might have been able to wangle a research assistant post to someone, but I'd be doing all of the dull stuff. None of the exploration; certainly none of the puzzle-solving. That would be as far as I could go; an RA job takes too much time to study for a Doctorate. I'd have been locked inside the Institute walls, even if my boss went out on digs himself. Because when you need someone to mind the store at home, you don't hire someone extra, you leave your RA behind."

"Oh, I see why you didn't do that," she replied. "But why the Academy?"

"Standards for scholarships to the Academy are—a little different," he told her. "The Scholarship Committees aren't just looking for poor but brilliant people—they're looking for competent people with a particular bent, and if they find someone like that, they do what it takes to get him. And the competition isn't as intense; there are a lot more scholarships available to the Academy than there are to any of the university Archeology and History Departments I could reach. All two of them; I'd have *had* to go to a local university; I couldn't afford to go off-planet. Space

Academy pays your way to Central; university History scholarships don't include a travel allowance. I figured if I couldn't go dig up old bones on faraway worlds, I'd at least *see* some of those faraway worlds. If I put in for A and E I'd even get to watch some of the experts at work. And while I was at it, I might as well put in for brawn training and see what it got me. Much to my surprise, my personality profile matched what they were looking for, and I actually found myself in brawn training, and once I was out, I asked to be assigned to A and E."

"So, why are you insisting on partnering me?" she asked, deciding that if he had manipulated her, she was going to be blunt with him, and if he couldn't take it, he wasn't cut out to partner her. No matter what he thought. Hmm, maybe frankness could scare him away. . . .

He blinked. "You really don't know? Because you are you," he said. "It's really appallingly simple. You have a sparkling personality. You don't try to flatten your voice and sound like an AI, the way some of your classmates have. You aren't at all afraid to have an opinion. You have a teddy bear walled up in your central cabin like a piece of artwork, but you don't talk about it. That's a mystery, and I love mysteries, especially when they imply something as personable as a teddy bear. When you talk, I can hear you smiling, frowning, whatever. You're a shell*person*, Hypatia, with the emphasis on *person*. I like you. I had hoped that you would like me. I figured we could keep each other entertained for a long, long time."

Well, he'd out-blunted her, and that was a fact. And—startled her. She was surprised, not a little flattered, and getting to think that Alex might not be a bad choice as a brawn after all. "Well, I like you," she replied hesitantly, "but . . ."

"But what?" he asked, boldly. "What is it?"

"I don't like being manipulated," she replied. "And you've been doing just that: manipulating me, or trying."

He made a face. "Guilty as charged. Part of it is just something I do without thinking about it. I come from a low-middle-class neighborhood. Where I come from, you either charm your way out of something or fight your way out of it, and I prefer the former. I'll try not to do it again."

"That's not all," she warned. "I've got—certain plans—that might get in the way, if you don't help me." She paused for effect. "It's about *what* I want to hunt down. The homeworld of the Salomon-Kildaire Entities."

"The EsKays?" he replied, sitting up, ramrod-straight. "Oh, my—if this weren't real life I'd think you were telepathic or something! The EsKays are my favorite archeological mystery! I'm *dying* to find out why they'd set up shop, then vanish! And if we could find the homeworld—Hypatia, we'd be holo-stars! Stellar achievers!"

Her thoughts milled about for a moment. This was very strange. Very strange indeed.

"I assume that part of our time Out would be spent checking things out at the EsKay sites?" he said, his eyes warming. "Looking for things the archeologists may not find? Looking for more potential sites?"

"Something like that," she told him. "That's why I need your cooperation. Sometimes I'm going to need a mobile partner on this one."

He nodded, knowingly. "Lovely lady, you are looking at him," he replied. "And only too happy to. If there's one thing I'm a sucker for, it's a quest. And this is even better, a quest at the service of a lady!"

"A quest?" she chuckled a little. "What, do you want us to swear to find the Holy Grail now?"

"Why not?" he said lightly. "Here—*I'll* start." He stood up, faced not her column but Ted E. Bear in his illuminated case, and held his hand as if he were taking the Space Service Oath. "I, Alexander Joli-Chanteu, do solemnly swear that I shall join brainship Hypatia One-Oh-Three-Three in a continuing and ongoing search for the homeworld of the Salomon-Kildaire Entities. I swear that this will be a joint project for as long as we have a joint career. And I swear that I shall give her all the support and friendship she needs in this search, so help me. So let it be witnessed and sealed by yon bear."

Tia would have giggled, except that he looked so very solemn.

"All right," he said, when he sat down again. "What about you?"

What about her? She had virtually accepted him as her brawn, hadn't she? And hadn't he sworn himself into her service, like some kind of medieval knight?

"All right," she replied. "I, Hypatia One-Oh-Three-Three, do solemnly swear to take Alexander Joli-Chanteu into my service, to share with him my search for the EsKay homeworld, and to share with him those rewards both material and immaterial that come our way in this search. I pledge to keep him as my brawn unless we both agree mutually to sever the contract. I swear it by— by Theodore Edward Bear."

He grinned, so wide and infectiously, that she wished she could return it. "I guess we're a team, then," she said.

"Then here—" he lifted an invisible glass "—is to our joint career. May it be as long and fruitful as the Cades'."

He pretended to drink, then to smash the invisible glass in an invisible fireplace, little guessing that Tia's silence was due entirely to frozen shock.

The Cades? How could *he—*

But before she vocalized anything, she suddenly realized that he could not possibly have known who and what she really was.

The literature on the Cades would never have mentioned their paralyzed daughter, nor the tragedy that caused her paralysis. That simply wasn't done in academic circles, a world in which only facts and speculations existed, and not sordid details of private lives. The Cades weren't stellar personalities, the kind people made docudramas out of. There was no way he could have known about Hypatia Cade.

And once someone went into the shellperson program, their last name was buried in a web of eyes-only and fail-safes, to ensure that their background remained private. It was better that way, easier to adjust to being shelled. The unscrupulous supervisor could take advantage of a shellperson's background for manipulation, and there were other problems as well. Brainships were, as Professor Brogen had pointed out, valuable commodities. So were their cargoes. The ugly possibilities of using familial hostages or family pressures against a brainship were very real. Or using family ties to lure a ship into ambush. . . .

But there was always the option for the shellperson to tell trusted friends about who they were. Trusted friends—and brawns.

She hesitated for a moment, as he saluted Ted. Should she tell him about herself and avoid a painful gaffe in the future?

No. No, I have to learn to live with it, if I'm going to keep chasing the EsKays. If he doesn't say anything, someone else will. Mum and Dad may have soured on the EsKay project because of me, but their names are still linked with it. And besides—it doesn't matter. The EsKays are mine, now. And I'm not a Cade anymore, even if I do find the homeworld. I won't be listed in the literature as Hypatia Cade, but as Hypatia One-Oh-Three-Three. A brainship. Part of the AH team—

She realized what their team designation looked like. "Do you realize that together our initials are—"

"'Ah'?" he said, pronouncing it like the word. "Actually, I did, right off. I thought it was a good omen. Not quite 'eureka,' but close enough!"

"Hmm," she replied. "It sounds like something a professor says when he thinks you're full of lint but he can't come up with a refutation!"

"You have no romance in your soul," he chided mockingly. "And speaking of romance, what time is it?"

"Four thirty-two and twenty-seven point five nine seconds," she replied instantly. "In the morning, of course."

"Egads," he said, and shuddered. "Oh-dark-hundred. Let this be the measure of my devotion, my lady. I, who *never* see the sun rise if I can help it, actually *got up* at *four in the morning* to talk to you."

"Devotion, indeed," she replied with a laugh. "All right, Alex— I give in. You are hereby officially my brawn. I'm Tia, by the way, not Hypatia, not to you. But you'd better sneak back to your dormitory and pretend to be surprised when they tell you I picked you, or we'll both be in trouble."

"Your wish, dearest Tia, is my command," he said, rising and bowing. "Hopefully I can get past the gate-guard going out as easily as I got past going in."

"Don't get caught," she warned him. "I can't bail you out, not officially, and not yet. Right now, as my supervisor told me so succinctly, I am an expensive drain on Institute finances."

He saluted her column and trotted down the stair, ignoring the lift once again.

Well, at least he'll keep in shape.

She watched him as long as she could, but other ships and equipment intervened. It occurred to her then that she could listen in on the spaceport security net for bulletins about an intruder—

She opened the channel, but after a half an hour passed, and she heard nothing, she concluded that he must have made it back safely.

The central cabin seemed very lonely without him. Unlike any of the others—except, perhaps, Chria Chance—he had filled the entire cabin with the sheer force of his personality.

He was certainly lively enough.

She waited until oh-six-hundred, and then opened her line to CenCom. There was a new operator on, one who seemed not at all curious about her or her doings; seemed, in fact, as impersonal as an AI. He brought up Beta's office without so much as a single comment.

As she halfway expected, Beta was present. And the very first words out of the woman's mouth were, "Well? Have you picked a brawn, or am I going to have to trot the rest of the Academy past you?"

Hypatia stopped herself from snapping only by an effort. "I made an *all-night* effort at considering the twelve candidates you presented, Supervisor," she said sharply. "I went to the considerable trouble of accessing records as far back as lower schools."

Only a little fib, she told herself. *I did check Alex, after all.*

"And?" Beta replied, not at all impressed.

"I have selected Alexander Joli-Chanteu. He can come aboard at any time. I completed all my test-flight sequences yesterday, and I can be ready to lift as soon as CenCom gives me clearance and you log my itinerary." *There,* she thought, smugly. *One in your eye, Madame Supervisor. I'll wager you never thought I'd be that efficient.*

"Very good, AH-One-Oh-Three-Three," Beta replied, showing no signs of being impressed at all. "I wouldn't have logged Alexander as brawn if I had been in your shell, though. He isn't as . . . professional as I would like. And his record is rather erratic."

"So are the records of most genius-class intellects, Supervisor," Tia retorted, feeling moved to defend her brawn. "As I am sure you are aware." *And you aren't in my shell, lady,* she thought, with resentment at Beta's superior tone smoldering in her, until she altered the chemical feed to damp it. *I will make my own decisions, and I will thank you to keep that firmly in mind.*

"So they say, AH-One-Oh-Three-Three," Beta replied impersonally. "I'll convey your selection to the Academy and have CenCom log in your flight plan and advise you when to be ready to lift immediately."

With that, she logged off. But before Tia could feel slighted or annoyed with her, the CenCom operator came back on.

"AH-One-Oh-Three-Three—congratulations!" he said, his formerly impersonal voice warming with friendliness. "I just wanted you to know before we got all tangled up in official things that the operators here all think you picked a fine brawn. Me, especially."

Tia was dumbfounded. "Why—thank you," she managed. "But why—"

The operator chuckled. "Oh, we handle all the cadets' training-flights. Some of them are real pains in the orifice—but Alex always has a good word and he never gripes when we have to put him in a holding pattern. And—well, that Donning character tried to get me in trouble over a near-miss when he ignored what I told him and came in anyway. Alex was in the pattern behind him— he saw and heard it all. He didn't *have* to log a report in my defense, but he did, and it kept me from getting demoted."

"Oh," Tia replied. Now, that was interesting. Witnesses to near misses weren't required to come forward with logs of the incident— and in fact, no one would have thought badly of Alex if he hadn't. His action might even have earned him some trouble with Donning. . . .

"Anyway, congratulations again. You won't regret your choice," the operator said. "And—stand by for compressed data transmission—"

As her orders and flight-plan came over the comlink, Tia felt oddly pleased and justified. Beta did *not* like her choice of brawns. The CenCom operators did.

Good recommendations, both.

She began her pre-flight check with rising spirits, and it seemed to her that even Ted was smiling. Just a little.

All right Universe, brace yourself. Here we come!

CHAPTER FOUR

"All right, Tia-my-love, explain what's going on here, in words of one syllable," Alex said plaintively, when Tia got finished with tracing the maze of orders and counter-orders that had interrupted their routine round of deliveries to tiny two- to four-person Exploratory digs. "Who's on first?"

"And What's on second," she replied absentmindedly. Just before leaving she'd gotten a datahedron on old-Terran slang phrases and their derivation; toying with the idea of producing that popular-science article. If it got published on enough nets, it might well earn her a tidy little bit of credit—and no amount of credit, however small, was to be scorned. But one unexpected side-effect of scanning it was that she tended to respond with the punch lines of jokes so old they were mummified.

Though now, at least, she knew what the CenCom operator had meant by "hang onto your bustle" and that business about the wicked witch who'd had a house dropped on her sister.

"What?" Alex responded, perplexed. "No, never mind. I don't want to know. Just tell me whose orders we're supposed to be following. I got lost back there in the fifth or sixth dispatch."

"I've got it all straight now, and it's dual-duty," she replied. "Institute, with backup from Central, although they were coun-termanding each other in the first four or five sets of instructions.

One of the Excavation digs hasn't been checking in. Went from their regular schedule to nothing, not even a chirp."

"You don't sound worried," Alex pointed out.

"Well, I am, and I'm not," she replied, already calculating the quickest route through hyperspace, and mentally cursing the fact that they didn't have Singularity Drive. But then again, there wasn't a Singularity point anywhere near where they wanted to go. So the drive *wasn't* the miracle of instantaneous transportation some people claimed it was. *Hmm, and some brainships too, naming no names.* All very well if there were Singularity points littering the stellarscape like stars in the Core, but out here, at this end of the galactic arm, stars were close, but points were few and far between. One reason why the Institute hadn't opted for a more expensive ship. "If it were an Exploratory dig like my—like we've been trotting supplies and mail to, I would worry a *lot.* They're horribly vulnerable. And an Evaluation dig is just as subject to disaster, since the maximum they can have is twenty people. But a Class Three— Alex, this one had a complement of two hundred! That's more that enough people to hold off any trouble!"

"Class Three Excavation sites get a lot of graduate students, don't they?" Alex said, while she locked things down in her holds for takeoff with help from the servos. Pity the cargo handlers hadn't had time to stow things properly.

"Exactly. They provide most of the coolie labor when there aren't any natives to provide a work force—that's why the Class Three digs have essentially the same setup as a military base. Most of the personnel are young, strong, *and* they get the best of the equipment. This one has—" she quickly checked her briefing "—one hundred seventy-eight people between the ages of twenty-five and thirty-five. That's plenty to set up perimeter guards."

Alex's fingers raced across the keypads in front of him, calling up data to her screens. "Hmm. No really nasty native beasties. Area declared safe. And—my. Fully armed, are we?" He glanced over at the column. "I had no idea archeologists were such dangerous beings! They never told me that back in secondary school!"

"Grrr," she responded. She flashed a close-up of the bared fangs of a dog on one of the screens he wasn't using. In the past several weeks she and Alex had spent a lot of time talking, getting to know each other. By virtue of her seven years spent mobile, she was a great deal more like a softperson than any of her classmates,

and Alex was *fun* to be around. Neither of them particularly
minded the standard issue beiges of her interior; what he had done,
during the time spent in FTL, was to copy the minimalist style
of his *sensei*'s home, taking a large brush and some pure black
and red enamel, and copying one or two Zen ideographs on the
walls that seemed barest. She thought they looked very handsome—
and quietly elegant.

Of course, his cabin was a mess—but she didn't have to look
in there, and she avoided doing so as much as possible.

In turn, he expressed delight over her "sparkling personality."
No matter what the counselors said, she had long ago decided that
she had feelings and emotions and had no guilt over showing them
to those she trusted. Alex had risen in estimation from "partner"
to "trusted" in the past few weeks; he had a lively sense of humor
and enjoyed teasing her. She enjoyed teasing right back.

"Pull in your fangs, wench," he said. "I realize that the only
reason they get those arms is because there are no sentients down
there. So, what's on the list of Things That Get Well-Armed Archeologists? I have the sinking feeling there were a lot of things they
didn't tell me about archeology back in secondary school!"

"Seriously? It's a short list, but a nasty one." She sobered. "Lock
yourself in; I'm going to lift, and fast. Things are likely to rattle
around." With drives engaged, she pulled away from her launch
cradle, acknowledged Traffic Control and continued her conversation, all at once. "Artifact thieves are high on that list—if you've
got a big dig, you can bet that there are things being found that
are going to be worth a lot to collectors. They'll come in, blast
the base, land, kill everyone left over that gets in their way, grab
the loot and lift, all within hours." *Which was why the hidey was
so far from our dome, and why Mum and Dad told me to get in it
and stay in it if trouble came.* "But *normally* they work an area,
and *normally* they don't show up anyplace where Central has a
lot of patrols. There haven't been any thieves in that area, and it
is heavily patrolled."

"So—what's next on the list?" Alex asked, one screen dedicated
to the stats on the dig, his own hands busy with post-lift chores
that some brawns would have left to their brains. Double-checking
to make sure all the servos had put themselves away, for instance.
Keeping an eye on the weight-and-balance in the holds. Just another
example, she thought happily, of what a good partner he was.

She was clear of the cradle and about to clear local airspace. Nearing time to accelerate "like a scalded cat." *Now that's a phrase that's still useful. . . .* "Next on the list is something we don't even have to consider, and that's a native uprising."

"Hmm, so I see." His eyes went from the secondary screen where the data on the dig was posted and back to the primary. "No living native sophonts on the continent. But I can see how it could be the Zulu wars all over again."

He nodded, acknowledging her logic, and she was grateful to *his* self-education in history.

"Precisely," she replied. "Throw enough warm bodies at the barricades, and any defense will go down. In a native uprising, there are generally hordes of fervent fanatics willing to die in the cause and go straight to Paradise. Accelerating, Alex."

He gave her a thumbs-up, and she threw him into his seat. He merely raised an eyebrow at her column and kept typing. "There must be several different variations on that theme. Let's see—you could have your Desecration of Holy Site Uprising, your Theft of Ancient Treasures Uprising, your Palace Coup Uprising, your Local Peasant Revolution Uprising. Uh-huh. I can see it. And when you've overrun the base, it's time to line everyone up as examples of alien exploitation. Five executioners, no waiting."

"They normally don't kill except by accident, actually, or in the heat of the moment," she told him. "Most native sophonts are bright enough to realize that two hundred of Central Systems' citizens, a whole herd of their finest minds *and* their dependents, make a much better bargaining chip as hostages than they do as casualties."

"Not much comfort to those killed in the heat of the moment," he countered. "So, what's the next culprit on the list?"

"The third, last, and most common," she said, a bit grimly, and making no effort to control her voice-output. "Disease."

"Whoa, wait a minute—I thought that these sites were declared free of hazard!" He stopped typing and paled a little, as well he might. Plague was the bane of the Courier Service existence. More than half the time of every CS ship was spent in ferrying vaccines across known space—and for every disease that was eradicated, three more sprang up out of nowhere. Nor were the brawns immune to the local plagues that just might choose to start at the moment they planeted. "I thought all these sites were sprayed down to a fare-thee-well before they let anyone move in!"

"Yes, but that's the one I'm seriously concerned about." *And not just because it was a bug that got me.* "That, my dear Alex, is what they *don't* tell you bright-eyed young students when you consider a career in archeology. The number one killer of xeno-archeologists is disease." *And the number one crippler, for that matter.* "Viruses and proto-viruses are sneaky sons-of-singularities; they can hibernate in tombs for centuries, millennia, even in airless conditions." She flashed up some Institute statistics; the kind they *didn't* show the general public. There was a thirty percent chance that a xeno-archeologist would be permanently disabled by disease during his career; a twenty percent chance that he would *die.* And a one hundred percent chance that he would be seriously ill, requiring hospitalization, from something caught on a dig, at some point in his life.

"So the bug hibernates. Then when the intrepid explorer pops the top off—" Alex looked as grim as she felt.

"Right. Gotcha." She laughed, but it had a very flat sound. "Well, sometimes it's been known to be fortuitous. The Cades actually *met* when they were recovering *from* Henderson's Chorea—ah— or so their biographies in *Who's Who* say. There could be worse things than having the Institute cover your tropic vacation."

"But mostly it isn't." His voice was as flat as her laugh had been.

"Ye-es. One of my—close friends is Doctor Kennet on the *Pride of Albion.* He's gotten to be a specialist in diseases that get archeologists. He's seen a lot of nasty variations over the years— including some really odd opportunistic bugs that are not only short-lived after exposure to air, but require a developing nervous system in order to set up housekeeping."

"Developing—oh, I got it. A kid, or a fetus, provided it could cross the placental barrier." He shivered, and his expression was very troubled. "Brr, that's a really nasty one."

"Verily, White Knight." She decided not to elaborate on it. *Maybe later. To let him know I'm not only out for fortune and glory.* "I just wanted you to be prepared when we got there, which we will in—four days, sixteen hours, and thirty-five minutes. Not bad, for an old-fashioned FTL drive, I'd say." She'd eliminated the precise measurements that some of the other shellpersons used with their brawns in the first week—except when she was speaking to another shellperson, of course. Alex didn't need that kind of precision, most of the time; when he did, he asked her for it. She had worried at first that she might be getting sloppy—

No, I'm just accommodating myself to his world. I don't mind. And when he needs precision, he lets me know in advance.

"Well, let me see if I can think of some non-lethal reasons for the dig losing communications—" He grinned. "How about—'the dinosaur ate my transmitter?'"

"Cute." Now that their acceleration had smoothed and they were out of the atmosphere, she sent servos snooping into his cabin, as was her habit whenever a week or so went by, and he was at his station, giving her non-invasive access. "Alex, don't you ever pick up your clothes?"

"Sometimes. Not when I'm sent hauling my behind up the stairs with my tail on fire and a directive from CS ordering me to report back to my ship *immediately*." He shrugged, completely unrepentant. "I wouldn't even have *changed* my clothes if that officious b—"

"Alex," she warned. "I'm recording, I have to. Regulations." Ever since the debacle involving the Nyota Five, *all* central cabin functions were recorded, whenever there was a softperson, even if only a brawn, present. That was regulation even on AI drones. The regs had been written for AI drones, in fact; and CS administration had decided that there was no reason to rewrite them for brainships—and every reason why they *shouldn't*. This way no one could claim "discrimination," or worse, "entrapment."

"If that officious *bully* hadn't insisted I change to uniform before lifting." He shook his head. "As if wearing a uniform was going to make any difference in how well *you* handled the lift. Which was, as always, excellent."

"Thank you." She debated chiding him on his untidy nature and decided against it. It hadn't made any difference before, it probably wouldn't now. She just had the servos pick up the tunic and trousers—wincing at the ultra-neon purple that was currently in vogue—and deposited them in the laundry receptacle.

And I'll probably have to put them away when they're clean, too. No wonder they wanted him to change. Hmm. Wonder if I dare "lose" them? Or have a dreadful accident that dyes them a nice sober plum?

That was a thought to tuck away for later. "Getting back to the dinosaur—com equipment breaks, and even a Class Three dig can end up with old equipment. If the only fellow on the dig quali-fied to fix it happens to be laid up with broken bones—in case you hadn't noticed, archeologists fall down shafts and off cliffs a lot—or double-pneumonia . . ."

"Good point." He finished his "housekeeping chores" with a flourish and settled back in his chair. "Say, Tia, they're all pro-fessorial types—do they ever just get so excited they forget to transmit?"

"Brace yourself for FTL—" The transition to FTL was nowhere near as distressing to softpersons as the dive into a Singularity, but it required some warning. Alex gripped the arms of the seat, and closed his eyes, as she made the jump into hyperspace.

She never experienced more than a brief shiver—*like ducking into a freezing-cold shower*—but Alex always looked a little green during transition. Fortunately, he had no trouble in hyper itself.

And if I can ever afford a Singularity Drive, his records say he takes those transitions pretty well. . . .

Well, right now, that was little more than a dream. She picked up the conversation where it had left off. "That has happened on Class One digs and even Class Two, but usually somebody realizes the report hasn't been made after a while when you're dealing with a big dig. Besides, logging reports constitutes publication, and grad students need all the publication they can get. Still, if they just uncovered the equivalent of Tutankhamen's tomb, they *might* all be so excited—and busy documenting finds and putting them into safe storage—that they've forgotten the rest of the universe exists."

He swallowed hard, controlling his nausea. It generally seemed to take his stomach a couple of minutes to settle down. *Maybe the reason it doesn't hit me is because there's no sensory nerves to my stomach anymore. . . .*

But that only brought back unpleasant memories; she ruthlessly shunted the thought aside.

"So—" he said finally, as his color began to return. "Tell me why you aren't in a panic because they haven't answered."

"Artifact thieves would probably have been spotted, there aren't any natives to revolt, and disease *usually* takes long enough to set in that *somebody* would have called for help," she said. "And that's why CS wasn't particularly worried, and why they kept counter-manding the Institute's orders. But either this expedition has been out of touch for so long that even *they* think there's something wrong, or they've got some information they didn't give us. So we're going in."

"And we find out when we get there," Alex finished; and there wasn't a trace of a smile anywhere on his face.

Tia brought them out of hyper with a deft touch that rattled Alex's insides as little as possible. Once in orbit, she sent down a signal that should activate the team's transmitter if there was anything there to activate. As she had told Alex several days ago, com systems broke. She was fully expecting to get no echo back.

Instead—

You are linked to Excavation Team Que-Zee-Five-Five-Seven. The beacon's automatic response came instantly, in electronic mode. Then came the open carrier wave.

"Alex, I think we have a problem," she said, carefully.

"Echo?" He tensed.

"Full echo—" She sent the recognition signal that would turn on landing assistance beacons and alert the AI that there was someone Upstairs—the AI was supposed to open the voice-channel in the absence of humans capable of handling the com. The AI came online immediately, transmitting a *ready to receive instructions* signal.

"Worse, they've got full com. I just got the AI go-signal."

She blipped a compressed several megabytes of instructions to give her control of all external and internal recording devices, override any programs installed since the base was established, and give her control of all sensory devices still working.

"Get the AI to give me some pictures," he said, all business. "If it can."

"Coming up—ah, external cam three—this is right outside the mess hall and—*oh shellcrack*—"

"I'll second that," Alex replied, just as grimly.

The camera showed them—somewhat fuzzily—a scene that was anything but a pretty sight.

There were bodies lying in plain view of the camera; from the lack of movement they could not be live bodies. They seemed to be lying where they fell, and there was no sign of violence on them. Tia switched to the next camera the AI offered; a view inside the mess hall. Here, if anything, things were worse. Equipment and furniture lay toppled. More bodies were strewn about the room.

A chill that had nothing to do with the temperature in her shell held her in thrall. Fear, horror, helplessness—

Her own private nightmares—

Tia exerted control over her internal chemistry with an effort; told herself that this could *not* be the disease that had struck her. These people were taken down right where they stood or sat—

She started to switch to another view, when Alex leaned forward suddenly.

"Tia, wait a minute."

Obediently, she held the screen, sharpening the focus as well as the equipment, the four-second lag-to-orbit, and atmospheric interference would allow. She couldn't look at it herself.

"There's no food," he said, finally. "Look—there's plates and things all over the place, but there's not a scrap of food anywhere."

"Scavengers?" she suggested. "Or whatever—"

Whatever killed them? But there are no signs of an invasion, an attack from outside—

He shook his head. "I don't know. Let's try another camera."

This one was outside the supply building—and this was where they found their first survivors.

If that's what you can call them. Tia absorbed the incoming signal, too horrified to turn her attention away. There was a trio of folk within camera range: one adolescent, one young man, and one older woman. They paid no attention to each other, nor to the bodies at their feet, nor to their surroundings. The adolescent sat in the dirt of the compound, stared at a piece of brightly colored scrap paper in front of him, and rocked, back and forth. There was no sound pickup on these cameras, so there was no indication that he was doing anything other than rocking in silence, but Tia had the strange impression that he was humming tunelessly.

The young man stood two feet from a fence and shifted his weight back and forth from foot to foot, swaying, as if he wanted to get past the fence and had no idea how. And the older woman paced in an endless circle.

All three of them were filthy, dressed in clothes that were dirt-caked and covered with stains. Their faces were dirt-streaked, eyes vacant; their hair straggled into their eyes in ratty tangles. Tia was just grateful that the cameras were not equipped to transmit odor.

"Tia, get me another camera, please," Alex whispered, after a long moment.

Camera after camera showed the same view; either of bodies lying in the dust, or of bodies and a few survivors, aimlessly wandering. Only one showed anyone doing anything different; one young woman had found an emergency ration pouch and torn it open. She was single-mindedly stuffing the ration-cubes into her mouth with both hands, like—

"Like an animal," Alex supplied in a whisper. "She's eating like an animal."

Tia forced herself to be dispassionate. "Not like an animal," she corrected. "At least, not a healthy one." She analyzed the view as if she were dealing with an alien species. "No—she acts like an animal that's been brain-damaged—or maybe a drug addict that's been on something so long there isn't much left of his higher functions."

This wasn't "her" disease. It was something else—deadly—but not what had struck her down. What she felt was not exactly relief, but she was able to detach herself from the situation, to distance herself a little.

You knew, sooner or later, you'd see a plague. This one is a horror, but you knew *this would happen.*

"Zombies," Alex whispered, as another of the survivors plodded past without so much as a glance at the woman eating, who had given up eating with her hands and had shoved her face right down into the torn-open ration pouch.

"You've seen too many bad holos," she replied absently, sending the AI a high-speed string of instructions. She had to find out when this happened—and how long these people had been like this.

It was too bad that the cameras weren't set to record, because that would have told her a lot. How quickly the disease—for a plague of some kind would have had an incubation time—had set in, and what the initial symptoms were. Instead, all she had to go on were the dig's records, and when they had stopped making them.

"Alex, the last recorded entry into the AI's database was at about oh-two-hundred, local time, a week and a half ago," she said. "It was one of the graduate students logging in pottery shards. Then— nothing. No record of illness, nothing in the med records, no one even using a voice-activator to ask the AI for help. The mess hall computer programmed the synthesizer to produce food for a few meals, then something broke the synthesizer."

"One of them," Alex hazarded.

"Probably." She looked for anything else in the database and found nothing. "That's about all there is. The AI has been keeping things going, but there's been no interaction with it. So forget what I said about diseases taking several days to set in—it looks like this one infected and affected everyone on the base between— oh—some time during the night, and dawn."

If she'd had a head, she would have shaken it. "I can't imagine how something like that could happen to *everyone* at the same time without someone at least blurting a few words to a voice pickup!"

"Unless . . . Tia, what if they had to be asleep? I mean, there's things that happen during sleep, neuro transmitters that initiate dream-sleep—" Alex looked up from the screen, with lines of strain around his eyes. "If they had to be asleep to catch this thing—"

"Or if the first symptom *was* sleep . . ." She couldn't help herself; she wanted to shiver with fear. "Alex, I have to set down there. You can't do anything for those people from up here."

"No argument." He strapped himself in. "Okay, lady—get us down as fast as you can. There's one thing I *have* to do, quick, before we lose any more."

She broke orbit with a sudden acceleration that threw him into the back of his seat; he didn't bat an eye. His voice got a little more strained, but that was all.

"I'll have to put on a pressure-suit and get into the supplies; put out food and pans of water. They're starving and dehydrated. Spirits of space only know what they've been eating and drinking all this time—could be a lot of them died of dysentery, or from eating or drinking something that wasn't food." He was thinking out loud; waiting for Tia to put in her own thoughts, or warn him if he was planning to do something really stupid. "No matter what else we do, I *have* to do that."

"Open up emergency ration bags and leave pans of the cubes all over the compound," she suggested, as her outer skin heated up to a glowing red as she hit the upper atmosphere. "Do the same with the water. Like you were feeding animals."

"I am feeding animals," he said, and his voice and face were bleak. "I have to keep telling myself that. Or I'll do something really, really stupid. You get a line established to Kleinman Base, ASAP."

"Already in the works." A hyperwave comlink that far wasn't the easiest thing to establish and hold—

But that was why she was a brainship, not an AI drone.

"Hang on," she said, as she hit the first of the turbulence. "It's going to be a bumpy burn down!"

The camera and external mike on Alex's helmet gave her a much clearer view of the survivors than Tia really wanted. Of the complement of two hundred at this base, no more than fifty survived, most of them between the ages of fifteen and thirty.

They avoided Alex entirely, hiding whenever they saw him—but they came out to huddle around the pans of food and water he put out, stuffing food into their faces with both hands. Alex had gotten three of the bodies he'd found in their beds into the medcenter, and the diagnosis was the same in all three cases; complete systemic collapse, which might have been stroke. The rest—the ones that had not simply dropped in their tracks—had died of dysentery and dehydration. Of the casualties, it looked as if half of the dead had keeled over with this collapse, all of them the oldest members of the team.

After the third, Alex called a halt to it; instead he loaded the bodies into the base freezer. Someone else would have to come get them and deal with them. Tia had recorded his efforts, but could not bring herself to actually watch the incoming video.

He completed his grisly work and returned to caring for the living. "Tia, as near as I can guess, this thing hits people in one of two ways. Either you get a stroke or something and die, or you turn into—that." She saw whatever he was looking at by virtue of the fact that the helmet-camera was mounted right over his forehead. And "that" was something that had once been a human boy, scrambling away out of sight.

"That seems like a good enough assumption for now," she agreed. "Can you tell what happened with the food situation? Are they so—far gone that they can't remember how to get into basic supplies?"

"That's about it," he agreed, wearily. "Believe it or not, they can't even remember how to pop ration packs—they seem to have a vague memory of where the food was stored, but they never even tried to open the door to the supply warehouse." He trudged across the compound to one of the pans he had set out. It was already empty, without even crumbs. He poured ration-cubes into it from a bag he carried under his arm. She caught furtive movement at the edge of the camera-view; presumably the survivors were waiting for him to go away so that they could empty the pan again. "When they found the emergency pouches they tore them open, like that woman we watched. But a lot of times, they don't even seem to realize that the pouch has food in it."

"There's two kinds of victims; the first lot, who got hit and died in their sleep or on the way to breakfast," he continued, making his way to the next pan. "Then the rest of them died of dehydration and dysentery because they were eating half-rotten food."

"Those would go hand-in-hand, here," she replied. "With nothing to stop the liquid loss through dysentery, dehydration comes on pretty quickly."

"That's what I figured." He paused to fill another pan. "There'd be more of them dead, of exposure and hypothermia, except that the temperature doesn't drop below twenty Celsius at night, or get above thirty in the daytime. Shirtsleeve weather. Tia—see when this balmy weather pattern started, would you?"

"Right." He must have had an idea—and it didn't take her more than a moment to interrogate the AI. "About a week before the last contact. Does that sound as suspicious to you as it does to me?"

"Yeah. Maybe something hatched." Alex scanned the area for her, and she noted that there were a fair number of insects in the air.

But native insects wouldn't bite humans—or would they? "Or sprouted—this could be a violent allergic reaction, or some other kind of interaction with a mold spore or pollen." Farfetched, but not entirely impossible.

"But why wouldn't the Class One team have uncovered it?" he countered, filling another pan with ration-cubes. "Kibble," the brawns called it. The basic foodstuff of the Central System worlds; the monotonous ration-bars handed out by the PTA to client-planets cut up into bite-sized pieces. Tia had never eaten it; her parents had always insisted on real meals, but she had been told that while it looked, smelled, and tasted reasonable, its very sameness would drive you over the edge if you had to eat it for very long. But every base had emergency pouches of the stuff cached all over, and huge bags stockpiled in the warehouse, in case something happened to the food-synthesizers.

Those pouches must have been what kept the survivors going— until they ran out of pouches that were easy to find.

The dig records were, fortunately, quite clear. "Got the answer to your question—Class One dig was here for winter, only—they found what they needed to upgrade to Class Three within a couple of days of digging. They really hit a big find in the first test trench, and the Institute pushed the upgrade through to take advantage of the good weather coming."

"And initial Survey teams don't *live* here, they live on their ships." Alex had a little more life in his voice.

"They were only here in the fall," she said. "There's never been a human here during spring and summer."

"Tia, you put that together with an onset of this thing after dark, and what do you get?"

"An insect vector?" she hazarded. "Nocturnal? I must admit that the pattern for venomous and biting insects is to appear after sunset."

"Sounds right to me. As soon as I get done filling the pans again, I'm going to go grab some bedding from one of the victims' beds, seal it in a crate, and freeze it. Maybe it's something like a flea. Can you see if there's anything in the AI med records about a rash of insect bites?"

"Can do," she responded, glad to finally have something, *anything*, concrete to do.

The sun was near the horizon when Alex finished boxing his selection of bedding and sealing it in a freezer container. He came back out again after loading the container into one of Tia's empty holds. She saw to the sealing of the hold, while he went back out to try and catch one of the Zombies—a name he had tagged the survivors with over her protests.

She finally established the comlink while he was still out in the compound, fruitlessly chasing one after another of the survivors and getting nowhere. He was weighted down with his pressure-suit; they were weighted down by nothing at all and had the impetus of fear. He seemed to terrify them, and they did not connect the arrival of food in the pans with him, for some reason.

"They act like I'm some kind of monster," he panted, leaning over to brace himself on his knees while he caught his breath. "Since they don't have that reaction to each other, it has to be this suit that they're afraid of. Maybe I should—"

"*Stay in the suit,*" she said, fiercely. "You make one move to take that suit off, and I'll sleepygas you!"

"Oh, Tia—" he protested.

"I'm not joking." She continued her conversation with the base brain in rapid, highly compressed databursts with *horribly* long pauses for the information to transmit across hyperspace. "You stay in that suit! We don't know what caused all this—"

Her tirade was interrupted by a dreadful howling and the external camera bounced as Alex moved violently. At first she thought that something awful had happened to Alex—but then she realized that the sound came from his *external* suit-mike, and that the movement of the camera had been caused by his own violent start of surprise.

"*What the*—" he blurted, then recovered. "Hang on, Tia. I need to see what this is, but it doesn't sound like an attack or anything."

"Be careful," she urged fearfully. "Please—"

But he showed no signs of foolhardy bravery; in fact, as the howling continued under the scarlet light of the descending sun, he sprinted from one bit of cover to another like a seasoned guerrilla-fighter.

"Fifty meters," Tia warned, taking her measurement from the strength of the howls. "They have to be on the other side of this building."

"Thanks." He literally crept on all fours to the edge of the building and peeked around the corner.

Tia saw exactly what he did, so she understood his sharp intake of breath.

She couldn't count them, for they milled about too much, but she had the impression that every survivor in the compound had crowded into the corner of the fence nearest the sunset. Those right at the fence clung to it as they howled their despair to the sun; the rest clung to the backs of those in front of them and did the same.

Their faces were contorted with the first emotion Tia had seen them display.

Fear.

"They're scared, Tia," Alex whispered, his voice thick with emotions that Tia couldn't decipher. "They're afraid. I think they're afraid that the sun isn't going to come back."

That might have been the case—but Tia couldn't help but wonder if their fear was due to something else entirely. Could they have a dim memory that something *terrible* had happened to them in the hours of darkness, something that took away their friends and changed their lives into a living hell? Was that why they howled and sobbed with fear?

When the last of the light had gone, they fell suddenly silent— then, like scurrying insects, they dropped to all fours and scuttled away, into whatever each, in the darkness of his or her mind, deemed to be shelter. In a moment, they were gone. All of them.

There was a strangled sob from Alex. And Tia shook within her shell, racked by too many emotions to effectively sort out.

"You have two problems."

Tia knew the name to put to the feeling she got when her next transmission from the base was not from some anonymous CS doctor but from Doctor Kenny.

Relief. Real, honest, relief.

It flooded her, making her relax, clearing her mind. Although she could not speak directly with him, if there was *anyone* who could help them pull this off, it would be Doctor Kenny. She settled all of her concentration on the incoming transmission.

"You'll have to catch the survivors and keep them alive—and you'll have to keep them from contaminating your brawn. After that, we can deal with symptoms and the rest."

All right, that made sense.

"We went at this analyzing your subjects' behavior. You were right in saying that they act in a very similar fashion to brain-damaged simians."

This was an audio-only transmission; the video portion of the signal was being used to carry a wealth of technical data. Tia wished she could see Doctor Kenny's face—but she heard the warmth and encouragement in his voice with no problem.

"We've compiled all the data available on *any* experiments where the subjects' behavior matched your survivors," Doctor Kenny continued. "Scan it and see if anything is relevant. Tia, I can't stress this enough—no matter *what* you think caused this disease, *don't let Alex get out of that suit.* I can't possibly say this too many times. Now that he's gone out there, he's got a contaminated surface. I want you to ask him to stay in the suit, sleep in the suit, eat through the suit-ports, use the suit-facilities. I would prefer that he stayed out in the compound or in your airlock even to sleep—every time he goes in and out of the suit, in and out of your lock, we have a chance for decontamination to fail. I know you understand me."

Only too well, she thought, grimly, remembering all that time in isolation.

"Now, we've come up with a general plan for you," Doctor Kenny continued. "We don't think that you'll be able to catch the survivors, given the way they're avoiding Alex. So you're going to have to trap them. My experts think you'll be able to rig drop-traps for them, using packing crates with field generators across the front and rations for bait. The technical specs are on the video-track, but I think you have the general idea. The big thing will be not to frighten the rest each time you trap one."

Doctor Kenny's voice echoed hollowly in the empty cabin; she damped the sound so that it didn't sound so lonely.

"We want one, two at most, per crate. We're afraid that, bunched together, they might hurt each other, fight over food—they're damaged, and we just don't know how aggressive they might get. That's why we want you to pack them in the hold in the crates. Once you get them trapped, we want you to put enough food and water in each crate to last the four days to base—and Tia, at that point, leave them there. Don't do anything with them. Leave them alone. I trust you to exercise your good sense and not give in to any temptation to intervene in their condition."

Doctor Kenny sighed, gustily. "We bandied around the idea of tranking them—but they *have* to eat and drink; four days knocked out might kill them. You don't have the facilities to cold-sleep fifty people. So—box them, hope the box matches their ideas of a good place to hide, leave them with food and water and shove them in the hold. That's it for now, Tia. Transmit everything you have, and we'll have answers for you as soon as we're able. These double-bounce comlinks aren't as fast as we'd like, but they beat the alternative. Our thoughts are with you."

The transmission ended, leaving her only with the carrier-wave.

Now what? Give Alex the bad news, I guess. And calculate how many packing crates I can pack into my holds.

"Alex?" she called. "Are you having any luck tracking down where the survivors are?"

"I've turned on all the exterior lights," Alex said. "I hoped that I'd be able to lure some of them out into the open, but it's no good." She activated his helmet-camera and watched his gloved hand typing override orders into the keyboard of the main AI console. Override orders had to be put in by hand, with a specific set of override codes, no matter how minor the change was—that was to keep someone from taking over an AI with a shout or two. "Right now I'm giving myself full access to everything—I may not need it, but who knows?"

"I've got our first set of orders," she told him. "Do you want to hear them?"

"Sure." Typing in a pressure-suit was no easy task, and Tia did not envy him. It took incredible patience to manage a normal keyboard in those stiff gloves.

She retransmitted Doctor Kenny's message and waited patiently for his response when she finished.

"So I have to stay in the suit." He sighed gustily. "Oh, well. It could be worse, I suppose. It could be two weeks to base, instead of four days." He typed the last few characters with a flourish and was rewarded by the "Full Access, Voice Commands accepted" legend. "No choice, right? Look, Tia, I know you're going to be lonely, but if I have to stay in this suit, I might just as well sleep out here."

"But—" she protested, "—what if they decide you're an enemy or something?"

"What, the Zombies?" He snorted. "Tia, right now they're all crammed into some of the darnedest nooks and crannies you ever saw in your life. I couldn't pry them out of there with a forklift. I know where they all are, but I'd have to break bones to get them. *Their* bones. They're terrified, even with all the floodlights on. No, they aren't going to come after me in the dark."

"All right," she agreed reluctantly. She knew he was right; he'd be much more comfortable out there—there was certainly more room available to him there.

"I'll be closer to the Zombies," he said wearily, "and I can barricade myself in one of the offices, get enough bedding from stores to make a reasonable nest. I'll plug the suit in to keep everything charged up, and you can monitor the mike and camera. I snore."

"I know," she said, in a weak attempt to tease him.

"You would." He turned, and the camera tracked what he was seeing. "Look, I'm here in the site supervisor's office. There's even a real nice couch in here and—" He leaned down and fiddled with the underside of the piece of furniture. "Ah hah. As I thought. There's a real bed in the couch. Bet the old man liked to sneak naps. Look—" He panned around the office. "No windows. One door. A full-access terminal. I'll be fine."

"All right, I believe you." She thought, quickly. "I'll look over those plans for traps and transmit them to the AI, and I'll find out where everything you'll need is stored. You can start collecting the team tomorrow."

What's left of them, she thought sadly. *What isn't already stored in the freezer.*

"See what you can do about adding some sleepygas to the equation," he suggested, yawning under his breath. "If we can knock them out once they're in the boxes, rather than trapping them with field generators, that should solve the problem of frightening the others."

That was a good suggestion. A much better one than Doctor Kenny's. *If* she had enough gas. . . .

But wait; this was a fully-stocked station. There might be another option. Crime *did* exist wherever there were people, and mental breakdowns—sometimes it was necessary to immobilize someone for his protection and the protection of others.

She interrogated the AI and discovered that, indeed, there were several special low-power needlers in the arms locker. And with them, full clips of anesthetic needles.

"Alex," she said, slowly, "how good a shot are you?"

"When this is over, I'm requisitioning an ethological tagging kit," she said fiercely, as Alex crouched on the roof of the mess hall and waited for his subject's hunger to overcome her timidity. She hesitated, just in front of the crate—she smelled the food, and she wanted it, but she was afraid to go inside after it. She swayed from side to side, like one of the first three survivors they'd seen; that swaying seemed to be the outward sign of inner conflict.

"Why?" he asked. The woman stopped swaying and was creeping, cautiously, into the crate. Alex wanted her to be all the way inside before he darted her, both to prevent the rest from seeing her collapse and to avoid having to haul her about and perhaps hurt her.

"Because they have full bio-monitor contact-buttons in them," she replied. "Skin adhesive ones. They're normally put inside ears, or on a shaved patch."

After a bit more consultation with Kleinman Base and Doctor Kenny, darting the survivors had been given full approval—and since they were going to be out, a modification in the setup had been arranged for. There would be shredded paper bedding in the crates as well as food and water—and each victim would wear a contact-button glued to the spine between the shoulder blades with surgical adhesive. With judicious reprogramming, a minimal amount of medical information could come from that—heart rate, respiration, skin temperature. Tia had reprogrammed the buttons; now it was her brawn's turn to live up to his title.

"I sure never thought my marksmanship would ever be an asset," he said absently. The woman had only a foot or so to go. . . .

"I never thought I was going to be packing my hold with canned archeologists." The packing crates would fit—but only if they were stacked two deep. Alex had already set up the site machine shop servos to drill air holes in all of the crates, and there would be an unbreakable bio-luminescent lightstick in each. They were rated for a week of use. Hopefully that much light would be enough to keep their captives from panicking.

"That's a good girl," Alex crooned to the reluctant Zombie. "Good girl. Smell the nice food? It's really good food. You're hungry, aren't you?" The woman took the last few steps in a rush and fell on the dish of ration-cubes. Alex darted her in the same moment.

The trank took effect within seconds, and she didn't even seem to realize that she'd been struck. She simply dropped over on her side, asleep.

Alex left the needler up on the roof where he'd rigged a sniper-post with a tripod to hold the gun steady. He trotted down the access steps to the first floor and hurried to get out where he could be seen before someone else smelled the food and came after it. As he burst out into the dusty courtyard, a hint of movement at the edge of the camera-field told Tia there *was* another Zombie lurking out there.

After many protests, she had begun calling the survivors "Zombies," too—it helped to think of them as something other than humans. She admitted to Doctor Kenny that without that distancing it was hard to keep working without strong feelings getting in the way of efficiency.

"That's all right, Tia," he soothed on his next transmission. "Even I have to stop thinking of my patients as people and start thinking of them as 'cases' or 'case studies' sometimes. That's the nature of this business, and we'll both do what we have to in order to get as many of these people back alive as we can."

She would have liked to ask him if he'd ever thought of *her* as a "case study," but she knew, in her heart of hearts, that he probably had. But then, look what he had done for her. . . .

No, calling these poor people "Zombies" wasn't going to hurt them, and it would keep her concentrating on what to do for them, and not on *them*.

Alex had been boxing Zombies all morning, and now he had it down to a system. Wheeling out of the warehouse, under the control of the AI, came a small parade of servos laden with the supplies that would keep the woman—hopefully—alive and healthy in her crate for the next five or six days. A bag of finely shredded paper, to make a thick nest on the bottom of the box. A whole bag of ration-cubes. A big squeeze-bottle of water. A tiny chemical toilet, on the off-chance she *might* remember how to use it. The bio-luminescent lightstick. Inside of fifteen minutes, Alex had his set up. The big bottle of water was strapped to one wall, the straps glue-bonded in place, the bottle bonded to the straps. The toilet was bonded to the floor in the corner of the six foot by six foot crate. The bag of ration-cubes was opened at the top, and strapped and bonded into the opposite corner. Paper was laid in a soft bed over the entire floor, and the unconscious woman rolled onto it, with the contact-button glued to her back. Lastly, the bio-luminescent tube was activated and glue-bonded to the roof of the crate, the side brought up and fastened in place, and the crate was ready for the loader.

That was Tia's job; she brought the servo-forklift in from the warehouse under her control rather than the AI's. Alex did not trust the AI to have the same fine control that Tia did. The lift bore the now-anonymous crate up her ramp, and she stored it with the rest, piled not two but three high and locked in place. Each crate was precisely eight inches from the ones next to it, to allow for proper ventilation on four sides. There were twelve crates in the hold now. They hoped to have twelve more before nightfall. If all went well.

Thirty minutes for each capture. . . .

They couldn't have done it if not for Tia's multitasking abilities and all the servos under her control. Right now, a set of servos were setting up crates all over the compound, near the hiding places of the Zombies. The Zombies seemed just as frightened of the servos as they were of Alex in his suit. By running the servos all over the compound, they managed to send every one of the Zombies into hiding. They ran servos around each hiding place until they were ready to move to that area for darting and capture. By now, the Zombies were getting hungry, which was all to the good, so far as Alex and Tia were concerned. One trap was being baited now—and Alex was on his way to the hidden sniper position above it. Meanwhile, the rest of the servos were patrolling the compound *except* in the area of that baited crate, keeping the Zombies pinned down.

A second hair-raising moment had occurred at dawn, bringing Alex up out of his bed with a scream of his own. The Zombies had gathered to greet the rising sun with another chorus of howls, although this time they seemed more—well, not joyous, but certainly there was no fear in the Zombie faces.

Once the first servo appeared, and frightened the Zombies into hiding again, the final key to their capture plan was in place.

They would catch as many of the Zombies as possible during the daylight hours. Alex had marked their favorite hiding places last night, and by now those patrolling servos had those that were not occupied blocked off. More crates would be left very near those blocked-off hiding holes. Would they be attractive enough for more of the Zombies to hide in them? Alex thought so. Tia hoped he was right—for every Zombie cowering in a crate meant one more they could dart and pack up—one more they would not have to catch tomorrow.

One less half-hour spent here. If they could keep up the pace—if the Zombies didn't get harder to catch.

Alex kept up a running dialogue with her, and she sensed that he was as frightened and lonely as she was, but was determined not to show it. He revealed a lot, over the course of the day; she built up a mental picture of a young man who had been just different enough that while he was mildly popular—or at least, not unpopular—he had few close friends. The only one who he really spoke about was someone called Jon—the chess and games player he had mentioned before. He spent a lot of time with Jon—who had helped him with his lessons when he was younger, so Tia assumed that Jon must have been older than Alex.

Older or not, Jon had been, and still was, a *friend*. There was no mistaking the warmth in Alex's voice when he talked about Jon; no mistaking the pleasure he felt when he talked about the message of congratulation Jon had sent when he graduated from the academy—

Or the laughter he'd gotten from the set of "brawn jokes" Jon had sent when Tia picked Alex as her partner.

Well, Doctor Kenny, Anna, and Lars were my friends—and still are. Sometimes age doesn't make much of a difference.

"Hey, Alex?" she called. He was waiting for another of the timid Zombies to give in to hunger. The clock was running.

"What?"

"What do you call a brawn who can count past ten?"

"I don't know," he said good-naturedly. "What?"

"Barefoot."

He made a rude noise, then sighted and pulled the trigger. One down, how many more to go?

They had fifty-two Zombies packed in the hold, and one casualty. One of the Zombies had not survived the darting; Alex had gone into acute depression over that death, and it had taken Tia more than an hour to talk him out of it. She didn't dare tell him then what those contact-buttons revealed; some of their passengers weren't thriving well. The heart rates were up, probably with fear, and she heard whimpering and wailing in the hold whenever there was no one else in it but the Zombies. The moment any of the servos or Alex entered the hold, the captives went utterly silent. Out of fear, Tia suspected.

The last Zombie was in the hold; the hold was sealed, and Tia had brought the temperature up to skin-heat. The ventilators were at full-strength. Alex had just entered the main cabin.

And he was reaching for his helmet-release.

"Don't crack your suit," she snapped. How could she have forgotten to tell him? Had she? Or had she told him, and *he* had forgotten?

"What?" he said—then—"Oh, *decom* it. I forgot."

She restrained herself from saying what she wanted to. "Doctor Kenny said you have to stay in the suit. Remember? He thinks that the chance we might have missed something in decontamination is too much to discount. He doesn't want you to crack your suit until you're at the base. All right?"

"What if something goes wrong for the Zombies?" he asked, quietly. "Tia, there isn't enough room in that hold for me to climb around in the suit."

"We'll worry about that if it happens," she replied firmly. "Right now, the important thing is for you to get strapped down, because *their* best chance is to get to Base as quickly as possible, and I'm going to leave scorch-marks on the ozone layer getting there."

He took the unsubtle hint and strapped himself in; Tia was better than her word, making a tail-standing takeoff and squirting out of the atmosphere with a blithe disregard for fuel consumption. The Zombies were going to have to deal with the constant acceleration to hyper as best they could—at least she knew that they were all sitting or lying down, because the crates simply weren't big enough for them to stand.

She had been relaying symptoms—observed and recorded—back to Doctor Kenny and the med staff at Kleinman Base all along. She had known that they weren't going to get a lot of answers, but every bit of data was valuable, and getting it there ahead of the victims was a plus.

But now that they were on the way, they were on their own, without the resources of the abandoned dig or the base they were en route to. The med staff might have answers—but *they* likely would not have the equipment to implement them.

Alex couldn't move while she was accelerating—but once they made the jump to FTL, he unsnapped his restraints and headed for the stairs.

"Where are you going?" she asked, nervously.

"The hold. I'm in my suit—there's nothing down there that can get me through the suit."

Tia listened to the moans and cries through her hold pickups; thought about the contact-buttons that showed fluttering hearts and unsteady breathing. She knew what would happen if he got down there.

"You can't do anything for them in the crates," she said. "You know that."

He turned toward her column. "What are you hiding from me?"

"N-nothing," she said. But she didn't say it firmly enough.

He turned around and flung himself back in his chair, hands speeding across the keyboard with agility caused by days of living in the suit. Within seconds he had called up every contact-button and had them displayed in rows across the screen.

"Tia, what's going on down there?" he demanded. "They weren't like this before we took off, were they?"

"I think—" She hesitated. "Alex, I'm not a doctor!"

"You've got a medical library. You've been talking to the doctors. What do you think?"

"I think—they aren't taking hyper well. Some of the data the base sent me on brain-damaged simians suggested that *some* kinds of damage did something to the parts of the brain that make you compensate for—for things that you know should be there, but aren't. Where you can see a whole letter out of just parts of it— identify things from split-second glimpses. Kind of like maintaining a mental balance. Anyway, when that's out of commission—" She felt horribly helpless. "I think for them it's like being in Singularity."

"For *four days*?" he shouted, hurting her sensors. "I'm going down there—"

"And do what?" she snapped back. "What are you going to do for them? They're afraid of you in that suit!"

"Then I'll—"

"You do, and I'll gas the ship," she said instantly. "I *mean* that, Alex! You put *one finger* on a release and I'll gas the whole ship!"

He sat back down, collapsing into his chair. "What can we do?" he said weakly. "There has to be something."

"We've got some medical supplies," she pointed out. "A couple of them can be adapted to add to the air supply down there. *Help* me, Alex. Help me find something we can do for them. Without you cracking your suit."

"I'll try," he said, unhappily. But his fingers were already on the keyboard, typing in commands to the med library, and not sneaking towards his suit-releases. She blanked for a microsecond with relief—

Then went to work.

Three more times there were signs of crisis in the hold. Three more times she had to threaten him to keep him from diving in and trying to save one of the Zombies by risking his own life. They lost one more, to a combination of anti-viral agent and watered-down sleepygas that they *hoped* would act as a tranquilizer rather than an anesthetic. Zombie number twenty-seven might have been allergic to one or the other, although there was no such indication in his med records; his contact-button gave all the symptoms of allergic shock before he died.

Alex stopped talking to her for four hours after that—twenty-seven had been in the bottom rank, and a shot of adrenaline would have brought him out—*if* it had been allergic shock. But his crate was also buried deep in the stacks, and Alex would have had to peel the whole suit off to get to him. Which Tia wouldn't permit. They had no way of knowing if this was really an allergic reaction, or if it was another development of the Zombie Bug. Twenty-seven had been an older man, showing some of the worst symptoms.

Although Alex wasn't talking to her, Tia kept talking at him, until he finally gave in. Just as well. His silence had her convinced that he was going to ask for a transfer, and that he hated her—if a shellperson could be in tears, she was near that state when he finally answered.

"You're right," was all he said. "Tia, you were right. There are fifty more people there depending on both of us, and if I got sick, that's the mobile half of the team out." And he sighed. But it was enough. Things went back to normal for them. Just in time for the transition to norm space.

Kleinman Base kept them in orbit, sending a full decontamination team to fetch Alex as well as the Zombies, leaving Tia all alone for about an hour. It was a very lonely hour. . . .

But then another decontamination team came aboard, and when they left again, two days later, there was nothing left of her original fittings. She had been fogged, gassed, stripped, polished, and refitted in that time. All that was left—besides the electronic components— were the ideographs painted on the walls. It still looked the same, however, because everything was replaced with the same standard-issue, psychologically approved beige—

Only then was she permitted to de-orbit and land at Kleinman Base so that the decontamination team could leave.

No sooner had the decontamination team left, when there was a welcome hail at the airlock.

"Tia! Permission to come aboard, ma'am!"

She activated her lock so quickly that it must have flown open in his face, and brought him up in the lift rather than waiting for him to climb the stairs. He sauntered in sans pressure-suit, gave her column a jaunty salute, and put down his bags.

"I have good news and better news," he said, flinging himself into his chair. "Which do you want to hear first?"

"The good news," she replied promptly, and did *not* scold him for putting his feet up on the console.

"The good news is all personal. I have been granted a clean bill of health, and so have you. In addition, since the decontamination team so rudely destroyed my clothing and anything else that they couldn't be sure of, I have just been having a *glorious* spending-spree down there at the Base, using a CS unlimited credit account!"

Tia groaned, picturing more neon-purple, or worse. "Don't open the bags, or they'll think I've had a radiation leak."

He mock-pouted. "My dear lady, your taste is somewhere back in the last decade."

"Never mind my taste," she said. "What's the better news?"

"Our patients are on their way to full recovery." At her exclamation, he held up a cautionary hand. "It's going to take them several months, maybe even a year. Here's the story—and the reason why they stripped you of everything that could be considered a fabric. Access your Terran entomology, if you would. Call up something called a 'dust mite' and another something called a 'sand flea.'"

Puzzled, she did so, laying the pictures side by side on the central screen.

"As we guessed, this was indeed a virus, with an insect vector. The culprit was something like a sand flea, which, you will note, has a taste for warm-blooded critters. But it was about the size of a dust mite. The fardling things don't hatch until the temperature is right, the days are long enough, and there's been a rainstorm. Once they hatch, the only thing that kills them is really intense insecticide or freezing cold for several weeks. They live in the dust, like sand fleas. Those archeologists had been tracking in dust ever since the rainstorm, and since there'd been no sign of any problems, they hadn't been very careful about their decontamination protocols. The bugs all hatched within an hour, or so the entomologists think. They bit everything in sight, since they always wake up hungry. *But*—here's the catch—since they were so small, they didn't leave a bite mark, so there was nothing to show that anyone had been bitten." He nodded at the screen. "Every one of the little beggars carries the virus. It's like *E. coli*, the human bacillus, living in their guts the way it does in ours."

"I assume that everyone got bitten about the same time?" she hazarded.

"Exactly," he said. "Which meant that everyone came down with the virus within hours of each other. Mostly, purely by coincidence, in their sleep. The virus itself invokes allergic shock in most people it infects. Which can look a lot like a stroke, under the right circumstances."

"So we didn't—" She stopped herself before she went any further, but he finished the statement for her.

"No, we didn't kill anyone. It was the Zombie Bug. And the best news of all is that the Zombie state is caused by interference with the production of neurotransmitters. Clean out the virus, and eventually everyone gets back to normal."

"*Oh Alex*—" she said, and he interrupted her.

"A little more excellent news—first, that we get a bonus for this one. And second, my very dear, you saved my life."

"I did?" she replied, dumbfounded.

"If I had cracked my suit even once, the bugs would have gotten in. They were everywhere, in your carpet, the upholstery; either they got in the first time we cracked the lock, or the standard decontamination didn't wash them all off the suit or kill them. And I am one of those seventy-five percent of the population so violently allergic to them that—" He let her fill in the rest.

"Alex—I'd rather have you as my brawn than all the bonuses in the world," she said, after a long pause.

"Good," he said, rising, and patting her column gently. "I feel the same way."

Before the moment could get maudlin, he cleared his throat, and continued. "Now the bad news: we're so far behind on our deliveries that they want us out of here yesterday. So, are you ready to fly, bright lady?"

She laughed. "Strap on your chair, hotshot. Let's show 'em how to burn on out of here!"

CHAPTER FIVE

"Well, Tia," Doctor Kenny said genially, from his vantage point in front of her main screen. "I have to say that it's a lot more fun talking to you face-to-column than by messages or double-bounce comlink. Waiting for four hours for the punchline to a joke is a bit much."

He faced her column, not the screen, showing the same courtesy Alex always did. Alex was not aboard at the moment; he was down on the base spending his bonus while Tia was in the refit docks in orbit. But since the *Pride of Albion* was so close, Doctor Kenny had decided that he couldn't resist making a visit to his most successful patient.

The new version of his chair had been perfected, and he was wearing it now. The platform and seat hid the main power-supply, a shiny exoskeleton covered his legs up to his waist, and Tia thought he looked like some kind of ancient warrior-king on a throne.

"Most of my classmates don't get the point of jokes," she said, with a chuckle. "They just don't seem to have much of a sense of humor. I have to share them with you softies."

"Most of your classmates are as stiff as AIs," he countered. "Don't worry, they'll loosen up in a decade or two—that's what Lars tells me, anyway. He says that living around softies will contaminate even the most rule-bound shellperson. So, how's life with a partner?

As I recall, that was one of your worst worries, that you'd end up with a double-debt like Moira for playing brawn-basketball."

"I really like Alex, Kenny," she said slowly. "Especially after the Zombie Bug run. I hate to admit this, but—I even like him more than you, or Anna, or Lars. And that's what I wanted to talk to you about when you called the other day. I really—trust your judgment."

He nodded, sagely. "And since I'm not in the brain-brawn program, *I* am not bound by regs to report you when you tell me how much you are attracted to your brawn." He sent an ironic wink toward her column.

She let herself relax a little. "Something like that," she admitted. "Kenny, I just don't know what to think. He's sloppy, he's forgetful, he's a little impulsive—he has the *worst* taste in clothes—and I'd rather have him as a partner than anyone else in the galaxy. I'd rather talk to *him* than my classmates, and being classmates is supposed to be the strongest bond a shellperson can have!" Supposed to be—that was the trick, wasn't it? There was very little in her life that had happened the way it was supposed to. At this point, she should have been entering advanced studies under the auspices of the Institute—not working for it. She should have been a softie—not a shellperson.

But you didn't deal with life by dwelling on what "should" have happened. You handled it by making the best out of what *had* happened.

"Well, Tia, you spent the first seven of your most formative years as a softperson," Kenny pointed out gently. His next words echoed her own earlier thoughts. "You never thought you'd wind up in a shell, where your classmates never knew anything but their shells and their teachers. Just like when a chick hatches—what it imprints on is what it's going to fall in love with,"

"I—I didn't say I was in love," she stammered, suddenly alarmed.

Kenny held his peace. He simply stared at her column with a look she remembered all too well. The one that said she wasn't entirely telling the truth, and he knew it.

"Well—maybe a little," she admitted, in a very soft voice. "But—it's not like I was another softie—"

"You can love a friend, you know," Kenny pointed out. "That's been acknowledged for centuries—even among stuffy shellperson Counselors. Remember your Greek philosophers—they felt there were three kinds of love, and only one of them had anything to do with the body. *Eros, filios,* and *agape.*"

"Sexual, brotherly, and religious," she translated, feeling a little better. "Well, okay. *Filios,* then."

"Lars translates them as 'love involving the body,' 'love involving the mind,' and 'love involving the soul.' That's even more apt in your case," Kenny said comfortably. "Both *filios* and *agape* apply here."

"I guess you're right," she said, feeling sheepish.

"Tia, my dear," Kenny said, without a hint of patronization, "there is nothing wrong with saying that you love your brawn— the first words you transmitted to me from your new shell, in case you've forgotten, were 'Doctor Kenny, I love you.' Frankly, I'm a lot happier hearing *this* from you than something 'appropriate.' "

"Like what?" she asked curiously.

"Hmm. Like this." He raised his voice an octave. "Well, Doctor Kennet," he said primly, "I'm quite pleased with the performance of my brawn Alexander. I believe we can work well together. Our teamwork was quite acceptable on this last assignment."

"You sound like Kari, exactly like Kari." She laughed. "Yes, but imagine trying to have this conversation with one of my BB Counselors!"

He screwed up his face and flung up his hands. "Oh, *horrors!*" he exclaimed, his expression matching the outrage in his voice. "How *could* you confess to feeling *anything*? AH-One-Oh-Three-Three, I am going to *have* to report you for *instability!*"

"Precisely," she replied, sobering. "Sometimes I think they just want us to be superior sorts of AIs. Self-aware and self-motivating, but someone get out a scalpel and excise the *feeling* part before you pop them in their shells."

"There's a fine line they have to tread, dear," he told her, just as soberly. "Your classmates lack something you had—the physical nurturing of a parent. They never touched anything; they've never known anything but a very artificial environment. They don't really understand emotions, because they've never been allowed to experience them or even see them near at hand. I don't think there's any question in *my* mind what that means, when they first come out into the real world of us softies. It means they literally enter a world as foreign and incomprehensible as any alien culture. In some ways, it would be better if they all entered professions where they never had to deal with humans one-on-one."

"Then why—" She picked her words with care. "Why don't they put adults into shells?"

"Because adults—even children—often can't adapt to the fact that their bodies don't work anymore, and that—as you pointed out yourself—they will never have that human *touch* again." He sighed. "I've seen plenty of that in my time, too. You are an exception, my love. But you always have been special. Outstandingly flexible, adaptable." He sat back in his chair and thought; she didn't interrupt him. "Tia, there are things that I don't agree with in the way the shellperson training program is run. But you're out of the training area now and into the real world. You'll find that even the Counselors can have an entirely different attitude out here. They're ready to accept what works, not just what's in the rule books."

She paused a moment before replying. "Kenny, what do I do if—things creep over into *eros*? I mean, I'm not going to crack my column or anything, but . . ."

"Helva," Kenny said succinctly. "Think of Helva. She and her brawn had a romance that still has power over the rest of known space. If it happens, Tia, let it happen. If it *doesn't*, don't mourn over it. Enjoy the fact that your brawn is your very best friend; that's the way it's supposed to be, after all. I have faith in your sense and sensibility; I always have. You'll be fine." He coughed a little. "As it—ah—happens, I have a bit of fellow-feeling for you. Anna and I have gotten to be something of an item."

"Really?" She didn't even try to modulate the glee out of her voice. "It's about time! What did she do, tip your chair over to slow you down and seduce you on the spot?"

"That's just about word for word what Lars said," Kenny replied, blushing furiously. "Except that he added a few other pointed remarks."

"I can imagine." She giggled. Lars was over two centuries old, and he had seen a great deal in that time. Every kind of drama a sentient was capable of, in fact—he was the chief overseer of one of the largest hospital stations in Central Systems. If there was ever a place for life-and-death drama, a hospital station was it—as holo-makers across the galaxy knew. From the smallest incident to the gravest, Lars had witnessed—and sometimes participated in—all of it.

He had been in charge of the *Pride of Albion* since it was built—he had been built into it. He would never leave, and never wanted to. Cynical, brilliant—with an unexpectedly kind heart. That was Lars. . . .

He could be the gentlest person, soft- or shell-, that Tia had ever met. Though he never missed an opportunity to jab one of his softperson colleagues with his sharp wit.

"But Kenny—" She hesitated, eaten alive with curiosity, but unsure how far she could push. "Kenny, how nosy can I be about you and Anna?"

"Tia, I know everything there is to know about you, from your normal heart rate to the exact composition of the chemicals in your blood when you're under stress. *My* doctor knows the same about me. We're both used to being poked and prodded—" he paused "—and you are my very dear friend. If there is something you are really curious about, please, go ahead and ask." His eyes twinkled. "But don't expect me to tell you about the birds and the bees."

"You're—when we first met, you called yourself a 'medico on the half-shell.' You're half machine. How does Anna—feel about that?" If she could have blushed, she would have, she felt so intrusive.

He didn't seem to feel that she was intruding, however. "Hmm, good questions. The answer, my dear, is one that I am afraid can't apply to you. I'm only 'half machine' when I'm strapped in. When I'm not in my chair, I'm—an imperfect, but entirely human creature." He smiled.

"So it's like comparing rocks to bonbons." That was something she hadn't anticipated. "Or water to sheet-metal."

"Good comparisons. You're not the first to ask these questions, by the way. So don't think you're unique in being curious." He stretched and grinned. "Anna and I are doing a lot of—hmm—personal-relations counseling of my other handicapped patients."

"At least I'm not some kind of—would-be voyeur." That was nice to know.

"You, however, were and are in an entirely different boat than my other patients," he warned. "What applies to them does not apply to you." He shook his head. "I'm going to give this to you straight and without softening. You have no working nerves, sensory or motor control, below your neck. And from what I've seen, there was some further damage to the autonomic system as well before we stabilized you. What with the mods they made to you when you went into the shell, you're dependent on life-support now. I don't think you could survive outside your shell—I know you wouldn't be happy."

"Oh. All right." In a way, she was both disappointed and relieved. Relieved that it was one more factor she wouldn't have to consider in her ongoing partnership. Disappointed—well, not that much. She hadn't really thought there would ever be any way to reverse the path that had brought her into her column.

"I did bring some records of the things I've been working on to show you—devices that are helping out some of our involuntary amputees. I thought you'd be interested, just on an academic basis." He slipped a datahedron into her reader, and she brought up the display on her central screen. "This young lady was a professional dancer—she was trapped under several tons of masonry after an earthquake. By the time medics got to her, the entire limb had suffered cell-death. There was no saving it."

The video portion of the clip showed a lovely young lady in leotards and tights trying out what looked like a normal leg— except that it moved very stiffly.

"The problem with the artificial limbs we've been giving amputees is that while we've fixed most of the weight and movement problems, they're still completely useless for someone like a dancer, who relies on sensory input to tell her whether or nor her foot is in the right position." Kenny smiled fondly as he watched the girl on the screen. "That's Lila within a few minutes of having the leg installed. At the hip, may I add. The next clip will be three weeks later, then three months."

The screen flickered as Tia found her attention absorbed by the girl. Now she was working out in what were obviously ballet exercises, and doing very well, so far as Tia could tell. Then the screen flickered a third time—

And the girl was on stage, partnered in some kind of classic ballet piece—and if Tia had not known her left leg was cyborged, she would never have guessed it.

"Here's a speed-keyer who lost his hand," Kenny continued, but he turned towards the column. "Between my work and Moto-Prosthetics, we've beaten the sensory input problem, Tia," he said proudly. "Lila tells me she's changed the choreography so that she can perform some of the more difficult moves on her left foot instead of her right. The left won't get toe-blisters or broken foot-bones, the tendons won't tear, the knee won't give, and the ankle has no chance of buckling. The only difference that *she* can see between the cyborged leg and the natural one is that the cyborg is a little heavier—not enough to make any difference to her if she can change the choreography—and it's a lot sturdier."

A few more of Doctor Kenny's patients came up on the screen, but neither of them were paying attention.

"There have to be some problems," Tia said, finally. "I mean, nothing is perfect."

"We don't have *full* duplication of sensory input. In Lila's case, we have it in the entire foot and the ankle and knee-joints, and we've pretty much ignored the stretches of leg in between. Weight is the other problem. The more sensory nerves we duplicate, the higher the weight. A ten-kilo hand is going to give someone a lot of trouble, for instance." Kenny shifted a little in his chair. "But all of this is coming *straight* out of what's going on in the Lab Schools, Tia! And most of it is from the brainship program—the same thing that gives you sensory input from the ships' systems are what became the sensory linkups for those artificial limbs."

"That's wonderful!" Tia said, very pleased for him. "You're quite something, Doctor Kennet!"

"Oh, there's a lot more to be done," he said modestly. "I haven't heard any of Lila's fellow dancers clamoring to have double-amputations and new legs installed. She has her problems, and there's some pain involved, even after healing is completed. In a way, it's a good thing for us that our first leg-installation was for a dancer, because Lila was used to living with pain—all dancers are. And it's *very* expensive; she was lucky, because the insurance company involved judged that compensating her for a lost—very lucrative—career was more expensive than an artificial limb. Although—given the life expectancy of you shellpersons, and compare it to those of us still in our designed-by-genetics containers—well, I can foresee a day when we'll all have our brains tucked into minishells when the old envelope starts to decay, and instead of deciding what clothes we want to wear, we have to decide what body to put on."

"Oh, I don't think it'll come to that, really," Tia said decisively. "For one thing, if it's expensive for one limb, a whole body would be impossible."

"It is that," Kenny agreed. "But to tell you the truth, right now the problem besides expense isn't technical—we could put the fully-functioning body together—and do it today. It's actually easier to do that than just one limb. Oh, by that, I mean one with full sensory inputs."

He didn't say anything, but he winked, and grinned wickedly. "And by 'full sensory input,' I mean exactly what you're thinking, you naughty young lady."

"Me?" she said, with completely feigned indignation. "I have *no* idea what you're talking about! I am as innocent as—as—"

"As I am," Kenny said. "You were the one who was asking about me and Anna."

She remained silent, pretending dignity. He continued to grin, and she knew he wasn't fooled in the least.

"Well, anyway, the problem is having a life-support system for a naked brain." He shrugged. "Can't quite manage that—putting a whole body into a life-support shell is still the only way to deal with trauma like yours. And we can't fit *that* into a human-sized body."

"Oh, you could make us great *big* bodies and create a whole race of giants," she joked. "That should actually be easier, from what you've told me."

He cast his eyes upwards, surprising her somewhat with his sudden flare of exasperation. "Believe it or not, there's a fellow who wants to do something like that, for the holos. He wants to create giant full-sensory bodies of—oh, dinosaurs, monsters, whatever—hire a shellperson actor, and use the whole setup in his epics."

"No!" she exclaimed.

"I swear," he said, placing his hand over his heart. "True, every word of it. And believe it or not, he *has* the money. Holostars make more than you do, my love. I think the next time some brain wants to retire from active ship-service, especially one that's bought out his contract, this fellow just might tempt them into the holos."

"Amazing. Virtual headshaking here." She thought for a moment.

"What would the chances be of creating a life-sized body with some kind of brainstem link to the shell?"

"Like a radio?" he hazarded. "Hmm. Good question. A real problem; there is a *lot* of information carried by these nerves—you'd need separated channels for everything, but—well, the effective range would be very, very short, otherwise you run the risk of signal breakup. That turned out to be the problem with this rig," he finished, nodding at his armored legs. "It has to stay in the same room with me, otherwise—Greek frieze time."

She laughed.

"Anyway, the whole rig would probably cost as much as a brainship, so it's not exactly practical," he concluded. "Not even for me, and they pay me very well."

Not exactly practical for me, either, she thought, and dismissed the whole idea. Practical, for a brainship, meant buying out her contract. After all, if she wanted to be free to join the Institute as an active researcher and go chasing the EsKays on her own, she was going to have to buy herself out.

"Well, money—that's the other reason I wanted to talk to you," she said.

"And the bane of the BB program rears its ugly head," he intoned, and grinned. "Oh, they're going to hate you. You're just like all the rest of the really good ones. You want to buy that contract out, don't you?"

"I don't think there are too many CS ships that *don't* plan on doing it someday," she countered. "We're people, not AI drones. We like to have a choice of where we go. So, do you have any ideas of how I can start raising my credit balance? Moira has kind of cornered the market on spotting possible new sites from orbit and entry."

"Gave her the idea, did you?" Kenny shook his finger at her. "Don't you know you should never give ideas away to the competition?"

"She wasn't competition, then," Tia pointed out.

"Well, you have a modest bonus from the Zombie Bug run, right?" he said, scratching his eyebrow as he thought. "What about investing it?"

"In what?" she countered. "I don't know anything about investing money."

"Operating on my own modest success in putting my own

money into Moto-Prosthetics—and not in paper stock, my dear, but in shares in the company itself—if you use your own knowledge to choose where to invest, the results can be substantial." He tapped his fingers on the side of his chair. "It's not insider trading, if you're thinking that. I would consider putting your money where your interest and expertise is."

"Virtual headshaking," she replied. "I have *no* idea what you're getting at. What do *I* know?"

"Look—" he said, leaning forward, his eyes bright with intensity. "The one thing an archeologist is *always* cognizant of is the long term—especially long-term patterns. And the one thing that most often trips up the sophonts of any race is that they are *not* thinking in the long term. Look for what a friend of mine called 'disasters waiting to happen,' and invest in the companies that will be helping to recover from that disaster."

"Well, that sounds good in theory," she said doubtfully. "But in practice? How am I going to find situations like that? I'm only one person, and I've already got a job."

"Tia, you have the computing power of an entire brainship at your disposal," Kenny told her firmly. "And you have access to Institute records for every inhabited planet that also holds ruins. Use both. Look for problems the ancients had, then see if they'll happen again at current colonies."

Well, nothing sprung immediately to mind, but it *would* while away some time. And Kenny had a point.

He glanced at his wrist-chrono. "Well, my shuttle should be hailing you right about—"

"Now," she finished. "It's about to dock: four slots from me, to your right as you exit the lock. Thanks for coming, Kenny."

He directed his Chair to the lift. "Thank you for having me, Tia. As always, it's been a pleasure."

He turned to look back over his shoulder as he reached the lift, and grinned. "By the way, don't bother to check my med records. Anna has never complained about my performance yet."

If she could have blushed . . .

While Alex spent his time with some of his old classmates—presumably living up to what he had told her was the class motto, "The Party Never Ends"—she dove headlong into Institute records. The Institute gave her free, no-charge access to anything she

wanted; perhaps because they counted her as a kind of member-researcher, perhaps because of her part in the Zombie Bug rescue—or perhaps because brainship access was one hole in their access system they'd never plugged because they never thought of it. Normally they charged for every record downloaded from the main archives. It didn't matter to her; there was plenty there to look into.

But first—her own peculiar quest. She caught up on everything having to do with the old EsKay investigations in fairly short order. There wasn't much of anything new from existing digs, so she checked to see what Pota and Braddon were doing, then went on to postings on brand new EsKay finds.

It was there that she came across something quite by accident.

It was actually rather amusing, when it came down to it. It was the report from a Class Two dig, from the group taking over a site that had initially gotten a lot of excitement from the Exploration team. *They* had reported it as an EsKay site—the first ever to be uncovered on a non-Marslike world. And an EsKay Evaluation team was sent post-haste.

It turned out to be a case of misidentification; not EsKays at all, but another race entirely, the Megalt Tresepts, one of nowhere near as much interest to the Institute. Virtually everything was known about the Megalts; they had sent out FTL ships in the far distant past, and some of the colonies they had established still existed. Some of their artifacts looked like EsKay work, and if there was no notion that the Megalts had been in the neighborhood, it was fairly easy to make the mistake.

The world was surprisingly Terran—which would have made an EsKay site all the more valuable *if* it really had been there.

Although it was not an EsKay site after all, Tia continued reading the report out of curiosity. Largo Draconis was an odd little planet—with an eccentric orbit that made for one really miserable decade every century or so. Other than that, it was quite habitable; really pleasant, in fact, with two growing seasons in every year. The current settlements were ready for that dismal decade, according to the report—but also according to the report, the Megalts had been, too.

Yet the Megalt sites had been abandoned, completely. Not typical of the logical, systematic race.

During the first year of that wretched ten years, every Megalt

settlement on the planet (all two of them) had been abandoned. And not because they ran out of food, either, which was her first thought. They had stockpiled more than enough to carry them through, even with no harvests at all.

No, not because the *settlers* ran out of food—but because the native rodents did.

Curious about what had happened, the Evaluation team had found the settlement records, which outlined the entire story, inscribed on the thin metal sheets the Megalts used for their permanent hardcopy storage. The settlements had been abandoned so quickly that no one had bothered to find and take them.

It was a good thing the Megalts used metal for their records; nothing else would have survived what had happened to the settlement. The rodents had swarmed both colonies; a trickle at first, hardly more than a nuisance. But then, out of nowhere, a swarm, a flood, a *torrent* of rodents had poured down over the settlement. They overwhelmed the protections in place—electric fences—and literally ate their way into the buildings. Nothing had stopped them. Killing them in hordes had done nothing. They merely ate the bodies and kept moving in.

The evidence all pointed to a periodic change in the rodents' digestive systems that enabled them to eat *anything* with a cellulose or petrochemical base, up to and including plastic.

The report concluded with the Evaluation team's final words on the attitude of the current government of Largo Draconis, in a personal note that had been attached to the report.

"Fred: I am just glad we are getting *out* of here. We told the Settlement Governor about all this, and they're ignoring us. They think that just because I'm an archeologist, I have my nose so firmly in the past that I have no grasp on the present. They told me in the governor's office that their ward-off fields should be more than enough to hold off the rats. Not a chance. We're talking about a feeding-frenzy here, furry locusts, and I don't think they're going to give a ward-off field a second thought. I'm telling you, Fred, these people are going to be in trouble in a year. The Megalts threw in the towel, and they weren't anywhere near as backward as the governor thinks they were. *Maybe* this wonder ward-off field of his will keep the rats off, but I don't think so. And I don't want to find out that he was wrong by waking up under a blanket of rats. They didn't eat the Megalts—but they ate their *clothes*. I don't fancy piling into a shuttle with my derriere bared to the gentle breezes—which by that time should be, oh, around fifty kilometers per hour, and minus twenty Celsius. So I may even beat this report home. Keep the beer cold and the fireplace warm for me."

Well. If ever there was something that matched what Doctor Kenny had suggested, this was it.

Just to be certain, she checked several other sources—not for the veracity of the report, but to see just how prepared the colony was for the "rats" as well as the worsening weather.

Everything she found bore out what the unknown writer had told "Fred." Ward-off generators were standard issue, not heavy-duty. Warehouses had metal doors—and many had plastic or wooden siding. Homes were made of native stone and well-insulated against the cold, but had plastic or wooden doors. Food had been stockpiled, but what would the colonists do when the "rats" ate through the warehouse sides to get at the stockpiled rations? The colony had been depending on food grown on-planet for the past twenty years. There were no provisions for importing food and no synthesizers of any real size. They had protein farms—but what if the "rats" got into them and ate the yeast-stock along with everything else? What would they do when the stockpiled food was gone? Or if they managed to save the food, what would they do when—as Fred had suggested—the "rats" ate through their doors and made a meal off their clothing, their blankets, their furniture. . . .

So much for official records. Was there *anyone* on-planet that could pull these people out of their disaster?

It took a full day of searching business-directories before she had her answer. An on-planet manufacturer of specialized protection equipment, including heavy-duty ward-off and protection-field generators, could provide protection once the planetary governor admitted there was a problem. Governmental resources might not be able to pay for all the protection the colonists needed—but over eighty percent of the inhabitants carried hazard insurance, and the insurance companies should pay for protection for their clients.

That was half of the answer. The other half?

Another firm with multi-planet outlets, and a load of old-fashioned synthesizers in a warehouse within shipping distance. They didn't produce much in the way of variety, but load them up with raw materials, carbon from coal or oil, minerals, protein from yeast and fiber from other vat-grown products, and you had something basic to eat—or wear—or make into furnishings—

She set her scheme in motion. But *not* through Beta, her supervisor, but through Lars and his.

Before Alex returned, she had made all the arrangements; and she had included carefully worded letters to the two companies she had chosen—plus all of the publicly available records. She tried to convey a warning without sounding like some kind of crazed hysteric.

Of course, the fact that she was investing in their firms should at least convey the idea that she was an hysteric with money. . . .

If they had any sense, they would be able to put the story together for themselves from the records, and they would believe her. Hopefully, they would be ready.

She transmitted the last of the messages, just as Alex arrived at her airlock.

"Permission to come aboard, ma'am," he called cheerfully, as she opened the lock for him. He ran up the stairs two at a time, and when he burst into the main cabin, she told herself that fashions would surely change, soon—he was dressed in a chrome yellow tunic with neon-red piping, and neon-red trousers with chrome-yellow piping. Both bright enough to hurt the eyes and dazzle the pickups, and she was grateful she could tune down the intensity of her visual receptors.

"How was your reunion?" she asked, once his clothes weren't blinding her.

"There weren't more than a half dozen of them," he told her, continuing through the hall and down to his own cabin. He pitched both his bags on his bed, and returned. "We just missed Chria by a hair. But we had a good time."

"I'm surprised you didn't come back with a hangover."

He widened his eyes with surprise. "Not me! I'm the Academy designated driver—or at any rate, I make sure people get on the right shuttles. Never touch the stuff, myself, or almost never. Clogs the synapses."

Tia felt irrationally pleased to hear that.

"So, did you miss me? I missed you. Did you have enough to do?" He flung himself down in his chair and put his feet up on the console. "I hope you didn't spend all your time reading Institute papers."

"Oh," she replied lightly, "I found a few other things to occupy my time. . . ."

The comlink was live, and Alex was on his very best behavior—including a fresh, and only marginally rumpled, uniform. He sat quietly in his chair, the very picture of a sober Academy graduate and responsible CS brawn.

Tia reflected that it was just as well she'd bullied him into that uniform. The transmission was shared by Professor Barton Glasov y Verona-Gras, head of the Institute, and a gray-haired, dark-tunicked man the professor identified as Central Systems Sector Administrator Joshua Elliot-Rosen y Sinor. Very high in administration. And just now, very concerned about something, although he hid his concern well. Alex had snapped to a kind of seated "attention" the moment his face appeared on the screen.

"Alexander, Hypatia—we're going to be sending you a long file of stills and holos," Professor Barton began. "But for now, the object you see here on my desk is representative of our problem."

The "object" in question was a perfectly lovely little vase. The style was distinctive; skewed, but with a very sensuous sinuosity, as if someone had fused Art Nouveau with Salvador Dali. It seemed—as nearly as Tia could tell from the transmission—to be made of multiple layers of opalescent glass or ceramic.

It also had the patina that only something that has been buried for a very long time achieves.

Or something with a chemically faked patina. But would the professor himself have called them if all he was worried about were fake antiquities? Not likely.

The only problem with the vase—if it was a genuine artifact—was that it did not match the style of any known artifact in any of Tia's files.

"You know that smuggling and site-robbing has always been a big problem for us," Professor Barton continued. "It's very frustrating to come on a site and find it's already been looted. But this—this is doubly frustrating. Because, as I'm sure Hypatia has already realized, the style of this piece does not match that of any known civilization."

"A few weeks ago, hundreds of artifacts in this style flooded the black market," Sinor said smoothly. "Analysis showed them to be quite ancient—this piece for instance was made some time when Ramses the Second was Pharaoh."

The professor was not wringing his hands, but his distress was fairly obvious. "There are *hundreds* of these objects!" he blurted. "Everything from cups to votive offerings, from jewelry to statuary! We not only don't know where they've come from, but we don't even know anything *about* the people that made them!"

"Most of the objects are not as well-preserved as this one, of course," Sinor continued, sitting with that incredible stillness that only a professional politician or actor achieves. "But besides being incredibly valuable, and not incidentally, funneling money into the criminal subculture, there is something else rather distressing associated with these artifacts."

Tia knew what it *had* to be as soon as the words were out of the man's mouth. Plague.

"Plague," he said solemnly. "So far, this has not been a fatal disease, at least, not to the folk who bought these little trinkets. *They* have private physicians and in-house medicomps, obviously."

High Families, Tia surmised. *So the High Families are mixed up in this.*

"The objects really aren't dangerous, once they've been through proper decontam procedures," the professor added hastily. "But whoever is digging these things up isn't even bothering with a run under the UV gun. He's just cleaning them up—"

Tia winced inwardly, and *saw* Alex wince. To tell an archeologist that a smuggler had "cleaned up" an artifact, was like telling a coin collector that his nephew Joey had gotten out the wire brush and shined up his collection for him.

"—cleaning them up, putting them in cases, and selling them." Professor Barton sighed. "I have no idea why his helpers aren't coming down with this. Maybe they're immune. Whatever the reason, the receivers of these pieces *are*, they are not happy about it, and they want something done."

His expression told Tia more than his words did. The High Families who had bought artifacts they must have known were smuggled and possibly stolen, and some members of their circle had gotten sick. And because the Institute was the official organization in charge of ancient relics, they expected the Institute to find the smuggler and deal with him.

Not that any of them would tell us how and where they found out about these treasures. Nor would they ever admit that they knew they were gray market, if not black. And if they'd stop buying smuggled artifacts, they wouldn't get sick.

But none of that meant anything when it came to the High Families, of course. They were too wealthy and too powerful to ever find themselves dealing with such simple concepts as *cause* and *effect.*

Hmm. Except once in a great while—like now—when it rises up and bites them.

"In spite of the threat of disease associated with these pieces, they are still in very high demand," Sinor said.

Because someone in the High Families spread the word that you'd better run the thing through decontamination after you buy it, so you can have your pretty without penalty. But there was something wrong with this story. Something that didn't quite fit. But she couldn't figure out what it was.

Meanwhile, the transmission continued. "But I don't have to tell either of you how dangerous it is to have these things out there," Professor Barton added. "It's fairly obvious that the smugglers are not taking even the barest of precautions with the artifacts. It becomes increasingly likely with every piece sold at a high price that someone will steal one, or find out where the source is, or take one to a disadvantaged area to sell it."

A slum, you mean, Professor. Was he putting too much emphasis on this?

Tia decided to show that both she and her brawn *were* paying attention. "I can see what could happen then, gentlemen," she countered. "Disease spreads very quickly in areas of that sort, and what might not be particularly dangerous for someone of means will *kill* the impoverished."

And then we have a full-scale epidemic and a panic on our hands. But he had to know how she felt about this. *He* knew who she was—there weren't too many "Hypatias" in the world, and he had been the immediate boss of Pota and Braddon's superior. He had to know the story. He was probably trading on it.

"Precisely, Hypatia," said Sinor, in an eerie "answer" to her own thoughts.

"I hope you aren't planning on using us as smuggler hunters," Alex replied, slowly. "I couldn't pass as High Family in a million years, so I couldn't be in on the purchasing end. And we aren't allowed to be armed—I know I don't want to take on the smuggling end without a locker full of artillery!"

In other words, gentlemen, "we ain't stupid, we ain't expendable, and we ain't goin'." But this was all sounding a little too pat, a little too contrived. If Sinor told them that they *weren't* expected to catch the smugglers themselves . . .

"No—" Sinor said soothingly—and a little too hastily. "No, we have some teams in the Enforcement Division going at both ends. *However,* it is entirely possible that the source for these artifacts is someone—or rather, several someones—working on Exploration or Evaluation teams. Since the artifacts showed up in this sector first, it is logical to assume that they originate here."

Too smooth. Too pat. This is *all a story. But why?*

"So you want us to keep our eyes peeled when we make our deliveries," Alex filled in.

"You two are uniquely suited," Professor Barton pointed out. "You both have backgrounds in archeology. Hypatia, you know how digs work, intimately. Once you know how to identify these artifacts, if you see even a hint of them—shards, perhaps, or broken bits of jewelry—you'll know what they are and where they came from."

"We can do that," Tia replied, carefully. "We can be a little snoopy, I think, without arousing any suspicions."

"Good. That was what we needed." Professor Barton sounded very relieved. "I suppose I don't need to add that there is a bonus in this for you."

"I can live with a bonus," Alex responded cheerfully.

The two VIPs signed off, and Alex turned immediately to Tia.

"Did that sound as phony to you as it did to me?" he demanded.

"Well, the objects they want are certainly real enough," she replied, playing back her internal recording of the conversation and analyzing every word. "But whether they really are artifacts is another question. There's definitely more going on than they're willing to tell us."

Alex leaned back in his chair and put his hands behind his head. "Are these things financing espionage or insurrection?" he hazarded. "Or buying weapons?"

She stopped her recording; there was something about the artifact that bothered her. She enhanced the picture and threw it up on the screen.

"What's wrong with this?" she demanded. Alex leaned forward to have a look.

"Is that a hole bored in the base?" he said. "Bored in, then patched over?"

"Could be." She enhanced her picture again. "Does it seem to you that the base is awfully thick?"

"Could be," he replied. "You know . . . we have only *their* word that these are 'alien artifacts.' What if they are nothing of the sort?"

"They wouldn't be worth much of anything then—unless—"

The answer came to her so quickly that it brought its own fireworks display with it. "Got it!" she exclaimed, and quickly accessed the Institute library for a certain old news program.

She remembered this one from her own childhood; both for the fact that it had been an ingenious way to smuggle and because Pota had caught her watching it, realized what the story was about, and shut it off. But not before Tia had gotten the gist of it.

One of the Institute archeologists had been subverted by a major drug-smuggler who wanted a way to get his supply to Central. In another case where there were small digs on the same planets as colonies, the archeologist had himself become addicted to the mood-altering drug called "Paradise," and had made himself open to blackmail.

The blackmail came from the supplier-producer himself. Out there in the fringe, it was easy enough to hide his smuggled supplies in ordinary shipments of agri-goods, but the nearer one got to civilization, the harder it became. Publicly available transport was out of the question.

But there were other shipments going straight to the heart of civilization. Shipments that were so innocent, and so fragile, they never saw a custom's inspector. Such as . . . Institute artifacts.

So the drug-dealer molded his product in the likeness of pottery shards. And the archeologist on-site made sure they got packed like any other artifacts and shipped—although they were never cataloged. Once the shipment arrived at the Institute, a worker inside the receiving area would set the crates with particular marks aside and leave them on the loading dock overnight. They would, of course, disappear, but since they had never been cataloged, they were never missed.

The only reason the archeologist in question had been caught was because an overzealous graduate student *had* cataloged the phony shards, and when they came up missing at the Institute, the police became involved.

Tia ran the news clip for Alex, who watched it attentively. "What do you think?" she asked, when it was over.

"I think our friend in the dull blue-striped tunic had a strangely fit look about him. The look that says 'police' to yours truly." Alex nodded. "I think you're right. I think someone is trying the artifact-switch again, except that this time they're coming in on the black market."

She did a quick access to the nets, and began searching for a politician named Sinor. She found one—but he did *not* match the man she had seen on the transmission.

"The trick is probably that if someone sees a crate full of smuggled glassware, they don't think of drugs." Tia felt very smug over her deduction, and her identification of Sinor as a ringer. Of course, there was no way of knowing if her guess was right or wrong, but still. . . . "The worst that is likely to happen to an artifact-smuggler is a fine and a slap on the wrist. They aren't taken very seriously, even though there's serious money in it and the smugglers may have killed to get them."

"That's assuming inspectors even find the artifacts. So where were *we* supposed to fit in to all this?" Alex ran his hand through his hair. "Do they think we're going to find this guy?"

"I think that they think he's working with one of the small-dig people again. By the way, you were right about Sinor. Or rather, the Sinor we saw is not the one of record." Another thought occurred to her. "You know—their story may very well have been genuine. There's not a lot of room in jewelry to hide drugs. Whoever is doing this may have *started* by smuggling out the artifacts, freelance—got tangled up with some crime syndicate, and now he's been forced to deal the fake, drug-carrying artifacts along with the real ones."

"Now *that* makes sense!" Alex exclaimed. "That fits all the parameters. Do we still play along?"

"Ye-es," she replied slowly. "But in a severely limited sense, I'd say. We aren't trained in law enforcement, and we don't carry weapons. If we see something, we report it, and get the heck out."

"Sounds good to me, lady," Alex replied, with patent relief. "I'm not a coward—but I'm not stupid. And I didn't sign up with the BB program to get ventilated by some low-down punk. If I wanted to do *that*, all I have to do is stroll into certain neighborhoods and flash some glitter. Tia—why all that nonsense about plague?"

"Partially to hook us in, I think," she said, after a moment. "They know we were the team that got the Zombie Bug—we'll feel strongly about plague. And partially to keep us from touching these objects. If we don't mess with them, we won't know about the drug link."

He made a sound of disgust. "You'd think they'd have trusted us with the real story. I'm half tempted to blow this whole thing off, just because they didn't. I won't—" he added hastily, "but I'm tempted."

He began warming up the boards, preparatory to taking off. Tia opened a channel to traffic control—but while she did so, she was silently wondering if there was even more to the story than *she* had guessed.

There was something bothering Alex, and as they continued on their rounds, he tried to put his finger on it. It was only *after* he replayed the recorded transmission of Professor Barton and the bogus "Sinor" that he realized what it was.

Tia had known that Professor Barton was genuine—without checking. And *Barton* had said things that indicated he knew who she was.

Alex had never really wondered about her background. He'd always assumed that she was just like every other shellperson he'd ever known; popped into her shell at birth, because of fatal birth-defects, with parents who would rather forget she had ever been born. Who were just as pleased that she was someone else's problem.

What was it that the professor had said, though? *You both have backgrounds in archeology. Hypatia, you know how digs work, intimately.*

From everything that Jon Chernov had said, the shellperson program was so learning-intensive that there *was* no time for hobbies. A shellperson only acquired hobbies after he got out in the real world and had leisure time for them. The Lab Schools' program was so intensive that even play was scheduled and games were choreographed, planned, and taught just like classes. There was no room to foster an "interest" in archeology. And it was not on the normal course curriculum.

The only way you knew how digs worked "intimately" was to work on them yourself.

Or be the child of archeologists who kept you on-site with them.

That was when it hit him; something Tia had said. *The Cades met while they were recovering from Henderson's Chorea.* That kind of information would not be the sort of thing someone who made a hobby of archeology would know. Details of archeologists' lives were of interest only to people who knew them.

Under cover of running a search on EsKay digs, he pulled up the information on the personnel—backtracking to the last EsKay dig the Cades had been on.

And there it was. C-121. Active personnel, Braddon Maartens-Cade, Pota Andropolous-Cade. Dependent, *Hypatia* Cade, age seven.

Hypatia Cade; evacuated to station-hospital *Pride of Albion* by MedService AI-drone. Victim of some unknown disease. Braddon and Pota put in isolation—Hypatia never heard from again. Perhaps she died—but that wasn't likely.

There could not be very many girls named "Hypatia" in the galaxy. The odds of two of them being evacuated to the same hospital-ship were tiny; the odds that *his* Tia's best friend, Doctor Kennet Uhua-Sorg—who was chief of Neurology and Neurosurgery—would have been the same doctor in charge of that other Tia's case were so minuscule he wasn't prepared to try to calculate them.

He replaced the file and logged off the boards feeling as if he had just been hit in the back of the head with aboard.

Oh, spirits of space. When she took me as brawn, I made a toast to our partnership—"may it be as long and fruitful as the Cades'." Oh, decom it. I'm surprised she didn't bounce me out the airlock right then and there.

"Tia," he said carefully into the silent cabin. "I—uh—I'd like to apologize—"

"So, you found me out, did you?" To his surprise and profound relief, she sounded *amused.* "Yes, I'm Hypatia Cade. I'd thought about telling you, but then I was afraid you'd feel really badly about verbally falling over your own feet. You do realize that you can't access any data without my being aware of it, don't you?"

"Well, heck, and I thought I was being so sneaky." He managed a weak grin. "I thought I'd really been covering my tracks well enough that you wouldn't notice. I—uh—really am sorry if I made you feel badly."

"Oh, Alex, it would only have been tacky and tasteless—or stupid and insensitive—if you'd done it on purpose." She laughed; he'd come to like her laugh, it was a deep, rich one. He'd often told her BB jokes just so he could hear it. "So it's neither; it's just one of those things. I assume that you're curious now. What is it you want to know about me?"

"Everything!" he blurted, and then flushed with embarrassment. "Unless you'd rather not talk about it."

"Alex, I don't mind at all! I had a very *happy* childhood, and frankly, it will be a lot more comfortable being able to talk about Mum and Dad—or *with* Mum and Dad—without trying to hide them from you." She giggled this time, instead of laughing. "Sometimes I felt as if I was trying to hide a secret lover, only in reverse!"

"So you still stay in contact with your parents?" Alex was fascinated; this went against *everything* he'd been told about shellpersons, either at the academy or directly from Jon Chernov. Shellpersons didn't have families; their supervisors and their classmates were their families.

"Of course I still stay in contact with them. I'm their biggest fan. If archeologists can have fans." Her center screen came up; on it was a shot of Pota and Braddon, proudly displaying an ornate set of body-armor. "Here's something from their latest letter; they just uncovered the armory, and what they found is going to set the scholastic world on its collective ears. That's iron plates you see on Bronze Age armor."

"No—" He stared in fascination, and not just at the armor. At Pota and Braddon, smiling and waving like any other parents for their child. Pota pointed to something on the armor, while Braddon's mouth moved, explaining something. Tia had the sound off, and the definition wasn't good enough for Alex to lip-read.

"That's not *my* real interest though," she continued. "I was telling you the truth. I'm after the EsKay homeworld, but I want it because I want to *find* the bug that got me." The two side-screens came up, both with older pictures. "Before you ask, dear, there I am. The one on the right is my seventh birthday party, the one on the left, as you can see, is a picture of me with Theodore Bear and Moira's brawn Tomas—Ted was a present from both of them." She paused for a moment. "Just checking. Yes, that's the last good picture that was taken of me. The rest are all in the hospital, and I wouldn't inflict them on anyone but a neurologist."

Alex studied the two pictures, each of which showed the same bright-eyed, elfin child. An incredibly *pretty* child, dark-haired, blue-eyed, with a thin, delicate face and a smile that wouldn't stop. "How did you get into the shellperson program?" he asked. "I thought they didn't take anyone after the age of one!"

"They didn't, until me," she replied. "That was Doctor Kenny's doing, and Lars, the systems manager for the hospital; they were convinced that I was flexible enough to make the transition—since I was intelligent enough to *understand* what had happened to me, and what it meant. Which was—" she added, "—complete life-support. No mobility."

He shuddered. "I can see why you wouldn't want that to happen to anyone else ever again."

"Precisely." She blanked the screens before he had a chance to study the pictures further. "After I turned out so well, Lab Schools started considering older children on a case-by-case basis. They've taken three, so far, but none as old as me."

"Well, my lady—as remarkable as you are now, you must have been just as remarkable a child," he told her, meaning every word.

"Flatterer," she said, but she sounded pleased.

"I mean it," he insisted. "I interviewed with two other ships, you know. None of them had your personality. I was looking for someone like Jon Chernov; *they* were more like AI drones."

"You've mentioned Jon before—" she replied, puzzled. "Just what does *he* have to do with us?"

"Didn't I tell you?" he blurted—then hit himself in the forehead with his hand. "*Decom* it, I didn't! Jon's a shellperson too; he was the supervisor and systems manager on the research station where my parents worked!"

"Oh!" she exclaimed. "So *that's* why—"

"Why what?"

"Why you treat me like you do—facing my column, asking permission to come aboard, asking me what kind of music I want in the main cabin—"

"Oh, you bet!" he said with a grin. "Jon made darn sure I had good shellsoft manners before he let me go off to the Academy. He'd have verbally blistered my hide if I *ever* forgot you're here—and that you're the part of the team that can't go off to her own cabin to be alone."

"Tell me about him," she urged.

He had to think hard to remember the first time he ever started talking to Jon. "I think I first realized that he was around when I was about three, maybe two. My folks are chemtechs at one of the Lily-Baer research stations—there weren't a lot of kids around at the time, because it was a new station and most of the personnel were unattached. There weren't a lot of facilities for kids, and I guess what must have happened was that Jon volunteered to sort of babysit while my parents were at work. Wasn't that hard—basically all he had to do was make sure that the door to my room stayed locked except when he sent in servos to feed me and so forth. But I guess I kind of fascinated him, and he started talking to me, telling me stories—then directing the servos in playing with me." He laughed. "For a while my folks thought I was going through the 'invisible friend' stage. Then they got worried, because I didn't grow out of it, and were going to send me to a headshrinker. That was when Jon interrupted while they were trying to make the appointment and told them that *he* was the invisible friend."

Tia laughed. "You already knew that Moira and I have known each other for a long time—well, she was the CS ship that always serviced my folks' digs, that was how I got to know her."

"Gets you used to having a friend that you can't see, but can talk to," he agreed. "Well, once I started preschool, Jon lost interest for a while, until I started learning to play chess. He is *quite* a player himself; when he saw that I was beating the computer regularly, he remembered who I was and stepped in, right in the middle of a game. I *was* winning until he took over," he recalled, still a little aggrieved.

"What can I say?" she asked rhetorically.

"I suppose I shouldn't complain. He became my best friend. He was the one that encouraged my interest in archeology—and when it became obvious my parents weren't going to be able to afford all the university courses that would take, he helped get me into the Academy. Did you know that a recommendation from a shellperson counts twice as much as a recommendation from anyone but a PTA and up?"

"No, I didn't!" She sounded surprised and amused. "Evidently they trust our judgment."

"Well, you've heard his messages. He's probably as pleased with how things turned out as I am." He spread his hands wide. "And that's all there is to know about me."

"Hardly," she retorted dryly. "But it does clear up a few mysteries."

When Alex hit his bunk that night, he found he was having a hard time getting to sleep. He'd always thought of Tia as a person— but now he had a face to put with the name.

Jon Chernov had shown him, once, what Jon would have looked like if he could have survived outside the shell. Alex had known that it was going to be hideous, and had managed not to shudder or turn away, but it had taken a major effort of will. After that it had just been easier not to put a face with the voice. There were completely nonhuman races that looked more human than poor Jon.

But Tia had been a captivatingly pretty child. She would have grown up into a stunning adult. *Shoot, inside that shell, she probably is a stunning adult. A stunning, lifeless adult. Like a puppet with no strings; a sex-companion android with no hookups.*

He had no desire to crack her column; he was not the sort to be attracted by anything lifeless. Feelie-porn had given him the creeps, and his one adolescent try with a sex-droid had sent him away feeling dirty and used.

But it made the tragedy of what had happened to her all the more poignant. Jon's defects were such that it was a relief for everyone that he was in the shell. Tia, though . . .

But she was happy. She was as happy as any of his classmates in the Academy. So where was the tragedy? Only in his mind.

Only in his mind. . . .

CHAPTER SIX

Alex would have been perfectly happy if the past twelve hours had never happened.

He and Tia returned to Diogenes Base after an uneventful trip expecting to be sent out on another series of message-runs, only to learn that on *this* run, they would be carrying passengers. Those passengers were on the way from Central and the Institute by way of commercial liner and would not arrive for another couple of days.

That had given him a window of opportunity for a little shore leave, in a base-town that catered to some fairly heavy space-going traffic, and he had taken it.

Now he was sorry he had . . . oh, not for any serious reasons. He hadn't gotten drunk, or mugged, or into trouble. No, he'd only made a fool out of himself.

Only.

He'd gone out looking for company in the spaceport section, hanging around in the pubs and food-bars. He'd gotten more than one invitation, too, but the one he had followed up on was from a dark-haired, blue-eyed, elfin little creature with an infectious laugh and a nonstop smile. "Bet" was her name, and she was a fourth-generation spacer, following in her family's footloose tradition.

He hadn't wondered what had prompted his choice—hadn't even

140

wondered why he had so deviated from his normal "type" of brown-haired, brown-eyed and athletic. He and the girl—who it turned out was the crew chief of an AI-freighter—had a good time together. They hit a show, had some dinner—and by mutual agreement, wound up in the same hotel room.

He *still* hadn't thought about his choice of company; then came the moment of revelation.

When, in the midst of intimacy, he called her "Tia."

He could have died, right then and there. Fortunately the young lady was understanding; Bet just giggled, called him "Giorgi" back, and they went on from there. And when they parted, she kissed him, and told him that his "Tia" was a lucky wench, and to give her Bet's regards.

Thank the spirits of space he didn't have to tell her the truth. All she'd seen was the CS uniform and the spacer habits and speech patterns; he could have been anything. She certainly wasn't thinking "brawn" when she had picked him up, and he hadn't told her what he did for the Courier Service.

Instead of going straight back to the ship, he dawdled; visited a multi-virtual amusement park, and took five of the wildest adventures it offered. It took all five to wash the embarrassment of his slip out of his recent memory, to put it into perspective.

But nothing would erase the meaning of what he had done. And it was just his good fortune—and Tia's—that his partner hadn't known who Tia was. Brawns had undergone Counseling for a lot less. CS had a nasty reputation for dealing with slips like that one. They wouldn't risk one of their precious shellpersons in the hands of someone who might become so obsessed with her that he would try to get at the physical body.

He returned to the docks in a decidedly mixed state of mind, and with no ideas at all about what—if anything—he could do about it.

Tia greeted her brawn cheerfully as soon as he came aboard, but she left him alone for a little while he got himself organized— or as organized as Alex ever got. "I've got the passenger roster," she said, once he'd stowed his gear. "Want to see them, see what we're getting for the next couple of weeks?"

"Sure," Alex replied, perking up visibly. He had looked tired when he came in; Tia reckoned shrewdly that he had been celebrating his shore leave a little too heavily. He wasn't suffering from a hangover, but it looked to her as if he'd done his two-day pass to the max, squeezing twenty-two hours of fun into every twenty-four hour period. He dropped down into his chair and she brought up her screens for him.

"Here's our team leader, Doctor Izak Hollister-Aspen." The Evaluation team leader was an elderly man; a quad-doc, as thin as a grass stem, clean-shaven, silver-haired, and so frail-looking Tia was half-afraid he might break in the first high wind. "He's got four doctorates, he's published twelve books and about two hundred papers, and he's been head of twenty-odd teams already. He also seems to have a pretty good sense of humor. Listen."

She let the file-fragment run. "I must admit," Aspen said, in a cracked and quavery voice, "there are any number of my colleagues who would say that I should sit behind my desk and let younger bodies take over this dig. Well," he continued, cracking a smile. "I am going to do something like that. I'm going to sit behind my desk in my dome, and let the younger bodies of my team members take over the digging. Seems to me that's close enough to count."

Alex chuckled. "I like him already. I was afraid this trip was going to be a bore."

"Not likely, with him around. Well, this is our second-in-command, double-doc Siegfried Haakon-Fritz. And if this lad had been in charge, I think it might have been a truly dismal trip." She brought up the image of Fritz, who was a square-jawed, steely-eyed, stern-faced monument. He could have been used as the model for any ortho-Communist memorial statue to The Glorious Worker In Service To The State. Or maybe the Self-Righteous In Search Of A Convert. There was nothing like humor anywhere in the man's expression. It looked to her as if his head might crack in half if he ever smiled. "This is all I have, five minutes of silent watching. He didn't say a word. But maybe he doesn't believe in talking when it's being recorded."

"Why not?" Alex asked curiously. "Is he paranoid about being recorded or something?"

"He's a Practical Darwinist," she told him.

"Oh, *brother*," Alex replied with disgust. The Practical Darwinists had their own sort of notoriety, and Tia was frankly surprised to find one in the Institute at all. They were generally concentrated in the soft sciences—when they were in the sciences at all. Personally, Tia did not consider political science to be particularly scientific. . . .

"His political background is kind of dubious," she continued, "but since there's nothing anyone can hang on him, it simply says in the file that his politics have not always been those of the Institute. That's bureaucratic double-talk for someone they would rather not trust, but have no reason to keep them out of positions of authority."

"Got you." Alec nodded. "So, we'll just not mention politics around him, and we'll make sure it's one of the forbidden subjects in the main cabin. Who's next?"

"These are our post-docs; they have their hard science doctorates, and now they're working on their archeology doctorates." She split her center screen and installed them both on it at once. "On the right, Les Dimand-Taylor, human; on the right, Treel rish-Yr nal-Leert, Rayanthan. Treel is female. Les has a Bio Doc, and Treel Xenology."

"Hmm, for Treel wouldn't Xenology be the study of *humans*?" Alex pointed out. Les was a very intense fellow, thin, heavily tanned, very fit-looking, but with haunted eyes. Treel's base-type seemed to be cold-weather mammalian, as she had a pelt of very fine, dense brown fur that extended down onto her cheekbones. Her round, black eyes stared directly into the lens, seeing everything, and giving the viewer the impression that she was cataloging it all.

"No audio on the post-docs, just static file pictures," she continued. "They're attached to Aspen."

"Not to Old Stone Face?" Alex asked. "Never mind. Any grad student or post-doc he'd have would be a clonal copy of himself. I can't imagine any other type staying with him for long."

"And here are our grad students." Again she split the screen. "Still working on the first doctorate. Both male. Aldon Reese-Tambuto, human; and Fred, from Dushayne."

"*Fred?*" Alex spluttered. Understandably. The Dushaynese could not possibly have looked *less* human; he had a square, flat head— literally. Flat on top, flat face, flattened sides. He was bright green and had no mouth, just a tiny hole below his nostril slits. Dushaynese were vegetarian to an extreme; on their homeworld they lived on tree sap and fruit juice. Out in the larger galaxy they did very well on sucrose-water and other liquids. They had, as a whole, very good senses of humor.

"*Fred?*" Alex repeated.

"Fred," she said firmly. "Very few humans would be able to reproduce his real name. His vocal organ is a vibrating membrane in the top of his head. He does human speech just fine, but we can't manage his." She blanked her screens. "I'll spare you their speeches; they are very eager, very typical young grad students and this will be their first dig."

"Save me—" Alex moaned.

"Be nice," she said firmly. "Don't disillusion them. Let the next two years take care of that."

He waved his hands vigorously. "Far be it from me to let them know what gruesome fate awaits them. What was the chance of death on a dig? Twenty percent? And there's six of them?"

"The chance of catching something non-fatal is a lot higher," she pointed out. "Actually, the honor of being the fatality usually goes to the post-docs or the second-in-command; they're the ones doing the major explorations when a dig hits something like a tomb. The grad students usually are put to sifting sand and cataloging pottery shards."

Alex didn't get a chance to respond to that, for the first members of the team arrived at the lock at that moment, and he went down the lift to welcome them aboard, while Tia directed the servos in storing most of their baggage in the one remaining empty hold. As they came up the lift, both the young "men" were chattering away at high speed, with Alex in the middle, nodding sagely from time to time and clearly not catching more than half of what they said. Tia decided to rescue him.

"Welcome aboard, Fred, Aldon," she said, cutting through the chatter with her own, higher-pitched voice.

Silence, as both the grad students looked around for the speaker.

Fred caught on first, and while his face remained completely without expression, he had already learned the knack of displaying human-type emotions with his voice. "My word!" he exclaimed with delight, "you are a brainship, are you not, dear lady?"

As a final incongruity, he had adopted a clipped British accent to go along with his voice.

"Precisely, sir," she replied. "AH One-Oh-Three-Three at your service, so to speak."

"Wow," Aldon responded, clearly awestruck. "We get to ride in a brainship? They've actually put us on a brainship? Wow, PTAs don't even get rides from brainships! I've never even seen a brainship before—Uh, hi, what's your real name?" He turned slowly, trying to figure out which way to face.

"Hypatia, Tia for short," she replied, tickled by the young beings' responses. "Don't worry about where to look, just assume I'm the whole ship. I am, you know. I even have eyes in your quarters—" she chuckled at Aldon's flush of embarrassment "—but don't worry, I won't use them. Your complete privacy is important to us."

"I can show you the cabins, and you can pick the ones you want," Alex offered. "They're all the same; I'm just reserving the one nearest the main cabin for Doctor Hollister-Aspen."

"Stellar!" Aldon enthused. "Wow, this is better than the liner coming in! I had to share a cabin with Fred and two other guys."

"Quite correct," Fred seconded. "I enjoyed Aldon's company, but the other two were—dare I say—spoiled young reprobates? High Family affectations without the style, the connections, or the Family. Deadly bores, I assure you, and a spot of privacy will be welcome. Shall we, then?"

The two grad students were unpacking their carry-on baggage when the two post-docs arrived, this time singly. Treel arrived first, accepted the greetings with the calm, intense demeanor of a Zen Master, and took the first cabin she was offered.

Les Dimand-Taylor was another case altogether. It was obvious to Tia the moment he came aboard—*without* the automatic salute he made to her column—that he was ex-military. He confirmed her assumption as soon as Alex offered him a cabin.

"Anything will do, old man," he said, with a kind of nervous cheer. "Better than barracks, that's for sure. Unless—lady Tia, you don't have anything that makes an unexpected noise in the middle of the night, do you? I'm afraid—" he laughed a little shakily "—I'm afraid I'm just a little twitchy about noises when I'm asleep. What they euphemistically call 'unfortunate experiences.' I'll keep my door locked so I don't disturb anyone but—"

"Give him the cabin next to Treel, Alex," she said firmly. "Doctor Dimand-Taylor—"

"Les, my dear," he replied, with a thin smile. "Les to you and your colleagues, always. Pulled me out of a tight spot, one of you

BB teams did. Besides, when people hear my title they tend to start telling me about their backs and innards. Hate to have to tell them that I'd only care about their backs if the too, too solid flesh had been melted off the bones for the past thousand years or so."

"Les, then," she said. "I assume you know Treel?"

"Very well. A kind and considerate lady. If you have her assigned as my neighbor, she's so quiet I never know she's there." He seemed relieved that Tia didn't press him for details on the "tight spot" *he'd* been in.

"That cabin and hers are buried in the sound-proofing around the holds," Tia told him. "You shouldn't hear anything—and I can generate white-noise for you at night, if you'd like."

He relaxed visibly. "That would be charming of you, thanks awfully. My superior, Doc Aspen, told the others about my little eccentricities, so they know not to startle me. So we should be fine."

He went about his unpacking, and Alex returned to the main cabin.

"Commando," Tia said succinctly.

"That in his records?" Alex asked. "I'm surprised they left that there. Not saying where, though, are they?"

"If you know where to look and what to look at, the fact that he was a commando *is* in his records," she told her brawn. "But where—that's not in the Institute file. It's probably logged some-where. Remember not to walk quietly, my dear."

"Since I'd rather not get karate-chopped across the throat, that sounds like a good idea." He thought for a moment and went off to his cabin, returning with what looked like a bracelet with a bell on it. "These things went into fashion a couple of months ago, and I bought one, but I didn't like it." He bent over to fasten it around his boot. "There. Now he'll hear me coming, in case I forget to stamp." The bell was not a loud one, but it was definitely producing an audible sound.

"Good idea—ah, here's the Man himself—Alex, he's going to need some help."

Alex hurried down to the lift area and gave Doctor Aspen a hand with his luggage. There wasn't much of it, but Doctor Aspen was not capable of carrying much for long. Tia wondered what could have possessed the Institute to permit this man to go out into the field again.

She found out, once he was aboard. His staff immediately clustered around him, fired with enthusiasm, as soon as he was settled in his cabin. He asked permission of Tia and Alex to move the convocation into the main cabin and use one of her screens.

"Certainly," Tia answered, when Alex deferred to her. She was quite charmed by Doctor Aspen, who called her "my lady," and accorded to her all the attention and politeness he gave his students and underlings.

As they moved into main room, Doctor Aspen turned toward her column. "I am told that you have some interest and education in archeology, my lady Tia," he said, as he settled into a seat near one of the side screens. "And you, too, Alex. Please, since you'll be on-site with us, feel free to participate. And if you know something we should, or notice something we miss, feel free to contribute."

Alex was obviously surprised; Tia wasn't. She had gleaned some of this from the records. Aspen's students stayed with him, went to enormous lengths to go on-site with him, went on to careers of their own full of warm praise for their mentor. Aspen was evidently that rarest of birds: the exceptional, inspirational teacher who was also a solid researcher and scientist.

Within moments, Aspen had drawn them all into his charmed circle, calling up the first team's records, drawing his students— and even Alex—into making observations. Tia kept a sharp eye out for the missing member of the party, however, for she had the feeling that Haakon-Fritz had deliberately timed his entrance to coincide with the gathering of Aspen's students. Tia figured that he wanted an excuse to feel slighted. She wasn't going to give it to him.

She could—and did—hook herself into the spaceport surveillance system, and she spotted Haakon-Fritz coming long before he was in range of her own sensors. Plenty of time to interrupt the animated discussion with a subtle, "Gentlebeings, Doctor Haakon-Fritz is crossing the tarmac."

Treel and Les exchanged a wordless look, but said nothing. Aspen simply smiled, and rose from his chair, as Tia froze the recording they had been watching. Alex hurried down the stairs to intercept Haakon-Fritz at the lift.

So instead of being greeted by the backs of those deep in discussion, the man found himself greeted by the Courier Service brawn, met at the top of the lift by the rest of his party, and given an especially hearty greeting by his superior.

His expression did not change so much as a hair, but Tia had the distinct feeling that he was disgruntled. "Welcome aboard, Doctor Haakon-Fritz," Tia said, as he shook hands briefly with the other members of his party. "We have a choice of five cabins for you, if you'd care—"

"If you have more than one cabin available," Haakon-Fritz interrupted rudely, speaking not to Tia, who he ignored, but to Alex, "I would like to see them all before I make a choice."

Tia knew Alex well enough by now to know that he was angry, but he covered it beautifully. "Certainly, Professor," he said, giving Haakon-Fritz the lesser of his titles. "If you'll follow me—"

He led the way back into the cabin section, leaving Haakon-Fritz to carry his own bags.

Treel made a little growl that sounded like disgust; Fred rolled his eyes, which was the closest he could come to a facial expression. "My word," Fred said, his voice ripe with surprise. "*That* was certainly rude!"

"He ees a Practical Darweeneest," Treel replied, with a curl to her lip. "Your pardon, seer," she said to Aspen. "I know that you feel he ees a good scienteest, but I am glad he ees not the one in scharge."

Fred was still baffled. "Practical Darwinist?" he said. "Does someone want to explain to a baffled young veggie just what that might be and *why* he was so rude to lady Tia?"

Les took up the gauntlet with a sigh. "A Practical Darwinist is one who believes that Darwin's Law applies to *everything*. If someone is in an accident, they shouldn't be helped, if an earthquake levels a city, no aid should be sent, if a plague breaks out, only the currently healthy should be inoculated; the victims should be isolated and live or die as the case may be."

Fred's uneasy glance toward her column made Tia decide to spare Les the embarrassment of stating the obvious. "And as you have doubtless surmised, the fanatical Practical Darwinists find the existence of shellpersons to be *horribly* offensive. They won't even acknowledge that we exist, given the option."

Professor Aspen shook his head sadly. "A brilliant scientist, but tragically flawed by fanaticism," he said, as he took his seat again. "Which is why he has gotten as far as he will ever go. He had a chance—was given a solo Exploration dig—and refused to consider any evidence that did not support his own peculiar partyline. Now he is left to be the chief clerk of digs like ours." He looked soberly into the faces of his four students. "Let this be a lesson to you, gentlebeings. Never let fanatic devotion blind you to truth."

"Or, in other words," Tia put in blithely, "the problem with a fanatic is that their brains turn to tofu and they accept nothing as truth except what conforms to their ideas. What makes them dangerous is not that *they'll* die to prove their truth, but that they'll let *you* die—or take you with them—to prove it."

"Well put, my lady." Doctor Aspen turned his attention back to the screen. "Now since I know from past experience that Haakon-Fritz will spend the time until takeoff sulking in his cabin—shall we continue with our discussion?"

The Exploration team had left the site in good shape; equipment stowed, domes inflated but sealed, open trenches covered to protect them. The Evaluation team erected two new living domes and a second laboratory dome in short order, and settled down to their work.

Everything seemed to be under control; now that the team was on-site, even the sulky Haakon-Fritz fell to and took on his share of the duties. There would seem to have been no need for AH One-Oh-Three-Three to remain on-planet when they could have been making the rounds of "their" established digs.

But that was not what regulations called for, and both Tia and Alex knew why, even if the members of the team didn't. Regulations for a CS ship attached to Institute duty hid a carefully concealed second agenda, when the ship placed a new Exploration or Evaluation team.

Archeological teams were put together with great care; not only because of the limited number of personnel, but because of their isolation. They were going to be in danger from any number of things—all of the hazards that Tia had listed to Alex on their first mission. There was no point in exposing them to danger from within.

So the prospective members of a given team were probed, tested, and Psyched to a fare-thee-well, both for individual stability and for interactive stability with the rest of the team. Still, mistakes could be made, and had been in the past. Sometimes those mistakes had led to a murder, or at least, an attempted murder.

When a psychological problem surfaced, it was usually right at the beginning of the stint, after the initial settling in period was over, and once a routine had been established and the stresses of the dig started to take their toll. About that time, if something was going to go wrong, it did. The team had several weeks in cramped quarters in transit to establish interpersonal relations; ideal conditions for cabin fever. Ideal conditions for stress to surface, and that stress could lead to severe interpersonal problems.

So regulations were that the courier, whether BB or fully-manned, was to manufacture some excuse to stay for several days, with the ship personnel staying inside and out of sight, but with the site being fully monitored from inside the ship. The things they were to look for were obvious personality conflicts, new behavioral quirks, or old ones going from "quirk" to "psychosis." Making sure there was nothing that might give rise to a midnight axe murder. It would not have been the first time that someone snapped under stress.

Alex was most worried about Les, muttering things about post-trauma syndrome and the fragility of combat veterans. Tia had her own picks for trouble, *if* trouble came—either Fred or Aldon, for neither one of them had ever been on-site in a small dig before, and until he went to the Institute, Aldon had never even been off-planet. Despite his unpleasantness to *her*, Haakon-Fritz was brilliant and capable, and he had been on several digs before without any trouble surfacing. And now that they were all on-site, while he was distant, he was also completely cooperative, and his behavior in no way differed from his behavior on previous digs. There was no indication that he was likely to take his fanatic beliefs into his professional life. Fred and Aldon had only been part of a crew of hundreds with an Excavation team—where there were more people to interact with, fewer chances for personality stress, and no real trials to face but the day to day boredom of repetitive work.

For the first couple of days, everything seemed to be just fine, not only as far as the personnel were concerned, but as far as the conditions. Both Tia and Alex breathed a sigh of relief.

Too soon by half.

For that night, the winter rains began.

✧   ✧   ✧

Tia had been sifting through some of the records she'd copied at the base, looking for another potential investment prospect like Largo Draconis. It was late; very late—the site was quiet and dark, and Alex had called it a night. He was in his cabin, just about at the dreaming stage, and Tia was considering shutting down for her mandated three hours of DeepSleep—when the storm struck.

"Struck" was the operative word, for a wall of wind and rain hit her skin hard enough to rattle her for a moment, and that was followed by a blast of lightning and thunder that shook Alex out of bed.

"What?" he yelped, coming up out of sleep with a shout. "How? Who?"

He shook his head to clear it, as another peal of thunder made Tia's walls vibrate. "What's going on?" he asked, as Tia sank landing-spikes from her feet into the ground beneath her, to stabilize her position. "Are we under attack or something?"

"No, it's a storm, Alex," she replied absently, making certain that everything was locked down and all her servos were inside. "One incredible thunderstorm. I've never experienced anything like it!"

She turned on her external cameras and fed them to her screens so he could watch, while she made certain that *she* was well-insulated against lightning strikes and that all was still well at the site. Alex wandered out into the main cabin and sat in his chair, awestruck by the display of raw power going on around them.

Multiple lightning strikes were going on all around them; not only was the area as bright as day, it was often brighter. Thunder boomed continuously, the wind howled, and sheets—no, entire linen-closets—of rain pounded the ground, not only baffling any attempt at a visual scan of the site, but destroying any hope of any other kind of check. With this much lightning in the air, there was no point even in trying a radio call.

"What's happening down at the site?" Alex asked anxiously.

"No way of telling," she said reluctantly. "The Exploration team went through these rains once already, so I guess we can assume that the site itself isn't going to wash away, or float away. For the rest—the domes are insulated against lightning, but who knows what's likely to happen to the equipment? Especially in all this lightning."

Her words proved only too prophetic; for although the rain

lasted less than an hour, the deluge marked a forty-degree drop in temperature, and the effects of the lightning were permanent.

When the storm cleared, the news from the site was bad. Lightning had not only struck the ward-off field generator, it had slagged it. There was nothing left but a half-melted pile of plasteel and duraloy. Tia didn't see how one strike could have done that much damage; the generator must have been hit over and over. The backup was corroded beyond any repair, though Haakon-Fritz and Les labored over it for most of the night. Too many parts had been ruined—probably while it sat in its crate through who-knew-how-many transfers. Never once uncrated and checked—and now Doctor Aspen's team paid the price for that neglect.

Tia consulted with Doctor Aspen in person the next morning. There was little sign of the damage from where they sat, but the results were undeniable. No ward-off generator. No protection from native fauna, from insectoids to the big canids. And if the huge grazers, the size of moose, were to become aggressive, there would be no way to keep them out of the camp. Ordinary fences would not hold against a herd of determined grazers; the last team had proved that.

"I don't have a spare in the holds," Tia told the team leader. "I don't have even half the parts you need for the corroded generator. There were no storms like the one last night mentioned in the records of the previous team, but we should assume there are going to be more. How many of them can you handle? Winter is coming on, and I can't predict what the native animals are going to do. Do you want to pull the team out?"

Doctor Aspen pursed his lips thoughtfully. "I can't think of any reason why we should, my lady," he replied. "The only exterior equipment that had no protection was the ward-off generator. The first team stayed here without incident all winter—there's nothing large enough to be a real threat to us, so far as I can tell. We'll have a few insects, perhaps, until first hard frost—I imagine those jackal-like beasts will lurk about and make a nuisance of themselves. But they're hardly a threat."

Alex, feet up on the console as usual, agreed with the archeologist. "I don't see any big threat here, either. Unless lightning takes out something a lot more vital."

Tia didn't like it, but she didn't challenge them, either. "If that's the way you want it," she agreed. "But we'll stay until the rains are over, just in case."

Stay they did; but that was the first and the last of the major storms. After the single, spectacular downpour, the rains came gently, between midnight and dawn, with hardly a peal of thunder to wake Alex. She had to conclude that the first storm had been a freak occurrence, something no one could have predicted, and lost a little of her ire over the lack of warning from the previous team.

But that still didn't excuse the corroded generator.

Still, the weather stayed cold, and the rain left coatings of ice on everything. It would be gone by midmorning, but the difficulty in walking around the site meant that the team changed their working hours—beginning around ten-hundred and finishing about twenty-two-hundred. Despite his recorded disclaimer, Doctor Aspen insisted on working alongside his students, and no one, not even Haakon-Fritz, wanted him to risk a fall on the ice.

Meanwhile, Tia made note of a disturbing development. The sudden cold had sent most of the small game and pest animals into hiding or hibernation. That left the normally solitary jackal-dogs without their usual prey, and in what appeared to be seasonal behavior, they began to pack up for the winter, so that they could take down the larger grazers.

The disturbing part was that a very large pack began lurking around the camp.

Now Tia regretted her choice of landing areas. The site was between her and the camp; that was all very well, especially for observing the team at work, but the dogs were lurking in the hills around the *camp*. And with no ward-off generator to keep them out of it—

She mentioned her worry to Alex, who pointed out that the beasts always scattered at any sign of aggression on the part of a human. She mentioned it again to Doctor Aspen, who said the animals were probably just looking for something to scavenge and would leave the camp alone once they realized there was nothing to eat there.

She never had a chance to mention it again.

With two moons, both in different phases, the nights were never dark unless it was raining. But the floodlights at the site made certain that the darkness was driven away. And lately, the nights were never silent either; the pack of jackal-dogs wailed from the moment the sun went down to the moment the rains began. Tia quickly became an expert on what those howls meant; the yipping social-howl, the long, drawn-out rally-cry, and most ominous, the deep-chested hunting call. She was able to tell, just by the sounds, where they were, whether they were in pursuit, and when the quarry had won the chase, or lost it.

Tia wasn't too happy about them; the pack numbered about sixty now, and they weren't looking too prosperous. Evidently the activity at the site had driven away the larger grazers they normally preyed on; that had the effect of making all the smaller packs join up into one mega-pack—so there was always some food, but none of them got very much of it. They weren't at the bony stage yet, but there was a certain desperate gauntness about them. The grazers they did chase were escaping five times out of six—and they weren't getting in more than two hunts in a night.

Should I suggest that the team feed them? Perhaps take a grav-sled and go shoot something and drag it in once every couple of days? But would that cause problems later? That would be giving the pack the habit of dependence on humans, and that wouldn't be good. Could they lure the pack into another territory that way, though? Or—would feeding them make them lose their fear of humans? She couldn't quite make up her mind about that, but the few glimpses she'd had of the pack before sunset had put her in mind of certain Russian folktales—troikas in the snow, horses foaming with panic, and wolves snapping at the runners. Meanwhile, the pack got a little closer each night before they faded into the darkness.

At least it was just about time for the team to break off for the night. Once they were in their domes, they'd be safe.

As if in answer to her thought, the huge lights pivoted up and away from the site, as they were programmed to do, lighting a clear path for the team from the site to the camp. When everyone was safely in the domes, Les would turn them off remotely. So far, the lights alone had kept the jackal-dogs at bay. They lurked just outside the path carved by the lights, but would not venture inside.

As if to answer that thought, the pack howled just as the first of the team members emerged from the covered excavation area. It sounded awfully close—

Tia ran a quick infrared scan.

The pack *was* awfully close—right on the top of the hill to the right of the site!

The beasts stared down at the team—and the leader howled again. There was *no* mistaking that howl, not when all the rest answered it. It was the hunt-call. Quarry sighted; time to begin the chase.

And the leader was staring right at the archeologists. The team stared back, sensing that there was something different tonight. No one stirred; not archeologists, nor jackal-dogs. The beasts' eyes glared red in the darkness, reflection from the work lights, but no less disturbing for having a known scientific explanation.

"Alex," she said tightly. "Front and center. We have a situation."

He emerged from his cabin as if shot from a gun, took one look at the screen, and pelted for the hold where they kept the HA grav-sled.

Then the pack poured down the hillside in a furry avalanche.

Haakon-Fritz took off like a world-class sprinter, leaving the rest behind. For all the attention that he paid them, the rest of his team might just as well have not existed.

Shellcrack! Aspen can't run—

But Les and Treel were not about to leave Aspen to become the a la carte special; as if they had rehearsed the move, they each grabbed one arm and literally picked him up off his feet between them and started running. Fred and Aldon grabbed shovels to act as some kind of flank-guard. With the jackal-dogs closing on them with every passing moment, the entire group pelted off for the shelters.

They were barely a quarter of the way there, with the jackals halfway down the hill and gaining momentum, when Haakon-Fritz reached the nearest shelter. He hit the side of the dome with a crash and pawed the door open. He flung himself inside—

And slammed it shut; the red light coming on over the frame indicating that he had locked it.

"*Alex!*" Tia cried in anguish, as the jackal-dogs bore down upon their prey. "Alex, *do* something!" She had never felt so horribly helpless.

Grav-sleds made no noise—but they had hedra-players and powerful speakers, meant both to entertain their drivers and to broadcast prerecorded messages on the fly. A blast of raucous hard-wire shatter-rock blared out from beneath her—she got her underbelly cameras on just as Alex peeled out in the sled at top speed, music screaming at top volume.

The unfamiliar shrieks and howls behind them startled the pack for a moment, and they hesitated, then came to a dead halt, peering over their shoulders. The rock music was so unlike anything they had ever heard before that they didn't know how to react; Alex plowed straight through the middle of them and they shied away to either side.

He was never going to be able to make a pickup on the five still running for their lives without the pack being on all of them—but while he was on the move with music caterwauling, the jackal-dogs hesitated to attack him. And while he was harassing them, their attention was on him, not on their quarry.

That must have been what he had figured in the first place—that he would startle them enough to give the rest of the team a chance to get to safety inside that second dome. While the archeologists ignored what was going on behind them and kept right on to the second shelter, Alex kept making dives at the pack—scattering them when he could, keeping the sled between them and the team. It was tricky flying—stunt-flying with a grav-sled, pulling crazy maneuvers less than a meter from the ground. Not a lot of margin for error.

He cornered wildly; rocking the sled up on one side, skewing it over in flat spins, feinting at the pack leader and gunning away before the beast had a chance to jump into the sled. Over the sound of the wild music, the warning signals and overrides screamed objection for what Alex was doing. Alex challenged the jackal-dogs with the only weapon he had; the sled. Tia longed for her ethological pack; still not approved for the Institute ships. With a stun-needler, they could have at least knocked some of the pack out.

The animals assumed that the attack was meant to drive them off or kill them. They must have been hungrier than any of them had guessed, for when nothing happened to hurt or kill any of the pack, they began making attempts to mob the sled, and they seemed to be trying to think of ways to pull it down.

Tia knew why, then, in a flash of insight. Alex had just gone from "fellow predator" to "prey"; the jackal-dogs were used to grazer-bulls charging them aggressively to try to drive them away. Alex was imitating the behavior of the bulls, though he did not know it—and in better times, the pack probably *would* have responded by moving to easier prey. But these were lean times, and any imitation of prey-behavior meant they would try to catch and kill what was taunting them.

Alex was now in real danger.

But Alex was a better flyer than Tia had ever thought; he kept the sled just out of reach of a strong jump, kept it moving in unpredictable turns and spins.

Then, one of the biggest beasts in the pack leapt—and landed, feet scrabbling on the back bumper of the sled.

"*Alex!*" Tia shrieked again. He glanced back over his shoulder and saw his danger.

He sent the sled into a spin; the sled's protection overrides objected strenuously, whining as they fought him. The jackal-dog fought, too, hind-claws skidding against the duraloy of the bumper. Alex watched desperately over his shoulder as the beast's claws found a hold, and it began hauling itself over the bumper toward him.

In what was either a burst of inspiration or insanity, he jammed on the braking motors. The sled stopped dead in mid-spin, flinging him sideways against his safety-belts—

And flinging the jackal-dog off the back of the sled entirely, sending it flying into the pack, and tumbling at least a dozen of them nose-over-tail.

At that moment the team reached the second dome.

The flash of light as they opened the door told Alex they were safe, and he no longer had to make a target of himself. Alex burned air back towards Tia; she dropped open a cargo-bay, activated restraint-fields and hoped he'd be able to brake in time to keep from hitting the back wall. At the speed he was coming—the restraint-fields, meant to keep the sled from banging around too much in rough flight, wouldn't do much.

He didn't even slow down as he hit the bay door, which she slammed down behind him. Instead, he killed the power and skidded to a halt on the sled's belly in a shower of sparks. The sled skewed sideways and crashed into the back wall—but between Alex's own maneuver and the restraint-fields, the impact wasn't bad enough to do more than dent her hold-wall. Once again, Alex was hurled sideways against his seat-belts. There were a half-dozen impacts on the cargo door, indicating the leaders of the pack hitting it, unable to stop.

He sat there for a moment, then sagged over the steering wheel, breathing heavily. Nothing on Tia's pickups made her think he was hurt, so she waited for him to catch his breath.

When his breathing slowed, and he looked up, she focused on his face. He was flushed, but showed no shock, and no sign of pain.

"Well," she said, keeping her voice calm and light, "you certainly know how to make an entrance."

He blinked—then leaned back in his seat, and began laughing.

It was no laughing matter the next day, when Haakon-Fritz emerged from his shelter and was confronted by the remainder of his team. He had no choice; Tia had threatened to hole his dome if he didn't, giving the beasts a way inside. It was an empty threat, but he didn't know that; like any other fanatic Practical Darwinist, he had never bothered to learn the capabilities of brainships.

Les took charge of him before he had a chance to say anything; using some kind of commando-tactics to get a hold on the man that immobilized him, then frog-marching him into the ship.

By common consent, everyone else waited until Les and Tia had secured Haakon-Fritz in one of her cabins, with access to what was going on in the main cabin, but no way of interrupting the proceedings. Any time he started in on one of his speeches, she could cut him off, and he'd be preaching to the bare walls.

As the others gathered in the cabin, Doctor Aspen looking particularly shaken and worn, Tia prepared to give them the news. It wasn't completely bad . . . but they weren't going to like part of it.

"We aren't pulling you out," she said, "although we've got that authority. We understand your concern about leaving this dig and losing essentially two years, and we share it."

As she watched four of the five faces register their mix of relief and anticipation, she wished she could give them unmixed orders.

"That's the good news," Alex said, before anyone could respond. "Here's the bad news. In order to stay here, we're going to order you to stay in your domes until the next courier shows up with your new generator and parts for the old one. We ordered one for you when the old one slagged; the courier should arrive in about a month or two with the new one."

"But—" Doctor Aspen started to object

"Doctor, it's that, or we pull you right this moment," Tia said firmly. "We *will not* leave you with those canids on the prowl unless you, each of you, pledge us that. You didn't see how those beasts attacked Alex in his sled. They have no fear of humans now, and they're hungry. They'll attack you without hesitation, and I wouldn't bet on them waiting until dark to do it."

"What's better?" Alex asked shrewdly. "Lose two months of work, or two years?"

With a sigh, Doctor Aspen gave his word, as did the rest—although Fred and Aldon did so with visible relief.

"If they'd just supply us with damned guns . . ." Les muttered under his breath.

"There are sophonts on the other continent. I didn't make the rules, Les," Tia replied, and he flushed. "I didn't make them, but I *will* enforce them. And by the letter of those rules, I should be ordering you to pack right now."

"Speaking of packing—" Alex picked up the cue. "We need you to bundle Haakon-Fritz' things and stow them in the hold. He's coming back with us."

Now Les made no attempt to hide his pleasure, but Doctor Aspen looked troubled. "I don't see any reason—" he began.

"Sorry, Doctor, but we do," Alex interrupted. "Haakon-Fritz finally broke the rules. It's pretty obvious to both of us that he attempted to turn his politics into reality."

In his cabin, the subject of discussion got over his shock and began a shouted tirade. As she had threatened, Tia cut him off—but she kept the recorders going. At the moment, they couldn't *prove* what had been on the man's mind when he locked his colleagues out. With any luck, his own words might condemn him.

"Doctor, no matter what his motivations were, he abandoned us," Les said firmly. "One more fighter might have made a difference to the pack—and the fact remains that when he reached shelter, instead of doing anything helpful, he ran inside and *locked the door.* The former might only have been cowardice—but the latter is criminal."

"That's probably the way the Board of Inquiry will see it," Tia agreed. "We'll see to it that he has justice, but he can't be permitted to endanger anyone else's life this way again."

After a bit more argument, Doctor Aspen agreed. The team left the shelter of the ship, gathered what they could from the dig, and returned to the domes. Well before sunset, Les and Fred returned with a grav-sled laden with Haakon-Fritz' belongings stowed in crates—and by the rattling they were making, the goods hadn't been stowed any too carefully.

Tia didn't intend to expend too much effort in stowing the crates either.

"You'll keep everyone in the domes for us, won't you?" Tia asked Les anxiously. "You're the one I'm really counting on. I don't trust Doctor Aspen's common sense to hold his curiosity at bay for too long."

"You read him right there, dear lady," Les replied, tossing the last of the crates off the sled for the servo to pick up. "But the rest of us have already agreed. Treel was the most likely hold-out, but even she agrees with you on your reading of the way those jackal-dogs were acting."

"What will happen to the unfortunate Haakon-Fritz?" Fred asked curiously.

"That's going to depend on the board," she told him. "I've got a recording of him ranting in his cabin about survival and obsolescence, and pretty much spouting the extremist version of the Practical Darwinism party line. That isn't going to help him any, but how much of it is admissible, I don't know."

"Probably none of it to a court," Les admitted after thought. "But the board won't like it."

"All of it's been sent on ahead," she told him. "He'll probably be met by police, even if, ultimately, there's nothing he can be charged with."

"At the very least, after this little debacle, he'll be dropped from the list of possible workers for anything less than a Class Three dig," Fred observed cheerfully. "They'll take away his seniority, if *they* have any sense, and demote him back to general worker. He'll spend the rest of his life with us undergrads, sorting pot-shards."

"Assuming he can *find* anyone who is willing to take a chance on him," Alex responded. "Which I would make no bets on."

He patted Tia's side. "Just be grateful you're not having to go back with us," he concluded. "If you thought the trip out was bad with Haakon-Fritz sulking, imagine what it's going to be like returning."

CHAPTER SEVEN

There was a message waiting for Tia when they returned to the main base at Central, with Doctor Haakon-Fritz still confined to quarters. A completely mysterious message. Just the words, "Call this number," a voice-line number for somewhere in the L-5 colonies, and an ID-code she recognized as being from Lars.

Now what was Lars up to?

Puzzled, she left the message in storage until Alex completed the complicated transfer of their not-quite-prisoner, and accompanied him and duplicate copies of the records involving him down to the surface. Only then, when she was alone, did she make the call.

"Friesner, Sherman, Stirling and Huff," said a secretary on the first ring. There was no delay, so Tia assumed that the office was somewhere in one of the half-dozen stations or L-5 colonies nearby. "Investment brokers."

"I was told to call this number," Tia said cautiously. "I—my name is Hypatia Cade—" She hesitated as she almost gave her ship-numbers instead of her name.

"Ah, Miz Cade, of course," the secretary said, sounding pleased. "We've been waiting for you to call. Let me explain the mystery; Friesner, Sherman, Stirling and Huff specialize in investments for shellpersons like yourself. A Mister Lars Mendoza at *Pride of Albion* opened an account for you here to manage the investments you had already made. If you'll hold, I'll see if one of the partners is free—"

Tia *hated* to be put on hold, but it wasn't for more than a microsecond. "Miz Cade," said a hearty-sounding male voice, "I'm Lee Stirling; I'm your broker if you want to keep me on, and I have good news for you. Your investments at Largo Draconis have done *very* well. Probably much better than you expected."

"I don't know about that," she replied, letting a little humor leak through. "My expectations were pretty high." There was something about that voice that sounded familiar, but she couldn't identify it. Was it an accent—or rather, lack of one?

"But did you expect to triple your total investment?" Lee Stirling countered. "Your little seed money grew into quite the mighty oak tree while you were gone!"

"Uh—" she said, taken so much by surprise that she didn't know what to say. "What do you mean by total investment?"

"Oh—your companies split their bonds two times while you were gone; you had the option of cash or bonds, and we judged you wanted the bonds, at least while the value was still increasing." Stirling was trying to sound matter-of-fact, but couldn't keep a trace of gloating out of his voice. "Those bonds are now worth three times what they were after the last split."

"Split?" she said faintly. "I—uh—really don't know what that means. I'm—new at this."

Patiently Stirling walked her through exactly what had happened to her investment. "Now the question you have in front of you is whether you want to sell out now, while the value of the bond is still increasing, or whether you want to wait."

"What's happening on Largo Draconis?" she asked. After all, *her* investment had been based on what was going to happen in the real world, not the strange and unpredictable universe of the stock market. And from the little she had seen, the universe of the stock market seemed to have very little to do with "real" reality.

"I thought you'd ask that. Your companies have pretty much saturated their market," Stirling told her. "The situation has stabilized—just short of disaster, thanks to them. The bond prices are going up, but a lot more slowly. I think they're going to flatten out fairly soon. I'd get out, if I were you."

"Do it," she said flatly. "I'd like you to put everything I earned into Moto-Prosthetics, preferred stock, with voting rights. Hold onto the seed money until I contact you."

"Taking care of it now—there. All logged in, Hypatia. I'm looking forward to seeing what you're going to invest in next." Stirling sounded quite satisfied. "I hope you'll stay with us. We're a new firm, but we're solid, we have a lot of experience, and we intend to service our clients with integrity. Miz Friesner was formerly a senior partner in Weisskopf, Dixon, Friesner and Jacobs, and the rest of us were her handpicked proteges. She's our token softie."

"Token—oh! You're all—"

"Shellpersons, right, all except Miz Friesner. Oh, we all worked on the stock, bond, and commodity exchanges, but as systems managers. We couldn't do any investments while we were systems managers, but Miz Friesner agreed to join us when we bought out our contracts." Stirling chuckled. "We've been planning this for a long time. Now we're relying on grapevine communications within the shell-net for those like us who want to invest, for whatever reasons—and would rather not go through either their Counselors, their Supervisors, or their Advocates." He sent her a complicated burst of emoticons conveying a combination of disgust, weariness, annoyance, and impatience. "We *are* adults, after all. We can think for ourselves. Just because we're rooted to one spot or one structure, it doesn't follow that all of us need keepers."

She sent back a burst that mirrored his—with the addition of amusement. "Some of us do—but not anyone who's been out in the world for more than fifty years or so, *I* wouldn't think. Well, I'll tell a couple of friends of mine about you, that's for certain."

"Word of mouth, as I said." Stirling laughed. "I have to tell you, after that phenomenal start, we're all very interested in your next investment choice."

"I'll have it in a couple of days at most," she promised, and signed off.

Well, now it was certainly time to start digging for that second choice, and she couldn't hope to happen on it the way she had the last time.

This time, it was going to take a combination of stupidity on someone's part, and her own computational power. So she concentrated on sorting out those colonies that had been in existence for less than a hundred years. It was probably fair to assume that anything repetitive that *she* would be able to take advantage of would have to take place within that kind of cycle.

That narrowed the field quite a bit—but it meant that she was going to have to concentrate her search by categories. Floods were the first things that came to mind, so she called up geological and climatological records on all of her candidates and ran a search for flood patterns.

Meanwhile she and Alex were also dealing with the authorities on the Haakon-Fritz case—which looked likely to put the Practical Darwinists out of business, at least with the general public—and the Institute in regards to resupply. Tia was determined not to leave port this time without that ethological tagging kit. Alex was tired of dealing with each crisis barehanded.

He demanded a supply of firearms—locked up until authorized if necessary, but he wanted to have *something* to enforce his decisions or to defend himself and others.

"What if Haakon-Fritz had gone berserk?" he asked. "What if those canids had been more aggressive?"

Courier Services was agreeable, but the Institute was fighting him; their long-time policy of absolute pacifism was in direct conflict with any such demand. The ban was clear; on any site where there were nearby sophonts with an Iron Age civilization or above—and "nearby" meant on the same continent—absolutely no arms were to be permitted in association with any Institute personnel, not even those under contract. And since the couriers hit at least one dig on every run that came under the ban, they were not allowed *any* weaponry at any time. Tia backed her brawn, and she was lobbying with CS and the Lab Schools to help. After all, *her* well-being was partially dependent on his. The Institute, on the other hand, was balking because there were those who would take the presence of even small arms on board the courier in the worst possible interpretation.

Tia could see their point—but Institute couriers were the only ones not carrying some kind of hand weaponry. They were likely at any time to run into smugglers, who absolutely *would* be armed. If CS made a ruling on the subject, there would be no way the Institute could get around it.

Meanwhile, on the subject of Haakon-Fritz, things were definitely heating up. The recordings of his Olympic sprint to shelter had somehow gotten leaked to the media—fortunately, long *after* Tia had locked down her copies—along with the following recording of Alex's heroic dash to the rescue via grav-sled. Alex was a minor celebrity for a day—but he successfully avoided the media, and they soon grew tired of his self-deprecating attitude, and his refusal to make himself photogenic. Haakon-Fritz did not avoid the media, he sought them out—and he became everyone's favorite villain. The Institute could not keep the incident quiet. The Practical Darwinists came to their proponent's rescue, and only made things worse with their public statements of support and their rhetoric. People did not care to hear that they were weaklings, failures, and ought to be done away with for the good of the race. It began to look as if there was going to be a public trial, no matter how hard the Institute tried to avoid one.

It was on the eve of that trial that Tia finally found her next investment project.

In the Azteca system, the third planet—predictably Terran—known as Quetzecoatl.

Interstellar Teleson, one of the major communications firms in their quadrant with cross-contracts and reciprocal agreements across known space, had just relocated their sector corporate headquarters on Quetzecoatl. The location had a great deal to be said for it—central, in the middle of a stable continental plate, good climate. That, however, was not why they had relocated there.

It was one of those secretly negotiated High Family contracts, and Tia had no doubt that there was a lot more at stake than just the area. Someone owed someone else a favor—or else someone wanted something else kept quiet, and this was the price.

She was doubly sure when the location came up red-flagged on her geological search. According to the survey records, that lovely, flat plain was a flood basin. Quetzecoatl did not have the kind of eccentric orbit that Largo Draconis did—just a little tilt. One that didn't affect anyone in the major settlements at all. But once every hundred years, that tilt angled the north pole into the solar plane for a bit longer than usual. The glaciers would start to melt. The plain below wouldn't exactly "flood"—or at least, not all at once. It would just get very, very soggy, slowly—then, when the spring rains came, the water would rise over the course of a week or two. Eventually the entire plain would be under about two inches of water, and would remain that way for about three years, gradually drying again for the fourth as the glaciers in the north grew.

But Interstellar Teleson's Corporate Standards dictated that the most sensitive records and delicate instruments, and all their computer equipment, be installed permanently in sub-basements no less than four stories below surface level, to avoid any possibility of damage. Corporate Standards had been set to guard against human interference, not nature's. Corporate Standards evidently did not consider nature to be important.

Whoever was in charge of this project apparently completely disregarded the geological survey. Engineers complained about seepage and warned of flooding; the reaction was to order extra sump pumps. Sump pumps were keeping the sub-basements tolerably dry *now*, but Tia guessed that they were going constantly just to keep up with ordinary ground water. They were not going to handle the flood.

Especially not when flood waters were seeping in through the ground floor walls and creeping over the doorsills.

According to the meteorological data, the glaciers were melting, and the spring rains were only a couple of months away.

Meanwhile, half a continent away, there was a disaster recovery firm that specialized in data and equipment recovery. They advertised that they could duplicate an existing system in a month, and recover data from devices that had been immersed in saltwater for over a year, or through major fires with extensive smoke damage. Interstellar Teleson was going to need them, and they didn't even know it. Besides, Tia liked the name. Whoever these people were, they had one heck of a sense of humor.

Chuckling to herself, Tia called Lee Stirling and made her investment—then sent out another carefully worded letter to Crash and Burn Data Recovery, Limited.

The public trial of Doctor Haakon-Fritz was a ten-day circus— but by then, Tia and Alex had far more serious things on their minds and no time to waste on trivialities.

Tia's recordings—both at the site and in the main cabin— were a matter of public record now, and that was the only stake they had in the trial. The Institute only wanted to keep from looking too foolish. In return for the supply of small arms Alex demanded, they asked that he not testify at the trial, since anything he could say would only corroborate those records. They both knew what the Institute people were thinking: records were one thing, but a heroic participant, who just *might* sound impassioned—no, that was something they didn't want to see. *He* was willing—he reckoned it was a small price to pay. Besides, there was little he could add, other than becoming another source of media attention.

So while the media gathered, the quiet Institute lawyers and spokesmen tried to downplay the entire incident, Alex got his arms-locker, and Tia her ethological kit as the price for their non-participation. And as they prepared to head out on a new round of duties, there came an urgent message.

The Institute contract was on hold; CS had another use for them as the only BB ship on base.

And they suddenly found themselves, not only with a new agenda—but an entirely new employer.

"Kenny, what is all this about?" Tia asked, when the barrage of orders and follow-up orders concluded, leaving them with a single destination, an empty flight plan, and a "wait for briefing" message. So here they were, docked with the *Pride of Albion*, and the briefing was coming from Doctor Kennet Uhua-Sorg.

"This," Doctor Kennet replied, grimly, sending the live-cam view of one of the isolation rooms.

Alex gasped. Tia didn't blame him.

The view that Doctor Kennet gave them of this, the *Pride of Albion's* newest isolation patient, was blessedly brief. It had been a human at one point. Now it was a humanoid-shaped mass of suffering. Somewhere in the mass of open sores were eyes, a mouth, a face. Those had been hands, once—and feet.

Tia was the first to recover. "Who is that," she asked sharply, "and what happened to him?"

"Who—we don't know," Kenny replied, his face completely without expression. "He was from a tramp freighter that left him when he didn't get aboard by lift-off time. We don't know if they expected something like this, or if they were just worried because one of their bogus crew turned up missing, but they burned out of Yamahatchi Station with a speed that simply didn't match their rather shabby exterior. He was under false papers, of course—and there isn't enough of his fingers or retinas left to identify him. And unless he's ever been a murder or crime-of-violence suspect, his DNA patterns could take years to match with his birth-records."

Alex nodded. It wouldn't have been too difficult to deduce his ship; anyone logging into a station hostel or hotel had to list his ship-of-origin as well as filing his papers. That information was instantly cross-checked with the ship; the ship had to okay the crewman's ID before he would be allowed to check in. Passengers, of course, used an entirely separate set of hotels.

"That kind of speed probably means a pirate or a smuggler," Alex said.

"I don't think there's much doubt of that," Kenny replied. "Well, when his logged time at the cheap hostel he'd checked into ran out, they opened the door to his room—found *that*—and very wisely slammed the door and reported him."

"What about the hostel personnel?" Tia asked.

"We have them all in isolation, but so far, thank the deity of your choice, none of them are showing any signs of infection."

"For which favor, much thanks," Alex muttered.

"Just what is it that he's got?" Tia asked, keeping her voice even and level.

Kenny shrugged. "Another plague with no name. Symptoms are simple enough. Boils which become suppurating sores that seem to heal only to break open again. A complex of viruses and bacteria, reinforced with modified immune deficiency syndrome. So far, no cure. Decontamination sterilized the hostel room completely, and we haven't seen anyone else come down with this thing. And, thank the spirits of space, once he checked into the hostel, door records show he never left his room."

"There is no reason for a pirate to come down with something like that," Tia pointed out, "but an artifact smuggler—"

"Precisely why I asked for you two," Kenny replied, "and precisely why the Institute loaned you to us. Oh, Alex, in case you wondered, I'm in this because, despite my specialty, I seem to have become the expert in diseases associated with archeology."

Alex cast an inquiring glance at her column. Tia knew what he was asking. Could this be the same disease their mysterious "Sinor" had told them about? Could it be that the man had given them a true story, though not his true name?

She printed her answer under Dr. Kenny's image. *It's a*

coincidence. Not the same as Sinor's phony plague—he would have been frantic if he truly had this to contend with.

He signaled his question with his eyes. Why?

Immune deficiency. Contact or airborne. Think about it.

His eyes widened, and he nodded, slowly. The nightmare that had haunted the human world since the twentieth century; the specter of an immune deficiency disease communicated by an airborne or simple-contact vector. No one wanted to think about it, yet in the minds of anyone connected to the medical professions, it was an ever-present threat.

"You two are a unique combination that I think has the best chance to track this thing to its source," Kenny said. "Medical Services will have more than one team on this—but you're the only BB team available. The Institute doesn't want any of their people to stumble on the plague the hard way, so they subcontracted you to Medical for the duration. I'm delegating the planning of search patterns to you. Got any ideas on how to start?"

"Right," Alex replied. "Then if that's what you want, let's do this the smart way, instead of the hard way. First off, what's the odds this could have come off a derelict—station *or* ship—out in hard vacuum?"

"Odds? Not likely. Hard vacuum kills all of the bugs involved. That *does* eliminate anything like an asteroid or EsKay situation though, doesn't it?" Kenny looked fairly surprised, as well as pleased. "Let me get Lars in on this, he's been monitoring the poor devil."

It took a few moments for Lars to clear his boards enough to have attention to devote to a vocal circuit. During that time, Tia thought of a few questions she'd like to ask.

"Lars, has he *said* anything?" she asked, as soon as Lars joined the conference call. "Something that could give us clues?"

"Ravings mostly—do you think you can get anything out of that?" Lars sounded fairly dubious. "It's not as if he was an astrogator or anything. Mostly he's been yammering on about the weather, besides the usual; either pain and hallucinations, or about treasure and gold."

"The weather?" Tia responded immediately. "What about it?"

"Here, I'll give you what I've got—cleaned up so you can understand it, of course."

A new voice came over the circuit; harsh, with a guttural accent. "Treasure . . . gold . . . never saw s'much. Piles'n'piles . . . no moon, *frag* it, how c'n a guy see anythin' . . . anythin' out there. No moon. Dark 's a wormhole. Crazy weather. Nothin' but crazy weather . . . snow, rain, snow, sleet, mud—how ya s'pposed t' dig this stuff up in this?"

"That's basically it," Lars said, cutting the recording off. "He talks about treasure, moonless, dark nights, and crazy weather."

"Why not assume he's complaining about where he was? Put that together with an atmosphere and—?" Tia prompted. "What do you get?"

"Right. Possible eccentric orbit, probably extreme tilt, third-in Terra-type position, and no satellites." Lars sounded pleased. "I'll get Survey on it."

"What about the likely range of the ship that left him?" Tia asked. "Check with CenSec and Military; the docks at Yamahatchi had to have external specs and so forth on that ship. What kind of fuel did they take on, if any? Docks should have external pictures. Military ought to be able to guess at the range, based on that. That should give us a search area."

"Good." Kenny made notes. "I've got another range—how long it probably took for our victim to come down with the disease once he was infected. Combine that one with yours, and we should have a sphere around Yamahatchi."

"Kenny, he couldn't possibly have shown any symptoms while he was *in* space—they'd have pitched him out the airlock," Tia pointed out. "That means he probably went through incubation while they were in FTL and only showed symptoms once they hit port."

"Right. I'll have that calculated for you and get you the survey records for that sphere, then it'll be up to you and the other teams." Kenny signed off, and Alex swiveled his chair to face Tia's column.

"There's an information lag for that area," Alex pointed out. "Yamahatchi is on the edge of known space. Survey is still working out there—except for really critical stuff, it's going to take weeks, months, even years for information to make it here. We need a search *net*, not just a couple of search teams."

"So—how about if we have Kenny call in not just Medical Services, but Decontamination?" she asked. "They don't have any BB teams either, but they do have the AI drones and the med teams assigned to them. They can run the net as well as we can. Slower, but that may not be so bad."

"I'll get on it," Alex replied instantly. "He can be mobilizing every free ship and team they've got while we compute the likely targets."

"And Intelligence!" she added, as Alex got back on the horn with Kenny and his team. "Get Kenny to get in touch with Intel, and have their people inside that sphere be on the watch for more victims, rumors of plague or of plague ships, or ships that have mysteriously lost half their crews!"

That would effectively increase their available eyes and ears a hundred-thousandfold.

"Or of ships that vanish and don't come into port," Alex said grimly. "Somewhere along the line that so-called tramp freighter is going to do just that; go into hyper and never come out again. Or come out and drift with no hand on the helm."

Tia wished she could still shiver; as it was, she felt rather as if her hull temperature had just dropped to absolute zero.

No computer could match the trained mind for being able to identify or discard a prospect with no data other than the basic survey records. Alex and Tia each took cone-shaped segments of the calculated sphere and began running their own kind of analysis on the prospects the computer search came up with.

Some were obvious; geologic instability that would uncover or completely bury the caches unpredictably. Weather that did not include snow, weather that did not include rain. Occupied planets with relatively thick settlements, or planets with no continents, only tiny island chains.

Some were not so obvious. Terrain with no real landmarks or landmarks subject to change. Terrain with snow and rain, but with snow piling up twelve feet thick in the winter; too deep to dig in. The original trove must have been uncovered by accident—perhaps during the construction of a rudimentary base—or by someone just outside, kicking around dirt.

Places with freelance mining operations *were* on the list; agri-colonies weren't. Places marked by the Institute for investigation were, places with full Institute teams weren't. While Tia would not have put it past someone with problems to sell out to smugglers, she didn't think that they'd care to cover up a contagious disease *this* hideous.

As soon as they finished mapping a cone, it went out to a team to cover. They had another plan in mind for themselves: covering free-trade ports, looking for another victim. They could cover the ports a lot faster than any of the AI or softperson-piloted ships; the only one faster would have been someone with a Singularity Drive. Since *those* were all fully occupied—and since, as yet, they had only one victim and not a full-scale plague in progress—there was no chance of getting one reassigned to this duty. So AH One-Oh-Three-Three would be doing what it could—and trying to backtrack the "freighter" to its origin point.

They were running against the clock, and everyone on the project knew it. If this disease got loose in a large, space-going population, the chances of checking it before millions died were slender.

"Alex," Tia called for the third time, raising the volume of her voice a little more. This time he answered, even though he didn't turn his dark-circled eyes away from his work.

"What, m'love?" he said absently, his gaze glued to a topographical map on the screen before him, despite the fact that he could hardly keep his eyes open.

She overrode the screen controls, blanking the one in front of him. He blinked and turned to stare at her with weary accusation.

"Why did you do that?" he asked. "I was right in the middle of studying the geography—"

"Alex!" she said with exasperation. "You hadn't changed the screen in half an hour; you probably hadn't really looked at it in all that time. Alex, you haven't eaten anything in over six hours, you haven't slept in twenty, and you haven't *bathed* or changed your clothes in forty-eight!"

He rubbed his eyes and peered up at the blank screen. "I'm fine," he protested feebly.

"You're not," she countered. "You can hardly hold your head up. Look at your hand shake! Coffee is no substitute for sleep!"

He clenched his fist to stop the trembling of his hand. "I'm fine," he repeated, stubbornly.

She made a rude noise and flashed her screens at him, so that he winced. "There, see? You can't even control your reactions. If you don't eat, you'll get sick, if you don't sleep, you'll miss something vital, and if you don't bathe and change your clothes I'm turning you over to Decontam."

"All right, love, all right," he sighed, reaching over and patting her column. "Heat me up something; I'll be in the galley shortly."

"How shortly?" she asked sharply.

"As long as it takes for a shower and fresh clothes." He pried himself up out of his chair and stumbled for his room. A moment later, she heard the shower running—and when she surreptitiously checked, she discovered that as she had suspected, he was running it on cold.

Trying to wake up, hmm? Not when I want you to relax. She overrode the controls—not bringing it all the way up to blood-heat, but enough that he wasn't standing in something one degree above sleet. It must have worked; when he stumbled out into the galley, freshly clothed, he was yawning.

She fed him food laden with tryptophane; he was too tired to notice. And even though he punched for it, he got no coffee, only relaxing herbal teas.

He patted her auxiliary console—this time as if he were patting someone's hand to get her attention. He'd been doing that a lot, lately—that and touching her column like the arm of an old and dear friend. "Tia, love, don't you realize we're almost through with this? Two cones to go—three if you count the one I'm working on now—"

"Which I can finish," she said firmly. "I don't need to eat, and I only need three hours of DeepSleep in twenty-four. Yes, I knew. But you aren't going to get teams out there any faster by killing yourself—and if you work yourself until you're exhausted, you are going to miss what might be *the* important clue."

"But—" he protested, and was stopped by a yawn.

"No objections," she replied. "I can withhold the data, and I will. No more data for another eight hours. Consider the boards locked, brawn. I'm overriding you, and if I have to, I'll get Medical to second me."

He was too tired to be angry, too tired even to object. In the past several days he had averaged about four hours in each sleep period, with nervous energy waking him long before he should have reawakened. But the strain was taking its toll. She had the feeling he was going to get that eight solid hours this time, whether or not he intended to.

"You aren't going to accomplish anything half-conscious," she reminded him. "You know what they say in the Academy; do it right, or don't do it."

"I give up." He threw his hands up in the air and shook his head. "You're too much for me, lover."

And with that, he wandered back into his cabin and fell onto his bunk, still fully clothed. He was asleep the moment he was prone.

She did something she had never done before; she continued to watch him through her eye in his cabin, brooding over him, trying to understand what had been happening over the past several days.

She had forgotten that she was encased in a column, not once, but for hours at a time. They had talked and acted like—like ordinary people, not like brain and brawn. Somehow, during that time, the unspoken, unconscious barriers between them had disappeared.

And he had called her "love" or "lover" no less than three times in the past ten minutes. He'd been calling her by that particular pet name quite a bit

He had been patting her console or column quite a bit, these past few days—as if he were touching someone's hand to gain attention, soothe, or emphasize a point.

She didn't think he realized that he was doing either of those things. It seemed very absentminded, and very natural. So she wasn't certain what to make or think of it all. It could simply be healthy affection; some people used pet names very casually. Up until now, Alex hadn't, but perhaps until now he hadn't felt comfortable enough with her to do so. How long had they known each other anyway? Certainly not more than a few months—even though it felt like a lifetime.

No, she told herself firmly. *It doesn't mean a thing. He's just finally gotten to know me well enough to bring all his barriers down.*

But the sooner they completed their searches and got out into space again, the sooner things would go back to normal.

Let's see if I can't do two of those three cones before he wakes up. . . .

Predictably, the port that the mysterious tramp freighter had filed as its next port of call did not have any record of it showing up. Tia hadn't really expected it to; these tramps were subject to extreme changes of flight plan, and if it had been a smuggler, it *certainly* wouldn't log where it expected to go next.

She just hoped that it had failed to show up because the captain had lied—and not because they were drifting out in space somewhere. She let Alex do all the talking; he was developing a remarkable facility for playing a part and very cleverly managed to tell the absolute truth while conveying an impression that was entirely different from the whole truth.

In this case, he left the station manager with the impression that he was an agent for a collection agency—one that meant to collect the entire ship, once he caught up with it

Alex shut down the com to the station manager, and turned his chair to face her screen and the plots of available destinations.

"How do you do that?" she asked, finally. "How do you make them think something entirely different from the real truth?"

He laughed, while she pulled up the local map and projected it as a holographic image. "I've been in theater groups for as long as I can remember, once I got into school. My *other* hobby, the one I never took too seriously, even though they said I was pretty good. I just try to imagine myself as the person I want to be, and figure out what of the truth fits that image."

"Well," she said, as they studied the ship's possible destinations, "if I were a smuggler, where would I go?"

"Lermontov Station, Presley Station, Korngold Station, Tung Station," he said, ticking them off on his fingers. "They might turn up elsewhere, but the rest all have Intel people on them; we'll know if they hit there."

"Provided whoever Intel has posted there is worth his paycheck. Why Presley Station?" she asked. "That's just an asteroid-mining company headquarters."

"High Family in residence," he replied, leaning back in his chair, and lacing his fingers behind his head. "Money for valuable artifacts. Miners with money—and not all of them are rock-rats."

"I thought miners were all—well, fairly crude," she replied.

He shook his head. "Miners are people, and there are all kinds out there. There are plenty of miners looking to make a stake— and some of them outfit their little tugs in ways that make a High Family yacht look plain. *They* have money for pretties, and they don't much care where the pretty came from. And one more thing; the Presley-Lee y Black consortium will buy ore hauls from anyone, including tramp prospectors, so we have a chance that someone may actually stumble on the trove itself. We can post a reward notice there, and it'll be seen."

"Along with a *danger* warning," she told him. "I only hope these people believe it. Lermontov first, then Tung, then Presley?"

"Your call, love," he replied comfortably, sending a carefully worded notice to the station newsgrid. They didn't want to cause a panic, but they *did* want people to turn in any clue to the whereabouts of the freighter. And they didn't want anyone infected along the way. So the news notice said that the ship in question might have been contaminated with Anthrax Three, a serious, but not fatal, variant of old Terran anthrax.

He finished posting his notice, and turned back to her. "You're the pilot. I'm just along for the ride."

"It's the most efficient vector," she replied, logging her flight plan with Traffic Control. "Three days to Lermontov, one to Tung, a day and a half to Presley."

Despite Alex's disclaimer that he was only along for the ride, the two of them did not spend the three days to Lermontov idle. Instead, they sifted through all the reports they'd gotten so far from the other teams, looking for clues or hints that their mystery ship could have made port anywhere else. Then, when they hit Lermontov, Alex went hunting on-station.

This time his cover was as a shady artifact dealer; looking for entire consignments on the cheap. There were plenty of people like him, traders with negotiable ethics, who would buy up a lot of inexpensive artifacts and forge papers for them, selling them on the open market to middle-class collectors who wanted to have something to impress their friends and bosses with their taste and education. Major pirates wouldn't deal with them—at least, not for the really valuable things. But crewmen, who might pick up a load of pottery or something else not worth the bigger men's time, would be only too happy to see him. In this case, it was fortunate that Tia's hull was that of an older model without a Singularity Drive; she looked completely nondescript and a little shabby, just the sort of thing such a man would lease for a trip to the Fringe.

Lermontov was a typical station for tramp freighters and ships of dubious registration. Not precisely a pirate station, since it *was* near a Singularity, it still had station managers who looked the other way when certain kinds of ships made port, docks that accepted cash in advance and didn't inquire too closely into papers, and a series of bars and restaurants where deals could be made with no fear of recording devices.

That was where Alex went—wearing one of his neon outfits. Tia was terrified that he would be recognized for what he was, but there was nothing she could do about it. He couldn't even wear a contact-button; the anti-surveillance equipment in every one of those dives would short it out as soon as he crossed the threshold. She could only monitor the station newsgrids, look for more clues about "their" ship, and hope his acting ability was as good as he thought it was.

Alex had learned the trick of drinking with someone when you wanted to stay sober a long time ago. All it took was a little sleight of hand. You let the quarry drain his drink, switch his with yours, and let him drain the second, then call for another round. After three rounds, he wouldn't even notice you weren't drinking, particularly not when *you* were buying the drinks.

Thank the spirits of space for a MedService credit account.

He started out in the "Pink Comet," whose neon decorations more than outmatched his jumpsuit. He learned quickly enough there that the commodities *he* wanted weren't being offered—although the rebuff was friendly enough, coming from the bartender after he had already stood the whole house a round. In fact, the commodities being offered were more in the line of quasi-legal services, rather than goods. The bartender didn't know who might have what he wanted—but he knew who would know and sent Alex on to the "Rimrunners."

Several rounds later, he suffered through a comical interlude where he encountered someone who thought he was buying feelie-porn and sex-droids, and another with an old rock-rat who insisted that what he wanted was not artifacts but primitive art. "There's no money in them arty-facts no more," the old boy insisted, banging the table with a gnarled fist. "Them accountants don't want arty-facts, the damn market's *got glutted* with 'em! I'm tellin' ya—primy-tive art is the *next* thing!"

It took Alex getting the old sot drunk to extract himself from the man—which might have been what the rock-rat intended in the first place. By then he discovered that the place he really wanted to be was the "Rockwall."

In the "Rockwall" he hit paydirt, all right—but not precisely what he had been looking for.

The bar had an odd sort of quiet ambience; a no-nonsense non-human bartender, an unobtrusive bouncer who outweighed Alex by half again his own weight, and a series of little enclosed table-nooks where the acoustics were such that no sound escaped the table area. Lighting was subdued, the place was immaculately clean, the prices not outrageously inflated. Whatever deals went on here, they were discrete.

Alex made it known to the bartender what he was looking for and took a seat at one of the tables. In short order, his credit account had paid for a gross of Betan funeral urns, twenty soap-stone figurines of Rg'kedan snake-goddesses, three exquisite little crystal Kanathi skulls that were probably worth enough that the Institute and Medical would forgive him anything else he bought, and—of all bizarre things to see out here—a Hopi kachina fig-ure of Owl Dancer from old Terra herself. The latter was prob-ably stolen from another crewman; Alex made a promise to himself to find the owner and get it back to him—or her. It was not an artifact as such, but it might well represent a precious bit of tribal heritage to someone who was so far from home and tribe that the loss of this kachina could be a devastating blow.

His credit account had paid for these things—but those *he* did business with were paid in cash. Simply enough done, as he dis-covered at the first transaction. The seller ordered a "Rock'n'Run"— the bartender came to the table with a cashbox. Alex signed a credit chit for the amount of sale plus ten percent to the bar; the bar-tender paid the seller. Everyone was happy.

He'd spoken with several more crewmen of various odd ships, prompting, without seeming to, replies concerning rumors of disease or of plague ships. He got old stories he'd heard before, the *Betan Dutchman,* the *Homecoming,* the *Alice Bee.* All ships and tales from previous decades; nothing new.

He stayed until closing, making the bartender stretch his "lips" in a cheerful "smile" at the size of the bills he was paying—and making the wait-beings argue over who got to serve him next with the size of his tips. He had remembered what Jon Chernov had told him once about Intel people: *They have to account for every half-credit they spend, so they're as tightfisted as a corporate accoun-tant at tax time. If you're ever doing Intel work, be a big spender.*

They'll never suspect you. And better a docked paycheck for over-spending than a last look at the business end of a needler.

Just before closing was when the Quiet Man came in. As unobtrusive as they came, Alex didn't realize the man was in the bar until he caught a glimpse of him talking with the bartender. And he didn't realize that he was coming towards Alex's table until he was standing there.

"I understand you're buying things," the Quiet Man breathed. "I have some—things."

He opened his hand, briefly, to display a miniature vase or bottle, a lovely thing with a rainbow sheen and a style that seemed oddly familiar, although Alex couldn't place it. As if one had fused Art Nouveau with Salvadore Dali, it had a skewed but fascinating sinuosity.

"That's the sort of merchandise I'm interested in, all right," Alex said agreeably, as he racked his brain, trying to place where he had seen a piece like it before. "The trouble is, it looks a little expensive for my pocket."

The Quiet Man slid in opposite Alex at a nod. "Not as expensive as you think," the Quiet Man replied. "The local market's glutted with this stuff." The Quiet Man's exterior matched his speech; gray jumpsuit, pale skin, colorless eyes and hair, features that were utterly average. "I have about a hundred little pieces like this and I haven't been able to unload them, and that's a fact."

"I appreciate your honesty," Alex told him, allowing his surprise to show through.

The Quiet Man shrugged. "You'd find it out sooner or later. The bosses only wanted the big stuff. Some of the other guys took jewelry; I thought they were crazy, since it was only titanium, and the pieces weren't comfortable to wear and a little flimsy. But some of the earlier crews must have brought back these perfume bottles, because I haven't been able to dump even one. I was hoping if you were buying for another sector, you'd be interested. I can give you a good deal on the lot."

"What kind of a good deal?" Alex asked.

The Quiet Man told him, and they began their bargaining. They ended it a good half hour after the bar was officially closed, but since Alex was willingly paying liquor prices for fruit juice—all that was legal after-hours—the bartender was happy to have him there. The staff cleaned up around them, until he and the Quiet Man shook hands on the deal.

"These aren't exactly ancient artifacts," the Quiet Man had admitted under pressure from Alex. "They can be doctored to look like 'em with a little acid-bath, though. They're—oh—maybe eight, nine hundred years old. Come from a place colonized by one of the real early human slowships; colony did all right for a while, then got religion and had themselves a religious war, wiped each other out until there wasn't enough to be self-sustaining. We figured the last of them died out maybe two hundred years ago. Religion. Go figure."

Alex eyed his new acquisition with some surprise. "This's human-made? Doesn't look it!"

The Quiet Man shrugged. "Beats me. Bosses said the colonists were some kind of artsy-craftsy back-to-nature types. Had this kind of offshoot of an earth-religion with sacramental hallucinogenics thrown in to make it interesting, until somebody decided *he* was the next great prophet and half the colony didn't see it that way. I mean, who knows with that kind? Crazies."

"Well, I can make something up that sounds pretty exotic," Alex said cheerfully. "My clients won't give a damn. So, what do you want to do about delivery?"

"You hire a lifter and a kid from SpaceCaps," the Quiet Man said instantly. "I'll do the same. They meet here, tomorrow, at twelve-hundred. Your kid gives mine the credit slip, mine gives yours the box. Make the slip out to the bar, the usual."

Since that was exactly the kind of arrangement Alex had made for the gross of funeral urns, with only the time of delivery differing, he agreed, and he and the Quiet Man left the bar and went their separate ways.

When he returned to the ship, he took the stairs instead of the lift, still trying to remember *where* he had seen the style of the tiny vase.

"You look cheerful!" Tia said, relief at his safe return quite evident in her voice.

"I feel cheerful. I picked up some artifacts on the black market that I'm sure the Institute will be happy to have." He emptied his pockets of everything but the "perfume bottle" and laid out his "loot" where Tia could use her close-up cameras on the objects. "And this, I suspect, is stolen—" He unwrapped the kachina. "See if you can find the owner, will you?"

"No problem," she replied absently. "I've been following your credit chit all over the station; that's how I figured out how to keep track of you. Alex, the two end skulls are forgeries, but the middle one is real, and worth as much as everything you spent tonight."

"Glad to hear it." He chuckled. "I wasn't sure what I was going to say to the Institute and Medical if they found out I'd been overtipping and buying rounds for the house! All right, here's my final find, and I have a load of them coming over tomorrow. Do *you* remember what the devil this is?"

He placed the warped little vase carefully on the console. Tia made a strange little inarticulate gargle.

"Alex!" she exclaimed. "That's one of SWOT's artifacts!"

He slapped his forehead with the heel of his hand. "Of course! That's why I couldn't remember what book I'd seen it in! Spirits of space—Tia, I just made a deal with the crewman of the ship that's running these things in for a whole load of them! He said— and I quote—'the bosses only wanted the bigger stuff.' They're not really artifacts, they're from some failed human art-religious colony."

"I'm calling the contact number Sinor gave us," she said firmly. "Keep your explanations until I get someone on the line."

Tia had been ready to start sending her servos to pick lint out of the carpet with sheer nerves until she figured out that she could trace Alex's whereabouts by watching for his credit number in the station database. She followed him to three different bars that way, winding up in one called "Rockwall," where he settled down and began spending steadily. She called up the drink prices there, and soon knew when he had made an actual artifact purchase by the simple expedient of which numbers didn't match some combination of the drink prices. A couple of times the buys were obvious; no amount of drinking was going to run up numbers like he'd just logged to his expense account.

She had worried a little when he didn't start back as soon as the bar closed—but drinks kept getting logged in, and she figured then, with a little shiver of anticipation, that he must have gotten onto a hot deal.

When he returned, humming a little under his breath, she *knew* he'd hit paydirt of some kind.

The artifacts he'd bought were enough to pacify the Institute— but when he brought out the little vase, she thought her circuits were going to fry.

The thing's identification was so obvious to *her* that she couldn't believe at first that he hadn't made the connection himself. But then she remembered how fallible softperson memory was. . . .

Well, it didn't matter. That was one of the things she was here for, after all. She grabbed a com circuit and coded out the contact number Sinor had given her, hoping it was something without *too* much of a lag time.

She could not be certain where her message went to—but she got an answer so quickly that *she* suspected it had to come from someone in the same real-space as Lermontov. No visual coming through to them, of course—which, if she still had been entertaining the notion that this was really an Institute directive they were following, would have severely shaken her convictions. But knowing it was probably the Drug Enforcement Arm—she played along with the polite fiction that the visual circuit on their end was malfunctioning, and let Alex repeat the details of the deal he had cut, as she offered only a close-up of the little vase.

"Go through with it," their contact said, when Alex was done. "You've done excellent work, and you'll be getting that bonus. Go ahead and receive the consignment; we'll take care of the rest and clear out the debits on that account for you. And don't worry; they'll never know you weren't an ordinary buyer."

There was no mention of plague or any suggestions that they should take precautions against contamination. Alex gave her a significant look.

"Very well, sir," he only said, with careful formality. "I hope we've accomplished something here for you."

"You have," the unknown said, and then signed off.

Alex picked up the little vase and turned it around and around in his hands as he sat down in his chair and put his feet up on the console. Tia made the arrangements for the two messengers to come to the ship for the credit chits and then to the bar for the pickups—fortunately, not at the same time. That didn't take more than a moment or two, and she turned her attention back to Alex as soon as she was done.

"Was that stupid, dumb luck, coincidence, or were we set up?" she asked suspiciously. "And where *was* that agent? It sounded like he was in our back pocket!"

"I'm going to make some guesses," Alex said, carefully. "The first guess is that we *did* run into some plain good luck. The Quiet Man had tried all the *approved* outlets for his trinkets—outlets that the Arm doesn't know about—and found them glutted. He was desperate enough to try someone like me. I suspect his ship pulls out tomorrow or the next day."

"Fine—but why go ahead and sell to you if he didn't know you?" Tia asked.

"Because I was in the right bar, making all the right moves, and I didn't act like the Arm or Intel." Alex rubbed his thumb against the sides of the vase. "I was willing to go through the barkeep to pay, which I don't think Intel would do. I had the right 'feel,' and I suspect he was watching to see if any of his buddies got picked up after they sold to me. And lastly, once again, we were lucky. Because *he* doesn't know what his bosses are using the phony artifacts for. He thought the worst that could happen is a wrist-slap and fine, for importing art objects without paying customs duty on them."

"Maybe *his* bosses aren't using the artifacts for smuggling," she pointed out, thinking out all the possibilities. "Maybe they are just passing them on to a second party."

"In this station, that's very possible." Alex put the vase down carefully. "At any rate, I think the Arm suspected this cluster of stations all along, and they've got a ship out here somewhere— which is why we got an answer so quickly. I *thought* that was a ship-contact number when I saw it, but I didn't say anything."

"Hmm." Tia ran through all the things *she* would have done next and came up with a possible answer. "So now they just find the messenger that goes to 'Rockwall' at noon from a ship that isn't ours, and tags the ship for watching? Or is that too simple?"

Alex yawned and stretched. "Probably," he said, plainly bored with the whole game now. "He probably won't send the messenger from his ship. They'll do their spy-work somehow; we just gave them what they didn't have in the first place, a contact point. It's out of our hands, which is just as well, since I'd rather not get involved in a smuggler versus Intel shoot-out. I'm *tired*."

"Then you should get some rest," she said immediately. "And get that jumpsuit out of my cabin before it burns out my optics."

He laughed—but he also headed straight for his bed.

Tia didn't even bother to wake her brawn as she approached Presley Station and hailed their traffic control. She expected the usual automated AI most mining stations had; she got a human. Although it was audio-only, there was no doubt that this was a real human being and not an AI-augmented recording.

Because, from the strain in the voice, it was a very nervous and unhappy human.

"AH-One-Oh-Three-Three, be advised we are under a Code Five quarantine," the com officer said, with the kind of hesitation that made her think he wasn't on a microphone very often. "We can let you dock, and we can refuel you with servos, but we can't permit you to open your airlock. And we'd like you to move on to some other station if you have the reserves."

He can't deny us docking under a Code Five, but he's frightened. And he really wants us to go away.

Tia made a quick command decision. "Presley Station, be advised that we are on assignment from CenCom Medical. References coming now." She sent over her credentials in a databurst. "We're coming in, and we'd appreciate Presley Station's cooperation. We'd like to be connected to your Chief Medical Officer while we maneuver for docking, please."

"Uh—I—" There was a brief muttering, as if he was speaking to someone else, then he came back on the mike. "We can do that. Stand by for docking instructions."

At that point the human left the com, and the AI took over; she woke up Alex and briefed him, then gave him a chance to get dressed and gulp some coffee while she dealt with the no longer routine business of docking. As she followed the AI's fairly simple instructions, she wondered just what, exactly, was going on at Presley Station.

Was this the start of the plague, or a false alarm?

Or—was this just one outbreak among many?

She waited, impatiently, for the com officer to return online, while Alex gulped down three cups of coffee and shook himself out of the fog of interrupted sleep. It took forever, or at least it seemed that way.

Finally the com came alive again. "AH-One-Oh-Three-Three, we have the Chief Medical Officer online for you now." It was a different voice; one with more authority. Before Tia could respond, both voice and visual channels came alive, and she and Alex found themselves looking into the face of a seriously frightened man, a man wearing medical whites and the insignia of a private physician.

"Hello?" the man said, tentatively. "You—you're from Med-Services? You don't look like a doctor."

"I'm not a doctor," Alex said promptly. "I've been authorized by CenCom MedServices to investigate a possible outbreak of a new infectious disease that involves immune deficiency syndrome. We had reason to believe that there's an infectious site somewhere in this sphere, and we've been trying to track the path of the last known victim."

There was no doubt about it; the doctor paled. "Let me show you our patient," he whispered, and reached for something below the screen. A second signal came in, which Tia routed to her side screen.

The patient displayed suppurating boils virtually identical to Kenny's victim; the only difference was that this man was not nearly so far gone as the first one.

"Well, he matches the symptoms of the victim we've been tracking," Alex said, calmly, while Tia made frantic adjustments to her blood-chemistry levels to get her heart calmed down. "I trust you have him in full isolation and quarantine."

"Him *and* his ship," the doctor replied, visibly shaking. "We haven't had any new cases, but *decom* it, we don't know what this is or what the vector is or—"

"I've got a contact number coming over to you right now," Alex interrupted, typing quickly. "As soon as you get off the line with me, get onto this line; it's a double-bounce link up to MedServices and a Doctor Kennet Uhua-Sorg. He's the man in charge of this; he has the first case in his custody, and he'll know whatever there is *to* know. What we'd like is this; we're the team in charge of tracking this thing to its source. Do you know anything about where this patient came from, what he was doing—"

"Not much," the doctor said, already looking relieved at the idea that someone at CenCom was "in charge" of this outbreak. Tia didn't have the heart to let him know how little Kenny knew; she only hoped that since they'd left, he'd come up with something more in the way of a treatment. "He's a tramp prospector; he came in here with a load we sealed off, and sick as a dog—crawled into port under his own power, but he collapsed on the dock as soon as he was out of the ship, yelling for a medic. We didn't know he was sick when we let him dock, of course—"

The man was babbling, or he wouldn't have let that slip. Interstellar law decreed that victims of disease be given safe harborage within quarantine, but Tia had no doubt that if traffic control *hadn't* been an AI, the prospector would have never gotten a berth. At best, they would have denied him docking privileges; at worst, they'd have sent a fighter out to blast him into noninfectious atoms. She made a mental note to send that information on to Kenny with their initial report.

"—when he collapsed and one of the dockworkers saw the sores, he hit the alarm and we sealed the dock off, sent in a crew in decontam suits to get him and put him into isolation. I sent off a Priority One to our PTA, but it takes so long to get an answer from them—"

"Did he say where he thought he caught this?" Alex said, interrupting him again.

The doctor shook his head. "He just said he was out looking for a good stake when he stumbled across something that looked like an interstellar rummage sale, and he figures that was where he got hit. What he meant by 'interstellar rummage sale' he won't say. Just that it was a lot of 'stuff' he didn't recognize."

Well, that matched their guess as to the last victim.

"Can we talk to him?" Tia asked.

The doctor shrugged. "You can try. I'll give you audiovisual access to the room. He's conscious and coherent, but whether or not he'll be willing to tell you anything, I can't say. He sure won't tell us much."

It was fairly obvious that he was itching to get to a comset and get in contact with MedServices, thus, symbolically at least, passing the problem up the line. If his bosses cared about where the miner had picked up the infection, they hadn't told *him* about it.

Not too surprising. He was a company doctor. He was supposed to be treating execs for indigestion, while his underlings patched up miners after bar fights and set broken bones after industrial accidents. The worst he was ever supposed to see was an epidemic of whatever new influenza was going around. He was *not* supposed to have to be dealing with a plague, at least, not by his way of thinking. Traffic control was supposed to be keeping plague ships from ever coming near the station.

"Thanks for your cooperation, Doctor," Alex said genially. "Get that link set up for us, if you would, and we'll leave you to your work."

The doctor signed off—still without identifying himself, not that Tia was worried. Her recordings were enough for any legal purposes, and at this point, now that he had passed authority on to them, he was a nonentity. They didn't need to talk to him anymore. What they needed was currently incarcerated in an isolation room on that station—and they were going to have to figure out how to get him to talk to them.

"Okay, Alex," she said when the screen was safely blank. "You're a lot closer to being an expert on this than I am. How do we get a rock-rat to tell us what we want to know?"

"Hank, my name's Alex," the brawn said, watching the screen and all the patient-status readouts alongside. "I'm a brawn from CS, on loan to MedServices; you'll hear another voice in a moment, and that's my brainship, Tia."

"Hello, Hank," she said, very glad that she was safely encased in her column with no reactions for Hank to read. Alex was doing a good job of acting; one she knew she would never be able to match. Just looking at Hank made her feel—twitchy, shivery, and quite uncomfortable; sensations she hadn't known she could still have. "I don't know if anyone bothered to tell you, but we were sent out here because there's someone else with what you've got; it's very contagious, and we're trying to keep it from turning into a plague. Will you help us?"

"*Give him the straight story,*" Alex had said; Kenny had agreed to that when they got hold of him, right after the company doctor had called him. "*There's no point in trying to trick him. If he knows how bad off he is, he just might be willing to cooperate.*"

The sores only grew worse when you bandaged them, so Hank was lying in a gel-bed—a big pan full of goo, really, with a waterbed mattress beneath the goo. Right now only the opaque green gel covering him was keeping him from outraging modesty. The gel was a burn-treatment, and something Kenny had come up with for the other man. *He* was still alive, but no better than when they had left. They still had no idea who or what he was, besides horribly unlucky.

Hank peered up at the screen in the corner of his room, through a face grotesquely swollen and broken-out. "These company goons won't give me any kind of a straight story," he said hoarsely. "All they do is try an' brush me off. How bad off am I?"

"There's no cure," Alex said, flatly. "There's one other known victim. The other man is worse than you, and they haven't found anything to reverse his condition. That's the truth."

Hank cursed helplessly for about four or five minutes straight before he ran out of breath and words. Then he lay back in the gel-bed for another couple of minutes with his eyes closed.

Tia decided to break the silence. "I don't know how you feel about the rest of the universe, Hank, but—we need to know where you came down with this. If this got loose in any kind of population—"

" 'Sall right, lady," he interrupted, eyes still closed. "You're preachin' to the choir. Ain't no percentage in keeping my mouth shut now." He sighed, a sound that sounded perilously close to a sob. "I run across this place by accident, and I ain't sure how I'd find it again—but you guys might be able to. I give you what data I got. I'd surely hate t' see a kid in the shape I'm in right now."

"Thanks, Hank," Alex said, with quiet gratitude. "I wish there was something we could do for you. Can you think of anything you'd like?"

Hank shook his head just a little. "Tell you what; I got some serious hurt here, an' what they're given me ain't doin' much, 'cause they're 'fraid I'm gonna get hooked. You make these bozos give me all the pain meds I ask for—if I ever get cured up, I'll dry out *then*. You think you can do that for me?"

"I'll authorize it," Tia said firmly. At Alex's raised eyebrow, she printed: *Kenny's authorizations include patient treatments. We've got that power, and it seems cruel not to give him that much relief.*

Alex nodded. "Okay, Hank, my partner says she can boss the docs here. So, fire away; we're recording. Unless you want something now."

"Naw. I wanta stay on this planet long enough t' give you what little info I got." Hank coughed. "First off, my boat's an old wreck; falls outa hyper all the time, and the recorder don't always work when she takes a dive. Basically, what happened was she fell out, and there was a Terra-type planet not too far from where she dropped. My holds was pretty empty, so I figured I'd see if there was anything around. Registered somethin' that looked like wrecked buildings in one spot, went down t' take a look-see."

"That was where you caught this thing?" Alex asked.

"I'm gettin' to that. Weren't no signs of life, okay? But there was some buildings there, old and kinda busted up, round, like them flyin' saucers people used to see—I figgered maybe I'd hit some place where the archies hadn't got to, mebbe I could pick up somethin' I could peddle. I went ahead an' landed, okay? Only I found somethin' that looked like somebody else had been there first. Looked like—I dunno, like somebody'd been collectin' and hoardin' for a long, long time, buryin' the stuff in caves by the buildings, stashin' it in the buildings that wasn't busted up. Some of it was dug up already, some of it somebody'd just started t' dig up."

"How do you mean?" Alex asked.

"Like—somebody's kid's idea of a treasure place. Caves, lots of 'em, some of 'em dug up, all of 'em prob'ly had stuff in 'em." Hank's voice started to slur with fatigue, but he seemed willing to continue, so Tia let him.

"Anyway, I got down there, grabbed some of the good stuff, took lots of holos so if I ever figured out where it was, I could stake a legal claim on it." He sighed. "I was keepin' my mouth shut, partly 'cause I don't trust these company goons, partly 'cause I figured on goin' back as soon as I got cured." He coughed, unhappily. "Well, it don't much look like I'm gonna get cured up any time soon, does it?"

"I can't promise anything but the pain meds, Hank," Tia said softly.

"Yeah." He licked cracked and swollen lips with a pale tongue. "Look, you get into my ship. See if the damn recorder was workin' at all. Get them holos, see if you can figure out where the devil I was from 'em. You guys are CS, ev'body knows you can trust CS—if there's anything I can get outa this, see what you can do, okay?" The last was more of a pathetic plea than anything else.

"Hank, I can guarantee you this much—since you've cooperated, there's some kind of reward system with MedService for people who cooperate in closing down plagues," Alex said, after a few moments of checking with regs. "It includes all medical covered—including prosthetics and restorations—and full value of personal possessions confiscated or destroyed. That should include your ship and cargo. We'll itemize the *real* value of your cargo if we can."

Hank just sighed—but it sounded relieved. "Good," he replied, his voice fading with exhaustion. "Knew I could . . . trust CS. Lissen, can I get some'f that pain med now?"

Tia logged the authorization and activated the servo-nurse. "Coming up, Hank," she said. The man turned his head slightly as he heard the whine of the motor, and his eyes followed the hypospray until it touched his arm. "From now on, you just voice-activate the servo—tell it 'DM-Tia' and it will know what to give you." There was a hiss—then for one moment, what was left of his swollen lips curved in something like a smile. Tia closed down the link, after locking in the "on-demand" authorization. It would take someone from CenCom MedServices to override it now.

Meanwhile, Alex had been arguing with Dock Services, and finally had to pull rank on them to get access to the controls for the dock servos and remotes. Once that was established, however, it was a matter of moments for Tia to tie herself in and pick out a servo with a camera still inside the quarantined area to send into the ship.

She selected the most versatile she could find; one with a crawler base, several waldos of various size and strength, and a reasonable optical pickup. "We aren't going to tell them that hard vacuum kills the bugs yet, are we?" she asked, as she activated the servo and sent it crawling towards the abandoned dock.

"Are you kidding?" Alex snorted. "Given the pass-the-credit attitude around here, I may never tell them. Let Kenny do it, if he wants, but I'd be willing to bet that the moment we tell them, they'll seal off the section and blow it, then go in and help themselves to whatever's on Hank's ship before we get a chance to make a record of it."

"I won't take that bet," she replied, steering the crawler up the ramp and into the still-gaping airlock.

Hank hadn't exaggerated when he'd said his ship was a wreck; it had more patches and make-dos on it than she had dreamed possible on a ship still in space and operating. Half the wall-plates were gone on the inside of the lock; the floor-plates were of three different colors. And when she brought the crawler into the control cabin, it was obvious that the patchworking probably extended to the entire ship.

Exposed wiring was everywhere; the original control panels had long ago been replaced by panels salvaged from at least a dozen other places. Small wonder the ship had a tendency to fall out of hyper; she was surprised it ever managed to stay *in* hyper, with all the false signals that should be coming off those boards.

"You think the recorder caught where he went?" Alex asked doubtfully, peering at the view in the screen. The lighting was in just as poor shape as everything else, but Tia had some pretty sophisticated enhancement abilities, and the picture wasn't too bad. The ship's "black box" recorder, that *should* have registered everything this poor old wreck had done, was in no better shape than the rest of the ship.

"Either it did, or it didn't," she said philosophically. "We'll have a pattern of where he was supposed to *be* going, though, and where he thought he was heading when he left our little plague-spot. We should be able to deduce the general area from that."

"Ah, and since we know the planetary type, if Survey ever found it, we'll know where it is." Alex nodded as his hands raced across the keyboards, helping Tia with the complex servo. "Look, there's the com, I think. Get the servo a little closer, and I'll punch up a link to us."

"Right." She maneuvered the crawler in between two seats with stuffing oozing out of cracks in the upholstery, and got the servo close enough to the panel that Alex could reach it with one of the waldos. While he punched in their access com-code, she activated the black box, plugged the servo into it, and put it on com uplink mode with another waldo. She would have shaken her head, if she could have. Not only was all of this incredibly jury-rigged, it actually looked as if many of the operations that should have been automatic had deliberately been made manual.

"I can't believe this stuff," she said, finally. "It must have taken both hands and feet to fly this wreck!"

"It probably did," Alex observed. "A lot of the old boys are like that. They don't trust AIs, and they'll tell you long stories about how it's because someone who was a friend of a friend had trouble with one and it nearly killed him or wrecked his ship. The longer they stay out here, the odder they get that way."

"And CenCom worries about *us* going loonie," she replied, making a snorting sound. "Seems to me there's a lot more to worry about with one of these old rock-rats—"

"Except that there's never been a case of one of them going around the bend in a way that endangered more than a couple of people," Alex replied. Just about then, one of Tia's incoming lines activated. "There. Have I got you live, lover?"

"Yes, and I'm downlinking now." The black box burped its contents at her in a way that made her suspect more than one gap in its memory-train. *Oh well. Maybe well get lucky.* "Should we go check out the holds now?"

"Not the holds, the cabin," Alex corrected. "The holds will probably be half-full of primary-processed metals, or salvage junk. He'll have put his loot from the site in the cabins, if it was anything good."

"Good enough." She backed the servo out, carefully, hoping to avoid tangling it in anything. Somehow she actually succeeded; she wasn't quite sure how. She had no real "feeling" from this servo; no sense of where its limbs were, no feedback from the crawler treads. It made her appreciate her shipbody all that much more. With the kinesthetic input from her skin sensors and the internals, she knew where everything was at all times, exactly as if she had grown this body herself.

There were two cabins off the main one; the first was clearly Hank's own sleeping quarters, and Tia was amazed at how neat and clean they were. Somehow she had expected a rat's nest. But she recalled the pictures of the control room as she turned the servo to the other door, and realized that the control room had been just as neat and clean—

It was only the myriad of jury-rigs and quick-fix repairs that had given the impression of a mess. There wasn't actually any garbage in there—the floor and walls were squeaky-clean. Hank ran as clean a ship as he could, given his circumstances.

The second door was locked; Alex didn't even bother with any kind of finesse. Hank's ship would be destroyed at this point, no matter what they did or didn't do. One of the waldos was a small welding torch; Alex used it to burn out the lock.

The door swung open on its own, when the lock was no longer holding it. Tia suddenly knew how Lord Carnavon felt, when he peeked through the hole bored into the burial chamber of Tutankhamen.

" 'Wonderful things!' " she breathed, quoting him half-unconsciously.

Hank must have worked like a madman to get everything into that cabin. This *was* treasure, in every sense of the word. There was nothing in that cabin that did not gleam with precious metal or the sleekness of consummate artistry. Or both. The largest piece was a statue about a meter tall, of some kind of stylized winged creature. The smallest was probably one of the rings in the heaps of jewelry piled into the carved stone boxes on the floor—which were themselves works of high art. If Hank could claim even a fraction of this legally, he could buy a new ship and still be a wealthy man.

If he lived to enjoy his wealth, that is.

He had stowed his loot very carefully, Tia saw, with the same kind of neat, methodical care that showed in his own cabin. Every box of jewelry was carefully strapped to the floor; every vase was netted in place. Every statue was lying on the bunk and held down by restraints. The cabin had been crammed as full as possible and still permit the door to open, but every single piece had been neatly stowed and then secured, so that no matter what the ship did, none of it would break loose. And so that none of it would damage anything else.

"Have we got enough pictures?" Alex asked faintly. "I'm being overcome by gold-fever. I'd like to look for those holos before my avarice gets the better of my common sense, and I go running down there to dive into that stuff myself."

"Right!" Tia said hastily, and backed the servo out again. The door swung shut after it, and Alex heaved a very real sigh of relief.

"Sorry, love," he said apologetically. "I never thought I'd ever react like that."

"You've never been confronted with several million credits'-worth of gold alone," she replied soothingly. "I don't even want to think what the real value of all of that is. Do you think he'd keep the holos in his cabin?"

"There's no place to stash them out in the control room," Alex pointed out.

Once again, Hank's neat and methodical nature saved the day for them, and Tia knew why he hadn't bothered to tell them where he'd put his records. Once they entered his cabin, there next to a small terminal was a drawer marked "Records," and in the drawer were the hardcopy claim papers he'd intended to file and the holos he'd taken in a section marked "Possible Claims."

"Luck's on our side today," Alex marveled. Tia agreed. It would have been *far* more likely that they'd have gotten some victim who'd refuse to divulge anything, or one who'd been half-crazed— or one who simply hadn't kept any kind of a record at all.

Luck was further on their side; he'd made datahedron copies of everything, including the holos, and *those* could be uplinked to AH-One-Oh-Three-Three. There would be no need to bring anything out of the quarantined dock area.

It took them several hours to find a way to bring up the reader in the control cabin, then link the reader into the com system, but once they got a good link established, it was a matter of nano-seconds and the precious recordings were theirs.

She guided the servo towards the lock and swiveled the optic back for a last look—and realized that *she* still had control over a number of the ship's functions via the servo.

"Alex," she said slowly, "it would be a terrible thing if the airlock closed and locked, wouldn't it? That would mean even if station ops blew the section to decontaminate it, they wouldn't be able to get into the ship—or even get it undocked. They'd never know *exactly* what was on board."

Alex blinked in bewilderment for a moment—then slowly grinned. "That *would* be terrible, wouldn't it?" he agreed. "Well, goodness, Tia, I imagine that they'd probably dither around about it until somebody from CenCom showed up—somebody with authority to confiscate it and hold it for decontamination and evaluation."

"Of course," she continued smoothly, sending a databurst to the servo, programming it to get the airlock to shut and lock up. "And you know, these old ships are *so* unreliable—what if something happened to the ship's systems that made it vent to vacuum? Why then, even if the station managers decided to try and short-circuit the lock, they couldn't get it open against a hard vacuum. They'd have to bring in vacuum-welders and cut the locks open—and that would damage their own dock area. That would just be such an inconvenience."

"It certainly would—" Alex said, stifling a laugh.

She sent further instructions to the ship and noted with glee the ship proceeding to vent out the spaceward side. The servo noted hard vacuum on one of its sensors in a fairly reasonable length of time.

Satisfied that no one was going to be able to break into Hank's ship and pilfer his treasure, she sent a last set of instructions to the servo, shutting it down until she sent it an activation key. No one was going to get into that ship without her cooperation.

Hank would get a finder's fee, if nothing else, based on the value of the artifacts he had found. But now it would be based on the *true* value of what he had found, and not just what was left after the owners of Presley Station took their pick of the loot. Assuming they left anything at all.

"Well," she said, when she had finished. "We'd better get to work. Are *you* any good at deciphering black box recordings?"

"Tolerably," Alex replied. "Tell you what; you analyze the holos while I diddle the black box data, then we'll switch."

"Provided you don't get gold-fever again," she warned him, opening the data on his screens.

The holos showed exactly what Hank had reported; a series of caves—caves that looked to have been artificially cut into the bluffs beside the ruined buildings. The nearest were completely dug up, and plainly emptied, but beyond them, there was another series of caves that were open to the air and still held treasures. But this wasn't like anything Tia had ever seen before. Each one of those caves, rather than being some kind of grave or other archeological entity, was clearly nothing more than a cache—and each one held precious objects from an entirely different culture than the one next to it. The two nearest the camera in the first holo held sacred objects from two cultures that were light-years apart—and from ages when neither civilization had attained even interplanetary flight, much less starflight.

Furthermore, the more Tia studied the holos, the more she came to the conclusion that the original caches were old; never mind who was digging them up now. The kind of weathering of the surface and layering of detritus she saw in the holos took hundreds, perhaps thousands of years to build up. And the buildings in one of the other holos were *very* old.

Nor did she recognize who could have constructed them.

So who could have been responsible for collecting all these treasures in the first place? Why had they buried them? Where did they get it all—and above all, why didn't they come back after it?

There was some evidence around the caves that the current looters had attempted to rebury their finds. But had they done so in an attempt to hide it again—or had they done it to try and kill the disease? How many of the looters were exposed? From the number of caves that had been broken into, it looked as if there had been quite a few people at work there. . . .

Tia wished she could sit back and chew a nail or something. All she had now were questions and no answers. And the lives of other people might hang in the balance.

There was only one way to answer all those questions. They were going to have to find Hank's mystery planet and find out for themselves.

CHAPTER EIGHT

Tia didn't entirely trust the integrity of the Presley Station comcenter. She *certainly* expected that whatever she sent out would be monitored by the owners and their underlings. Unfortunately, there had been no provision for the need for secrecy in this mission; she had no codes and no scramblers. There had been no real reason to think that they would ever need such secrecy, so she was forced to send in the clear. Just to be on the safe side, she uplinked on her own and double-sent everything, but she knew that whatever she sent off that way would be subject to delays as it bounced from remote hyperwave relay-station to relay-station, taking the long way "home."

As she had expected, the owners of the station were quick to move on the information that Hank's ship contained treasure, despite the fact that no one should have read her messages back to Kenny and the rest. She was just grateful that the owners' first thought was to grab what they could from the nearby trove, and *not* to try and figure out where Hank came from—or attempt to force him to tell them.

The first intimation that the communications had been leaked was when the station ops tried to claim the ship and all its contents for themselves; filing confiscation papers in the Central Systems Courts. When they discovered that Tia had already tied the ship and its contents up legally on Hank's behalf, they moved on the principle that "possession is nine-tenths of the law, and the fellow arguing the other tenth has to prove it with a lawyer."

They sent crews into the docks, to try and get into the ship to strip it of as much as they could. Tia's cleverness thwarted them, as they worked their way—slowly—through every step she'd expected.

She figured that by the time they were in a position to actually threaten Hank's possessions, the CS authorities would be on the scene in person. Meanwhile, she and Alex had some figuring to do—*where* was Hank's cache-world? Same problem as before, except that this time the possible search area was smaller, and cone-shaped rather than spherical.

Unfortunately, there were some other people who wanted to get their hands on that same information.

And unknown to either of them, those people had decided that Alex and Tia were already privy to it.

Tia kept a careful eye on the activity around her slip just on general principles, even when she wasn't feeling nervous—but given their current circumstances, and the fact that they were the *only* Central Systems ship out here at the moment, she couldn't help but feel a bit, well, paranoid. At the moment, only three people knew for certain that she was a brainship; Hank, the traffic control officer who brought them in, and that doctor. She was pretty certain that the doctor hadn't mentioned it to his superiors; she knew Hank hadn't told anyone, and as jittery as the other man had been, he'd probably forgotten it.

No one addressed *her* when they called, at any rate, and she took pains to make callers think that she was an AI. So far, they seemed to be falling in with the deception. This wasn't a bad state of affairs; no one expected an AI to recognize dangers the way a real sentient could. She could tap into the optical scanners in the dock area around the ship and no one would have any notion that she was keeping watch. She made sure to schedule her three or four hours of DeepSleep while Alex was awake; normally taking them during his "morning," while he was still rather grumpy and uncommunicative and she'd rather not talk to him anyway. And she scanned the recordings she made while she was under, just to be sure she didn't miss anything.

That was why, a few days after their interview with Hank,

she noticed the man in the dock-crew uniform coverall who seemed to be working double shifts. Except that no one else was working double shifts . . . and what was more, there was currently a company prohibition against overtime as a cost-cutting measure.

Something wasn't right, and he never left the immediate area of her slip. What was he doing there? It wasn't as if she was either a freighter with goods to load or unload, or a passenger liner. She didn't need servicing either. He never got close enough that she could see exactly what he was up to—but it seemed to her that he was doing an awful lot of make-work. . . .

She kept a close eye on him as he wandered around the dock area—purposefully, but accomplishing nothing that she could see. Gradually though, he worked his way in closer and closer to *her* slip, and little mental alarms began going off as she watched him and the way he kept glancing at her lock out of the corner of his eye.

Around sixteen-hundred she watched him removing control-panel plates and cleaning in behind them, work too delicate to trust to a servo.

Except that he'd just cleaned that same area two hours ago.

That was senseless; regs stated that the panels only had to be cleaned once every two *weeks*, not every two hours.

Furthermore, there was something not quite right with his uniform. It wasn't exactly the same color of gray as everyone else's; it looked crisply new, and the patches were just a little too bright. There were plenty of dockworkers' uniforms in Presley storage, there was no reason for someone to have had a new one made up unless he was an odd size. And this man was as average as anyone could possibly be. He was so *very* unremarkable that she noticed his uniform long before she noticed him.

That was bad enough—but just as seventeen-hundred passed and everyone else in the dock-crew went on supper break, another man in that too-new uniform showed up, while the first man kept on puttering about.

"Alex?" she said, unhappily. "There's something going on out there I don't like."

He looked up from his perusal of Hank's holos; he had prints made from them spread out all over the floor and was sitting on his heels beside them. "What's up?"

She filled him in quickly, as a third and a fourth person in that same uniform ambled into the dock.

There were now four crewmen in the docks during break. All four of them in a dock area where there were no ships loading or unloading and no new ships expected to dock in the next twenty-four hours.

"Tia, I don't like this either," he said, much to her relief, standing up and heading for the main console. "I want you to get the station manager online and see what—"

Abruptly, as if someone had given the four men a signal, they dropped everything they were pretending to do and headed for her docking slip.

Tia made a split-second decision, for within a few seconds they were going to be in her airlock.

She slammed her airlock shut, but one of the men now running for her lock had some kind of black box in his hands; she couldn't trust that he might not be able to override her own lock controls. "Alex!" she cried, as she frantically hot-keyed her engines from cold-start. "They're going to board!"

As Alex flung himself at his acceleration couch, she sent off a databurst to the station manager and hit the emergency override on *her* side of the dock.

The dockside airlock doors slammed shut, *literally* in the faces of the four men approaching. Another databurst to the docking-slip controls gave her an emergency uncouple—there weren't too many pilots who knew about that kind of override, still in place from the bad old days when captains had to worry about pirates and station-raiders. She gave her insystem attitude thrusters a kick and shoved free of the dock altogether, frantically switching to external optics and looking for a clear path out to deep space.

As her adrenaline-level kicked up, her reactions went into over-drive, and what had been real-time became slow motion. Alex sailed ungracefully through the air, lurching for his chair; to her, the high-speed chatter of comlinks between AIs slowed to a drawl. Calculations were going on in her subsystems that she was only minimally aware of; a kind of background murmur as she switched from camera to camera, *looking* for the trouble she knew must be out there.

"The *chair* Alex—" she got out—just in time to spot a bee-craft, the kind made for outside construction work on the station, heading straight for her. Behind it were two men in self-propelled welder-suits. Someone had stolen or requisitioned station equipment, and they were going to get inside her no matter what the consequences were.

Accidents in space were so easy to arrange....

Alex wasn't strapped down yet. She couldn't wait.

She spun around as Alex leapt for his couch, throwing him off-balance, and blasted herself out of station-space with a fine disregard for right of way and inertia as he grabbed and caught the arm of the chair.

Alex slammed face-first into the couch, yelped in pain at the impact, and clung with both hands.

There was another small craft heading for her with the purposeful acceleration of someone who intended to ram. She poured on the speed, all alarms and SOS signals blaring, while Alex squirmed around and fastened himself in, moaning. His nose dripped blood down the side of his face, and his lip poured scarlet where he'd bitten or cut it.

She dove under the bow of a tug, delaying her pursuer.

Who was in on this? Was this something the High Families were behind?

Surely not—

Please, not—

She continued to accelerate, throwing off distress signals even onto the relays, dumping real-time replays into message bursts every few seconds. Another tug loomed up in front of her; she sideslipped at the last moment, skimming by the AI-driven ship so close that it shot attitude thrusters out in all directions, the AI driven into confusion by her wild flying.

The ship behind was still coming on; no longer gaining, but not losing any ground either.

But with all the fuss that Tia was putting up, even Presley Station couldn't ignore the fact that someone was trying to 'jack her. Especially not with Central Systems investigators due any day, and with the way she was dumping her records onto the relays. If "they" were allied with the station, "they" wouldn't be able to catch everything and wipe it. If AH-One-Oh-Three-Three disappeared, she was making it very hard for the claim of "accident" to hold any water—

I hope.

As Tia continued to head for deep space, a patrol craft finally put in an appearance, cutting in between her and her pursuer, who belatedly turned to make a run for it.

Tia slowed, and stopped, and held her position, as the adrenaline in her blood slacked off.

I remember panting. I remember shivering. I'd do both right now, if I could. As it was, errant impulses danced along her sensors, ghost-feelings of the *might-have-been* of weapons' fire, tractor beams. . . .

Slow heart. It's all right. Gradually her perception slowed back down to real-time, and the outside world "sped up." That was when the station manager himself hailed her.

"*Of course* I'm sure they were trying to break in," she snapped in reply to his query, re-sending him her recordings, with close-ups on suspicious bulges under the coveralls that were the right size and placement for needlers and other weapons. She followed that with the bee-craft and the two men in the welding-suits—headed straight for her. "And those pursuit-craft certainly were *not* my imagination!" She raised her voice, both in volume and pitch. "I happen to be a fully trained graduate of Lab Schools, you know! I'm not in the habit of imagining things!"

Now her adrenaline kicked in again, but this time from anger. They'd been in real danger—they could have been killed! And this idiot was talking to her as if she was some kind of—of joy-riding tweenie!

"I never said they were, ma'am," the station manager replied, taken somewhat aback. "I—"

"Just what kind of station are you running where a CS craft can be subject to this kind of security breach?" she continued wrathfully, running right over the top of him, now that she had the upper hand and some verbal momentum. "I'm reporting this to the Central Worlds Sector Coordinator on my *own* comlink!"

"You don't need to do that ma—"

"*And furthermore,* I am standing off-station until you can give me a *high-security* slip!" she continued, really getting warmed up and ready to demand all the considerations due a PTA. "My poor brawn is black and blue from head to toe from the knocking around he took, and lucky it wasn't worse! I want you to *catch* these people—"

"We're taking care of that, ma—"

"And I want to know *everything* you learn from them *before* I dock again!" she finished, with a blast of feedback that punctuated her words and made him swear under his breath as the squeal pierced his ears. "Until then, I am going to *sit* out here and dog your approach lanes, and I don't particularly care whether or not you like it!"

And with that, she put him on "record" and let him splutter into a datahedron while she turned her attention to Alex.

He had a wad of tissues at his face, trying to staunch the blood from nose and lip, and his eyes above the tissues were starting to puff and turn dark. He was going to look like a raccoon before too long, with a double set of black eyes.

Obviously the first thing that had impacted with the couch was his face.

"Alex?" she said timidly. "Oh, Alex, I'm so sorry—I didn't mean—there wasn't time—"

"Ith awright," he replied thickly. "You di okay. Din hab mush shoice. Hanneled ev'thing great, hanneled him great. You arn gon moof for wile?"

She correctly interpreted that as praise for her handling of the situation and a query as to whether or not she planned on moving.

"No, I don't *plan* on it," she replied, dryly. "But I hadn't *planned* on any of this in the first place."

He simply grunted, pried himself up painfully out of the acceleration couch and headed for their tiny sickbay to patch himself up.

She sent in a servo, discreetly, to clean up the blood in the sickbay and a second to take care of the mess in the main cabin, thanking her lucky stars that it *hadn't* been worse. If Alex had been standing when she pulled that spin and acceleration instead of heading in the direction of the couch—

She didn't want to think about it. Instead, she ordered the kitchen to make iced gel-packs. Lots of them. And something soft for dinner.

They left as soon as the CS contingent arrived and spent a little time debriefing them. The CS folk showed up in a much fuller force than even Tia had expected. Not only Central Systems Medical and Administrative personnel—but a CenSec Military brainship, the CP-One-Oh-Four-One. Bristling with weaponry—

And with the latest and greatest version of the Singularity Drive, no doubt, she thought, a little bitterly. *Heaven only knows what their version can do. Bring its own Singularity point with it, maybe.*

Whatever the administrators of Presley Station had *thought* they were going to get away with, they were soon dissuaded. The first person off the CenSec ship was a Sector Vice-Admiral; right behind him was an armed escort. He proclaimed the station to be under martial law, marched straight into the station manager's office, and within moments had the entire station swiftly and efficiently secured.

Tia had never been so happy to see anyone in her life. Within the hour all the witnesses and guilty parties had been taken into military custody, and Tia confidently expected someone to call them and take their depositions at any time.

Alex still looked like someone had been interrogating him with rubber hoses, so when the brainship hailed them, she took the call, and let him continue nursing his aching head and bruises.

The ship-number was awfully close to hers, although the military might not use standard CS brainship nomenclature. Still. . . . *One-Oh-Four-One. That's close enough for the brain to have been in my class—*

"Tia, that is you, isn't it?" were the first words over the comlink. The "voice"—along with the sharp overtones and aggressive punch behind them—was very familiar.

"Pol?" she replied, wondering wildly what the odds were on *this* little meeting.

"In the shell and ready to kick some tail!" Pol responded cheerfully. "How the heck are you? Heard you had some trouble out here, and the Higher Ups said 'go,' so we came a-running."

"Trouble—you could say so." She sent him over her records of the short—but hair-raising, at least by her standards—flight, in a quick burst. He scanned them just as quickly, and sent a wordless blip of color and sound conveying mingled admiration and surprise. If he had been a softie, he would have whistled.

"Not bad flying, if I do say so myself!" he said. "Like the way you cut right under that tug—maybe you should have opted for CenSec or Military."

"I don't think so," she replied. "That was more than enough excitement for the next decade for me."

"Suit yourself." Pol laughed, as if he didn't believe her. "My brawn wants to talk to your brawn. It's debriefing time."

She called Alex, who had been flat on his back in his bunk with an ice-gel pack on his black eyes. He staggered out to his chair and plopped down into it. For once, she thought, no one was going to notice his rumpled uniform—not with the black-blue-purple and green glory of his bruised face staring out of a screen.

"Line's open," she told Pol, activating the visual circuit.

As she had half-expected, given her impressions of the candidates when she had been picking a brawn, it was Chria Chance who stared out of the screen, with surprise written all over her handsome features. She was still wearing her leather uniforms, Tia noticed—which argued powerfully for "Chria" being High Family. Little eccentricities like custom-tailored uniforms could be overlooked in someone who was both a High Family scion and had an excellent record of performance. Tia had no doubt that Chria's record was outstanding.

Tia noted also one difference between the Courier Service ships and the CenSec Couriers besides the armament. Directly behind Chria was another console and another comchair; this one held a thin, sharp-featured man in a uniform identical to Chria's, with an ornamental leather band or choker circling his long throat. He looked just as barbaric as she did. More, actually. He had the rangy, take-no-prisoners look of someone from one of the outer systems.

In short, he and Chria probably got along as if they had been made for each other.

"Frigging novas!" Chria exclaimed, after the first few seconds of staring. "Alex, what in blazes happened to *you*? Your dispatches never said anything about—did they—"

"Nobody worked me over, Brunhilde," Alex said tiredly, but with a hint of his customary humor. "So don't get your tights in a knot. This is all my own fault—or maybe just the fault of bad timing. It's the result of my face hitting my chair at—what was that acceleration, Tia?"

"About two gees," she said apologetically.

Chria shook her head in disbelief. "Huh. Well, shoot—here I was getting all ready to go on-station and dent some heads to teach these perps some manners." She sat back in her chair and grinned at him. "Sorry about that, flyboy. Next time, strap in."

"Next time, maybe I'll have some warning," he replied. "Those clowns tried to 'jack us with no advance notice. New regs should require at least twenty-four hours warning before a hijacking. And forms filed in quad."

Chria laughed. "Right. You two have been making my people very happy, did you know that? Their nickname for you is 'Bird-dog,' because you've been flushing so much game out for us."

"No doubt." Alex copied her stance, except that where she steepled her hands in front of her chin, he rubbed his temple. "Do I assume that this is not a social call? As in, 'debriefing time'?"

"Oh, yes and no." She shrugged, but her eyes gleamed. "We don't really need to debrief you, but there's a couple of orders I have to pass. First of all, I've been ordered to tell you that if you've figured out where your rock-rat's treasure trove is, transmit the coordinates to us so we know where you're going, but get on out there as soon as you can move your tail. We'll send a follow-up, but right now we've got some high-level butts to bust here."

"Generous of you," Alex said dryly. "Letting us go in first and catch whatever flack is waiting. Are we still a 'bird-dog,' or have we been elevated to 'self-propelled trouble magnet'?"

Chria only laughed.

"Come on, flyboy, get with the team. There's still a Plague-spot out there, and you're the ones most likely to find it; we don't know what in Tophet we're looking for." She raised an eyebrow at him, and he nodded in grudging agreement. "Then when you find it, *you* know how to handle it. I kind of gather that your people want the plague stopped, but they also want their statues and what-all kept safe, too. What're Neil and I going to do, shoot the bug down? He's hot on the trigger, but he's not up to potting microbes just yet!"

Behind her, the sharp-faced man shrugged in self-deprecation and grinned.

"So, if you've got a probable, let us know so we can keep an eye on you. Otherwise—" she spread her hands "—there's nothing we need you for. Fly free, little birds—the records you so thoughtfully bounced all over the sector are all we need to convict these perps, wrap them up, and stick them where they have to pump in daylight."

"Here's what we have," Tia said before Alex could respond. She sent Pol duplicates of their best guesses. "As you can see, we have narrowed it down to three really good prospects. Only one of those has a record of sentient ruins, so that's the one we think is the most likely—I wish they'd logged something besides just 'presence of structures,' but there it is."

"Survey," Pol said succinctly. "Get lots of burnout cases in Survey. Well, what can you expect, going planet-hopping for months on end, dropping satellites, with nothing but an AI to keep you company? Sometimes surprised they don't go buggy, all things considered. I would."

Pol seemed much more convivial than Tia recalled him ever being, and completely happy with *his* brawn, and Chria had that relaxed look of a brawn with the perfect partner. But still—Chria had been an odd one, and Military and Central Security didn't let their brainships swap brawns without overwhelming reasons. *Was* Pol happy?

"*Pol,*" Tia sent only to him, "*did you get a good one?*"

Pol laughed, replying the same way. "*The best! I wouldn't trade off Chria or Neil for any combo in the Service. We three-up over here, you know—it's a double-brawn and brain setup; it's a fail-safe because we're armed. Chria's the senior officer, and Neil's the gunnery-mate, but Neil's been studying, and now he can double her on anything. Fully qualified. That's not usually the case, from what I hear.*"

"*Why didn't he get his own brainship, then?*" she asked, puzzled. "*If he's fully qualified, shouldn't he get a promotion?*"

"*Who can figure softies?*" Pol said dismissively. "*He and Chria share her cabin. Maybe it's hormonal. How about you—you were saying you planned to be pretty picky about your brawns. Did they rush you, or did you get a good one?*"

There were a hundred things she could have said—many of which could have gotten her in a world of trouble if she answered as enthusiastically as she would have liked. "*Oh, Alex will do—when he's not shoving his face into chairs,*" she replied as lightly as she could. Pol laughed and made a few softie jokes while Alex and Chria tied up all the loose ends that needed to be dealt with.

They were the only ship permitted to leave Presley space—Chria hadn't been joking when she'd said that there was going to be a thorough examination of everything going on out here. On the other hand, not having to contend with other traffic was rather nice, all things considered.

Now if only they had a Singularity Drive. . . .

Never mind, she told herself, as she accelerated to hyper. *I can manage without it. I just hope we don't have any more "help" from the opposition.*

This place didn't even have a name yet—just a chart designation. Epsilon Delta 177.3.3. Pol had called it right on the nose—whoever had charted this place must have been a burnout case, or he would have at least tried to name it. That was one of the few perks of a Survey mission; most people took advantage of it.

It certainly had all the earmarks of the kind of place they were looking for; eccentric tilt, heavy cloud cover that spoke of rain or snow or both. But as Tia decelerated into the inner system, she suddenly knew that they *had* hit paydirt without ever coming close enough to do a surface scan.

There should have been a Survey satellite in orbit around their hot little prospect. This was a Terra-type planet; even with an eccentric tilt, eventually someone was going to want to claim it. The satellite should have been up there collecting data on planet three, on the entire system, and on random comings and goings within the system, if any. It should have been broadcasting warnings to incoming ships about the system's status—charted but unexplored, under bio-quarantine until checked out, possibly dangerous, native sentients unknown, landing prohibited.

The satellite was either missing or silent.

"Accidents do happen," Alex said cautiously, as Tia came in closer, decelerating steadily, and prepared to make orbit. "Sometimes those babies break."

She made a sound of disbelief. "Not often. And what are the odds? It should at *least* be giving us the navigational bleep, and there's nothing, nothing at all." She scanned for the satellite as she picked her orbital path, hoping to pick something up.

"Oh, Tia—look at that rotation, that orbit! It could have gotten knocked out of the sky by something—" he began.

"Could have, but wasn't. I've got it, Alex," she said with glee. "I found it! And it's deader than a burned-out glow-tube."

She matched orbits with the errant satellite, coming alongside for a closer look. It was about half her size, so there was no question of bringing it inside, but as she circled it like a curious fish, there was one thing quite obvious.

Nothing was externally wrong with it.

"No sign of collision, and it wasn't shot at," Alex observed, and sighed. "No signs of a fire or explosion inside, either. You've tried reactivating it, I suppose?"

"It's not answering," she said firmly. "Guess what? You get to take a walk."

He muttered something under his breath and went after his pressure-suit. After the past few days in transition, his face had begun to heal, turning from black, blue and purple to a kind of dirty green and yellow. She presumed that the rest of him was in about the same shape—but he was obviously feeling rather sorry for himself.

Do I snap at him, or do I kind of tease him along? she wondered. He hadn't been in a particularly good mood since the call from Chria. Was it that he was still in pain? Or was it something else entirely? There were so many signals of soft-person body language that she'd never had a chance to learn, but there had been something going on during that interview—not precisely between Alex and Chria, though. More like, going on *with* Alex, *because* of Chria.

Before she had a chance to make up her mind, he was at the airlock, suited up and tethered, and waiting for her to close the inner lock for him.

She berated herself for wool-gathering and cycled the lock, keeping an anxious eye on him while she scanned the rest of the area for unexpected—and probably unwelcome—visitors.

It would be just our luck for the looters to show up right about now.

He jetted over to the access-hatch of the satellite and popped it without difficulty.

Wait a moment—shouldn't he have had to unlock it?

"Tia, the access hatch was jimmied," he said, his breath rasping in the suit-mike as he worked, heaving the massive door over and locking it down. "You were right, green all the way. The satellite's been sabotaged. Pretty crude work; they just disconnected the solar-cells from the instrument pack. It'll still make orbital corrections, but that's all. Don't know why they didn't just knock it out of the sky, unless they figured Survey has some kind of telltale on it, and they'd show up if it went down."

"What should we do?" she asked, uncertainly. "I know you can repair it, but should you? We need some of the information it can give us, but if you repair it, wouldn't they figure that Survey had been through? Or would they just not notice?"

"I don't want to reconnect the warn-off until we're ready to leave, or they'll definitely know someone's been eating their porridge," he replied slowly, as he floated half-in, half-out of the hatch. "If the satellite's telling them to take a hike as soon as they enter orbit, there won't be much doubt that someone from the authorities has been here. But you're right, and I not only want to know if someone shows up in orbit while we're down on the ground, I want the near-space scans it took before they shut it down, and I want it to keep scanning and recording. The question is, am I smart enough to make it do all that?"

"I want the planetary records," she told him. "With luck, the ruins may show up on the scans. We might even see signs of activity where the looters have been digging. As for, are you smart enough—if you can get the solar arrays reconnected, I can reprogram every function it has. I'm CS, remember? We do work for Survey sometimes, so I have the access codes for Survey satellites. Trust me, they're going to work; Survey never seems to think someone might actually want to sabotage one of their satellites, so they never change the codes."

"Good point." He writhed for a moment, upside-down, the huge blue-white globe behind him making an impressive backdrop. "Okay, give me a minute or two to splice some cable." Silence for a moment, except for grunts and fast breathing. "Good; it wasn't as awful as I thought. There. Solar array plugged back in. Ah, I have the link to the memory established. And—yes, everything is powering up, or at least that's what it looks like in here."

She triggered memory-dump, and everything came over in compressed mode, loud and clear. All the near-space scans and all the geophysical records that had been made before the satellite was disabled. Surface-scans in all weathers, made on many passes across the face of the planet.

But then—nothing. Whoever had disabled the satellite had known what he was doing—the memory that should have contained records of visitors was empty. She tried a number of ways of accessing it, only to conclude that the data storage device had been completely reformatted, nonsense had been written over all the memory, and it had been reformatted again. Not even an expert would have been able to get anything out of it now.

"Can you hook in the proximity-alert with our com-system?" she asked.

"I think so." He braced himself against the hatch and shoved himself a little farther inside. "Yes, it's all modular. I can leave just that up and powered, and if they aren't listening on this band, they won't know that there's been anyone up here diddling with it."

A few moments more, and she caught a live signal on one of the high-range insystem comlinks, showing a nearby presence in the same orbit as the satellite. She felt her heart jump and started to panic—

—then she scolded herself for being so jumpy. It was the satellite, registering *her* presence, of course.

Alex closed the hatch and wedged it shut as it had been before, reeling himself back in on the tether. A moment later, her lock cycled, and he came back into the main cabin, pulling off his helmet and peeling off his suit.

Tia spent some time reprogramming the satellite, killing the warn-off broadcast, turning all the near-space scanners on and recording. Then she turned her attention to the recordings it had already made.

"So, what have we got?" he asked, wriggling to get the suit down over his hips. "Had any luck?"

"There's quite a few of those ruins," she said carefully, noting with a bit of jealousy that the survey satellite array was actually capable of producing sharper and more detailed images than her own. Then again, what it produced was rather limited.

"Well, that's actually kind of promising." He slid out of the suit and into the chair, leaving the pressure-suit in a crumpled heap on the floor. She waited a moment until he was engrossed in the screen, then discretely sent a servo to pick it and the abandoned helmet up.

"I'd say here or here," he said at last, pointing out two of the ruins in or near one of the mountain ranges. "That would give us the rain-snow pattern the first victim raved about. Look, even in the same day you'd get snow in the morning, rain in the afternoon, and snow after dark during some seasons."

She highlighted those—but spotted three more possibilities, all three in areas where the tilt would have had the same effect on the climate. She marked them as well, and was rewarded by his nod of agreement.

"All right. This *has* to be the planet. There's no reason for anyone to have disabled the satellite otherwise. Even if Survey or the Institute were sending someone here for a more detailed look, they'd simply have changed the warn-off message; they wouldn't have taken the satellite off-line." He took a deep breath and some of the tension went out of his shoulders. "Now it's just going to be finding the right place."

This was work the computers could do while Tia slept, comparing their marked areas and looking for changes that were not due to the seasons or the presence or absence of snow. Highest on the priority list was to look for changes that indicated disturbance while there was snow on the ground. Digging and tramping about in the snow would darken it, no matter how carefully the looters tried to hide the signs of their presence. That was a sign that *only* the work of sentients or herd-beasts would produce, and herd-beasts were not likely to search ruins for food.

Within the hour, they had their site—there was no doubt whatsoever that it was being visited and disturbed regularly. Some of the buildings had even been meddled with.

"Now why would they do that?" Tia wondered out loud, as she increased the magnification to show that one of the larger buildings had mysteriously grown a repaired roof. "They can't need that much space—and how did they fix the roof within twenty-four hours?"

"They didn't," Alex said flatly. "That's plastic stretched over the hole. As to *why*—the hole is just about big enough to let a twenty-man ship land inside. Hangar and hiding place all in one."

They changed their position to put them in geosynchronous orbit over their prize—and detailed scans of the spot seemed to indicate that no one had visited it very recently. The snow was still pristine and white, and the building she had noted had a major portion of its roof missing again.

"That's it," Alex said with finality.

Tia groaned. "We know—and we can't prove it. We know for a fact that someone is meddling with the site, but we can't prove the site is the one with the plague. Not without going down."

"Oh, come on, Tia, where's your sense of adventure?" Alex asked, feebly. "We knew we were probably going to have to go down on the surface. All we have to do is go down and get some holos of the area just like the ones Hank took. Then we have our proof."

"My sense of adventure got left back when I was nearly hijacked," she replied firmly. "I can do without adventure, thank you."

And she couldn't help herself; she kept figuratively glancing over her shoulder, watching for a ship—

Would it be armed? She couldn't help but think of Pol, bristling with weaponry, and picturing those weapons aimed at her.

Unarmed. Unarmored. Not even particularly fast.

On the other hand, she was a *brainship*, wasn't she? The product of extensive training. Surely if she couldn't outrun or outshoot these people, she could out-think them—

Surely.

Well, if she was going to out-think them, the first thing she should do would be to find a way to keep them from spotting her. So it was time to use those enhanced systems on the satellite to their advantage.

"What are you doing?" Alex asked, when she remained silent for several minutes, sending the manual-override signal to the satellite so that she could use the scanners.

"I'm looking for a place to hide," she told him. "Two can play that game. And I'm smaller than their ship; I shouldn't need a building to hide me. I'll warn you, though, I may have to park a fair hike away from the cache sites."

It took a while; several hours of intense searching, while Alex did what he could to get himself prepared for the trip below. That amounted mostly to readying his pressure-suit for a long stay; stocking it with condensed food and water, making certain the suit systems were up to a week-long tour, if it came to that. Recharging the power-cells, triple-checking the seals—putting tape on places that tended to rub and a bit of padding on places that didn't quite fit—everything that could be done to his suit, Alex was doing. They both knew that from the time he left her airlock to the time he returned and she could purge him and the lock with hard vacuum, he was going to have to stay in it.

Finally, in mid-afternoon by the "local" time at the site below them, she found what she was looking for.

"I found my hiding place," she said into the silence, startling him into jumping. "Are you ready?"

"As ready as I'll ever be," he said, a little too jauntily. Was it her imagination, or did he turn a little pale? Well, if she had been capable of it, she'd have done the same. As it was, she was so jittery that she finally had to alter her blood-chemistry a little to deal with it.

"Then strap down," she told him soberly. "We're heading right into a major weather system and there's no getting around it. This is going to be tricky, and the ride is likely to be pretty rough."

Alex took the time to strap down more than himself; he made a circuit of the interior, ensuring that anything loose had been properly stowed before he took his place in the comchair. Only then, when he was double-strapped in, did Tia make the burn that began their descent.

Their entry was fairly smooth until they were on final approach and hit thick atmosphere and the weather that rode the mid-levels. The wild storm winds of a blizzard buffeted her with heavy blows; gusts that came out of nowhere and flung her up, down, in any direction but the one she wanted. She fought her way through them with grim determination, wondering how on earth the looters had gotten this far. Surely with winds like this, the controls would be torn right out of the grip of a softperson's hands!

Of course, they could be coming down under the control of an AI. Once the course had been programmed in, the AI would hold to it. And within limits, it would deal with unexpected conditions all the way to the surface.

Within limits: that was the catch. Throw it too far off the programmed course, and it wouldn't know what to do.

Never mind, she told herself. *You need to get down there yourself!*

A little lower, and it wasn't just wind she was dealing with, it was snow. A howling blizzard, to be precise—one that chilled her skin and caked snow on every surface, throwing off her balance by tiny increments, forcing her to recalculate her descent all the way to the ground. A strange irony—she who had never seen weather as a child was now having to deal with weather at its wildest. . . .

Then suddenly, as she approached the valley she had chosen, the wind died to a mere zephyr. Snow drifted down in picture perfect curtains—totally obscuring visuals, of course, but that was why she was on instruments anyway. She killed forward thrusters and went into null-grav; terribly draining of power, but the only way she could have the control she needed at this point. She inched her way into her chosen valley, using the utmost of care. The spot where she wanted to set down was just big enough to hold her—and right above it, if the readings she'd gotten from above were holding true, there was a big buildup of snow. Just enough to avalanche down and cover her, if she was very careful not to set it off prematurely.

She eased her way into place with the walls of the valley less than a hand-span away from her skin; a brief look at Alex showed him clenching teeth and holding armrests with hands that were white-knuckled. He could read the instruments as well as she could. Well, she'd never set down into a place that was quite this narrow before. And certainly she had never set down under conditions that might change in the next moment. . . .

If that blizzard behind them came howling up this valley, it could catch her and send her right into the valley wall.

There. She tucked herself into the bottom of the valley and felt her "feet" sink through the snow to the rock beneath. Nice, solid rock. Snow-covered rocks on either side.

And above—the snowcrest. Waiting. *Here goes—*

She activated an external speaker and blasted the landscape with shatter-rock, bass turned to max.

And the world fell in.

"Are you going to be able to blast free of this?" Alex asked for the tenth time, as another servo came in from the airlock to recharge.

"It's not that bad," she said confidently. She was *much* happier with four meters of snow between her and the naked sky. Avalanches happened all the time; there was nothing about this valley to signal to the looters that they'd been discovered, and that a ship was hiding here. Not only that, but the looters could prance around *on top of her* and never guess she was there unless they found the tunnel her servos were cutting to the surface. And she didn't think any of them would have the temerity to crawl down what *might* be the den-tunnel of a large predator.

"If it's not that bad," Alex said fretfully, "then why is it taking forever to melt a tunnel up and out?"

"Because no one ever intended these little servos to have to do something like that," she replied, as patiently as she could. "They're *welders*, not snow clearers. And they have to reinforce the tunnel with plastic shoring-posts so it doesn't fall in and trap you." He shook his head; she gave up trying to explain it. "They're almost through, anyway," she told him. "It's about time to get into your suit."

That would keep him occupied.

"This thing is getting depressingly familiar," he complained. "I see more of the inside of this suit than I do my cabin."

"No one promised you first-class accommodations on this ride," she teased, trying to keep from showing her own nervousness. "I'll tell you what; how about if I have one of the servos make a nice set of curtains for your helmet?"

"Thanks. I think." He made a face at her. "Well, I'll tell you this much; if I have to keep spending this much time in the blasted thing, I'm going to have some comforts built into it—or demand they get me a better model." He twisted and turned, making sure he still had full mobility. "The sanitary facilities leave a lot to be desired."

"I'll report your complaints to the ship's steward," she told him. "Meanwhile—we have breakout."

"Sounds like my cue." Alex sighed. "I hope this isn't going to be as cold as it looks."

Alex crawled up the long, slanting tunnel to the surface, lighting his way with the work-lamp on the front of his helmet. Not that there was much to see—just a white, shiny tunnel that seemed to go on forever, reaching into the cold darkness . . . as if, with no warning, he would find himself entombed in ice forever. The plastic reinforcements were as white as the snow; invisible unless you were looking for them. Which was the point, he supposed. But he was glad they were there. Without them, tons of snow and ice could come crashing down on him at any moment. . . .

Stop that, he told himself sharply. *Now is not the time to get claustrophobia.*

Still, there didn't seem to be any end to the tunnel—and he was cold, chilled right down to the soul. Not physically cold, or so his readouts claimed. Just chilled by the emptiness, the sterility. The loneliness . . .

You're doing it again. Stop it.

Was the surrounding snow getting *lighter*? He turned off his helmet light—and it was true, there was a kind of cool, blue light filtering down through the ice and snow! And up ahead—yes, there was the mouth of the tunnel, as promised, a round, white "eye" staring down at him!

He picked up his pace, eager to get out of there. The return trip would be *nothing* compared to this long, tedious crawl—just sit down and push away, and he would be able to slide all the way down to the airlock!

He emerged into thickly falling snow and saw that the servos had wrought better than he and Tia had guessed, for the mouth of the tunnel was outside the area of avalanche, just under an overhanging ridge of stone. That must have been what the snow had built up upon; small wonder it buried Tia four meters under when she triggered it! Fortunately, snow could be melted; when they needed to leave, she could fire up her thrusters *and* increase the surface temperature of her skin, and turn it all to water and steam. Well, that was the theory, anyway.

That was assuming it didn't rain and melt away her cover before then.

By Tia's best guess, it was late afternoon, and he should be able to get to the site and look around a little before dark fell. At that point, the best thing he could do would be to get under cover somewhere and curl up for the night. *This* time he had padded all the uncomfortable spots in the suit, and he'd worn soft, old, exercise clothing. It shouldn't be any less comfortable than some of his bunks as a cadet.

He took a bearing from the heads-up display inside his helmet and headed for the site.

"Tia," he called. "Tia, come in."

"Reading you loud and clear, Alex," she responded immediately. Funny how easy it was to think of her as a person sitting back in that ship, eyes glued to the screens that showed his location, hands steady on the com controls—

Stop that. Maybe it's a nice picture, but it's one that can get you in more trouble than you already have. "Tia, we have the right place, all right." He toggled his external suit-camera and gave her a panoramic sweep from his vantage point above the valley holding the site. It was fairly obvious that this place was subject to some pretty heavy-duty windstorms; the buildings were all built into the lee of the hills, and the hills themselves had been sculpted by the prevailing winds until they looked like cresting waves. No doubt either why the entities who built this place used rounded forms; less for the winds to catch on.

"Does this look like any architecture in your banks?" he asked, panning across the buildings. "I sure as heck don't recognize it."

"Nothing here," she replied, fascination evident in her voice. "This is amazing! That's not metal, I don't think—could it be ceramic?"

"Maybe some kind of synthetic," Alex hazarded. "Plague or not, there are going to be murders done over the right to excavate this place. How in the name of the spirits of space did that Survey tech just dismiss this with 'presence of structures'?"

"We'll never know," Tia responded. "Well, since there can't be two sites like this in this area, and since these buildings match the ones in Hank's holos, we can at least assume that we have the right planet. Now—about the caches—"

"I'm going down," he said, feeling for footholds in the snow. It crunched under his feet as he eased down sideways, one careful step at a time. Now that he was out of Tia's valley, there were signs everywhere of freeze-thaw cycles. Under the most recent layer of snow, the stuff was dirty and covered with a crust of granular ice. It made for perilous walking. "The wind is picking up, by the way. I think that blizzard followed us in."

"That certainly figures," she said with resignation.

As he eased over the lip of the valley, he saw the caves—or rather, storage areas—cut into the protected side of the face of a lower level canyon cutting through the middle of the valley. There were more buildings down there, too, and some kind of strange pylons—but it was the "caves" that interested him most. Regular, ovoid holes cut into the earth and rock that were then plugged with something rather like cement, a substance slightly different in color from the surrounding earth and stone. Those nearest him were still sealed; those nearest the building with the appearing–disappearing roof were open.

He worked his way down the valley to the buildings and found to his relief that there was actually a kind of staircase cut into the rock, going down to the second level. Protected from the worst of the weather by the building in front of it, while it was a bit slippery, it wasn't as hazardous as his descent into the valley had been.

It was a good thing that the contents of Hank's cabin and the holos the man had taken had prepared him for what he saw.

The wall of the valley where the storage caves had been opened looked like the inside of Ali Baba's cave. The storage caches proved to be much smaller than Alex had thought; the "window" slits in the nearby building were tiny, as might have been expected in a place with the kind of punishing weather this planet had. That had made the caches themselves appear much larger in the holos. In reality, they were about as tall as his waist and no deeper than two or three meters. That was more than enough to hold a king's ransom in treasure. . . .

Much hadn't even been taken. In one of the nearest, ceramic statuary and pottery had been left behind as worthless—some had been broken by careless handling, and Alex winced.

There were dozens of caches that had been opened and cleaned out; perhaps a dozen more with less-desirable objects still inside. There were dozens more, still sealed, running down the length of the canyon wall—

And one whose entrance had been sealed with some kind of a heat-weapon, a weapon that had been turned on the entrance until the rock slagged and melted metal ran with it, mingling and forming a new, permanent plug.

"Do you think that's where the plague bug came from?" Tia asked in his ear.

"I think it's a good bet, anyway," he said absently. "I sure hope so, anyway."

Suddenly, with the prospect of contamination looming large in his mind, the shine of metal and sheen of priceless ceramic lost its allure. *Whether it is or isn't, there is no way I am going to crack this suit, I don't care what is out there.* Hank and the other man drifted in his memory like grisly ghosts. The suit, no longer a prison, had just become the most desirable place in the universe.

Oh, I just love this suit. . . .

Nevertheless, he moved forward towards the already-opened caches, augmenting the fading light with his suit-lamp. The caches themselves were very old; that much was evident from the weathering and buildup of debris and dirt along the side of the canyon wall. The looters must have opened up one of the caches out of sheer curiosity or by accident while looking for something else. Perhaps they had been exploring the area with an eye to a safe haven. Whatever had led them to uncover the first, they had then cleared away the buildup all along the wall, exposing the rest. And it looked as if the loot of a thousand worlds had been tucked away here.

He began taking careful holos of every thing that had been left behind, Tia recording the tiniest details as he covered every angle, every millimeter. At least this way, if anything more was smashed there would be a record of it. Some things he picked up and stashed in his pack to bring back with him—a curious metal book, for instance—

Alex moved forward again, reaching out for a discarded ceramic statue of some kind of winged biped—

"*Alex!*" Tia exclaimed urgently. He started back, his hand closing on empty air.

"What?" he snapped. "I—"

"Alex, you have to get back here *now*," she interrupted. "The alarms just went off. They're back, and they're heading in to land right now!"

"Alex!" Tia cried, as her readouts showed the pirates making their descent burn and Alex moving *away* from her, not back in. "Alex, what are you doing?"

Dusk was already making it hard to see out there, even for her. She couldn't imagine what it was like for him.

"I'm going to hide out in the upper level of one of these buildings and watch these clowns," Alex replied calmly. "There's a place up on this one where I can get in at about the second-story level—see?"

He was right; the structure of the building gave him easy hand- and foot-holds up to the window-slits on the second floor. Once there, since the building had fallen in at that point, he would be able to hide himself up above eye-level. And with the way that the blizzard was kicking up, his tracks would be hidden in a matter of moments.

"But—" she protested. "You're all alone out there!" She tried to keep her mind clear, but a thousand horrible possibilities ran around and around inside her thoughts, making her frantic. "There's no way I can help you if you're caught!"

"I won't be caught," he said confidently, finding handholds and beginning his climb.

It was already too late anyway; the pirates had begun entry. Even if he left now, he'd never make it back to the safety of the tunnel before they landed. If they had heat-sensors, they couldn't help but notice him, scrambling across the snow.

She poured relaxants into her blood and tried to stay as calm as he obviously felt, but it wasn't working. As the looters passed behind the planet's opposite side, he reached the top of the first tier of window-slits, moving slowly and deliberately—so deliberately that she wanted to scream at him to hurry.

As they hit the edge of the blizzard, Alex reached the broken place in the second story. And just as he tumbled over the edge into the relatively safe darkness behind the wall, they slowed for descent, playing searchlights all over the entire valley, cutting pathways of brightness across the gloom and thickly falling snow.

Alex took advantage of the lights, moving only after they had passed so that he had a chance to see exactly what lay in the room he had fallen into.

Nothing, actually; it was an empty section with a curved inner and outer wall, one door in the inner wall, and a wall at either end. Roughly half of the curving roof had fallen in; not much, really. Dirt and snow mounded under the break, near the join of end wall and outer wall the windows were still intact, and the floor was relatively clean. That was where Alex went.

From there he had a superb view of both the caches and the building that the looters were slowly lowering their ship into. Tia watched carefully and decided that her guess about an AI in-system pilot was probably correct; the movements of the ship had the jerkiness she associated with AIs. She kept expecting the looters to pick up Alex's signal, but evidently they were not expecting anyone to find this place—they seemed to be taking no precautions whatsoever. They didn't set any telltales or any alerts, and once they landed the ship and began disembarking from it, they made no effort to maintain silence.

On the other hand, given the truly appalling weather, perhaps they had no reason to be cautious. The worst of the blizzard was moving in, and not even the best of AIs could have landed in *that* kind of buffeting wind. She was just glad that Alex was under cover.

The storm didn't stop the looters from sending out crews to open up a new cache, however. . . .

She could hardly believe her sensors when she saw, via Alex's camera, a half-dozen lights bobbing down the canyon floor coming towards his hiding place. She switched to IR scan and saw that there were three times that many men, three to a light. None of them were wearing pressure-suits, although they were bundled up in cold weather survival gear.

"I don't believe they're doing that," Alex muttered.

"Neither do I," she replied softly. "That storm is going to be a killing blizzard in a moment. They're out of their minds."

She scanned up and down the radio wavelengths, looking for the one the looters were using. She found it soon enough; unmistakable by the paint-peeling language being used. While Alex huddled in his shelter, the men below him broke open yet another cache and began shoveling what were probably priceless artifacts into sacks as if they were so many rocks. Tia winced, and thought it likely that Alex was doing the same.

The looters were obviously aware that they were working against time; their haste alone showed the fact that they knew the worst of the storm was yet to come. Whoever was manning the radio back at the ship kept them appraised of their situation, and before long, he began warning them that it was time to start back, before the blizzard got so bad they would never be able to make it the few hundred meters back to their ship.

They would not be able to take the full fury of the storm—but Alex, in his pressure-suit, would be able to handle just about anything. With his heads-up helmet displays, he didn't need to be able to see where he was going. Was it possible that he would be able to sneak back to her under the cover of the blizzard?

It was certainly worth a try.

The leader of the looters finally growled an acknowledgement to the radio operator. "We're comin' in, keep yer boots on," he snarled, as the lights turned away from the cache and moved slowly back up the canyon. The operator shut up; a moment later a signal beacon shone wanly through the thickening snow at the other end of the tiny valley. Soon the lights of the looters had been swallowed up by darkness and heavy snowfall—then the beacon faded as the snow and wind picked up still more.

"Alex," she said urgently, "do you think you can make it back to me?"

"Did you record me coming in?" he asked.

"Yes," she assured him. "Every step. I ought to be able to guide you pretty well. You won't get a better chance. Without the storm to cover you, they'll spot you before you've gone a meter."

He peered out his window again, her camera "seeing" what he saw—there was nothing out there. Wind and snow made a solid wall just outside the building. Even Tia's IR scan couldn't penetrate it.

"I'll try it," he said. "You're right. There won't ever be a better chance."

Alex ignored the darkness outside his helmet and concentrated on the HUD projected on the inner surface. This was a lot like fly-by-wire training—or virtual reality. Ignore what your eyes and senses wanted you to do and concentrate on what the instruments are telling you.

Right now, they said he was near the entrance to the valley hiding Tia.

It had been a long, frightening walk. The pressure-suit was protection against anything that the blizzard flung at him, but if he made a wrong step—well, it wouldn't save him from a long fall. And it wouldn't save him from being crushed by an avalanche if something triggered another one. Snow built up quickly under conditions like this.

It helped to think of Tia as he imagined her; made him feel warm inside. She kept a cheerful monologue going in his left ear, telling him what she had identified from the holos they'd made before the looters arrived. Sometimes he answered her, mostly he just listened. She was warmth and life in a world of darkness and cold, and as long as he could think of her sitting in the pilot's seat, with her sparkling eyes and puckish smile, he could muster the strength to keep his feet moving against the increasingly heavy weight of the snow.

Tired—he was getting so tired. It was tempting to lie down and let the snow cover him for a while as he took a little rest.

"Alex—you're here—" she said suddenly, breaking off in the middle of the sentence.

"I'm where?" he said stupidly. He was so tired—

"You're here—the entrance to the tunnel is somewhere around there—" The urgency in her voice woke him out of the kind of stupor he had been in. "Feel around for the rock face—the tunnel may be covered with snow, but you should be able to find it."

That was something he hadn't even thought of! What if the entrance to the tunnel had filled in? He'd be stuck out here in the blizzard, nowhere to go, out alone in the cold!

Stop that! he told himself sternly. *Just stop that! You'll be all right. The suit heaters won't give out in this—they're made for space, a little cold blizzard isn't going to balk them!*

Unless the cold snow clogged them somehow . . . or the wind was too much for them to compensate for . . . or they just plain gave up and died. . . .

He stumbled to his right, hands out, feeling frantically in the darkness for the rock face. He stumbled into it, cracking his faceplate against the stone. Fortunately the plate was made of sterner stuff than simple polyglas; although his head rang, the plate was fine.

Well, there was the rock. Now *where*—

The ground gave away beneath his feet, and he yelled with fear as he fell—the back of his head smacked against something and he kept falling—

No—

No, he wasn't falling, he was sliding. He'd fallen into the tunnel!

Quickly he spread hands and feet against the wall of the tunnel to slow himself and toggled his headlamp on; it had been useless in the blizzard. Now it was still pretty useless, but the light reflecting from the white ice above his face made him want to laugh with pleasure. Light! At last!

Light—and more of it down below his feet. The opposite end of the tunnel glowed with warm, white light as Tia opened the airlock and turned on the light inside it. He shot down the long dark tunnel and into the brightness, no longer caring if he hit hard when he landed. Caring only that he was coming home.

Coming home. . . .

CHAPTER NINE

The whisper of a sensor-sweep across the landscape—like the brush of silk across Tia's skin, when she'd had skin. Like something not-quite-heard in the distance.

Tia stayed quiet and concentrated on keeping all of her outputs as low as possible. *We aren't here. You can't find us. Why don't you just fill your holds and go away?*

What had been a good hiding place was now a trap. Tia had shut down every system she could; Alex moved as little as possible. She had no way of knowing how sophisticated the pirates' systems were, so they were both operating on the assumption that anything out of the ordinary would alert the enemy to their presence, if not their location.

Whether or not the looters' initial carelessness had been because of the storm or because of greed—or whether they had been alerted by something she or Alex had done—now they were displaying all the caution Tia had expected of them. Telltales and alarms were in place; irregular sensor sweeps made it impossible for Alex to make a second trip to the ruins without being caught.

And now there were two more ships in orbit that had arrived while the blizzard still raged. One of those two ships had checked the satellite. Had they found Alex's handiwork, or were they simply following a procedure they had always followed? She had no way of knowing.

Whatever the case, those two ships kept her from taking off—and she wasn't going to transmit *anything* to the satellite. It was still broadcasting, and they only hoped it was because the pirates hadn't checked that closely. But it could have been because the pirates wanted them lulled into thinking they were safe.

So Tia had shut off all nonessential systems, and they used no active sensors, relying entirely on passive receptors. Knowing that sound could carry even past her blanket of snow, especially percussive sounds, Alex padded about in stocking feet when he walked at all. Three days of this now—and no sign that the looters were ready to leave yet.

Mostly he and Tia studied holos and the few artifacts that he had brought out of the cache area—once Tia had vacuum-purged them and sterilized them to a fare-thee-well.

After all, she kept telling herself, the pirates couldn't stay up there forever. Could they?

Unless they had some idea that Tia was already here. *Someone* had leaked what they knew about Hank and his cargo when they were on Presley Station. The leak could have gone beyond the station.

She was frightened and could not tell him; strung as tightly as piano strings with anxiety, with no way to work off the tension.

She knew that the same thoughts troubled Alex, although he never voiced them. Instead, he concentrated his attention completely on the enigmatic book of metal plates he had brought out of the cache.

There were glyphs of some kind etched into it, along the right edge of each plate, and a peculiarly matte-finished strip along the left edge of each. But most importantly, the middle of each page was covered with the pinprick patterns of what could only be stellar configurations. Having spent so much time studying stellar maps, both of them had recognized that they *were* nav-guides immediately. But to what—and far more importantly, what was the reference point? There was no way of knowing that she could see.

And who had made the book in the first place? The glyphs had an odd sort of familiarity about them, but nothing she was able to put a figurative finger on.

It was enough of a puzzle to keep Alex busy, but not enough to occupy her. It was very easy to spend a lot of time brooding over her brawn. Slumped in his chair, peculiarly handsome face intent, with a single light shining down on his head and the artifact, with the rest of the room in darkness—or staring into a screen full of data—

Like a scene out of a thriller-holo. The hero, biding his time, ready to crack under the strain but not going to show his vulnerability; the enemies waiting above. Priceless data in their hands, data that they dared not allow the enemy to have. The hero, thinking about the lover he had left behind, wondering if he will ever see her again—

Shellcrack. This was getting her nowhere.

She couldn't pace, she couldn't bite her nails, she couldn't even read to distract herself. Finally she activated a single servo and sent it discretely into his cabin to clean it. It hadn't been cleaned since they'd left the base; mostly Alex had just shoved things into drawers and closets and locked the doors down. She couldn't clean his clothing now—but as soon as they shook the hounds off their trail—

If they shook the hounds off their trail—if the second avalanche and the blizzard hadn't piled too much snow on top of them to clear away. There were eight meters of snow up there now, not four. Much more, and she might not be able to blast free.

Stop that. We'll get out of this.

Carefully she cleaned each drawer and closet, replacing what wasn't dirty and having the servo kidnap what was. Carefully, because there were lots of loose objects shoved in with the clothing.

But she never expected the one she found tumbled in among the bedcoverings.

A holocube—of her.

She turned the cube over and over in the servo's pinchers, changing the pictures, finding all of them familiar. Scenes of her from before her illness; the birthday party, posing with Theodore Bear—

Standing in her brand new pressure-suit in front of a fragment of wall covered with EsKay glyphs—that was a funny one; Mum had teased Dad about it because he'd focused on the glyphs out of habit. She'd come out half out of the picture, but the glyphs had been nice and sharp.

It hit her like a jolt of current. The glyphs. *That* was where she had seen them before! Oh, these were carved rather than inscribed, and time and sandstorms had worn them down to mere suggestions. They were formed in a kind of cursive style, where the ones on the book were angular—but—

She ran a quick comparison and got another jolt, this time of elation. "Alex!" she whispered excitedly. "Look!"

She popped the glyphs from the old holo up on her screen as he looked up, took the graphic of the third page of the book, and superimposed the one over the other. Aside from the differences in style, they were a perfect match.

"EsKays," he murmured, his tone awestruck. "Spirits of space— this book was made by the EsKays!"

"I think these caches and buildings must have been made by some race that knew the EsKays," she replied. "But even if they weren't—Alex, how much will you wager that this little set of charts shows the EsKay homeworld, once you figure out how to deci- pher it?"

"It would make sense," he said, after a moment. "Look at this smooth area on every page—always in the same place along the edge. I bet this is some kind of recording medium, like a datahedron—maybe optical—"

"Let *me* look at it," she demanded. "Put it in the lab." Now she had something to keep *her* attention. And something to keep her mind off him.

Alex had nothing more to do but read and brood. While Tia bent all the resources at her disposal on the artifact, he was left staring at screens and hoping the pirates didn't think to scan for large masses of metal under the snow.

Reading palled after too long; music was out because it could be detected, even if he were wearing headphones, and he hated headphones. He'd never been much of a one for entertainment holos, and they made at least as much noise as music.

That left him alone in the dark with his thoughts, which kept turning back towards Tia. He knew her childhood very well now— accessing the data available publicly and then doing the unthink- able, at least for anyone in the BB program: contacting Doctor Kennet and Doctor Anna and pumping them for information. Not with any great subtlety, he feared, but they hadn't taken it amiss. Of course, if anyone in CS found out what he'd been doing, he would be in major trouble. There was an ugly name for his feel- ing about Tia.

Fixation.

After that single attempt at finding a temporary companion in port, Alex had left the women alone—because he kept picking ones who looked like Tia. He had thought it would all wear off after a while; that sooner or later, since nothing could be done about it, the fascination would fade away.

And meanwhile, or so he'd told himself, it only made sense to learn as much about Tia as he could. She was unique; the oldest child ever to have been put into a shell. He had to be very careful with someone like that; the normal parameters of a brain-brawn relationship simply would not apply.

So now he knew what she had looked like—and, thanks to computer-projection, what she would have looked like if she had never caught that hideous disease and had grown up normally. Why, she might even have wound up at the Academy, if she hadn't chosen to follow in her famous parents' footsteps. He knew most of the details, not only of her pre-shell life, but of her life at Lab Schools. He knew as much about her as he would have if she had been his own sibling—except that his feelings about her had been anything but brotherly.

But he had told himself that they were brotherly, that he was not falling in love with a kind of ghost, that everything would be fine. He'd believed it, too.

That is, up until he ran into Chria Chance and her gunner.

There was no doubt in his mind from the moment the screen lit up that Chria and Neil were an item. The signs were there for anyone who knew how to read body language, especially for someone who knew Chria as well as Alex did. And his initial reaction to the relationship caught him completely by surprise.

Envy. Sheer, raw, uncomplicated envy. Not jealousy, for he wasn't at all interested in Chria and never had been. In some ways, he was very happy for her; she had been truly the poor little rich girl—High Family with four very proper brothers and sisters who were making the Family even more prestige and money. She alone had been the rebel; she of all of them had wanted something more than a proper position, a place on a board of directors, and a bloodless, loveless, high-status spouse. After she threatened to bring disgrace on all of them, blackmailing them by swearing she would join a shatter-rock synthocom band under her real name, they had permitted her the Academy under an assumed one.

No, he was happy for Chria; she had found exactly the life and partners that she had longed for.

But he *wanted* what she had—only he wanted it to be Tia sitting back there in the second seat. Or Tia in the front and himself in the back; it didn't much matter who was the one in command, if he could have had her *there*.

The strength of his feelings had been so unexpected that he had not known what to do with them—so he had attempted, clumsily, to cover them. Fortunately, everyone involved seemed to put his surliness down to a combination of pain from his injuries and wooziness due to the pain-pills he'd gulped.

If only it had been . . .

I'm in love with someone I can't touch, can't hold, can't even tell that I love her, he thought with despair, clenching his hand tightly on the armrest of his chair. *I—*

"Alex?" Tia whispered, her voice sounding unnaturally loud in the silence of the ship, for she had turned even the ventilation system down to a minimum. "Alex, I've decoded the storage-mode. It's old-fashioned hard-etched binary storage and I think that it's nav directions that relate to the stellar map on the page. Once I find a reference point I recognize, I'm pretty sure I can decode it all eventually. I got some ideas, though, since I was able to match some place-name glyphs—and we were right—I'm positive that these are directions to all the EsKay bases from the homeworld! So if we could just find a base—"

"And trace it back!" This was what she'd been looking for from the beginning, and excitement *for* her shoved aside all other feelings for the moment. "What's the deal—why the primitive navcharts? Not that it isn't a break for us, but if they were space-going, why limit yourself to a crawl?"

"Well, the storage medium is pretty hard to damage; you wouldn't believe how strong it is. So I can see why they chose it over something like a datahedron that a strong magnetic field can wipe. As for why the charts themselves are so primitive, near as I can make out, they didn't have Singularity Drive and they could or would only warp *between* stars, using them as navigational stepping-stones. I don't know why; there may be something there that would give the reason, but I can't decode it." There was something odd and subdued about her voice—

"What, hopping like a Survey ship?" he asked incredulously. "You could spend years getting across space that way!"

"Maybe they didn't care. Maybe hyper made them sick." Now he recognized what the odd tone in her voice was; she didn't seem terribly excited, now that she had what she was looking for.

"Well, *we* don't have to do that," he pointed out. "Once we get out of here, we can backtrack to the EsKay homeworld, make a couple of jumps, and we'll be stellar celebs! All we have to do is—"

"Is forget about our responsibilities," she said, sharply. "Or else 'forget' to turn in this book with the rest of the loot until we get a long leave. Or turn it in and hope no one else beats us to the punch."

Keeping the book was out of the question, and he dismissed it out of hand. "They won't," he replied positively. "No one else has spent as much time staring at star-charts as we have. You've said as much yourself; the archeologists at the Institute get very specialized and see things in a very narrow way. I don't think that there's the slightest chance that anyone will figure out what this book means within the next four or five years. But you're right about having responsibilities; we *are* under a hard contract to the Institute. We'll have to wait until we can buy or earn a long leave—"

"That's not what's bothering me," she interrupted, in a very soft voice. "It's—the ethics of it. If we hold back this information, how are we any better than those pirates out there?"

"How do you mean?" he asked, startled.

"Withholding information—that's like data piracy, in a way. We're holding back, not only the data, but the career of whoever is the EsKay specialist right now—Doctor Lana Courtney-Rai, I think. In fact, if we keep this to ourselves, we'll be *stealing* her career advancement. I mean, we aren't even *real* archeologists!" There was no mistaking the distress in her voice.

"I think I see what you mean." And he did; he could understand it all too well. He'd seen both his parents passed over for promotions in favor of someone who hadn't earned the advancement but who "knew the right people." He'd seen the same thing happen at the Academy. It wasn't fair or right. "We can't do everything, can we?" he said slowly. "Not like in the holos, where the heroes can fight off pirates while performing brain surgery."

Tia made a sad little chuckle. "I'm beginning to think it's all we can do just to get our real job done right."

He leaned back in his chair and stared at the ceiling. "Funny. When this quest of ours was all theoretical, it was one thing—but we really can't go shooting off by ourselves and still do our duty, the duty that people are expecting us to do."

She didn't sigh, but her voice was heavy with regret. "It's not only a question of ethics, but of priorities. We can simply go on doing what we do best—and Chria Chance really put her finger on it, when she pointed out that she and Neil and Pol wouldn't know how to recognize our plague spot, and we would. *She* knows when she should let the experts take over. I hate to give up on the dream—but in this case, that dream was the kind of thing a kid could have, but—"

"But it's time to grow up—and let someone else play," Alex said firmly.

"Maybe we could go pretend to be archeologists," Tia added, "but we'd steal someone else's career in the process. Become second-rate—but very, very lucky amateur pot-hunters."

He sighed for both of them. "They'd hate us, you know. Everyone we respected would hate us. And we'd be celebrities, but we wouldn't be real archeologists."

"Alex?" she said, after a long silence. "I think we should just seal that book up with our findings and what we've deduced about it. Then we should lock it up with the rest of the loot and go on being a stellar CS team. Even if it does get awfully boring running mail and supplies, sometimes."

"It's not boring now," he said ruefully, without thinking. "I kind of wish it was."

Silence for a long time, then she made a tiny sound that he would have identified as a whimper in a softperson. "I wish you hadn't reminded me," she said.

"Why?"

"Because—because it seems as if we're never going to get out of here—that they're going to find us eventually."

"Stop that," he replied sharply, reacting to the note of panic in her voice. "They can't hover up there forever. They'll run out of supplies, for one thing."

"So will we," she countered.

"And they'll run out of patience! Tia, think—these are pirates, and they don't even know there's anyone else here, not for certain, anyway! When they don't find anything, they'll give up and take their loot off to sell!" He wanted, badly, to pace—but that would make noise. "We can leave when they're gone!"

"If—we can get out."

"What?" he said, startled.

"I didn't want you to worry—but there's been two avalanches since you got back, and all the snow the blizzard dropped."

He stared at her column in numbed shock, but she wasn't finished.

"There's about eleven meters of snow above us. I don't know if I can get out. And even if CenSec shows up, I don't know if they'll hear a hail under all this ice. I lost the signals from the surface right after that last avalanche, and the satellite signals are getting too faint to read clearly."

He said the first thing that came into his head, trying to lighten the mood, but without running it past his internal censor first. "Well, at least if I'm going to be frozen into a glacier for all eternity, I've got my love to keep me warm."

He stopped himself, but not in time. *Oh, brilliant. Now she thinks she's locked in an iceberg with a fixated madman!*

"Do—" Her voice sounded choked, probably with shock. "Do you mean that?"

He could have shot himself. "Tia," he began babbling, "it's all right, really, I mean I'm not going to go crazy and try to crack your column or anything, I really am all right, I—"

"Did you *mean* that?" she persisted.

"I—" *Oh well. It's on the record. You can't make it worse.* "Yes. I don't know, it just sort of—happened." He shrugged helplessly. "It's not anything crazy, like a fixation. But, well—I just don't want any partner of *any* kind but you. If that's love, then I guess I love you. And I really, really love you a lot." He sighed and rubbed his temples. "So there it is, out in the open at last. I hope I don't offend or frighten you, but you're the best thing that ever happened to me, and that's a fact. I'd rather be with you than anyone else I know, or know of." He managed a faint grin. "Holostars and stellar celebs included."

The plexy cover to Ted Bear's little "shrine" popped open, and he jumped.

"I can't touch you, and you can't touch me, but—would you

like to hug Theodore?" she replied softly. "I love you, too, Alex. I think I have ever since you went out to face the Zombie Bug. You're the bravest, cleverest, most wonderful brawn I could ever imagine, and I wouldn't want to be anyone's partner but yours."

The offer of her childhood friend was the closest she could come to intimacy—and he knew it.

He got up, carefully, and took the little fellow down out of his wall-home, hugging the soft little bear once, hard, before he restored him again and closed the door.

"You have a magnificent lady, Theodore Bear," he told the solemn-faced little toy. "And I'm going to do my best to make her happy."

He turned back to her column and cleared his throat, carefully. Time, and more than time, to change the subject. "Right," he said. "Now that we've both established why we've been touchy—let's see if we can figure out what our options are."

"Options?" she replied, confused.

"Certainly." He raised his chin defiantly. "I intend to spend the rest of my life with you—and I don't intend *that* to be restricted to how long it takes before the pirates find us or we freeze to death! So let's figure out some *options*, hang it all!"

To his great joy and relief, she actually laughed. And if there was an edge of hysteria in it, he chose to ignore that little nuance.

"Right," she said. "Options. Well, we can start with the servos, I guess. . . ."

"Tia snuggled down into his arms, and turned into a big blue toy bear. The bear looked at him reproachfully.

He started to get up, but the bedcoverings had turned to snowdrifts, and he was frozen in place. The bear tried to chip him out, but its blunt arms were too soft to make an impression on the ice-covered drifts.

Then he heard rumbling—and looked up, to see an avalanche poised to crash down on him like some kind of slow-motion wave—

The avalanche rumbled, and Tia-the-bear growled back, interposing herself between him and the tumbling snow—

"*Alex, wake up!*"

He floundered awake, flailing at the bedclothes, hitting the light button more by accident than anything else. He blinked as the light came up full, blinding him, his legs trapped in a tangle of sheets and blankets. "What?" he said, his tongue too thick for his mouth. "Who? Where?"

"Alex," Tia said, her voice strained, but excited. "Alex, I have been trying to get you to wake up for fifteen minutes! There's a CenSec ship Upstairs, and it's beating the tail off those two pirates!"

CenSec? Spirits of space—

"What happened?" he asked, grabbing for clothing and pulling it on. "From the beginning—"

"The first I knew of it was when one of the pirates sent a warning down to the ship here to stay under cover and quiet. I got the impression that they thought it was just an ordinary Survey ship, until it locked onto one of them and started blasting." Tia had brought up all of her systems again; fresher air was moving briskly through the ventilator, all the lights and boards were up and active in the main cabin. "That was when all the scans stopped—and I started breaking loose. I ran that freeze-thaw cycle you suggested, and a couple of minutes ago, I fired the engines. I can definitely move, and I'm pretty sure I can pull out of here without too much trouble. I might lose some paint and some bits of things on my surface, but nothing that can't be repaired."

"What about Upstairs?" he asked, running for his chair without stopping for shoes or even socks, and strapping himself down.

"Good news and bad news. The CenSec ship looks like its going to take both the pirates," she replied. "The bad news is that while I can receive, I can't seem to broadcast. The ice might have jammed something, I can't tell."

"All right; we can move, and the ambush Upstairs is being taken care of." Alex clipped the last of his restraint belts in place; when Tia moved, it could be abruptly, and with little warning. "But if we can't broadcast, we can't warn CenSec that there's another ship down here—we can't even identify ourselves as a friend. And we'll be a sitting duck for the pirates if we try to rise. They can just hide in their blinds and ambush the CenSec ship, then wait to see if we come out of hiding—as soon as we clear their horizon they can pot us."

Alex considered the problem as dispassionately as he could. "Can we stay below their horizon until we're out of range?"

Tia threw up a map as an answer. If the pirate chose to pursue them, there was no way that she could stay out of range of medium guns, and they had to assume that was what the pirate had.

"There has to be a way to keep them on the ground, somehow," Alex muttered, chewing a hangnail, aware that with every second that passed their window of opportunity was closing. "What's going on Upstairs?"

"The first ship is heavily damaged. If I'm reading the tactics right, the CenSec ship is going to move in for the kill—provided the other pirate gives him a chance."

Alex turned his attention back to their own problem. "If we could just cripple them—throw enough rocks down on them or— wait a minute. Bring up the views of the building they're hiding in—the ones you got from my camera."

Tia obeyed, and Alex studied the situation carefully, matching pictures with memory. "Interesting thing about those hills—see how some of them look broken-off, as if those tips get too heavy to support after a while? I bet that's because the winds come in from different directions and scour out under the crests once in a while. Can you give me a better shot of the hills overhanging those buildings?"

"No problem." The viewpoint pulled back, displaying one of those wave-crest hills overshadowing the building with the partial roof. "Alex!" she exclaimed.

"You see it too," he said with satisfaction. "All right girl, think we can pull this off?"

For answer, she revved her engines. "Be a nice change to hit back, for once!"

"Then let's lift!"

The engines built from a quiet purr to a bone-deep, bass rumble, more felt than heard. Tia pulled in her landing gear, then began rocking herself by engaging null-grav, first on the starboard, then on the port side, each time rolling a little more. Alex did what he could, playing with the attitude jets, trying to undercut some of the ice.

Her nose rose, until Alex tilted back in his chair at about a forty-five degree angle. That was when Tia cut loose with the full power of her rear thrusters.

"*We're moving!*" she shouted over the roar of her own engines, engines normally reserved only for in-atmosphere flight. There was no sensation of movement, but Alex clearly heard the scrape of ice along her hull, and winced, knowing that without a long stint in dry dock, Tia would look worse than Hank's old tramp-freighter. . . .

Suddenly, they were free—

Tia killed the engines and engaged full null-gee drive, hovering just above the surface of the snow in eerie silence.

"CenSec got the first ship; the other one jumped them. It looks pretty even," Tia said shortly, as Alex heard the whine of the landing gear being dropped again. "So far, no one has noticed us. Are you braced?"

"Go for it," he replied. "Is there anything I can do?"

"Hold on," she said shortly.

She shot skyward, going for altitude. She knew the capabilities of her hull better than Alex did; he was going to leave this in her hands. The hill they wanted was less than a kilometer away—when they'd gotten high enough, Tia nosed over and dove for it. She aimed straight for the crest, as if it were a target and she a projectile.

Sudden fear clutched at his throat, his heart going a million beats per second. *She can't mean to ram—*

Alex froze, his hands clutching the armrests.

At the last minute, Tia rolled her nose up, hitting the crest of the hill with her landing gear instead of her nose.

The shriek and crunch of agonized metal told Alex that they were not going to make port anywhere but a space station now. The impact rammed him back into his chair, the lights flickered and went out, and crash-systems deployed, cushioning him from worse shock. Even so, he blacked out for a moment.

When he came to again, the lights were back on, and Tia hovered, tilted slightly askew, above the alien city.

Below and to their right was what was left of the roofless building—now buried beneath a pile of ice, earth, and rock.

"Are you all right?" he managed, though it hurt to move his jaw.

"Space-worthy," she said, and there was no mistaking the shakiness in her voice. "Barely. I'll be as leaky as a sieve in anything but the main cabin and the passenger section, though. And I don't know about my drives—hang on, we're being hailed."

The screen flickered and filled with the image of Neil, with Chria Chance in the background. "AH-One-Oh-Three-Three, is that you?

I assume you had a good reason for playing 'chicken' with a mountain?"

"It's us," Alex replied, feeling all of his energy drain out as his adrenaline level dropped. "There's another one of your playmates under that rockpile."

"Ah." Neil said nothing more, simply nodded. "All right, then. Can you come up to us?"

"We aren't going to be making any landings," Tia pointed out. "But I don't know about the state of our drives."

Chria leaned over her partner's shoulder. "I wouldn't trust them if I were you," she said. "But if you can get up here, we can take you in tow and hold you in orbit until one of the transports shows up. Then you can ride home in their bay."

"It's a deal," Alex told her—then, with a lift of an eyebrow, "I didn't know you could do that."

"There's a lot you don't know," she told him. "Is that all right with you, Tia?"

"At this point, just about anything would be all right with me," she replied. "We're on the way."

Tia was still a little dizzy from the call she'd gotten from the Institute. *When you're refitted, we'd like you to take the first Team into what we think is the EsKay homeworld. You and Alexander have the most experience in situations where plague is a possibility of any other courier on contract to us.* It had only made sense; to this day no one knew what had paralyzed *her.* She had a vested interest in making sure the team stayed healthy, and an even bigger one in helping to find the bug.

Of course, they knew that. And they knew she would never buy out her contract until *this* assignment was over. Blackmail? Assuredly. But it was a form of blackmail she could live with.

Besides, if her plan worked, she would soon be digging *with* the Prime Team, not just watching them. It might take a while, but sooner or later, she'd have enough money made from her investments—

Once she paid for the repairs, that is. From the remarks of the techs working on her hull, they would not be cheap.

Then Stirling stunned her again, presenting her with the figures in her account.

"So, my dear lady," said Stirling, "between an unspecified reward from the Drug Enforcement Arm, the bonus for decoding the purpose of the EsKay navbook, the fine return from your last investment, and the finders' fee for that impressive treasure trove, you are *quite* a wealthy shellperson."

"So I see," Tia replied, more than a little dazed. "But what about the bill for repairs—"

"Covered by CenSec." Stirling wasn't precisely gloating, but he was certainly enjoying himself. "And if you don't mind my saying so, that was *my* work. I merely repeated what you had told me about the situation—pointed out that your damages were due entirely to a civilian aiding in the apprehension of dangerous criminals—and CenSec seemed positively eager to have the bills transferred over. When I mentioned how you had kept *their* ship from ambush from the ground, they decided you needed that Singularity Drive you've always wanted."

She suspected he had done more than merely mention it . . . perhaps she ought to see if she could get Lee Stirling as her Advocate, instead of the softperson she had, who had done *nothing* about the repairs or the drive! So, she would not have to spend a single penny of all those bonuses on her own repairs! "What about my investments in the prosthetics firm? And what if I take my bonus money and plow it back into Moto-Prosthetics?"

"Doing brilliantly. And if you do that—hmm—do you realize you'll have a controlling interest?" Stirling sounded quite amazed. "Is this something you wanted? You *could* buy out your contract with all this. Or get yourself an entire new refit internally and externally."

"Yes," she replied firmly. She was glad that Alex wasn't aboard at the moment, even though she felt achingly lonely without the sounds of his footsteps or his tuneless whistling. This was something she needed absolute privacy for. "In fact, I am going to need a softperson proxy to go to the Board of Directors for me."

"Now?" Stirling asked.

"As soon as I have controlling interest," she replied. "The sooner the better."

And it can't be soon enough to suit me.

Alex looked deeply into the bottom of his glass and decided that this one was going to be his last. He had achieved the state of floating that passed for euphoria; any more and he would pass it, and become disgustingly drunk. Probably a weepy drunk, too, all things considered. That would be a bad thing; despite his civilian clothing, someone might recognize him as a CS brawn, and that would be trouble. Besides, this was a high-class bar as spaceport bars went; human bartender, subdued, restful lighting, comfortable booths and stools, good music that was not too loud. They didn't need a maudlin drunk; they really didn't need any drunk. No point in ruining other people's evening just because his life was a mess. . . .

He felt the lump in his throat and knew one more drink would make it spill over into an outpouring of emotion. The bartender leaned over and said, confidingly, "Buddy, if I were you, I'd cut off about now."

Alex nodded, a little surprised, and swallowed back the lump. Had liability laws gotten to the point where bartenders were watching their customers for risky behavior? "Yeah. What I figured." He sniffed a bit and told himself to straighten up before he became an annoyance.

The bartender—a human, which was why Alex had chosen to drink away his troubles here, if such a thing was possible—did not leave. Instead, he polished the slick pseudo-wooden bar beside Alex with a spotless cloth, and said, casually, "If you don't mind my saying so, buddy, you look like a man with a problem or two."

Alex laughed, mirthlessly. The man had no idea. "Yeah. Guess so."

"You want to talk about it?" the bartender persisted. "That's what they hire me for. That's why you're paying so much for the drinks."

Alex squinted up at the man, who was perfectly ordinary in a way that seemed very familiar. Conservative haircut, conservative, casual clothing. Nothing about the face or the expression to mark him except a certain air of friendly concern. It was that "air" that tipped him off—it was very polished, very professional. "Counselor?" he asked, finally.

The bartender nodded to a framed certificate over the three shelves of antique and exotic bottles behind the bar. "Licensed. Confidential. Freelance. Been in the business for five years. You probably can't tell me anything I haven't heard a hundred times before."

Freelance and confidential meant that whatever Alex told him would stay with him, and would not be reported back to his superiors. Alex was both surprised and unsurprised—the Counselor-attended bars had been gaining in popularity when he had graduated. He just hadn't known they'd gotten *that* popular. He certainly hadn't expected to find one out here, at a refit station. People tended to pour out their problems when they'd been drinking; someone back on old Terra had figured out that it might be a good idea to give them someone to talk to who *might* be able to tender some reasonable advice. Now, so he'd heard, there were more Counselors behind bars than there were in offices, and a large number of bartenders were going back to school to get Counselor's licenses.

Suddenly the need to unburden himself to *someone* was too much to withstand. "Ever been in love?" he asked, staring back down at the empty glass and shoving it back and forth a little between his index fingers.

The bartender took the glass away and replaced it with a cup of coffee. "Not personally, but I've seen a lot of people who are— or think they are."

"Ah." Alex transferred his gaze to the cup, which steamed very nicely. "I wouldn't advise it."

"Yeah. A lot of them say that. Personal troubles with your significant?" the bartender-*cum*-Counselor prompted. "Maybe it's something I can help out with."

Alex sighed. "Only that I'm in love with someone that—isn't exactly reachable." He scratched his head for a moment, trying to think of a way to phrase it without giving too much away. "Our— uh—professions are going to keep us apart, no matter what, and there's some physical problems, too."

The habit of caution was ingrained too deeply. Freelance Counselor or no, he couldn't bring himself to tell the whole truth to this man. Not when telling it could lose him access to Tia altogether, if the wrong people heard all this.

"Can't you change jobs?" the Counselor asked, reasonably. "Surely a job isn't worth putting yourself through misery. From everything I've ever seen or heard, it's better to have a low-paying job that makes you happy than a high-paying one that's driving you into bars."

Alex shook his head, sorrowfully. "That won't help," he sighed hopelessly. "It's not just the job, and changing it will only make things worse. Think of us as—as a Delphin and an Avithran. She can't swim, I can't fly. Completely incompatible lives."

And that puts it mildly.

The Counselor shook his head. "That doesn't sound promising, my friend. Romeo and Juliet romances are all very well for the holos, but they're hell on your insides. I'd see if I couldn't shake my emotional attachment, if I was you. No matter how much you think you love someone, you can always turn the heat down if you decide that's what you want to do about it."

"I'm trying," Alex told him, moving the focus of his concentration from the coffee cup to the bartender's face. "Believe me, I'm *trying*. I've got a couple of weeks extended leave coming, and I'm going to use every minute of it in trying. I've got dates lined up; I've got parties I'm hitting—and a friend from CenSec is planning on taking me on an extended shore leave crawl."

The bartender nodded, slowly. "I understand, and seeing a lot of attractive new people is one way to try and shake an emotional attachment. But friend—you are not going to find your answer in the bottom of a bottle."

"Maybe not," Alex replied sadly. "But at least I can find a little forgetfulness there."

And as the bartender shook his head, he pushed away from his seat, turned, took a tight grip on his dubious equilibrium, and walked out the door, looking for a little more of that forgetfulness.

Angelica Guon-Stirling bint Chad slid into her leather-upholstered seat and smiled politely at the man seated next to her at the foot of the huge, black marble table. He nodded back and returned his attention to the stock market report he was reading on the screen of his datalink. Other men and women, dressed in conservative suits and the subdued hues of management, filed in and took the remaining places around the table. She refrained from chuckling. In a few more moments, he might well be more interested in her than in anything that datalink could supply. She'd gotten entry to the meeting on the pretext of representing her uncle's firm on some unspecified business—they represented enough fluid wealth that the secretary had added her to the agenda and granted her entry to the sacred boardroom. It was a very well-appointed sacred boardroom; rich with the scent of expensive leather and hushed as only a room ringed with high-priced anti-surveillance equipment could be. The lights were set at exactly the perfect psychological hue and intensity for the maximum amount of alertness, the chair cradled her with unobtrusive comfort. The colors of warm white, cool black, and gray created an air of efficiency and importance, without being sterile.

None of this intimidated Angelica in the least. She had seen a hundred such board rooms in the past, and would probably see a thousand more before her career had advanced to the point that she was too busy to be sent out on such missions. Her uncle had not only chosen her to be Ms. Cade's proxy because they were related; he had chosen her because she was the best proxy in the firm. And this particular venture was going to need a very delicate touch, for what Ms. Cade wanted was not anything the board of directors of Moto-Prosthetics was going to be ready for. *They* thought in terms of hostile takeovers, poison pills, golden parachutes. Ms. Cade had an entirely different agenda. If this were not handled well and professionally, the board might well fight, and that would waste precious time.

Though it might seem archaic, board meetings still took place in person. It was too easy to fake holos, to create a computer-generated simulacrum of someone who was dead or in cold sleep. That was why she was here now, with proxy papers in order and properly filed with all the appropriate authorities. Not that she minded. This was exciting work, and every once in a while there was a client like Hypatia Cade, who wanted something so different that it made everything else she had done up to now seem like a training exercise.

The meeting was called to order—and Angelica stood up before the chairman of the board could bring up normal business. Now was the time. If she waited until her scheduled turn, she could be lost or buried in nonsense—and as of this moment, the board's business was no longer what had been scheduled anyway. It was hers, Angelica's, to dictate. It was a heady brew, power, and Angelica drank it to the dregs as all eyes centered on her, most affronted that she had "barged in" on their business.

"Gentlemen," she said smoothly, catching all their attentions. "Ladies. I believe you should all check your datalinks. If you do, you will see that my client, a Miz Hypatia Cade, has just this moment purchased a controlling interest in your preferred stock. As of this moment, Hypatia Cade *is* Moto-Prosthetics. As her proxy, she directs me to put the normal business before the board on hold for a moment."

There was a sudden, shocked moment of silence—then a rustle as cuffs were pushed back—followed by another moment of silence as the members of the board took in the reality of her statement, verified that it was true, wondered how it had happened without them noticing, then waited for the axe to fall. All eyes were on Angelica; some of them desperate. Most of the desperate were those who backed risky ventures within the company, and were wondering if their risk-taking had made them into liabilities for the new majority owner.

Ah, power. I could disband the entire board and bring in my own people, and you all know it. These were the moments that she lived for; the feeling of having the steel hand within the velvet glove—knowing that she held immense power, and choosing not to exercise it.

Angelica slid back down into her seat and smiled—smoothly, coolly, but encouragingly. "Be at ease, ladies and gentlemen. The very first thing that my client wishes to assure you of is that she intends no shakeups. She is satisfied with the way this company is performing, and she does not intend to interfere in the way you are running it."

Once again, the faces around the table changed. Disbelief in some eyes, calculation in others. Then understanding. It would be business as usual. Nothing would change. These men and women still had *their* lives, *their* power, undisturbed.

She waited for the relief to set in, then pounced, leaning forward, putting her elbows down in the table, and steepling her hands before her. "But I must tell you that this will be the case only so long as Miz Cade is satisfied. And Miz Cade *does* have a private agenda for this company."

Another pause, to let the words sink in. She saw the questions behind the eyes—what kind of private agenda? Was it something that this Cade person wanted them to do—or to make? Or was it something else altogether?

"It's something that she wants you to construct; nothing you are not already capable of carrying off," Angelica continued, relishing every moment. "In fact, I would venture to say that it is something you *could* be doing now, if you had the inclination. It's just a little personal project, shall we say. . . ."

Alex's mouth tasted like an old rug; his eyes were scratchy and puffed, and his head pounded. Every joint ached, his stomach churned unhappily, and he was not at all enjoying the way the room had a tendency to roll whenever he moved.

The wages of sin were counted out in hangovers, and this one was one of monumental proportions.

Well, that's what happens when you go on a two-week drunk.

He closed his eyes, but that didn't help. It hadn't exactly been a two-week drunk, but he had never once in the entire span been precisely sober. He had chosen, quite successfully, to glaze his problems over with the fuzz and blurring of alcohol.

It was *all* that had happened. He had not shaken his fixation with Tia. He was just as hopelessly in love with her as he had been before he started his binge. And he had tried everything short of brain-wipe to get rid of the emotion; he'd made contact with some of his old classmates, he'd gone along with Neil and Chria on a celebratory spree, he'd talked to more bartender-Counselors, he'd picked up girl after girl. . . .

To no avail whatsoever.

Tia Cade it was who was lodged so completely in his mind and heart, and Tia Cade it would remain.

So, besides being hung over, he was still torn up inside. And without that blur of alcohol to take the edge off it, his pain was just as bad as before.

There was only one thing for it: he and Tia would have to work it all out, somehow. One way or another.

He opened his eyes again; his tiny rented cubicle spun slowly around, and he groaned as his stomach protested.

First things first; deal with the hangover. . . .

It was just past the end of the second shift when he made his way down the docks to the refit berth where CenSec had installed Tia for her repair work. It had taken that long before he felt like a human being again. One thing was certain; that was *not* something he intended to indulge in ever again. One long binge in his life was enough.

I just hope I haven't fried too many brain cells with stupidity. I don't have any to spare.

He found the lock closed, but there were no more workers

swarming about, either inside the bay or out. That was a good sign, since it probably meant all the repairs were over. He'd used the day-and-night noise as an excuse to get away, assuming Tia would contact him if she needed to.

As he hit the lock controls and gave them his palm to read, it suddenly occurred to him that she hadn't made any attempt at all to contact him in all the time he'd been gone.

Had he frightened her?

Had she reported him?

The lock cycled quickly, and he stepped onto a ship that was uncannily silent.

The lights had been dimmed down; the only sounds were of the ventilation system. Tia did not greet him; nothing did. He might as well have been on an empty, untenanted ship, without even an AI.

Something was wrong.

His heart pounding, his mouth dry with apprehension, he went to the main cabin. The boards were all dark, with no signs of activity.

Tia wasn't sulking; Tia didn't sulk. There was nothing functioning that could not be handled by the stand-alone redundant micros.

He dropped his bag on the deck, from fingers that had gone suddenly nerveless.

There could be only one cause for this silence, this absence of activity. Tia was gone.

Either the BB authorities had found out about how he felt, or Tia herself had complained. They had come and taken her away, and he would never see or talk to her again.

As if to confirm his worst fears, a glint of light on an open plexy window caught his eye. Theodore Edward Bear was gone, his tiny shrine empty.

No—

But the evidence was inescapable.

Numb with shock, he found himself walking towards his own cabin. Perhaps there would be a note there, in his personal database. Perhaps there would be a message waiting from CS, ordering him to report for official Counseling.

Perhaps both. It didn't matter. Tia was gone, and very little mattered anymore.

Black despair washed into him, a despair so deep that not even tears would relieve it. Tia was gone. . . .

He opened the door to his cabin, and the light from the corridor shone inside, making the person sitting on his bunk blink.

Person sitting on my—

Female. It was definitely female. And she wasn't wearing anything like a CS uniform, Counselor, Advocate, or anything else. In fact, she wasn't wearing very much at all—a little neon-red Skandex unitard that left nothing to imagine.

He turned on the light, an automatic reflex. His visitor stared up at him, lips creasing in a shy smile. She was tiny, smaller than he had first thought; dark and elfin, with big blue eyes, the image of a Victorian fairy—and oddly familiar.

In her hands, she gently cradled the missing Ted Bear. It was the bear that suddenly shook his brain out of inactive and into overdrive.

He stared; he gripped the side of the door. "T-T-Tia?" he stammered.

She smiled again, with less shyness. "Hi," she said—and it was Tia's voice, sounding a bit—odd—coming from a mouth and not a speaker. "I'm sorry I had to shut so much down, I can't run *this* and the ship, too."

It was Tia—*Tia!*—sitting there in a body, a human body, like the realization of his dream!

"This?" he replied cleverly.

"I hope you don't mind if I don't get up," she continued, a little ruefully. "I'm not very good at walking yet. They just delivered this today, and I haven't had much practice in it yet."

"It?" he said, sitting heavily down on his bunk and staring at her. "How—what—"

"Do you like it?" she asked, pathetically eager for his approval. He wasn't sure what he was supposed to approve of—the body?

"How could I *not* like it—you—" His head was spinning as badly as it had a few hours ago. "Tia, what on earth *is* this?"

She blinked, and giggled. "I keep forgetting. You know all that bonus money we've been getting? I kept investing it, then reinvesting the profits in Moto-Prosthetics. But when we got back here, I was thinking about something Doctor Kenny told me, that they had the capability to make a body like this, but that there was no way to put a naked brain in it, and there was so *much* data-transfer needed to run it that the link could only be done at very short distances."

"Oh." He couldn't help but stare at her; this was his dream, his daydream—his—

Never mind.

"Anyway," she continued, blithely unaware that she had stunned him into complete silence, "it seemed to me that the body would be perfect for a brainship, I mean, we've got all the links already, and it wouldn't be any harder to control a body from inside than a servo. But he was already an investor, and he told me it wasn't likely they'd ever build a body like that, since there was no market for it, because it would cost as much as a brainship contract buy-out."

"But how—"

She laughed aloud. "That was why I took all my share of the bonuses and bought more stock! I bought a controlling interest, then I told them to build me a body! I don't need a buy-out— I don't really want a buy-out—not since the Institute decided to give us the EsKay homeworld assignment."

He shook his head. "That simple? It hardly seems possible . . . didn't they argue?"

"They were too happy that I was letting them keep their old jobs," she told him cynically. "After all, as controlling stockholder, I had the right to fire them all and set up my own Board of Directors. But I have to tell you the funniest thing!"

"What's that?" he asked.

Her hands caressed Theodore's soft fur. "Word of what I was doing leaked out, and now there *is* a market! Did you have any idea how many shellpersons there are who've earned a buy-out, but didn't have any place to go with it, because they were happy with their current jobs?"

He shook his head, dumbly.

"Not too many ships," she told him, "but a lot of shellpersons running installations. Lots of them. And there were a lot of inquiries from brainships, too—some of them saying that they'd be willing to skip a buy-out to have a body! Moto-Prosthetics even got a letter of protest from some of the Advocates!"

"Why?" he asked, bewildered. "Why on earth would they care?"

"They said that we were the tools of the BB program, that we had purposely put this 'mechanical monster' together to tempt brainships out of their buy-out money." She tilted her head to one side, charmingly, and frowned. "I must admit that angle had never occurred to me. I hope that really isn't a problem. Maybe I should have Lars and Lee Stirling look into it for me."

"Tia," he managed, around the daze surrounding his thoughts, "what is this 'mechanical monster' of yours?"

"It's a cybernetic body, with a wide-band comlink in the extreme shortwave area up here." She tapped her forehead. "What's different about it is that it's using shellperson tech to give me full sensory input from the skin as well as output to the rest. My range isn't much outside the ship, but my techs at Moto are working on that. After all, when we take the Prime Team out to the EsKay homeworld, I'm going to want to join the dig, if they'll let me. What with alloys and silicates and carbon-fibers and all, it's not much heavier than you are, even though it outmasses a softperson female of this type by a few kilos. *Everything* works, though, full sensory and well—everything. Like a softperson again, except that I don't get muscle fatigue and I can shut off the pain-sensors if I'm damaged. That was why I took Ted out; I wanted to feel him, to hug him again."

She just sat there and beamed at him, and he shook his head. "But why?" he asked, finally.

She blinked, and then dropped her eyes to the bear. "I—probably would have gone for a buy-out, if it hadn't been for you," she said shyly. "Or maybe a Singularity Drive, except that CenSec decided that maybe they'd better give me one and threw it in with the repairs. But—I told you, Alex. You're the most special person in my life. How could I know this was possible, and *not* do it for— for both of us?"

He dared to touch her then, just one finger along her cheek, then under her chin, raising her eyes to meet his. There was nothing about those lucent eyes that looked mechanical or cold; nothing about the warmth and resiliency of the skin under his hand that said "cybernetic."

"You gave up your chance of a buy-out for me—for us?" he asked.

She shrugged. "Someone very wise once said that the chance for happiness was worth giving up a little freedom for. And really, between the Advocates and everybody, they really can't *make* us do anything we don't want to."

"I guess not." He smiled, and she smiled back. "You do realize that you've actually done the BB program two favors, don't you?"

"I have?" She blinked again, clearly bewildered.

"You've given shellpersons something *else* to do with their buy-out money. If they don't have Singularity Drives, they'll *want* those first—and *then* they'll want one of these." He let go of her chin and tapped her cheek playfully. "Maybe more than one. Maybe one of each sex, or in different body types. Some brainships may never buy out. But the other problem—you've solved fixation, my clever lady."

She nodded after a moment. "I never thought of that. But you're right! If you have a *body,* someone to be with and—ah—everything—you won't endanger the shellperson. And if it's just an infatuation based on the dream instead of the reality—well—"

"Well, after a few rounds with the body, it will cool off to something manageable." He chuckled. "Watch out, or they'll give you a bonus for that one, too!"

She laughed. "Well, I won't take it as a buy-out! Maybe I'll just build myself a second body! After all, if we aren't going to be exploring the universe like a couple of holo-heroes, we have the time to explore things a little—closer to hand. Right?"

She posed, coyly, looking at him flirtatiously over her shoulder. He wondered how many of her entertainment holos she'd watched to find *that* pose. "So, what would you like, Alex? A big, blond Valkyrie? An Egyptian queen? A Nubian warrior-maid? How about a Chinese princess or—"

"Let's learn about what we have at hand, shall we?" he interrupted, sliding closer to her and taking her in his arms. Her head tilted up towards his, her eyes shining with anticipation. Carefully, gently, he took the bear out of her hands and placed him on the shelf above the foot of the bed, as her arms slid around his waist, cautiously, but eagerly.

"Now," he breathed, "about that exploration . . ."

-END-

PARTNERSHIP

by Anne McCaffrey & Margaret Ball

CHAPTER ONE

To ordinary human ears the slight crackle of the speaker being activated would have been almost inaudible. To Nancia, all her sensors fine-tuned for this signal, it sounded like a trumpet call. Newly graduated and commissioned, ready for service—and apprehensive that she would not be able to live up to her family's high Service traditions—she'd had little to do but wait.

He's coming aboard now, she thought in the split second of waiting for the incoming call. And then, as the unmistakable gravelly voice of CenCom's third-shift operator rasped across her sensors, disappointment flooded her synapses and left her dull and heavy on the launching pad. She'd been so sure that Daddy would find time to visit her, even if he hadn't been able to attend the formal graduation of her class from Laboratory Schools.

"XN-935, how soon can you be ready to lift?"

"I completed my test flight patterns yesterday," Nancia replied. She was careful to keep her voice level, monitoring each output band to make sure that no hint of her disappointment showed in the upper frequencies. CenCom could perfectly well have communicated with her directly, via the electronic network that linked Nancia's ship computers with all other computers in this subspace—and via the surgically installed synaptic connectors that linked Nancia's physical body, safe behind its titanium shell, with the ship's computer—but it was a point of etiquette among most of the operators to address brainships just as they would any other human being. It would have been rude to send only electronic instructions, as if the brainships were no more human than the AI-controlled drones carrying the bulk of Central Worlds' regular traffic.

Or so the operators claimed. Nancia privately thought that their insistence on voice-controlled traffic was merely a way to avoid the embarrassing comparison between their sense-limited communication system and a brainship's capabilities of multi-channel communication and instantaneous response.

In any case, it was equally a point of pride among shellpersons to demonstrate the control over their "voices" and all other external comm devices that Helva had shown to be possible, nearly two hundred years ago. Nancia knew herself to lack the fine sense of musical timing and emphasis that had made Helva famous throughout the galaxy as "The Ship Who Sang," but this much, at least, she could do; she could conceal her disappointment at hearing CenCom instead of a direct transmission from Daddy to congratulate her on her commissioning, and she could maintain a perfectly professional facade throughout the ensuing discussion of supplies and loading and singularity points.

"It's a short flight," CenCom told her, and then paused for a moment. "Short for *you*, that is. By normal FTL drive, Nyota ya Jaha is at the far end of the galaxy. Fortunately, there's a singularity point a week from Central that will flip you into local space."

"I *do* have full access to my charts of known decomposition spaces," Nancia reminded CenCom, allowing a tinge of impatience to color her voice.

"Yes, and you can read them in simulated 4-D, can't you, you lucky stiff!" CenCom's voice showed only cheerful resignation at the limitations of a body that forced him to page through bulky books of graphs and charts to verify the mapping Nancia had already created as an internal display: a sequence of three-dimensional spaces collapsing and contorting about the singularity point where local subspace could be defined as intersecting with the subspace sector of Nyota ya Jaha. At that point Nancia would be able to create a rapid physical decomposition and restructuring of the local spaces, projecting herself and her passengers from one subspace to the other. Decomposition space theory allowed brainships like Nancia, or a very few expensive AI drones equipped with metachip processors, to condense the major part of a long journey into the few seconds they spent in Singularity. Less fortunate ships, lacking the metachips or dependent upon the slow responses of a human pilot who lacked Nancia's direct synaptic connections to the computer, still had to go through long weeks or even months of conventional FTL travel to cover the same distance; the massive parallel computations required in Singularity were difficult even for a brainship and impossible for most conventional ships.

"Tell me about the passengers," Nancia requested. When they came aboard, presumably one of her passengers would have the datahedron from Central specifying her destination and instructions, but who knew how much longer she would have to wait before the passengers boarded? She hadn't even been invited to choose a brawn yet; that would surely take a day or two. Besides, picking CenCom's brains for information on her assignment was better than waiting in tense expectation of her family's visit. They would certainly come to see her off . . . wouldn't they? All through her schooling she had received regular visits from one family member or another—mostly from her father, who made a point of how much time he was taking from his busy schedule to visit her. But Jinevra and Flix, her sister and brother, had come too, now and then; Jinevra less often, as college and her new career in Planetary Aid administration took up more and more of her time.

None of them had attended Nancia's formal graduation, though; no one from the entire, far-flung, wealthy House of Perez y de Gras had been there to hear the lengthy list of honors and awards and prizes she'd gained in the final, grueling year of her training as a brainship.

It wasn't enough, Nancia thought. *I was only third in my class. If I'd placed first, if I'd won the Daleth Prize. . . .* No good would come of brooding over the past. She knew that Jinevra and Flix had grown up and had their own lives to lead, that Daddy's crowded schedule of business and diplomatic meetings didn't leave him much time for minor matters like school events. It really wasn't important that he hadn't come to see her graduate. He would surely make time for a personal visit before liftoff; that was what really counted. And when he did come, he should find her happy and busy and engaged in the work for which she had trained. "About the passengers?" she reminded CenCom.

"Oh, you probably know more about them than I do," the CenCom operator said with a laugh. "They're more your sort of people than mine. High Families," he clarified. "New graduates, I gather, off to their first jobs."

That was nice, anyway. Nancia had been feeling just a bit apprehensive at the thought of having to deal with some experienced, high-ranking diplomatic or military passengers on her first flight. It would be pleasant to carry a group of young people just like her—well, not *just* like her, Nancia corrected with a trace of internal amusement. They would be a few years older, maybe nineteen or twenty to her sixteen; everybody knew that softpersons suffered from so many hormonal changes and sensory distractions that their schooling took several years longer to complete. And they would be softpersons, with limited sensory and processing capability. Still, they'd all be heading off to start their careers together; that was a significant bond.

She absently recorded CenCom's continuing instructions while she mused on the pleasant trip ahead. "Nyota ya Jaha's a long way off by FTL," he told her unnecessarily. "I expect somebody pulled some strings to get them a Courier Service ship. But it happens to be convenient for us too, being in the same subspace as Vega, so that's all right."

Nancia vaguely remembered something about Vega subspace in the news. Computer malfunctions . . . why would that make the newsbeams? There must have been something important about it, but she'd received only the first bits of the newsbyte before a teacher canceled the beam, saying something severe about the inadvisability of listening to upsetting newsbytes and the danger of getting the younger shellpeople upset over nothing. Oh, well, Nancia thought, now that she was her own ship she could scan the beams for herself and pick up whatever it had been about Vega later. For now, she was more interested in finding out what CenCom knew about her newly assigned passengers.

"Overton-Glaxely, del Parma y Polo, Armontillado-Perez y Medoc, de Gras-Waldheim, Hezra-Fong," CenCom read off the list of illustrious High Family names. "See what I mean?"

"Umm, yes," Nancia said. "We're a cadet branch of Armontillado-Perez y Medoc, and the de Gras-Waldheims come in somewhere on my mother's side. But you forget, CenCom, I didn't exactly grow up in those circles myself."

"Yes, well, your visitor will probably be able to give you all the latest gossip," CenCom said cheerfully.

"Visitor!" *Of course he came to see me off. I never doubted it for an instant,*

"Request just came in while I was looking up the passenger list. Sorry, I forgot to route it to you. Name of Perez y de Gras. Being a family member, they told him to go right on out to the field. He'll be at the launching pad in a minute."

Nancia activated her outside sensors and realized that it was almost night . . . not that the darkness made any difference to her, but her infrared sensors picked up only the outline of a human form approaching the ship; she couldn't see Daddy's face at all. And it would be rude to turn on a spotlight. Oh, well, he'd be there any minute. She opened her lower doors in silent welcome.

CenCom's voice was an irritation now, not a welcome distraction. "XN? I asked if you can lift off within two hours. Your provision list is more than adequate for a short voyage, and these pampered brats are kvetching about having to wait around on base."

"Two hours?" Nancia repeated. That wouldn't give her much time for a visit—well, be realistic; it was probably more time than Daddy could spare. But there were other problems with leaving so soon. "Are you out of your mind? I haven't even picked a brawn yet!" She intended to get to know the available brawns over the next few days before choosing a partner. The selection process was not something to be rushed through, and she certainly didn't want to waste the precious minutes of Daddy's visit choosing a brawn!

"Don't you young ships ever catch the newsbeams? I told you Vega. Remember what happened to the CR-899? Her brawn's stranded on his home planet—Vega 3.3."

"What a dreary way to name their planets," Nancia commented. "Can't they think of any nice names?"

"Vegans are . . . very logical," CenCom said. "The original group of settlers were, anyway—the ones who went out by slowship, before FTL. I gather the culture evolved to an extremely rigid form during the generations born on shipboard. They don't make a lot of allowances for human frailty, little things like names being easier to remember than strings of numbers."

"Makes no difference to *me*," Nancia said smugly. Her memory banks could encode and store any form of information she needed.

"You should get along just great with the Vegans," CenCom told her. "Anyway, this brawn is out in Vegan subspace, no ship, nothing in the vicinity but a couple of old FTL drones. OG Shipping ought to be able to divert their metachip drone from Nyota, but as usual, we can't contact the manager. So it's either waste months of Caleb's service term by sending him home FTL, or provide our own transport. You're it. You can drop off your friends and relations on the planets around Nyota ya Jaha—I'll transmit a databurst of your orders after we get through chatting—and then proceed to Vega 3.3 to pick up your first brawn. Very neat organization. Psych records suggest the two of you ought to make a great team."

"Oh, they do, do they?" said Nancia. She had her own opinion of the Psych branch of Central and the intrusive tests and questionnaires with which they bombarded shellpersons, and she had no intention of being hustled by Central into forgoing her right to choose a brawn just because some shelltapper in a white coat thought they knew how to pick a man for her—and because she was a convenient free ride for a brawn who'd already lost one ship. Nancia was about to turn up her beam to CenCom and favor the operator with a few choice words on the subject when she felt her visitor stepping aboard. Well, there'd be time for that argument later; she could think about it on the way out. Agreeing to transport the CR-899's stranded brawn back to Central wouldn't commit her to a permanent partnership, and when she returned from this voyage she'd have plenty of time to choose her next brawn . . . and to tell Psych what they could do with their personality profiles.

Meanwhile, her visitor had ignored the open lift doors in favor of climbing the stairs to the central cabin, taking the last steps two at a time; Daddy made a point of keeping in shape. Nancia activated her stairway sensors and speakers simultaneously.

"Daddy, how nice of you—"

But the visitor was Flix, not Daddy. At least, from what Nancia could see of his face behind the enormous basket of flowers and fruit, she assumed it was her little brother: spiky red hair in an old-fashioned punk crown, one long peacock's feather dangling from the right earlobe, fingertips callused from hours of synthcom play. It was her little brother, all right.

"Flix." She could keep her vocal registers level, to conceal her disappointment; but she couldn't for the life of her think of any words to add.

"'S'okay," Flix said, his voice coming slightly muffled from the stack of Calixtan orchids and orange Juba apfruits that threatened to topple over him from the insecurely stacked basket. Nancia slid out a tray from a waist-level cabinet just in time. Flix staggered into the tray, dropped the basket on it and sat backwards on the floor with a look of mild surprise. Two glowing orange apfruits fell off the towering display and rolled towards Nancia's command console, revealing a bottle of Sparkling Hereot in the center of the basket. "Know you'd rather have Daddy. Or Jinevra. Somebody worthy of the honor you do House Perez y de Gras. You deserve 'em, too," he added after a sprawling dive to retrieve the Juba apfruits. "Deserve a brass marching band and a red carpet instead of this thing." He brushed one hand across the soft nap of the sand-colored, standard-issue synthorug with which Nancia's internal living areas were carpeted.

"You—you really think I didn't disgrace the House?" Nancia asked. She *had* been wondering if that was why nobody had come to see her graduated and commissioned. Daddy had always spoken of her graduation with the words, "When you win the Daleth—" And she hadn't done that.

Flix turned his head toward the titanium column and gave Nancia the same disbelieving, slightly contemptuous look he'd bestowed on the beige synthorug. "Stupid," he mourned. "Only member of the family I can stand to talk to, our Nancia; only one who doesn't give me hours of grief about giving up my synthcomposing for a Real Career, and it turns out she has worse problems than a few little malfunctioning organs. If you hadn't been popped into your shell at birth I'd suspect you were dropped on your head as a baby. *Of course* you've done the House proud, Nancia, what do you think? Third in academics and first in Decom Theory and taking so many special awards they had to restructure the graduation ceremony to make time for your presentations—"

"How did you know about that?" Nancia interrupted.

Flix looked away from the titanium column. Of course she could still see his expression perfectly well from her floor-level sensors, but it would have been rude to remind him of that. He looked embarrassed enough as it was. "Had a copy of the program," he mumbled. "Meant to show up, as long as I happened to be on

Central anyway, but . . . well, I met these two girls when I was doing a synthcom gig in the Pleasure Palace, and they taught me how to mix Rigellian stemjuice with Benedictine to make this wonderful fizzy drink, and . . . well, anyway, I didn't wake up until the graduation ceremony was about over."

He scowled at the carpet for a moment longer, then brightened up. "Another thing I like about you, Nancia, you're the only relative I've got who won't burst into a long diatribe about how I could lower myself by playing synthcom at the Pleasure Palace. Of course, I don't suppose you have any idea what those places are like. Still, neither does Great Aunt Mendocia, and that doesn't stop *her* from sounding off."

He got to his feet and began pulling things out of the basket. "So . . . since I was unavoidably detained at the Pleasure Palace . . . and Jinevra's off at the tail end of nowhere investigating a Planetary Aid fraud, and Daddy's in a meeting, I thought I'd just drop by while you were waiting for assignment and we'd have a little private party."

"What meeting?" Nancia asked before she could stop herself. "Where?"

Flix looked up from the basket, surprised. "Huh?"

"You said our father was in a meeting."

"Yes, well, isn't he always? *No,* I don't know where; it's just a logical deduction. You know how full his dayplanner program is. Y'know, I often wondered," Flix rattled on as he unpacked the basket, "just how the three of us got born. Well, conceived, anyway. Do you suppose he sent Mother a memo? *Please come by my office this morning. Can work you in between ten and ten-fifteen. Bring sheets and pillow.*" He reached the bottom of the basket and pulled out two scratched and faded datahedra. "There! I know you think I'm a selfish bastard, bringing fruit and champagne to somebody who doesn't eat or drink, but actually I have covered all contingencies. These are my latest synthcompositions—here, I'll drop them in your reader. Background music for the party, and you can play them on the trip to entertain yourself.

As the jangling sounds of Flix's latest experimental composition rang out in the cabin, he held up a third datahedron and smiled. Unlike the first two well-worn hedra, this was a glittering shape with a slick commercial laser-cut finish that spattered rainbows of light across the cabin. "And here—"

"Let me guess," Nancia interrupted. "You've finally found some-body to make a commercial cut of your synthcompositions."

Flix's smile dimmed perceptibly. "Well, no. Not exactly. Although," he said, brightening, "I do know this girl who knows a chap who used to date a girl who did temporary office work for the second VP of Sound Studios, so there *are* distinct possi-bilities in the offing. But this is something quite different. This," he said, sounding almost reverent, "is the new, improved, vastly more sophisticated version of SPACED OUT, not due for public release until the middle of next month, and I won't tell you what I had to do to get it."

Nancia waited for him to tell her what the thing was about, but Flix paused and beamed as if he was expecting some immediate reaction from *her.*

"Well?" he said after a few seconds. His spiky red hair began to droop around the edges.

"I'm sorry," Nancia confessed, "but I have no idea what you're talking about."

Flix shook his head mournfully. "Never heard of SPACED OUT? What *do* they teach them at these academies? No, no, don't tell me." He held up one hand in protest. "I know. Decomposition theory and subspace astrogation and metachip design and a lot of other things that make my head hurt. But I do think they could have let you have a little time off to play games."

"We *did* play," Nancia told him. "It was in the schedule. Two thirty-minute periods daily of free play to improve synapse/tool coordination and gross propulsion skills. Why, I used to love playing Stall and PowerSeek when I was in my baby shell!"

Flix shook his head again. "All very improving, I'm sure. Well, *this* game"—he grinned—"is absolutely, one hundred percent guaranteed *not* to improve your mind. In fact, Jinevra claims playing SPACED OUT can cause irreversible brain damage!"

"It can?" Nancia slid her reader slots shut with a click as Flix approached. "Look, Flix, I'm not sure—"

"Consider our big sister," Flix said with his sunniest smile. "Go ahead, just call up an image from her last visit. Don't you think anything she disapproves of must be worth a try?"

Nancia projected a lifesize Jinevra on the screen that filled the center wall of the cabin. Her sister might have been standing beside Flix. Trim and perfect as ever, from the hem of her navy blue

Planetary Technical Aid uniform to the smooth dark hair that fell
perfectly straight to just the regulation 1/4 inch distance from her
starched white collar, she was the pattern of reproach to every
disorderly element in the universe. Nancia couldn't remember just
what had caused the disapproving glint in Jinevra's eyes or the
tight, pinched look at the corners of her mouth at the moment
this image had been stored, but in this projection she seemed to
be glaring right at Flix. One of the red spikes of his retro-punk
hair crown wilted under the withering gaze of the projection.

Nancia felt sorry for him. Jinevra had never bothered to conceal her opinion that their little brother was a wastrel and a disgrace to the family. Daddy, she suspected, felt much the same way.
The weight of the Perez y de Gras clan's disapproval would have
been crushing to her. How could she join them in condemning
Flix? She'd heard stories enough about his wild tricks—there were
times when Jinevra and Daddy seemed to have nothing else to
discuss on their brief visits—but to her he was still the tousle-
headed toddler who'd hugged her titanium shell every time he came
for a visit, who'd waved and yelled as enthusiastically as if she were
a real flesh-and-blood sister who could cuddle him on her lap,
who'd screamed with glee when she carried him around the school
track for a quick round of PowerSeek with her classmates.

And what harm could it do her to try the stupid game?

"You'd like it, Nancia," Flix said hopefully as the projected image
of Jinevra faded into a blank screen. "Really. It's the best version
SpaceGamers has ever released. It's got sixty-four levels of hidden
tunnels, and simulated Singularity space, and holodwarfs. . . ."

"*Holodwarfs?*"

"Just look." Flix dropped the glittering datahedron into the
nearest reader slit—funny, Nancia couldn't remember having
decided to open that reader, but she must have done so. There
was a soft whirring noise as the contents of the datahedron were
read into computer memory, then Flix said, "Level 6, holo!" and
a red-bearded dwarf appeared in the middle of the cabin, bran-
dishing a curved broadsword whose hilt glittered with a shower
of refracted colored light. Flix dropped to one knee as the dwarf's
broadsword slashed through the space where his head had been,
rolled towards a control panel and shouted, "Space Ten laser
armor!"

A shape of light beams bent into impossible curved paths around

him. The dwarf bent and thrust his sword through a gap between
the rapidly weaving lights—

And vanished.

So did the lights.

Flix got to his feet, aggrieved. "You cut the game off! And I was
winning!"

"I, umm, I don't think I'm quite ready for the holodwarfs,"
Nancia apologized. "I have this automatic reaction to seeing people
I love attacked."

Flix nodded. "Sorry. I guess we'll have to bring you up to speed
slowly. Want to start at Level 1, no holos?"

"That sounds . . . better."

And it was better. In fact, after a few rounds, Nancia found
herself actually enjoying the silly game, although she still had
trouble making sense of the rules.

"What am I supposed to do with the Laser Staff?"

"It helps you walk uphill through the gravity well."

"That's dumb. Lasers don't have anything to do with gravity."

"Nancia. It's a *game*. Now, be sure to ask the simugrif for the
answers to the Three Toroid Triples; you'll need them after you
reach the trolls' bridge. . . ."

As Flix instructed her in the rudiments of the game, Nancia
discovered that the actual game program used very little of her
computing power. She was easily able to scan CenCom's databurst
about her coming passengers while they played. At the same time
she activated the ship's enhanced graphics mode to fill the three
wall-size screens in the central cabin with color images of the game
and of their play icons. Flix had chosen to be, of all things, a
brainship, careening through imaginary asteroid belts in search of
the Mystic Rings of Daleen. Nancia preferred to imagine herself
as Troll Slayer, the long-limbed, bold explorer who strode through
gravity wells and over mountain ranges with laser staff and
backblasters.

"Nancia, you can't slay that troll yet!"

"Why not?"

"Because he's in ambush behind the rocks. I can see him, but
you can't."

"I can so. I can see *everything* in this game. It's part of my main
memory now, remember?"

"Well, your play icon can't. He's just a man. He hasn't got multi-D vision. And you see that blinking blue light? The program rules are warning you that he's going to die of hypothermia if you don't get him into some kind of shelter soon."

"Why doesn't he just increase his fuel—oh, I remember. You softpersons certainly are limited in your fuel allocation capabilities." Nancia went ahead and bent her laser staff to take out the hiding troll, as well as three of his fellows, then sent her play icon under the trolls' snow bridge. Behind three hidden doors and through a labyrinth there was a nice warm cave, now uninhabited, where Troll Slayer could rest and refuel.

"Nancia, you're cheating!" Flix accused. "How did you find that place so quickly, without making any mistakes?"

"How could I *not* find it? The game maps are in my main memory too, remember? All I had to do is look."

"Well, couldn't you *not* look? To be fair?"

"No, I could not," Nancia said in a tone that should have effectively closed off further discussion. Cut off her consciousness from a part of the ship's computer memory? The single worst experience of her entire life had been the partial anesthesia required while experts completed her synaptic connections to the ship. There was nothing, absolutely nothing a shellperson hated more than losing connections! Flix ought to understand that without her telling him.

"Just shut down that memory node for a little while," Flix wheedled.

He never did know when to stop. And the idea of shutting down her own nodes made Nancia so uncomfortable that she couldn't bear to discuss it with him.

"Listen, softshell, I'd have to cut off more than one node to bring myself down to your computational level!"

"Oh, yeah? Come outside and say that again!"

"Sure, I'll come outside. I'll take you right up to the Singularity point and let you find your own way out of the decomposition!"

"Aah, relying on brute force again. It's not fair." Flix appealed to the ceiling. "Two big sisters, and they both pick on me all the time!"

"We had to do *something* to keep you under control—" Nancia shut down her vocal transmissions abruptly. There was an incoming beam from Central.

"XN? Message relay from Rigellian subspace." A brief pause, then the image of Nancia's father appeared on the central screen opposite her pillar. On the left-hand screen Flix's brainship icon flipped and rotated in an endless, mindless loop against the glittering stars of deep space; on the right, Troll Slayer stood frozen with one foot lifted to step across the threshold of the hidden cave. Between them, a tired man in a conservative green and blue pinstripe tunic smiled at Nancia.

"Sorry I couldn't come to your graduation, Nancia dear. This meeting on Rigel IV is vital to keeping Central's economy on the planned graph for the next sixteen quarters. I couldn't let them down. Knew you'd understand. Hey, congratulations on all those awards! I didn't have time to read the program in detail yet, but I'm sure you've done House Perez y de Gras proud, as always. And I think you'll like your first assignment. It'll be a chance for you to get to know some of the younger members of the High Families—a very fitting start for our own Courier Service star. Eh? What's that?" He turned towards his left, so that he seemed to be speaking to the frozen Troll Slayer icon. "The Secretary-Particular? Oh, very well, send him in. I'll need to brief him before the next session."

Eyes front again. "You heard that, I suppose, Nancia? Sorry, I have to go now. Good luck!"

"Daddy, wait—" Nancia began, but the screen went blank for a moment. The old image of the snow bridge and the trolls reappeared and she heard the voice of the CenCom operator.

"Sorry, XN. That was a canned message beam. There's no more. And your passengers are ready to board now."

"Thank you, Central." Nancia discovered to her horror that she had lost all control over her vocal channels; the trembling overtones that surrounded her speech made her emotional state all too apparent. *A Perez y de Gras does not weep.* And a brainship *could not* weep. And Nancia had been well trained to repress the sort of unseemly emotional displays that softpersons indulged in. All the same, she very much did not want to talk to anybody just now.

Flix seemed to have sensed her mood; he silently packed up the basket of fruit and sparkling wine and patted Nancia's titanium column as if he thought that she could feel the warmth of his hand. For a moment she had the illusion that she did feel it.

"I'd better get out of the way now," he said. "Can't have a Perez y de Gras brainship caught *partying* on her maiden voyage, can we?"

He paused on the stairs. "Y'know, Nancia, there's no regulation says you have to greet your passengers the minute they step aboard. Let 'em find their cabins and unpack on their own. There'll be plenty of time for social chitchat on the way out."

Then he was gone, a redheaded blur vanishing into the darkness, a whistled melody lingering on the night air outside; and moments later, the bright lights of a spacepad transport shone in Nancia's ground-level sensors and a party of young people tumbled out, laughing and talking all at once and waving glasses in the air. One of them stumbled and spilled the liquid over Nancia's gleaming outer shell; from a fin sensor she could see the snail-trail of something green and viscous defacing her side. The boy swore and shouted, "Hey, Alpha, we need a refill on the Stemerald over here!"

"Wait till we're inside, can't you?" called back a tall girl with ebony skin and features sharp and precise as an antique cameo. Right now her handsome face was etched with lines of anger and dissatisfaction, but as the fair-haired boy looked back over his shoulder at her she gave him a bright smile that wouldn't have deceived Nancia for a minute.

They were all still talking—and drinking that sticky green stuff— as they crowded into the airlock lift without even asking permission to board. Well, she *had* left the entry port open after Flix's departure; maybe they considered that an implied welcome. And Nancia had heard that softpersons—at least those outside the Academy— didn't observe the formality that governed greetings and official exchanges in the Courier Service and other branches of Central's far-flung bureaucracy. She wasn't one to take offense yet, not when she herself was hardly ready for introductions to this bunch of strangers.

As they trooped out of the airlock and into the central cabin, Nancia played a game of matching faces to the names Central had given her. The short red-haired boy with a face like a friendly gargoyle had Flix's coloring and the flashing smile that reeled girls in to Flix like trout on a hook; he must be one of the two related to Nancia's family. "Blaize?" the black girl called. "Blaize, I can't *open* this." She held out a plastic pouch full of shimmering green liquid, and Nancia winced in anticipation as the redhead tore off the sealstrip with two short, strong fingers. But not a drop spilled on her new, official-issue beige carpeting—not now, anyway.

"Here you are, Alpha," the boy said as he handed it back, and

Nancia matched their faces with the names and descriptions that had come in CenCom's databurst. The red-haired boy must be Blaize Armontillado-Perez y Medoc, of a family so high that they barely deigned to recognize the Perez y de Gras connection. And for some puzzling reason his first posting was to a lonely Planetary Technical Aid position on the remote planet of Angalia; she would have expected anybody from a three-name Family to start off somewhere near the top of whatever Central bureaucracy he chose. As for the ebony princess, with her sharp clever face that would have been beautiful if not for the discontented expression, she had to be Alpha bint Hezra-Fong. The short burst transmitted from CenCom identified her as a native of the warm, semi-desert world of Takla, with high marks in her medical research program, and no hint as to why she'd chosen to take a five-year sabbatical in the midst of training to run the Summerlands Clinic on Bahati.

As they passed the pouch of Stemerald back and forth, Nancia was able to identify the other three from their casual conversation without having to introduce herself. The slightly pudgy boy with a halo of overlong brown curls clustering around his red face was Darnell Overton-Glaxely, going to Bahati to take charge of OG Shipping from the cousin who'd been administering the business during Darnell's minority. The other girl, the sleek black-haired beauty whose delicate bones and slightly tilted eyes suggested a family connection with the Han Parma branch of the family, would be Fassa del Parma y Polo. The del Parma y Polo clan controlled all the major space construction in this subspace, and now it appeared they were sending this delicate little thing out to establish the family's rights in Vega subspace as well. The girl was probably, Nancia reflected, stronger than she looked. At any rate she was the only one refusing the pouch of Stemerald as it went around the circle, and that was a good sign.

And the last one—Nancia let her sensors take in the full glory of Polyon de Gras-Waldheim, the cousin she'd never met. From the crown of his smoothly cropped yellow hair to the gleaming toes of his black regulation-issue shoes, he was the epitome of the perfect Space Academy graduate: standing straight but not stiff, eyes moving in full awareness of what each of his companions was doing, even in this moment of repose conveying a sense of dangerous alertness. Like Nancia, he was newly graduated and commissioned. And like her, he'd ranked high in his class but not first; first in technical grades, the databurst said, but only second overall because of an inexplicable low mark in Officer Fitness—whatever that might be.

When she'd first scanned the databurst, during Flix's silly computer game, Nancia had been looking forward to meeting her cousin Polyon. He was the only one of the group with whom she felt that she had much in common. As two High Families members trained for a life of service to Central, just setting out to meet their destinies, they should have felt an instant sense of kinship. Now, though, she felt strangely reluctant to introduce herself to Polyon. He was so tense, so watchful, as though he considered even this laughing group of other young people in the light of potential enemies.

And, she reminded herself, he had personally consumed at least two-thirds of the recently opened pouch of Stemerald, plus Central only knew what else before coming on board. No, it wasn't a good time to introduce herself and tell Polyon of their family connections. She would just have to wait.

"Hey, guys, look at the welcoming committee!" Blaize interrupted the chatter. He was staring past Nancia's titanium column, at the triple-screen display of the SPACED OUT game that Nancia had absentmindedly left up after Flix's abrupt departure. The concealed visual sensors between the screens showed Blaize's freckled, snub-nosed face alight with pure, uncomplicated joy.

Blaize moved slowly across the soft carpet until he sank into the empty pilot's chair that should have been reserved for Nancia's brawn. "This," he said reverently, "has got to be the biggest, best SPACED OUT I've ever seen. Two weeks will go like nothing with this setup to play with." The game control channels were still open, and as Blaize identified himself and took control of the brainship icon, Nancia let the underlying game program alter the brainship's course to zoom in on Troll Slayer's world. The brilliance of the graphic display drew the other passengers to look over Blaize's shoulder, and one by one, with half-ashamed comments, they let themselves be drawn into the game.

"Well, it beats watching a bunch of painbrains dose themselves silly in the clinic," Alpha murmured as she took a seat beside Blaize.

Nancia had hardly recovered from the shock of this callous comment when Darnell, too, joined the game. "I'll have to copy the mastergraphics off this program and have somebody install it on all OG Shipping's drones," he said, animating Troll Slayer. "Anybody know how to break the code protection?"

"I," said Polyon de Gras-Waldheim, "can break any computer security system ever installed." He favored Darnell with a slanting, enigmatic side glance. "If it's worth my while . . ."

Oh, you can, can you? thought Nancia. *We'll see about that.* Software game piracy wasn't exactly a major crime, but a newly commissioned Space Academy officer ought to have a stronger ethical sense than some commoner who hadn't had the benefit of a High Families upbringing and an Academy training. She felt distinctly less eager than she had been to introduce herself to her handsome cousin.

Polyon turned his head and treated Fassa del Parma y Polo, still lingering beside the door, to a brilliant smile. "Now you, little one, could make just about anything worth my while."

Fassa moved towards the game controls with a sinuous, gliding motion that riveted Blaize and Darnell's attention as well as Polyon's. "Forget it, yellowtop," she said in a voice as sweet as her words were stinging. "A second-rate Academy officer with a prison-planet posting doesn't have enough to keep me interested. I'm saving it for where it'll do me some good."

Nancia briefly shut down all the cabin's sensors. How had she gotten stuck with these greedy, amoral, spoiled brats? She had a good mind to put off introducing herself indefinitely. From the freedom of their comments, they must be assuming she was only a drone ship with no power to understand or act on anything but a limited set of direct commands.

But she would still need to know what they were up to. She opened one auditory channel and heard Blaize leading Darnell and Polyon in a raucous chorus of, "She never sold it, she just gave it away!" while Fassa glowered and slithered off to her cabin.

Nancia had the feeling this would be one of the longest two-week voyages any brainship had ever endured.

CHAPTER TWO

Polyon

Nancia watched curiously as Polyon de Gras-Waldheim sauntered into the central cabin. The other passengers were still sleeping off their departure-night Stemerald party, snoring and thrashing as the last doses of the stimulant worked its way out of their exhausted bodies. Polyon had recovered remarkably early. Like any good Academy graduate, he'd been up at 0600 ship's time, washed in the shower cubicle and dressed in his neatly pressed undress grays before presenting himself in public. Nancia had shut down visual sensors in the cabins to allow her passengers the privacy they would be expecting, but the auditory sensors brought her enough small sounds to enable her to follow Polyon through his early-morning routine.

Nancia caught her first glimpse of Polyon as he swung down the passageway to the central cabin. This was public space; she had no compunction about leaving all sensors activated here. And Polyon de Gras-Waldheim was certainly a treat for the sensors. Just a shade under two meters tall, with his golden hair ruthlessly cropped in the Academy bristle cut, he was a happy blend of the best in the Waldheim and de Gras family lines: Waldheim height and rugged strength, de Gras refinement and quick awareness.

Nancia felt a moment of regret. Polyon was a Space Academy graduate; he might have been her brawn.

A de Gras-Waldheim? jeered an inner voice. *What are you dreaming of, girl?* A young man who combined those two bloodlines could look *far* higher than command of a single brainship. He should have been destined for a staff position somewhere, being groomed for high command.

The short databurst of information about her passengers and their destinations didn't explain why, instead of joining a Fleet General staff, Polyon was headed out to be the technical overseer for a prison metachip plant in a remote subspace. *Oh, well, there must be some good reason for the assignment. Maybe there's more going on in Vega subspace than I realized.* Nancia remembered that interrupted newsbyte about Vega and her resolve to study it in depth, now that she was her own ship. *I'm Courier Service now; I'd better start keeping up with public affairs.* But just at the moment, watching her cousin was more interesting than pulling up files of old newsbeams.

Polyon glanced about the cabin and his body relaxed imperceptibly as he scanned the area; a human observer might not have noticed the slight change, but Nancia—by now scanning for muscle tension and autonomic nervous system response as well as for the usual visual and auditory cues—was immediately aware of his relaxation. That must be Academy training, that alertness upon entering any unfamiliar territory. She should have expected no less of one trained in the High Families' tradition of service; just as she should not have been surprised that Polyon wakened at a regulation hour, no matter what he'd been indulging in the night before. The other passengers might be soft and self-indulgent, but this one, at least, was a credit to his training. *That's the de Gras blood in him,* she thought with a trace of smugness; Daddy had always stressed the value of Nancia's connection, through her mother, with the House of de Gras.

Polyon glanced once more around the room—if he hadn't been a de Gras-Waldheim, Nancia would have described his second look as *furtive*—and then sat down, not in the pilot's chair facing the central console, but in one of the spectator seats to the side of the room. He nodded once, sharply, as if to say, "That's all right, then," and spoke in a low voice that no softperson could have heard.

"Computer, open master file, pass 47321-Aleithos-Hex242."

The automatic security system that guarded the ship's main computer acknowledged Polyon's command. Hardly believing what she observed, Nancia let the computer act without overriding it. How had Polyon learned the master file password? Perhaps there was a secret side to her mission, something only another member of the High Families could be trusted to know and to reveal at the proper time. That would explain Polyon's near-furtive way of approaching the cabin. It would also explain his crude behavior last night; naturally, as an undercover agent, he'd have to be sure to blend in with his fellow passengers.

Or . . . there might be no such explanation forthcoming. Now that he had master file access, Polyon was typing, moving the touchscreen icons, and issuing verbal commands in a rapid low stream that rivaled even a shellperson's multi-channel capacity. And he still hadn't acknowledged her as anything more than a droneship. What *was* going on? Nancia waited and watched, following Polyon's maneuverings through her computer system while her external sensors kept track of his bodily movements.

Piece of cake, Polyon thought as his fingers darted from keyboard to touch-screen, setting up his user account with system privileges that would allow him access to any data in the ship's computer. *Easy as debugging a kid's first program.* Now for the tricky stuff—persuading the security system to treat him as a privileged user on the Net. Once linked to that subspace-wide communications system, he would be able to find out anything he wanted to know about anybody who'd ever linked into the Net.

Voice commands wouldn't work here; just as well, he didn't want to be overheard by any of those smalltime snoops he was stuck with on this voyage. His fingers flashed over the keys, rattling out commands as fast as his excellent brain could analyze the results. Hmm, security block here . . . but having already granted himself user privileges on the ship's system, he could take a look at the object code in the blocking program itself. He could even "fix" it. "Here a patch, there a patch," Polyon hummed as he entered a slightly revised version of the object code, "everywhere a trap-door, dum-de-dum-de-dum." As the system accepted and ran the revised program, Polyon's humming switched to a triumphant version of, "I'm the man who broke the bank at Monte Carlo!"

Not quite accurate, of course; he intended to win far, far more than the proceeds of a single night's old-Earth-style gambling. He would show them—all of them. Starting with—but definitely not finishing with—the lamebrains who'd shipped out with him. Polyon knew why *he* was being posted to a second-rate assignment in a third-rate solar system—his memories skittered like frightened mice over the surface of that ugly scene with the Dean—but there must be some reasons why all these other pampered darlings of the High Families were going into semi-exile. He would start by finding those little secrets, and then . . . well, then maybe even these rich brats could be useful in the Grand Plan.

And after them . . . the Nyota system. All of Vega subspace. *Central.* Why not? Polyon thought, dazzled by the grandeur of his own desires. If there was one thing he'd learned while he was growing up, it was that you could get away with nearly anything if you did most of it while people weren't watching and used your charm when they did watch.

And where charm didn't work . . . there were other means of persuasion. Polyon smiled grimly and tapped into Alpha bint Hezra-Fong's med school files.

What *could* Polyon be doing? Nancia watched and waited as he redefined the ship's security system, reached out to the Net, scanned his fellow-passengers' files. Ought she to stop him? Discretion was the first thing a Courier Service brainship learned, the first and last component of duty. She hadn't been briefed on what to do with a passenger who started manipulating the Net as if it were part of his personal comsystem. He was redefining the security parameters now . . . no matter, she could change those back whenever she chose. So far he hadn't touched her personal data areas, didn't show any signs of knowing that her synaptic connections to the ship's computer allowed her to follow everything he was doing.

Could it be that he really thought her a drone ship? Maybe not. At least, he wasn't sure. Now that he was through playing with the Net, Polyon sent out an exploratory tendril of code to report on other activities linked into the ship's computer . . . a patch that would reveal the exact location and extent of Nancia's connections within the ship.

A little late to check that, my lad! Didn't the Space Academy teach you to look for ambushes before *you started maneuvers?* Self-protection was an automatic response, more deeply ingrained even than discretion. Nancia closed down pathways and redefined access codes in a single, instinctive wave of activity that left Polyon staring at a blank screen and touching a keyboard that no longer responded to his search commands.

Darnell

Darnell Overton-Glaxely moaned gently as he caught sight of his puffy face, a distorted reflection in the polished curve of synthalloy along the ship's central corridor. It was too early in the morning to face mirrors, especially curving ones that made his reflection swell and shrink and ripple like waves on the damned ocean. Darnell moaned again and reminded himself that the artificial gravity of space was practically like being on Earth; it was only his imagination making him feel sick. This was really nothing like being aboard one of the old-style oceangoing vessels that had been the start of OG Shipping, back when they were still a planetbound local corporation. His old man had made him go on one of those monsters once, with some crap about remembering the family's roots. Darnell had taken a lot more crap from the old man when he puked his guts out before the ship left harbor.

Well, there wouldn't be any more of *that*! Dear Papa was history now, and so was the unexplained space-station collapse that had killed him and left OG Shipping in the hands of its directors until Darnell finished school. And last night's Stemerald debauch was also history—if only he could convince his queasy stomach and pounding head of that!

It wasn't fair that he should suffer like this after what had only been a perfectly reasonable indulgence to celebrate the end of schooling and the start of his new career. A pity neither of the girls had seen fit to continue the celebration in the logical manner. Well, they had two weeks to planetfall; they'd come around and see his attractions soon enough. After all, it wasn't as if he had any serious competition on this droneship. De Gras-Waldheim was handsome enough, but a cold fish if Darnell had ever seen one. Something frightening about him, with those intense blue eyes burning like dry ice under the stiff Academy haircut. As for the Medoc boy, Blass or Blaze or whatever his name was, no girl was going to waste time on a kid with a face like a friendly gargoyle. No, it would be old Darnell to the rescue again, the only man on board with the social skills to entertain two lovely ladies all the way to their destination planets around Nyota ya Jaha.

And he could hear sounds in the central cabin. Was one of the girls up and about already? Darnell sucked in his gut, threw his shoulders as far back as they would go, and glanced at his reflection in the synthalloy wall once again. His face wasn't really soft and puffy like that; he told himself; it was a trick of the distorted reflection. Made him look middle-aged and flabby and tired. Nonsense. He was the handsome young heir to OG shipping and he was fit to take on anybody or anything. . . .

But not, maybe, that cold fish, Polyon de Gras-Waldheim. Darnell clutched at the doorway and tried to stop his impulsive movement into the central cabin. His legs kept going while his arms tried to haul him back.

"Oh, come on in, OG," Polyon said impatiently, his back to the door. "Don't just cling to the doorframe waving your tentacles like a seasick jellyfish."

Seasick.

Jellyfish.

Darnell gulped down a wave of nausea and reminded himself again that space travel on a grav-enhanced drone was *not* like being on an actual moving, swaying, shifting oldstyle sea vessel.

"What are you doing?"

Polyon released the chair controls and spun slowly round to face Darnell, long limbs relaxed as if to emphasize his comfort in this environment. "Just . . . playing games," he said with a queer smile. "Just a few little games to pass the time."

"What'd you do, crash the SPACED OUT gameset so badly you lost the screens?"

"Something like that," Polyon agreed. "You can help me start it up again, if you like."

It was the closest thing to a friendly overture Darnell had heard from Polyon since they met the previous night. Maybe, he thought forgivingly, maybe the poor guy didn't know *how* to make friends. Coming from a stiff-backed upper-crust lot like the de Gras-Waldheims, spending his life at military boarding schools, you

couldn't expect him to have the *savoir vivre* and easy social manners
that Darnell prided himself on displaying. Well, he'd help old
Polyon out, be his friend on this little jaunt.

"Sure thing," he said, walking on into the room with a careful
soft step that didn't jar his aching head. He sank into one of the
cushioned passenger chairs. "Nothing to it. I used to play this stuff
all the time in prep school. Tell you what—if I help you get into
the computer, maybe you'll help me get into something else?" He
winked laboriously at Polyon.

"What exactly did you have in mind?" The man didn't have a
clue how to make light conversation.

"Two of us," Darnell explained cheerfully, tapping away at the
console keys. "Two of them. The black one is more your size. But
I need a strategy to get into the del Parma skirt's pants. Tactics,
maneuvers, advance and retreat—Got any suggestions?" Not,
Darnell thought, that he really needed any help, but there was
nothing like a round of good, bawdy male-to-male bonding talk
to cement a friendship. And since Polyon evidently wanted to be
friends, Darnell was more than ready to meet him halfway.

"I'm afraid you're on your own there," Polyon said distantly.
"I've . . . never had occasion to study the problem." He flicked an
invisible speck of dust off his pressed sleeve and affected to study
the SPACED OUT screens as Darnell brought them back to fill
the walls of the cabin.

The implication was clear; he'd never *needed* to work out tactics with the ladies. Well, of course not. With the de Gras-Waldheim
name and fortune behind him—and that muscle-bound, oversized
physique—still, he had no call to sneer at somebody who was just
trying to be friendly. Darnell glowered at the console and tapped
the commands that would set the game at—hmm, not Level 10,
his reflexes weren't quite up to the interactive holowarriors just
yet. Level 6. That should be high enough to scramble Polyon's
moves and let him see what it was like dealing with an expert.

"It's a new version," Polyon said in surprise. "I don't remember that asteroid belt."

"I'll bet five credits there's a clue to the Hidden Horrors of
Holmdale somewhere in the new asteroids," Darnell offered.

"No bet on that. But I'll lay you five credits that if it's there,
I'll find it first. Choose your icon!"

Darnell chose one of the play icons displayed along the bottom of the central screen. He always liked to be Bonecrush, the cyborg monster who stalked the lower tunnels of the labyrinth but occasionally blasted out into space with his secretly installed jetpacks and personal force shield. Polyon, he noticed with pleasure, was taking the icon for Thingberry the Martian Mage, a wimp of a character if there ever was one. This game should be over in no time.

"So what brings you out to the Nyota system?" Polyon asked after a few minutes of seemingly idle maneuvering and pointless commands.

Darnell scowled at the screen. How had Thingberry managed to surround two-thirds of the asteroid belt with a charm of impenetrability? Very well, he would let Bonecrush turn around and use his internal jetpacks as a weapon; that should blast through sneaky Thingberry's magic. "Taking up the old inheritance," he replied as he tapped in the commands that would give Bonecrush maximum blasting power. "OG Shipping, you know. Can't think why old Cousin Wigran moved the firm's headquarters out to Vega subspace, but I'm sure he'll explain everything when I get there."

"If he can," Polyon agreed. "You have that much faith in him?"

Darnell stealthily maneuvered Bonecrush into range. That idiot Polyon was looking at him, not at the screen; he could get away with murder if he could keep Polyon's attention away from the game for a few more seconds.

"What d'you mean?" he asked, not really listening for the answer. "Why shouldn't I have faith in Wigran?"

Polyon looked shocked, and for a moment Darnell was afraid he'd noticed Bonecrush's moves on the central game screen. "My dear chap! You mean you haven't heard? *Decom* it," he cursed in a low vicious tone. "I didn't realize—Look, Darnell, I shouldn't be the one to tell you this. Haven't you been paying attention to the newsbytes from Vega?"

"Management bores me," Darnell told him. "I'll be perfectly happy to draw the profits from the company and let Cousin Wigran keep running the store." His hands were resting on the key that would activate Bonecrush's jet packs. Any minute now he'd execute a controlled power surge that should blast a hole right through Thingberry's defenses. But he wanted Polyon to be watching in the moment of defeat, not babbling on about some boring accountant's trial in the Vega system.

"Well, I suppose you'd have to know pretty soon anyway," Polyon was saying now. "I hate like hell to be the one to tell you, though." He was watching Darnell's face more closely than he'd ever looked at the game screens.

"Tell me what?" For the first time Darnell felt a chill of apprehension creep over him.

"It's all been coming out in the trial," Polyon said. "That accountant who was skimming his clients' credits to play Lotto-Roids? OG Shipping was one of his biggest accounts. And your cousin Wigran knew exactly what the fellow was doing. He even helped him—for a share in the cash. Together, they've gambled away more than ninety per cent of OG Shipping's assets. I'm afraid all you're going to inherit on Bahati is one over-age AI drone and a bunch of debts."

Darnell's sweaty fingers slipped and punched the power key harder than he'd intended. Bonecrush's jet packs released their maximum thrust. The blast rebounded harmlessly off Thingberry's invisible charm-shield and propelled Bonecrush, too depleted of power to activate his personal force-shield, into the blackness of deep space. His cyborg body exploded into a million stars of synthalloy debris.

"Wow," Polyon said, finally glancing at the dazzling light effects on the screen. "This *is* a great game! Will you look at those graphics? What is it, a supernova?"

"Me," said Darnell Overton-Glaxely. A gentleman knew when to bite the bullet. "I owe you five credits."

Blaize

Oh, no, not another one!

Nancia briefly shut down all her internal sensors as Blaize Armontillado-Perez y Medoc stirred in his cabin. She had come to the conclusion that her passengers were most bearable when they were sleeping it off. If only she could flood all their cabins with sleepgas and keep them unconscious until they reached the Nyota ya Jaha system. . . . Nancia caught herself in mid-thought. She was becoming as bad as they were! How could she even think such a thing? Hadn't she made perfect marks in all her Integrity and Shell Ethics classes? She should have been doubly guarded, by family heritage and Academy training, against even imagining such a betrayal of her ideals.

There was nothing to stop her from leaving her internal sensors inactive until they reached Nyota ya Jaha, though. Nancia considered this briefly before deciding against it. True, her passengers wouldn't notice anything, since they already assumed she was a droneship programmed to carry them in privacy to their destination. And it was also true that she would rather perform the Singularity transformations that carried them through decomposition space without the irritating distraction of these . . . *brats.* But she shrank from the idea of spending days, more than a week, in the isolation of space, with nothing to see but the wheeling stars, no other brain to communicate with—for if she opened a beam to Central, her cousin Polyon, with his propensity for snooping through the ship's computer systems, would be bound to notice the comm activity. Brainships were as human as any softpersons; Nancia knew that it would be unwise to expose herself for so long to the strain of partial sensory deprivation.

Besides, she wanted to know what her passengers were up to.

When Nancia reactivated the central cabin's sensors, Darnell was already stalking down the hall to his cabin and Polyon, lips taut with rage, was about to follow him. "I don't care for that name," he told Blaize.

Nancia hastily scanned the cabin's automatic recording system. Blaize had been teasing his cousin by calling him "Polly." Academy records on Polyon de Gras-Waldheim mentioned this nickname as the basis for several vicious fights that had occurred during Polyon's Academy training, including one in which Polyon's opponent was so badly injured that he had to drop out of the officer training program. Witnesses had attested that Polyon went on twisting the boy's bones and listening to them splinter long after his opponent was begging for mercy.

Following that incident, Polyon's file had been flagged with warning signals that would forever preclude his being assigned to a responsible military post . . . and he had been verbally notified of this decision in an interview with retired General Mack Erricott, Dean of the Space Academy—

What was she doing? Nancia closed down all her information channels momentarily. Where had all this private information come from? She reopened her channels and traced the dataflow. It came through the Net, and she shouldn't have had access to any of this material; it came from the Space Academy's private personnel files. Somehow the Net had responded to her momentary curiosity by opening up material that should have been shielded under the Dean's personal password.

After a moment's confusion, Nancia realized what had happened. Polyon's meddling with the ship's security system had extended to some very sophisticated tampering in the Net itself. He had, in effect, defined Nancia as the node of origin for a system controller with unlimited powers to access and change files and codes in any computer on the Net. Nancia's instinctive intervention had then made the "System Controller" identity unavailable to Polyon himself . . . but had left the node definition in place, allowing her access to all the files he had scanned, and a great deal more besides.

Nancia felt as embarrassed as if she'd been caught peeking into an anesthetized classmate's open shell during synaptic remodeling . . . the invasion of privacy was that great. *I didn't realize what I was doing!* She defended herself, and hastily erased the superuser node definition before she could be tempted into looking at anybody else's private files.

But she couldn't forget the shocking and disturbing things she'd just read about Polyon. And she was relieved that he'd left the central cabin to Blaize, stalking back to his own cabin in a pose of offended dignity far more impressive than Darnell's pout.

Blaize looked directly at Nancia's titanium column and winked. "Bet you thought he was going to beat me up, didn't you?"

Nancia responded without thinking to this, the first direct address she'd received since her passengers boarded and she lifted off from Central. "I hope you weren't counting on me to protect you!"

Blaize gave a soft, satisfied chuckle. "Not at all, dear lady. Until this moment I wasn't even sure what—or who—you were." He lifted an imaginary cap and mimed an extravagant bow. "Allow me to introduce myself," he murmured as he straightened again. "Blaize Armontillado-Perez y Medoc. And you?"

It was too late to retreat into the silence that had protected her so far. Nancia gave a mental shrug—no more than a quick flashing of connectors—and decided that she might as well converse with the brat. She'd been starting to get lonely, anyway; the isolation of deep space was too great a contrast after her years of comfortable, constant multi-channel input and output with her classmates in Laboratory Schools. "XN-935," Nancia said grudgingly. And then, because the call letters seemed inadequate, "Nancia Perez y de Gras."

"A cousin, a veritable cousin!" Blaize crowed with unabashed delight. "So tell me, cousin, what's a nice girl like you doing convoying a rabble of riffraff like us?"

The question was uncomfortably close to Nancia's own opinion of her passengers. "How did you know I was a brainship?" she countered.

"The liftoff procedures *could* have been performed by an AI drone. But somehow I didn't really think the Medoc clan and the rest of our loving families would have sent us off to jaunt through Singularity on automatic. Wouldn't be fitting to the dignity of the High Families, y'know, to have a packet of metachips responsible for our safety instead of a human brain."

"You don't have much respect for your family, do you? No wonder they're sending you off to a fringe world. They're probably afraid you'll embarrass them."

For a moment Blaize's freckled face looked cold and hard and infinitely sad. Then, so quickly that a human eye would hardly have recognized the brief betrayal, he grinned and flashed a salute at Nancia's column. "Absolutely. Just one minor correction. They're not *afraid* I'll embarrass them. They're bloody sure of it!" Pulling out one of the padded chairs, he seated himself cross-legged in the middle of the cabin, arms folded, and beamed at Nancia's column as though he hadn't a care in the world. She retrieved the image of his face a moment earlier and projected it on interior space, comparing the bleak-eyed young man of the recording with the smiling boy in the cabin. What could be hurting him so deeply? Against her will, she felt a twinge of sympathy for this spoiled scion, this disgrace to the High Families.

"And do you intend to?" she asked in carefully neutral tones.

"What? Oh—disgrace them?" Blaize shrugged a little too gracefully. Nancia began to wonder how many of his seemingly casual gestures were rehearsed. "No, it's too late now. Sure, I had fantasies when I was a kid. But I'm a little old for running away now, don't you think?"

"What—to join the circus?"

For another split second, the mobile face before her matched

the bleak image she'd stored. "No. The Space Academy. Actually,"
Blaize said in a voice as carefully neutral as Nancia's own, "I used
to think I'd train as a brawn—Don't laugh; it was a kid's idea.
But I never could imagine anything better than working with a
brainship. To fly between the stars, saving lives and worlds,
partnered with a living ship to learn the dance of space. . . ." His
voice cracked on the last word. "I told you. Kids have dumb ideas."

"It doesn't seem like such a dumb idea to me," Nancia told him.
"Why did you give it up? Did somebody tell you brawns have to
be six feet tall and built like . . . like Polyon de Gras-Waldheim?"

"Give it up!" Blaize echoed. "I didn't give it up. I ran away three
times. The first time I actually got into the Space Academy, too.
Took the open tests, forged papers saying I was a war orphan, won
a scholarship. It was three weeks before my tutor found me." The
momentary, unguarded joy in his face as he remembered those
weeks wrenched at Nancia's heart. "The second and third times
they knew where I'd go; there was a squad of House Medoc private guards waiting for me at the Academy."

"Your family seems to have been rather violently against the
idea."

Blaize's mobile, ugly face twisted into a sneer. "Wouldn't do for
folks in our position, y'know. Not quite the thing. My cousin Jillia
is in line to be the next Planetary Governor of Kaza-uri, and my
buddy Henequin—m'father's best friend's son," Blaize explained
parenthetically, "is already in charge of the Vega branch of Planetary Technical Aid. A son who's in brawn training doesn't quite
match up with those stellar accomplishments for after-dinner
bragging."

"I wonder if my family feels that way," Nancia said. Was that
why Daddy hadn't made time for her graduation?

"Shouldn't think so. They sent you to Laboratory Schools, didn't
they?"

"They didn't," Nancia said, "have many options. I would not have
survived a normal birth."

"Oh. Well. Anyway," Blaize said carefully, "I don't think your
branch of the family is *quite* as snobbish as ours. And neither one
can beat the de Gras-Waldheims for exclusiveness. Polly got to go
to the Academy, but he was supposed to turn into a general, not
a lowly space jockey; I can't imagine what he's doing on his way
to administer a metachip plant on Shemali. Must have been some

scandal at the Academy. I thought I knew all the family gossip, but whatever he got into, they hushed it up exceedingly well. *You* probably have access to the files, though—or—anyway, I bet you could find out if you wanted to."

"I imagine," Nancia said, "they are in need of his technical expertise." She felt no impulse whatever to share the details of Polyon's Academy problems with this gossipy boy. Didn't the High Families train their softperson children in any kind of discretion? First Polyon, using his computer expertise to hack through security checks and find out the other passengers' secrets, and now Blaize, turning his charm on her to the same end.

"You don't approve of gossip, do you?" Blaize guessed. "All right. Have it your way. You will be a suitably discreet Courier Service brainship and a credit to the family, and I'll be a nice little PTA administrator on Angalia and try not to disgrace my side of the family, and we can all drift on in boredom forever."

"Planetary Technical Aid isn't so bad," Nancia told him. "My sister Jinevra is an area administrator, and she's only twenty-nine. You could rise rapidly—"

"From *Angalia*?" Blaize's eyebrows shot up like red exclamation marks, giving his face a look of comical astonishment. "Dear Cousin Nancia, you really *don't* pry, do you? If you'd read my file you would know better than to try and stir up my ambitions for Angalia. The sum total of civilization there consists of one PTA office, one corycium mine, and a bunch of humanoid natives with the collective IQ of a zucchini. A *small* zucchini. It's amazing they even qualify for Planetary Aid; somebody must have filled out the FCF wrong, and whoever later determined that they didn't have ISS forgot to correct the PTA data. The wheels of the bureaucracy grind on and on. . . . So here I go to Angalia, less than the dust beneath old Henequin's chariot wheels."

"You should do well enough," Nancia said. "You've certainly got the jargon of the bureaucracy down pat." She scanned her data files for translations of the initials Blaize had used. PTA was Planetary Technical Aid, of course, and FCF turned out to be a First Contact Form, and ISS—ah. Intelligent Sentient Status. Nancia had learned all the regulations for dealing with alien sentients in Basic Courier Diplomacy and Development 101, but she wasn't used to hearing the abbreviations tossed about so casually. Daddy, when he visited and told her about his work, was always careful to give each bureaucratic office its full name, each official his full title.

It was possible, Nancia thought, involuntarily contrasting Blaize's darting, hummingbird speech patterns with Daddy's measured delivery—it was possible that her father, Javier Perez y de Gras, was just a bit stuffy. No. That was ridiculous. She was getting corrupted by her passengers, straying into non-regulation and non-approved ways of thinking. Heaven knew what indiscretions Blaize would lure her into if they continued this conversation.

"Do you play SPACED OUT?" She filled the three wall-size screens with the displays that had tempted Polyon and Darnell into the game. "It'll have to be solitaire, I'm afraid."

"Why?"

"I can't *not* know the underlying structure," Nancia apologized. "You see, the game's part of my memory banks now. And I've never learned your softperson trick of selectively turning off awareness." She wasn't about to try, either. But she could, she told Blaize, make the solitaire game a little more challenging by redefining the maze of tunnels and Singularity nodes that connected one part of the SPACED OUT galaxy with another.

"Rules that change as you play?" Blaize hummed in delight. "Great idea. Polly will hate it, too."

That thought seemed to increase his pleasure in the game. And while he happily manipulated a solitary play icon through the traps and surprises set up by the designer, Nancia contemplated the vast loneliness of the stars around them and the distance she must travel before she could make private contact with another shellperson.

CHAPTER THREE

Alpha

When she awoke after the graduation "party," Alpha bint Hezra-Fong made her way to the main cabin and found her traveling companions engaged in one of those silly role-playing games. Medical school and a demanding research program had never given her the time to waste on such frivolities. *But there might be plenty of time where she was going.* Alpha pushed that thought to the back of her mind. She would find something productive to do; she always did. She might even find a way to continue her research.

For the present, her companions watched the game screens, and Alpha watched them. They were considerably more amusing than the game; especially Blaize and Polyon, stalking one another in an ongoing verbal battle. Blaize was obviously dying to know why someone like Polyon, destined by family and training for a high command post, was being sent out to start his career on a remote planet of no real military importance.

Alpha rather wanted to know the answer to that little puzzle herself. As part of the powerful and high-ranking de Gras-Waldheim clan, Polyon would seem like a good person to cultivate. And in some ways, Alpha thought, it would be a pleasure to make friends with Polyon. He was certainly the most attractive

man on this ship, the only one worth her time. But if he'd disgraced himself at the Academy and been disowned by his family,
she couldn't afford the risk of getting close to him. Some of that
scandal—whatever it could have been—might rub off on her. And
she couldn't afford any more blots on her record, not after the
way the medical school had overreacted to that trivial business
about her research protocols. No, she'd wait and find out a little
more about Polyon before she moved on him. And she'd let Blaize
Armontillado-Perez y Medoc, a born gadfly if ever there was one,
do the finding out.

"Shemali's such an *obscure* spot," Blaize hinted, "for a brilliant
young man on his way up."

Polyon stared into the display of distant mountain peaks for a
moment before he answered. Alpha could see a muscle twitching
in his jaw. *As well as all the muscles everywhere else . . . those Academy undress grays don't leave much to the imagination! Why doesn't
he just break the little pest in half?* But Polyon retained his control. "Yes, it's nearly as godforsaken as Angalia, isn't it? My brilliant little cousin-on-his-way-up," he added remotely.

"Ah, but we all know I'm the black sheep of the family," Blaize
countered, "a modern-day remittance man. You, on the other hand,
are supposed to be the pride of the de Gras-Waldheims, the last
and finest flower of those entwined family trees, bursting with
military potential and—umm—hybrid vigor."

"At least the Academy taught me not to mix my metaphors,"
Polyon said.

"It must be some super-secret military base," Blaize decided
aloud. "Nothing less would suit for a de Gras-Waldheim's first
posting. So classified even the droneship doesn't know why you're
going there."

Alpha noticed that his eyes flicked towards the central titanium
column as though he expected an answer through the ship's speakers. Well, she conceded, it was as likely that the drone would take
part in the conversation as that Polyon would tell his cousin
anything he didn't want to. Likelier.

She yawned and fiddled with the joyball, rolling the SPACED
OUT display from the Mountains of Momentum to Asteroid Hall
and back. This conversation was *boring*. Polyon wasn't going to
tell them anything. He wasn't even going to smash his cousin into
the wall. No information, no amusement. Alpha was about ready

to go back to her cabin and take a nap. There was little enough else to do on this stupid droneship.

"No secret military plans," Polyon said. "No secrets at all, Blaize, sorry to disappoint you. But if it'll shut you up, I'll try to explain what I'm going to do in terms you'll be able to understand. . . . Leaving out the technical terms, let's just say that I'm going to manage the metachip plant attached to the Shemali prison. Governor Lyautey is out of his depth. He knows how to run a prison. He doesn't know anything about metachip manufacturing. And the productivity record shows it. I'm going to set things straight, that's all."

Alpha sighed. The man's discretion was so perfect, she almost believed him; except that Blaize was right, it didn't compute for a de Gras-Waldheim to take a job as a factory manager.

"Ahh, *now* I understand," Blaize almost purred. "The governor is to take lessons from you in the finer points of chip manufacture, and you're to take lessons from him in the finer points of . . . ahhh . . . torture and degradation of prisoners? Or do I have it wrong? Maybe it's the other way round."

Polyon smiled. "If the governor wants an expert in nagging prisoners to death, I'll advise him to send for you."

"What a pity, though," Blaize prodded. "All that military training going to waste. Seems the family could have arranged something a little better for you. Unless there's something you're not telling us about your Academy record. . . ."

Polyon's perfectly shaped ears turned red and Alpha raised her head, suddenly alert. The flush of rage didn't improve Polyon's looks, but that was all right with her; if anything, his face in repose was a little too perfect. And now he looked ready to kill somebody—or tell something. Alpha mentally applauded. Blaize had finally hit on a nerve!

"And what better position might the family have arranged for *you*, dear cousin?" Polyon inquired. "Save a little of that pity for yourself. When your posting at Angalia is finished—if you ever do get off that godforsaken planet—you'll have nothing but your savings. Granted, they should be considerable, since there's nothing to spend money on there, but how much can a PTA-17's monthly salary add up to?"

"About as much as a factory supervisor's, I should imagine. Face the facts, Polyon. We've both been screwed over by our respective families. For once you're in the same boat I'm in, regardless of that pretty face and stiff back. I know why I'm here. What I'd dearly like to know is why they did it to you."

Alpha, too. She leaned forward, tensing slightly in anticipation of the answer, but Polyon chose to answer the first part of Blaize's goading speech rather than the second. "Oh, but I've no intention of trying to make it on my savings, dear coz."

"What, then?"

"Metachips," Polyon said meditatively, "are very expensive. Not to mention that they're in short supply."

"Tell me something I don't know," Blaize invited him.

"I plan," said Polyon, "to . . . improve on the current rationing system."

Unnoticed in her corner, Alpha nodded thoughtfully. Polyon had a good point. Metachips were exceedingly scarce and costly, and for good reason. The metachip manufacturing process involved at least three different acids so hazardous to the environment that most planets refused to harbor the plants, despite the unquestioned financial benefits. Shemali, inhospitable, cursed with the perpetual biting north wind that had given the planet its name, with its one land mass dedicated to a maximum-security prison, was the only major metachip manufacturing site in existence; Shemali, where nothing you did could make the environment much worse, and where the workers bought their lives one day at a time by laboring in the metachip plant.

Because who else could you use, in the final analysis, but convicts already under sentence of death? One of the acids involved, when used in the quantities required for manufacturing, released a gas whose effects on human tissue were slow, painful, deadly . . . and so far, irreversible. Alpha was an expert on those effects; her research at Central Med had been devoted to trying various drug therapies to reverse the effects of Ganglicide. She might have had a major paper out of the work if the school's Ethics Committee hadn't got so upset about her testing methods . . . Alpha clamped her lips down on the flare of anger that possessed her. That was all in the past. The present was Polyon and his plan, which he was explaining to Blaize with a wealth of patronizing detail about the adverse effects on the economy of the present rationing system.

"It's ridiculous to have metachips distributed by a committee of old men and do-gooders," he declared. "Sure, the military is entitled to first cut at the chips, but after our applications have been satisfied, the remaining chips ought to go where they'll do the most good."

"I thought that was the object of the rationing system," Blaize remarked. "Companies get Social Utility Marks for their intended use of the metachips, and the chips are distributed in proportion to the SUM. What's wrong with that?"

"Unrealistic," Polyon said promptly. "They're using chips for single-body operations like repairing kidneys or replacing damaged spinal nerves, when the same chips could go into, oh, applications that thousands of people could use at once. Dorg Jesen would pay *millions* for a handful of metas and a promise of steady supply."

Blaize began to laugh. "*Dorg Jesen? The feelieporn king? That's your idea of a SUM?*"

"Millions," Polyon repeated himself. "And if you don't believe I can think of a socially useful function for all that cash—"

"That," said Blaize, "I can believe. But just how do you think you'll sneak the feelieporn application past the advisory board?"

"I see no reason why the matter should ever come before the board. QA testing for the metachips is one of the areas Governor Lyautey asked me to supervise. Disposal of the chips that fail QA will presumably also fall within my duties." He looked so smug that Alpha felt the need to puncture his self-satisfaction.

"I wouldn't plan on selling defective chips to Dorg Jesen if I were you," she interrupted Polyon's gloating. "He's been known to rearrange the features of people who interfered with his business." Her shiver wasn't assumed; one of her first tasks in med research had been to diagram the facial injuries on a girl who'd refused Jesen's offer of employment. Alpha had eventually made a complete inventory of the damage, together with holosims of the girl's face before the attack and as she would look after plastifilm had replaced what used to be living flesh.

Eventually.

After she rushed out of the lab theater and threw up in front of the senior surgical advisor.

At the time, she'd thought it would be the most humiliating thing that could ever happen to her in med school.

Remembering, she barely heard Polyon's bland reply that he had no intention of selling defective chips to anybody.

Blaize gave a low, admiring whistle. "Of course. Fiddle the QA parameters one way for Governor Lyautey's reports, the other way for sales, and who knows what happens to the metachips in between? You could make a fortune in five years!"

"I intend to," said Polyon.

He was really *much* too self-satisfied, especially for a man who'd left the Academy under some kind of a cloud that he was afraid or ashamed to discuss. Alpha decided that it would be doing humanity a favor to wipe that smug smile off Lieutenant de Gras-Waldheim's face. He really shouldn't smirk like that. Spoiled his looks.

"I do hope you'll still be able to enjoy your fortune by then," she cooed sweetly at Polyon. "Better stay out of the way of your convict laborers, though. Nasty accidents are *so* easy to arrange in a D-class facility, aren't they? But don't let it worry you. Even if you do get a little spot of Ganglicide on your precious skin, I'm sure Governor Lyautey will rush you to Bahati for medical treatment. And you're lucky to have an expert in Ganglicide therapy right there at the Summerlands clinic."

"You." Polyon nodded stiffly. "That was to be your thesis topic, wasn't it?"

Alpha suppressed a start. How had Polyon known of her research? Oh, well, the High Families were such an inbred group. Probably her aunt Leona had been gossiping over the chai tables. But Polyon wouldn't know much more than the title of her projected paper; the symptoms of Ganglicide exposure were hardly fit material for chai-table gossip. She relaxed and prepared to enjoy her project of wiping that superior smirk off Polyon's face.

"I had some success with chemical treatments for the skin decay," she told him. "Halted the disintegrating process, anyway. I'm afraid we couldn't do much to reverse the effects, though. The skin shreds like paper and turns sort of blue-green. And it spreads very rapidly. If you get a drop of Ganglicide on one finger while you're on Shemali, your arm will look like it's been through a paper shredder by the time the shuttle delivers you to Bahati. *Do* try to keep it away from your pretty face."

Polyon's handsome features betrayed only slight uneasiness, but there was a knowing look in his eyes. "You—had to interrupt your research rather suddenly, didn't you?"

Alpha silently cursed all interfering, gossiping old relatives and friends. Never mind. "More's the pity," she sighed. "I was just getting into the most *interesting* cases. You know, when Ganglicide goes into its gaseous form it attacks nerves and brain synapses. Has much the same effects on them that it has on the skin; we dissected a really fascinating case, a senior assembly tech from Shemali, as it happens. The inside of his head looked like a wet blue sponge. Of course, by the time the Ganglicide got that far he was too far gone to know or care what was happening to him. A mercy, really. Not that we'll ever really know how long he felt the pain. Ganglicide goes straight to the pain receptors, you know; we can't block the effects with drugs. And towards the end he was screaming continuously. Like an animal dying under torture." She licked her lips and regarded Polyon. He was standing quite still, two fingers beating a nervous tattoo on the command panel behind him. The dance of his fingertips on the sensitive pressure pads made the SPACED OUT screen on the far side of the room shift back and forth jerkily, displaying alternate images of deep space and of a flaming labyrinth where molten lava menaced the hapless play icons.

"If you're nice to me," Alpha added, "I'll promise to kill you before the Ganglicide eats out your brains. No human being should have to die like that."

"Oh, I'll be nice to you," Polyon said. His voice was still even; he thrust off from the control panel with two fingers and floated across the room. As he came closer, Alpha recognized the look in his eyes. Not frightened. Wary. Like a hunter waiting for his quarry to burst from cover. And as he reached out to encircle her wrist with strong, blunt fingers, the look changed to a light of triumph. "I think we can be *very* nice to one another, lovely Alpha. It's so kind of you to take an interest in my career." His voice changed on the last words, mocking, savagely amused. "But enough about me. Tell us about yourself, why don't you?" He gestured towards Darnell and Fassa, floating through the open door to join them. "We'd all like to hear about your interrupted research. And why one of the school's brightest young medical researchers chose to donate five years of public service to an obscure clinic on Bahati. You're too modest, Alpha."

Alpha tossed her head and tried to pull away from Polyon, but he was too strong for her. "There's nothing to tell, really. I was tired—wanted a change of scene. That's all."

"*Is* it?" Polyon murmured. "Funny. The way I heard it, there were some other people who wanted to change your scene. The news-nibblers never beamed the story, did they? Can't have scandals about a High Families girl going out as entertainment bytes. But I fancy our friends on board here would find the story *very* entertaining."

Alpha stared up at Polyon, looking for a hint of compassion in the sharp planes of his face and the ice-blue eyes that had seemed so attractive a moment ago. "I did nothing to be ashamed of," she whispered. "The tradition of scientific experiments—"

"Does *not* include testing Ganglicide on unwitting subjects." His voice was so low the others could not hear it.

"Charity cases," Alpha defended herself. "Street bums. Some of them were so far gone on Blissto they didn't even know what was happening to them. They were incurable—nothing but an expense to the state as long as they lived. I did them a favor, making sure their lives ended for some purpose."

"Somehow," Polyon murmured, "I don't think the court would have seen it that way. But then, you never did come to trial, did you? Hezra clan and Fong tribe wouldn't let that happen. Private settlement in the med school offices, records sealed."

"How—did you find out?" Alpha gasped. He was very close to her now, his voice the subtlest vibration of sound from lips that almost brushed her cheek. The raw power of his will and his anger wrapped about her. She felt weak from the spine out. His smile made her shiver.

"That's my little secret," he told her, still smiling. His face and gestures might have been those of a courtship; Alpha realized that the others in the room might imagine they were flirting. That was a relief. Anything was preferable to having her humiliation made public before these people who were to be her constant companions for the next two weeks—having them see her as the disgraced failure she was, instead of the successful young researcher with a social conscience she pretended to be. "You were lucky to get off with five years of community service on Bahati, weren't you?" Polyon commented, stroking her cheek with his free hand. "A commoner would have been doing time. *Hard* time. Who knows, gorgeous, you might even have wound up on Shemali—getting a chance to check out Ganglicide at first hand, so to speak. Wouldn't our innocent little friends love to hear the story?"

But he was still speaking in a low voice, head partially turned away from Fassa and Blaize and Darnell, who had grouped together in the far corner of the cabin and were pretending deep interest in a round of SPACED OUT.

"What—do you want?"

"Cooperation," Polyon said. "Only a little—cooperation."

Blindly, drowning in a sea of air that somehow gave her nothing to breathe, Alpha turned her face up to meet Polyon's parted lips.

"Not that sort of cooperation," Polyon told her, laughing gently, "not yet." His eyes measured her with a cold glance that made her more afraid than ever—and, somehow, more excited too. "Maybe later, if you're a good girl. You were too uppity before, you know that, Alpha? Now you're the way I like my women. Quiet. And respectful. Stay that way, and we won't have to discuss any— ah—painful subjects with the others. Come with me and follow my lead. That's all I expect of you—for now."

Submissive, head bowed, Alpha drifted towards the three SPACED OUT gamers in Polyon's wake. They were still pretending to be totally involved in the game, but she felt sure they had avidly witnessed her humiliation.

She would pay them back. That was certain, she vowed. Fassa, Darnell, Blaize—they would all learn not to laugh at her.

She didn't even think of retaliating against Polyon.

Nancia quietly transferred the recording of the scene she'd just witnessed to an offline storage hedron. Having those bits in her system made her feel . . . dirty. As if *she* were somehow implicated in Polyon's sadistic games.

Perhaps she should have interfered. But how . . . and why? Alpha was just as bad as Polyon, worse even, to judge from what he'd revealed of her unauthorized medical experiments. The two of them deserved each other. Blaize was the only one of the bunch she would care to talk to. The little redhead reminded her of Flix— and unlike the others, he didn't seem to have anything wrong with him that a few years away from family pressures wouldn't cure.

And what, exactly, will you say if you do *interrupt?* Nancia couldn't answer her own question. She was a Courier Service Ship, not a diplomat! She wasn't supposed to interfere with her passengers! She should have had a brawn on board—an *experienced* brawn—to break up nasty scenes like the one she'd just witnessed, to keep these spoiled young passengers happy and away from one another's throats for the two weeks of the trip. *It's not fair! Not on my very first voyage!*

But there was nobody to hear her plaint. They were still five days away from Singularity and the decomposition into Vega subspace.

At least I can keep evidence recordings going, Nancia thought grimly. *If one of the little brats drives another over the edge, there'll be plenty of datahedra to show what happened.* But at the moment, the five passengers seemed to be getting along reasonably well. Perhaps his sadistic games with Alpha had momentarily satiated Polyon's need for command and control; he had taken a play icon and seemed absorbed in that silly role-playing game. Nancia relaxed . . . but she kept her datacorders running.

CHAPTER FOUR

"**W**hy can't I get past the Wingdrake of Wisdom?" Darnell griped. He had chosen Bonecrush again, but his mighty-thewed play icon was backed into a corner where a winged serpent hissed menacingly at him every time he tried to move.

"You should have bought some intelligence for Bonecrush at the Little Shop of Spiritual Enlightenment," Polyon commented. His fingers flicked carelessly at the screen as he spoke, sending Thingberry the Martian Mage to spin an apparently pointless web in the night sky above Asteroid 66.

"I didn't know you *could* buy intelligence." Darnell's lower lip protruded in a definite pout. "That wasn't in the rule book."

"A lot of things aren't in the rule book," Polyon said, "including most of what you need to survive. And information is always for sale . . . if you know the right price. Anything from the secrets of Singularity to the origins of planet names."

"Oh. Encyclopedias. Libraries. Anybody can buy the Galactic Datasource on fast-hedra," Darnell whined. "But who has time to read all that crud?"

"The price of some kinds of information," Polyon said, "is more than the cost of a book and the time to read it. I could print out the rules of Singularity math for you, but you haven't paid the price of understanding it—the years of space transformation algebra and the intelligence to move the theories into multiple dimensions."

"Oh, come on," Blaize challenged him. "It's not that complicated. Even I know Baykowski's Theorem."

"A continuum C is said to be locally shrinkable in M if, and only if, for each epsilon greater than zero and each open set D containing C, there is a homeomorphism h of M onto M which takes C onto a set of diameter less than epsilon and which is the identity on M – D," Polyon recited rapidly. "And it's not a theorem, it's a definition."

Nancia quietly followed the discussion with mild interest. The mathematics of Singularity was nothing new to her, but at least when her brat passengers were talking mathematics they weren't trying to drive each other crazy. And she was impressed that Polyon had retained enough Singularity theory to be able to recite Baykowski's Definition from memory; common gossip among the brainships in training was that no softperson could *really* understand multidimensional decompositions.

"The real basis for decom theory," Polyon lectured his audience, "is what follows that definition. Namely, Zerlion's Lemma: that our universe can be considered as a collection of locally shrinkable continua each containing at least one non-degenerating element."

Fassa del Parma pouted and jabbed her play icon across the display screen in a series of short, jerky moves. "Very useful information, I'm sure," she said in a sarcastic voice, "but do the rest of us have to pay the price of listening to it? All this theoretical mathematics makes my head hurt. And it's not as if it were good for anything, like stress analysis or materials testing."

"It's good for getting us to the Nyota system in two weeks instead of six months, my dove," Polyon told her. "And it's really quite simple. In layman's terms, Singularity theory just shows us how to decompose two widely separated subspace areas into a sequence of compacted dimensionalities sharing one non-degenerating element. When the subspaces become singular they will appear to intersect at that element—and when we expand from the decomposition, pop! out of Central subspace and into Vega space we go."

Nancia felt grateful that she'd resisted her impulse to join in the conversation. Her Lab Schools classmates had been right about softpersons. Polyon knew all the right words for Singularity mathematics, but he'd gotten the basic theory hopelessly scrambled.

And clearly he didn't understand the computational problems underlying that theory. Pure topological theory might prove the existence of a decomposition series, but actually forcing a ship through that series required massive linear programming optimizations, all performed in realtime with no second chances for mistakes. No wonder softpersons weren't trusted to pilot a ship through Singularity!

"I agree with you," Alpha told Fassa. "Bo-ring. Even the history of Nyota is better than studying mathematics."

"You'd think so, of course," Fassa said, "seeing that it was discovered and named by your people." The small grin on her face told Nancia that this was a jab of some sort at Alpha. Hastily she scanned her data notes on the Nyota system, but nothing there explained why the Hezra-Fong family should take a particular interest in it.

"Swahili is a slave language," Alpha said haughtily. "It has nothing to do with the Fong tribe. My people come from the other side of the continent—and we were *never* enslaved!"

"Will somebody give me a map of this conversation?" Darnell said plaintively. "I'm more lost than I was during Polyon's math lecture."

"This particular information," Alpha told him, "is free." She drew herself up to her full height, several inches taller than Fassa, and favored the top of her sleek, dark head with a withering glare. "The system we're going to was discovered by a Black descendant of the American slaves. In a burst of misguided enthusiasm, he decided to give the star and all the planets names from an African language. Unfortunately, he was so poorly educated that the only such language he knew was Swahili, a trade language spread along the east coast of Africa by Arab slavers. He called the sun Nyota ya Jaha—Lucky Star. The planets' names are fairly accurate descriptions, too. Bahati means Fortune, and it's a reasonably decent place to live—green, mild climate, lots of nice scenery that stays put. Shemali means North Wind."

Polyon groaned appreciatively. "I know. Unlike some of us, I did read up on my destination. The place is called North Wind because that's what you get for thirteen months out of the year."

"*Thirteen* months you have in the year? Oh—I get it! Longer rotation period, right?" Darnell beamed with pride at his own cleverness.

"Shorter, as it happens," Polyon said. His voice sounded remarkably hollow. "Shemali has a year of three hundred days, divided into ten months for convenience. I was being sarcastic about the fact that there is *no* good season."

"Never mind," Alpha told him almost kindly, "it's better than Angalia. Actually the full name is Angalia! with an exclamation point at the end. It means Watch out!"

"Dare I ask what *that* means?" Blaize inquired.

"It means," Alpha told him, "that the scenery—unlike that of Bahati—doesn't stay put."

Blaize and Polyon stared at one another, briefly companions in misery.

Polyon was the first to recover himself. "Oh, well," he said, turning back to the game screen, "you see the value of information, Darnell—and the fact that it isn't always in the Galactic Datasource. And some of the information that isn't—ah—publicly available—is the most valuable of all." With delicate gestures he nudged the joyball while the fingers of his left hand tapped out codes to enlarge and strengthen Thingberry's magical net. "You need to think of ways to trade for that kind of information. For instance, your shipping company—such as it is—could offer discreet transport for parcels that *don't* get on the cargo list, or that go by a slightly misleading name—in some cases, disinformation or the lack of information is as valuable as actual data."

"Who'd want that?" Darnell objected. "And who cares, anyway? Can't we just play the game?"

Polyon favored him with a dazzling smile. "Dear boy, this is the game—and a far more rewarding one than SPACED OUT. Why, I can think of any number of people who might want a—suitably discreet—cargo carrier service. Myself, for starters."

"Why you?"

"Let's just say that not all the metachips going off Shemali are going to be in the SUM rationing board's records," Polyon said.

"So? What's it worth to me to oblige you?"

"I could pay you back with Net contacts. I can work the Net like no hacker since the days of the first virus breeders. It's an unsecured hedron to me. How soon could you rebuild OG Shipping if you knew ahead of time about every big contract about to be let in Vega subspace . . . and what your opponents' sealed bids were?"

Darnell's pout vanished to be replaced by a look of stunned calculation. "I could be rich again in five years!"

"But not, I fancy, as rich as I could be from selling metachips," Polyon murmured. Thingberry's web glistened on the screen above him, strings of jeweled light looping and floating above the play icons on the surface of Asteroid 66. "What would you say to a friendly wager? The five of us to meet and compare notes, once a year—to see how we're each doing at making lemonade out of the lemons of assignments our dear families have landed us with? Winner to take a twenty-five percent share in each of the losers' operations—business, goods, or cold credits?"

"When do we decide to stop and make the final evaluation?" Darnell asked.

"Five years—that's the end of most of our tours of duty, isn't it?"

"You know it is," said Alpha quickly. "Standard tour. And," she went on under Polyon's firm gaze, "I think it's a marvelous idea. I've got my own plans, you know."

"What?" Darnell demanded.

Alpha gave him a slow, lazy smile. "Wouldn't you like to know?"

"I'm sure we would *all* like to know," Polyon put in. A deft twist of the joyball set Thingberry's jeweled web spinning over the top half of the display screen. "Will you enlighten them, Alpha, or shall I—er—contribute my own scraps of information?" He crooked his finger, beckoning to her, and she moved closer to his control chair.

"Nothing much," Alpha said. "But . . . Summerlands is a double clinic. One side for the paying customers—mostly VIPs—and one side for charity cases, to improve their SUM rating. I've got some ideas for an improvement on Blissto—something we can give addicts in controlled doses. They won't get locked into a cycle of craving and ever-increasing hits of street drugs."

"Hey, *I* like Blissto," Darnell protested, "and I don't get into that cycle."

"Good," Alpha told him. "You're not an addictive personality. Some people aren't that lucky. You've seen Blissed-Out cases? Big enough doses, over a long enough period of time, until their nervous systems look like shredded wheat? *My* version won't do that. We'll be able to take Blissed-Out cases out of the hospital and send them out to do useful work as long as they stay on their meds. And I'm the one who did all the preliminary design work on this drug. Actually, it was a side-effect of my work on—well, there's no need to discuss all the boring details of my research," she concluded with a sidelong glance at Polyon. "What matters is that I've got the formulas and all the lab notes on hedra."

"But won't Central Meds hold the patent, if you did the work there?"

"When—and if—it's patented," Alpha agreed.

"And you can't sell it until it's passed the trials and been patented—so it's no good to you!"

Alpha's eyes met Polyon's over Darnell's head. "Quite true," she agreed gravely, "but I think I may find a way to profit from the situation anyway."

"What about you, Fassa?" Polyon asked. The girl had been very quiet since her jab about the slave names of the Nyota system. "You going to take this boondocks construction company Daddy handed you *lying down*?" His tone invested the question with a wealth of obscene possibilities.

"Double profit on every job," Fassa announced calmly. "I've got a degree in accounting. I can fix the books in ways an auditor will never catch."

Darnell whistled appreciatively. "But if you *are* caught—"

Fassa coiled herself on the other side of Polyon's chair in a series of languorous, sinuous movements that drew all eyes to her. "I think," she said dreamily, "that I can distract any auditors who *may* think about checking the books. Or any building inspectors who need to sign off on materials quality." Her slow, dreamy smile promised a world of secret delights. "There's a lot of money in construction . . . if you go about it the right way."

The four of them made a tight grouping now: Polyon in the control chair, Darnell standing behind him, Fassa and Alpha seated on either side of him. Four pairs of eyes gazed expectantly at Blaize.

"Well," he said, swallowed, and started over again. "Ah—PTA doesn't offer quite as much scope for creativity as the rest of your outfits, does it now?"

"You're with us or against us," said Polyon. "Which is it to be, little cousin?"

"Ah—neutrality?"

"Not good enough." Polyon glanced around at the other three. "He's heard our plans. If he doesn't join us, he could have some idea of informing . . ."

Alpha leaned forward, smiling sweetly. Her teeth looked long and very white against her dark skin. "Oh, you wouldn't do that, would you, Blaize dear?"

"I wouldn't even think about it," Darnell put in, tapping one pudgy fist against his open palm.

Fassa licked her lips and smiled like a child anticipating a treat. "This could be *interesting*," she murmured to no one in particular.

Blaize glanced around the circle of faces, then looked towards Nancia's titanium column. She kept her silence. Nothing had actually happened yet; if these brats attempted violence, she could stop it in seconds with a flood of sleepgas. And Blaize knew that as well as she did. Nancia saw no reason to give up her anonymity just to reassure him. He'd been brave enough when he was picking on Polyon alone; why, for heaven's sake, couldn't he stand up to the rest of them?

"But then, Blaize never did have the guts to do something as decisive as *telling*," Polyon dismissed his cousin with a brief nod. "We'll let him think it over . . . all the way to Angalia. It'll be a long couple of weeks, little cousin, with nobody to talk to. And a much longer five years on Angalia. Hope you enjoy life among the veggie-heads. I shouldn't think anybody else in the Nyota system will have much to do with you." He swiveled to face the SPACED OUT display, and the other three turned with him.

"Oh—don't leap to assumptions so fast. I'm with you, definitely with," Blaize babbled. "There *are* possibilities—I just haven't had time to think them over yet. The corycium mine, for instance—it hasn't been properly developed—maybe I could get a part interest in that. And PTA makes regular food drops to Angalia, who's to say how much of the food gets distributed to the natives and how much gets transshipped to some place that can pay for it . . ." He spread his hands and shrugged jerkily. "I'll think of something. You'll see. I'll do as well as any of you!"

Polyon nodded again. His fist closed over the joyball and Thingberry's jeweled web spiraled down to enclose Asteroidland, trapping the others' play icons in a tissue of glittering strands. "Done, then. Five of us together. Here, we'd better each have a record." He drew a handful of minihedra from the pocket of his Academy grays and dropped them into the datareader. One by one, Alpha, Fassa, Darnell and Blaize identified themselves by hand and retina print and spoke aloud the terms and conditions of the wager they'd agreed to. Polyon retrieved the minihedra after the recording was over and handed one faceted black polyhedron to each of them, keeping the last for himself. "Better store them someplace safe," he suggested.

Fassa clipped her minihedron inside a silver wire cage that hung from her charm bracelet among tinkling bells and glittering bits of carved prismawood. She alone seemed in no particular hurry to escape Polyon's influence; while the others jostled to reach the exit door, Fassa fiddled with her charm bracelet and tried out the shining black minihedron in various places, as if her only concern was to see where it would show to best advantage.

As Alpha, Darnell and Blaize left the central cabin, Nancia wondered whether Polyon's quick actions and mesmerizing personality had made them forget that he alone, of the five, had not recorded his intentions on the minihedra. Or were they simply afraid to challenge him?

Not that it mattered. She had the entire scene recorded. From several angles.

"You'll see," Blaize repeated over his shoulder as he left. "I'll do better than any of you."

"Small time, little man," Alpha sneered on her way down the corridor, "small-time plans for a small person. You'll be the loser, but who cares? *Somebody* has to lose."

"She's wrong, you know," Polyon commented to Fassa. "*Four* of you have to lose. There'll be only one winner in this game." And he too left, twiddling his black minihedron between two fingers and humming quietly to himself.

Fassa

The gleaming black surfaces of the minihedron flashed in the central cabin lights as Fassa turned her arm this way and that, admiring the effect of the stark blackness against the jumble of silver and prismawood trinkets. The hedron was as black as Fassa's own sleek hair and tip-tilted eyes, an admirable contrast to the whiteness of her creamed and pampered skin. In its hard glossy perfection she saw a miniature of herself... beautiful, impenetrable...

A shell full of dangerous secrets.

Fassa stared at the mirror-smooth surfaces of the minihedron and saw her face reflected and distorted in half a dozen directions at once, a shattered self looking out, trapped in the black mirrors that distorted her lovely features to a mask of pain and a silent scream.

No! That's not me—that can't be me. She dropped her arm; the jingling silver bells on the bracelet tinkled a single discordant peal. Pushing off from the strange titanium column that wasted so much cabin space, Fassa floated into a corner between display screens and a storage locker. "Blank screens," she ordered the ship.

The dazzling display of SPACED OUT graphics faded away, to be replaced by a black emptiness like the surfaces of the minihedron. Fassa stared into the flat screen, lips parted, until the reflection of her own beauty reassured her. Yes, she was still as lovely as she'd always believed. The distorted reflections from the minihedron had been an illusion like the dreams that troubled her sleep, dreams in which her lovely face and perfect body peeled away to reveal the shrunken, miserable creature underneath.

Reassured, she stroked the charm bracelet with two fingers until she touched the sharp faceted surface of the minihedron. *I keep my secrets, and you keep yours, little sister.* As long as she had the shield of her perfect beauty between herself and the world, Fassa felt safe. Nobody could see beyond that to the worthless thing inside. Very few tried; they were all too mesmerized by the outer facade. Men were rutting fools, and they deserved no better than to have their own folly turned back on them. If she could use their desire for her to enrich herself, so much the better. Gods knew her beauty had cost her too much in the past!

Mama, mama, make him stop, wailed a child's voice from the recesses of her mind. Fassa laughed sourly at the memory of that folly. How old had she been then? Eight, nine? Young enough to think her mother could stand up to a man like Faul del Parma y Polo, could make him give up anything he really wanted—like his daughter. Mama had closed her eyes and turned her head away. She didn't want to know what Faul was doing to their lovely little girl.

Ugly little girl. Dirty little girl, whispered another of the voices.

All the same, it had been Mama who stopped it, in a way. Too late, but still—her spectacular and public suicide had ended Faul's private games with his daughter. Jumping from the forty-second story balcony, Mama had shattered herself on the terraces of the Regis Galactic Hotel in the middle of Faul del Parma's annual company extravaganza, the one *all* the gossipbyters attended. And the news and gossip and rumor and innuendo that surrounded the suicide of del Parma's wife had been splashed all over the newsbeams for weeks thereafter. Why should she kill herself? Faul del Parma could give a woman everything. There was no history of mental instability. And everyone knew Faul del Parma never so much as looked at another woman, he only cared for his wife— well, one didn't hear so much about the wife, did one? A homebody type. But he went everywhere with that lovely little daughter at his side, only thirteen but a heartbreaker in the making. . . .

It occurred to a dozen gossipbyters at once that the daughter should be interviewed. And *that* had stopped it. Faul del Parma had whisked his daughter into a very exclusive, very private boarding school where no gossipbyters could find her and ask inconvenient questions.

Fassa twisted the minihedron on its clasp. *Thank you, Mama.* Even now, six years later, the story of the del Parma wife's suicide still made an occasional gossipbyte. Even now, Faul del Parma didn't want to risk having Fassa anywhere near him. So now that she was graduated from the expensive, exclusive school, he'd found a position for her with the least of his companies, Polo Construction, based on a planet in Vega subspace. And Fassa had practiced her bargaining skills for the first time.

I'll take it. But not as your subordinate. Make over Polo Construction to me, and I'll go out to Bahati and manage the company and never trouble you again. Call it a graduation present."

Call it a bribe for going into exile, Fassa thought, twisting the minihedron back and forth until the sharp angles of the facets bit into her thumb and forefinger. Because when Faul had balked at giving her complete ownership of the company, Fassa had leaned elegantly on his desk and speculated aloud about her chances of getting a position with one of the major newsbeamers. "They're all *very* interested in me," she teased her father.

"Interested in picking up sleazy gossip about our family," Faul snapped. "They've no interest in you for your own abilities."

Fassa smoothed her gleaming black hair back from her face. "*Some* of my abilities are very interesting," she told him. She let her voice drop down into the husky lower register that seemed to produce such an effect on her male teachers. "And the del Parma y Polo family is always news. I bet some of the major newsbeam companies would just love to serialize a book by me. I could tell them all the secrets I learned from my father. . . ."

"All right. It's yours!" Faul del Parma y Polo slapped his hand on the palmscanner beside his deskcomp, jabbed the hardcopy pad with his free thumb and ejected the finished minihedron with a glare for his daughter.

"You won't object if I scan it first?"

"Use a public scanner. You can't be sure of mine," Faul pointed out. "I might have programmed it to give a false readout. You'd better start thinking smarter if you want to make a success of this business, Fassa. But don't worry—it's all there. Ownership transfer and my palmprint to back it up. I wouldn't cheat you. I don't want you coming back to this office."

"*Don't* you, Daddy dear?" Fassa twisted forward over the desk, sinuous and flowing in her formfitting sheath of Rigellian spiderspin. She leaned close enough to let Faul breathe in the warmth and subtle perfume of her skin . . . and was rewarded by a flash of pain and desire in his eyes.

"Ta-ta, Daddy dearest." She slid from the desk and clasped the minihedron inside a corycium heart that dangled from her charm bracelet. "See you around . . . *I don't think.*"

"I wonder," Faul said hoarsely, "how many of those little charms contain men's hearts and souls."

"Not many—yet." Fassa paused at the door and gave him a sparkling smile. "I'm starting the collection with you."

Now, three days out from Central, she had already added a second hedron to the collection. Fassa jingled the charm bracelet reflectively. Each of the sparkling bits of jewelry was a clasp or a cage or an empty locket, waiting to receive some trinket. She'd collected the charms over those lonely years at boarding school, spending the lavish birthday and Christmas checks from Faul on expensive custom-made baubles. One for each time that Faul had come to her room at night. Only twenty-three in all; strange, she thought, that less than two dozen carefully chosen nights over a period of four or five years could make you rot away from the inside. Twenty-three shining jewels, each as perfect and beautiful in its own way as Fassa was in hers; each as empty inside as she was.

No, not any more. Two of them are filled. Fassa pushed off from the wall with the tips of her fingers and floated gently through the main cabin, twirling the charms around her wrist. Before she was done, she'd fill every charm with something . . . appropriate.

And then what?

No answers to that, no conceivable end to the future she'd mapped out for herself.

Blaize

The central cabin was empty; Polyon's buddies had all slunk off to their cabins to think over their wager and its probable consequences. Good. Blaize knew he could perfectly well have talked to Nancia from the privacy of his own cabin, but somehow it seemed more real to come here and speak directly to the titanium column that contained her shell.

Besides, she wasn't answering him from the cabin. He thought maybe she'd turned off the cabin sensors to give her passengers privacy.

He cleared his throat tentatively. Now that he was here, and not so confident of his welcome, it seemed rather strange to be talking to the walls. Sort of thing that got you shipped off for a nice rest in a place like Summerlands Care, Inc. Blaize shivered. Not for him, thank you. If he ever *did* need medical treatment, he'd make sure to go to a clinic where that snake Alpha bint Hezra-Fong was *not* operating.

"Nancia? Can you hear me?"

The silence was as absolute as that of the empty, black space outside the brainship's thin skin.

"I know you're listening," Blaize said desperately. "Watching, too. You *have* to be. *I* wouldn't close my eyes or turn my back on somebody like Cousin Polyon, and I don't believe you'd risk letting him sneak into your control cabin unobserved."

His wild gestures as he made the last statement almost over-balanced him in the ship's light grav field. He grabbed at a handrail and made a dancer's turn into the center of the cabin, recovering from the near-stumble as gracefully as a cat correcting a mistimed jump. Nancia's titanium column coruscated in rainbow reflections of the cabin lights, sparkling and dancing around him. And she did not reply.

"Look, I know what you're thinking, but it's not like that. Really." Blaize grasped a chair back to steady himself. "I mean, what could I do? Did you expect me to call them all criminals and wrap myself in my own integrity? They could've *spaced* me before we got to Angalia, and called it an unfortunate accident."

Silence.

"All right," Blaize conceded. "They probably wouldn't have spaced me. Especially if I told them you were a brainship and could bear witness against them."

Silence.

This was worse than the time he'd been locked in his room for a month.

"But that would have meant telling on *you*," Blaize pointed out, "and you didn't really want them to know you've been listening, did you?"

Silence.

"Well, what did you expect me to do, anyway? They'd all have hated me." Blaize's voice cracked. "Isn't it bad enough I have to go out to Angalia and spend the next five years handing out PTA boxes to some walking veggies? Do I have to start by losing my only friends in the whole star system?"

Nancia answered at last, "They are not your friends, and you know it."

Blaize shrugged. "Best imitations I've got. Look, I've spent my whole life being the family black sheep, the one nobody bothers with, the one nobody likes much, nobody respects. Can you blame me for wanting to change that? Just once in my life I want to *belong*."

"You do," Nancia told him. "As far as I'm concerned, you do indeed belong with the rest of this amoral brat-pack. And as for respect . . . you can add me to the list of people who don't respect you. I don't believe you ran away from home three times, either. You haven't got the gumption to cross the street without somebody holding your hand."

"I did so!"

Silence.

"Once, anyway. And if I *had* run away again, it would've been just like I said. They'd have been waiting for me at the Academy.

So what was the point? And what difference does it make? Worked out the same as if I'd actually done it, didn't it?"

Silence.

Blaize decided to go back to his cabin before somebody drifted in here and caught him talking to the walls.

"One more thing," he called as he pushed off for the return. "I *did* win that scholarship. Under the name of Blaize Docem. You can check Academy records on that!"

Nancia maintained her silence. All the way to Angalia.

CHAPTER FIVE

Singularity

The neighborhood of the brainship collapsed inward on itself, spiraling down tornado-like to the Singularity point where Central Worlds subspace could momentarily be defined as intersecting Vega subspace. The ship's metachip-augmented parallel processors solved and optimized the set of equations represented in a thousand-square matrix of subspace points, dropped out of that subspace into Decomposition, rode the collapsing funnel of spaces with a new optimization problem to choose and resolve every tenth of a second. To Nancia, Singularity was how she envisioned the ancient Earth sport called "surfing"; balanced at the non-degrading point where decomposing subspaces met, she recognized and evaluated local paths so quickly that the massive optimization problems blurred together into a sense of skimming over a wave that was always just about to crash beneath her.

The Singularity field test she'd taken at the Academy had been simpler than this. There, she'd had to deal with only one set of parallel equations; here, the sequence of equations and diminishing subspaces streamed past her in an incessant flow. It was challenge, danger, joy: it was what she had been trained for. She swept over matrices of data and guided them to the ship's processors, choosing and resolving the ever-changing paths to Singularity with an athlete's single-minded concentration.

The same newsbeam that showed Nancia the sport of "surfing" had also had a section on a diving competition. The clean lines of the divers' movements, the seconds during which they hurtled through the air as though they could give their bodies the lift and freedom of brainships, fascinated Nancia; she'd viewed the beam over a dozen times, marveling at what softpersons would go through for a few seconds of physical freedom. "Didja see how he ripped that dive!" the newsbyter had jabbered after one athlete's performance, then explaining that the term referred to the clean way the diver had entered the water without a single splash.

Nancia ripped a perfect dive through Singularity and came out into Vega subspace.

For her passengers, with nothing to do during Singularity and no way to filter the barrage of sensory data, the transition was markedly less pleasant. The few seconds of decomposition and reformation seemed like hours of wading through air gone viscous, picking their way among shapes distorted out of all recognition, in a place where colors hummed on the air and light bent around corners.

They gasped with relief when the ship broke through into normal space again.

Nancia watched them staggering and rubbing their eyes and ears. She was rather surprised by the intensity of their reactions; the trainer who'd accompanied her through her Singularity test had not seemed to be bothered by the few seconds of sensory distortion. Perhaps practice made a difference to how softpersons took Decomposition. Polyon's first words after the return to normal space suggested this might be the case.

"Well, *mes enfants,*" said Polyon, "how did you like your first Decomposition? It's been so long since *my* first training flights that I've forgotten how it affects newcomers."

"Once is enough," said Darnell with feeling. "If I ever go home again, I'll *take* the six months of travel by FTL. Or better yet, I'll *walk.*"

Fassa nodded vigorous agreement, then winced as if she wished she hadn't moved her head so soon.

"Have a Blissto," Alpha offered. "Works on hangovers—ought to help with Singularity headaches too."

Darnell snatched the small blue pills out of her hand and downed six of them in a single desperate gulp. Fassa started to shake her head and then obviously thought better of it. She waved Alpha's hand away with a languid gesture. "Never touch drugs."

"More fool you," said Alpha. "I know more about side effects than any of you, and I promise you a few blues won't do any harm. Just wish I'd thought of it before we entered Singularity. Blaize?"

"Excellent idea," Blaize said hollowly, accepting the offered pills. Unlike Darnell, he made his way to the far side of the cabin and found a half-empty bottle of Stemerald to help him choke down the pills. "Almost as good an idea as walking. Don't think I ever really *appreciated* Earth before." His skin was pale green under the spattering of freckles.

Polyon chuckled. "May have been a blessing in disguise that you weren't allowed to go in for brawn training, little one. Apparently you haven't the stomach for it. Now when you imagine combining frequent Decom hops with Mil Spec meals of boiled synthoprot and anonymous vitacaps that all smell like cabbage—"

Fassa clapped a hand over her mouth and ran for the door. Darnell swallowed convulsively two or three times. "Would you mind very much not mentioning food just now?" His last words were slurred and relaxed; the Blissto was already taking effect.

"At least not till I've had my own blues," Alpha added, pouring a handful of the shiny blue pills down her throat.

Fassa didn't quite make it to the privacy of her cabin. Silently, Nancia extruded probes that captured and vaporized the resulting mess. She activated the release latch on Fassa's cabin door so that it irised open in front of the girl.

"T-thank you," Fassa hiccuped into the wet cloth Nancia's second probe held out. "I mean—I know you're just a droneship, so this is silly, but—oh, thank you anyway." She collapsed on her bunk, a huddle of misery. Nancia closed down the cabin sensors, transmitted a shut command to the door iris, and left Fassa to recover on her own. At least, she thought, the girl had the strength of character to abstain from mind-rotting drugs. And the manners to thank whoever helped her, even a supposedly inanimate droneship. Her stated intention of using sex to get concessions for her company was appalling, as were her manners in general; but maybe she was a shade less repellent than the rest of Nancia's young passengers.

They had completely ignored Fassa's distress, Nancia noted. Polyon was playing a solitaire round of SPACED OUT and the other three were giggling over a new bottle of Stemerald. Nancia wondered uneasily what the mix of stimulants and depressants was likely to do to a softperson's nervous system—and what else Alpha might have smuggled aboard. Maybe it had been a mistake to turn off the cabin sensors; these people didn't *deserve* privacy.

But then, what business was it of hers if they wanted to drug themselves into a stupor? They'd be much nicer that way, after all. Nancia herself could conceive of nothing more horrible than voluntarily scrambling one's synapses, but softpersons did, by all reports, have very strange tastes.

Besides, they were much easier to put up with now that they were too doped to do anything but giggle softly and spill their Stemerald. Nancia's housekeeping probes mopped up the green puddles on the cabin floor; her passengers ignored the probes and their cleanup activity, and she, as far as possible, ignored the passengers.

Because now, at last, there was somebody else to talk to.

Within seconds of her emergence from Singularity, Nancia had initiated a tightbeam contact with Vega Base. By the time Fassa was cleaned up in her cabin and the other passengers busy with their own peculiar amusements, she had gone through the recognition Sequences and the official messages and was happily chatting with Simeon, the managing brain of Vega Base.

"So how did you like your first voyage?" Simeon inquired.

"Singularity was . . ." Nancia couldn't find words for it; instead she transmitted a short visual burst of colors melting and expanding like soap bubbles, iridescent trails of light joyously spiraling around one another. "I can't wait to jump again."

Simeon chuckled. "You're one of the lucky ones, then. From all I hear, it doesn't take everyone that way."

"My passengers didn't seem to enjoy it much," Nancia conceded, "but who cares?"

"Even brainships don't always get such a kick out of Singularity," Simeon told her.

Nancia found that hard to believe, but she remembered that Simeon was a stationary brain. Embedded in the heart of Vega Base, his only experience of travel would have been the jump that brought him here from Laboratory Schools—as a passenger, like any softperson. Perhaps she shouldn't go on about the joys of Singularity to someone who could never experience the thrill of managing his own jumps.

Besides, Simeon wanted to pursue something else.

"You don't seem to care much for your passengers' comfort."

Again words failed Nancia. She damped the colors of her visual burst to a muddy swirl of greenish browns and grays. "They're not ... very nice people," she finally answered. "Some of the things I overheard them discussing on the trip ... Simeon, could I ask you a hypothetical question? Suppose a brainship happened to learn that some people had unethical plans. Should she report them?"

"You mean, like a plot to murder somebody? Or high treason— an attempt to overthrow Central?"

"Oh, goodness, no, nothing like *that!*" How could Simeon sound so calm while discussing such dreadful things? "At least, I don't think—I mean, suppose they weren't planning to hurt anybody, but what they meant to do was morally wrong? Even illegal?" Alpha's plans to profit from a drug that should have been credited to Central Meds, Polyon's idea of creating a black market in metachips—no, Nancia assured herself, her passengers were nasty and corrupt as all get-out, but at least they weren't violent.

"Hmm. And how might this brainship have found out about her passengers' plans?"

"I—they thought she was a droneship," Nancia said, "and they discussed everything quite freely. She has datacordings of it all, too."

"I *see.*" Simeon sounded quite disapproving, and for a moment Nancia thought he shared her shock at her passengers' plans. "And has it occurred to you, young XN-935, that masquerading as a droneship in order to eavesdrop on High Families' conversations is a form of entrapment? In fact, given that the passengers involved *are* High Families and very close to CenCom, the act of taking surreptitious datacordings could even be interpreted as treason. What if they'd been discussing vital military secrets?"

"But they weren't—I didn't—Listen, VS-895, *they're* the criminals, not me!" Nancia shouted.

"Ouch."

Simeon's reply was almost an electronic whisper.

"Turn down your waveforms, would you? That nearly jolted me out of my shell."

"Sorry." Nancia controlled her impulses and channeled a clean, tight beam at Simeon. "But I don't see what you're accusing *me* of."

"Me? Nothing, XN, I assure you. I'm just trying to warn you that the courts may see things rather differently. Now, I don't know what your young passengers have been up to, and I don't particularly care to know. You haven't seen much of the world yet, or you'd realize that most softpersons have some way or other to get a little extra out of every situation in which they find themselves."

Nancia mulled that over. "You mean—are they *all* corrupt, then?"

Simeon chuckled. "Not all, Nancia, just enough to make it interesting. You have to understand the poor things. Short lifespan, limited to five senses, single-channel comm system. I expect they feel cheated when they compare themselves with us. And some of them translate that feeling into trying to get extra goodies for themselves."

Nancia had to agree that what Simeon said made a lot of sense. She tried to emulate his attitude of lofty detachment while she went about the business of landing her passengers at their assigned stations in the Nyota ya Jaha system. Since four of them still thought her a droneship and the fifth knew she wasn't speaking to him, it was easy enough to remain aloof.

Nancia made each planetary landfall an exercise in split-second timing and perfect orbit-matching. It was good practice, it kept her concentrating on her own business and not on that of her passengers, and if the rapid maneuvers involved gave them a bumpy ride—well, so much the worse. She took pride in making the actual moments of touchdown as gentle as the landing of a feather. At least, Bahati and Shemali went that way. When she reached Angalia, she couldn't quite restrain her impulse to give Blaize a good shaking on the way down. He was pale and sweating by the time they came to a bumpy halt on the mesa that served as Angalia's spacefield.

"That," he said as he collected his baggage, "was not necessary."

Nancia preserved an icy silence—literally. Each moment that Blaize delayed, she lowered her internal temperature by several degrees.

"You could at least send a housekeeping probe to help me with all this stuff," he complained, gripping a box of novelhedra with fingers that were rapidly turning blue with cold.

"You're not my mother, you know," he said while leaning on

the button to the lift. "Nobody asked *you* to pass judgment on my moral standards. Just like nobody asked *me* if I wanted to come out to this godforsaken place."

"I guess it would be too much to expect anybody to have a little sympathy," he said as the lift sped downward.

Nancia tilted the hatchway floor so that Blaize's carefully stacked boxes of supplies tumbled out as soon as he stepped onto the surface of Angalia.

"I know what you're thinking," he shouted from the red dust of the mesa top, "but you're wrong about me! You're all wrong! I'll show you!"

Nancia was pleased that her assignment made no mention of collecting the previous PTA administrator, the one whom Blaize had been sent to relieve. Apparently, not being a member of the High Families, he was expected to wait for the regularly scheduled PTA transport rather than taking advantage of a brainship for the Courier Service. Hard on him, Nancia thought, but quite appropriate. She would proceed directly to Vega 3.3, collect this stranded brawn, and return to Central for a *real* assignment—with a brawn of her own choosing. Thank goodness she was through being used as a substitute droneship for the convenience of the rich and powerful!

She discovered her error when she was halfway from Nyota ya Jaha to Vega 3.

"What do you *mean*, another little errand?" she blasted poor Simeon.

"Turn it down," came Simeon's low-intensity reminder. "It wasn't my idea and you don't have to shout like that. Anyway, what difference does it make? You were going to Vega 3 anyway."

"I was going to 3.3, not 4.2," Nancia pointed out, and this reminded her of another grievance. "Why can't these people give their suns and planets real names, anyway? This Vega numbering system makes me feel like a machine."

"They're great believers in efficiency," Simeon said. "And logic. You'll see what I mean when you pair up with Caleb."

"Hmph. You mean, when I transport the man—for that's all I've agreed to. Efficiency!" Nancia grumbled. "That's a new word for misuse of the Courier Service. Why, it's a whole different solar system and an extra stop to pick up this governor Thrixtopple and his family, not to mention having to feed them all the way back to Central. Time and fuel and ship's stores wasted. My fuel belongs to the Courier Service," she said, "and so does my time."

"What about your soul?" inquired Simeon, returning to a normal-intensity beam. "Oh, never mind. I keep forgetting how new you are, XN. Wait till you've been around the subspaces a few hundred years. You'll start understanding how the rules have to be bent to accommodate people."

"You mean, to accommodate *softpersons*," Nancia corrected proudly. "I've never asked for an exception or a favor in my life, and I'm not about to start now."

Simeon's responding burst of discordant waves and clashing colors was the electronic equivalent of an extremely rude word. "I can see why Psych thought you and Caleb would be a good match," he said. Infuriatingly, he shut down transmissions on that comment, leaving Nancia to wonder all the way to Vega 3.3. Why *did* Psych see fit to match her with a brawn whose major accomplishment so far had been the loss of his first brainship? Was there something wrong in her profile, some instability that made it appropriate to assign her an incompetent brawn? This Caleb softperson was probably going to be stuck doing interplanetary hops and minor errands—like picking up Governor Thrixtopple—for the rest of his Service. And Central Psych wanted to stick *her* with *him* and his flawed record! It *wasn't fair.* Nancia brooded about it all the way to Vega 3.3.

Her first sight of Caleb did nothing to restore her confidence in this assignment. Courier Service records said that he was only twenty-eight—young for a softperson—but he walked slowly and carefully, as if he were already old and tired. His Service uniform looked as if it had been designed for a larger man; the tunic hung loosely from broad but bony shoulders, the trousers flapped about his shins. *Short, scrawny and sour-faced,* Nancia mentally catalogued as he made his halting way up the stairs. *And why couldn't he use the lift, if he's too out of shape to walk up one flight of stairs?*

His greeting to her was correct but lifeless. Nancia responded in the same tone. Listlessly, they went through the Service formulas until Nancia displayed the orders beamed from Vega Base.

Caleb exploded. "Detouring to pick up that lard-bottomed junketer and his family? *That's* not a Courier Service job. Why can't Thrixtopple wait for the next scheduled passenger transport like anyone else?"

Nancia sent a ripple of muddy brown rings across the screen where their orders were displayed. "Nobody told me anything," she responded verbally for Caleb's benefit. "Stop here, go there, take these kids to the Nyota system, collect a stranded brawn on Vega 3.3, pick up the governor of 4.2 and take him back to Central. *I* don't know why he rates a special deal; he's not even High Families."

"No, but he's been working this subspace for a long time," Caleb told her. "Probably has more pull than half a dozen empty-headed aristos with their double-barreled names."

"We are not all," Nancia said, "empty-headed. Perhaps you failed to read your orders in detail?" She flashed her full name on the screen to get his attention.

"Oh, well, you can't help your birth," Caleb said absent-mindedly, "and I suppose a good Lab Schools training will make up for a lot. Are you ready for liftoff? We can't waste time gossiping if we have to fit this extra stop into the itinerary."

I give him ten minutes after we reach Central to get himself and his bags off me and make room for a brawn with some manners, Nancia vowed to herself as she drove her engines through a harder and faster takeoff than she would normally have imposed on a softperson passenger. *No, that's too generous. Five minutes.*

She felt slightly regretful when she peeked through Caleb's cabin sensors and saw him struggling to sit up after the takeoff, white and shaken. But she wasn't sorry enough to change her basic position on brawn assignments.

"There's one thing we should have settled before liftoff," she announced without preamble.

"Yes?" Caleb didn't bother turning his head to look at the cabin speaker. Of course, he was an experienced—if incompetent—brawn; he would know that she would be able to pick up his words from any direction. Still, Nancia felt vaguely ruffled—as if she were being ignored even as he replied to her.

"Transporting you back to Central Worlds is my official assignment, and I cannot refuse it. But I do not wish you to construe this as formal acceptance of you as my brawn. I have no intention of waiving my rights to free choice of my own brawn just because this match is convenient for Central."

Now what ailed the man? He had just begun to regain some color after the high-G lift-off; now his face was drained again, still as a mask—or a corpse. Nancia began to wonder if this brawn would live to see Central. *If he wasn't fit enough to make the journey, somebody should have warned me.*

"Of course," said Caleb in a voice so level and drained of meaning that it could have issued from any housekeeping drone, "no one would expect you to waive that right. Particularly for me." He turned his head and for the first time looked directly at the sensor. "Shut down sensors to this cabin, please, XN. I wish to rest. In privacy," he emphasized. He lay down again with one arm flung over his face. After a moment he rolled over and lay facedown on the bunk, as if he didn't trust Nancia not to peek at him.

"Simeon? Shellcrack, Simeon, I know you're picking up my beams. TALK TO ME!"

"You're an excessively demanding young thing, XN-935, and you're shouting again."

"Sorry." Nancia was so glad to have got some response from the Vega Base brain that she immediately lowered the intensity of her beam to match Simeon's almost inaudible burst. "Simeon, I need to know about this brawn they've saddled me with."

"So scan the newsbeam files."

"I did. There's nothing in them. Not what I need to know, anyway." The files had been enlightening in their own way, with their lurid stories of a ship and a man almost destroyed by a sudden radiation burst, the brawn's limping, months-long journey homeward in his crippled, brainless ship and the hero's welcome he had received when he arrived at Vega 3.3 with the survey data he'd been sent to gather. The tale of what Caleb had gone through, the months of solitude and deprivation and the lingering effects of radiation poisoning, had done much to reshape Nancia's feelings towards the pallid brawn who'd boarded her on Vega 3.3. She felt a grudging respect for the man she saw spending hours in her exercise facility, working out with gyroweights and spring resistors to restore wasted muscles.

The man who had accepted her initial hostile attitude as no more than his due, who'd shut her out of his mind at once and had not spoken a word to her since. They had traveled in silence through the three days it took to move between the suns of Vega 3 and Vega 4, while Nancia waited impatiently for Simeon to resume communications so that she could ask what she wanted to know. Finally she'd begun battering at the Vega Base brain's frequencies with ever-increasing bursts of communication that must have given him the equivalent of a softperson's "headache."

Nancia condensed the newsbytes she'd read and transmitted them in three short bursts to Simeon, just to convince him she'd done her homework.

"So what else do you want to know?"

"How. Did. He. Lose. His. Ship?" Nancia punctuated each word with a burst of irritated static.

"You read the newsbytes."

"WE'RE SHIELDED AGAINST—sorry." She started over at normal intensity. "We're shielded against radiation. He shouldn't have been harmed, unless he was being careless—leaving the ship without checking radiation levels? And there's no way his ship could have been affected. What could have got through her column?"

"*His* column, in this case," Simeon corrected, as if that mattered.

Unless Caleb used the access code to open his brainship's shell. That was the nightmare, that was what she wanted reassurance about. No brawn was supposed to know both the syllables and the musical tones that comprised his brainship's access codes. One sequence was given to the brawn on assignment, the other deeply classified in CenCom's codes. But Polyon's casual dabbling in the Net had left Nancia deeply suspicious of computer security systems. Any code invented could be broken . . . and how else could the CL-740 have been lost to something as minor as a radiation burst?

"Nothing did get through the column," Simeon told her. "The CL-740 was one of the first Courier Service ships commissioned, though. Three hundred years ago they didn't know as much as we do about shielding the synapse connectors. The radiation burst they were subjected to wasn't enough to harm the major ship's systems, but it fried the connections to the shell, leaving CL-740 in total isolation—unable to communicate or to receive signals, completely unable to control the ship. Caleb brought the ship back on manual controls, but by the time they got to Vega the CL-740 had gone mad from sensory deprivation."

"But the Helva System—" Nancia protested. It had been a long, long time since any brainship had been subjected to sensory deprivation; shell-internal metachips, named for the legendary brainship who'd survived the ordeal and suggested the modification, should have been invulnerable to any outside interference.

"The Helva modifications are not universal, though God knows they should be." Simeon sounded very tired. "It's a traumatizing procedure for those of us who aren't lucky enough to have it built into our first design, young'un. Some of the older brainships, those who'd paid off and continued in the Courier Service as free agents, had a right to refuse retrofitting. CL . . . exercised that right."

"Oh." It was a brain's worst nightmare, that being cut off from the world with a thoroughness no softperson could even imagine. Nancia closed down all her sensors for a moment, imagining that absolute blackness. How long would *she* be able to bear it? No wonder her supervisor at Lab Schools had canceled the first newsbyte about the CL-740. No wonder the newsbyte files made available to her now had been censored. No one wanted a brainship to start thinking about the worst that could happen. Nancia didn't want to think about it any longer. With an internal shudder she threw open all her sensors and comm channels at once.

The minor clatter of everyday life was a warm, reassuring tide about her, connecting her with the rest of humanity, the rest of all sentient life. Nancia catalogued the details with surprise and gratitude. *How strange and wonderful all this is . . . to see, hear, feel, think, know . . . and I have been taking it all for granted!* For a moment, the smallest input was precious to her, a gift of life. Caleb was hanging between two spring-resistors in the gym, the display screens in the central cabin were dancing with their elegant geometric screensaver patterns, the stars outside burned with their distant fire, Vega 4 was a ruddy glow before her, someone was chattering between Vega 4.3 and 4.2 about Central synthsilk fashions. Someone else was crying into a satellite link. . . .

And Simeon was still talking. "Levin." The databits transmitted like a whisper. "His name wasn't CL-740. His name was Levin, and he was my friend."

At Vega 4.2, Governor Thrixtopple and his family spilled aboard Nancia like a pack of cruise passengers, dropping their luggage anywhere for the patient servants who followed to pick up, commenting loudly on any feature of Nancia's interior that caught their attention.

"Hey! Look at these display screens!" The youngest Thrixtopple, a weasel-faced brat in his early teens, lit up on sight of the three wall-size display screens in the central cabin. "Sis, where's my SPACED OUT hedron? I could play all the way home—"

"*I* don't have to keep track of where you drop all your junk," his older sister whined. "Mama, there's only one storage bin in my cabin. My Antarxian ruffs will get all wrinkled!"

"Who cares? They still won't make any difference to your ugly face!" Thrixtopple Junior stuck out his tongue at his sister. She hurled a globe of something pink and slushy at him; he ducked out of the way and Caleb caught the globe in a neat one-handed catch.

"Now, kiddies," Thrixtopple Senior mumbled, "mustn't upset your mother or the servants." He held out one skinny hand to receive the pink globe his daughter had thrown; glance and gesture included Caleb among those "servants." Nancia bristled. He might not be her official brawn, she might still have her reservations about the way Psych was trying to throw the two of them together for the convenience of CenCom, but Caleb was still a trained brawn and deserving of more respect than that!

"Governor Thrixtopple, I'm afraid I will have to ask all of you to enter your personal cabins and strap down for lift-off now," Caleb said tonelessly.

"*Already?* Why, these clumsy servants haven't begun to unpack for me yet! I'm not nearly ready to send them away!" Trixia Thrixtopple complained without a word of gratitude or farewell to the servants who had, presumably, waited on her through the twenty years of Governor Thrixtopple's service. It was clear where her daughter had learned that penetrating whine.

"My apologies, ma'am," Caleb said, still without any inflection that they could react to, "but I am bound by regulations. Section 4, subsection 4.5, paragraphs ii to iv. Courier Service ships are not permitted to dally for any reason; a prolonged stop here could upset urgently needed communications elsewhere."

He personally escorted the Thrixtopple family to their bunks and made sure each of them was secured against the high-grav stresses of lift-off. Nancia kept the cabin sensors open to double-check every move, but Caleb made no mistakes.

Once the passengers were strapped down and their luggage stowed, Caleb returned to the central cabin and waved one hand towards the door. "Would you close us off, please, XN?" He sighed with exaggerated relief. "If only we could keep them out of here for the entire flight. People like that are a disgrace to Vega. Why, they didn't even have the manners to greet you!"

"Neither did the passengers I took on the way out," Nancia told him. "I was beginning to feel invisible."

"Not to me," Caleb told her. His eyes scanned the entire cabin with a look of longing that surprised Nancia. "Never to me. . . . If I don't get a new assignment, this could be my last voyage on a brainship. And we had to be saddled with these, these . . ." He threw up his hands as though words failed him.

"It is a pity," Nancia agreed, "but there's no reason *we* can't be professional about doing our jobs, is there?" While she made conversation with Caleb, she was rapidly reviewing the volumes of Courier Service regulations with which her data banks had been loaded upon commissioning. There should have been something in the third megahedron. . . . Ah, there it was. Precisely what the situation called for. But she wouldn't mention it now. Caleb was eager to escape the surface of Vega 4.2 before the Thrixtopple family started complaining about their restraints, and she couldn't blame him.

In deference to Caleb's weakened condition, Nancia made this lift-off as slow and gentle as she could. After all, it wasn't his fault that Psych Central was practically forcing their personal codes into one datastream. And she didn't want to kill the man on the way home.

When they entered freefall again, Caleb unlatched himself from the support chair and moved about the cabin with none of the languor he'd shown after the previous lift-off. "Being gentle with the civilians?" he inquired. "I seem to recall that you can lift considerably faster than that when you're so inclined, XN."

"I . . . um . . . I didn't see any need to hurry," Nancia muttered. Damn the man! Too stiff-necked to admit that he, too, could benefit from a slightly gentler takeoff!

Caleb looked faintly amused. "No. Considering that now there's no excuse to keep them strapped in, and we'll probably have the brats in our laps until you reach Singularity. . . . I wouldn't have wanted to hurry, either."

As if on cue, the Thrixtopple boy punched through the iris-opening of the door. Nancia winced at the damage to her flexible membranes. She left the door iris open so that Governor Thrixtopple, proceeding down the corridor at a stately pace behind his son, wouldn't inflict further violence on her.

"OK, we're in space now, lemme play with the computer!" the boy demanded.

Nancia slid her datareaders shut as the boy approached and deliberately blanked her screens. "I'm sorry, young sir. Courier Service Regulations, volume XVIII, section 1522, subsection 6.2, paragraph mcmlii, strictly prohibit allowing unauthorized passengers access to the ship's computer or free movement within the central cabin. The prohibition is intended as a protection against illegal interference with Courier Service property."

"Hear now, you—you talking shell, that's not meant to apply to people like us!" Governor Thrixtopple blustered as he entered the cabin.

"The official orders which were transmitted to me by CenCom at the beginning of this voyage make no reference to your family, Governor Thrixtopple," Nancia replied. She paused slightly between words and gave her voice a slight metallic overtone to make the Thrixtopples feel they were talking to a machine that could not be threatened or bribed. "I am not myself authorized to change such orders save on direct beam from Central Command."

"But Vega Base *told* you to ferry us to Central!"

"And I am always happy to do my good friends at Vega Base a favor," Nancia replied. "Nevertheless, it is not in my power to change regulations. Should Central Command retroactively authorize you to access my computers, I will—retroactively—permit you to have done so. In the meantime, I must request that you return to your personal cabin areas. I should be reluctant to enforce the order, but you must know that I retain the power to flood all life support areas with sleepgas."

Governor Thrixtopple grabbed his son's collar and dragged him out of the central cabin. The iris of the door membrane slid together.

"That," said Caleb reverently, "was brilliant, XN. Positively brilliant. Ah—I suppose there is such a regulation?"

"Of course there is! You don't think I'd *lie*?"

"My deepest apologies, ma'am. It was only that I had no personal recollection of the paragraph in question—"

"I understand that softperson brains are quite limited in their storage and retrieval powers," Nancia said loftily. Then she relented. "It took me several minutes of scanning to find something applicable, actually. And I never would have thought of it if you hadn't quoted regulations to get them out of here before lift-off."

"If it weren't for meals," Caleb reflected aloud, "we wouldn't have to speak to them again all the way back to Central. . . ."

"I have the capacity to serve meals from any room in the living quarters," Nancia informed him. *Unlike the older models . . .* She cut that thought off before voicing it. It would be sheer cruelty to remind Caleb of what he had lost.

"Okay, XN, try this one." Caleb manipulated the joyball to bring up a display of a double torus containing two simple closed curves. Three disks labeled A1, B, and A2 contained sections of the torus. "You're in A1; A2 is your target space. Find the Singularity points and compute the decompositions required."

"No fair," Nancia protested. "It's never even been proved that there *is* a decom sequence that'll navigate that structure. Satyajohi's Conjecture." She quoted from her memory banks, "If h is a homeomorphism of E3 onto itself that is fixed on E3 − T, need one of h(J1), h(j2) contain an arc with four points of A+B such that no two of these points which are adjacent on the arc belong to the same one of A and B? If so, the decomposition space H does not yield E3. And in this application," she reminded Caleb, "E3 is equivalent to normal space."

Caleb blinked twice. "I didn't expect you to know Satyajohi's Conjecture, actually. Still—let me point out, XN, it's only a conjecture, not a theorem."

"In one hundred and twenty-five years of deep-space mathematics it's never been disproved," Nancia grumbled.

"So? Perhaps you'll be the first to find a counterexample."

Nancia didn't think there was much point in even trying, but she set an automatic string-development program to race through the display, illuminating various possible Singularity paths as lines of brilliant blue light, then letting them fade out as the impossibility of one after the other was proved. There was something else on which she very much wanted Caleb's advice, and now—with the Thrixtopple family intimidated into staying in their cabins, and Caleb in as good a mood as she'd ever seen him after his demonstration of Satyajohi's Conjecture—now was the best time she could have to bring it up.

"I haven't been commissioned very long, you know, Caleb," she began.

"No, but you're going to be one of the best," Caleb told her.

"I can see it in the way you handle little things. I wouldn't have thought of finding a regulation to get the Thrixtopples out of our hair. And I don't think I'd have tested Satyajohi's Conjecture the way you're going about it right now, either." Two possible Singularity lines flashed bright blue and then vanished from the screen as he spoke, while a third snaked through A1 and into the B disk around the double torus.

"Some things," Nancia said carefully, "get more complicated than that. In mathematics a conjecture either is or isn't true."

"The same is true of Courier Service Regulations," Caleb pointed out.

"Yes, well . . . not everything. They don't tell you what to do if a brainship happens to hear her passengers making illegal plans."

"If you've been eavesdropping on Governor Thrixtopple in his cabin," Caleb said sternly, "that's a dishonorable action and I hereby formally request you to stop it immediately."

"Oh, I haven't," Nancia assured him. "But what if—if a brainship had some passengers who *didn't know* she was sentient, and they liked to sit in the central cabin and play SPACED OUT, and they just happened to discuss some possibly illegal plans while they were doing it?"

"Oh—a hypothetical case?" Caleb sounded relieved, and Nancia felt the same way. At least he hadn't guessed immediately, as Simeon had, that she was talking about her own previous experience. Everything Nancia had learned or seen of Caleb—the newsbeams of his heroic solo return to Vega, the dedication with which he put himself through a grueling exercise program, his respect for Courier Service regulations—made her think of him as a man of supreme integrity, one whose word she could trust under any circumstances. She would not have wanted to hear him laugh at her as Simeon had done, or suggest—as Simeon had done—that her own actions in this instance had been morally culpable.

"Well, in such a case—if it ever arises—you should remember that a sentient ship is morally obliged to identify herself as such to her passengers at the first opportunity."

"That's not in the regulations," Nancia defended herself against a charge Caleb didn't know he had made.

"No, but it's common sense. Anything else would be like—like me hiding in a closet to catch Governor Thrixtopple counting his ill-gotten gains from bribes while in public office." Caleb said this with so much disgust in his voice that Nancia shrank from pursuing the subject.

So, evidently, did Caleb. He looked up at the central display screen, where a network of dim gray lines showed Nancia's repeated attempts to compute a path of Singularity points through the topological configuration he'd defined.

"Let's just take it that Satyajohi's Conjecture is upheld in this particular case," he suggested, "and now it's your turn to put up a problem. I don't know why we're discussing hypothetical ethical problems that are never likely to arise when we could both be improving our Decom Math skills. Nor do I understand why—" He bit his lip and blanked out the screen with a swift roll of the joyball.

"Why what?" Nancia asked.

"Your turn to pose a problem," Caleb reminded her.

"Not until you finish that sentence."

"All *right*! I don't understand why you're asking for ethical guidance from a brawn whose greatest achievement to date has been the loss of his first ship!" Caleb bit out the words with a frustrated savagery that aroused Nancia's sympathy. She remembered Simeon's grief for his lost friend Levin, the CL-740. How stupid she had been.

"I'm sorry," she told Caleb. "I should have realized that discussing such issues would remind you of Levin. Do you miss him so very much?"

Caleb sighed. "It's not that, XN. Levin was a good, competent brainship, and he trained me when I was a new brawn, and I'll always owe a debt of gratitude to him. But we weren't—we never just talked, like this, you know? Five years I served with him, and I don't feel I ever really got to know him. No, I'm not in mourning for Levin. But he had a right to look forward to hundreds more years of service, and I lost him that time. And I myself had rather hoped to spend more than five years as a brawn."

"You may yet," Nancia pointed out. "Just because you haven't got a ship assignment yet—"

"And what brainship is going to accept the brawn who let the CL-740 die?" Caleb snapped back. "You yourself have made that little point tolerably clear, XN. Now drop it. Next problem, please!"

✧   ✧   ✧

Nancia started transmitting to CenCom—on a private beam—the moment she exited Singularity and entered Central Worlds subspace. She wanted to have everything arranged, with no possibility of argument, before Caleb was ready to leave the ship.

All proceeded as planned. Dahlen Rahilly, her Service Supervisor, requested permission to enter even before the Thrixtopple family had gathered their numerous items of luggage and departed.

"Arrogant snit," Rahilly commented as they watched the last of Governor Thrixtopple's bony shoulders through Nancia's ground viewport. "He could at least have credited you with a bonus for doing him the favor of this quick transport home."

"I didn't expect it," Nancia replied with perfect truth. The only bonus she expected—or wanted—was still in his cabin, using the cabin comm board to enter a job application letter that somehow kept getting wiped from his personal file storage area. This was his third attempt, and Nancia could tell by the emphatic way Caleb's voice snapped out the words for the dictaboard that he was losing patience. If she didn't get matters settled soon, he would quit trying to use the ship's comm system and make his application personally, at CenCom offices. And that wouldn't suit her at all.

"Well . . . there will have to be a few changes. Paperwork," Rahilly said. "We . . . weren't expecting this, you know, XN. In fact, VS at Vega seemed quite certain that you had formally refused the assignment."

"He . . . may have misinterpreted my words," Nancia said demurely. "How soon can it be arranged?" Shellcrack! While she was talking to Rahilly, Caleb had managed to dictate the complete text of his application letter. He was getting ready to transmit it to CenCom. That mustn't happen . . . not yet. Nancia shut down all outgoing beams at once.

"Oh, we can finish the paperwork in a day. If you're sure that's what you want?"

"I am," Nancia said firmly. There was another party to be consulted, but Rahilly didn't seem to think that would be necessary.

Caleb stalked into the central cabin, brows drawn together. "XN, what do you mean by shutting down my beam to CenCom?"

"*Your* beam?" Nancia replied. "Oh, dear. All my external beams seem to have lost power for a moment."

"We'll have a tech out to fix the malfunction immediately," Rahilly promised.

"Oh . . . I don't think that will be necessary," Nancia told him. "I've been investigating while we talk, and I believe I have found the source of the problem. It should be easy enough to correct internally." All she needed to do was reopen the power gate. . . .

"Very well, CN-935." Rahilly sketched a Service salute in the general direction of Nancia's titanium column. "The remaining paperwork will be completed within the day, and then you and Brawn Caleb will be requested to hold yourselves ready for a new assignment—there was one pending, actually; Central will be happy not to have to wait while you choose a brawn."

He left as soon as the last word was snapped out, and Nancia was grateful for that. Caleb was staring around the cabin with an expression she could not read. If he was going to be angry with her for going behind his back, she'd just as soon have it out in private.

"I . . . don't understand," he said slowly. "You aren't waiting to choose a new brawn? You're going to go out solo again?"

"Hardly that," Nancia told him. "I've had enough of solo voyages, thank you very much; I find that I much prefer to travel with a partner."

"Then . . ."

"Didn't you hear the man? From now on I'm the CN-935. I've decided that Psych Central was *right,*" Nancia said. It was a struggle to keep her voice projections calm and even. "We make a very good team."

Caleb was still speechless, and Nancia felt her one fear approaching.

"If . . . if that's all right with you?"

"All right, all *right, all right!*" Caleb exploded. "The woman gives me back my life—and with the perfect brain partner—and she wants to know if it's *all right?* I—Nancia—oh, wait a minute, would you? There's something I've got to take care of before you restore external beam transmissions."

He hurried off to his cabin, presumably to erase the job application letter that had taken so long to create, and Nancia permitted herself a small coruscating display of stars and comets across her three wide screens. It was going to be all right.

More than all right. "Nancia," she repeated to herself. "He finally called me Nancia."

CHAPTER SIX

Angalia, Central Date 2750:
Blaize

Blaize Armontillado-Perez y Medoc stared in disbelief at his new home as the exit port of the XN-935 slid shut behind him. The mesa top that had served Nancia as a landing field was the only level bit of solid ground in sight. Behind the mesa was a wall of crumbly, near-vertical rock that rose in jagged peaks to block out the morning sun. The long black shadows of the mountains fell across the mesa and down into a sea of oozing *glop* that looked like the Quagmire of Despair as displayed in the latest version of SPACED OUT. The only variation in the brownish sea was that at a few locations large, lazy bubbles rose from the glop and burst with a sulfurous stink.

At the very edge of the mesa, cantilevered precariously out over the Quagmire of Despair, was a gray plastifilm prefab storage facility. Bulging brown sacks stenciled with the initials of Planetary Technical Aid hung from hooks on one side of the shack, dangling right out over the sea of glop. On the side of the shanty nearest Blaize, the plastifilm roof had been extended with some sort of woven fronds to create a sagging awning. Beneath this awning lounged an immensely fat man wearing only a pair of sweat-stained briefs.

Blaize sighed and picked up the nearest two pieces of his kit. Staggering slightly under a gravity considerably higher than ship's norm, he made his way towards the obese guardian of Angalia.

"PTA tech-trainee Armontillado-Perez y Medoc, sir," he introduced himself. *Who is this guy? He's got to be one of the corycium miners. They're the only humans on Angalia—except, of course . . .*

"And the top of the morning to you, Sherry, me lad," said the sweating man-mountain cordially. "Never was so glad to see anybody in m'life. Hope you enjoy the next five years here."

"Ah—PTA Grade Eleven Supervisor Harmon?" Blaize hazarded. *Except my new boss.*

A richly alcoholic wheeze almost knocked him off his feet. "You see anybody else around here, kid? Who d'you *think* I am?"

"The corycium mine—"

"Dead. Defunct. Abandoned. *Kaput,* all gone splash, stinko," Grade 11 Supervisor Harmon said with relish. "Went bust. Owner sold the mine to me for a case of spirits before he pulled out."

"What went wrong?"

"Labor. Company couldn't keep miners here for love nor money. Not that they offered much love—even a corycium miner ain't desperate enough to try and get it on with a Loosie, heh, heh, heh." Another wave of alcohol-flavored breath washed over Blaize.

"Loosie?"

"*Homosimilis Lucilla Angalii* to you, m'boy. The veg-heads Lucilla Sharif discovered, damn her soul, and reported as possibly intelligent on the FCF, double-damn her, and for her sins we're stuck administering Planetary Technical Aid to a bunch of walking zucchini. All the company I've had since they closed the mine. And all *you'll* have for the next five years. Next PTA transport comes by here is taking me off-planet." Harmon looked enviously at the sleek length of the XN-935, her tip now gleaming in the sun that peeked over the jagged mountains. "Nice perks you High Families kids get, transport like that. I don't suppose you could persuade that brainship—"

"I doubt it," Blaize said.

Harmon chortled. "No, didn't much sound like it, way you come out yelling and screaming over your shoulder, with it dumping your luggage after you. You musta pissed it off real handsome. No matter. Next PTA shipment oughta be along any day now. And when it comes, my new assignment should be ready." He stretched luxuriously, took a deep drink from the bottle beside him, and sighed with anticipated contentment. "Reckon I've earned myself a nice long tour of duty on Central, in a nice office tower with air conditioning and servos and no need to pay any bloody attention to bloody nature unless you happen to feel like looking out the window. Sit down, Madeira y Perez, and don't look so miserable. Do your five years and maybe they'll post you back in civilization. You're in luck, coming when you did."

"I am?" The sun was over the mountain by now, and it was *hot* on the mesa. Blaize pulled his largest grip under the shade of the awning and sat down on it.

"Sure. Today's feeding time at the zoo. Put on a real show for you, the Loosies will." Harmon waved again, this time as if beckoning the cliff that towered above them to come on down. Blaize stared in shock as craggy bits of mountain broke loose and trickled down to the mesa top, shambling like crazy puppets made of rocks and wire. Strange costumes—no, they were naked; that was their *skin* he was looking at.

"Yaohoo! Feeding time! Whoee!" Harmon yodeled, simultaneously jerking the cord that ran along the side of the PTA prefab. One of the sacks overhanging the muddy basin opened and brownish-gray ration bricks spilled out in a torrent, piling up in the mud below the mesa.

The Loosies scurried to the edge of the mesa and let themselves down into the muddy sea, fingers and toes clinging to crevices in the rocks. The first ones down threw themselves on the ration bricks as if they were greeting a long-lost lover; the later arrivals piled on top of them, swinging uncoordinated limbs and wriggling to burrow into the muddy heap of rations.

Blaize felt a rumbling vibration coming up through the soles of his feet.

"Look out!" Harmon roared.

Blaize jumped and Harmon chuckled. "Sorry to startle you, kid. You wouldn't want to miss the other big show of Angalia." He pointed to the western horizon.

It seemed to be moving.

It was a wall of water. No, mud. No—Blaize struggled for the right word and could only find the one that had first occurred to him: *glop*.

The "Loosies" had ignored Harmon's shout as if they were deaf, but something—perhaps the rumbling vibration that Blaize felt—alerted those still at the bottom of the quagmire. They swarmed up the sides of the mesa, clutching their ration bricks in teeth and fingers. The last one got out of the way just before the advancing tide of glop struck the mesa.

The whole desperate, squirming consumption of ration bricks had taken place in total silence. Now, less than three minutes later, it was over and the mesa was surrounded by a sucking, slimy tide of glop. As Blaize watched, the tide receded, sliding back down the sides of the mesa until the new mud melted into the same soggy configuration of puddles and bubbles that had greeted him on arrival.

"That was a small one," Harmon said with regret. "Oh, well, there'll likely be some better ones before you go. Bound to be, in fact."

In response to Blaize's questions he explained, without much interest, that the erratic climatic pattern of Angalia produced a constantly moving band of thundershowers in the mountains which surrounded this central basin. Whenever the storms stayed in the same place for a while, the rainfall built up into a flash flood which raced across the plain, picking up mud as it went, and sweeping away anything that might be foolish enough to remain in its path.

"Terraforming," Blaize mused. "Dams to catch the rainfall and release it slowly . . ."

"Expensive, and who'd bother? Nothing here to repay the investment. Besides," Harmon explained, "*it's fun.* Damn sure ain't much else to watch out here!"

Blaize gathered that one of Harmon's amusements was trying to predict the times of the mud-floods so that he could feed the natives just before one, forcing them to scramble first for ration bricks and then to save themselves from the tide of mud.

"Ain't it the damnedest thing?" he demanded as the rock-like natives climbed back to their mountain heights, some clutching a few ration bricks for later consumption, some still chewing the last mouthfuls of their haul. "You ever see anything like it?"

"Never," Blaize admitted. *Are the—the Loosies starving? Is that why their skin hangs loose like that? Or is that their normal appearance? And how does this fat creep get away with putting them through such a degrading performance?*

"I know what you're thinking, Port-Wine y Medoc," the fat man said, "but wait'll you've done six months out here, you'll forget all the PTA regs about respecting the natives' dignity and all that crapola. Damned Loosies don't have any dignity to respect, anyway. They're a bunch of animals. Never developed agriculture— or clothing—or even language."

"Or lies," commented Blaize.

"What?" For a moment Harmon looked startled, then he chuckled and wheezed with amusement. "Righto. No language, no lies— gotta say that for them, anyway! But they're not *people*, young Claret-Medoc. Waste of resources, this whole operation—some paperpusher's mistake. Only encourages the veg-heads to breed more little veggies. We oughta pull outa here and let 'em starve on their own, y'ask me."

"Maybe they could be trained to work the mine," Blaize suggested.

Harmon snorted. "Yeah, sure. I did hear about some prisoners in olden times who amused themselves trying to train their pet rats to run errands. You could do that sooner'n you could teach a Loosie anything, kid. I tell you, there's just three amusements on Angalia: feedin' time for the Loosies, drinkin' time for me, and playing computer games. And I've mapped every damn level of the Maze of the Minotaur so many times I can't stand to look at it no more."

Blaize felt in his pocket. The datahedron recording the wager wasn't the only item he'd copied from Nancia's computer. "Does your computer—"

"Yours now, Sake-Armontillado," Harmon interrupted with a cheerful belch. "PTA issue."

"Does it have enough memory and display graphics to run SPACED OUT? Because," Blaize said, "I just happen to have a copy of the latest version here. Pre-release—it's not even on sale at Central yet." He winked at Harmon.

"Is that so!" Harmon oozed to his feet. "C'mon inside, Burgundy-Champagne. Pass the time in a li'l friendly game until my transport gets here." He scratched his bare chest, squinting at Blaize with the rudiments of a thoughtful expression on his face. "Have to name some stakes, of course. No fun playing for nothing."

"My sentiments exactly," Blaize agreed. "Lead the way."

Five days later, exactly as scheduled, the PTA transport touched down to deliver new supplies and to pick up Supervisor Grade

11 Harmon for the months-long FTL journey to his new assignment. Blaize remained behind with the Loosies and his winnings: two partially depleted cases of Sapphire Ruin, Supervisor Grade 11 Harmon's hand-woven palm-frond sun hat, and the title to an abandoned corycium mine.

Deneb Subspace, Central Date 2750: Nancia and Caleb

"That," said Caleb as he and Nancia left Deneb Spacebase, "was one of our more satisfying assignments."

"Out of a grand total of two?" Nancia teased him. But she agreed. Their first scheduled run out of Central, delivering medical supplies to a newly settled planet, had been worthwhile but hardly challenging. And they had both been apprehensive about this assignment: transporting some semi-retired general, another High Families representative, into the middle of a particularly nasty conflict between Central Worlds settlers and Capellan traders. But General Micaya Questar-Benn had proved completely different from the spoilt High Families children Nancia had taken out to Vega subspace on her first assignment. Short, competent, unassuming, the general had won Caleb's heart at once with her in-depth knowledge of Vega's complex history. She'd proceeded to spend much of the short run to Deneb subspace talking shop with Nancia; half the general's body parts and several major organs were cyborg replacements, and she was interested in the possibility of improving her liver functions with one of the newer metachip implants such as kept Nancia's physical body healthy within its shell. Nancia had never envisioned herself discussing something so personal with anybody, let alone a high-ranking army officer, but something about General Questar-Benn's unassuming manner made intimate talk unthreatening and easy.

Nancia wasn't too surprised to learn that before she and Caleb had even prepared for the return journey, General Questar-Benn had drawn human and Capellan antagonists into negotiations and worked out a settlement that would allow each side to feel they had "won."

"And here I thought we were warmongering, delivering

somebody with authority to send in the heavy armored divisions!"
Caleb went on.

Nancia chuckled. "The galaxy could do with a few more 'war-mongers' like Micaya Questar-Benn. Ready for Singularity, partner? Central should have a new assignment for us by now."

Bahati, Central Date 2751: Alpha

Alpha bint Hezra-Fong stared down in distaste at the writhing body of her experimental subject. What had gone wrong? The molecular variations of Blissto which she'd been preparing should have rendered the patient calm and tractable. Instead he was contorting his limbs and moaning uncontrollably, trying to break the restraint straps on his stretcher.

Alpha tightened the straps until the patient stopped thrashing and passed a medscanner over his forehead. She frowned at the results. Instead of generating soothing hormones, Blissto.Rev.2 was invading and replicating itself within the man's nervous system like a cancer gone wild.

"Damn! I haven't got *time* for this," she muttered. Quickly she considered her options. If she could keep the patient alive and in isolation for a few days, perhaps she would be able to find out what was causing this invasive replication and find a way to stop it. But if anybody questioned her work—

The man's convulsions increased. One leg broke the reinforced restraint strap and kicked out wildly.

"Too dangerous," Alpha decided. She pressed a hypospray to the man's neck and watched his body sag back against the stretcher. His eyes rolled upwards and the thrashing stopped.

So did all other movement.

Alpha had papers prepared for just such an emergency. The clinic director was an old fool, too lazy to check her reports; nobody else would dare to question her. Charity Patient B.342.iv would be listed as having died of heart failure brought on by a preexisting medical condition which the clinic had not had time to reverse.

The only trouble was, that made the third such death in the

year since Alpha had begun testing her improved version of Blissto. Sooner or later, if she didn't get the drug dosage right, somebody was going to notice the string of identical sudden-death reports and ask questions.

Alpha seriously considered returning to experimenting on rabbits. But rabbit cages stank, and taking care of the beasts was a lot of work, and there was even more probability that somebody would question her sudden interest in raising pets.

She'd just have to think up a few more excuses for sudden deaths on the charity wing. A little variation in the paperwork would help disguise these unfortunate accidents.

Procyon Subspace, Central Date 2751: Caleb and Nancia

"This is boring," Nancia complained as she watched workers on Szatmar II unload the cases of vaccine she and Caleb had transported there.

"It is important to see that children's vaccinations are kept up regularly," Caleb told her.

"Yes, but it's hardly an emergency. At least, it wouldn't have been one if PTA would keep its records up to date." A horrified bureaucrat had discovered that some incompetent named Harmon, working out of PTA on Central Worlds, had forgotten to ship last year's supplies of vaccine to any PTA client planets in the Procyon subsystem. In consequence, Nancia and Caleb were getting an extended tour of that subsystem, delivering measles and whooping-cough vaccine to several dozen settlements on widely scattered planets. "I've got a good mind to speak to my sister about this idiot Harmon," Nancia grumbled. "Jinevra would never tolerate such inefficiency in her own branch of PTA; maybe she can get Central to transfer Harmon to a spot where he can't do any harm."

"Nancia, you wouldn't seriously consider using your family connections for personal interest!"

Caleb sounded shocked. Nancia apologized immediately. She hadn't realized that trying to get an incompetent bureaucrat ousted came under the heading of "personal interests." But Caleb was doubtless right; he always was. And she felt quite guilty as he lectured her about the consequences of being flighty and expecting glamorous assignments. He was right about that, too. Service loyalty demanded not only that she go where she was needed, but that she do so willingly and cheerfully.

Nancia closed her loading dock and tried to lift off for their next vaccine delivery with a willing and cheerful heart.

Bahati, Central Date 2752: Darnell

Darnell leaned back in his upholstered stimuchair and activated the interoffice transmitter. "You may send Hopkirk in now, Julitta m'lovely."

"Oh, Mr. Overton-Glaxely!" Julitta's delighted giggles came clearly through the transmitter. Darnell activated the double display screens as well and enjoyed two views of his secretary. The top screen showed her tossing her pretty yellow curls and preening with delight at his compliment; the lower screen displayed her shapely legs, crossing and recrossing restlessly beneath the desk. Darnell noted with pleasure that Julitta's petiskirt had ridden up almost to her waist. *Such a delightful, twitchy little girl.*

Darnell considered Julitta, like the second display screen and the vibrostim units in his executive chair and the view of Bahati from his glass-walled executive office, to be one of the perks appropriate to a Man Who Had Made It. He let Hopkirk wait awkwardly in front of his desk while he contemplated with equal delight his own rapid success, his immediate plans for Julitta, the view of her legs in the lower display screen, and the fact that Julitta didn't know about the second screen.

"Hopkirk, I've got a job for you," Darnell ordered. "Productivity in the glimware plant dropped by three thousandths of a percent last month. I want you to get out there and send me a full report of any contributing factors."

"Yes, Mr. Overton-Glaxely," the man called Hopkirk murmured.

"It's probably cumulative worker fatigue due to the poor design of the assembly line," Darnell continued. Ah, that was better; a flash of pain crossed Hopkirk's features. Six months ago the man had owned, designed, and managed Hopkirk Glimware, producers of

fine novelty prismaglasses for the luxury trade. And managed it
damn poorly, too, Darnell thought; the place would have gone
bankrupt soon enough anyway, even without his interference. Now
it was a profitable, if small, addition to Darnell's revitalized OG
Shipping (and other) Enterprises.

"Questions, Hopkirk?" Darnell snapped as the man remained
standing instead of speeding to his task.

"I was just wondering why you did it this way," Hopkirk said.

"Did it what way?"

Hopkirk shrugged. "You know and I know that Hopkirk Glimware would have done all right if you hadn't manipulated the Net
to bring my stock prices down and cut off my credit."

"That's a matter of opinion," Darnell told him. "Admit it,
Hopkirk. You're an engineer, not a manager, and you didn't know
how to run the company. It would have crashed eventually in any
case. All I did was help it along."

"But why do it this way? Why ruin me when you could have
bought the company for a fair price and still made your profit?"

Darnell was pleased that the man didn't argue the basic point.
He'd been an incompetent manager and he knew it.

"You're a brilliant businessman," Hopkirk went on. "Look at how
you turned OG Shipping around in just a year!"

With a little help from my friends . . . Darnell quashed that
thought. Sure, Polyon's ability to hack into the Net and get advance
information had been useful. But it was also true that Darnell had
discovered within himself a true talent for efficiency. Cut out the
deadwood! Fire the incompetent, the lazy, and those who've merely
failed to get results! And know everything! Those were Darnell's
new mottoes. Those who'd been fired talked about the Reign of
Terror. Those who hadn't been fired yet didn't dare to talk. And
OG Shipping prospered . . . leaving Darnell free to amuse himself
again.

There was Julitta, of course. There were an infinite number of
Julittas. But Darnell had discovered that no number of willing girls
could give him quite the thrill of victory that his business
manipulations brought.

He regarded Hopkirk thoughtfully. The man seemed to intend
no offense; perhaps he honestly wanted to understand the work-
ings of Darnell Overton-Glaxely's brilliant mind. A laudable
impulse; he deserved an honest answer.

"Sure, I could have done it straight," he said at last. "Would have taken a little longer. No prob. But," he winked at Hopkirk, "it wouldn't have been as much fun . . . and that way I wouldn't have had you working for me, would I? Get on with the job, Hopkirk. I've got another assignment for you when you get back."

Now that he'd as good as admitted his illegal use of the Net to Hopkirk, Darnell thought, the man had to go. It had been fun to keep him around for a little while, using him as a clerk and gofer, but one couldn't risk disgruntled victims getting together to compare notes. Once OG Glimware was taken care of, Darnell would "reward" Hopkirk with a free vacation at Summerlands Clinic. The Net revealed, among other things, that Alpha bint Hezra-Fong's patients on the charity side of Summerlands had an unusually high death rate. He'd "suggest" to Alpha that it would be convenient for both of them if Hopkirk never came back from Summerlands. That way nobody would talk about Darnell's use of the Net; and in return, he'd get Polyon to fix the Net records so that nobody would raise inconvenient questions about the number of charity patients Alpha had lost.

Achernar Subspace, Central Date 2752: Caleb and Nancia

"I wonder if he'll really be able to resolve anything," Nancia said thoughtfully as she and Caleb watched their latest delivery being greeted at Achernar Base on Charon. The short, spare man whom they'd brought halfway across the galaxy wasn't doing much to take control of his first meeting with the Charonese officials. He was just standing there on the landing field, listening to the speeches of welcome and accepting bouquets of flowers.

"None of our business," Caleb reminded her. "Central said, take Unattached Diplomatic Agent Forister to Charon, and do it fast. They didn't say to evaluate his job performance. And we've got another assignment waiting."

"Don't we always?" But the little group of pompous Charonese officials that surrounded Forister was moving off now, leaving the spacefield clear for Nancia's liftoff.

"It's just that I like to feel we've accomplished something," she lamented as Caleb strapped down for liftoff, "and I do feel this Charonese situation calls for somebody a bit more . . . more forceful." Somebody like Daddy, for instance. With his brisk, nononsense manner and willingness to enforce his decisions, Javier Perez y de Gras would have made short work of Charon's seven feuding factions, the continual war between the Tran Phon guerrillas and all seven provisional governments, and the consequent destruction of Charon's vital quinobark forests. He'd have been using Nancia's comm facilities and working the Net every minute they weren't in Singularity, preparing for his descent on the Charonese, arming himself with every last detail of the conflict, softening up the principal offenders with stern warning messages.

This Forister had spent the three days of the voyage reading ancient books—not even disks, but some account of an Old Earth war too minor to have been transcribed to computer-readable format. And when he wasn't reading about this place called Viet Nam, he wasted his time in relaxed, casual conversation with her and Caleb, chatting about their families and upbringing, their hopes and dreams. Too soft to stop a war, Nancia thought contemptuously. Oh, well, Caleb was right—the results were none of their business. They were Courier Service; they went where they were sent, quickly and efficiently. Sticking around to report on the failure of the resulting mission was not in the CS job description.

Bahati, Central Date 2753: Fassa

"You can't just leave me like this!"

Fassa del Parma y Polo paused at the door and blew a mocking kiss at the gray-faced, potbellied man who was looking at her with such pain in his eyes. "Watch me, darling. Just watch me." She touched her left index finger to the charm bracelet on her wrist. There'd been an empty prismawood heart there, just the right size to hold the minihedron recording this stupid bureaucrat's sign-off on the Nyota ya Jaha Space Station contract. "Our business is *done*." *All* their business, including those boring maneuvers on the man's synthofur rug. At least it hadn't taken too long. These old guys had dreams of grandeur, but they really couldn't do much when they did get the chance. *You're past it, sweetheart, and the future belongs to me.* Something uncomfortable writhed under the triumphant thought, some question as to why she exulted so much in the moral destruction of a small-time civil servant old enough to be her father; but Fassa pushed the question away with the ease of long practice. She had got what she wanted. It was as simple as that.

"But we were going to live together. You were going to quit this messy, unfeminine job, now that you've got enough money to pay for your sister's metachip prosthesis, and we were going to retire to Summerlands . . ."

Fassa laughed out loud. "What, me? Spend my last hundred years tending to some old man in a Summerlands retirement cottage? You've been popping too much Blissto, my friend." She paused to let the rejection sink in before delivering her final warning. "And don't even think about blowing the whistle on me. Remember, you've got more to lose than I have." She always set it up that way.

There was an unwelcome surprise waiting for her when she reached her offices. Two, in fact. One was minor; some kid was slumped in the corner sackback chair in the outer office, fiddling with forms. Employment applications were supposed to be handled in a different office; the kid should have been sent there to begin with.

Before she had time to point this out, her secretary lowered his head and apologetically informed her that Bahati CreditLin insisted on one more palmprint before they would release the final payment for the space station construction into her Net account. Just a formality, the secretary quoted the CreditLin officials.

Fassa's brows snapped together as the man assured her there was nothing to worry about. "Inspection? What inspection? Everything's been passed and signed by Vega Base." Or rather, by the befuddled old fool she'd just left, who hadn't even bothered to take a transport up to the station and walk its corridors in person, much less assign a qualified engineer to the task of a detailed structural inspection.

"That's what I told them," the secretary said, "and I'm sure this will take no time at all, since Vega's engineering division has already signed off on all the main structural elements. Just a formality," he repeated. "It seems there's been a new law passed; CreditLin is obliged to send one of its own independent inspectors to verify that our construction meets standards before they can transfer the credits."

A new law . . . Damn! I thought all the Bahati Senators had been paid off. Do I have to do everything myself?

Fassa suppressed the thought with a quick frown. She'd deal with the legislature later. For now—so there was one more fool of a man to deal with, to wheedle and distract and please into forgetting the obvious checks that would reveal her substandard materials. Annoying, that was all. She didn't like surprises. But it would, after all, be one more minihedron to fill her charm bracelet.

Fassa caught a flicker of movement in the corner, just enough to distract her for a moment. The kid in the sackback was stretching, rising out of the enveloping chair. *Not now. Go away. I have other things to think about.*

"Miss del Parma y Polo?"

Not such a kid; a man grown, older than she was herself—but not by so very much. Fassa took in his appearance with growing appreciation. Broad shoulders, legs long enough to carry off his outrageously psychepainted Capellan stretchpants, black hair and eyes whose blue was set off by slashing streaks of ochre face paint. *A pretty peacock of a man. Maybe I'll hire him after all, even if he did bypass the employment office. Who cares whether he can do anything? Keep him around just to look at.*

"I should introduce myself now, I guess." He smiled down at her and enveloped her hand in his. "Sev Bryley, chief inspector for Bahati CreditLin. I reckon it'll be a pleasure working with you, Miss del Parma."

Cor Caroli Subspace, Central Date 2753: Caleb and Nancia

Caleb slammed one fist into the opposite palm and paced the width of the central cabin, growling deep in his throat. He paused opposite a purple metalloy bulkhead with silver-gilt stenciled borders and raised his fist again.

"Don't even think about it," Nancia warned him. "You'll only hurt your hand and damage my nice new paint job."

Caleb lowered his fist. A reluctant smile twitched at the corners of his lips. "Don't tell me you *like* the paint job?"

"No. But it seemed suitable for our role. And I don't wish to return to Central looking as if I'd been through a clawing match with some of Dorg Jesen's popsies, thank you very much."

They had been undercover for this mission, Caleb posing as a debauched young High Families scion who wanted a cut of Dorg Jesen's secret metachip supply. In return, he was to have offered the feelieporn king secret information on certain of his High Families customers.

"Could be dangerous," Rahilly had warned them, back on Central Base. "Jesen doesn't like awkward questions. Try to keep the meetings on shipboard. Nancia, you'll have to protect yourself and Caleb if Jesen tries anything."

But they hadn't even lured Jesen into one shipboard meeting. He'd taken one look at Caleb's vidcom image, listened to Caleb's stiff delivery of the speech he'd been assigned to make, and burst out laughing. "Pull the other one, it's got bells on," he taunted Caleb. "And next time Central decides to send someone to investigate me, tell them not to make it an Academy boy with a Vega accent you could cut with a knife, in a brainship with a tarted-up central cabin. If you're High Families, I'll eat my . . ."

Nancia cut the sound transmission at that point.

"Perhaps," she said now, "undercover work is not our *metier*."

"I hate lies and spying," Caleb confirmed moodily. "We should have refused this mission." He looked up with a glimmer of hope in his eyes. "Unless . . . did you get anything?"

Nancia had used the brief minutes of the vidcom link to insert feelers into Jesen's private computer system, so private that it didn't even have a Net connection. Central had surmised he might have such a system in addition to the open accounts he maintained via Net, but nothing could be checked until they arrived planetside.

"Nothing," she told him. "I did get into his supply acquisition database, but all the metachips in the records there show perfectly legitimate Shemali Base control numbers."

Caleb made a fist again. "Then you didn't get into the right records. Somebody's counterfeiting metachips, and Jesen could lead us to the source . . . could have led us. He must be keeping *three* sets of books. Do you think if I got him on vidcom again . . ."

An incoming transmission reached Nancia, and she activated her central display screen. Dorg Jesen's narrow face appeared. "Been doing a little research of my own," he announced, almost pleasantly. "Got your Central ID now to add in to my report. CN-935, lift your Courier Service tailfins offplanet in fifteen minutes and we'll forget this episode ever happened. Otherwise I'll file a formal complaint with CS, charging you and your brawn with entrapment."

"You can't win them all," Nancia tried to soothe Caleb when they were offplanet and on their way back to Central. "We do many things well. Lying doesn't happen to be among them, that's all." *But I'm lying, right now, by saying nothing.* Nancia made an internal playback of the datacordings she'd made four years earlier, on her maiden voyage. There was Polyon, cheerfully announcing his plan to slip metachips past the SUM board and sell them to unauthorized operations like Dorg Jesen's feelieporn empire. If only Caleb knew what she knew, he could make a report to Central that would send them straight to Shemali.

Except . . . he wouldn't do it. In the four years of their partnership, Caleb had never once wavered or compromised his moral principles. He would never stoop to using a datacording made without the knowledge or consent of the passengers. And he would never respect Nancia again, once he knew what she'd done on that first voyage.

Sadly, Nancia ended the replay and slapped five more levels of security classifications on the datacording. Caleb must never know. But there must be some way to point Central's investigations towards Shemali, to stop them thinking in terms of counterfeit metachips and start them thinking about the prison factory.

Shemali, Central Date 2754:
Polyon

Polyon slapped the palmboard built into his armchair and activated a vidcom link with Bahati.

"Summerlands Clinic, Alpha bint Hezra-Fong, private transmission, code CX22." That would scramble his message so that only someone with the CX22 decoding hedron would be able to see and hear anything but gibberish. "Alpha, my sweet, you were just a tad premature in announcing that you'd finished your Seductron research. The free sample you sent up has one of my key techs too blissed-out to do any useful work. I've no idea when he'll stop contemplating his toenails, so you'd better find out—and fast. Unless you want to be the next test subject." He smiled sweetly into the vidcom unit. "I *can* arrange it, you know."

The next message went to Darnell, using a similar scrambling technique. In a few words Polyon informed Darnell that Intra-Manager, the small commlink manufacturing company Darnell was presently trying to take over, was not to be touched. "It's one of mine," he said pleasantly. "I'm sure you wouldn't have made a takeover move if you'd known that, would you now? By the way— did I show you the latest vids of the metachip line?" A tap of his fingers on the palmboard called up a datacording from the lowest circles of Hell: suited and masked workers toiling amid clouds of poisonous green steam. This was the last and most dangerous phase of metachip assembly, when the blocks between the poly-printed connection patterns were burned off with a quick dip into vats of acid. The burn-off process released a gaseous form of Ganglicide into the atmosphere. Before Polyon's time, this phase had been handled—rather badly—by automated servos that mis-judged the depth and timing of the burnoff phase, dropped metachip boards, and quickly self-destructed in the poisonous atmosphere. Expensive and wasteful. By contrast, prison workers in protective suits could process more than three times as many metachips in a session, and only a few of them were lost each year to leaks in the suit sealing.

"See the third man from the left, Darnell?" Polyon spoke into the vidcom while the images unreeled. "He used to be High Fami-lies. Now he's a Shemali assembly worker. How are the mighty fallen, eh?"

He cut the connection on that—an implied threat was ever so much more effective than a specific one. Actually, Polyon had no idea who the masked workers on the line might be. They were the scum of the prison system, the expendables who had neither tech training nor business sense to justify keeping them in the safer areas of design and preprocessing. And while there was indeed a High Families convict on Shemali, the man had been sent there for a particularly revolting series of crimes involving the torture of small children. Polyon didn't really think he could frame Darnell for something like that and make it stick; anybody would see the rich boy didn't have the guts to torture anybody.

But I won't need to, will I? The threat will be enough to keep old Darnell in line.

The last call was to Fassa. He was lucky enough to catch her in person. Polyon enjoyed the sight of Fassa's eyes widening while he explained in detail just how unhappy he felt about the collapse of his new metachip assembly building, how personally hurt he was to discover that Polo Construction had supplied the substandard materials used in the building, and exactly what he might do to assuage his sense of loss and betrayal. The only trouble with the live connection, Polyon thought, was that he didn't get to finish outlining the list of things he could do to Polo Construction as a company and to Fassa personally. Before he was half through, she was stammering apologies and practically begging to be allowed to rebuild the assembly facility. Free of charge, naturally.

Polyon graciously accepted the offer.

Just one more item of business to clear up. "Send in 4987832," he commanded.

A few minutes later, a pale-faced man in the prison uniform of green coveralls came into the office. He gave Polyon a confident smile. "Thought it over, have you?"

"I most certainly have," Polyon agreed. He smiled and shrugged with palms outspread. "Can't say I'm altogether happy about the idea—but I see you leave me no choice. You're a clever fellow, 4987832. Who were you, before?"

"James Masson," the prisoner said. "Head of research for Zectronics—you've heard of them? No? Well, it's a large galaxy. But it so happens I personally directed the metachip design effort there. That's how I happened to recognize the changes you've introduced in the chips."

"My hyperchips will be faster and more powerful than the old metachips by at least two orders of magnitude," Polyon said. "They'll revolutionize the industry. It didn't take any genius to recognize that. The genius was in figuring out how to do it."

"And that's not all the hyperchips will do, is it, de Gras-Waldheim? Industry isn't the only thing about to suffer a . . . revolution."

Polyon inclined his head slightly. "You'll have a glass of Stemerald with me, to celebrate our arrangement?"

Masson's eyes widened and he licked his lips. "Why, I haven't tasted Stemerald in—in—well, it must be ten years! Not since I came here! I must say, de Gras-Waldheim, I didn't think you'd take our little arrangement so well."

Polyon's back was to Masson as he poured out the Stemerald into two sparkling globes from OG Glimware.

"A lot of men would be petty about cutting me in on the profits," Masson babbled on, accepting his globe and draining it between words, "but that's you High Families type, you know how to accept defeat graciously. And after all, giving me a small cut isn't much when you think of what it would do to your plans if I told Governor Lyautey about *all* the hyperchips' programming." He swallowed the last drops of Stemerald, ran his tongue round his lips once more to savor the taste, then sat back with the slightly dazed expression of a man who'd just had his first strong drink in ten years.

"As I said," Polyon repeated, "you leave me no choice in the matter." He frowned quickly. "You have honored your end of the agreement, haven't you, Masson? No word to anyone else?"

"No word," Masson agreed. He spoke more slowly now. "I wouldn't . . . want . . . anyone else . . . cutting in . . ." His eyes glazed over and he sat staring into space with a blissful smile on his face.

"Very good. Now, Masson, I have a special task for you." Polyon leaned forward. "Hear and repeat! You will go to the dip chambers."

"I . . . will . . . go . . . to . . . the . . . dip . . . chambers," Masson droned.

"I want you to make a surprise inspection. You will not announce yourself."

". . . not . . . announce . . . 'self."

"You do not need a protective suit."

Masson nodded and smiled. All the intelligence had left his face now. Polyon felt a twinge of regret. The man had been brilliant; would be again, if the Seductron wore off. He could have been a useful subordinate if he hadn't made the mistake of trying to blackmail Polyon. But as it was . . . well, there was no point in waiting, was there? Damn Alpha. If she'd only developed the controlled Seductron she kept promising, with doses ranging from ten-minute zaps to a state of mindless, permanent bliss, there would be no need for this last distasteful step.

Polyon finished his orders to Masson and snapped a dismissal. "Go. Now!"

Masson stood unsteadily and left Polyon's inner office. Polyon sat back and began sketching a metachip linkage plan with one forefinger, tracing glowing paths across the design screen.

Five minutes later, his vidcomm lit up to show the face of the afternoon shift supervisor. "Lieutenant de Gras-Waldheim? Sir? There's been a terrible accident. One of your designers just . . . the man must have gone mad, he walked right into the dip room without a suit . . . if only he'd knocked they could have kept him waiting in the outer lock until the gases were cleared out . . . they didn't even know he was there. . . . The room was filled with Ganglicide in gaseous form, he didn't have a chance. . . ." Screams sounded in the background. "Oh, sir, it's terrible!"

"A most distressing accident," Polyon agreed. "Begin the paperwork, 567934. And don't blame yourself. Sometimes it just takes them like that, you know, the lifers. Better any death than a lifetime on Shemali, they think, and who knows? Perhaps they're right. Oh, sorry, I forgot—you're a lifer too, aren't you?"

He didn't start laughing until the connection was broken.

CHAPTER SEVEN

Spica Base, Central Date 2754:
Caleb and Nancia

Nancia limped into Spica Base on half power, dependent on Caleb for reports on the lower deck damage where her sensors had self-destructed to preserve her from shock when the asteroid struck them.

"Freak accident," commented the Tech Grade 7 who came out to survey the damage in person.

Nancia mourned the sleek gloss of her exterior finish, now pitted and gouged around the torn metal shreds of the entrance hole. "I should have taken a different route."

"Freak ship." The tech snapped his IR-Sensor goggles down, hiding his eyes behind a band of black plastifilm. "Ain't natural. Ship talks, pilot don't."

"The correct terms, as I'm sure you are aware, are 'brainship' and 'brawn,'" Nancia said frostily. "Caleb is . . . it's none of your business. Just leave him alone, okay?" She'd seen him plunged into these unreasoning depressions before, whenever one of their missions was less than one hundred percent successful. He'd retreated into himself without speaking for a week after the disastrous undercover assignment with Dorg Jesen, while Nancia tried to tempt his appetite with fancy dishes from the galley and interesting tidbits of news picked up from the gossipbeams.

"I'll need somebody at the other end to help me link the hyperchips into the ship's system," the tech protested. "Somebody who knows the ship. My guys are good, but this is a small base. They ain't never worked on a talking ship before. And nobody's got that much experience with hyperchips. They might not interface with these sensor setups just like the old metachips did."

"Then," said Nancia, "perhaps you should explain to them that a talking ship can, in fact, *talk.* There's no need to trouble my brawn for information; I'll manage the installation myself." She didn't feel nearly so cheerful and carefree as she tried to sound; the thought of some dolt like this tech fooling around with her synaptic connectors made her feel sick and weak. But she did *not* want him bothering Caleb. One thing she'd learned in the last four years of partnership was that Caleb only stayed depressed longer if he was forced to talk to people before he was ready to.

The tech grunted acquiescence and twiddled something she couldn't see. "Sensor connection to OP-N1.15, testing."

"If you mean can I see what you're doing," Nancia responded, "the answer is no."

The tech gaped but recovered himself quickly. "Hah! OP-N1 series . . . optic nerve connections? Sorry, lady—ship—whatever you are. What I'm looking at, see, it's just schematics. I didn't think . . ." His voice trailed off for a moment. "Awesome, really, when you think about it that way. That there's a *person* somewhere inside this steel and titanium."

"Correction," Nancia said. She was becoming used to this tendency among softpersons; they insisted on equating her with the body curled inside the titanium column, as if that was all there was to her. "I *am* a person. That's my lower deck vision you're twiddling with now, and I'd very much like to have it—Thank you!" A partial visual field opened as she spoke. Now she could see the tech again, and one gloved hand reaching up into the tangle of fused metal and wires that had been her lower deck sensory system.

"OP-N1.15 restored," the tech noted. "Now if—say, this is going to be easy. Don't need this stuff" He clipped a test meter to his belt and used both hands to rejoin severed wires. "OP-N1.16 functioning now? Good. 17?" He worked through the full series rapidly, while Nancia kept him informed of the status of each repair.

"Thank you," she said again when he'd restored her full optic series for the lower deck. "It's . . . most troubling, being unable to look at a part of myself."

"Imagine it would be," the tech agreed. "Glad to help a lady, any time."

Nancia noted that in the course of one short repair session she had advanced from "unnatural talking ship," to "person" to, apparently, "lady in distress." *By the time the repairs are finished, he'll be wanting to sign up for brawn training . . . and most distressed to learn he's over age.*

"And this is just the beginning," the tech promised. "We'll have you fixed up good as new in a day or so. *Better* than new, really. You had any hyperchips installed before? Thought not. They're— I dunno—about a thousand times better than the old line meta-chips. You're gonna like this, ma'am." His fingers twisted, seating one of the new chips. It felt strange to see the movements without feeling the slight pressure and hearing the click as the chip slid into place.

"Can you feel anything when I do this?"

"No—yes. Oh!"

"Hurt you?"

"No. Just—surprised." Nancia felt as if her sensors had been turned up to full volume, without sacrificing the slightest accuracy. Every movement was clear; the world sparkled like crystal around her. "How many more of those do you have? Can you replace my upper deck sensor chips too?"

The tech shook his head regretfully. "Sorry, ma'am. It's a new design out of Shemali. There's not enough hyperchips out yet to go around to all the folks who need them for repairs, let alone bringing in functional equipment and retrofitting it. Shemali Plant estimates it'll be a good three-four years before they can produce enough to retrofit all the Fleet ships."

"Oh. Of course." Nancia remembered the plan Polyon had described on her maiden voyage. "I suppose," she said, feeling very crafty, "I suppose a lot of the chips are failing QA tests? It being a new design, and all," she added hastily.

The tech shook his head. "No, ma'am. Actually, these new chips don't fail in testing near as often as the old design. Pretty near the full production run is being cleared for distribution, most times. It's just that even a year's full production runs out of Shemali don't amount to that much when you consider all the places the chips have to go these days. It's not just the Fleet, y'know. Hospitals, Base brains, cyborg replacements, defense systems—seems like we just about couldn't run the galaxy without 'em!"

Nancia felt first disappointed, then relieved. She had expected to hear that the new design somehow caused a great many metachips to fail in the QA phase and that nobody knew what became of the substandard chips rejected by the SUM ration board. That would have been evidence she could mention to Caleb, something to steer his mind in the direction of Polyon's illicit activities without revealing that she already knew about the plan.

Instead, it seemed that Polyon had given up his plan altogether. He *was* brilliant. Perhaps the hyperchip design was his idea; and perhaps, Nancia thought optimistically, he had forgotten his original notion of stealing metachips in favor of the honest pleasure of seeing his design accepted and used galaxy-wide.

Angalia, Central Date 2754

The third annual progress meeting of the Nyota Five was held on Angalia, an arrangement which pleased no one—least of all the host.

"It was *your* idea to rotate the annual meetings," Alpha bint Hezra-Fong pointed out, somewhat snappishly, when Blaize apologized for the primitive accommodations. "We could have been comfortably settled in a Summerlands conference room, but nooo, you and Polyon had to fuss that it wouldn't be fair if you two had to travel to Bahati every time just to suit the three of us who had the good luck to be stationed there. So we have to rotate. Two nice meetings on Bahati, now this godforsaken dump, and next time, stars help us, Shemali. You and your bright ideas! Send someone to unpack for me—you must have *some* help around the place, surely?"

"'Fraid not," Blaize said with a sunny smile. He was beginning to enjoy the prospect of Alpha's discomfort on Angalia. Rotating the meeting sites had really been Polyon's idea, not his, but Alpha was obviously afraid to take out her bad temper on Lieutenant de Gras-Waldheim. Blaize glanced sidelong at Polyon, very straight and correct in his Academy dress blacks, and admitted to himself that he didn't blame Alpha. Given a choice of tongue-lashing the enigmatic technical manager of Shemali MetaPlant, or the little red-haired runt from PTA, who wouldn't choose to lash out at the PTA wimp?

But this understanding didn't make him love Alpha—or the rest of the Nyota Five, including himself—any better.

"Welcome," Blaize said with a sweeping bow that included all four of his guests, "to the Angalia Tourist Center. A modest facility, as you can see—"

Darnell's snort of laughter testified to the truth of that statement.

"—but vastly improved from its humble beginnings," Blaize finished. "If the winner were to be chosen on the basis of progress rather than of absolute wealth, I'd have no doubt of succeeding next year." And that, by God, was the absolute and unvarnished truth! The rest of them might sneer at Blaize's long, low bungalow with its thatched roof and thatch-shaded balcony, the garden of native ferns and grasses and the paved path leading from there to the corycium mine. Never mind. *He* knew what it had taken to create these amenities from the mud-hole that Supervisor Harmon had left him with.

"All done with native labor?" Fassa interrupted his explanation. "But everybody knows the Loosies are too stupid to do anything useful."

Blaize put one finger to the side of his nose and winked, a gesture borrowed from an old tri-D show called *Fagin and His Gang*. "Amazing what even a veg-head can do with the proper . . . incentive," he drawled.

"Where d'you store the whips and spiked sticks?" That was pudgy Darnell, bright-eyed as if he actually expected Blaize to produce a panoply of torture instruments and demonstrate their use.

"You've no subtlety, Overton-Glaxely," Blaize reproved the man. "Think. The—er—Loosies were starving when I came here, kept alive only by PTA ration bricks. The task of distributing the ration bricks, naturally, belonged to the PTA representative on Angalia. Me."

"So?" Darnell really was amazingly slow. Not for the first time,

Blaize wondered how he'd made such a success out of OG Shipping and the smaller corporations that OG Enterprises had swallowed up over the years.

"So," Blaize drawled, "I saw no reason to *give* away PTA ration supplements when they could perfectly well be used to train the natives. We have a simple rule of life now on Angalia, my friends— no work, no eat." He pointed towards the entrance to the corycium mine. "And it's not just applied to building the master's bungalow. I hold the title to that mine. United Spacetec abandoned it because they couldn't keep human miners on Angalia. *I* use the native resources to mine the native resources, so to speak—you'll see the day shift coming out in a few minutes."

"And you pay them with ration bricks, which come free via PTA?" Alpha gave Blaize an approving smile that chilled him to the bone. "I must admit, Blaize, you're not as stupid as you look. Anything you make from the corycium mine is profit, free and clear."

Blaize opened his mouth wide in simulated shock. "Dr. Hezra-Fong! Please! I am deeply shocked and disillusioned that you should think such a thing of me. Any profits accruing from the corycium mine naturally belong to the natives of Angalia." He waited a beat before continuing. "Of course, since the natives of Angalia do not have Intelligent Sentient Status, they can't have bank accounts— so the credits do, perforce, go into a Net account in my name. But held in trust for the Loosies—you understand?"

The others chuckled knowingly and all agreed that they did indeed understand, and that Blaize was a clever lad to have found such a good way of covering his tail in the event of a PTA inspection. All but Polyon de Gras-Waldheim, who was tapping one finger against the seam of his black trousers and staring at the thunderclouds on the horizon.

"You've done pretty well, considering," Darnell admitted, "but with creatures as dumb as these, surely you have—er—discipline problems?" He was getting that whips-and-chains expression again.

"If he does, maybe regulated doses of Seductron would be the answer," cooed Alpha. "I've just about got the bugs worked out of the dosage schedule now, and it might be interesting to test it on non-humans."

Blaize forced himself to smile. Time for his demonstration. He'd planned it beforehand, in case there was need to make an additional impression on the others, but had hoped it wouldn't be necessary. Messy, it would be. And wasteful. But apparently they still weren't convinced of his firm control over the Loosies.

"Thanks, Alpha, but Seductron wouldn't quite do the trick; the Loosies are passive and malleable enough already. What they need is occasional stimulation, and that," he said with a low laugh, "that I can arrange for myself." He raised one hand in the air and brought it down with a swift chopping motion.

Two of the tall rock pillars beside the garden wall moved forward in the shambling, awkward gait characteristic of the Loosies. With movement, their features and humanoid shapes could be dearly seen, although until a moment earlier they had blended in with the real stones making up the rest of the wall. Between them they hauled a third "rock," a native whose double-jointed legs sagged under him and whose flapping liplike folds of skin opened and closed with a mimed display of silent terror.

"They may not talk," said Blaize, "but they've learned to understand simple sign commands quite well. Most of them have, anyway. This fellow in the middle dropped a serving dish when he was waiting on me at dinner yesterday. I've been saving him to make an example of in front of the miners, but since there's an audience here already"—he allowed his eyes to roam lazily over his four co-conspirators—"why wait any longer for the pleasure?"

He pointed over the side of the mesa with a deliberate downward motion, three times repeated. The two Loosie guards bobbed their square heads and half carried, half dragged their prisoner over the edge.

"You make 'em throw themselves over the cliff?"

"Not at all," Blaize cackled. "Too fast, that'd be. Come and watch!"

By the time everybody had crowded around the low wall at the mesa's edge, the three Loosies were already down on the mud flats, approaching one of the areas where bubbles rose and burst in the glop with a stench of sulfur. The two guards hauled the prisoner to the edge of this bubbling area and thrust him into the soft mud. As he writhed and struggled to escape, they picked up the long sticks that had marked the site of the bubbles and used them to thrust him back into the steaming mud.

"Natural hot springs under there," Blaize explained. "Very hot. Takes a couple of hours to cook 'em through. Fortunately, the

Loosies are real patient. Those two I use as guards will keep pushing him down until he quits trying to get out, even if it takes most of the evening."

He turned away from the spectacle of torture and bowed once again to his guests. "Well, ladies and gentlemen," he inquired with a benign smile, "shall we begin the business meeting?"

Even Polyon, Blaize noted, was pale against the dead black of his uniform; while the other three were shocked into silence. So much the better. It would be a while, he thought, before any of them underestimated little Blaize again.

After the shocking scene Blaize had just provided, the third annual progress meeting began more quietly than the previous meetings had gone. The underlying tensions in the group were still present, however, and all the sharper for another year's fermenting.

As host, Blaize claimed the honor of giving the initial report. While Polyon gazed over his head in unfeigned boredom and the two girls sat pale and silent, he began reciting facts and figures to back up his earlier assertions. In earlier years he'd had little to report. This year he was at last coming into his own. He fancied a glimmer of respect in Polyon's eyes as Blaize explained how he was using the first profits from the corycium mine to finance the purchase of heavy mining equipment that would open up even more of the planet for exploitation. Darnell twitched and muttered to himself during this part of the report, but he didn't explode until Polyon pointedly inquired as to how Blaize had financed the initial startup costs of the mine.

"Reselling surplus PTA shipments," Blaize replied promptly.

"Dear me," commented Polyon, "I thought the—ah—'Loosies' were starving. Didn't this move reduce your potential worker population somewhat?"

"Waste not, want not," Blaize waved his hand in vague circles. "There's a lot of surplus in any bureaucracy. I just—as you might say—cut the fat out."

It was perhaps unfortunate that his eyes met Darnell's at this moment, and that the airy circles his hand was sketching could have been taken for an indication of Darnell's growing paunch.

"The hell you did!" Darnell exploded, surging to his feet on a wave of red-faced fury. "Cut it right out of *my* hide, you mean!"

He turned to the others as if appealing for their sympathy. "Little bastard blackmailed me to ship extra food here—*free*—while he was selling the supplies that ought to've gone to the natives!"

This accusation did not have quite the effect he might have been hoping for.

"Really, Darnell?" asked Polyon with bright-eyed interest. "And what were you doing that he could blackmail you for, I wonder?"

Darnell puffed and stammered and Alpha interrupted him. "Who cares? I'm delighted *somebody* finally nailed you. Ever since you took over Pair-a-Dice I've wanted to pay you back!"

"What do you care whether I buy out a crummy casino?"

"That 'crummy casino,'" Alpha informed him, "just happened to be my primary outlet for Seductron at street prices. The gambling was only a front—once you pay the Bahati cops off for a gambling operation, they're too dumb to check and see if that's really where all the money is coming from. Pair-a-Dice—Paradise—get it, stupid? That's the street name for Seductron."

"I thought you didn't have the dosage schedules worked out yet!" Fassa sounded appalled.

Alpha shrugged thin, elegant shoulders. Her face was sharp as a knife under the elaborate Nueva Estrella style of tight braids piled high in a prismawood spiral frame. "So a few Blissto addicts go out happy. Who cares? I've got to start making something off Seductron before next year. Even if I work around all the side effects, it's too late to patent it now. So it's street deals or nothing." This reminded her of her grievance. "And since *you* took over my best outlet, Pudge-face, it's been nothing. You owe me!"

"So do you," Fassa told Blaize. "Del Parma was low bidder on the corycium processing plant. By government regulations you ought to've given us the job. How much did the winning contractor slip you under the table?"

"That," Blaize replied stiffly, "is between the two of us, and nothing to do with you, Fassa! Besides, knowing what I do about del Parma's construction methods, what made you think I'd be fool enough to let you build a latrine trench on Angalia?"

"Huh! Angalia already *is* a latrine trench! Ha-ha-ha!"

Nobody except Fassa paid the least attention to Darnell's lame jest. She whirled and stabbed a long iridescent corycium-sheathed fingernail at his chest. "And you! Remember the Procyon run? That's the last time OG Shipping gets any del Parma business!"

Darnell smoothed down his green synthofur jacket and smirked. "Can't see what you're complaining about," he replied. "Switching good construction materials for substandard ones is standard practice for del Parma."

"Only," Fassa said, "when *I* keep the profit. I'm not running a charitable association for the benefit of OG Shipping."

"Can't see why not," Darnell leered. "The word is you've been charitable to enough of Bahati's male population already."

Fassa sat down abruptly, holding her head in her hands. "Don't remind me," she wailed, "as if you and everybody else cheating me weren't enough, can't I at least forget about that inspector from CreditLin for a little while? I gave him what he wanted, the space station's paid for, I can't understand why he won't go *away.*"

"I can," suggested Blaize helpfully. "Fraudulent QA records, shoddy materials, slipshod building practices, non-union workers . . ."

"Cheat!"

"Bloodsucker!"

"Shark!"

The meeting dissolved into the usual chaos while Polyon sat back, arms crossed, and murmured, "Naughty children."

CHAPTER EIGHT

Kailas, Procyon Subspace, Central Date 2754

The Central Diplomatic Services office tower was a lacework of steel and titanium needles, wrapped in translucent green synthofilm that trapped and redistributed natural light in a soft, unchanging glow. Midnight or noon, the CDS offices on Kailas were lit by a gentle, slightly green-tinged light that was energy-efficient, situation-appropriate, and psychologically proven to be simultaneously soothing and inspirational.

It made Sev Bryley feel as if he was about to suffer a recurrence of the jungle rot that had attacked his skin on Capella Four. He tried not to think about the light. It was a minor matter, not worth wasting the precious minutes this important man had granted him.

"You hate this, too, don't you?" the important man said.

"Sir?"

An impatient grunt. "The blasted light. Something Psych and EcoTech dreamed up between them. Makes me feel as if I were back on Capella Six."

"For me it was Four," Sev confessed.

Another grunt. "Different war, same jungle. I'd open a window if this place *had* windows. Can't peel plastifilm open, more's the pity."

"It's very good of you to make time to see me at all, sir," Sev said cautiously. So they had a common background—service in

359

the Capellan Wars? Was that why this highly placed diplomat had given a mere private investigator ten minutes out of his crowded schedule?

"Not at all. Do the same for any friend of the family who needed help. So. What's your problem, d'Aquino?"

Sev stiffened. "I didn't intend to call on family connections, sir—"

"Then you're a damned young fool," said the gray-haired man in the conservative blue tunic. "I've been checking your Net records. Your full name is Sevareid Bryley-Sorensen d'Aquino—why didn't you use it when you requested this appointment? You could have gotten in to see me three days sooner. And why me, if you didn't mean to call on High Families connections?"

"I was not aware that there was a relationship between our families. Sir," Sev said stiffly. "I came to Kailas because it was the nearest world with any CDS representatives high-ranking enough to deal with my problem. And I approached you because you have the reputation of being one of the two Central Worlds officials on this planet who cannot be bribed, threatened, or suborned."

"So you found two honest men, my Diogenes? I'm flattered."

"Sir. My name is Bryley, not Dio—whatever."

"A classical reference. No matter. What do they teach them in University these days? But then, you didn't finish your schooling. Why didn't you cash in your veteran's benefits after Capella IV to complete your education at Central's expense?"

Sev tried without success to conceal his surprise.

"The Net can supply—um—rather a lot of detail," his interlocutor explained gently. "Even about a rather obscure private investigator who's recently lost his position with Bahati CreditLin—yes, I found out about that too. Something about a gambling scandal at the Pair-a-Dice, wasn't it?"

"It was a lie!" Sev leaned forward, burning with indignation at the memory. "My supervisor—he had anonymous letters about me. I know who sent them, but I can't prove it."

"And who might that be?"

"The same man who transferred credits into my Net account and played under my name at Pair-a-Dice—or maybe he sent one of his flunkies to play the part. When I went to the casino, they wouldn't tell me anything about the man who used my name."

"No. They beat you—rather badly—and threw you out into the

ecocycler in the back alley." The gray-eyed man surveyed Sev with eyes that took in every faint mark of healing bruises and scraped skin. "Lucky you didn't wind up being recycled into somebody's rose garden; we suspect that's what has happened to a few other people who annoyed the proprietor of that particular establishment. So. You came to your senses, crawled out of the ecocycler before it began its chop sequence, got treatment for your more obvious wounds from some shady blacklisted ex-doctor among your underworld friends, and . . . came halfway across the galaxy to wait three days for an interview with me. Want me to get you reinstated with Bahati CreditLin, is that it? Favor for a friend? Teach them not to act on anonymous accusations against a High Families lad—even one who's rebelled against his background and is working incognito?"

"Sir!"

"It can be arranged, you know," said the gray-eyed man, watching Sev closely. "A word from this office, and Bahati CreditLin will reinstate you, full back pay, no questions asked. If that's what you want . . ."

"No, sir."

The gray-eyed man nodded briskly. "Good. I didn't think so, but one has to be sure. You want to track down the people who framed you, then."

"More than that." Sev dropped his eyes. "I think I know who framed me. And why. But it's a long story, and there are High Families involved. That's why I came to you, sir. Somebody without that background might be tempted to shove everything under the carpet for fear of offending someone powerful. And of those in Central Administration who are High Families—well—" He spread his hands helplessly. "I don't know the lineages and their reputations. The only two people whose integrity everyone is absolutely sure of are you and General Questar-Benn—and she's on some kind of secret assignment, nobody would tell me where."

"How flattering," purred the gray-eyed man.

Belatedly, Sev realized the implications of his words. "Sir. I didn't mean—I am most grateful that you agreed to see me, truly I am."

"Take that as read. Now why don't you tell me what's going on?"

Sev's cheekbones reddened. His tongue felt like a wad of cotton in his mouth. Where could he begin? In this cool green-lit office, the madness that had seized him on Bahati seemed like a dream.

"There was—a girl."

"Ahh. You know, there quite often is, in such cases. And you—made a fool of yourself?" He looked at Sev sympathetically. "You know, I *can* remember the urge to make a fool of oneself over a young lady. I'm not so old and dried-up as all that. But if this story is going to be personal, perhaps you'd feel easier continuing it in a less formal environment? Sometimes I go across town for lunch—there's a cafe in Darkside. Nothing fancy. But at least it gets one out of this damned jungle light."

Fifteen minutes later, feeling somewhat as if he'd actually been through the ecocycler's processing sequence, Sev and the man he'd come to see were seated at a table in the back of a cavernous, dimly lit cafe. The one window that might have admitted a little sunlight was curtained by dusty streamers of glitzribbon and prismawood light-dangles. In one corner of the room, a weedy boy with long red hair tied in a black velvet bow tinkered with his synthocom set, producing occasional bursts of strident sound that grated on Sev's eardrums.

Even his sleazy story seemed no more than normal, here. He wondered if that was why they'd come to this dingy place. It seemed an odd setting for a man who spent his working life meeting with presidents and kings and generals.

"It's quiet here," said the only honest man on Kailas, "and more to the point, I know there won't be any unauthorized datacordings made of our conversation; I'm acquainted with the proprietor of this place. She has quite a number of visitors who don't want their discussions overheard or recorded."

"I can believe it," said Sev with feeling.

"So. If that answers your curiosity about why we came here—why don't you tell me about this girl?"

"She was—" Sev stopped, swallowed, searched again for a place to begin. "She is head of a construction company based on Bahati. Their most recent contract was for a space station to catch Net signals and route small-package traffic between Vega subspace and Central. As part of my routine duties for Bahati CreditLin, I was asked to do a final walk-through inspection of the station. It was—it should have been just a formality; the head of Contracts Administration had already signed off on the work."

"I take it," murmured the gray-eyed man, "there were, in fact, some deficiencies in the construction methods?"

"It was a *joke*." Sev's hands moved freely and he forgot his nervousness as he sketched the discoveries he'd made. "Oh, everything looked good enough on the outside. Fresh new perm-alloy surface skin. Interior corridors painted and glowlit, shiny new sensor screens to scan the exteriors. But once I opened up a few panels and started looking at what was behind the fresh paint—" He shook his head, remembering. "She tried to distract me. No. That's not fair. She...did distract me. For a while." Three days and nights in Fassa del Parma's private cubicle on her personal transport ship, wheeling around the space station, watching the blazing dance of the stars through the clear walls above and below and around their own dance...

Sev felt himself on fire again, remembering. And regretting. Even now, some part of him wanted nothing better than to be back on the *Xanadu* with Fassa del Parma y Polo. Whatever the cost.

"She was...annoyed," he said slowly, "when I told her I'd have to complete the inspection according to form." He looked up at the man seated across the table, searching for a hint of condemnation in the level gray eyes. "I should have done the inspection immediately. I'd given her three days." *No, she gave them to me. Three days I'll never forget.* "She'd had her people working overtime to conceal their cheap work. Panels behind panels. Fake safety numbers stenciled on the recycled supporting beams. Warning signs about chemical danger areas in front of the rats' nests they called an electronic system—as though that would've stopped me!" Sev snorted.

"If *I* had put up signs warning of chemical dangers," the other man commented, "I would have made sure that you did indeed run into such dangers the first time you removed a panel. Nothing fatal, of course. Certainly nothing really nasty, like gaseous Ganglicide. Maybe a little sinoidal stimulant. Or Capellan fungus spores."

"She thought of that," said Sev grimly. "So, unfortunately for her, did I...I wore a chem-pro suit and gas mask while I checked out the electronics."

"And?"

"The place never should have passed the most cursory inspection," Sev said tonelessly. "It *didn't* pass mine. I transmitted a full report via the Net—enough to stop payment on the space station and put Polo Construction under investigation. The lady was, ummm—not pleased when I told her what I'd done." A reminiscent smile tugged at one corner of his mouth and he rubbed absentmindedly at the four parallel scratches under his right ear. Nothing more than the faint memory of scars now, but the lines still tingled whenever he thought of Fassa. Being clawed by Fassa del Parma wasn't nearly as much fun as the things they'd done on the *Xanadu*, but it was still a remarkably stimulating experience. Even now, Sev reckoned he would rather have a fight with Fassa than party with any six other girls of his acquaintance.

Not that the opportunity was likely to come his way again. . . .

"You said your report should have shut down the space station," his companion prompted gently. "Instead . . . ?"

"Damned if I know." Sev spread his hands. "When I got back planetside, my report was gone. All my files had been erased by some freak computer malfunction, and nobody had bothered to copy it to a datahedron first . . . or so they said. And I was up on charges of sexual harassment. Specifically, failing to complete a scheduled inspection, and threatening Fassa del Parma y Polo with a bad inspection report if she didn't comply with my perverted desires."

"She got there first," the other man murmured.

"She's fast," Sev admitted grudgingly. "And smart. And . . . well, it doesn't matter. Not now." *I'll never get back on the* Xanadu *now. And if I did, she'd nail me to a wall and flay me. Slowly.*

"It was her word against mine, no evidence on either side. Or so my supervisor told me. A second inspection, a second *honest* inspection, would have found the same flaws I detailed in my report. But they weren't going to send me, not after her complaints. And while they were waffling around looking for somebody else with the technical background to do the inspection, Senator Cenevix pushed a special bill through his committee. He's in charge of the Ethics Committee," Sev explained. "This bill made second inspections in the same class as trying a man twice for the same crime—placed a construction company under the protection of the old double jeopardy rule. So we weren't allowed to go back and collect the evidence. *Then* the letters started coming—about me gambling at the Pair-a-Dice—and, well, you know the rest of it."

"What I don't know, though, is what you expect me to do about it. You've said you don't want me to get you reinstated at Bahati

CreditLin—and I think that's a good idea; if you went back to the Nyota ya Jaha system, I don't think your life would be worth much. And you must know Central doesn't interfere with other worlds' internal legislative affairs. If this young lady has bribed a senator, that's most deplorable, but we must wait for the people of Bahati to recognize the fact and remove him by due electoral process."

"Not," said Sev grimly, "if I can get incontrovertible evidence of what she's been up to."

"My dear boy, you'll never get close to a Polo Construction job again. From what you've told me, I'm quite sure she's too bright to let you anywhere near her operations."

"True," Sev agreed, "*I* haven't a chance of catching her now. And there aren't many investigators—male or female—whom I'd guarantee to be immune to Fassa's, umm, methods of distraction." He paused for a moment of brief, intense, almost painful memory. "Maybe none," he concluded, opening his eyes again. "But a brainship would be safe enough, don't you think?"

"Tell me," said the gray-eyed man, "exactly what you have in mind." He hadn't moved by so much as the flicker of an eyelash, but Sev could sense the suddenly heightened interest. He outlined his plan, accepted several corrections and emendations to the basic strategy, and all but held his breath with hope and excitement. It had been a long shot, coming to this man, and one he hadn't really expected to pay off.

"I think it can be done," was the final verdict. "I think it should be done. And I do believe I can arrange it."

"Then it only remains to find a brainship capable of carrying out the plan."

"Any Courier Service ship would be *capable*." There was a hint of reproof in the level, passionless voice. "But we can do better than that. You want integrity, brains, diplomatic skills, and the ability to pass as a droneship. There's one ship fairly recently commissioned—about five years—that should suit your purposes. I can guarantee her personal integrity, you see, and that's what is most important in this operation. For the rest—" a brief, ironic smile that puzzled Sev—"well, let's just say I've been following this particular ship's career with some interest."

He stood, and Sev followed suit. As they passed the music platform, the synthocommer broke into a raucous burst of primitive melody—annoying, far too loud, but with a compelling rhythm behind the raw sounds. Sev rather liked it, but his companion closed his eyes and shuddered faintly.

"I apologize," he said as the door closed behind them, "for the music. It's not one of the cafe's attractions, in my opinion. Still, it is the other reason why I come here."

Sev frowned in puzzlement.

"You'd think a young man of High Families stock, with a good education and a family eager to help him get started in a worth-while profession, could find some better career than playing synthocom in a dusty bar on the wrong side of town, wouldn't you?"

It was clearly a rhetorical question. Sev nodded his head in agreement.

"So," said the only honest man on Kailas, "so would I. But evidently my son is of a different opinion."

CHAPTER NINE

Rahilly, Nancia's CS supervisor, ordered her to take it easy while she was getting used to the hyperchip implants. "Cruise back to Central and take your time about it," he ordered her. "You'll have several assignments to pick from when you get here, but there's nothing urgent and no reason for you to strain yourself with too many Singularity transitions while you're getting up to speed with your new capabilities." So Nancia chose a lengthy return route that required only one very small transition through Singularity, while she reveled in the enhanced clarity and speed of thought she enjoyed wherever the hyperchips had been installed.

After the jump she was inclined to grumble at the caution displayed by the Courier Service.

"That was the best jump I've ever made," she told Caleb. "Did you feel how cleanly I ripped that dive into Central subspace?"

"Ripped a dive?" Caleb inquired.

Nancia realized that in all their time together, she'd never discussed how she felt about Singularity, or mentioned the Old Earth-style athletic metaphors that came to her when she was diving through decomposing three-space. "It's . . . a term athletes use," she explained. "There were some newsbytes of the Earth Olympics once . . . anyway. I just meant it was a perfectly wonderful jump. Don't you think so?"

"It was over faster than most," Caleb allowed. "Let's see what our next assignment is."

They had a choice of three, but as soon as Nancia scanned the beam she knew there was only one she wanted to take. A brainship was needed for an undercover assignment investigating the methods of BLEEP Construction Company on planet in the star system CENSORED. The matter must be handled with extreme discretion; details would be available only to the brainship accepting the assignment.

"Two weeks travel. One major Singularity point. I bet I know where it is," Nancia said.

"That could describe any number of routes," Caleb pointed out.

"Yes, but . . ." Nancia created a pattern of dancing lightstrings on her central panel. She would have been willing to bet her four years' accumulated pay and bonuses that at least one of the spoiled brats she'd carried out to the Nyota ya Jaha system was implementing the plans she'd discussed. Fassa del Parma y Polo. Polo Construction. Bahati. Hadn't there been something on the newsbytes about a delay in financing the new space station off Bahati, some question about the inspection? . . . It had to be Fassa's company. And here, at last, was Nancia's chance to stop one of the unethical little beasts. "Caleb, let's take this one. I like it."

Caleb sniffed disapprovingly. "Well, I don't. Undercover—that's next door to espionage. Vega Ethical Code considers it the same thing, in fact. I didn't sign on to Courier Service to become a dirty, sneaking *spy*." He made the word sound obscene. "And look at this." He overrode Nancia's pattern of dancing lights to display a copy of the assignment description on the central screen. A laser pointer highlighted the wait-code inconspicuously marked on the top left corner of the message header. "See that? Somebody specifically routed this assignment to us, even if it meant waiting three weeks for us to come back from Spica subspace by the longest route. With a little checking the Net we could probably find out who—no, that would be unethical," Caleb conceded with a small sigh. "But I don't like it, Nancia. Smells of High Families meddling and pulling strings. I think we ought to take one of the other two assignments. Something that's presented in a straightforward manner, something we can do without compromising our integrity."

But even Caleb couldn't work up much enthusiasm for their other two choices.

The first, they were warned, might be a relatively long-term assignment. A ship was required to transport the Planetary Technical Aid inspection committee on its five-yearly rounds, remaining at each planet while the committee inspected the situation and prepared a report.

"I guess there are worse chores," he said. "And maybe it wouldn't take so long. If they do this trip every five years, the last inspection ship should have been coming back just before you were commissioned. Want to check the records and find out how long the round trip took?"

Nancia began checking the Courier Service's open records while Caleb studied the third assignment choice. "Taking a bull to Cor Caroli subspace? This is a Courier Service assignment?"

"Improving agriculture," Nancia suggested, and then, "but they can't be serious. Surely all we'd have to take out is a sperm sample."

But it turned out, when they checked, that nobody had ever successfully taken a sperm sample from Thunderbolt III, the prize bull buffalo of the Central Worlds Zoo. And since the only surviving cow buffalo was on Cor Caroli VI, and since the zoo keeper there claimed Shaddupa suffered from terrible Singularity stress and couldn't possibly handle spaceflight, the preservation of the species required that Thunderbolt III be transported to Cor Caroli VI.

"I think even a PTA committee would be better company than Thunderbolt Three," Caleb commented. "Nancia, isn't there any CS record of how long the previous inspection tour lasted?"

"I just found it," Nancia told him. She'd had to check through more years of records than she anticipated.

"And?"

"And they should be returning some time next year. They're still out in Deneb subspace. I've been reading the interim reports. It seems the PTA bylaws prohibit the inspection committee from leaving any planet until they have all agreed to and signed the report for that planet."

"And?"

This time Nancia did sigh. "Caleb, it's a *committee*."

Three hours later Sevareid Bryley-Sorensen d'Aquino came aboard to explain his plan in detail.

"I don't like the paint job," Nancia complained when the retrofitting was done.

Caleb glared at her control panel. She wished he would turn around and look at her central column, now hidden behind fake bulkheads. "It was your idea to travel under false colors. Don't complain now."

"It's not being disguised as an OG Shipping droneship I mind," Nancia said. "It's Darnell's choice of colors. Puce and mauve, ugh!"

That wasn't quite true. She did mind the OG Shipping logos stenciled on her sides; it gave her a creepy feeling to know that strangers would look at her and see part of Darnell Overton-Glaxely's rapidly growing empire. But she wasn't about to admit that to Caleb, not after arguing so hard to convince him that they should take the assignment.

Sev Bryley's plan had been simplicity itself. Fassa del Parma seduced men when she needed to, but she was economical with herself as with all Polo Construction's resources: very few strangers were allowed close enough to the construction company's operations to become any sort of a threat. Her workers were fanatically loyal to her—

"Let's not discuss that part," Caleb had interrupted Sev at this point. "It's not fit for Nancia to hear."

"I believe," Sev said carefully, "that their loyalty is purchased by stock options and high financial bonuses. Not to mention the fact that a number of them are rumored to be wanted by Central under other IDs; somebody seems to be doing a fine business in supplying Fassa with fake Net identities for her workers."

Polyon. Nancia remembered the ease and dexterity with which he'd hacked into the Net accounts via her own computer. And that had been five years before. He was probably much, much better at it now. She could tell Sev Bryley where to look for the Net forger . . . or just drop him a hint. A hint might be enough for this determined young man; look how quickly he'd dredged up the connection between Polo Construction and OG Shipping, the very basis for their hastily executed plan.

Fassa's business required heavy transport facilities. For the most part Polo Construction ran their own ships, but when she had too many contracts Fassa rented droneships from OG Shipping. The drones were the safest way for her to transport illicitly acquired materials; there would be no witnesses except her own men, loading materials at one end, and the customer's men unloading at the other end of the run. Neither would be inclined to bear witness against a system that brought them so much profit.

Sev had worked out all this from a combination of studying partial Net records, interviewing anybody with even casual interest in Polo Construction, and putting the bits together with his own flashes of brilliant insight. He lacked just one thing: the testimony of an unimpeachable eyewitness to confirm his deductions. Somebody needed to *see* the substitution of materials going on . . . somebody whose integrity could not be questioned . . . somebody who could get close to operations without warning Fassa.

The integrity of Courier Service brainships was beyond question. And Fassa, accustomed to the services of the patient, silent, brainless OG droneships, would hardly suspect that behind painted bulkheads and empty loading docks there resided a human brain with the sensor capacity to hear and see all that went on aboard the ship . . . and the intelligence to testify about it later.

"It's a brilliant plan," Nancia declared when Sev first explained it.

"I don't like it," Caleb glowered. "Sending Nancia out alone—without me to tell her how to do things? What if she panics?"

"I won't panic." Nancia made her voice as calm and soothing as possible.

"And I'll be with her," Sev pointed out "I won't risk coming out where they can see me, but I'll track everything via Nancia's sensor screens and send her cues if she needs help."

Caleb folded his arms. "That," he said grimly, "is not a satisfactory solution. Why can't I go too? I'm her brawn. I should be wherever she is."

"Minimizing the risks," Sev said briefly. Actually, his original plan had called for the brainship to go completely unattended, just like a drone. But he was damned if he would miss out on the culmination of his careful plans. He trusted himself to have the self-control to stay out of sight until Fassa had completely incriminated herself; he didn't trust Caleb to display the same good sense. But explaining all that would hardly mollify the brawn.

Caleb appealed directly to Nancia. "You're too young," he said. "You're too innocent. You won't recognize their dirty tricks until too late. You—"

"*Caleb.*" Sev Bryley's voice cracked like a gunshot. The brawn stopped his compulsive pacing around the narrow perimeter of the remodeled cabin. "You aren't helping Nancia," Sev said once he had Caleb's attention. "Don't make her nervous. Why don't you go to the spaceport bar and have a drink? I'll join you as soon as Nancia and I have run through her final checklist of instructions."

Caleb opened his mouth for an angry retort and then shut it again. Nancia wished she had a sensor that could report on the rapid ticking of his brain. He was thinking something behind that quiet, tight-lipped exterior—but what?

"Consumption of intoxicating beverages is against the Vega Ethical Code," Caleb said at last, and Nancia relaxed connections that she hadn't realized were so tight. Whatever Caleb's thoughts, they weren't leading him into a fight with Sev that would very likely abort the mission at this late date. "I'll, I'll, I could have a vegosqueeze, though."

"You do that, then," Sev agreed. "See you in a few minutes."

He leaned against a fake bulkhead, arms folded. The temporary wall squeaked in protest and Sev straightened up quickly. "Crummy construction job they did on your interior," he remarked as Caleb's footsteps echoed down the central stairs.

"Then it should m-match the rest of the work around P-Polo Construction." Where had that stammer come from? Nancia ordered her vocal circuits to relax. They only tightened up farther, making the next sentence come out in a squeak. "What final checklist?"

"What? Hmm? Oh, there isn't one. I just wanted to get Caleb out of the way. He was making you nervous, wasn't he?"

"I'm fine," Nancia said, this time more gruffly than she had intended.

"You'll need to get better control over your vocal registers if you want to sound like a dronetalker," Sev warned. "Drones' synthesized voices don't wobble."

He sank to the cabin floor, long legs folding under him with no apparent strain, and gazed at the fake wall concealing Nancia's titanium column. "Undercover work is always a strain," he confided. "I used to do half an hour of yoga meditation before taking on a false identity."

Nancia rapidly scanned her data banks. Apparently *yoga* was an old-style Earth exercise designed to induce tranquility and spiritual enlightenment.

"Too bad you can't do the same thing," Sev commented.

"A brainship can do anything you softpersons can," Nancia snapped, "only better! Tell me about this *yoga*."

Sev grinned. "Well. Maybe you can. It just requires a little translation. Let's see, start with regular breathing . . . Not heavy," he said reprovingly as Nancia flushed clean air in and out through her ventilation ports, "just regular. Even. Smooth. That's the idea. Now close your . . . umm, deactivate your visual sensors."

Usually Nancia hated the blackness that accompanied temporary loss of visual sensor connections. But this time it was voluntary. And Sev's voice continued, low and soothing . . . and it *was* restful not to be scanning her remodeled interior.

Caleb must be exiting her lower entry port now, if she opened an external sensor she'd be able to see him walking across the landing field towards the spaceport central building . . . *no*. She wouldn't break the concentration of the exercise now; Sev's patient instructions were working. She felt perceptibly less nervous as she followed his suggestions to feel the energy in her lower engines and let it flow through her propulsion units without actually releasing it. A warm glowing sensation bathed her fins and exterior shell. Caleb's near-quarrel with Sev, the approaching confrontation off Bahati, even the exciting suspicion that Daddy had personally recommended her for this assignment . . . all these doubts and fears and hopes seemed very small and far away. Nancia contemplated herself, a tiny speck in the universe; as was the planet on which she sat, the sun that lit the sky around them. All little floating dots in an infinite pattern; dots winked out or came into existence, but the pattern swirled on and on forever. . . .

"Restore full sensor connections." Sev's calm order was like a gentle wake-up call. Nancia opened her sensors one by one, feeling anew the wonder of existence. The gritty spaceport floor beneath her landing gear, the smell of engine oil in the air outside, the sights and sounds of an ordinary working spaceport were all bright and trembling with new meaning.

"I think you'll do now," Sev said with satisfaction.

"I think so, too," Nancia agreed.

Out of habit, Nancia lifted off as gently as if she were carrying a full committee of Central Worlds diplomats. Just because she was decked out in the revolting colors of OG Shipping didn't mean she had to slam on- and off-world like a mindless drone. Besides, rapid movement would destroy the trance of peace in which she was still floating. *And,* she thought guiltily, it would also bounce Sev around. If Caleb had been aboard, his comfort would have been her first thought; Sev deserved the same consideration.

The work of outfitting her as an OG drone had been done at Razmak Base in Bellatrix subspace. Razmak possessed the very useful quality of being located just one hour's spaceflight away from a Singularity zone opening directly onto Vega subspace near Nyota ya Jaha; Nancia would not have to risk a long flight during which some authentic OG Shipping employee might notice and report her presence. She arced through the sky like a silver rainbow and made one sleek rolling dive into Singularity.

The disadvantage of this particular transition, from a softperson's point of view, was that the transition through Singularity was subjectively longer than usual. Sev had considered this a reasonable tradeoff for the advantages of Razmak Base; Nancia hoped he would feel the same way when they exited into Vega subspace.

For herself, Nancia had been looking forward to the jump. She skimmed the rolling waves of collapsing subspace, dove and surfaced and spiraled through the spaces until the decomposition funnel drew her whirling into its shrinking space. Systems of linear equations followed their orderly dance; space shrank and expanded about Nancia, colors sang to her and the inexorable regularity of the mathematical transformations unfolded with the beauty of a Bach fugue. She came out into Vega subspace with an exuberant shout of joy, the golden notes of a Purcell trumpet voluntary echoing through concealed passages and empty loading bays.

"CUT THAT OUT!"

The outraged shout, echoing where no human voice should have sounded, was like a spattering of high-frequency power along Nancia's synaptic connectors.

She opened all sensor connections at once. The world was a faceted diamond of images: painted bulkheads, pseudosteel corridors, Sev still strapped to his bunk for the Singularity transition, the central cabin viewed from three angles at once: all framed by the external sensor views of blackness spattered by the fire of distant suns.

And Caleb, coming from one of the angles where temporary

walls blocked Nancia's sensor view of her own interior, resplendent in his Courier Service full-dress uniform and still green in the face from the extended period in Singularity. Nancia closed down all the other sensors and expanded the image of Caleb. Her brawn wasn't usually inclined to Service fripperies; she had forgotten just how fine a man could look in the uncomfortable full-dress black and silver of the Courier Service, with the stiff collar forcing his jaw up and the silver-and-corycium braid winking in rainbow lightfires every time he drew a deep breath.

"You've developed a distaste for classical music?" It was the only thing she could think of to say—the only thing that was even remotely safe to say.

"You were half a tone flat on the high notes," Caleb informed her, using the same carefully remote voice that Nancia had employed. "And *much* too loud."

"I suppose I should apologize for the unintended assault on your delicate sensors," Nancia said. "I had turned off the cabin speakers, and I wasn't aware that there was another softshell aboard."

"*A what?*"

Had Caleb really spent four and a half years as her brawn without ever once hearing the slang term that shellpersons used for mobile humans? Nancia rapidly reviewed a selection of their communications. It was indeed possible. She had never realized how much of her communication she censored for Caleb's benefit, how careful she'd been to avoid offending against his standards of speech and action.

Maybe she'd been too careful, if he thought he could get away with a stunt like this.

"I think you can figure out what the term means," Nancia told him. Then, as she absorbed the emotional impact of what Caleb's action meant, her hard-won control cracked like a faulty shell. "Caleb, you idiot, you could have been *killed*! What if I'd lifted off at full speed? Hiding in that corner, you'd have been bounced around like three dice in a cup!"

"You never do bruising takeoffs or landings," Caleb pointed out. "Too fond of showing off your land-on-an-eggshell, turn-on-a-dime navigational skills."

Nancia was momentarily distracted. "What's a dime?"

"I'm not sure," Caleb admitted. "It's an Old Earth phrase. I think it refers to some kind of small insect. Want to check your thesaurus? We could call up the Old English language files via the Net, too. Something to pass the time."

"Stop trying to change the subject! *Why* didn't you tell me you were going to be aboard?"

"Would you have let me come?"

"Well . . . no," Nancia admitted. "I'd have had to tell Bryley. Your presence could compromise the mission, Caleb, don't you realize that? I'm supposed to be an unmanned droneship, remember?"

"I know," Caleb said. "Don't worry. I won't compromise the bloody mission. But I couldn't let you face this gang of thieves alone, Nancia. Don't you see that?"

She wasn't alone; she had Sev, who knew all about investigative work and undercover missions. But she couldn't very well berate Caleb for wanting to protect her, could she?

"Just keep out of sight," Nancia said finally. "Please, Caleb?" *Oh-oh. Sev is using his cabin. He isn't going to like that.* "Work it out with Sev. If one of you can hide, I guess two of you can. But— he's in charge for this mission. I agreed to that, and you'll have to do the same."

She took the set of his jaw and the brief upward jerk of his head for all the assent she was going to get.

"Oh. One other thing."

"Yes?"

"Why," Nancia inquired, "did you choose to wear full Service uniform for this little jaunt? Not that it isn't becoming, but I'd have thought something a little less conspicuous. . . ."

Caleb explained, patiently and at length, about traditions of honor on Vega. There seemed to be some connection in his mind between wearing uniform and being taken for a spy. Or not taken for a spy. Nancia couldn't quite follow the argument, and when he went from Vega history to Old Earth stories about somebody called Major André, she quit trying. Caleb was Caleb. His sense of honor wouldn't let him send his brainship without him into what he considered a dangerous and morally ambiguous situation. Apparently his sense of honor also wouldn't let him dress sensibly for the occasion. His sense of honor was a royal pain in the synapses at times, but it was part of Caleb. Part of what she respected in him.

While Caleb discussed the laws of war, the concept of a just war, the Truce of God, and the Geneva Conventions, Nancia found and activated her files of baroque brass music. With all speakers off, she ran the Purcell trumpet voluntary through her comm channels three times and was going on for a fourth before Caleb finally ran out of things to say.

Fassa del Parma paced the loading dock of Bahati SpaceBase II, biting her lip. Ever since that near-debacle over SpaceBase I, she had been unwilling to delegate the ambiguous details of her business. That had been a near thing. Who'd have thought Sev Bryley would be so persistent? She'd taken him aboard the *Xanadu* and given him what he wanted, hadn't she? And when that hadn't proved sufficient to shut the man up—Fassa stopped pacing and bit her lip. All she'd wanted from Darnell was to fake a minor gambling and embezzling record that would discredit Sev with his employers. There'd been no need to go as far as he had, even if Sev had come sniffing around the Pair-a-Dice to find out who was framing him. There were other ways to discourage people besides dumping their unconscious bodies in a recycling bin. She should have recognized Darnell's sadistic tendencies, she should have remembered the whispers about mysterious disappearances from the Pair-a-Dice.

Oblivious to the soft thump and the vibration through the base walls that announced the docking of Darnell's OG Shipping drone, Fassa leaned her head against the wall for a moment. It gave slightly where her forehead pressed against it; that was what happened when you replaced the contracted synthosteel with steel-painted plastifilm. Not that she cared. Not that anybody cared about anything. That was how the world was, and nobody bothered to stop any of the corruption. Why should she trouble herself about one man caught up in the general unfeeling way of the world? Nobody had ever cared about *her,* had they?

Certainly not Sev Bryley. All he'd been after was a scandalous case that would build up his career. He'd taken what she offered and then attacked her again as if none of it meant anything. Well, it didn't.

Did it?

Fassa blinked rapidly and activated the series of locks that would automatically check on the seal between an attached ship and the spacebase itself, equalize pressures and open the spacebase for loading and unloading. She hadn't economized on that part of the work. She was clever enough to keep well above standards on any part of a contract that might jeopardize her personal safety. Clever enough, she thought as the spacebase doors irised open, to handle any problem that came up . . . except, maybe, her own memories.

Which were no problem!

She was about to call the loading crew to shift the permasteel beams and other expensive materials onto Darnell's drone when a thought stopped her. You couldn't be too careful these days. She walked through the spaceport iris, through the extruded pressure chambers and into the empty loading bays of the OG Shipping droneship.

Everything seemed to be as it should. The loading layout was rather strange, but Darnell had a habit of taking ships from the other companies he acquired and retrofitting them to suit his own needs. Certainly there was plenty of space. And everywhere she looked, on columns and walls and internal panels, Fassa saw the puce-and-mauve logo of OG Shipping stenciled. Rather sloppily stenciled, in some cases: lines wobbled and droplets of paint spattered the borders of the stencils. Looked like a rush job. Darnell didn't take the trouble to oversee his people personally as she did hers, she thought, and the difference showed.

"Droneship, are you prepared to accept cargo?" she queried the air.

"Prepared. To accept. Cargo. Begin. Transfer." The answer came back from a speaker somewhere behind her, metallic and uninflected like all AI speech. Fassa remembered reading that AI linguists were perfectly capable of designing a more human-sounding speech system, especially with the help of the sophisticated metachips of Shemali design, but that marketing forces wouldn't let them release it. Drones and other AI devices weren't supposed to sound too human; it made people nervous.

"Credit transfer, please," Fassa requested briskly. Darnell had stiffed her on one load of supplies, reselling it and pocketing the profit himself and blandly denying that any of his drones had been anywhere near SpaceBase I. And her own excessive caution, her own refusal to leave any records behind, had given her no way to fight him. Now she demanded payment in advance before a single roll of synthosteel made it onto one of the bastard's drones.

"Your credit transfer will be. Approved. As soon as the. Loading is complete."

Fassa grinned to herself. That speech had sounded considerably more like human inflections than most dronetalk did. She wouldn't put it past Darnell to have diverted some of the new metachips for frivolous applications like improving dronetalk. He hadn't got it quite right, though. She could still tell she was talking to a machine.

And she wasn't about to let a damned droneship cheat her out of the rights to this expensive shipment!

"Credit transfer to be produced when loading is twenty-five percent complete," she said, "as by usual agreement. Or I stop loading there and you don't leave SpaceBase until the credit slip is approved."

"Agreed." The last word from the droneship had a very human sound of resignation to it. Darnell *had* been fooling with the Shemali metachips in his ships; Fassa was now willing to bet on it.

She still felt a vague unease about the operation, but brushed it off. She was just brooding over the Sev Bryley fiasco, that was all. No reason to suppose anything like that would happen again— not with the number of senators and bankers and inspectors Fassa now had personally dedicated to her welfare. Fassa activated the spacebase's comm link and called her hand-picked loading crew to complete the transfer.

With drone-powered lifters and other automated devices, loading the construction materials was a quick job, calling for no more than three men, all of them bound to Fassa by personal loyalty— and by the stock which they had vested in Polo Construction. Those stock options were an expense Fassa regretted, but it was necessary to ensure the absolute silence of her assistants. Once again, while the men went about their business, she cursed the underlying chauvinism of contractors who insisted on building their lifters to the specifications of a six-foot, muscular male body. There was no reason the lifters couldn't be designed so that their controls were within the reach and strength of a smallish woman; the real muscle involved here came from the machines, not from the men. But Fassa was too small to operate the machines. When she calculated what this one fact was costing her in stocks and bonuses to keep her loading crews silent, she was tempted to start her own heavy machinery factory, with lifters and forks and cranes all built so that anybody could operate them at the touch of a button.

Someday, she promised herself. *When I have enough money. When I feel strong enough . . . and secure enough . . . when I am enough.*

Somehow she felt that such a day would never arrive.

But the twenty-five percent mark on transfer had arrived . . . and it was time to claim her credit slip. Fassa motioned to the loading crew to stop. While they waited in position, lifters frozen in mid-arc, she walked back into the partially filled cargo bays of the droneship.

"Credit transfer," she rapped out. "Now!"

"Regret that I do not have facilities to issue credit slips in loading bay area," the droneship replied. "Request that del Parma unit transfer self to cabin area to receive payment."

The inflections were almost human, but the awkward wording was pure dronespeak. Smiling as she waved her hand before the lift-door sensors, Fassa reflected that she would have to recommend some better linguists to Darnell.

The lift-door irised open and Fassa, wrapped in her satisfied thoughts, took one step forward before she took in the glitter of silver and corycium braid against the deep-space black of a Courier Service uniform.

Startled, she flung herself backwards, but the uniformed man grabbed her sleeve just before she was out of reach. Fassa fell back onto the loading dock floor, dragging her assailant with her. He landed heavily on her midsection, knocking the breath out of her. Where were the damned loading crew? Couldn't they see something had gone wrong?

"Fassa del Parma—I arrest you—in the name of Central Worlds—for embezzlement of SpaceBase—construction and supplies," the bastard wheezed. Both his hands were around her wrists now, pinning her to the floor. Fassa gasped for breath, brought up a knee into the brute's crotch, and wriggled free in one movement. Her brain had never stopped working. So there was a witness! Darnell had double-crossed her? All right; dispose of the witness, that was the new problem, then she would deal with the rest.

"Kill that man!" she screamed at the dumbstruck idiots on her loading crew. She raced towards the safety of the spacebase.

The droneship's loading doors slammed shut. How had the bastard managed to transmit the command? He should still be writhing in agony.

He was. But as Fassa looked, he rose to his knees. "Under—arrest," he panted.

"That's what you think," Fassa said with her sweetest smile. What did this fool think, that she was too weak and sentimental to kill a man face to face? He was still on his knees, and she was standing, and the needler in her left sleeve slid into the palm of her hand with the cool solid feel of revenge. Time slowed and the air shimmered about her. The Courier Service brawn was lunging forward now, but he'd never reach her in time. Fassa aimed the needler until she saw a face neatly framed in the viewfinder. Who was he? It didn't matter. He was a total stranger, he was Sev, he was Senator Cenevix, he was Faul del Parma. All turning green around her, and her fingers almost too weak to squeeze the needler; what was happening? Fassa swayed on her feet, squeezed the needler handle and saw an arc of darts ripping wildly through the thick green clouds that surrounded them now. So dizzy . . . her eyes wouldn't stay open to track the darts to their target . . . but she'd been too close to miss. So close . . .

Fassa collapsed in the cloud of sleepgas with which Nancia had, just too late, flooded the closed loading bays. So did Caleb, going down just in front of Fassa with his black and silver uniform all spoiled by blood.

CHAPTER TEN

"Don't gas the lift! Don't gas the lift!"

The shouted commands, coming from a closed-off area behind the fake walls, startled Nancia. She shifted views rapidly, cursing the quick and dirty remodeling job that had left large areas of her own interior cut off from her visual sensors.

Sev Bryley, white-faced, appeared from behind one of the puce-and-mauve pseudoboard walls. "I'll get him out of the loading bay," he snapped without so much as a glance towards Nancia's sensor unit. "You can keep the sleepgas confined to that area?"

"Yes, but—"

"Don't have time for a mask." Bryley was in the lift now, and Nancia could watch him on the agonizingly slow passage down to the loading dock. His chest rose and fell rapidly as he took the deep, rapid breaths of clean air that would keep him going in the loading bay.

Nancia kept the lift door on three-quarter pressure, just enough to let Bryley squeeze through the flexible opening that shut behind him. At the same time she flushed the loading bay with the ventilation system on high power, replacing as much sleepgas as she could with clean air.

Sev's back and shoulders bulged awkwardly half through the lift door. Nancia released the flexible membrane just long enough to let him drag Caleb through into the lift. She kept the ventilation

382

system on high for the long seconds of the ride back. By the time the lift was at cabin level, she could find no measurable trace of sleepgas in the air. But Sev had inhaled enough to make him slump against the wall, too woozy to carry himself and Caleb farther.

"Antidote . . . ?"

"In the corridor," Nancia told him. "*In the corridor!*" She had no housekeeping servos within the lift itself. Sev had to stagger forward, out of the lift, fetching up against the freshly painted corridor wall with a thump. At least it was one of Nancia's true walls; only a few steps away from Sev was an opening from which the servos could dispense stimulants and medical aids. Sev took two gasping breaths of the clean air, reached into the shallow dish presented by the opening in the wall, grabbed a handful of ampules and crushed them under his nose.

"More," he commanded.

"You've already exceeded the recommended dosage."

"I need a clear head *now*," Sev growled.

Was there more blood on Caleb's uniform? Impossible to tell what he'd been hit with, or how bad the damage was. Nancia sent another set of stim ampules to the servo tray. Sev broke these more cautiously, one at a time. After the third deep breath of pungent stimulant, he dropped the rest back in the tray. "Medical supplies!"

"What?"

"I'll tell you when I know." He was on his knees, blocking Nancia's view as he peeled back the front of Caleb's spoiled uniform. "Something to stop bleeding . . . there shouldn't be so much from a needler . . . ahh. The . . ." he used a Vega slang term that was not in any of Nancia's vocabulary hedra. "She loaded it with anticoagulant. And . . . other things, I think. Analyze?" He dropped a torn and bloody strip of cloth into the servo tray. Nancia transferred it to the medical lab and replaced it with ampules of HyperClot which Sev injected directly into Caleb's veins.

"That's stopped the bleeding," he said finally, rising to his feet. "But I'm not happy about his color. Does that look like normal sleepgas pallor to you?"

"No." The one word was all Nancia could manage.

"Me neither. Can you analyze what else was in the needler?"

"No. Organics of some sort, but it's too complex for me." Concentrating on the technical problem helped to steady her voice.

"I haven't the facilities here. I am contacting Murasaki Base for Net access to medtechs."

But Murasaki Base could suggest only that she transport Caleb to the nearest planet-based clinic as quickly as possible. If Fassa's needler had been loaded with Ganglicide—

"It wasn't Ganglicide," Nancia said quickly. "He'd be dead by now. Besides, no one would do such a thing."

"You might be surprised," said the infuriatingly calm managing brain of Murasaki Base. "But I agree, probably not Ganglicide. There are, however, slower-acting nerve poisons which, untreated, can be just as fatal. From what you report of his convulsive reaction, I would suggest immediate medical treatment by someone experienced with nerve poisons and their antidotes."

"Thanks very much," Nancia snapped. Sev had wrapped Caleb in all the blankets he could collect, but nothing stopped Caleb's incessant nervous shivering. And every once in a while his spine arched backward while he cried out in delirium. "We came from Razmak Base in Bellatrix subspace. You're not seriously suggesting I take a man in this condition through Singularity, are you?"

"There happens to be an excellent clinic on Bahati," the Murasaki Base brain replied. "If you were calm enough to check the Net records I'm transmitting, CN, you'd see that the assistant director there has a strong background in nerve poison research. With your permission, I will alert the Summerlands clinic to receive an emergency patient for the direct care of Dr. Alpha bint Hezra-Fong."

Time stopped. Snatches of conversation forgotten for nearly four years echoed in Nancia's memory. *An expert in Ganglicide therapy right there at the Summerlands clinic . . . testing Ganglicide on unwitting subjects . . . so far gone on Blissto they didn't even know what was happening to them. . . .*

She had the full conversations recorded and safely stored away. She didn't need them. Her own human memory was mercilessly replaying words she'd tried to forget.

Did she dare put Caleb in Alpha bint Hezra-Fong's hands?

Did she dare *not* take him to the clinic?

There was really no choice.

They were only a few minutes from Bahati, but the time seemed like hours to Nancia. She blessed the multiprocessing capability that allowed her to perform multiple tasks at once. While one bank of processors controlled the landing computations, Nancia assigned two more to maintaining the comm link with Murasaki and opening a new link with Bahati. She reached the director of Summerlands and explained her requirements while simultaneously assimilating Murasaki Base's calm instructions.

The combination of Fassa's arrest and Caleb's wounds presented a complex political problem. Nancia was almost grateful for the complications; they gave her something to think about during the endless minutes before touchdown.

Courier Service policy strictly prohibited the transport of prisoners on a brainship with no brawn. Nancia thought it was a silly policy, born of fears that were decades out of date. Earlier, less cleverly designed brainships might have been vulnerable to passenger takeover, but she was well protected against any little tricks that Fassa might come up with. The auxiliary synaptic circuits known as the Helva Modification would prevent any attempt to close off her sensory contact with her own ship-body.

All the same, Murasaki Base informed Nancia, the regulations existed for good reason and it was not up to a brainship to pick and choose which Service regs she would obey.

"All right, all *right*." Had Caleb twitched again? Summerlands Clinic personnel were standing by to collect him as soon as they landed. Bahati Spaceport was issuing final landing instructions. "I'll hand Fassa del Parma over to Bahati authorities."

"That you will not," the Murasaki Base brain informed her. "I've been in contact with CenDip while you were fussing over your brawn. The young lady is a political hot potato."

"A what?"

"Sorry. Old Earth slang. Never thought about the literal meaning . . . let's see, I think a potato is some kind of tuber, but why anybody would try to ignite one . . . oh, well." Murasaki Base dismissed the intriguing linguistic question for later consideration. "What it means is that nobody really wants to handle her trial. Well, you can see for yourself, can't you, Nancia? If you're going to try a High Families brat and send her to prison, you don't do it out on some nowhere world at the edge of the galaxy. You bring her back to Central and you are very, very careful that all procedures are followed. To the letter. CenDip has strict instructions that *nothing* is to go wrong with this case; there's a certain highly placed authority who has taken a personal interest in stopping High Families corruption."

"You can tell your highly placed authority to—" Nancia transmitted a burst of muddy tones and discordant high-pitched sounds.

"Can't," said Murasaki Base rather smugly. "Softshells can't receive that kind of input. Fortunately for them, I might add. Where did a nice brainship like you pick up that kind of language?"

Nancia landed at Bahati Spacefield as gently as a feather floating in the breeze. She opened her upper-level cabin doors and waited for the spaceport workers to bring a floatube. They'd already been informed of the reason why she didn't want to open the lower doors; the equipment should have been ready and waiting—ah! There it was now.

"Well, then, just inform your 'highly placed authority,' that a few little things have *already* gone wrong with this operation," Nancia told Murasaki Base. "And if I can't transport del Parma without a brawn, and I can't hand her over to Bahati, what am I supposed to do with her?"

"Wait for your new brawn, of course," Murasaki Base informed her.

"And just how long will *that* take?" They were loading Caleb onto a stretcher now.

"About half an hour, if he can pack as quickly as he should."

"What?"

In answer, Murasaki Base transmitted the CenDip instruction bytes directly. "Senior Central Diplomatic service person Armontillado y Medoc, Forister, currently R&R at Summerlands Clinic, previous brawn status inactivated upon joining CenDip Central Date 2732, reactivated 2754 for single duty tour returning prisoner del Parma y Polo, Fassa, to Central Worlds jurisdiction."

Before taking Caleb away, the Summerlands medtechs were running tests and dosing him with all-purpose antidotes. Alpha bint Hezra-Fong had come personally to oversee the operation. Nancia's sensors caught her dark, sharp-featured face from several angles while she leaned over Caleb. Her expression showed nothing but keen professional interest: no hint of any evil plans to use Caleb as an unwitting experimental subject.

And no compassion.

And now he was going into the floatube, beyond Nancia's sensor range . . . beyond her help. *Where was Sev?* Nancia scanned the sensor banks until she located him in one of the passenger cabins that had been concealed behind her fake paneling. *He* was guarding a groggy Fassa who had just begun to come out of the sleepgas.

"Sev, I need you to go with Caleb," Nancia announced.

"CN-935, please acknowledge receipt of formal orders," Murasaki Base input on another channel.

"Can't," Sev answered without looking round. "Have to guard the prisoner. Check regulations."

Nancia knew he was right. The same stupid CS regs that forbade her to transport Fassa without a brawn would also forbid her to take sole charge of a prisoner. "Are regulations more important than Caleb's life?"

"Nancia, he's getting the best possible medical care. What are you *worried* about?"

"CN-935 RESPOND!" Murasaki Base shouted.

The floatube was a speck on the horizon. They weren't stopping at the spaceport; they were taking Caleb directly to Summerlands. Where Alpha bint Hezra-Fong could do anything, anything at all, to him, and Nancia wouldn't even know until it was too late—

"Instructions received and accepted," she transmitted to Murasaki Base in one short burst. "Now GET THAT BRAWN ON BOARD!" Forister Armontillado y Medoc? Nancia remembered the short, quiet man she'd transported somewhere, years earlier, to solve some crisis. The one who'd spent all his time on board reading. No matter what his records said, he wasn't her idea of a brawn. But who cared? The sooner he was here, the sooner Sev could be released from guard duty to go watch over Caleb.

Fassa was choking on the bottom of a lake. Weeds twined around her ankles, and the clear air was impossibly far away, miles above the green water that pressed her down and pushed at her mouth and ears and nose with gentle, implacable persistence. She tried to kick free of the weeds; they clung tighter, reaching up past ankle and calf and knee with green slimy fingers that pressed close against her thighs. When she looked down, the weeds shaped themselves into pale green faces with open mouths and closed eyes. All the men who'd given her their hearts and their integrity and pieces of their souls were there on the bottom of the lake, and they wanted to keep her there with them. Her chest was bursting with the need to breathe. If she gave back their souls, would they let her go?

She tried to strip off the charm bracelet on her left wrist, but the catch was stuck; tried to break the chain, but it was too strong. Green lake water seeped into her mouth with a bitter taste, and black spots danced before her eyes. She tugged the chain over her hand, scraping a knuckle raw, and flung it at the hungry ghosts. The sparkling charms of corycium and iridium floated lazily down among the muddy weeds, and Fassa was released to rise through rings of ever-lightening water until she broke the surface and breathed in the air that hurt like fire in her lungs.

She was lying on a bunk in a spaceship cabin. Sev Bryley was seated cross-legged on the opposite bunk, watching her with unsmiling attention. And the burning in her lungs was real, as was the throbbing pain in her head; sleepgas hangover. Now she remembered: surprise and violence and a fool who'd been where he had no business, and the gas flooding the cargo bay while she tried to hold her breath.

It all added up to a failure so crushing she could not bear to think about it yet. And Sev, the man who'd never given her a piece of his soul to keep in her charm bracelet—was he the one who'd engineered this disaster?

"What are you doing here?" she croaked.

"Making sure you came out of the sleepgas without complications," Sev said. His voice sounded thin and strained, as if he were trying to reach her from a great distance. "Some people have a convulsive reaction. It looked for a while like you were going to be one of them."

And that had worried him? Perhaps he still cared for her a little, then. Perhaps her experiment of taking him aboard the *Xanadu* hadn't been a total failure, after all. Fassa stretched, experimentally, and saw the way his eyes followed her movements. Perhaps something could yet be salvaged from this catastrophe. After all, they were alone on the droneship . . .

"Not convulsions," she said, languorously wriggling her toes and proceeding upward, muscle by muscle, to make certain that every inch of her own amazing body was back under her command again. "Just bad dreams."

"What sort of dreams?" Sev inquired.

Fassa sat up, rather more quickly than she had intended, and fell back against the cabin wall. "The sort that make you afraid to die."

"Thus conscience doth make cowards of us all," Sev agreed with no change of tone, and Fassa felt a stab of regret. She could have liked this man who so quickly picked up on her thoughts, capping her unvoiced quotations. If only he weren't so obstinately on the wrong side! Ah, well, perhaps that could be changed. It would damn well *have* to be changed if she hoped to get out of this, she reminded herself.

"Speak for yourself," she told him. "My conscience isn't all that troubled; I've done nothing more than what everybody does, just trying to get ahead by my own efforts." Wrong tone, wrong tone. She didn't want to argue with Bryley; she wanted to seduce him. No. Needed to seduce him. That was all.

And she wasn't going to get anywhere in her present condition. Fassa pushed sweaty, matted dark hair away from her forehead with a genuine moan of pain. "God, I must look like hell," she said. "Would you mind very much getting out of here so I can clean up?"

"Yes," said Sev, "I would. You're not to be left unguarded until we return to Central. Orders from CenDip."

Fassa moaned again. If CenDip was interesting itself in her case, she was worse off than she'd thought. Never mind. Central was a long way off. For the present she was alone on a droneship with this gorgeous hunk, and with any luck at all she'd make him change his allegiances before the official transports arrived to carry her to trial.

After only a little pouting and posing she managed to persuade Sev that propping himself against the wall outside her cabin would be adequate to fulfill his guard duty. It was, Fassa thought with satisfaction, a beginning. Now he would feel that this cabin was her territory. When he came in again, it would be at her invitation . . . and invitations could lead to all sorts of interesting things. She washed from head to foot, kicked her stained and crumpled clothes in a corner under the bunk, splashed a little extra cool water over her face, and wrapped a sheet around herself in lieu of fresh clothes. This would be a real test of her abilities. No cosmetics, hair combed straight with no styling, a scratchy Service-issue sheet instead of a clinging gown, and this bare cabin for a romantic setting!

"*Fossa baby, you're so sweet, I just can't resist you,*" Faul del Parma used to moan when he came into her room and buried himself in her. And she'd been an awkward, sullen little girl then, with her black hair in thin tight braids. She'd worn the ugliest, plainest clothes she could find, but that didn't put Faul off.

For the first time Fassa deliberately summoned up the memories she'd tried for so long to bury, seeking the confidence she needed to go on. She really was irresistible to men. Faul del Parma had proved that, hadn't he? Even knowing it was wrong, even knowing she hated it, he'd still refused to let her alone.

"It's everything about you, the way you walk, the way you smile up at me with those big sooty lashes half covering your eyes."

Instead of giving her confidence, the memories made Fassa feel grimy. She must have invited him, not with words, but with something about the way she walked and looked at him. Somehow she'd made Daddy want her without even knowing it. She was a bad little girl and if Mama ever found out . . .

Somewhere in the back of her mind, Mama screamed and fell endlessly through the glittering interior atrium of the hotel, tumbling in a cloud of gauzy draperies. And it was all her fault. Fassa cried out once and threw something across the cabin with all her might, and Sev Bryley burst through the unlatched door.

"What's the matter? What happened?"

His arms went around her and Fassa rested against the fresh starched fabric of his shirt, feeling the strong beat of his heart beneath her face. For some reason she was crying; she couldn't stop crying for long minutes while Sev just held her. Not easing her backwards towards the bunk, not letting his hands slide artfully downward in a disguised caress. Just holding her.

"Well," Fassa said finally, gulping down the last of her sobs, "I told you; I have bad dreams."

"You seemed wide awake when I left you."

Fassa drew a shaky deep breath. "I—I'm afraid to be alone just now," she said. It happened to be true. "Could you stay with me?"

"As it happens," Sev told her, "I was going to anyway." He released her, as if sensing that she was recovered for the moment, and moved a step backward. Fassa sighed again, with a little more forethought this time, and watched his eyes. Yes, he was aware of what those deep breaths were doing to the sliding knot that held the sheet together between her breasts, and he couldn't take his eyes off the creamy skin that contrasted with the stark white of the sheet. Good. She had a job to do, here; she had best think about that and nothing else, or she'd never win this man to her side before she was taken away for trial.

"Oh, that's right," she said, allowing a tear to creep into the corner of one eye; not difficult, in her present shaky mood. "I forgot; you're my jailer, aren't you?"

Sev looked uncomfortable at this assessment, as she'd wanted him to. "I wouldn't put it quite like that. But someone does have to stay with you until . . ."

"Until the end," Fassa finished for him. "What sort of sentences are in favor these days? Will it be hard labor, do you think?" She tossed her head and gave him her Christian-facing-the-lions look, all nobility and virgin defiance. At the same time she moved slightly so that the sheet molded over one thigh, giving him (she hoped) visions of what sort of *hard labor* she might be good for.

"You'll have a fair trial," Sev told her, "and a chance to speak in your own defense."

"*Will* I?" Fassa challenged him. "Look at me. Don't you think there'll be some old judge who'd just love to see me mindwiped? They'll be thinking what a pity it is to waste such a beautiful body, keep the body, just wipe out the personality and start over."

"Oh, I'm sure they won't do that," Sev said, but he sounded less righteously certain than he'd been a moment before. Fassa mentally applauded her own cleverness. There wasn't much point in trying to convince Sev that she was innocent of the charges against her, not when he was Central's prime witness. Much better to switch the topic to the corruption at all levels of government. Sev knew something about that. Let him stew over the assertion that she couldn't possibly get a fair trial, let him think—as he must be thinking now—about the danger that she'd end up as the mindwiped toy of some corrupt official.

"You know it happens," Fassa said in a low voice. "You know how much cheating there is in the government. Everybody wants something for himself. One of them will want *me*, and then—" She blew a kiss into the air with a mocking smile. "Bye-bye, Fassa del Parma!" Time to let the sheet fall to the ground, giving Sev a good look about what some dirty old man would get if he didn't get there first. She moved towards him, inch by inch, watching the color rise in his sharp features, watching the blue eyes darken with desire. "You could at least say good-bye properly, Sev, my love," she whispered.

She paused, eyes closed, awaiting the warmth of his arms about her and his mouth on hers.

"I think not," said Sev Bryley, and while Fassa's eyes flew open in shocked disbelief he took the two steps that brought him to the cabin door.

Once outside the cabin, Sev reactivated the guardlock mechanism that would prevent Fassa from leaving. He leaned against the wall and wiped his forehead with the back of one hand. It wasn't much help; he still felt as hot as if he'd just done a ten-mile run in the Capellan jungle. He needed a cold shower. And that ten-mile run might not be a bad idea, either, except he couldn't leave Nancia alone to guard Fassa.

He could get some extra help, though—and some insurance against temptation. "Nancia?" he said in a low voice, looking upward at the angle between ceiling and roof where her auditory sensors were installed. "Nancia, I think you'd better activate full sensors within Fassa's cabin. I know it's a breach of the prisoner's privacy, but this is a very dangerous woman. And, Nancia? You'd better keep the sensors on at all times. Even when I'm with Ms. del Parma."

Sev thought that over and decided he hadn't worded that last request strongly enough. "*Especially* when I'm with Fassa," he rephrased.

"I'd already done that, Sev," Nancia responded from the wall speaker. "Don't worry. Everything has been observed and recorded."

"Excellent," said Sev between his teeth. "I'm sure that little scene will be vastly amusing to somebody who's not troubled by hormonal urges. Now, if you don't mind, just keep watching Fassa and let me know if she tries anything. I'll be in the ship's exercise room."

"What for?"

"Taking care of my hormones," Sev said. He stamped off to improve his weight-lifting record.

"FN-935, Forister Armontillado y Medoc requests permission to come aboard."

"Permission granted."

Even to her own ears, Nancia sounded brusque. After a grudging nanosecond's thought she added formally, "Welcome aboard, Forister Armontillado y Medoc."

The short, spare man whom she'd last seen heading into the tangled planetary conflicts of the Tran Phon guerrillas on Charon dropped three heavy pieces of baggage onto the lift with a grunt of relief. *I'm getting an old man who can't even carry his own luggage without getting out of breath.* But as if to contradict the unspoken criticism, Forister waved the lift upwards with his luggage and took the circular stairs. Nancia watched his progress from sensor to sensor. He moved with quick, neat steps, economical of his motions. You couldn't say he was bounding up the stairs, but he did get to the top more quickly than she'd expected; and there wasn't a gray hair out of place or a drop of sweat on his forehead when he entered the central cabin.

"Greetings, Nancia," Forister said. Unlike Caleb, he looked directly at the titanium bulkhead that housed Nancia's human body and brain. His direct gaze was rather disconcerting to Nancia, who'd been used to Caleb wandering round the ship and addressing her without turning his head, counting on her efficient sensor system to pick up his words wherever he might be. She took a moment to look over this strange elderly brawn and prepare her response. Light eyes in a tanned face, with a network of crinkles around the eyes as if he were accustomed to looking deeply at whatever he saw; hints of red and ginger in the graying hair; a light, erect, relaxed stance, as if he were prepared to move in any direction at a moment's notice. *He may do. But he's not Caleb!*

"You seem remarkably fit for someone who's just been recuperating at Summerlands," Nancia said at last.

Forister grimaced. "Oh, I'm fit enough, if that's what's been worrying you, FN. The stay at Summerlands was not for any medical reasons."

"Then what? The orders I received said you were there for R&R."

"Um. Yes. Well, they would, wouldn't they?" Forister said, maddeningly, while Nancia wondered if the man ever gave a straight answer to anything. Maybe that was trained out of you in the diplomatic service.

At last he vouchsafed one more sentence that could be considered an explanation. "My last posting for CenDip was . . . shall we say, stressful, and things didn't work out as well as I'd hoped."

"Charon?" Nancia asked.

The brawn blinked once, surprised. "Why, no. Why—oh, I remember. I had the honor of being transported to Charon by you, didn't I? Some years ago—you were the CN-935 then, as I recall. My condolences on the loss of your partner."

"It's only temporary," Nancia said. "Which reminds me. I wouldn't wish to hurry your unpacking, but as soon as you're ready, I'd like you to take over guarding the prisoner. Sev Bryley is needed at Summerlands to look after my brawn."

"As you wish." Forister did not quite click his heels together as he executed a perfect bow in the direction of the titanium column. He wheeled, collected his bags from the open lift and marched down the hall to the brawn's cabin—*Caleb's cabin*—leaving Nancia with the feeling that she had been unpleasantly brusque. She opened a speaker in the cabin.

"If you don't object, we could continue our conversation while you unpack."

"No objection," said Forister. He was slightly out of breath now, after lifting the heavy bags to his bunk. What on Earth *did* the man travel with? A fortune in corycium bars buried beneath his underwear? The first things he drew out of the bags were commonplace enough: CenDip formal dress and spare shirts, toiletries and a handful of laser-printed datahedra.

He might not object, but he wasn't being very helpful either. Well, she hadn't been as friendly as she might; it was up to her to make the first move. "What was your last posting, then, if it wasn't Charon? And why did you pick Summerlands?"

"Summerlands has a very good reputation as a rest facility," Forister said. "I expect you're unduly worried about your former brawn; the medical staff there is top-quality."

"It's not their technical skills I'm worried about," Nancia told him. There was movement in Fassa's cabin. She had been keeping the sensors there down to monitor level; now she activated full pick-up and saw that Sev had gone in to talk to Fassa. The girl was fully dressed this time, and they were sitting on opposite bunks; she didn't think Sev would encounter any real problem. All the same, she captured their quiet conversation and listened to it with one ear while she watched Forister and wished he would hurry up with his unpacking. Now he had got to the bottom layer of the first bag, and she saw what had weighed his luggage down so: nothing but a lot of antiques. One antique book after another, kilos and kilos of them, and doubtless no more information in the lot of them than could be stored in a few facets of a data-hedron! There was no accounting for tastes.

"Isn't Summerlands rather remote for a man of your impor-tance?" Nancia probed. She knew she was being pushy, but she didn't care. If Forister was in with Alpha and her criminal friends, she didn't dare set him to guard Fassa—nor did she dare send him back to the clinic to watch over Caleb. She would have to get on the datastream to Murasaki Base at once.

"I've family in the Nyota system," Forister told her. "I was hoping to make a brief visit after I left Summerlands. And I'd a friend at the clinic."

"Alpha bint Hezra-Fong," Nancia surmised. She might as well face all the bad news at once.

"Good God, no!" Forister seemed genuinely startled. "If that's what you think of the company I keep, no wonder you've been so hostile. Somebody else entirely, I assure you."

"Who?"

"I'm not at liberty to say just now. If all goes well—" Forister broke off and rather fussily adjusted the portable folding shelf where he had stowed his books, tightening the spring-bindings that would keep them in place in case of any rapid ship's movements. "But whether it comes off or not," he said, more slowly, "I won't be here to help. *And* I won't have any free time afterwards to visit in this system. I'll be on my way back to Central with you, and once I land there, God knows what six urgent assignments will be waiting." He looked up, directly into Nancia's primary cabin sensor. "So you see, dear lady, this assignment is no more to my liking than it is to yours. I hope we can sink our differences for the duration—"

"*Hush.*" The conversation in Fassa's cabin had suddenly become very interesting; Nancia didn't want to have to wait and replay it, she wanted to know what was going on right now.

It appeared that Fassa was trying to plea bargain with infor-mation on some of the other young people who'd been involved in that vicious wager. She began by hinting to Sev that she might be able to inform on a whole gang of criminals in the Nyota system if doing so would get her a reduced sentence. Sev, quite properly, told her that he wasn't authorized to make such promises.

"Oh, what the hell," Fassa said wearily at last. "If I'm going down,

I won't go alone. You might as well know everything. At least then you'll see that I'm not the worst of the bunch by a long shot."

She began telling Sev all she knew about Darnell Overton-Glaxely and the ways in which he'd worked his illegal Net access, first to bring in shipping bids that were always just a shade lower than those of his competitors, then to destroy the credit and acquire the stock of any small businesses he felt like adding to his empire.

"All very interesting," Sev told her. "But if Overton-Glaxely is as clever as you say at accessing private Net datastreams, he'll have been clever enough to leave no traces of his taps."

"Oh, he's not clever at all," Fassa said. "He was taught how to tap into the datastream—"

"By?" Sev prompted gently.

Fassa shook her head. She had gone rather white about the lips. "It doesn't matter. Nobody you're likely to catch up with. Not me, if that's what you're thinking; I haven't got that kind of brains."

"I never suspected you had," Sev said, rather too solemnly. Fassa gave him a suspicious glance. His lips were twitching. She aimed a mock blow at him.

"That's right, insult my intelligence!"

Sev caught her wrist and held it for a long moment while Nancia wondered if it was time to interrupt. At last his fingers relaxed. Fassa subsided onto her bunk. There was a white ring about her wrist where Sev had held her; she rubbed it absently while she went on talking. "Never mind about the Net, then. There's other ways to prove it. One of the men Darnell ruined found out a little too much about his methods, and Darnell sent him to Summerlands."

At that point Nancia decided that Forister had better hear this too. Whatever she thought of the man as a replacement for her Caleb, he *was* a trusted CenDip senior civil servant. He had friends in Summerlands. And he seemed to share her opinion of Dr. bint Hezra-Fong. She piped the input from Fassa's cabin through her speakers in Forister's cabin. After a moment's stunned silence, Forister sat down amid the piles of antiques on his bunk and listened carefully.

"Darnell thought Alpha would kill the man for him. She'd had a bunch of accidents with the tests she ran on her charity patients; she was getting quite good at faking death certificates with innocent-seeming causes of death. She used to boast about it at our annual meetings. One more wouldn't have been any problem for her. But she didn't kill him. She keeps him so full of Seductron that he doesn't know who he is, and whenever she wants Darnell to do her a favor, she threatens to cut the man's Seductron dosage."

"His name?" Sev demanded.

Fassa looked down. "I'd like some assurances that you'll see my sentence reduced."

"You know I can't do that," Sev told her.

She twisted her fingers together. "You could lose the records of this last trip, though. Without your testimony and the recordings, there wouldn't be any hard evidence against me." She looked up, eyes brilliant with unshed tears. "*Please*, Sev? I thought you cared for me a little."

"You were wrong," said Sev in a voice as dead and even as any droneship's artificially generated speech.

"Then what do I have? Why should I give you a damned thing?" Fassa pounded on the yielding surface of the bunk in frustration. Her fists sank into the plasmaform and left momentary dents that smoothed out as soon as she lifted her hands. "Oh, all right. Go ahead and see me mindwiped, or sent to prison until I'm too old to care," she said wearily. "Why should the others get away with it when my life is ruined? The man's name is Valden Allen Hopkirk, and he used to own Hopkirk Glimware right here on Bahati. Is that enough for you, or would you like his Central Citizen Code as well?"

"Any little thing you can tell us would be much appreciated," said Sev carefully.

"Well, I don't happen to know his CCC, so you're out of luck!" Fassa snapped. "Wait—wait—there's more."

"There is?"

"Find Hopkirk, and you'll have evidence on Alpha and Darnell both," Fassa said rapidly. "But there's another one you ought to get. His name's Blaize. . . ."

In the brawn's cabin, Forister lowered his head to rest on his clenched hands. "Blaize Armontillado-Perez y Medoc," he whispered. "No. No."

I've family in the Nyota system . . . I was going to visit after I left Summerlands . . .

Nancia cut off the audio transmission to Forister's cabin and shut down her own sensors there. She listened alone while Fassa babbled out the details of Blaize's felonious career on Angalia; the diverting of PTA shipments, the slave labor and torture of the native population he was supposed to be guarding.

Some day Forister would have to know and face those details, but not yet. She would leave him alone until he requested the recordings of this conversation, and then she would let him listen in privacy.

And so Nancia was the only witness when Fassa's confessional came to an abrupt ending. After she finished the tale of Blaize's misdeeds, Sev probed her.

"I've looked up the records of that first voyage," he said, almost casually. "There were five of you in it together, weren't there? You, Dr. bint Hezra-Fong, Overton-Glaxely, Armontillado-Perez y Medoc, and one other. Polyon de Gras-Waldheim, newly commissioned from the Academy. What was his part in the wager?"

Fassa clamped her lips shut and slowly shook her head. "I can't tell you any more," she whispered. "Only—don't let them send me to Shemali. Kill me first. I know you never cared for me, but as one human being to another—kill me first. Please."

"You're wrong in thinking I never cared for you," Sev said after a long silence.

"You said so yourself."

"You asked if I liked you a little," he corrected her. "And I don't. You're vain and self-centered and you may have killed a good man and you've yet to show any interest at all in Caleb's fete. I don't much like you at all."

"Yes, I know."

"Unfortunately," he went on with no change of expression, "like it or not—and believe me, I'm not at all happy about the situation—I do seem to love you. Not," he said almost gently, "that it'll do either of us much good, under the circumstances. But I did think you ought to know."

CHAPTER ELEVEN

Caleb recovered with amazing speed. Two hours after his arrival at the clinic, forty minutes after Alpha bint Hezra-Fong had analyzed the poisons in his blood and slapped on stimpatches of the appropriate antidotes, the nervous convulsions had stopped. Nancia knew exactly when that happened, because by then she had thought to send Sev Bryley to Summerlands with a contact button discreetly replacing the top stud in his dress tunic and a second contact button to dip onto Caleb's hospital gown. While Forister remained on board as a nominal guard for Fassa, Sev lounged about the public rooms at Summerlands trying to look like a worried friend-or-relative and chatting up the recuperating VIPs. Nancia watched the clinic from two angles: the convulsive shuddering view of a cracked white ceiling, emanating from Caleb's contact button, and the repetitive views of artificial potted palms and doddering old celebrities to whom Sev talked. On the whole, the potted palms were more valuable than the celebrities; at least they didn't waste Sev's time with their reminiscences of events a century past.

"None of these people know anything about Hopkirk," she whispered through Sev's contact button.

"I've noticed," he replied as the senile director emeritus of the Bahati Musical College, aged one hundred seventy-five Standard Central Years, tottered away for his noon meds.

"Can't you do something more productive?"

"Give me time. We don't want to be obvious. And stop hissing at me. They'll think I'm talking to myself and hearing voices."

"From what I've seen of these befuddled gentry, that'll make you fit right in."

"Only," said Sev grimly, "if they don't hear the voices too."

Nancia hated to leave him with the last word in an argument, but she was distracted at that moment. Something had happened— or stopped happening. Caleb's sensor button was no longer transmitting a jiggling view of the cracks on the ceiling; the image was still and perfectly clear.

Not quite still. A regular, gentle motion assured her that he still breathed.

A moment later, two aides exchanged a flurry of rapid, low-voiced but mainly cheerful comments over Caleb's bed. Nancia gathered that the news was good; his (three-syllable Greek root) was up, his (four-syllable Latin derivation) was down, they were putting him on a regular dosage of (two-word Denebian form), and as soon as he was conscious they were to start him on a physical therapy routine.

She complained to Forister about the jargon.

"Now you know how the rest of the world feels about brains and brawns," he said soothingly. "You know, there are people who think decomposition theory is just a little hard to follow. They accuse us of mystifying the mathematics on purpose."

"Huh. There's nothing mystical about mathematics," Nancia grumbled. "This medical stuff is something else again."

"Why don't you translate the terms and find out what they mean?"

"I didn't have a classical education," Nancia told him. "I'm going to buy one when we get back to civilization, though. I want full datahedra of Latin, Greek, and medical terminology. With these new hyperchips I should be able to access the terms almost as fast as a native speaker."

Somebody shouted just out of visual range of Caleb's sensor button. The view of the hospital ceiling swayed, blurred, and was replaced by glass windows, green fields, and a white-clothed arm coming from the left. "Here," said a calm, competent voice just before Caleb bent over the permalloy bowl before him and gave up the contents of his last meal.

The contact button gave Nancia a very clear, sharply detailed close-up view of the results.

After that, though, he recovered his strength with amazing speed. Throughout the day Nancia followed his sessions with the physical therapist. At the same time she tracked Sev while he prowled the hallways of Summerlands Clinic and listened for any scrap of information about a patient named Valden Allen Hopkirk.

By mid-afternoon a new aide was able to assure Caleb that there would be no permanent nerve damage as a result of the attack.

"You're weak, though, and we'll need to retrain some of the nerve pathways; the stuff your space pirate used was a neural scrambler. Damage is reversible," the aide said briskly, "but I'd advise a prolonged course of therapy. You certainly won't be cleared to act as a brawn for some time. Has your ship been notified?"

"She knows everything that goes on here," said Caleb, placing one finger briefly on the edge of the contact button.

Nancia got a good look at the aide's face. The man looked thoughtful, perhaps worried. "I . . . see. And, um, I suppose the button has a dead-man switch? Some alarm if it's inactivated or removed?"

"Absolutely," Nancia responded through the contact button before Caleb could tell the truth. Some such arrangement would be a great safeguard for Caleb, and she wished Central had thought of it. But failing that, the illusion of the arrangement might give him some protection. She went on through the tiny speaker, ignoring Caleb's attempts to interrupt her. "Please notify all staff concerned of the arrangement. I would be sorry to have to sound a general alarm just because some ignorant staff member accidentally interfered with my monitoring system."

"That would indeed be . . . unfortunate," said the aide thoughtfully.

After he left, Caleb said quietly into the contact button, "That was a lie, Nancia."

"Was it?" Nancia parried. "Do you think you know *all* my capabilities? Who's the 'brain' of this partnership?"

"I see!"

Nancia rather hoped he didn't. At least she'd avoided lying directly to Caleb. That was something . . . but not enough.

She had never before minded her inability to move about freely on planetary surfaces. Psych Department's testing before she entered brainship training showed that she valued the ability to fly between the stars far more than the limited mobility of planet-bound creatures. "I could have told them that," Nancia responded when the test results were reported to her. "Who wants to roll about on surface when they could have all of deep space to play in? If I want anything planetside, they can bring it to me at the spaceport."

But they couldn't bring her Caleb. And she couldn't go to the Summerlands clinic to watch over him. Nancia could see and hear everything that passed within range of those buttons. She could even send instructions to the wearers. But she could not *act*. She was reduced to fretting over the slow progress they were making and worrying about the medications being inserted into Caleb's blood stream.

"Haven't you found anything yet?" she demanded of Forister. Since Fassa had spent the day crying quietly in her cabin, Forister interpreted his "guard" duties rather liberally. He was on board and available in case of any escape attempt, but he told Nancia that he saw no reason to waste his time sitting on a hard bench outside Fassa's cabin door. Instead, he sat before a touchscreen in the central cabin, inserting delicate computer linkages into Alpha's clinic records and scanning for some hint of where she'd put the witness they needed.

Forister straightened and sighed. "I have found," he told her, "four hundred gigamegs of patient charts, containing detailed records of all their medications, treatments, and data readouts."

"Well, then, why don't you just look up Hopkirk and find out what she's done with him?" Nancia demanded.

In response, Forister tapped one finger on the touchscreen and slapped his palm over Nancia's analog input. The data he had retrieved was shunted directly into Nancia's conscious memory stores. It felt like having the contents of a medical library injected directly into her skull. Nancia winced, shut down her instinctive read-responses, and opened a minuscule slit of awareness onto a tiny portion of the data.

It was an incomprehensible jumble of medical terminology, packed without regard for paragraphing or spacing, with peculiar symbolic codes punctuating the strings of jargon.

She opened another slit and "saw" the same tightly-packed gibberish.

"It's not indexed by patient name," Forister explained. "Names are encoded—for privacy reasons, I suppose. If the data is indexed by anything, it might be on type of treatment. Or it might be based on a hashed list of meds. I really can't find any organizing principle yet. Also," he added, unnecessarily, "it's compressed."

"We know he's being kept quiet by controlled overdoses of Seductron," Nancia said. "Why not . . . oh." As she spoke, she had been scanning the datastream. There was no mention of Seductron. "Illicit drug," she groaned. "Officially, there's no such treatment. She'll have encoded it as something else."

"I should have taken Latin," Forister nodded. "Capellan seemed so much more useful for a diplomat . . . Ah, well."

"Can you keep hacking into the records?" Nancia asked. "There might be a clue somewhere else."

Forister looked mildly offended. "Please, dear lady. 'Hacking' is a criminal offense."

"But isn't that what you're doing?"

"I may be temporarily on brawn service," Forister said, "but I am a permanent member of the Central Diplomatic Service. Code G, if that means anything to you. As such, I have diplomatic immunity. Hacking is illegal; whatever I do is not illegal; hence, it's not hacking." He smiled benignly and traced a spiraling path inward from the boundaries of the touchscreen, wiping the previous search and opening a new way into the labyrinth of the Summerlands Clinic records.

"*I* should have taken *logic*," Nancia muttered. "I think there's something wrong with your syllogism. Code G. That means you're a *spy*?" Caleb would never forgive her for this. Consorting with spies, breaking into private records . . . The fact that she was working as much to save him as to track down criminals wouldn't palliate her offense in his eyes.

"Mmm. You may call me X-39 if you like." Humming to himself, Forister smoothed out the path he had begun and traced a new, more complex pattern on the touchscreen.

"Isn't that rather pointless," Nancia inquired, "seeing that I already know your name?"

"Hmm? Ah, yes—there we go!" Forister chuckled with satisfaction as he opened his access to a new segment of Summerlands Clinic's computer system. "Supremely pointless, like most espionage. Most diplomacy, too, come to think of it. No, we don't use code names. But I've always thought it would be rather *fun* to be known as X-39."

"Have you indeed, fungus-brain?" Alpha bint Hezra-Fong muttered from the security of her inner office. "How'd you like to be known as Seductron Test Failure 106 Mark 7? If I'd known who you were—" She bit off the empty threats. She knew now. And if Forister made the mistake of coming back to Summerlands for any reason, she'd have her revenge.

Neither Forister nor Nancia had thought to check Nancia's decks for transmitters—and even if they had, they might not have recognized Alpha's personal spyder, a sliver-thin enhanced metachip device that clung to any permalloy wall and, chameleon-like, mimicked the colors of its surroundings. In all the fuss attendant on getting the wounded brawn into the floatube, Alpha had found it easy enough to leave one of the spyders attached to Nancia's central corridor. From there it picked up any conversation in the cabins, although the voices were distorted by distance and interference.

At the time, Alpha hadn't been exactly sure what instinct prompted her to plant the spyder; she had just felt that the amount of Net communications traffic concerning this particular brainship and brawn suggested they were more important than they looked. Infuriatingly, the datastreams coming from Central over the Net were in a code Alpha had not yet succeeded in breaking, so the spyder was her only source of information.

So far, though, it had proved a remarkably effective tool. Alpha preened herself on her cleverness in dropping one of the expensive spyders where it was most needed. She drummed her fingers on the palmpad of the workstation while she mentally reviewed what she'd done so far and the steps she'd taken to counteract the danger. The rhythm of her fingertips was repeated on the screen as a jagged display of colored lines, breaking and recombining in a hypnotic jazzy dance.

First had come the surprising sound of Fassa del Parma's voice. While admiring the dramatic range Fassa put into pleading with her captor, Alpha hadn't been too surprised when the girl rapidly broke down and began spilling what she knew about her competitors. She'd always felt the del Parma kid didn't have what it took to make it in the big time. Too emotional. She cried in her sleep and then she gloated over her victims. Real success came from being like Alpha or Polyon, cool, unmoved, above feeling triumph or fear, concentrating always on the desired goal.

Fortunately, Fassa didn't know much; she'd been too stupid to think much beyond her personal concerns. Alpha was willing to bet the little snip had never thought of compiling a dossier on each of her competitors, with good hard data that could be traded in emergency. All she had were gossip and innuendo and stories from the annual meetings. Blaize was nasty to the natives, Alpha had developed an illicit drug, Darnell was less than totally ethical in his business takeovers.

Hearsay! Without hard evidence to back up the stories, Central would never make charges like these stick, and they were too smart to try. Alpha grinned and slapped her open hand down on the palmpad, jolting the computer into a random display of medical jargon and meaningless symbols mixed with sentences pulled at random from patient reports. She'd prepared that program years ago, as protection against a computer attack like the one Forister was trying now. And to judge from the snippets of conversation between him and Nancia, it was working. They would waste all their energy trying to decipher a code that had no meaning.

And while they worked, Alpha would take steps to deal with the one piece of hard evidence Fassa had pointed out to them. Her fingers drummed faster; she slapped the palmpad again to enter voice mode.

"Send Baynes and Moss to my office—no, to Test Room Four," she said. Baynes could safely be pulled off the task of watching that brawn for a while; Caleb was too weak to be any danger, and anyway he was protected by his brainship's monitor button.

Alpha didn't think her office was infested with spyders; she was absolutely certain about Test Room 4, a gleaming permalloy shell with no crack in the walls, no furnishings but the permalloy benches and table. Alpha had commissioned the building of this room out of her profits from the first illicit street sales of Seductron. The official purpose of the lab room was for Alpha's experiments on bioactive agents; the extreme simplicity of its design was to aid in complete sterilization of the chamber after experiments were completed.

It served well enough for these purposes. And the contractor who'd installed nets of electronic impulse chargers behind the permalloy skin, making the room impervious to any known external monitors, had suffered a fatal overdose of Blissto shortly after the completion of the room. Alpha shook her head and sighed with everyone else that she'd never have guessed the man was an addict. And the secret of the room was safe.

Baynes and Moss really were addicts. Alpha had "cured" their Blissto addiction, found them jobs at the clinic, and then explained to them that the Blissto addiction had only been replaced by a much more serious drug, a variant of Seductron with the unfortunate side effect of causing complete nervous collapse in victims who were suddenly cut off from their regular dosage. Alpha had been experimenting with a mildly addictive form of Seductron that would create a captive market in anyone who ever tried the stuff; Seductron-B4 was an overresponse to the problem. She was afraid to release the stuff to street markets. But it was incredibly useful in creating willing servants. It had only taken one or two delicately timed delays in the Seductron-B4 doses to convince Baynes and Moss that their only hope of life lay in total loyalty to her. She had picked her tools carefully; they had enough medical background to be genuinely useful as aides in the clinic, but were far too stupid to replicate her work on Seductron. If she died or were incapacitated, Baynes and Moss would die too: inevitably, slowly, and painfully.

She felt quiet satisfaction, as always, at seeing two men to whom her life was, literally, as valuable as their own. *And for all that little snip Fossa vaunts her sex appeal, no man who's rutted after her cares about her life the way these two care about mine.*

She gave her instructions quickly and confidently, expecting nothing but instant obedience. The patient carried on Summerlands' lists as Varian Alexander was to be removed to the charity side of the clinic at once. There was an empty bed in Ward 6, where the recovering Blissto addicts and alcoholics were housed; he would do very well there for the moment.

"Excuse me, Doctor, but are you sure—" Baynes began.

"He'll stand the move," Alpha said.

"Yes, but—"

"It's simple enough even for your drug-logged brain, I should think!"

"It's not Alexander that worries him, Doctor," said the quicker

Moss. "It's that half-cyborg freak in Ward 6. Qualia Benton. Been asking a lot of questions, she has. Too many."

Alpha drummed her fingers on the permalloy table. Benton. Qualia Benton. Ah, yes. An interesting case. Presented as an alcoholic veteran of the Capellan Wars who was too shaky and brain-damaged to keep up her own periodic maintenance on her cyborg limb and organ replacements. All parts had appeared to be in good working order, but Alpha had approved the series of tests and maintenance anyway; Veterans' Aid would pay for the work, and if Qualia Benton was too far out of it to do her own maintenance, she'd never think to question whether the work the clinic charged was absolutely necessary—or whether it had even been done.

"What sort of questions?"

Baynes shrugged. "Anything. Everything. How do we like our jobs. How did we get our jobs. How many rooms are there in this wonderful big building, and what all goes on here besides taking care of poor old freaks like her. Supposing she wanted to get work at a nice clean place like this, would we put in a good word for her."

"No harm in all that."

"Yeah, but . . ." Baynes shifted his weight from one foot to the other and fell silent.

Moss took up the story. "Last Friday she was rolling about in her bed, claiming she had nervous pains something awful in her left foot, which it isn't there any more, Doctor, and nothing wrong with the prosthesis connections, I checked 'em out twice. Wouldn't go out for exercise with the rest of the winos, so I left her while we shoved the others out for their healthful walk around the park. Only thing is, I had to come back early on account of old Charlie Blissed-Out collapsed with chest pains and I wanted a floatube to bring him back. And I found her on the floor outside the staff room. She claimed she'd been trying to work the prosthesis and it collapsed on her."

"Possibly true," said Alpha.

"Yeah. But . . . the staff room door was unlocked. I swear I locked up like always, Doctor, but it was open then."

Alpha considered Moss's sweating face for a long moment. He could be trying to cover up his own carelessness in leaving the staff room door unlocked and a patient alone in the ward. But he hadn't had to tell her about the incident in the first place. He would only be risking her anger if he were afraid of something even worse—like a threat to her position at the clinic, something that would take her away and end his supply of Seductron-B4.

"Put the two of them in a private room," Alpha ordered.

"Aren't any on the charity side," Baynes objected glumly.

Moss rolled his eyes. "God give me strength," he pleaded. "Doctor *knows* that, Baynes. Forget about moving Victor Alexander to the charity side. We're to put Qualia Benton in a private room with him on the V.I.P. side, and don't worry about the fact that Veterans Aid won't pay; I reckon she won't be there long enough to run up much of a bill. Right, Doctor?"

He gave Alpha a conspiratorial smile which she did not return.

"Benton's is an interesting case," Alpha said neutrally. "I wish to investigate this prosthesis trouble myself. Any charges incurred will be billed to the experimental lab. Meanwhile, I wish you to keep an eye on the visitor Bryley. He's supposed to be here as escort to that brawn, but he's been spending entirely too much time talking to too many people in the public rooms."

Bryley might not be an immediate threat, but it wouldn't do any harm to have Baynes and Moss keep an eye on him. As for the other two, Alpha had no intention of leaving the disposal of her problems to this pair of bunglers, one stupid and the other trying to wriggle himself into her good graces. Nor did she intend to risk their being able to give direct evidence against her, if worst came to the worst.

Qualia Benton might be no more than an alcoholic old fool who couldn't keep from snooping into other people's business, or she might be considerably more than that. If the first, she would be no loss; if the second, she had to be disposed of immediately. As for Valden Allen Hopkirk—Alpha hated to waste a potential tool like Hopkirk, especially after going to the trouble of keeping him lightly drugged and available for all this time, but she prided herself on the ability to face facts and cut her losses. There were suddenly too many people asking too many questions around Summerlands.

Alpha dismissed Baynes and Moss and went back into her private storage room to prepare. "If you want a thing done well, do it yourself," she murmured as she prepared two stimpads, each loaded with a massive overdose of Seductron-B4.

❖   ❖   ❖

The woman known as Qualia Benton knew something was wrong when the two aides who were Doctor Hezra-Fong's shadows came to transfer her from the charity side of the clinic. She'd been ready to act then, fingers tensed against the side of her left-leg prosthesis, adrenalin keeping her unnaturally aware of every shadow and change of intonation.

And nothing happened. "You're moving to a private room," the big one called Baynes said.

"Who'll pay?" Qualia Benton demanded in the fretful, shrill tone to be expected from an old soak whose nerves were jangling for just one more drink.

"Doctor's interested in your case," said the little black-haired one, Moss. "She wants to run some special tests. On the clinic, if Veteran's Aid won't cover it. You could get into the next issue of the Medical Research Journal."

"I'm honored," said Qualia Benton politely. She let the men transfer her to a wheelchair and rode quietly down the long silent corridors of Summerlands clinic, watching the myriad reflections of herself and the aides in the polished tiles of floor and walls and ceiling, ready for the slightest move that would warn her it was time to act.

It won't happen in the halls. They'll move when I'm in a room alone, she told herself. But what if they expected her to count on that, and took her by surprise in one of these long empty hallways? She dared not relax.

Even when they wheeled her into a room with two beds, the one nearest the window already occupied, she was tense with expectation.

"Here now, you said I was getting a private room!" she whined. Qualia Benton would whine; what's more, she would be suspicious and distrustful like most recovering addicts, almost paranoid. God knew, it wasn't hard to fake that part.

"Might as well be private," said the one called Moss. "*He* won't bother you much. Will you, Varian?"

The patient in the other bed nodded and shook his head alternately, smiling with a loose, open-lipped grin that chilled her spirits. *Blissto addict. Or worse . . . if there is anything worse? And they're maintaining him in that condition, instead of trying to break the addiction. That's criminal!*

Qualia Benton, chronic alcoholic, too woozy to take proper care of her own prostheses and replacement organs, wouldn't care about somebody else's problems. She said nothing.

The aides helped her into the free bed.

"Here you go," said the small black-haired man cheerfully. He slapped a stimpad downwards; she recoiled but could not quite escape the stinging contact against her shoulder. "Just a little relaxation med before the tests," he said.

"Don't wanna relax," she muttered. The thickness in her speech was natural. She was suddenly finding it hard to think. Something was infiltrating her bloodstream, something soft as a cloud and warm as sunshine, floating her away to the Isles of the Blest— bless—bliss—Blissto! That was it!

The man in the other bed—was he really a Blissto addict, or had he been drugged in the same manner? Foolish, foolish not to have anticipated this. Once the aides had caught her out of bed and snooping where she had no business, she should have known her time at the clinic was limited.

She set her will to resisting the power of the drug. And not only her will. One thing about being underestimated, being seen as an old lush without the sense to care for her own artificial organs: Dr. Hezra-Fong hadn't, apparently, run any serious tests on those hyperchip-enhanced organs. The Blissto was carrying her away; but if she could only gain an hour or two, all might yet be well.

Did she have that hour's grace? No way to tell; she could only watch and wait, and that not very effectively. The hard hospital pillow beneath her head was soft as a Denebian flufftuff. Her left hand still rested against the smooth hard prosthesis, but she could barely feel the permaskin; the Blissto was interposing a fluffy cloud of blissful illusion between her and reality.

Doctor wants to run some tests . . . Was that truly all this meant? Surely not. So important a person as Dr. Hezra-Fong, assistant director of Summerlands, wouldn't go to all this trouble to prove that an old lush was faking disability. There had to be more going on here.

By late afternoon Sev noticed that the same two aides kept walking through the public visiting rooms. They were both rather striking in their appearance—one a burly, blue-chinned man with a lumbering walk, the other neat and quick and given to slicking down his black hair with short nervous strokes. And they would have looked more natural at a portside bar than in a luxury medical clinic.

Sev reckoned he was supposed to notice them and to be scared off. That was annoying. The doddering old CenDip widow he was talking to had finally mentioned a patient named Varian Alexander, a Blissto addict. That could be an alias for Valden Allen Hopkirk; the information that Alexander had just been moved to a semi-private room supported the theory. He was ready to get back to Nancia and check out the records on this Alexander, and he hated like hell to let these two petty thugs think they'd frightened him.

"You will *not* start anything with those two," Nancia instructed him when he muttered his complaints into the contact button. "They're minor. You get back and watch Caleb. I'll send Forister to take care of our friend Hopkirk."

"And who," Sev inquired sweetly, "will guard Fassa?"

Nancia assaulted his eardrums with a burst of static that attracted the attention of two other visitors. Glancing doubtfully at the artificial Capella fern beside Sev, they moved to the other side of the room and seated themselves well away from the strange, dour young man and his talking plant.

"You're attracting attention," Sev said sweetly. "Better let me handle this in my own way."

"Don't blame *me* if you end up in a recycler," Nancia grumbled in an undertone. "And don't expect me to send Forister to fish you out of trouble, either. After all, as you pointed out, somebody has to guard Fassa."

"I don't," said Sev loudly and clearly, "need anybody to get me out of trouble."

The other visitors whispered among themselves and somebody giggled. Sev felt his face turning red. Two shapes materialized at his elbows, one large and lumbering, one darting in quick as a hummingbird.

"Forgetting your meds again, sonny?" asked the small one in a kindly, concerned voice. He turned towards the other visitors in the room. "Sorry about the disturbance. He hears voices. Should improve with therapeu—ahh!"

Sev drove one fist into the small man's chin and wheeled to confront the big one. A hand like a small boulder descended on his head. The room whirled around him. An old lady screamed. He saw something sharp in the rock-like hand. *Should have guessed.*

The danger is never where you're looking. The hand came down for a second time, like an earthquake or an avalanche, vast, implacable, and as Sev twisted away the needle slid into flesh, quiet as a whisper, smooth as sleep.

When she heard the sounds of the fracas in the public waiting rooms, Alpha slipped into the semi-private room she'd assigned to Hopkirk and the snoopy derelict. Damn Baynes and Moss! Couldn't they handle a minor surveillance task without starting a fight? There must be something about Blissto that permanently destroyed the brain cells.

Oh, well, at least the disturbance in the waiting room would draw everybody's attention; there'd be no inconvenient witnesses to her actions here. Not that she expected to be here long enough for any problems to develop. Hopkirk was grinning in his usual loose-lipped, amiable way, and the derelict Benton was limp against her pillow in a Blissto dream. Better take care of her first; she knew Hopkirk was too sedated to give trouble.

As she pushed up the old lush's sleeve to apply the stimpad, Alpha wondered whether Qualia Benton were really a snoop, or just a brain-damaged bag lady who'd had the bad luck to stumble into private places at the wrong time. Not that it made much difference. She wouldn't be answering any questions now.

The stimpad slapped down on chill, firm flesh. The array of needles clicked but did not sink in. Alpha felt a moment's cold apprehension. *Something is wrong here. Something is very wrong.*

And Qualia Benton's dark eyes were wide open, watching her with amusement.

"The right arm prosthesis is real lifelike," she said cheerfully, "but you won't get stimpad needles through the plastiskin. And now— oh, no, dear. I wouldn't do that. I really wouldn't."

From under the bedclothes she had produced an ugly, snub-nosed needler. *Where did that come from? The old bitch isn't wearing anything but a hospital gown.*

"Whatever you had in that stimpad, the charge is wasted now," Qualia Benton informed her in that same cheerful tone. "There should be just enough left for a lab on Central to analyze. Please don't try to throw it away; I'll want to put it in an evidence bag for the trial."

"Trial," Alpha croaked. "Evidence bag." She backed up a step, frozen with horror, while her intended victim swung one real leg and one permalloy prosthesis out of bed, fussily straightened her gown, and produced a plastic bag from under the pillow.

"Just drop it in here, dear, and don't make any sudden moves. You wouldn't want to startle a poor nervous old woman. This needler is set on wide spray, and it's loaded with ParaVen. I don't really *want* to paralyze you," she said thoughtfully, "but if necessary..."

Two more backward steps brought Alpha to the door. She dropped and rolled into the corridor, momentarily out of range of the needler. "Baynes! Moss!" she shrieked. "32-A, patient out of control, Code Z, stat!"

Running feet pounded down the corridor and Alpha closed her eyes in momentary relief. That heavy tread had to belong to Baynes. Let this crazy snoop of a woman waste her needler charge on the aides—then Alpha would spirit her away to the violent ward. She promised herself a long and entertaining series of experiments on the bitch, once they got that damned needler away from her.

"Stop right there," the old woman called in a voice too clear for her apparent age. "I am a legally constituted representative of Central Worlds Internal Investigation. Any attack on my person is treason, punishable by law. You're under arrest."

"The hell I am," countered a voice that most certainly did not belong to the thick-witted Baynes. Alpha looked up and saw that Bryley man, the one she'd sent Baynes and Moss to take care of. "*I'm* the Central Worlds rep here, and *you're* under arrest. What have you done to my witness?"

"The guy in the next bed?" For the first time, the Benton woman sounded uncertain. "He's not going to be a lot of good to you. Too blissed-out to know his own name. But you're welcome to him, if you want him. I expect she was going to kill him next, after she took care of me."

"Kill? You?" Now Bryley sounded equally confused.

From her crouching position, Alpha saw the Benton woman bend and fumble along the side of her leg prosthesis. A crack opened and she drew out a thin holographic strip that shimmered with rainbow colors in the hallway lights. So *that's where she hid the needler....*

"General Micaya Questar-Benn," the woman introduced herself. She was standing straighter now, without the hunch and the bent leg that had made her look so small and helpless before. "Under-cover assignment for Central, checking out the suspiciously high death rate on the charity side of Summerlands. My colleague Forister Armontillado y Medoc should be somewhere around; he can vouch for me. And you?"

"Sevareid Bryley-Sorensen, on temporary assignment to investigate fraud in a Bahati construction company." He looked down at Alpha; she had a dizzying glimpse of blue eyes and an expression as if the cat had dragged in something better left in a back alley. "I think our cases may be connected. I was here to collect Valden Allen Hopkirk, witness to a case of criminal Net interference by one of the del Parma girl's friends. Apparently this 'lady' is another of the gang; she's been concealing the witness and—from what you say—keeping him too doped up to testify. You think she was going to kill him?"

"We'll have to wait until that stimpad in her hand has been analyzed for drug traces," General Questar-Benn said mildly, "but I certainly don't think she was dispensing routine meds. Fortunately, she slapped the stimpad on my upper-arm prosthesis. I think I was supposed to be too drugged to notice her; one of those thugs she uses for aides dosed me with Blissto, or something like it, about an hour ago."

Alpha slowly uncurled herself and stood up. If she was lost, she'd go with that much dignity. She was half a head taller than this Sev Bryley; it helped, a little, to look down on him.

"So what are you," she demanded, "a robot? Nobody's immune to Seduc—Blissto," she caught herself. No reason to give away information.

General Questar-Benn chuckled. "No, dear girl, I'm not quite as badly off as the Tin Woodman. The valves may be helped along by hyperchips, but I still have a heart—something that appears to have been left out of your makeup. But the liver and kidneys are replacements, and last year I had a new hyperchip-enhanced blood filtering function installed so that I could monitor my own internal prostheses. If you'd shown up right after your goon drugged me, I might have been in trouble. But an hour was more than enough time to filter the drug out of my bloodstream."

Alpha glowered at her and Bryley impartially. "And what about you?" she demanded of Bryley. "You looked like a *man*, but I guess you're another fucking cyborg freak."

"I am a man," Bryley said mildly. "I'm also fast—and I learned Capellan hand fighting in the war. Your big thug tripped over his own feet—with a little help—and slapped himself with the stimpad he was aiming at me. I don't know what was in it; perhaps you'd like to tell me whether he'll survive the experience? As for the little one, he collided with one of those big ceramic pots you've got decorating the waiting room. He'll have one hell of a headache when he wakes up, but he'll be in perfectly good shape to testify against you."

"No, he won't," Alpha snapped. "You don't know as much as you think you do! The man's addicted to—something you won't be able to supply. Without his next fix, he'll die in agony before the week's out!"

Bryley raised one eyebrow. "Then," he said cheerfully, "we'd better make sure to get his testimony on datahedron before he dies, hadn't we? Thanks for the warning."

CHAPTER TWELVE

"**H**ospitals!" General Questar-Benn made the word sound like an expletive. "No offense, Thalmark, but those damn gowns are just a plot to make patients helpless and submissive. Thanks for bringing my uniform, Bryley."

"I have a feeling it would take more than that to make you submissive, General," Galena Thalmark said with a slight inclination of her head.

Sev and Micaya had met in what used to be Alpha bint Hezra-Fong's office, now occupied by the administrative assistant who'd first alerted Central Worlds to the surprising death rate in Summerlands' charity wards. This morning Galena Thalmark looked ten years younger than the harried, overweight woman who'd greeted Micaya and smuggled her into the wards in the disguise of the alcoholic "Qualia Benton."

"I can't express my thanks to you both," she said, pushing dark curly hair away from her round face, "so I won't try. General Questar-Benn, you have my sincerest apologies for the dangers you experienced."

"Part of the job," said Micaya.

"All the same, we should have been more alert. I should have had staff I could trust watching you at all times," said Galena.

Micaya nodded without further comment. She was favorably impressed by Galena's quick command of the situation, even more

impressed by the fact that the young woman had taken full responsibility for problems which were hardly of her making. It wasn't
her fault that the aging director of Summerlands had left more
and more power in the hands of Dr. Hezra-Fong, allowing the
charity side to become disastrously understaffed and letting a
deplorable lack of discipline infect the whole clinic.

"Clinic's problems weren't your fault, Thalmark," Micaya said
at last, "but they're about to be your problem. The director must
have been senile to let all this go on under his nose. High Families, of course, politically unwise to fire him, but I've had one of
my aides compose a nice letter of resignation for him. Want the
spot? Can't guarantee it, you understand," she added, "but I've some
influence at Central."

Galena Thalmark flushed becomingly and murmured her thanks.
"Meanwhile," she said, shuffling papers until she'd recovered her
composure, "I'm glad to report that Mr. Hopkirk is responding quite
well to treatment. Dr. Hezra-Fong has supplied us with full details
of the drugs used to keep him sedated. We're steadily lowering the
dosage and watching him for seizures, but so far there have been
no complications. He should be quite lucid and competent to make
a deposition on datahedron within the next forty-eight hours."

"Good work!" Micaya exclaimed.

Galena Thalmark nodded. "Whatever her other failings, Dr.
Hezra-Fong is a brilliant biomedical researcher. I feel obliged to
tell you that without her full cooperation and guidance, we would
not have been able to reverse the effects of the treatment so rapidly." She looked up into Micaya's eyes. "She requested that this
fact be formally noted on her dossier."

"It will be," Micaya promised. "But I doubt that it'll bear much
weight against the rest of the record."

Galena bit her lip. "All those deaths," she murmured. "If only
I'd seen what was going on from the first . . ." Micaya nodded in
sympathy.

"Don't torture yourself," she told the younger woman. "You
weren't even at Summerlands when she began. You had every reason
to trust your superiors; it's to your credit that you suspected
something as soon as you did and called in the proper authorities to put a stop to it. Don't second-guess yourself!"

The last words were barked out in a parade-ground intonation
that made Galena's head snap up.

"I mean it," Micaya told her more gently. "My dear, I've commanded soldiers in battle. I've seen brave men and women die because of orders I gave; and sometimes those orders were wrong. You mourn the deaths, you do the best you can, and—you go on. Otherwise, you cannot be of service."

Galena Thalmark looked thoughtfully at the older woman, standing erect and composed in her plain green uniform. Some of her battle wounds were visible, the permalloy arm and leg. Others were buried in the surgical history that Galena had read: the internal replacements for kidneys and liver, the hyperchip implant in one heart valve and the blood-filtering function. And as a doctor, Galena could assess just how many hours of painful surgery and retraining had gone into reconstructing Micaya's body after she sustained each of the original wounds.

"You go on," Micaya repeated softly, "and . . . you serve as best you can. I believe that you will make an excellent director for Summerlands, Dr. Thalmark. Don't let regrets and hindsight cripple you; we need you here and now, not reliving a past that cannot be changed."

"I can see why you're a general," said Sev thoughtfully as they boarded the flyer that was to transport them from Summerlands. "If we'd had a commanding officer like you on Capella Four. . . ."

General Questar-Benn's high cheekbones flushed a shade darker. "Don't delude yourself. Making persuasive speeches is only a small part of the art of war."

"Oh? Seems to me I heard enough of them when I served on Capella. There may have been more going on in the staff rooms, but I never rose high enough in the army to see the whole picture. That's what I like about P.I. work," Sev added thoughtfully, "now I *am* the whole picture. Or was." He looked directly at Micaya. "I'll consider myself under your command for the rest of this operation."

"The rest—but my assignment's over," protested Micaya.

"Is it?"

It has been a long time since a young man looked at her so intently—and back then, Micaya thought with an amusement that she did not allow her features to reflect, the last man to look at her like that had wanted something quite different. Ah, well. They always wanted something, didn't they?

"Fassa del Parma and Alpha bint Hezra-Fong came out to the

Nyota system on the same transport," Sev went on. "So did Darnell Overton-Glaxely. They've all been helping each other get rich by the quickest and dirtiest means they could arrange. There were two others on that transport—Blaize Armontillado-Perez y Medoc, and Polyon de Gras-Waldheim. Fassa's already implicated Blaize— the one who was posted to Angalia. Don't you see? You're holding one thread into this tangle; I'm holding another one."

"You think that together we could unravel it?"

Sev gave her a flashing grin that was all but wasted on his present purpose. "Or take Alexander's solution, and cut the Gordian knot. This corruption ought to be cut off," he argued. "Don't tell me it's just a small part of what 'everybody does.' I don't care. This is the part I can see, that I can do something about. I *have* to see this through!" He stopped, looking momentarily embarrassed by his own intensity. "And I had hoped," he went on in a somewhat quieter voice, "I had hoped that you would want to join us. Lead us."

The flyer skated to a perfect landing just outside Nancia's opened entry bay.

"Come with me?" Sev suggested.

"I've got a scheduled transport to Kailas. Back to my desk job."

"You can change that," he said confidently, and grinned at her as he would at a contemporary. "Come on, Mic! You don't really want to go back to shuffling papers on Kailas, do you?"

Micaya rubbed the back of her neck. She felt generations older than this intense young man: tired, and dirty from the corruption of Summerlands, and not very interested in anything except a long bath and a massage. "Damn it," she said wearily. "You're not bad at persuasive speeches yourself, Bryley-Sorensen. I suppose you think I can get your brainship's orders changed so that we can go on to Angalia, instead of transporting del Parma straight back to Central?"

"It makes sense, doesn't it?"

"Sense," said Micaya, "has never been a compelling argument for any bureaucracy. All right. You win. I'll see what I can do towards persuading Central to reassign both Nancia and me. I must admit, I'd like to see the end of this case." Despite her weariness, she felt a smile beginning deep inside her. "Besides, your ship's brawn owes me a rematch at tri-chess."

"*Caleb?*"

"Forister," Micaya corrected him. "Nancia's been assigned a replacement brawn, remember? Forister Armontillado y Medoc. We were working together on this Summerlands business, until Central pulled him off the case to brawn Nancia back to Central." She stopped in the open landing bay. "Wait a minute. What did you say the other boy was called—the one who went to Angalia?"

Sev didn't have time to answer; a second flyer pounced down on the landing strip, and a messenger in the white uniform of Summerlands came running toward them.

"Tried to raise you in the air," he panted. "Your driver's comm unit must have been defective. Hopkirk's testified!"

"The devil he has! Already?"

"He seemed rather eager to do it. Dr. Thalmark thought it would do more harm to restrain him than to let him speak. His deposition's on datahedron—and there are a few honest men left on Bahati, Mr. Bryley; two of them are going to arrest Overton-Glaxely now. Since he'll likely be sent back to Central for trial, they'd like a representative of Central to accompany them now, just to make sure everything's in order."

"You mean, to make sure there's somebody else to blame if his family goes out for revenge," Sev muttered.

"I'll go," Micaya said. "No one will question my word."

"*I'll* go," Sev corrected her. "I've already annoyed so many High Families, one more makes no difference. You go catch up on your tri-chess."

"I always did like subordinates with plenty of initiative," Micaya said wryly. But she was tired, and worried about the possible connection between Blaize and Forister. Well, they'd have some privacy for a little while, with Sev Bryley off to collect his prisoner and Fassa del Parma locked in her cabin. She would have to ask Forister just how close the relationship might be—and whether he really wanted to brawn a ship headed for Angalia to arrest one of his relatives.

Forister was happily unpacking a special order from OG Glimware when Micaya Questar-Benn requested permission to board.

"We've got company coming," Nancia warned him. "And isn't there something unethical about buying something from a firm while you work to arrest its owner?"

"Can't think what," said Forister, whistling under his breath, "but if you find anything in CS regulations, be sure and let me know. Anyway, OG Glimware is the only company this side of Antares that does this particular specialty work." He peeled away the last opaque shrinkwrapping to display his purchase: a foot-high solido of a lovely young woman, every feature sharply delineated in the fragile prismatic carving. Her chin was lifted almost defiantly; she greeted the world with a smile whose reflection danced in her eyes; a short cap of curly hair, so finely carved it seemed the separate strands might lift in any passing breeze, crowned the uplifted head that gazed out at worlds beyond any human vision.

"Ah—very nice," Nancia said slowly, as Forister seemed to be waiting for some reaction. "Relative of yours?" *His records didn't say anything about a girlfriend, and isn't he rather old for this one?*

"A very distant connection, like most of the High Families scions. But she may become more than that—my friend, I hope. Perhaps my partner." Forister set the solido on the ledge above the pilot's control panel and turned to smile at Nancia's titanium column. "It's a genetic extrapolation, actually; shows what a certain young woman I know would have looked like if she'd grown up normally, without the one genetic anomaly that made her unable to survive outside a shell. Her name is . . . Nancia Perez y de Gras."

Nancia didn't know how to respond to that revelation. She couldn't respond. *Caleb never wondered what I would have looked like . . . never thought of me as a person.* Even thinking that was disloyal . . . but what *could* she say to Forister?

She was spared the necessity by the opening of the airlock. General Questar-Benn's somber face startled them both. "This part of the mission's completed," she announced. "Hezra-Fong's on her way here—under guard—and Bryley has gone off to arrest Overton-Glaxely. He's suggested that we should request a change in Nancia's orders, to investigate the other two passengers she brought to the Nyota system before returning to Central. Thought I should consult you first, Forister."

Forister's face went gray. "I will accept any orders issued by Courier Service as long as I brawn this ship."

"Know that," Micaya told him. "But I need to know more. Exactly what is the connection between you and this boy on Angalia? Distant relative? How much conflict of interest are we looking at?"

"He's my nephew." Forister dropped into the pilot's seat.

"Can I rely on you?"

Nancia watched and listened without intruding into the conversation. She had liked General Questar-Benn on their previous meeting, but now she felt the general was pushing Forister too hard. For the first time since he'd come on board, he was looking his age; the bristly graying hair lay flat, the sparkle of mischief that had made his face so familiar to Nancia had disappeared. Of course, she realized with a shock of recognition, that was why she felt as though she knew Forister already. It wasn't just his previous trip to Charon. It was the sparkle in his eyes as he hummed and hacked his way into Summerlands' medical records. That redheaded boy Blaize had just the same expression when he was planning mischief.

But Forister had the integrity so disastrously missing from Blaize's makeup. He hadn't tried to argue away Fassa's stories implicating his nephew, and now he would not evade the duty of confirming those stories.

"You don't have to come with us," Micaya told him. "We can get another brawn assigned to this ship. You're due a real R & R tour after that undercover work at Summerlands—"

Forister lifted his head and gazed at her with flat gray eyes. "You took all the risks at Summerlands," he said in a voice so drained of feeling that it made Nancia distinctly nervous. She increased the magnification of her local sensors until she could see the pulse throbbing in Forister's temple and hear the soft pounding of his heart. The man was under far too much strain.

"I WAS USELESS," his amplified voice crashed upon her, and Nancia hastily retreated to a normal sensor level, nerve endings twitching from the grating sounds. "Couldn't even find computer records to back you up. If anyone deserves a term of rest, Mic, it's you. And if anyone must prove my nephew's dishonor," he finished wearily, "let it be me. We won't be able to keep it in the family—I know that—but I need to know exactly what he's done and how we can make reparation."

"It's not good to be personally involved in your cases," General Micaya Questar-Benn murmured. "First rule of Academy."

Forister's spine straightened. "No. The first rule is . . . to serve. That's all I ask of you. A chance to serve, to make some reparation if any can be made. Besides," he added with just a trace of the old snap in his voice, "you won't find another brawn this side of Bellatrix subspace."

"Oh, come now," Micaya said. "You people with brawn training always overrate yourself. I'll wager there are half a dozen qualified brawns in Vega subspace alone."

Forister straightened another infinitesimal fraction of an inch. "Not qualified for the new hyperchip-enhanced brainships. Our Nancia's got the enhancements, haven't you, my dear?" As always, he turned his head towards the titanium column when addressing her, just as if he were inviting another softshell—soft*person*, Nancia corrected herself—to join in the conversation.

"My lower deck sensors and port side nav controls have the hyperchips," she told him, "and I'm using them in some of the processing banks. I'm on a waiting list for the rest."

"There you are, then," Forister told Micaya. "You need me. And I—need to do this."

"You need this assignment like I need another prosthesis," Micaya muttered, but she sat down again with the air of one who'd given up argument. "And just how do you happen to be qualified for the new chipships, anyway? You've been CenDip for—"

"More years than either of us chooses to specify," Forister interrupted her. "And the term is brainships, Mic, not 'chipships.' Let's not offend our lady."

"Its all right," Nancia cut in. "I'm not offended. Really."

"But I am," said Forister. He took a deep breath and straightened. Nancia could almost see him pushing the pain he felt deep inside, replacing his diplomat's mask. When he turned his head to speak directly to her, he looked almost untroubled— if you didn't focus your sensors on the tiny lines of strain and worry around his eyes. "You are *my* lady now, Nancia, at least for the duration of this mission. And no one speaks casually of my brainship."

Micaya blew out her pursed lips with an exasperated sigh. "You never answered my question. How come you're qualified for the newest models of brainships, when you've been out of the brawn service for . . . years?"

"I read a lot," Forister said with an airy wave of one hand. "Ancient guerrilla wars, new compunav systems, it's all grist to my mill. I'm a twentieth century man at heart," he told Micaya, referring to the Age of the First Information Explosion. "A man of many interests and unguessed-at talents. And I like to keep current in my field—*all* my fields."

"A man of unguessed-at bullshit, anyway," Micaya retorted. "Okay. You're in. At least I'll have someone to beat at tri-chess on the way over to Angalia."

Forister snorted. "You mean someone to beat you. Your ego has increased out of all proportion to your skill, General. Set 'em up!"

Nancia watched with curiosity as General Questar-Benn drew a palm-sized card from her pocket. Forister grinned. "Brought your portable game board, I see."

The general tapped the slight indentations on the surface of the card and it projected a hologram of a partitioned cube, shimmering with rainbow light at the edges. Another series of taps produced the translucent images of playing pieces aligned at two opposing edges of the cube. Nancia twiddled with her sensor magnification and focus until she could make out the details. Yes, those were the standard tri-chess pieces: she recognized the age-old triple ordering. Pawns in the first and lowest rank; above them, the King and Queen with their Bishops and Knights and Castles. Above them the highest rank was poised to swoop down over the gamecube, the Brainship and Brawn with their supporting pieces, the Scouts and Hovercraft and Satellites. The images were blurred and kept flickering in and out, giving Nancia a sensation of tight bands pulled across her sensor connections if she tried to look at them for any length of time.

"Pawn to Brain's Scout 4,2," Forister grunted a standardized opening move.

Nothing happened.

"My portable set isn't equipped with voice recognition," Micaya apologized. "You'll have to tap in the code."

As she indicated the row of fingertip-sized indentations, Nancia hummed softly—her substitute for the rasps and hawks of "throat-clearing" with which softshells began an unscheduled interruption. Both players looked up, and after a startled moment Forister inclined his head to Nancia's titanium column.

"Yes, Nancia?"

"If you'll give me a moment to study the configuration," Nancia suggested, "I believe I can replicate your play-holo with a somewhat clearer display. And I, of course, can supply the voice recognition processing."

Even as she spoke, she assigned a virtual memory space and a graphics co-processor to the problem. Before the sound of her voice had died away, a new and much clearer holographic projection shimmered beside the original one. Forister exclaimed in delight at the perfect detailing of the miniaturized pieces; Micaya put out her hand as if to touch a perfectly shaped little Satellite with its three living and storage globes, complete with tiny access doors and linking spacetubes.

"Beautiful," Forister sighed in delight. "But won't this take too much processing capability, Nancia?"

"Not when we're just sitting dirtside," Nancia told him. "I don't even use that processor when we're doing regular navigation. Might have to shut down briefly when we're in Singularity, that *does* take some concentration, but—"

Forister closed his eyes briefly. "That's perfectly all right, Nancia. To tell you the truth, it never occurred to me to play tri-chess in Singularity anyway."

"Me either," said Micaya, looking slightly green at the very thought. "You don't want to think about spatial relationships at a moment like that."

"*I* do," said Nancia cheerfully.

Less than two Central Standard Hours later, Sev interrupted the first tri-chess game to deliver a subdued Darnell Glaxely-Overton for transport to Central. "He broke when I showed him the hedron of Hopkirk's evidence," he told the others after Darnell had been confined in a cabin. "Funny—almost as if he'd expected somebody to come after him one of these days. Spent most of the flyer trip back telling all he knows about the other three. Here's the recording."

"Four," Nancia corrected Sev as he slid a datacard into her reader.

"Three," Sev said again. "Fassa. Alpha. And . . . Blaize." He carefully avoided looking at Forister as he pronounced the last name.

"Neither of them has said anything implicating Polyon de Gras-Waldheim?" Nancia couldn't believe this.

Sev shrugged. "Who knows? Maybe there isn't anything to say. You never know, there could be one good apple in this barrel of rotten ones."

Not Polyon. But Nancia refrained from voicing her protest. After the conversations she'd heard on her maiden voyage, she was convinced that Polyon de Gras-Waldheim was completely amoral. But would it be ethical to reveal those conversations? Caleb had been so adamantly against anything that even suggested spying, she'd never even thought of telling him.

But that had been five years ago. She had changed; she now saw shades of gray instead of the neat black and white of CS rules. Even Caleb might have changed; after all, he'd consented to this undercover mission.

Under protest.

He might feel doubly betrayed if she chose to violate his ethical code when he wasn't even here to censure her for it.

Perhaps she could put off the decision for a little longer. "It might be worth going by Shemali anyway," Nancia suggested. "You never know. We might find some evidence linking de Gras-Waldheim with the rest of the crew." *We'd have that evidence already, if they weren't all terrified to say a word against him.*

"Possibly," Sev agreed. "Meet me there, after Angalia?"

"I thought you were coming with us!" Micaya Questar-Benn half rose from her seat, putting one hand right through Nancia's tri-chess hologram.

"I was," Sev agreed. "I am. I'll meet you on Shemali. Something's come up."

He was gone before any of them could question him, taking the stairs three at a time and whistling as he went. Nancia briefly considered slamming her lower doors on him and holding him until he explained exactly what he was up to.

She wouldn't do that, of course. It would be an unethical and unconscionable abuse of her abilities, the sort of bullying she'd been warned against in the ethics classes that were part of every shellperson's training.

But it was a sore temptation.

"Something," Micaya said thoughtfully, "has made that young man extremely happy. I wonder what it was. Nancia, is there anything earth-shaking in that datacard of Darnell Overton-Glaxely's testimony?"

Nancia had started scanning just before Micaya spoke. "There isn't even anything interesting," she said, "unless a sordid record of petty bribes and corruption and bullying fascinates you."

"Ah. Overton-Glaxely did strike me as the cheap sort."

"You might want to examine his statement yourself," Nancia suggested. "You may see something I've overlooked."

Micaya nodded. "I'll do that. But I doubt I'll find anything. Bryley said there wasn't any evidence against de Gras-Waldheim, so whatever is taking him to Shemali, it can't be our business. Damn that boy! Oh, well, I suppose we'll find out when we reach Shemali."

"But first," Forister said, "we have a task to complete at Angalia." His face was gray and still again; the momentary animation brought on by the tri-chess game had vanished. *He looks like a man with a deadly disease. Is family honor so important to him?* Nancia wondered how she'd feel if her sister Jinevra were found to have corrupted her branch of PTA and embezzled the department's funds.

Impossible even to imagine such a thing. Well, then, what if Flix—she couldn't think what Flix might do, either, but what if he had got in with the wrong crowd—like Blaize—and had done something that would force her to hunt him down, arrest him, send him to Central for years of prison without his beloved music?

The pain of that thought shook Nancia so deeply that for a moment the even hum of the air stabilizers was broken and the co-processor handling the tri-chess hologram faltered. The game-cube image shivered, broke apart in rainbow fractures, then solidified again as Nancia gained control of herself and her systems.

If even imagining Flix in trouble hurt her so deeply, how could Forister face the reality of Blaize's crime? He couldn't, she decided, and it was up to her and Micaya to distract him whenever possible.

"General Questar-Benn, it's your move," she said.

"What? Oh—Scout to Queen's Bishop 3,3," Micaya said. The move took one of Forister's Satellites and left a probability path to his Brainship. Nancia calculated the possible moves without conscious effort.

"You have only two moves that will not put your Brainship in check within the next five-move sequence," she warned Forister.

"Two?" Forister's eyebrows shot up and he bent over the gamecube. "I saw only one."

"Foul!" Micaya complained. "I challenged the brawn, not the brain."

"We work as a team," Nancia told her.

She certainly hoped that was true. For Forister's sake—for both their sakes. He didn't need to get through this grief alone; she was there to steady him.

"Ah. I see what you mean." Forister bent over the board and surprised Nancia with a third move, one so apparently disastrous that she had not even considered it in her initial calculations.

With a subdued whoop of glee, Micaya Questar-Benn took Forister's second Satellite—and watched dumbfounded as he proceeded to shift an unconsidered knight from the second rank and place her Brainship in check.

"Thank you for the hint, Nancia," Forister said. "Until you forced me to consider the alternative move, I hadn't even thought of using the Jigo Kanaka advance in this situation."

"I . . . ah . . . you're quite welcome," Nancia managed to tell him between the three subsequent moves that brought the game to its slashing conclusion, with Micaya's forces immobilized, her Brawn taken and her Brainship checkmated.

Perhaps Forister didn't need quite so much help as she'd anticipated.

CHAPTER THIRTEEN

Nancia's landing on Angalia was one of the worst she'd ever executed. The planet took her completely by surprise.

Initial navigation maneuvers went normally. It wasn't until she was in visual range of the landing field that she became confused. The green terraced cliffs behind the mesa and the grassy basin surrounding it looked nothing at all like her memories of the landing five years ago. Could she possibly have miscalculated, come down in some hitherto unknown section of the planet?

Nancia called up her files from that first landing and superimposed the stored images on the green paradise below her. Yes, this had to be the Angalia landing field. The topographical features were a perfect match with her internal map. And there, at the edge of the mesa, was the plastifilm prefab hut with its sagging awning of woven grass, looking if anything slightly more derelict and tottering than it had appeared five years ago.

Intent on her image comparison, Nancia drained computing power from the navigation processor, forgot to monitor the approach, and came embarrassingly close to making a new crater on Angalia's landing field. She corrected the descent, hopped into mid-air, and came down more slowly the second time. Her auditory sensors picked up a variety of crashes, groans, and complaints from the cabins where Micaya and the three prisoners were housed.

"Apologies for the rough landing," she began, but Forister cut off her speakers for a moment and overrode her. "Local turbulence," he said. "Nancia recovered superbly, but even a brainship can't compensate for all the freak conditions on Angalia."

He swept his open hand over the palmpad with a caressing gesture, restoring speaker control to Nancia, and smiled at her benignly.

"I didn't need you to cover for me," Nancia transmitted a vibrant whisper through the main cabin speakers.

"Didn't you? I thought we were a team. If you can help me play tri-chess, I certainly have the right to preserve you from apologizing to those overindulged brats."

"I—well, thank you," Nancia conceded.

"Think nothing of it. By the way, what *did* happen just now?"

"I was distracted. This place doesn't look the way it did last time I landed." Nancia switched all her screens to external mode. Forister gazed appreciatively at the triple-screen display of a grassy paradise ringed by flowering terraces.

"What on earth is *that*?" Fassa cried from her cabin. Darnell and Alpha joined her exclamations of surprise.

Nancia was gratified by this response. The screens in the passenger cabins weren't as dramatic as her central cabin's display walls, but at least they showed enough of Angalia to confirm that she wasn't losing her mind—or if she was, she wasn't alone. None of the prisoners had been expecting Angalia to look like the Garden of Eden.

"Do I take it," she asked mildly, "that the planet has changed since your last visit?"

"It certainly has," Fassa said. "Are you sure it's the same place? Only last year—oh, I see."

A prolonged silence followed. For once in her life Nancia longed for a softperson's physical extrusions. It would be enormously satisfying to take Fassa by the shoulders and shake her out of the trance in which she had fallen. *Why* couldn't softpersons keep transmitting datastreams while they were processing?

She had to content herself with blinking Fassa's cabin lights and assaulting her with raucous bursts of music from Flix's latest sonohedron.

"Do I take it," she inquired when satisfied that she had the girl's attention, "that you recognize some salient features?"

"Yes ... I think so, anyway." Of course, Fassa would have no control over the visual detail, not to mention the accuracy, of whatever images she'd stored from her previous visit. She would be dependent on whatever her non-enhanced biological memory could provide. Recognizing this, Nancia didn't count on learning much.

"Those gardens on the side of the mountain," Fassa said. "He had the terraces in place a year ago, but nothing was planted. I thought it was something to do with the mine."

Nancia switched the signals going to Fassa's display screen to show the mine entrance. Blue-uniformed figures moved in and out, pushing wagons on railings that curved around the side of the mountain. A magnified display showed that the figures were shambling Angalia natives, neatly dressed in blue shorts and shirts and working together with the precision of a choreographed dance. One native heaved a sack from the mine entrance and tossed it over his head; another casually moved into place just in time to catch it; by the time he'd turned, a third native had backed his wagon down the rail system and into place to receive the load.

"Amazing," Nancia commented. "I thought the Angalians couldn't be trained."

"Blaize," Forister said hollowly, "has certainly been a busy little boy."

"It doesn't look all that bad so far," Nancia pointed out. "Fassa, do you—or the others—recognize anything else?"

She let the display screens sweep over a panoramic view of the mesa and the surrounding countryside. Suddenly Fassa gave a cry of recognition. "Oh, God, he's left the volcano!"

Nancia halted the display and studied it. An evil-looking bubble of brown and green mud heaved and burst and formed again, roiling continuously in the midst of the tall grass covering the rest of the basin.

"I don't suppose planting flowers would do much to disguise it," she agreed.

"You don't understand." Fassa sounded close to tears. "That's how he controls them—how he makes them do things for them. If the Loosies don't please him, he *cooks* them alive in that boiling mud! I saw it done last time—I'll never forget those screams."

"Alpha? Darnell?" Nancia queried the other two.

"That's right," Darnell told her. "Revolting."

Alpha nodded silently, the movement barely visible to Nancia's visual sensors.

She could think of no more encouraging words for Forister.

Micaya persuaded Forister to let her confront Blaize initially. "I'll wear a contact button," she promised him. "You and Nancia can see and hear everything that goes on."

"It's my duty—" Forister began.

"Mine too," Micaya interrupted him. "The young man is more likely to confess if he doesn't think he can bring family influence to bear."

"He can't," Forister said grimly. "I'm not here to intercede for him."

"Yes, but he doesn't know that," Micaya pointed out.

Nancia kept all her external sensors trained on Micaya as the general picked her way along a path of rounded volcanic stones to the door of the permalloy hut. On both sides of the path, feathery grasses and blazing tropical flowers grew in exuberant, uncontrolled patterning, throwing up their seed-heads and blooms above Micaya's crisp silver-sprinkled hair. Nancia recognized Old Earth species mixed with Denebian starflowers and the singing grasses of Fomalhaut II, a joyous blaze of pink and orange and purple flowers.

Micaya entered the hut and Nancia's field of vision contracted to the half-circle covered by the contact button. In the shadowy hut, stacked high with papers and bits of machinery, Blaize's red head glowed like a burning ember before the computer screen that held his attention.

"Blaize Armontillado-Perez y Medoc," Micaya said formally.

"Um. PTA shipment? I'll sign for it in a minute. Just got to finish this one thing. . . ."

The contact button's resolution wasn't enough for Nancia to read the words on the computer screen, but she recognized the seven-tone response code that chimed out when Blaize slapped his open hand on the palmpad. An interplanetary transmission— no, intersubspace; he had just sent something to . . . Nancia rummaged through her files and identified the code. To *Central Diplomatic* headquarters? What could they have to do with Angalia, a planet where no intelligent sentients existed? Had

Blaize's net of corruption drawn in some of her father's and Forister's own colleagues?

"There!" As the last notes of the code chimed out, Blaize swung round, a seraphic smile on his freckled face. "And what—"

His expression changed rapidly and almost comically at the sight of Micaya Questar-Benn in full uniform. "You," he said slowly, "are not PTA."

"Quite correct," said Micaya. "Your activities have attracted some attention in other quarters."

Blaize's jaw thrust out and his freckles seemed to take on a glowing life of their own. "Well, it's too late. You can't stop me now!"

"Can't I?" Micaya's tone was deceptively mild.

"I've sent a full report to CenDip. I don't care who your friends in PTA may be, they'll have to leave Angalia alone now."

"My dear boy," said Micaya, "haven't you got it backwards? *You're* the one employed by Planetary Technical Aid. Or rather, you were."

Nancia had been so caught up in the dialogue, she never noticed when Forister slipped out of her central cabin and made his way down the stairs. She was as startled as Blaize when Forister appeared in the doorway of the hut, just on the periphery of her view from the contact button.

"Uncle Forister!" Blaize exclaimed. "What's going on here? Can you help—"

"Don't call *me* uncle," Forister said between his teeth. "I'm here with General Questar-Benn to stop you, boy, not to help you!"

Blaize went green between the spattering of freckles. He closed his eyes for a moment and looked as if he wanted to be sick. "Not you too?"

"You didn't think family feeling would extend so far as helping you exploit and torture these innocents?"

"Torture? Exploit?" Blaize gasped. "I—oh, no. Uncle Forister, have you by any chance been talking to a girl named Fassa del Parma y Polo? Or Alpha bint Hezra-Fong? Or Darnell—"

"All three of them," Forister confirmed, "and—what the devil is so funny about that?"

For Blaize had all but doubled up, snorting with repressed laughter. "My sins come back to haunt me," he gasped between snorts.

"I don't see what's so funny about it." Forister's own face had gone white and there was a pinched look about the corners of his mouth.

"You wouldn't. Not yet. But when I—*Oh*, Lord! This is one complication I never—" Blaize sputtered into hysterical laughter that ended only when Forister slammed a fist into his belly. Blaize was still crowing and wheezing for breath when a second blow to the jaw knocked his head back and flung him in an undignified collapse against the rickety table where his computing equipment had been stacked. Blaize's legs folded under him and he slid gently to the floor. Behind him, the table rocked and wobbled dangerously. The palmpad skated to one corner of the table top and hung on a splinter. A shower of flimsy blue hardcopies fluttered down over Blaize in a gentle, rustling rain of reports and accounting figures and PTA instructions.

Forister snatched one sheet as it drifted down and studied the column of figures for a moment, brows raised. When his eyes reached the bottom of the page, he looked tired and gray and showed every year of his age.

"Proof positive," he commented as he passed the paper to Micaya, "if any was needed."

Micaya held the paper where Nancia could focus on it through the contact button. The figures wobbled and danced in Micaya's hand; grimly Nancia compensated for movement and enlarged the blurred letters and numbers until she too could read the flimsy.

It was a statement of Blaize's Net account balance for the previous month. The pattern of deposits and withdrawals of large sums made no immediate sense to Nancia, but one thing was clear: any single figure was considerably larger than Blaize's PTA salary, and the total at the bottom was damning—more than thirty times as much credit as he could have accumulated if he'd saved every penny of his legitimate pay.

"Uncle Forister," said Blaize from the floor, tenderly massaging his aching jaw, "you have got it all wrong. Trust me."

"After the evidence before my eyes," Forister spat out, "what could you possibly say that would incline me to trust you?"

Blaize grinned up at him. His lip was bleeding and one front tooth wobbled alarmingly. "You'd be surprised."

"If you were thinking of a small bribe out of your ill-gotten gains," Micaya told him, "you can think again." She lowered her head to speak directly into the contact button and Nancia hastily reduced the amplification. Softshells never could quite understand that they didn't need to shout at a conduct button; the speaker might be tinny, but the input lines were as powerful as any of a brainship's on-board sensors. "Nancia, please enter the Net with my personal ID code. That's Q-B76, JPJ, 450, MIC. Under that code you will be authorized to freeze all credit accounts under the personal code of, let me see...." She squinted at the top of the flimsy, peering to make out a code sequence that Nancia could read perfectly well with the vision correctors damping down movement and enhancing blurred letters. "Oh, never mind, I guess you can read it," Micaya recalled a moment later.

"Correct," Nancia sent a vocal signal over the contact link.

"Don't do that!" Blaize scrambled to his feet, swaying slightly. "You don't understand—"

Forister moved to one side more rapidly than Nancia had ever seen him step, a blur of motion that placed him between Blaize and Micaya with her copy of the account balance. "I understand that you've been exploiting nonintelligent sentients to enrich yourself," he said. "You can make your explanation to the authorities. Nancia, I want you to file a formal record of the charges now, just in case anything goes wrong here,"

"Done," Nancia replied.

Blaize shook his head and winced at the motion. "Ow. No. Uncle Forister, you really have got the wrong end of the story. And there's no way you can have me up on charges of—what did you say?— exploiting nonintelligent sentients. On the contrary. The Loosies are entitled to Intelligent Sentient Status and I can prove it—and nobody can stop me now; I've just sent the final documentation to CenDip. Even if you silence me, there'll be an independent CenDip investigation now."

"Silence you, *silence* you?" Forister looked at Micaya. His gray eyebrows shot up. "No question of that. We don't deal in coverups. You'll have the opportunity to say anything you like at your trial. And so will I, God help me," he murmured, so low that only Nancia's contact button picked up the words. "So will I."

"If you people would just *listen*," said Blaize, exasperated, "there wouldn't *be* any need for a trial. Didn't you hear what I said about the Loosies being intelligent?"

Micaya shook her head. "You've been here too long if you've

started to cherish that illusion. Face the facts. On the way here I downloaded the survey reports off the Net. The native species don't exhibit any of the key signs of intelligence—no language, no clothing, no agriculture, no political organization."

"They've always had language," Blaize insisted. "They've got clothing and agriculture now. As for a political organization, just think about PTA for a minute and then ask yourself if that's any proof of intelligence."

Micaya laughed in spite of herself. "You have a point. But we didn't come here to argue ISS certification standards—"

"Maybe not," said Blaize, "but since you *are* here, and—" He looked suspicious for a moment "You're not working with Harmon, are you?"

"Who?"

Micaya must have looked surprised enough to convince Blaize.

"My predecessor here—my supervisor now. Crooked enough to hide behind a spiral staircase," Blaize explained briefly. "He's the reason—well, one of the reasons—I had to do things in this way. Although even an honest PTA supervisor probably wouldn't have approved. I have bent a few regulations," he admitted. "But just do me the favor of taking a brief tour of the settlement. I think you'll understand a lot better after I show you a few things."

Micaya looked at Forister and shrugged. "I don't see any harm in it."

"I suppose if we don't go along, you'll apply for a mistrial on the grounds that you weren't allowed to show evidence in your defense?" Forister inquired.

Blaize's face turned almost as red as his hair. "Look. You're in contact with your brainship via that button. If it's inactivated, or if she sees anything she doesn't like, the full recording can go over the Net to Central at once. What will it cost you to listen to me for once in your life, Uncle Forister? God knows nobody else in our family ever bothered," he added, "but I used to think you were different."

Forister sighed. "I'm listening. I'm listening."

"Good! Just come this way, please." Blaize pushed between Forister and Micaya and flung the door of the hut open. Sunlight and gaudy flowers and a thousand shades of green danced before them, all the brighter for the contrast with the shabby interior of the hut. Blaize started down the path, talking a mile a minute over his shoulder as the other two followed him. Nancia activated the failsafe double recording system that would transmit every word and image directly to Vega Base as well as to her own storage centers.

"The Loosies never developed spoken language because they're telepaths," Blaize explained. "I know, I know, that's hard to prove directly, but just wait till you watch them work together! When the CenDip team gets here, they should bring some top Psych staff. Open-minded ones, who'll arrange tests without assuming from the start that I'm lying. Mind you, it took me a while to figure out myself," he babbled cheerfully, turning from the main path to a secondary one that wound through head-high reeds, "especially at the beginning, when they all looked alike to me. I was so damn bored, and those croaking noises they make got on my nerves, so I started trying to teach a couple of them ASL."

"What?" Micaya interrupted.

"It's an antique hand-speech, used for the incurably deaf back before we learned how to direct-install auditory synapses on metachip and hook them into the appropriate brain centers," Forister told her. "Blaize always did have strange hobbies. But teaching the Loosies a few signals in sign language doesn't prove they're intelligent, boy. A couple of twentieth-century researchers did that much with chimpanzees."

"Yeah, well, that's all I hoped to achieve in the beginning," Blaize said. "Believe me, after a couple of months on Angalia, a signing chimp would have seemed like real good company! But they picked it up like—like a brainship picks up Singularity math. That was the first surprise. I was teaching three of them who sort of hung around—Humdrum and Bobolin and Gargle." He flushed briefly. "Yeah, I know they're damn silly names, but I didn't know they were *people* then. I was just copying some of the strangled noises they made when I would talk to them and they'd try to talk back, before I realized they'd never developed the vocal equipment for true speech—that was when I started on the sign language—sorry, I'm getting mixed up. Where was I?"

"Teaching Humdrum to sign 'Where ration bar?'" Forister told him.

Blaize laughed. "Not bloody likely. His first sentence was more like, 'Why did Paunch Man throw ration bars in mud and treat us like animals, and why do you make stacks and hand them to us one at a time with proper respect?'"

He stopped and turned to face them, his freckled face dead serious for once. "Can you imagine how it felt to hear a question like that coming from somebody I'd been thinking of as—oh, like a trained spider to while away the hours of my prison sentence? I knew then that the Loosies weren't animals. Figuring out what to do about it," he said, resuming his progress through the reeds, "took a little longer."

"I deduced the telepathy when I noticed that a week after Humdrum caught on to ASL, *every* Loosie who showed up for rations was signing to me. Fluently. He couldn't have taught them the rudiments that fast; they had to have been picking the signs and the language structure out of his mind as the lessons progressed. In fact, they told me as much when I asked about it. Which wasn't all that easy. ASL doesn't *have* a sign for 'telepathy,' and since they don't know English, I couldn't spell it out. But eventually we got our signals straight."

"If they were as intelligent as you claim, and had a system of communication, they should have advanced beyond their primitive level without intervention," Micaya objected.

"Easy for *you* to say," Blaize told her. "I wonder how well you or any of us would do if we had evolved on a planet where the only surface fit for farming is rearranged by violent floods once a week, where the caves we used for shelter crumbled and were shattered by periodic quakes? They had a hunter-gatherer culture until a few generations ago—a small population, not more than the planet could support, ranging through the semi-stable marshlands on the far side of this continent."

"Then what?"

"Then," Blaize said, "they were discovered. The first survey thought they might be intelligent and requested Planetary Technical Aid support. By the time the second survey team came along, this PTA station had been handing out unlimited supplies of ration bricks for three generations, and the culture was effectively destroyed. Instead of small bands of hunter-gatherers, you had one large colony with no food-gathering skill. There were far too many for the existing marshlands to support, with nothing to do and no hope of survival except to collect the ration bricks. The second survey, not unnaturally, decided they weren't intelligent. After all, nobody on the survey team was stuck here long enough and lonely enough to try signing to them. But they recommended on humanitarian grounds, or kindness to animals, or whatever, that we not discontinue PTA shipments and starve them to death."

"But if they're intelligent—" Forister objected again.

"They are. And they can build for themselves. They just needed a—a place to start." Blaize pushed the last of the feathery reeds aside with both arms and stepped to one side, inviting Forister and Micaya to admire the view of the mine. "This was the first step."

From this vantage point, Nancia observed, they could see far more of the mine's operations than had been visible from the landing field. Teams of blue-uniformed workers were scattered across the hillside and grouped under the roofs of the unwalled processing sheds—twenty, forty, more than fifty of them, divided into groups of four or five individuals who worked at their chosen tasks with perfect unanimity and wordless efficiency.

"Could you train chimps to do *that*?" Blaize demanded.

Forister shook his head slowly. "And I suppose the mine is the source of your prodigious wealth?"

"It's certainly the source of the credits in that Net account," Blaize agreed.

"Exploiting intelligent sentients isn't any better than exploiting dumb animals."

Blaize ground his teeth; Nancia could pick up the clicks and grinding sounds through the contact button. "I. Am. Not. Exploiting. Anybody," he said. "Look, Uncle Forister. When I got here, the Loosies didn't have ISS. They couldn't be owners of record for the mine, they couldn't have Net accounts, they couldn't palmprint official documents. Of course my code is on everything! Who else could front for them?"

"And your code is also," Micaya pointed out, "associated with the illegal resale of PTA ration shipments that were supposed to be distributed to the natives."

Blaize nodded wearily. "Needed money to get the mine started again. I tried to get a loan, but the banks wanted to know what I was going to do with it. When I told them I was going to revive the Angalia mines they told me I couldn't do that because there was no source of labor on the planet, because the CenDip report said Angalia had no intelligent sentients. Without credits, I couldn't start the mine. And without the credits for the mine, I couldn't— well, we'll get to that in a while. Look, I falsified a few PTA reports. Said the population had tripled. Ration bars aren't exactly a hot item in international trade," he said dryly. "I had to have a *large* surplus to bargain with. Fortunately, I had an outlet right at hand. That bastard Harmon was keeping the Loosies at semi-starvation level so he could trade some of their ration bars for liquor. I had to have a little talk with the black market trader to convince him I wanted hard credits instead of hard liquor, but eventually he . . . um . . . came around to my way of thinking."

"Don't tell me how you persuaded him," Forister said quickly. "I don't want to know."

Blaize grinned. "Okay. Anyway, you've seen the mine; now I want to take you on a tour of Project Two. We'll have to go up the mountain for that, I'm afraid; I want you to get the long view."

The path up beside the mine was steep, but switchbacks and steps made it easier than it looked from a distance. As they passed the mine door, several Loosies looked up from their work to smile at Blaize. Their loose-skinned, grayish hands moved rapidly back and forth in flickering gestures that Nancia captured as imageflashes for later interpretation. For now, she was willing to accept Blaize's translation.

"They're asking who my mentally handicapped friends are, and whether you'd like a ride down to the processing sheds," he explained.

As he spoke, the team working at the mine's mouth filled a wagon with chunks of ore and poised it at the head of the rails swooping down into the valley. The three workers perched on top of the ore, hands gripping the sides of the wagon, and a member of the next team gave them a shove that started them off on a roller-coaster glide down the hill, swerving around rocks and dipping into hollows.

"Lost a few that way, at the start," Blaize commented, "before I remodeled the rail track so that the dips wouldn't throw anybody off."

The vegetation thinned out above the mine, giving them a view of the terraced gardens that replaced cliffs and rocks wherever a shovelful of soil could find a place. Micaya sniffed appreciatively and commented on the pungent aroma of the herbs growing in the mini-gardens.

At the top of the mountain they enjoyed a panoramic view of what had been the Great Angalia Mud Basin, now a grassland in which fields of grain shared space with brightly colored blossoms.

"This'll be our first year's crop," Blaize said. "I'd just finished the necessary preparations for planting last year, when those nitwits I came out with were here for the meeting. None of *them* noticed anything different, of course. But if your brainship can call up files of the first survey—"

"She can do better than that," Forister told him. "She's been here herself. Nancia, do you observe any changes here? Apart from the growing things, that is?"

Blaize paled between his freckles. "*Nancia?*"

"You have some problem with my brainship?" Forister inquired mildly.

"We . . . didn't part on the best of terms," Blaize confessed in a strangled voice.

Nancia was feeling rather more kindly towards Blaize now, but she wasn't quite ready to admit that to him. "Horizon shows changes between all major peaks," she reported in the neutral, tinny voice forced on her by the contact button's limitations. "Magnification of one area of variation shows new construction of rammed earth and boulders blocking a system of gullies that appears now to be under 17.35 meters of water. . . ."

"Lake Humdrum," Blaize said. "My first terraforming effort. Trouble was, I had to block *all* the outlets, and build up reservoir walls, before I could guarantee the floods wouldn't crash through the mud basin. Then we needed irrigation ditches down into the basin. And silt collection systems, so that the soil the floods used to carry down here would still reach the basin and renew its topsoil. You want to come back down now? I want to show you the grain samples and the test results. It's not quite ripe yet, of course," he chattered as he led the way down the path, "but it's going to be a prime crop. Amaranth-19-hyper-J Rev 2, if that means anything to you. High in protein, loaded with natural nutrients, super yield from that rich topsoil. We should be able to feed ourselves and have a surplus to sell. That's why I waited until now to claim Intelligent Sentient Status for the Loosies; I wanted to be sure we would be self-sufficient in case PTA decided to curtail the ration shipments. And I didn't dare start planting until the whole flood control system had been put in place and tested. The Loosies would never have trusted me again if they'd put in a crop and seen it washed away. We needed a lot of heavy-duty terraforming equipment; sucked up all the mine's profits for the first three years."

They reached the bottom of the mountain and Blaize set off at a brisk walk towards the hut. Forister took his arm and gently urged him away from the hut, towards the edge of the mesa. "I'd like to get a closer look at this grain crop of yours before we go inside," he suggested.

But they didn't wind up standing in the best place to assess the grain; they came to the edge of the mesa just above the ugly volcanic mud hole that disfigured the basin, with its lazy bubbles roiling and tumbling just before the sticky surface of the mud.

Forister eyed Blaize warily. "You've been forcing the natives to work in a corycium mine owned by you."

"Persuading," Blaize corrected.

"They believed your promises to use the profits for their own good?"

Blaize flushed. "I don't think they fully understood what I had in mind at the beginning. Most of them, anyway. Humdrum and Gargle got the idea, but they never believed it would work."

"Then . . . ?" Forister left the question dangling.

"I think," Blaize said almost inaudibly, "I think they did it because they like me a little."

"Other reasons have been suggested," said Forister.

Blaize looked blank for a moment, then noticed the direction of Forister's gaze. He was staring down at the volcanic mud bubble.

"Oh. Fassa del Parma again?"

"And Dr. Hezra-Fong," said Micaya, "and Darnell Overton-Glaxely. You've still to clear up their allegations of torture."

"I—I see." With a sudden leap, Blaize jumped away from Forister and Micaya to perch on a boulder sticking halfway out from the side of the mesa. "You want proof that I didn't torture Humdrum?"

"It won't do any good to produce some other native and claim he was the one you tortured publicly, and that he recovered," Micaya told him, "just in case you were thinking of that. You've no way to prove you didn't murder and bury the one witnesses saw you torturing."

"Well, it was Humdrum, all right, and he'll tell you so, but I see your point," Blaize agreed. He fumbled at the front of his tunic; the synthofilm sides parted and he folded the garment neatly. "My best tunic," he explained politely, "you'll understand I don't want to ruin it."

"What are you doing? Come back, boy!" Forister called, just too late; Blaize had skidded down a couple of feet and was clinging to a rock ledge barely out of reach.

"Just a minute," Blaize panted in between some strange contortions. His synthofilm trousers collapsed in a shining heap around his ankles; he kicked them upwards and they snagged on a thorn bush.

"Blaize, *don't do this.*" Micaya spoke in tones of quiet authority that seemed for a moment to weaken Blaize's will. He paused on the ledge, his milk-white skin almost glowing against the dull hues of the volcanic pool beneath him.

"I have to," he said calmly. "It's the only way."

Before either of them could argue further, he leapt from the ledge in a spiraling, awkward dive that ended with a resounding smack in the center of the heaving mud. White arms and legs splayed out, red head still, for a moment he seemed to have been stunned or killed outright by the fall. Then he kicked and wriggled vigorously, sinking deeper into the bubbling glop with each movement.

"Hold still," Forister called, "we'll get a rope to you—we'll do something—"

Blaize turned over onto his back. A thick layer of mud coated his body, barely preserving the decencies. He thrashed around in what Nancia belatedly recognized as an attempt at the backstroke.

"Come on in, Uncle Forister," he called up. "The mud's fine today!"

"Are you all right?" Micaya shouted while Forister, for once, struggled to find his voice.

"Couldn't be better. Mud's just at sauna heat today." Blaize stretched and wriggled luxuriously and grinned up at them through mud-spattered cheeks. "I don't usually dive from that high up—knocked the breath out of me for a minute—but I thought you needed the demonstration. Care to join me?"

Micaya looked quizzically at Forister. The brawn kicked off his shoes and rolled his trouser legs up. "Oh, I'm going down, all right," he said between clenched teeth. "It's the quickest way to get my hands on that boy. And then I'm going to—to—" Words failed him.

"Torture him in a boiling mud hole?" Micaya suggested.

CHAPTER FOURTEEN

Nancia deliberately slowed her speed for the short hop from Angalia to Shemali. She needed time to check her records, time to access the Net and look for evidence of Polyon's scam. Somewhere in all the past five years' records of metachip and hyperchip transactions there must be some clue to his criminal activities—for she could not believe he had totally given up on the plans he'd announced during her maiden voyage. Not Polyon de Gras-Waldheim.

Even Net access was not always instantaneous, particularly when one was gathering and collating all the public records on sale, transfer or use of hyperchips in the known galaxy. Nancia idled and hoped that her passengers would not notice how long the voyage was taking.

Fortunately, they all seemed wrapped up in their own concerns. Fassa, Alpha and Darnell were all being held in separate cabins, dealing with the long spells of solitary imprisonment in their own ways. Alpha requested medical and surgical journals from Net libraries and studied the technical material Nancia downloaded for her with intense concentration, just as if she thought she would be permitted to practice her chosen profession again. *Not if I have anything to say about it,* Nancia vowed silently. But the truth was, she didn't have much to say. She could record her testimony and the images she'd received via contact buttons, and those depositions would go into evidence at Alpha's trial. But after that, all would be up to those softpersons who controlled the high courts on Central. Most of them were High Families; half of them had some connection, kinship or financial, with the Hezra-Fong clan. Alpha might very well be free—not immediately, but in five years or ten or twenty, a mere blip in the life of a High Families girl with fewer than thirty chronological years behind her and access to the best rejuv technology to expand her life span close to two hundred years.

Not for me to decide, Nancia reminded herself, and turned her attention to the other two. As a safety precaution she kept sensors in all their cabins active at all times, but she tried not to pay too much attention unless the sensor receptors flashed to indicate unusual activity.

Darnell's activities were usual enough, Nancia supposed, for someone enslaved to a softperson's pitifully limited array of sense-receptors. He had requested Stemerald, Rigellian smokefowl and an array of Dorg Jesen's feelieporn hedra; Nancia had supplied nonalcoholic nearbeer, synthobird slices, and the hedra which Forister told her were the nearest things to porn in her library. Darnell spent most of his time reclining on his bunk, washing down synthobird and candied brancake with the nearbeer and watching a remake of an Old Earth novel over and over again. Nancia couldn't understand what he saw in the datacorded adventures of this Tom Jones, but then, it was none of her business.

Blaize was confined in the cabin opposite Darnell's. After half an hour's furious argument about who would look after "his" Loosies while he was being shipped back to Central, he'd accepted Nancia's promise to see that her sister Jinevra personally oversaw whoever was sent to replace him on Angalia. "One thing about the Perez line, they're hopelessly honest," he said in resignation. "Jinevra may not be creative, but at least she won't let that swine Harmon get his hooks into them again. You do realize that if this year's harvest fails, all my work will be wasted?"

"I realize, I realize," Nancia told him patiently. "Trust Jinevra." And as she sent out a general Net call to Jinevra and explained the situation to her sister, she wondered guiltily just how different she was from the rest of the High Families brats. Daddy had pulled strings to get her sent on this assignment. Now she was calling in favors owed her in Courier Service, and making her sister feel guilty, so that she could interfere in what should have been left to the normal channels of PTA administration.

But "normal channels" left the Loosies without the kind of aid they needed. Nancia sighed.

"Will there never be a bureaucracy that does what it's supposed to without sinking into corruption and inefficiency?" she asked Forister.

"Probably not," he replied.

"You sound like Simeon—advising me to accept corruption because it's everywhere!"

Forister shook his head. "Not in the least I'm advising you not to waste energy being surprised and shocked about the predictable. No system, anywhere, is proof against human failings. If it were—" he forced a tired smile—"we'd be computers. Your hyperchips may be foolproof, Nancia, but the human part of you makes mistakes—and so do all of us. Fortunately," he added, "humans can also recognize and correct mistakes—unlike computers, which just go on until they crash. Now if you'll excuse me, I'd like access to your comm system for a while. I want to see what I can do to prevent Blaize from crashing."

While Blaize's explanations had satisfied all of them on an emotional level, he still had some legal problems to face. No matter how excellent his motivation, the fact remained that he had falsified PTA reports, sold PTA shipments on the black market, and transferred the profits into his personal Net account. To leave him on Angalia while the others were shipped back for trial would have seemed like the worst kind of favoritism. All Forister could do was to make sure that *all* the facts were on record for the trial—not just how Blaize had obtained the money, but what he had done with it and how he had improved the lives of the people he was sent to aid.

"They *are* people," Forister reported to Blaize with satisfaction.

"Of course they are! Couldn't you tell that?"

"What I thought, or what you thought, is beside the point," Forister told him. "What counts is CenDip's decision. And there must be at least one intelligent man in CenDip, because your report has already been received and acted on. The Loosies have ISS as of yesterday. And the decision's palmprinted by no less a person than the CenDip Secretary-Universal, Javier Perez y de Gras."

Nancia heard that with great satisfaction and turned her

attention to her last prisoner. Fassa was spending most of this voyage just as she had spent the trip from Bahati to Angalia, crouched on her cabin floor, arms around her knees, staring at nothing and ignoring the food trays Nancia extruded at the dining slot. Untouched bowls of soup, baskets of sliced sweetbread, tempting fruit purees and sliced synthobird in glow-sauce went back into the recycling bins to be synthesized into new combinations of proteins and carbohydrates and fats. To all Nancia's gentle suggestions of food or entertainment Fassa replied with a dull "No, thank you," or "It doesn't matter."

"You must eat something," Nancia told her.

"Must I?" Fassa seemed obscurely amused. "No, thank you. I've had enough of men telling me what I must do and what I must be. Who cares if I get too skinny to appeal to anybody?"

"I'm not a man," Nancia pointed out. "I'm not even a softperson. And my only interest in your body is that I don't want you to get sick before . . ."

"Before my trial," Fassa finished calmly. "It's all right. You needn't be tactful. I'm going to prison for a long time. Maybe forever. As long as they don't put me on Shemali, I don't care."

"What's the matter with Shemali?" Nancia asked.

Fassa clamped her lips together and stared at the cabin wall. Her creamy skin was a little paler than usual, tinged with green shadows. "Nothing. I don't know anything about Shemali. I didn't say anything about Shemali."

Nancia gave up on Fassa for the moment. After all, there were other ways to find out what was up on Shemali. Reports on hyperchip production and sales should soon be coming in over the Net. A few invigorating hours of compiling evidence against Polyon would calm her and leave her better able to cheer up Fassa.

She felt a sneaking sympathy for the girl after reading her records. Growing up in the shadow of Faul del Parma couldn't have been easy. Losing her mother at thirteen, spending the next five years in a boarding school with not a single visit from her father, then sent out to Bahati to prove herself. . . . Nancia thought she understood how Fassa might feel. *But I didn't turn criminal to impress my family*, she argued with herself.

Your family, she replied, *wouldn't have been impressed*. Besides, she'd had it better than Fassa. Daddy and Jinevra and Flix had dropped in regularly during the eighteen years Nancia spent at

Laboratory Schools. It was only after graduation that Daddy had lost interest in her progress—

Softpersons could cry, and it was said that tears were a natural release of tension. Nancia looked up the biomed reports on the chemical components of tears, adjusted her nutrient tubes to remove those chemicals from her system, and concentrated on the Net records of hyperchip sales and transfer.

There was absolutely nothing there to incriminate Polyon. Two years after his arrival at Shemali, his new metachip design had been approved for production and christened the "hyperchip" in tribute to its improved speed and greater complexity. Since then, production of hyperchips had increased rapidly in each accounting quarter, so rapidly that Nancia couldn't believe Polyon was siphoning off any of the supply for his personal use. The manufactured hyperchips were subjected to especially stringent QA testing, but no more than the expected ratio failed the test . . . and all the failures were accounted for; they were sent off-planet for disposal and destroyed by an independent recycling company that had, so far as Nancia could discover, no links whatsoever with Polyon, the de Gras or Waldheim lines, or any other High Families. The hyperchips that passed QA were installed as fast as they were released, and every sale passed through the rationing board. Nancia knew from personal experience how difficult it was to get them; ever since her lower deck sensors and graphics coprocessors had been enhanced with hyperchips, she'd been pushing without success to get the hyperchips installed in the rest of her system. Micaya Questar-Benn, when questioned, told Nancia that her liver and heart-valve filter and kidneys all ran on hyperchips, installed when the metachip-controlled organs began to fail. But she, too, had been unable to get hyperchips to replace the smart chips in her external prostheses; that wasn't an emergency situation, and the ration board had refused to approve the surgery or the supplies.

Polyon had been nominated twice for the Galactic Service Award for the contributions his hyperchip design had made in areas as diverse as Fleet brainroom control, molecular surgery, and information systems. Even the Net, that ponderous, conservative communications system that linked the galaxy with news and information and records of everything ever done via computer— even the managers of the Net were slowly, conservatively augmenting key communications functions with hyperchip managers that had significantly speeded Net retrievals. The gossipbyters speculated openly that Polyon would receive the coveted GSA this year, the youngest man—and the handsomest, said Cornelia NetLink coyly—ever to hold one of the corycium statuettes. Speculation also ran rampant on which distinguished post he would surely accept after the presentation of the GSA. It seemed such a waste for such a talented young man—and so *handsome,* Cornelia inevitably added—to be stuck out at the back of beyond running a prison chip manufacturing plant. Yet so far, Polyon had refused with becoming modesty even to discuss offers of other positions.

"StarFleet assigned me to this post, and my honor is in serving where I am assigned," he declared whenever asked.

Nancia resisted the temptation to imitate a softperson raspberry at the files. Shellpersons, with near-total control over their auditory/speaker systems, didn't need to sink to such childish levels. . . .

"Thpfffft," she declared. There was *something* wrong on Shemali; she knew it, even if she couldn't prove it.

Perhaps their unannounced visit would give her the data she needed.

Despite her slowdown to cruising speeds, Nancia reached Shemali while she was still mulling over how to identify herself to the spaceport crew. Arrival of a Courier Service brainship was an unusual event on these remote planets; she didn't want to alert Polyon, give him a chance to cover up—whatever there was to cover up, and there must be *something*! Nancia thought.

In the event, the decision was made for her.

"OG-48, cleared for landing from orbit," the bored voice of a spaceport controller crackled over her comm link while Nancia hovered and wondered how to introduce herself without alarming anybody.

She quickly scanned her external sensor views. There were no other ships visible in orbit around Shemali, and any OG ship on the *far* side of the planet should have been out of commlink range. They must be speaking to her—oh, of course! Nancia chuckled to herself. Since the sting operation off Bahati, she'd been far too busy to demand a new paint job. The mauve-and-puce pseudowalls of an OG Shipping drone still cluttered her interior; the OG stencil was presumably still prominently displayed on her external skin.

Darnell Overton-Glaxely had a reputation for picking up and retrofitting ships from any possible source. Her sleek CS shape would be unusual for a shipping line's vessel, but apparently not unusual enough to rouse any suspicion in the spaceport controller. As he droned on with landing instructions, Nancia thought she recognized the calm, level, uninflected voice. Not that voice specifically, but the feeling of detachment from worldly cares. *Since when do Blissto addicts hold responsible spaceport positions? I knew something was very wrong here. And we—Forister and Micaya and I—are going to find out what!*

She settled on the landing pad with a sense of exultation and adventure. Then, as she took in her surroundings, the bubbles of joyous feelings went as flat as long-opened Stemerald.

"Ugh! What *happened* to this place?" Forister exclaimed as soon as Nancia cleared her display screens to give him a view of Shemali from the spaceport.

The permacrete of the landing pads was cracked and stained, and the edge of the 'crete had a ragged hole eaten into it, as though somebody had spilled a drum of industrial biocleaners and hadn't bothered to clean up the results before the microscopic biocleaners ate themselves to death on permacrete and paint. The spaceport building was a windowless permacrete block, grim and forbidding as any maximum-security prison—which, of course, described the whole planet.

Beyond the spaceport, clouds of green and purple smoke billowed into the air. Presumably they were the source of the greenish-black ashes which had drifted over every surface visible to Nancia.

While they waited for the spaceport controller to identify himself and welcome them to Shemali, a blast of wind shrieked across the open landing field, catching the ashes and tossing them into whirling columns of pollution that collapsed as rapidly as they had arisen.

Nancia's external monitors recorded the wind temperature at 5 degrees Centigrade.

"Shemali deserves its name," she murmured.

"What's that?"

"North Wind," Nancia said. "Alpha knows the language from which all the Nyota system names come. She mentioned the translations once . . . a long time ago."

"Is the rest of the planet like this?"

Nancia briefly replaced the view of the outside with magnified displays of the images she'd taken in while descending from orbit. At the time she'd been too exercised over the problem of an appropriate greeting formula to worry much about the surface problems of the planet. Now she and Forister gazed in horrified silence at stagnant pools in which no living thing stirred, valleys eroded from the brutal road cuts leading to new hyperchip plants, swirling clouds of dust and ash blanketing woods in which the trees died and no birds sang.

"I didn't know that one factory could do so much damage to a planet," Forister said slowly.

"Looks as if there are several factories operating now," Micaya pointed out. "All running at top capacity, I'd guess, with no concern for damage to the environment . . . and Shemali's winds will have distributed the polluting waste products planet-wide."

"Did nobody *visit* Shemali before recommending Polyon for a GSA? Probably not," Forister answered his own question. "Who wants to come to a prison planet in a minor star system? And his records are good, you said, Nancia?"

"The public records are excellent," Nancia replied. "It appears that Polyon de Gras-Waldheim has truly been making every effort to see that the maximum quantity of hyperchips is manufactured and that they are distributed as widely as possible." *At incalculable cost to the environment. But that's not a crime . . . not legally, not here anyway. If Central cared about Shemali, they wouldn't have located the prison metachip factory here to begin with.*

A pounding on the lower doors reverberated through Nancia's outer skin. She switched back to external auditory and visual sensors. The ones on her landing braces gave her a narrow view of whoever was making this commotion . . . a gaunt man wrapped in tattered rags that looked like the remnants of a prison uniform, gray smock and loose trousers, and with more rags draped over his head and bound about his fists.

He was calling her name. "Nancia! Nancia, let me in, quickly!"

On the edge of the landing field, two bulky figures in gleaming silvercloth protective suits moved slowly forward, awkward and menacing. The silver hoods covered their faces like helmets, the silver suits glittered around them like armor. But the weapons in their raised hands were not knightly lances, but nerve disrupters, bulky squat shapes more menacing than any iron lance point.

Nancia slid open the lower doors. The fugitive collapsed against the opening doors and fell into the cargo bay. As one of the silver-suited figures raised its nerve disrupter, Nancia slammed the doors shut again. The rays bounced harmlessly against her outer shell; she absorbed the energy without conscious thought. All her attention was on the ragged prisoner who was now pushing himself to his knees, slowly and painfully unwinding the rags from around his face.

"That may not have been a wise decision," Forister commented mildly. "We don't wish to become embroiled with the local authorities. Prison disputes aren't part of our mission."

"This man is," Nancia replied. She switched the display screens to show what her sensors were picking up in the cargo bay. Micaya Questar-Benn was the first to gasp in recognition.

"Young Bryley-Sorensen! How did he get into Shemali prison . . . and out again . . . and in such condition?"

"That," said Nancia grimly, "I should very much like to know."

Sev pulled himself upright by one of the support struts that crisscrossed the cargo bay. "Nancia, don't let anybody else in. There's—you don't know—terrible things on Shemali. Terrible," he repeated. His eyes rolled up and he slid to the floor again.

"Forister, Micaya, get him out of the cargo bay before those two guards or whatever come knocking on my doors," Nancia snapped. "No, wait. I have an idea. Take his clothes off first and leave them there."

"Why?"

"Don't have time to explain. Just do it!" She set her kitchen synthesizers to work and turned on the incinerator. What she had in mind would never work if Shemali were a decently run prison. But what she'd seen of the ravages wreaked on the planet matched what she remembered of young Polyon de Gras-Waldheim's ruthless personality, and Sev's last gasped words were all the confirmation she needed.

While Forister and Micaya stripped the unconscious Sev and manhandled him into the lift, Nancia expanded her sensor reception to examine him more closely. She recorded everything for future analysis, taking particular note of the horrible skin lesions that disfigured both Sev's arms and one leg. Dark bruises flowered in purple and blue and green on his ribs and stomach, and his back was crisscrossed with swollen weals that oozed red as the other two softpersons moved him. His breathing was shallow and irregular and he showed no sign of regaining consciousness while they dragged him to the lift.

What had they done to him on Shemali? Nancia knew how to treat the surface injuries; but this was a planet of nerve gas and acids. The lesions on his arms and legs frightened her. So did his desperate, ragged breath pattern. This went beyond the superficial injuries and known diseases she was qualified to treat. What they wanted was a doctor . . . and there happened to be one on board.

Nancia flashed her images of Sev to Alpha's cabin. There was a cry of dismay, then a strangled sob. Fassa's voice, not Alpha's. Nancia realized that in her hurry, she'd transmitted the same display to all the passenger cabins. Already Darnell was cursing about the interruption of his vid. She switched off the receptors from his cabin and displayed images of the other three prisoners so that she could watch their faces while she consulted with Alpha.

"Dr. Hezra-Fong," Nancia said formally, "we have just brought aboard a prisoner with the severe injuries you see. I fear Ganglicide poisoning. Can you treat him?"

"That's not Ganglicide," Alpha said confidently. "Minor acid burns, that's all. But there may be some lung damage. I can't be sure from these vids. And with the location of those bruises, I'm worried about kidney damage and internal bleeding. Transport him to the medtech center. I'll have a look."

She was cool and quick and competent; Nancia admired those qualities unwillingly. But could she be trusted with Sev's health?

Alpha pushed on the closed cabin door and turned back to the sensor port. Her fine, sharp-featured face was pinched with annoyance. "FN-935, I cannot diagnose and treat this man by remote control! If you're interested in his health, I strongly suggest you open this door and allow me to do my job!"

But what else would she do? Nancia wondered.

"Let me go with her," Blaize suggested.

"And me." Fassa's large eyes were filled with tears. Acting, or desperation? There was scant time to decide.

Nancia instinctively trusted Blaize, but she wasn't sure how reliable he might be. He tended to go along with the majority. And if she let both Fassa and Blaize out with Alpha, the prisoners would be the majority among the softpersons.

And whatever Fassa's crimes, Nancia somehow doubted that she would do anything to hurt Sev Bryley-Sorensen. Not after the scenes she had witnessed between them. Not after she'd watched Fassa sink into a depression between Bahati and Shemali, convinced that Sev had deserted her and that she would never see him again.

"Fassa del Parma y Polo will accompany and assist Dr. Hezra-Fong," Nancia announced with a mental prayer that she was making the right decision.

While the two women raced down the corridor to meet Forister and Micaya at the lift, Nancia slowly opened her lower cargo doors six inches. The silver-suited guard who stood outside had his fist raised to bang on the door; he lowered it now, but aimed his nerve disrupter into what he could see of the cargo bay.

"And what can I do for *you?*" Nancia asked icily.

"Drone OG-48, you are harboring an escaped prisoner," the guard said. "Return him to our custody now, or it'll be the worse for you. Your owner won't approve this, you know."

Nancia managed an icy laugh that chilled her own sensors. "This is not a drone. You'll meet us in good time. As for that diseased bundle of rags that begged entrance, it has been disposed of appropriately. It looked as if it had Capellan jungle rot and Altair plague—not to mention Old Earth lice. Did you think we'd leave something like that cluttering up this nice clean ship?"

"Don't try to lie to me," the guard warned. "This ship has been under surveillance from the moment of landing. The prisoner has not left the ship."

"Who said anything about leaving? There are its clothes—if you can call those rags clothes," Nancia added disparagingly. She slid the cargo doors open another ten inches, just enough to let the guard squeeze in edgewise. "And here's the rest of your fugitive." She opened the disposal slot and extruded the contents. A pitiful little heap of organic ash, partially burnt protein, and charred bone fragments spilled out onto the tray. The guard stepped back, every line of his body expressing horror. Nancia wished she could see his face behind the silver permafilm and the finely woven breath mesh.

"What's the matter?" she inquired. "He was dying anyway, you know."

The guard stumbled towards the doors, making retching sounds behind his mask. "I thought de Gras-Waldheim was a cold one," he said between gagging noises, "but you OG Shipping types are worse yet."

Nancia's last and most spine-chilling laugh followed him out onto the landing pad.

"Don't you want to take the remains back?" she called after him.

She slammed the cargo doors shut before he could answer, just in case he overcame his distaste and came back for the "remains." It would never do to let a lab get hold of the synthesized "bone" and algal-protein "flesh" that she had first created, then charred in the incinerator.

CHAPTER FIFTEEN

"Stimpad! Drug stores!" Alpha snapped over her shoulder. Nancia silently extruded the required equipment from her medtech drawers. Alpha's slim dark fingers darted among the ampules supplied and loaded the pad with a combination of drugs. Nancia recognized a general nervous stimulant, a breathing regulator, and at least two kinds of anesthetic.

"Er—are you sure those will work all right in combination?" she asked apologetically. Alpha was the doctor. But Nancia had been rigorously trained in the minor first aid and holding techniques she might expect to need until she could get an ailing brawn or passenger to a clinic; and one thing her instructor had been very, very firm about was the danger of unexpected side-effects from mixing two or more drugs.

"You wanted an expert," Alpha snapped, "you got one. I've got to stabilize his condition before I can treat the superficial lesions and check for internal damage. This should keep him breathing . . . if anything will. We haven't a lot of time to waste, you know."

Quietly, Fassa del Parma slid between Alpha and Sev's unconscious body, now prone on the padded examining bench that slid out of one wall in the narrow medtech chamber. "If the combination is harmless," she said, "try it on me first."

"Don't be silly," Alpha sneered, "you've less than half his body

456

mass. You'll be out of it for two days if I give you the same dose
I've prepared for Bryley!"

"Then just use half the stimpad," Fassa suggested. She pulled
one sleeve down over her shoulder, exposing an expanse of creamy
white skin, naked and vulnerable. "Here. I won't move. But I want
to see a demonstration before you stick anything into . . . Sev." She
gulped on his name, but otherwise her composure was unbroken.

Nancia, who alone had the luxury of viewing the scene from
several angles, thought she saw Sev's eyelids flutter at the sound
of Fassa's voice. Neither of the young women noticed; they were
too intent on one another. From the door, Micaya Questar-Benn
watched in concern. Behind her, Forister glanced up at one of
Nancia's hall sensors. "Time to intervene?" he mouthed soundlessly.

"Wait a minute," Nancia whispered back, the merest thread of
sound.

Alpha stared at Fassa's calm face and the exposed shoulder she
was offering. Her own face worked angrily. "I ought to take you
up on it," she said, "you interfering dolt. Always were soft on men,
weren't you? All right, then!" She tossed the loaded stimpad in the
general direction of a disposal chute; Nancia extended the chute's
wing-edges and caught the thing before it slid down into the
recycling chamber. She wanted to have an independent lab analyze the first mix when they got to a civilized planet.

Alpha prepared a second stimpad loaded with nothing more than
a common stimulant. "Happier with this?" she asked the air, brows
raised sarcastically.

"Yes, thank you," said Nancia and Fassa simultaneously. But Fassa
still insisted that Alpha inject her with a sample of each medica-
tion she used to treat Sev.

"You're a fool," Alpha muttered, too low for General Questar-
Benn to hear; Nancia had to amplify her audio sensors to catch
the thread of speech. Alpha bent over Sev as she spoke, swabbing
with short vicious strokes at the acid sores on his arms and legs.
"He was in bad enough shape . . . if he'd never waked up, there'd
be that much less evidence against you and me both. Do you feel
that grateful to him for doing his best to put you in prison?"

"I've already killed once," Fassa said. "That's enough for me.
What's that?"

"Antibiotic spray. Relax," Alpha told her. "We had our chance to
get rid of some evidence, you blew it, it's too late now. Got that

freak of a general and the old fart brawn peering over our shoulders, ready to slap me with a malpractice suit on top of everything else. I'll do my best to patch your detective up for you—and my best," she added with simple pride that was quite undiminished by her criminal record, "my best, Fassa dear, is very good indeed."

It was, too. Within the hour Sev was reclining on pillows, sipping camtea loaded with so much sugar and chalker that it was hardly recognizable, and explaining to Forister and Micaya the extent of what he'd uncovered on Shemali and why he'd been in such desperate straits when Nancia landed.

"I made a few mistakes," he admitted with a grimace. "Disguising myself as a prisoner on an incoming transport seemed like the only way to slip onto Shemali unnoticed. It worked, too. But there were a few things I hadn't counted on after that."

Sev had expected his faked "prison" records, showing expertise in metachip mathematics and computer network operation, to earn him a prison job somewhere in the administration, where he'd have a chance to poke around in Polyon's records and find what he was looking for. The position he was assigned to looked promising— but as soon as he started his search, everything had gone wrong.

"Ah—you didn't say exactly what you were looking for on Shemali," Forister hinted courteously.

Sev took a long gulp of his scalding camtea, coughed, gasped, and lay back looking a little weaker. "Not important. Important thing is, more going on than you can guess from outside. Don't have it all myself . . . but enough. . . ."

Polyon's entire computer system was laced with coded traps and alarms; the first time Sev tried to access secure data, Polyon and his trusties were alerted and caught him in the act before he'd more than downloaded a handful of innocuous records. Sev then showed them his Central Worlds pass and explained that he was on an investigative mission having nothing to do with Polyon or Shemali.

"They didn't believe me," he sighed. "Even though it happened to be true."

"Then what *were* you doing?" Micaya Questar-Benn demanded.

"Later." Sev went on with his story. The trusties had beaten him up, stripped him, located and disabled the thin sliver of spyderplate which he'd meant to use as a distress beacon to Nancia in case he got into trouble. "Those things are supposed to start emitting an all-frequencies distress signal hooking into the Net if they're damaged," Sev complained. "So at first I wasn't too worried. But then when you didn't come, and it got to be two days, I thought I might be on my own."

"De Gras-Waldheim must know some way to disable them," Forister nodded.

"Reasonable," Nancia put in from the speaker. "He invented them. They're essentially single-purpose hyperchips—and nobody knows more about hyperchips than Polyon."

Sev's next discovery was that Polyon had stepped up the new plants' production of hyperchips by ignoring all safety precautions. Sent to the hyperchip burnoff lines, where prisoners' life expectancy amid the clouds of nerve-destroying gas could be measured in days rather than years, Sev had resolved to make a break for freedom when the first ship touched down on Shemali—especially when he recognized the slim lines of Nancia's Courier Service hull behind the disguising frieze of OG Shipping logos and mauve stripes. The escape hadn't been too difficult; all the other prisoners had been terrorized out of even thinking about escape, and the guards were lazy and careless and unwilling to spend much time in the burnoff rooms.

"And besides," finished Forister with a grin, "nobody would expect a prisoner on the run to go to an OG Shipping drone for help. Nancia, your paint job has served us well. I don't suppose you'd consider keeping it after this is over?"

"Most certainly not!" Nancia told him. "And it wouldn't work, anyway. When we've finished in the Nyota system, there won't be any more OG Shipping. But—what do we do now?"

Sev's story had demonstrated enough irregularities to justify arresting Polyon twice over. But he was just one man, with no datacordings or computer records to exhibit in proof of his story. If they took Polyon away now without making sure of their evidence, Sev predicted that Shemali would be cleaned up by the time they got back.

"Impossible," said Forister with feeling.

Sev nodded weakly. "Not the planet's surface, I grant you. But you can be sure there'll be nothing inside the factories for an investigative committee to quarrel with. It'll all be clean assembly lines, strict safety features."

"And the prisoners who've already been damaged by exposure to acids and gases?"

"I don't think," said Sev somberly, "that any of them will be able to testify by that time."

"Then we'll have to go down now and get the evidence," Forister said.

Sev shook his head. "Won't work. He's clever—there's a VIP tour arranged—the disfigured prisoners and the dangerous work lines are all kept well out of sight. Mostly at the secondary plants hidden backplanet. I know how to find one of the worst plants. I was there. But without me, he'll whisk you from one end of the central prison factory to the other, and you won't see anything, and every time you try to turn around there'll be six guards in your way. I'll have to go with you." He tried to raise himself from the pillows, started coughing and fell back again.

"You can't!" Fassa exclaimed.

"May have to," said Micaya Questar-Benn. "Duty." She and Sev nodded at one another. "You two," she jerked her head at Fassa and Alpha—"back to your cabins now. Nothing to do with you—shouldn't have let you hear this much."

"Wait!" Fassa cried as Forister took her by the arm. "There has to be another way. It won't work, taking Sev with you, can't you see that? Even if he were stronger, the sight of his face will warn Polyon at once that there's something wrong. None of you—none of us will get away alive."

"Oh, come now," said Forister gently. "Your friend can't be that dangerous."

Fassa's face hardened. "If you don't believe me, ask the others. Alpha?"

Alpha bint Hezra-Fong nodded once, reluctantly.

Fassa looked up at the room sensor. "Nancia, can you connect us with Blaize and Darnell? Just for a moment?"

Both men agreed with Fassa's assessment of the situation.

"Then what *can* we do?" Forister demanded. "Damn it, I'm not going to turn tail and run off-planet for fear of some spoiled High Families brat who's got hold of some dangerous toys!"

"I think," Fassa said slowly, "that you're going to use me." She was very pale. "Take Alpha back to her cabin, and I'll explain what I think we can do." She looked apologetically at Alpha.

"Traitor! When Polyon finds out—"

Fassa's lips were pinched. She was not pretty at all, now. But she was almost beautiful, in a cold remote way. "I'll have to take that chance, won't I?"

"Better you than me," Alpha said. She turned to go. "All right. Lock me up. I don't even want to hear this plan. Maybe he won't hold it against me, if I'm not even here when you discuss it." She didn't sound too hopeful of that.

When Fassa explained her plan, there was a brief silence while Forister, Nancia and Micaya all thought it over.

"You think he'll fall for it?" Forister queried.

"He thinks Nancia is an OG drone," Fassa pointed out. "He believes her passengers cremated Sev for being a nuisance; if he hadn't swallowed that story, believe me, we'd be hearing from him by now." She gave them a strained smile. "Murderers in the escort of OG shipping—what better credentials could you have? And with me to front the introductions—"

"I won't let you!" Sev said hoarsely.

"Fassa stays on board Nancia," Micaya interrupted. "That's understood." She looked at the girl. "No offense, Fassa. But from the ship, we can monitor what you say. And I think you'd better wear these." She bent over briefly, fiddled with the prosthesis replacing her left leg, and straightened with two lengths of shining, thread-fine wire. "Hold out your wrists."

Fassa obeyed and Micaya encircled each wrist with a length of the wire. Where she twisted the ends shut, the wires seemed to collapse and seal invisibly upon themselves.

"Tanglefield? Is that really necessary?"

Micaya nodded. "Security measure, no more. Field won't be activated unless we run into trouble on Shemali. Clear, Nancia?"

"Affirmed."

Micaya touched her synthetic arm. "I've got a portable tanglefield generator built in here," she told Forister. "Might come in handy on Shemali. Want some wires?"

Forister took a handful of the gleaming wires and regarded them dubiously. "I prefer to solve my problems more elegantly than this."

"Me, too." Micaya tugged her dark green pants leg down over the prosthesis. "Isn't always possible, though. Everybody tells me there'll be terrible political complications if we harm a hair on the head of this High Families brat. So . . ." She patted her prosthetic leg again and straightened. "I've stashed the needler. Agree with you, taking him out straightaway would be simpler, but you insisted on doing this by the book."

"That wasn't," Forister said, "quite what I meant by an elegant solution."

Micaya regarded him with a hint of amusement on her solemn, dark face. "Know it. Usually is the most 'elegant' way, though. Leave little tyrants to run loose, they grow up into big tyrants. Then you get the Capellan mess, or something like. Wars," she pointed out, "aren't elegant." She nodded once to Fassa, by way of apology. "Understand, not accusing you of treachery, just not taking chances. Want you to be warned—"

"That a secret signal to Polyon will do me more harm than good," Fassa finished calmly. "You don't trust me. That's all right. *I* wouldn't trust me, either."

She was white to the lips now, and her hands were shaking, but she led the way from the medtech room without pausing.

Nancia could see that Sev was fretting enough to damage himself by trying to go after them, so she switched displays to give him visual and auditory sensor taps to the main cabin.

Fassa was still pale when Nancia initiated the signal sequence that would open a comm link with planetside authorities, but she managed the promised introductions with perfect composure. For Polyon's benefit Forister and Micaya became Forrest Perez and Qualia Benton, a pair of potential hyperchip customers with cash to invest in the operation. She hinted delicately that "Qualia Benton" was really a high-ranking general from Central, and Micaya started forward to stop her. Forister laid one hand on Micaya's arm. "Trust the young lady, Mic," he murmured. "She has—er—more experience in this sort of thing than you or I."

So it proved. Far from being alarmed by Micaya's military standing, Polyon accepted her presence with Fassa, on an OG ship, as proof that she was as corrupt as his friends. And he was clearly delighted to have made the contact. Within minutes he was arranging to meet Fassa's "friends" and give them a tour of the newest hyperchip plant.

"I don't know why, but Polyon's always been eager to get more hyperchips sold to the military," Fassa told the others after she cut the contact. "It's not the money, either; he offered Space Academy a cut rate once, but the Ration Board stopped him. I knew your rank would be the thing to draw him in, Micaya. A back door into the military supply system is Polyon's dream."

"I suppose he wants to impress his old teachers and classmates by making sure they all use his inventions," Forister surmised.

Nancia was confused. "But surely he doesn't imagine that selling hyperchips on the black market is the way to high standing in the Academy?"

All three softpersons laughed tolerantly, and Nancia heard a weak chuckle from the sensor link to the medtech cabin where Sev rested. "Investigate the sources of a few High Families fortunes some time, Nancia," Sev recommended to her. "Money washes clean of most any taint—and more rapidly than you'd believe possible."

"Not," Nancia said, "in the Academy. And not in House Perez y de Gras, either."

Nancia fussed over Forister and Micaya until the last minute, fitting them out with contact buttons, spyderplates, and every other remote protection device she could think of. "I don't know what good you think this will do," Forister complained. "De Gras-Waldheim disabled Sev's spyderplate without alerting anybody, didn't he?"

"Sev didn't have me monitoring him," Nancia pointed out.

She should have confined Fassa to her cabin before the other two left, but she didn't have the heart to. "Somebody should stay with Sev," Fassa pleaded.

"Oh, let the child stay with him," Forister put in unexpectedly. "She's not worth much as a hostage anyway. If even half of what Sev told us about the hyperchip factory conditions is true, Polyon de Gras-Waldheim is a murderer a dozen times over who'd think nothing of sacrificing a ship full of his former friends."

Fassa nodded. "Yes, that's about right. Except—I wouldn't say he'd 'think nothing of it.' He'd probably enjoy it."

"Why didn't any of you tell us about Polyon before this?" Nancia demanded. "You were all babbling your stupid heads off, pointing the finger at one another to get some credit for your own plea bargains, and you never warned us about Polyon."

"Afraid to," Fassa said sadly.

"So afraid that you let Sev go off to Shemali without a word of warning? I'd never have let him go unmonitored if I'd guessed."

"I didn't know Sev had gone to Shemali," Fassa defended herself. "Nobody told me anything. I didn't even know he wasn't on board when we left Bahati. All I knew was that he didn't come to see me again, and I thought, I thought . . . and quite right, too; why should he bother with someone like me?" Tears filled her eyes; Nancia thought that for once they were genuine.

"Fassa del Parma, you are a prime idiot!" Sev's weary, hoarse whisper startled all of them; Nancia had forgotten that she'd left the connections between the main cabin and the medtech room wide open. "Get in here and hold my hand and smooth my fevered brow. I'm an injured man. I need attention."

"Call Alpha. She's a doctor," Fassa gulped.

"I want *you*. Now are you coming, or do I have to get up and get you?"

Fassa fled. And Nancia watched, satisfied, and feeling only a little bit like an eavesdropper, as she burst through the door of the medtech room. Hadn't Sev given her explicit instructions to keep full sensors open whenever he was with Fassa del Parma?

Those two were too wrapped up in each other for Fassa to pose any danger to anybody. All the same, Nancia kept those sensors open while she concentrated most of her attention on the images and sounds coming in from Forister's and Micaya's contact buttons. Polyon was losing no time; he'd met them on the landing field in a flyer that swooped directly to the newest hyperchip production facility, a squat featureless building set in a valley that might have been beautiful before Polyon's construction teams sliced through the earth and the waste products from his factory killed off the trees. Now the building stood alone at the top of a sloping hill ringed round by stagnant, poisonous-looking waters and the broken stumps of dead trees. Nancia felt her sensors contracting in repulsion at the image.

"General, can you handle this flyer?" she murmured through Micaya's contact button.

"I'm glad to see you have such up-to-date equipment, de Gras," Micaya said loudly for Nancia's benefit. "I tested the prototype versions of this flyer recently, but I had no idea the model was in general distribution already."

Good. Micaya would be able to bring the three of them back. Nancia listened in on Sev's and Fassa's conversation while Polyon landed the flyer and took Forister and Micaya into the factory.

"You think too much," Sev was saying firmly to Fassa. "I meant what I told you before, and I still mean it. You idiot, I went to Shemali on your account!"

"On my account?" Fassa echoed, sounding as if she was unable to think at all.

Sev nodded. "Here I'd been pacing Nancia's corridors every night, trying to think out a way to save you, and then Darnell gave me a clue. He said you'd contracted to build a hyperchip factory for Polyon, and that when the original building collapsed you replaced it free of charge. I thought if I could prove that, your lawyer might argue that you never intended to do substandard work—that any problems with your buildings were the result of incompetence, of sending a young girl to manage a business she was unfamiliar with— and that he could prove it by demonstrating how willingly you'd made restitution when a problem was brought to your attention."

Fassa smiled through her tears. "It's a lovely, lovely argument, Sev. Unfortunately, not a word of that is true. I am," said Fassa, "or rather, I was an extremely competent contractor." She sniffed. "Damn Daddy. He accidentally sent me into a business I had a real talent for."

"That being the case," said Sev softly, "why the hell couldn't you just *be* a contractor, instead of slinking around in those dresses that kept falling off your shoulders and driving middle-aged men crazy?"

Fassa's face hardened. "Ask Daddy." She tried to turn away, but Sev had hold of both her hands.

"I guessed some time ago," he said. "And . . . I've been checking old gossipbytes. Was that why your mother killed herself?"

Fassa nodded. Tears were streaming down her face unchecked. "Well, then. You won't want to have anything more to do with me. I understand. I'm not, I'm not . . . it's not just Daddy, you know. There've been all those other men. . . ." She gulped down a sob.

For a man who'd been on the verge of collapse a few hours earlier, Sev demonstrated remarkable powers of recovery. Nancia was impressed by the strength with which he drew Fassa into his arms against her resistance. "You," he said deliberately, "are the woman I love, and nothing that happened before today matters in the slightest to me." He paused for a moment and Nancia blacked out her visual sensors. She didn't really think that the requirements of surveillance on Fassa included watching Sev Bryley-Sorenson kiss her as desperately as a man in vacuum gasping for oxygen.

On Shemali, Micaya Questar-Benn had finally persuaded Polyon to drop the sanitized V.I.P. tour of his factory. She didn't believe he could produce enough hyperchips to satisfy her requirements, she told him, and what was more, she didn't believe he would be able to extend the factory's production fast enough for her. The safety requirements mandated by the Trade Commission simply took too long to set up and maintain.

Polyon suggested that the Trade Commission could, collectively, do something anatomically impossible for the individual members. And if the General wanted to see just how fast he could turn out hyperchips, he added, she and her friend could just follow him. They'd have to wear protective gear, though, he said, struggling into a silvercloth suit himself as he spoke.

While Micaya and Forister put on the suits provided for guests, Micaya commented innocently that the cost of suiting up an entire production line of prisoners must be prohibitive, and that she didn't see how they maintained the dexterity necessary for the assembly process while working from inside the bulky silvercloth gloves.

Polyon chuckled and agreed that the difficulties posed were enormous.

On board, Sev and Fassa were talking again; Nancia discreetly tuned in to their conversation, but there wasn't much in it to require her attention. Fassa was gloomy about the prospect of years in prison. Sev wasn't any too cheerful about it himself, but he assured Fassa that he'd wait for her.

"I don't think they let murderers out," Fassa said. "Unless they decide to mindwipe me."

"Fassa, you are not a murderer. Caleb isn't dead."

Fassa's slender body became quite still. "He isn't?"

"You were right," Sev said. "Nobody tells you anything. He isn't dead. He isn't even seriously ill; he was in therapy for nerve damage when I left Bahati."

"Latest bulletins from Summerlands say that he should recover full function quite soon and will probably be restored to active brawn status within the next few weeks," Nancia confirmed.

Sev and Fassa broke apart and looked up at the overhead speaker.

"Nancia!" Sev exclaimed. "I didn't know you were listening."

"You gave me the orders yourself," Nancia reminded him.

"Oh. Well." Sev thought. "Can I cancel the orders? Will you obey me if I do?"

"I really shouldn't."

"Lock the door on us both," Sev suggested. "I don't mind. But please, could we have some privacy now? This voyage back to Central is likely to be my last chance to be alone with my girl for a long, long time."

Fassa looked ridiculously happy for someone facing trial and a stiff prison sentence. Nancia left them to it.

She didn't have much to occupy her on Shemali, either. Micaya and Forister hadn't waited to take the full tour of the hyperchip assembly line; a few images of prisoners working unshielded with skin-destroying acids, in rooms that leaked poisonous gas, were all the evidence they needed to bolster Sev's detailed eyewitness testimony. The datacordings were particularly damning when accompanied, as they were, by Polyon's pleasant, cultured voice explaining just how he had cut costs and speeded up production by condemning the prisoners in his care to lingering, painful deaths by industrial poisoning. By the time Nancia had scanned those images, Micaya had already slapped tanglewires around Polyon's wrists, ankles, and even his neck. With the ankle field activated, she read him the formal statement of arrest.

"You can't do this!" Polyon protested. "Do you know who I am? I'm a de Gras-Waldheim. And I have Governor Lyautey's approval for everything I've done here!"

"My brainship has already transmitted a request for drug testing on Lyautey and all other civilian personnel," Forister told him. "I suspected Blissto when I heard your spaceport controller talking. What did you do, make addicts of anybody who could blow the whistle on you?"

"You can't arrest *me*," Polyon repeated as though he hadn't understood a word.

Micaya Questar-Benn had a smile that would have chilled steel to the snapping point. "Want to bet, son? Walk in front of me. Slowly, now. Wouldn't want the tanglefield to think you're trying to escape and cut off your feet; it's too quick and easy a death for your sort." And when Polyon opened his mouth again, she activated the extended tanglefield from the neck wire to keep him from flapping his tongue about any more.

As they left the assembly lines, a ragged cheer went up from the prisoners behind them.

CHAPTER SIXTEEN

To Polyon's shock and amazement, the cyborg freak and her partner actually managed to convince Governor Lyautey that they were entitled to arrest a de Gras-Waldheim and take him away. "Convince" was probably too strong a word. Polyon recognized with rueful amusement that he'd been caught in his own trap. The governor, like all the civilians left on Shemali, was constantly dosed with Alpha bint Hezra-Fong's Seductron. Since Lyautey was in a nonessential job, Polyon kept his maintenance level of Seductron so high that the governor did little but nod amiably and agree with whoever spoke to him last.

Somebody must have figured that out and thought of this way to use it against him. With his mouth covered by tanglefield, Polyon could do nothing but listen while this Micaya Questar-Benn and her partner rattled off official-sounding words, flourished their forged credentials—they had to be forged—and took him away in the very flyer he himself had sent to pick them up at the spaceport.

They considerately removed the tanglefield from his mouth as soon as the flyer took off. Polyon maintained a dignified silence during the short flyer hop back to the spaceport, but his brain was working furiously. He refused to believe that this "arrest" was real. Real Central agents had their own transport, they didn't hitch a ride on an OG cruiser or get a conniving little whore like Fassa

del Parma to front for them. This had to be some trick cooked
up by Darnell and Fassa to get control of the hyperchips. He had
no intention of giving them or their friends the amusement of
seeing him struggle and protest. Later, when he'd figured out their
game, he would turn the tables and make them squirm. Darnell
would be easy to break, but Fassa . . . he smiled unpleasantly at
the thought of exactly how he'd take the pride out of her. He'd
never yet threatened Fassa physically. Maybe it was time to start.

Then, as the flyer came gently down on the landing pad, he
blinked and saw the ship for a moment silhouetted against the
bright sky, only sleek lines and smooth design, without the con-
fusing detail of the OG colors and logo, and he knew where he'd
seen a ship like that before.

"Courier Service," he groaned, and for the first time he began
to believe that he was really under arrest.

"Got it in one," said the spare, quiet man who'd accompanied
General Questar-Benn, offering Polyon his hand to help him to
the ground. "Time I introduced myself. Forister Armontillado y
Medoc, brawn to the FN-935."

"*You* a brawn, old man?" Polyon sneered. "I'll believe that when
I see it!" He refused the offer of the steadying hand and swung
himself out of the flyer, feet together, hands in front of him, still
with athletic grace. Even with his hands and feet constrained in
tanglefields, he still had his strength and his natural balance.

"You'll not have to wait long," Forister replied mildly. "I'll introduce you to my brainship as soon as we're aboard."

Polyon maintained a grim silence while these two escorted him
to the ship's lift, up to the passenger level and down a depress-
ing mauve-painted corridor to the cabin where he was to be
confined. Once there, he leaned against the wall and waited. The
brawn Forister and the cyborg Micaya withdrew, leaving him still
confined in the double tanglefield about wrists and ankles. "Wait!"
he cried out. "Aren't you going to—"

The door irised shut behind them with a series of clicks along
the concentric rings, and a moment later a sweet female voice spoke
from the overhead speaker.

"Welcome aboard the FN-935," she—it—said. "I am Nancia, the
brainship of this partnering. Your arrest is legal under Central
Code—" and she reeled off paragraphs and statute references that
meant nothing to Polyon. "As a prisoner awaiting trial on capital

crimes, you may legally be confined by tanglefield for the duration of the voyage, which will be approximately two weeks. General Questar-Benn has transferred the tanglefield control function
to my computer; if you will give me your word not to attempt
damage to me or to your fellow passengers, I will release the
tanglefield now and allow you the freedom of your cabin."

Polyon glanced over the narrow space and laughed sardonically.
"You have my word," he said. Words were cheap enough.

As soon as he spoke the electronic field ceased vibrating. His
wrists and ankles prickled with returning life; an uncomfortable
sensation, but *far, far* better than being electronically bound hand
and foot for the next two weeks.

The brainship blathered on with threats about sleepgas and other
restraints that could be applied if he gave it any trouble; Polyon
didn't bother to listen. He had too much to think about. Besides,
he didn't intend to do anything the brainship could see. He wasn't
that stupid.

Unobtrusively, under cover of flexing his wrists to restore full
movement, he patted his breast pocket and felt the reassuring lump
right where it should be, where he always carried a minihedron
with the latest test version of his master program. He *was* clever,
Polyon thought. Too clever by half for this pair to master for long.

Oh, he'd make some trouble for this interfering brainship and
its doddering brawn, all right, just as soon as he got the chance.
But it wasn't trouble that they would be able to see or hear coming,
and there wouldn't be a damned thing they could do about it once
he'd started. Damn them! He wasn't ready for this; he was still
two to three years short of having everything in place. How much
would it cost him to make his planned move ahead of schedule?

Impossible to calculate; he'd just have to go ahead and find out
later. Whatever the cost, it couldn't be as great as that of going
tamely back to Central for trial and imprisonment. It had always
been a gamble, Polyon comforted himself. He'd always known that
one day somebody might figure out about the hyperchips, and that
he'd have to move fast if that occurred.

At least now, even if the move was being forced on him, it was
forced by some ignoramuses who didn't even guess how he might
retaliate. He would have the advantage of surprise on his side.

If only he'd had time to implement Final Phase! Then he could
have started everything right now, with a spoken word of

command. As it was, he'd have to get this minihedron into a reader slot before he could make his move.

There weren't any reader slots in this cabin; and he was supposed to be confined here until they reached Central; and if he tried to break out of the cabin, the damned brainship would drop him with sleepgas or a tanglefield before he got to any place with reader slots.

Polyon bared his teeth briefly. He did love a challenge. He still had his voice, and his wits, and his charm, and sensor contact with the brainship and her brawn. He set to work with those tools to dig himself an impalpable tunnel to freedom, placing each word and each request as carefully as a miner shoring up the loose earth in the tunnel roof.

In the long dragging hours until they reached the Singularity point for transition into Central subspace, there wasn't much to do but play games or read. Forister and Micaya began another trichess contest; Nancia obligingly created the holocube for them and maintained a record of the moves, but warned them that some of the game data might be lost if she needed to call on that particular set of coprocessors during Singularity.

"That's all right," Forister said absently. "Mic and I have been interrupted by all sorts of things in our time. Aren't you partnering me, then?"

"I don't think I'd better," Nancia replied with real regret. "I think I should monitor our passengers. They've been allowed a great deal of freedom, you know."

Micaya snorted. "Freedom! They're free to move within their cabins, that's all. Granted, I wouldn't cut 'em that much slack, but—"

"That," said Forister, "is why you keep having political problems. You never cut the High Families any slack, and they resent it."

"Shouldn't," said Micaya. "I'm one of them."

"That doesn't help," Forister said, almost sadly. "Anyway, Mic, you're not seriously worried about a ship's mutiny?"

"From those spoiled brats?" Micaya snorted. "Ha! Even that de Gras boy, for all the others were so scared of him, trotted aboard like a little lamb. No, there's not a one of them has the brains— saving your Blaize, maybe—or the guts to try anything, now that we've cut off their special deals."

"Blaize wouldn't try anything," Forister said sharply. "He's a good boy."

Micaya patted Forister's arm. "I know, I know. Convinced me. But he did rip off PTA. And what's worse to my mind—he didn't speak up about the others. Have to answer for that, though it's less, all told, than the rest of this precious crew have to stand trial for."

"I understand," Forister said glumly.

Sev Bryley-Sorenson stretched out his long legs. "Think I'll work out for a while," he announced to no one in particular.

"You'd think it was him going back for trial, to look at the long face on the boy," Micaya commented as Sev whisked himself down the corridor to the exercise room.

"Can't be much fun," Forister said gently, "being in love with a girl who's likely to be unavailable for the next fifty Standard Years. And he doesn't have much to take his mind off it. He's not the type for tri-chess."

"Not bright enough, you mean. True," said Micaya with a trace of complacency. "And too bright for that silly game the prisoners are playing. Doesn't leave him much, you're right."

"Do you *really* have to monitor the prisoners all the time, Nancia?" Forister looked at her column with the smile that always melted her best resolutions. "Surely they'll do no damage while they're all wrapped up in that idiotic game. And if you think it's unfair to Micaya for you to partner me . . . we could play three-handed?"

Nancia had to concentrate a little harder for this display, but after a moment of intense processing the holocube shimmered, twisted, danced around its central core and reformed as a holohex, with three separate triple rows of pieces formed at opposing edges.

And in his cabin, Polyon de Gras-Waldheim stopped listening to the conversation in the central cabin and rejoined the SPACED OUT game that was currently helping his fellow prisoners to forget their troubles. Persuading Nancia to open the comm system so that the five of them could play from their cabins had been his first move. Now, at least, he could talk to the others. But he hadn't dared say anything beyond standard game moves while Nancia was conscientiously monitoring them.

The display screen showed that three of the game characters had managed to lose themselves in the Troll Tunnels. Polyon's own game icon was still at the mouth of the tunnels, awaiting a command from him. "I know how we can get out of the tunnels," he said.

"How? I've tried every exit the system shows. They're all blocked," Alpha complained.

"There's a secret key," Polyon told her. "I have it. But I can't get to the door it unlocks from here."

"I never heard anything about a secret key," Darnell announced. "I think you're bluffing." His game icon bounced angrily back along one of the Troll Tunnels, spitting sparks as it went.

"You wouldn't," Polyon said smoothly. "I'm the game master. This secret key can even override your character, Fassa."

Fassa had taken the Brainship icon for this game.

"I don't see how," Fassa responded. "Show me?"

"I *told* you. I can't get to where I can use it. If any of you can get me out of this blind alley, though—"

"You're not *in* a blind alley!" Darnell interrupted. "You're standing right at the entrance to the Troll Tunnels! Why don't you move your icon on into the tunnels?"

"And get lost like the rest of you? No, thanks." Polyon waved his hand over the palmpad and shut off the bickering voices of the gamesters. He brooded in silence for a while. Why had he ever bothered with such an inept bunch of conspirators? They were too stupid to pick up on his veiled hints. They thought he was interested in playing a *game*!

Blaize, now; Blaize was brighter than the others, and he'd taken no part in the brief exchange. Polyon tapped out a series of commands that would give him a private comm link to Blaize's cabin. At least he could hack into Nancia's system to that extent from the keyboard; though it was nothing to the power that would be his once he'd made his way to a reader slot with his minihedron.

While he thought out his approach to Blaize, he was startled by a crackle of sound. The idiot thought he'd achieved a private channel to the lounge! And what was he planning to do with it? Polyon scowled, then began to listen attentively. It seemed that Blaize was too bright to make a good tool.

But he might still be an excellent pawn, in a game whose moves he'd never see. . . .

"Uncle Forister?" Blaize switched comm channels to the lounge. "I need to talk to you."

"Talk," Forister grunted. He was just putting the final touches to a truly beautiful strategy, designed to pit Micaya's and Nancia's Brainship pieces against one another while he moved unopposed to control all vertices of the holohex.

"Privately."

"Oh, all right." Forister got up and stretched. "Nancia, can you store the holohex until I get back? I wouldn't want to tire you by asking you to maintain the display while we're not actually playing."

Nancia chuckled. "You mean you don't want to leave the holohex set up where we can study the positions and figure out what nasty trap you're getting ready to spring on us this time."

"Well . . ."

The holohex folded in upon itself and became a sheet, a line, a point of dazzling blue light that then winked out of existence. "All right. We're approaching the Singularity point, anyway; I really shouldn't be playing games now. Need to check my math," Nancia said cheerfully. "Be sure and get back in time to strap yourself in. You softpersons get so disoriented in Singularity."

"And you shellpersons get so uppity about it," Forister retorted. "All right. You'll warn us in plenty of time, I assume?"

"*And* monitor you while you're in the cabin," Nancia said. "Don't look like that; it's for Blaize's protection as well as yours. If you're left alone with him, the prosecution might try to discredit your testimony, say you'd been bribed or suborned."

"They won't have much respect for his uncle's good word anyway," said Forister gloomily, going on down the passageway to find out what Blaize had in mind. Nancia triggered the release mechanism on the door just long enough for him to slide through.

"I think Polyon's planning something," Blaize said as soon as Forister entered the cabin. He sat at the cabin console, one hand quivering over the palmpad without actually starting a program, all red-headed intensity like a fox at a rabbit hole.

"What?"

"I don't know. He wants to get out of his cabin. He keeps telling us that he can fix everything if only he could get out for a few minutes. Listen!" Blaize ran the heel of his hand over the palmpad and brought up a datacording of the last few transmissions between the SPACED OUT gamesters. From the cabin console he couldn't access enough memory to store images as well as voices; the players' words crackled out through the speaker, disembodied and robbed of half their meaning. Forister listened to the recorded exchange and shook his head.

"Just sounds like a few more moves in that dumb game of yours to me, Blaize."

"It's a move in a game, all right," Blaize said grimly, "but he's not playing the same game as the rest of us. Damn! I wish I'd been able to capture the images and the icon moves too. Then you'd see."

"See what?"

"That what Polyon was saying made absolutely no sense in the context of the actual game moves." Blaize dropped his hands in his lap and looked up at Forister. "Can Nancia keep Polyon under sleepgas until we reach Central?"

"She *can*," Forister replied, "but I've yet to see any reason why she *should*. This case is going to have all the High Families buzzing like uprooted stingherbs as it is; it'll only be worse if we give them some excuse to allege mistreatment of prisoners."

"But you heard him!"

"Didn't make any sense to me," Forister allowed, "but nothing about that silly game makes sense, in my humble opinion. Come on, Blaize. Can you seriously see me explaining to some High Court judge that I kept a prisoner stunned and unconscious for two solid weeks because something he said in the course of a children's game made me nervous?"

"I suppose not," Blaize agreed. "But—you'll be careful?"

"I am always careful," Forister told him.

"And—I don't think you should talk to him. The man's dangerous."

"I know you four are scared of him," Forister agreed, "but I think that's because you've been away from Central too long. He's nothing but an arrogant brat who was given more power than was good for him. Like some other people I could name. Now if you'll excuse me, it's nearly time to strap down for Singularity."

He nodded at the wall sensors and Nancia silently slid the door open for him.

Once he was in the passageway again, she spoke in a low voice.

"Polyon de Gras-Waldheim requests the favor of a private interview."

"He does, does he! And I suppose you think I ought to take

Blaize's warning seriously, and insist on having Micaya as a body-guard before I talk to him?"

"I think you're reasonably able to look after yourself," Nancia said, "especially with me listening in. It's not as if you were piloting a dumbship. But there's not much time; I'll be entering the first decomposition sequence in a few minutes."

"All the better," said Forister. "I won't have to spend too long with him. I'll talk with him until you sound the Singularity warning bell, if that's all right. Can't do much less. Visited Blaize—have to visit any of the others who request it."

When Forister entered, Polyon was lying on his bunk, arms folded behind his head. He turned at the soft sound of the slid-ing door, jumped to his feet and brought his heels together with a military precision that Forister found almost annoying.

"Sir!"

"I'm not," Forister said mildly, "your superior officer. You needn't click your heels and salute. You wanted to tell me something?"

"I—yes—no—I think not," Polyon said. His blue eyes looked haunted; he pushed a wayward strand of golden hair back from his forehead. "I thought——but he was my friend; I can't do it. Even to shorten my own sentence—no, it's impossible. I'm sorry to have disturbed you for nothing, sir."

"I think," Forister said gently, "you'd better tell me all about it, my boy." It was hard to reconcile the haunted creature before him with the monster who'd made Shemali prison into a living hell. Perhaps Polyon had some explanation he wished to proffer, some story about others who'd conceived the vicious factory system?

It took him a good five minutes of gentling Polyon's overac-tive sense of honor, all the time listening anxiously for the Sin-gularity warning bell, before he coaxed the boy into letting out a name.

"It's Blaize," Polyon said miserably at last. "Your nephew. I'm so sorry, sir. But—well, while we were playing SPACED OUT he was boasting to me of how he'd pulled the wool over your eyes, convinced you he was innocent of any wrongdoing—"

"Not quite," said Forister. He spoke very evenly to control the twist of pain that squeezed his chest. "He did sell PTA shipments on the black market. That's wrongdoing, in my book, and he'll be tried for it on Central."

Polyon nodded. His look of suffering had not abated. "Yes, he said that was the story he'd given you. Then I thought—if you didn't know—perhaps I could trade the information for a reduction in my own sentence."

"What information?" Forister asked sharply.

Polyon shook his head. "Never mind. It doesn't matter. I've enough on my conscience already," he said, raising his head and staring at the wall with a look of noble resignation that Forister found intensely irritating. "I won't compound my crimes by informing on a friend. It's all on this minihedron—well, never mind."

"What," asked Forister with the last vestiges of his patience, "what exactly is supposed to be on the minihedron?" He stared at the faceted black shape Polyon held in his hand, dark and baleful like the eye of an alien god.

"The true records of how Blaize made his fortune," Polyon said. "It's all there—he thought he'd concealed his tracks, but there were enough Net links for me to find the records. I'm very good with computers, you know," he said with a boy's naive pride. "But when I begged him to tell you the truth, he laughed at me. Said he had you convinced of his innocence and he saw no reason to change the situation. That was when I thought—but no," Polyon said, averting his face as he thrust out the minihedron towards Forister, "I don't want any favors."

Forister felt as queasy as though they had already entered Singularity. Was this why Blaize had tried so hard to keep him from talking to Polyon? He'd wanted to keep Polyon drugged and unconscious until they reached Central; he'd had that silly story about Polyon using the SPACED OUT game as a cover for some kind of plot. But what good would it do to keep Polyon from talking for two weeks, when his evidence—whatever it might be— would come out anyway at the trial?

"Just—you take this. Read it once. Then keep it safe—or wipe it if you want to," Polyon said, "*I* don't care. I just wanted to hand it over to—to somebody honorable." His voice broke slightly on the last word, and Forister thought there was a gleam of moisture in the corners of his eyes. "God knows, I can scarcely claim that for myself. You take it. You'll know what to do with the information."

"What is it?"

Polyon shook his head again. "I don't—I can't tell you. Go and read it in privacy. Just drop it into any of the ship's reader slots and have a look at the information. Then I'll leave it up to you to decide what should be done. And I don't," he said, almost savagely, "I *don't* want to profit from it, do you understand? Say you got it from somebody else. Or don't say where you got it. Or destroy it. Do what you want—it's off my conscience now, at any rate!"

He dropped back onto the bunk and buried his head in his arms. Overhead, the silvery chime of the first warning bell sounded. "Five minutes to Singularity," Nancia announced. "All passengers, please lie down or seat yourselves and secure free-fall straps. Tablets for Singularity sickness are available in all cabins; if you think you may be adversely affected by the transition, please medicate yourself now. Five minutes to Singularity."

Polyon fumbled without looking up, caught his free-fall strap and buckled it around himself. "Singularity," he said bitterly, "doesn't make me sick. But what's on that minihedron does."

Forister left the cabin with a sparkling black minihedron clutched in his hand, the facets cutting into his palms, his head awhirl with doubts.

"What a magnificent acting job!" Nancia commented with a low laugh.

"You think Polyon was lying?"

"I'm certain of it," she told him. "You know Polyon. You know Blaize. Is it credible for an instant that Blaize could have committed crimes that would turn Polyon's stomach?"

"I—don't know," Forister groaned. He dropped into the pilot's chair and stared unseeing at the console before him. Micaya Questar-Benn tactfully pretended to polish the gleaming buckle on her uniform belt. "Up to now, I'd have said—but I'm biased, you know."

"Well, I'm not," Nancia said decisively. "I don't know what Polyon's going on about, but whatever it is, I don't believe a word of it."

Forister laughed weakly. "You're biased too, dear Nancia." He stared at the sparkling surface of the minihedron, the polished opaque facets that gave nothing away, and sighed deeply. "I suppose I had better find out what this is."

"Can't it wait until after Singularity?" Nancia said, but too late. Forister had already dropped the datahedron into the reader slot.

Automatically, her mind already on the vortex of mathematical transformations ahead, Nancia absorbed the contents of the minihedron into memory. Something strange there, not like ordinary words, more like a tickle at the back of her head or an improperly positioned synaptic connector—

She rode the whirlwind down into Singularity, balancing and coasting along constantly changing equations that defined the collapsing walls of the vortex.

Something was wrong; she sensed it even before she lost her grasp on the mathematical transformations. She had never experienced a transition like this one. What was happening? Sounds as slimy as decaying weed whispered and snickered in her ears; colors beyond the edges of human perception rasped at her like fingernails being drawn over a blackboard. The balance of salts and fluids surrounding her shrunken human body swirled crazily, and a dozen alarm systems went off at once: *Overload! Overload! Overload!*

She couldn't optimize the path; spaces decomposed around her and shot off in an infinity of different recompositions, expanding in every path to lights and chaos that could tear her apart. The hyperchip-enhanced mathematics coprocessors returned gibberish. Her brain waves were strung out on the grid of a multi-dimensional matrix. Something was trying to invert the matrix. No computations matched previous results, and all directions held danger.

Nancia shut down all processing at once. The grating colors and stinking noises receded. She hung in blackness, refusing her own sensory inputs, balanced on the point of Singularity where decomposing subspaces intersected, with no way forward and no way back.

CHAPTER SEVENTEEN

Polyon was pacing the narrow space of his cabin, too impatient to strap himself in for Singularity, waiting for some sign that Forister had taken the bait, when the air shimmered and thickened around him.

He opened his mouth to curse his luck. The ship had entered Singularity before that thick-headed brawn ambled to a reader slot.

The air distorted into glassy waves, then became almost too thin to breathe. The cabin walls and furnishings receded to specks in the distance, then swam around him, huge menacing free-flowing shapes. Polyon's curses became a comical growl ending in a squeak.

Damn Singularity! There was no chance that Forister would drop the datahedron into a reader now, he'd be safely strapped into his pilot's chair like a good little brawn. By now, too, the ship's reader slots would probably be shut down for Singularity—and even if by some miracle he could persuade Nancia to accept the hedron, he still would not be able to enter the Net until the transformations were over and they had returned to normal space. No, he would have to wait until after the subspace transformation to implement Final Phase—and this transformation would bring the brainship into Central subspace, close to all the aid that Central Worlds and their innumerable fleets could give.

He reminded himself that this made no difference whatsoever.

The basic nature of the gamble remained the same. Either his plan had advanced far enough to succeed despite the way they were forcing his hand, or it hadn't. If it had, then the fleets of Central would be obedient to him and not to their former masters. If it hadn't—well, then, annihilation would be a little quicker than if he'd moved from the remote spaces around Nyota, that was all.

He had only to sit and wait. And waiting out a single transformation through Singularity should be nothing to him. He had already spent patient years waiting on Shemali, planting his seeds, watching them grow, seeding the universe, ever since he had the flash of brilliance which at once conceived the hyperchip design and saw how it could be twisted to his own ends.

But this waiting was harder than all those years in which he had at least been doing *something* to further those ends; and it seemed longer; and there was something disturbing about this particular ship's decomposition. Singularity wasn't supposed to be this bad. Polyon breathed and gagged on a sickly swirl of colors and smells and textures, looked down at the wavering distortions of his own limbs and closed his eyes momentarily. That was a mistake; Singularity sickness heaved through his guts. What was the matter? He'd been through plenty of decompositions during his Academy training, not to mention passing through this very same Singularity point on the way out to Vega subspace. Had he so completely lost conditioning in the five years on Shemali, to be gagging and puking like any new recruit now?

No. Something else was wrong. This decomposition was lasting too long. And some of the visual distortions looked oddly familiar. Polyon fixed his eyes on one small sector of the cabin, where braces supporting an extruded shelf formed a simple closed curve of permalloy and plastifilm. As he watched, the triangle of brace, wall and shelf elongated to a needle-shape with one thin eye, stretched out into an open eye as big as the wall, squeezed into a rotating pinpoint of light with absolute blackness at its center, and opened again into the original triangle. Needle, eye, pinpoint, triangle; needle, eye, pinpoint, triangle. They were caught in a subspace loop, perpetually decomposing and reforming in a sequence which preserved topological properties but which made no progress towards the escape sequence leading to Central subspace.

A loop like that couldn't have happened, shouldn't have

happened, unless the ship's processors had shut down. Or—a wild hope tantalized him—unless the ship's processors were too busy with some other problem to navigate them out of Singularity.

A problem like assimilating a worm program which would turn over all control to a single user, effectively cutting the brain off from her own body and its processing.

Polyon swallowed his unspoken curses and plunged across the cabin. He had some trouble locating the palmpad and holding his hand steady over it, but eventually he managed to match his shrinking and bending arm with the erratic loop of the ballooning palmpad. He slapped the surface twice. "Voice control mode!"

His own voice boomed oddly in his ears, the soundwaves distorted by the perpetual twisting of space around him, but evidently there was something unchanging in the voice patterns which his worm program still recognized. "Voice control acknowledged," an undulant voice boomed and twittered from the speakers.

"Unlock this cabin door." The first time the words came out as an unrecognizable squeak; the next, something close to his normal speaking voice emerged and the computer acknowledged the command. But nothing happened. A moment later the quavering vocal signal of the program responded with a shrill squeak that gradually became a groaning boom.

"Unable to identify designated entity."

Polyon was beginning to catch on to the rhythm of the subspace loop. If he kept his eyes fixed on any known point, like the triangle of shelf and wall and brace, he could recognize when they were passing through the decomposition closest to normal space. If he spoke then, residual subspace transformations still distorted his voice, but at least the computer could recognize and accept his orders.

He waited and spoke when the moment was right.

"Identify this cabin."

Lights flashed on the cabin control panel, rose and fluttered like fireflies trailing the liquid surface of the panel, swam into elongated hieroglyphics of an unknown language, and sank back into the panel's surface to become a pattern signaling failure.

"No such routine found."

Polyon cursed under his breath, and the subspace transformation loop twisted his words into a grating snarl. Something was wrong with his worm program. Somehow it had failed to complete its takeover of the ship's computer functions.

"General unlock," he snapped on the next loop through normal space.

His cabin door irised halfway open, then screeched and wobbled back and forth as the smooth internal glides had jammed on something. Polyon dove through, misjudged distances and clearance in the perpetual liquid shifting of the transformations, cracked a solid elbow on the very solid edge of the half-open door, landed on a bed of shifting sand, rolled, and found his feet in what was again, briefly, the solid passageway outside the cabin.

"Out! Everybody out!" The loop stretched his last word into a howl. *At least it got their attention.* A green slug oozed through one of the other doors and became Darnell, vomiting. Farther away, Blaize's red head blazed under lights that kept changing from electric blue to artificial sun to deepest shadow. Fassa was a china doll, white and neat and compact and perfect, but as the loop progressed she grew to her normal stature.

"What's happening?" The loop snatched away her words, but Polyon read her lips before the next phase stretched them into rubber. He waited for the next normal-space pass.

"Get Alpha. Don't want to have to explain twice."

Fassa nodded—Polyon thought it was a nod—and ducked into the cabin nearest hers. Darnell quivered and resumed his form as a giant green slug. The passageway elongated into a tunnel with Blaize at the far end, somehow aloof from the group.

Fassa reappeared, shaking her head. "She won't move. I—" She was bright, Fassa del Parma was; in mid-sentence, as space shifted around her, she waited until the next normspace pass to complete her sentence. "—think she's too frightened, I'm scared too. What's—"

Polyon didn't have time to waste listening to obvious questions. When the next normspace passed through them, he was ready to seize the moment. "I'm taking over the ship, is what's happening," he said over the tail-end of Fassa's question. "Any function on this ship that uses my hyperchips is under my command now. The reason—"

Shift, stretch, contract, waver, back to normal for a few seconds.

"—for this long transition is that the ship's brain is nonfunctional, can't get us out of Singularity."

Darnell wailed and vomited more loudly than before, drowning out Polyon's next words and wasting the rest of that normspace pass. Polyon waited, one booted foot contracting as he tapped it, stretching and looping over itself like a snake, then deflating again into the normal form of a regulation Academy boot.

"I can pilot us out of Singularity," he announced. "But I need to be at the control console. May have some trouble there. You'll have to help me take out the brawn and the cyborg."

"Why should we?" Blaize demanded.

Polyon smiled. "Afterwards," he said gently, "I won't forget who my friends are."

"What good—" Darnell, predictably, wanted to know, but the transformation loop washed away his question. And when normspace came round again, Blaize was closer to the rest of them; close enough to answer for Polyon.

"What good will his favor do? Quite a lot, I should imagine. It's not just the hyperchips on this ship, is it, Polyon? All the hyperchips Shemali has been turning out so fast have the same basic flaw, don't they?"

"I wouldn't," said Polyon, "necessarily define it as a flaw. But you're right. Once we're out of Singularity and ready to access the Net again, this ship's computer will broadcast Final Phase to every hyperchip ever installed. I'll have—"

They'd all caught on to the rhythm of the transformation loop by now; the wait through three distorted subspaces was becoming part of normal conversational style.

"—control of the universe," he finished on the next pass through normspace. Blaize had come closer yet; stupid little runt, trying to move during transformations.

"And we'll be your loyal lieutenants?" Blaize asked.

"I know how to reward service," Polyon said noncommittally. *Into a Ganglicide vat with you, troublemaker, as soon as I have the power.*

"Not if I know it," Blaize mouthed as normspace slid away into the first distortion. He swung a fist at Polyon, but before it landed his hand had shrunk to the size of a walnut, and on the next dip through normspace Polyon was ready for him with a return blow that sent Blaize to the deck. By the time he landed, it was soft as quicksand, a pool in which Blaize swirled, too dizzy to rise immediately.

"Stop me," Polyon said to the other two as normspace passed through, "and you die here, in Singularity, because nobody else can get us out of it. Try to stop me and fail," and he smiled again, very sweetly, "and you'll wish you *had* died here. Are you with me?"

Before they could answer, a new element entered the game; a hissing cloud of gas, invisible in normspace, dearly delineated as a pink-rimmed flood of rosy light in the first transformational space. It engulfed Blaize and he stopped twitching, lay like one dead in the yielding transformations of the deck.

Sleepgas. And he couldn't shout through the loop to warn them. Polyon clapped both hands over his mouth and nose, saw that Fassa did the same, jerked his head towards the central cabin. That door too was half open. He made for it, staggering through mud and quicksand, swimming through air gone thick as water, lungs aching and burning for a breath. Fell through, someone pushing behind him, Fassa, and Darnell after her. Forget Blaize, the traitor, and Alpha, by now sleepgassed in her cabin. Polyon gasped and with his first burning breath called, "General lock!"

The control cabin door irised shut with a strange jerky motion, as if it were fighting its own mechanism, and Polyon found his feet and surveyed his new territory.

Not bad. The only passenger he'd been seriously worried about was Sev Bryley-Sorensen. But Bryley wasn't here. Good. He was locked out, then, with Alpha and Blaize; probably sleepgassed, like them. The other two were bent over their consoles, probably still trying to figure out why doors were opening and closing without their command, trying to flood the passenger areas with sleepgas—well, they'd succeeded there, but much good it would do them now! Through the transitions he saw them turning in their seats, open mouths stretching like taffy in the second subspace, then shrinking to round dots in the third. Normspace showed the cyborg freak making a move that wasn't part of the transformation illusion, right arm darting towards her belt. Polyon snapped out a command and the freak's prosthetic arm and leg danced in their sockets, twisting away from the joining point; her flesh-and-blood torso followed the agonizing pull of the synthetic limbs and she rotated half out of her seat. Another command, and the prostheses dropped lifeless and heavy to the floor, dragging the body down with them. Her head cracked against the support pillar under the seat. Polyon stepped forward to take the needler before she recovered. Space stretched away from him, but his arm stretched with it, and the solid heavy feel of the needler reassured him that his fingers, even if they momentarily resembled tentacles, had firm hold of the weapon.

With the next normspace pass he was erect again, holding the needler on Forister. "Over there." With a jerk of his head he indicated the central column. Somewhere behind there the brain of the ship floated within a titanium shell, a shrunken malformed body kept alive by tubes and wires and nutrient systems. Polyon shuddered at the thought; he'd never understood why Central insisted on keeping these monsters alive, even giving them responsible positions that could have been filled by real people like himself. Well, the brain would be mad by now, between sense deprivation and the stimuli he'd ordered its own hyperchips to throw at it; killing it would be a merciful release. And it would be appropriate to kill the brawn at the foot of the column.

But not yet. Polyon was all too aware that he didn't know everything there was to know about navigating a brainship. He would need full support from both computers and brawn if he was to get them out of this transition loop alive.

He studied the needler controls, spun the wheel with his thumb, glanced at Darnell and Fassa. Which of them dared he trust? Neither, for choice; well, then, which was more afraid of him? Fassa had been showing an uppity streak, asking him questions when she should have been listening. Darnell was still green-faced but appeared to be through vomiting. Polyon tossed him the needler; it floated through normspace and Darnell caught it reflexively just before the transition shrunk it to a gleaming line of permalloy.

"If either of them makes a move," Polyon said pleasantly, "needle them. I've set it to kill . . . slowly." In fact he'd left the needler as Micaya had it, set to deliver a paralyzing but not lethal dose of paravenin; but there was no need to reassure his captives overmuch. "Now . . ." He removed his uniform jacket, draped it neatly over the swivelseat where Micaya had been sitting, and sat down in Forister's chair before the command console. Transitions exaggerated the slight flourish of his wrists into a great ballooning gesture, spun out his sleeves into white clouds of fabric that floated over and dwarfed the other occupants of the cabin.

"What do you think you're doing?" Forister cried. His voice

squeaked through the fourth transition space and fell with a thud on the last word.

Polyon smiled. He could see his own teeth and hair gleaming, white and gold, in the mirror-bright panel. "I," he said gently, "am going to get us out of Singularity. Don't you think it's time somebody did it?"

His reflection narrowed, gave him a squashed face like a bug, dulled the bright gold of his hair and turned his teeth to green rotting stumps. The control panel shrank under his hands, then swelled and heaved like a storm-tossed sea. As normspace approached Polyon darted in, tapping out one set of staccato commands with his right hand, passing the left over the palmpad to call up Nancia's mathematics coprocessors, rattling out the verbal commands that would bring the whole ship around, responsive to his commands and ready to sail the subspaces out of this Singularity.

She was sluggish as any water-going vessel lacking a rudder and taking in water, half the engines obeying his commands, the other half canceling them. The mathematics co-processors came online and then disappeared before he'd entered the necessary calculations, shrieking gibberish and sliding away in a jumble of meaningless symbols. The moment of normspace passed and Polyon ground his teeth in frustration. In the second transformation the teeth felt like squishy, rotting vegetables inside his mouth, then in the third they became needles that drew blood, and by the time normspace returned he had learned not to give way to emotion.

He made two more attempts at controlling the ship, waited out three complete transition loops, before he pushed the pilot's chair back from the control panel.

"Your brainship is fighting me," he told Forister on the next pass through normspace.

"Good for her!" Forister raised his voice slightly. "Nancia, girl, can you hear me? Keep it up!"

"Don't be a fool, Forister," Polyon said tiredly. "If your brainship were conscious and coherent, she'd have brought us out of Singularity herself."

He used the remaining seconds in normspace to tap out one more command. The singing tones of Nancia's access code rang through the room. Forister's face went gray. Then the transition spaces whirled about them, monstrously transforming the cabin and everything in it, and Polyon could not tell which of the distorted images before him showed the opening of Nancia's titanium column.

On the next pass through normal space he saw that the column was still closed. Transition must have garbled the last sounds in the access sequence. He typed in the command again; again the musical tones rang out without their accompanying syllables; again nothing happened.

"You'd better tell me the rest of the code," he said to Forister on the next normspace pass.

Forister smiled—briefly; something in the expression reminded Polyon of his own ironic laughter. "What makes you think I have it, boy? The two parts are kept separate. I didn't even know how to access the tone sequence from Nancia's memory banks. The syllables probably aren't encoded in her at all; they'll be on file at Central."

"Brawns are supposed to know the spoken half of the code," Polyon snapped in frustration.

"I asked to have it changed just before this run," Forister claimed. "Security reasons. With so many prisoners on board, I feared a takeover attempt—and with good reason, it seems."

"I do hope you're lying," Polyon said. He clamped his mouth shut and waited through the transition loop, marshaling his arguments. "Because if Central's the only source for the rest of the code, we're all dead. I can't tap the Net and hack into the Courier Service database from Singularity—and I can't get us out of Singularity without neutralizing the brain."

"You mean, without killing Nancia," Forister said in a voice emptied of feeling. His eyes flickered once to the cabin console. Polyon followed the man's gaze and felt a moment of fear. A delicate solido stood above the control panels, the image of a lovely young woman with an impish smile and clustering curls of red hair.

Polyon had heard of brawns who developed an emotional fixation on their brainship, even to the point of having a solido made from the brainship's genotype that would show how the freakish body might have matured without its fatal defects. He hadn't guessed that Forister was the sentimental type, or that he'd have had time to grow so attached to Nancia. The idiot might actually think that he'd rather die than kill his brainship.

"There's no need to clutter the problem with emotionalism," Polyon told him. How could he jolt Forister out of his sentimental fixation? "With partial control of the ship to me and partial control to Nancia, neither of us can navigate out of Singularity."

Damn the transition loop! Forister had caught on to the rhythm by now; and the necessary wait while three distorted subspaces composed and decomposed around them gave him time to think.

"I've a better suggestion," the brawn said. "You *say* you can navigate us out; well, we all *know* Nancia can. Restore full control to her, and—"

"And what? You'll drop charges, let me go back to running a prison factory? I've got a better career plan than that now."

"I wasn't," said Forister mildly, "planning to make that offer."

The rhythm of collapsing and composing subspaces was becoming natural to them all; the necessary pauses in their conversation no longer bothered Polyon.

"I had something like your own offer in mind," Forister continued at the next opportunity. "Release Nancia's hyperchip-enhanced computer systems, and she'll get us out of Singularity—and you'll live."

"How did you guess?"

Forister looked surprised. "Logical deduction. You designed the hyperchips; you tricked me into running a program that did something peculiar to Nancia's computer systems; the failure reports I read just before you came in showed precisely the areas where she has had hyperchips installed, the lower deck sensors and the navigation system; you've since exercised voice control on Micaya's hyperchip-enhanced prostheses. Clearly your hyperchip design includes a back door by which you can personally control any installation that uses your chips."

"Clever," Polyon said. "But not clever enough to get you out of Singularity. I assure you I'm not going to restore full computing power to a brainship who is probably mad by now."

"What makes you think that?"

Polyon raised his brows. "We all know what sensory deprivation does to shellpersons, Forister. Need I go into the details?"

"Take more than a few minutes in the dark to upset my Nancia," Forister said levelly.

Polyon bared his teeth. "By now, old man, she's had considerably more than that to deal with. The first thing my hyperchip worm does is to strike at any intelligence linked to the computers in which it finds itself. The sensory barrage would make any human break the link at once. I'm afraid that 'your' Nancia, not being able to escape the link that way, will have gone quite mad by now. So—I think—if you want to live—you'll tell me, *now*, the rest of the access code."

"I think not," Forister said calmly. "You've made a fatal error in your calculations."

The transition loop stifled all talk for the endless winding, looping moments of passage through shrinking and distorting spaces. Polyon ignored the sensory tricks of spatial transformations and thought furiously. When normspace returned, he reached up from his chair to grasp the solido of Nancia as a young woman. Deliberately, watching Forister's face, he dropped the solido on the deck and ground the fragile material to shards under his boot-heel.

"*That's* what's left of 'your' Nancia, old man," he said. "Are you going to let your love for a woman who never lived kill us all?"

Forister's face was lined with pain, but he spoke as evenly as always. "My—feelings—for Nancia have nothing to do with the matter. Your error is much more basic. You think I'd rather set you free with the universe in your control than die here in Singularity. This is incorrect."

He spoke so calmly that it took Polyon a moment to understand the words, and in that moment the transition loop warped the room and disguised the movements in it. When they passed through normspace again, Fassa del Parma was standing between Forister and Darnell, as if she thought she could shield the brawn from a direct needler spray.

"He's right," she said. "I didn't have time to think before. You're a monster."

Polyon laughed without humor. "Fassa, dear, to righteous souls like Forister and General Questar-Benn we're all monsters. I should have remembered how you sucked up to them before, helping them trick me. Did you think that would save you? They'll use you and throw you away like your father did."

Fassa went white and still as stone. "We don't all take such a simple-minded view of the universe," Forister said. "But, Fassa, you can't—"

Darnell's fingers were twitching. Polyon nodded. Slowly, too slowly, Darnell raised the needler. He gave Forister ample time to grasp Fassa by the shoulders and spin her out of danger. As Forister moved, the cabin seemed to lurch and the lights dimmed. Gravity fell to half-normal, then to nothing, and as Fassa spun into midair the reaction of Forister's thrust pushed him in the opposite direction. The spray of needles went wide, but one bright line on the far edge of the arc stung through Forister's sleeve and bloodied his wrist. The blood danced out across the cabin in bright droplets that the transition loop pulled out into bloody seas; Polyon watched a bubble the size of a small pond float inexorably toward him, settle around him with a clammy grip, then shrink to a bright button-sized stain on his shirt front.

Fassa floated back to grasp Forister's flaccid body and cry, "Why did you do that? I wanted to save you!"

"Wanted him—to kill me," Forister breathed. The paravenin was fighting the contractions of his chest. "Without me—no way to get Nancia's code. Trapped here, all of us—better than letting him go? Forgive me?"

"Death before dishonor." Polyon put a sneering spin on the words, letting the maudlin pair hear what he thought of such brave slogans. "And it will be death, too. See how the ship's systems are failing? What do you think will go next? Oxygen? Cabin pressure?"

In the absence of direct commands, gravity and lighting should have been controlled by Nancia's autonomic nervous functions. Forister groaned as the meaning of this latest failure came through to him.

"She's dying anyway. With or without your help," Polyon drove the point home. "And *you're* not dead yet. I lied to you. The needler was only set to paralyze. Now let's have the access code before Nancia stops breathing and kills us all."

Forister shook his head with slow, painful twitches.

"Come here, Fassa, dear," Polyon ordered.

"No. I stay with him."

"You don't really mean that," Polyon said pleasantly. "You know you're far too afraid of me. Remember those shoddy buildings you put up on Shemali? You replaced them free of charge, remember, and I didn't even have to do any of the interesting things we discussed. But if I'd threaten you with flaying alive for cheating me over a factory, Fassa, just think for a moment what I'll do to you for interfering with me now."

The transition loop was almost a help; the pauses it forced gave Fassa time to consider her brave stand.

"Go on, Fassa," Forister urged when normal speech was possible again. "You can't help me now, and I've no wish to see you hurt for my sake."

"Thank you for the information," Polyon said with a courteous bow. "Perhaps I'll try that next. But I think we'll begin with an older and dearer friend for quick results. Darnell, bring the freak—no, I'll do it; you keep the needler on Fassa, just in case she gets any silly ideas."

Holding onto the pilot's chair to keep himself in place, Polyon turned and aimed a loose kick at Micaya Questar-Benn. The cessation of ship's gravity had freed her of the artificially weighted prostheses that held her down, but the arm and leg were still flopping loose, free of her control. She was as good as a cripple— she was a cripple, disgusting sight.

"I want Forister to get a good view of this," he told her politely. "Lock prostheses."

This to the computer; a signal to the hyperchips clamped Micaya's artificial arm and leg together.

"Lay a finger on Mic—" Forister threatened, struggling vainly against the effects of the paravenin.

"I won't need to," Polyon said with a brilliant smile. "I can do it all from here."

A series of brisk verbal commands and typed-in codes caused the portion of the ship's computer that Polyon controlled to transmit new, overriding instructions to the hyperchips controlling Micaya's internal organ replacements. The changes had the full duration of a transition loop to take effect. When they returned to normspace, Micaya's face was colorless and beads of sweat dotted her forehead.

"It's amazing how painful a few simple organic changes can be," Polyon commented gaily. "Little things like fiddling with the circulation, for instance. How's that hand, Mic, baby? Bothering you a bit?"

"Come a little closer," Micaya invited him, "and find out." But now Polyon had drawn attention to her one remaining hand; they could all see how it had changed color. The fingernails were almost black, the skin was purplish and swollen.

"Keep it like that for a week," Polyon said, "and she'll have a glorious case of gangrene. Of course, we don't have a week. I could trap even more blood in the hand and burst the veins, but that might kill her too fast. So I'll just leave it like that while you think it over, Forister, and maybe we'll start working on the foot as well. Fortunately, the heart's one of her cyborg replacements, so we don't have to worry about it failing under the increased demands; it'll go on working . . . as long as I want it to. Want to hear how well it works now?"

A word of command amplified the sound of Micaya's artificial heart beating vehemently, the pulse rate going up to support the demands Polyon was making on the rest of her system. The desperate, ragged double beat echoed through the cabin, droned and drummed and shrilled through a complete transition loop, and no one spoke or moved.

For a heartbeat, no more, Nancia found silence and darkness a welcome relief from the stabbing pain of the input from her rogue sensors. *Is this what Singularity is like for softpersons?* But no, it was worse than that. In the confused moments before she shut down all conscious functions and disabled her own sensor connections, she had been aware of something much worse than the colorshifts and spatial distortions of Singularity; the malevolence of another mind, intimately entwined with her own, striking at her with deliberate malice.

He means to drive me mad. If I enable my sensors again, he'll do it. And if I stay floating in this darkness, that will do it too. The bleak desperation of the thought came from somewhere far back in her memories. When, how, had she ever felt so utterly abandoned before? Nancia reached out, unthinking, to search her memory banks—then stopped before the connection was complete. If sensors could be turned into weapons to use against her, could not memory, too, be infiltrated? Access the computer's memory banks, and she might find herself "knowing" whatever this other mind wanted her to believe.

Is it another mind? Or a part of myself? Perhaps I'm mad already, and this is the first symptom. The flashing, disorienting lights and garbled sounds, the sickening whirling sensations, even the conviction that she was under attack by another mind—weren't all these symptoms of one of those Old Earth illnesses that had ravaged so many people before modern electrostim and drug therapy restored the balance of their tortured brains? Nancia longed to scan just one of the encyclopedia articles in her memory banks; but that resource was denied her for the moment. Paranoid schizophrenia, that was it; a splitting off of the mind from reality.

Let's see, now—she reasoned. *If I'm mad, then it's safe to look up the symptoms and decide that I'm mad, except that presumably I won't accept the evidence. And if I'm not mad, I daren't check memory to prove it. So we'd better accept the working hypothesis that I am sane, and go on from there.* The dry humor of the syllogism did something to restore her emotional balance. *Although how long I will remain sane, under these circumstances . . .*

Better not to think about that. Better, too, not to remember Caleb's first partner, who had gone into irreversible coma rather than face the emptiness that surrounded him after the synaptic connections between his shell and the outside world had been destroyed. As a matter of sanity, as well as survival, Nancia decided, she would make the assumption that somebody had done this to her, and concentrate on solving the puzzle of who had done it and how they could be stopped.

A natural first step would be to reopen just one sensor, to examine the bursts of energy that had come so close to disrupting her nervous system. . . . *I can't!* the child within her shrieked in near-panic. *You can't make me, I won't, I won't, I'll stay safe in here forever.*

That's not an option, Nancia told herself firmly. She wanted to say it aloud, to reassure herself with the sound of her own voice; but she was mute as well as deaf and blind and without sensation, floating in an absolute blackness. Somehow she had to conquer that panic within herself.

Poetry sometimes helped. That Old Earth dramatist Sev and Fassa were so fond of quoting; she had plenty of his speeches stored in her memory banks. *On such a night as this . . .* Nancia reached unthinking for memory, stopped the impulse just in time. She *didn't* know that speech; she had stored it in memory. Quite a different thing. Try something else, then. *I could be bounded in a nutshell, and count myself king of infinite space, were it not that I have bad dreams. . . .* Not a good choice, under the circumstances. Maybe . . . did she know anything else? What was she, without her memory banks, her sensors, her powerful thrusting engines? Did she even exist at all?

That way lies madness. Of course she existed. Deliberately Nancia filled herself with her own true memories. Scooting around the Laboratory Schools corridors, playing Stall and Power-Seek with her friends. Acing the math finals, from Lobachevski Geometry up through Decomposition Topology, playing again, with all the wonderful space of numbers and planes and points to wander in. Voice training with Ser Vospatrian, the Lab Schools' drama teacher, who'd taught them to modulate their speaker-produced vocalizations through the full range of human speech with all its emotional overtones. That first day they'd all been shy and nervous, hating the recorded playbacks of their own tinny artificial voices; Vospatrian had made them recite limericks and nonsense poems until they broke down in giggles and forgot to be self-conscious. Goodness, she could still remember those silly poems with which he'd started off every session. . . .

And quite without thinking or calling on her artificially augmented memory banks, Nancia was off.

> *"The farmer's daughter had soft brown hair,*
> *Butter and eggs and a pound of cheese,*
> *And I met with a poem, I can't say where,*
> *Which wholly consisted of lines like these. . . ."*

> *"There was a young brainship of Vega. . . ."*

> *"Fhairson swore a feud against the clan M'Tavish;*
> *Marched into their land to murder and to ravish,*
> *For he did resolve to extirpate the vipers*
> *With four-and-twenty men and five-and-thirty pipers . . ."*

Nancia went through Ser Vospatrian's entire repertoire until she was giggling internally and floating on the natural high of laughter-produced endorphins. Then, floating quite calmly in her blackness, she set about testing her sensor connections one by one.

She got the mental equivalent of burned fingers and light-blinded eyes more than once during the testing process, but it wasn't as bad as she had feared. The lower-deck sensors were completely useless, as were her navigation computer and the new mathematics and graphics co-processors she'd just invested in. *Everything, in fact, that contains hyperchips from Shemali . . .* and with that deduction, Nancia knew just who was striking at her and why.

She opened the upper deck sensors one by one, first taking in the sleeping bodies tumbled in the passageway and cabins. Sev, slumped over the isometric spring set in the exercise room with his hands and feet still in the springholders; Alpha, strapped in her cabin; Blaize, floating just above the passageway deck, with an angelic expression on his sleeping face and a nasty bruise coming up on his chin.

Mutiny. And somebody released sleepgas. But which side? She opened the control cabin sensors slowly, cautiously. The port side sensors wavered and gave an erratic display. Somehow Polyon's hyperchips must be working to contaminate the entire computer system. *I don't have much time. . . .*

Even less time than she'd thought, Nancia realized as she took in the standoff in the control room. General Questar-Benn disabled—*of course, the hyperchips in her prostheses*—and Darnell holding her needler on a defiant Forister while Polyon sat in the pilot's chair and played his commands on the computer console. That, at least, she could do something about. Nancia struck back, sending her own commands to the computer, disabling the console section by section, garbling Polyon's commands as they came in. He tapped out a sequence she did not know; she traced it to its source and with shock recognized her own access code. The musical tones were already sounding in the cabin. But the accompanying syllables weren't stored in the same location. . . . *They have to be somewhere, though. In some part of memory not accessible to my conscious probe. Otherwise my shell wouldn't recognize and open to them.* Nancia felt proud of herself for figuring that out, then cold and sick as she wondered how long it would take Polyon to make the same deduction. *And if the syllables aren't where I can consciously retrieve them, how can I block Polyon against doing so?*

She felt queasy from the repeated looping through four decomposition spaces, but there was no safe way to leave the loop until she regained full computing and navigational facility. *First, let's repair the damage. . . .* Nancia worked furiously, permanently disabling the sections of her computer system that had been contaminated by the Shemali hyperchips, finding alternative routings to access the processors that remained untouched. At the same time the worm program unleashed by Polyon squirmed deeper into her system, changing and mutating code as it went, erasing its own tracks so that she could only tell where it had been by the sudden flares of disorienting sense input or the garbled mathematics where it had been. She had to find and stop that code before she could do anything else.

Deep in the intricacies of her own system, Nancia agonized as Darnell struck down Forister.

Don't listen. Don't think about that. She would need all her concentration to disable Polyon's rogue code, more concentration than she'd ever brought to bear on the comparatively trivial problems of subspace navigation. Nancia remembered Sev Bryley's training in relaxation and deliberately, slowly calmed herself, drawing energy away from her extremities and centering her consciousness on the internal core of light where she existed independent of computer and shell and ship. With some remote part of her awareness she sensed the failure of gravitational systems and the dimming of lights, the shock and concern of her passengers, but she could not afford to divert consciousness to those semi-automatic functions now.

The automatic datacording routines Nancia had set up continued to operate as Polyon began Micaya's torture. Nancia could not counter his commands without breaking her trance; she could not even restore gravity and lights to reassure Forister. Ignoring Micaya's pain was the hardest thing she had ever done. *For the moment, Micaya does not exist. Nothing exists outside this place, this moment, this center.* There was the rogue code; she annihilated it in a blaze of energy, destroying deep memory in the process; like an amputation, she thought, the shaft of pain and the nagging ache afterwards. Now to restore lost functions . . . Ruthlessly she cut back on the frills and luxuries of her programming, reducing the power that normally fed her autonomic functions. Lights dimmed even further in the control cabin, and the softpersons made comments about an acrid smell in the air. They would just have to put up with it; she needed that processing power to restore her crippled nav programs. Three of the four major math coprocessors were lost; the graphics processor could double for one of them. No time to think about the others. Nancia erased unnecessary programs and dumped others to datahedron, making space in what little remained of her memory for the processes she had to have. Would that be enough? No chance for tests, no time for second thoughts. She struck back, once, with everything she had; felt hyperchips shriveling to blank bits of permalloy, felt inactive sensors and processors become dead weights instead of living systems.

Some animals will gnaw off their own limbs to get out of a trap....

No time to mourn, either. With the "death" of the hyperchips within Nancia's system, the transmissions that tortured Micaya's cyborgans ceased. The sound of her amplified heartbeat ended between one drum beat and the next. Forister groaned. *He thinks I'm dead.* He would be reassured in a moment. Nancia activated full artificial gravity; Darnell fell to the deck from his wall perch, Fassa went to her knees. Polyon staggered but remained standing. Nancia beamed commands to the tanglefield wires. Darnell, Polyon and Fassa were frozen in place, nets of moving lights encompassing the tanglefield keys at their wrists and ankles and necks. Finally, Nancia spared a little power to bring up the cabin lights and freshen the air.

"FN-935 reporting for duty," she said. "I apologize for any temporary inconvenience...."

"Nancia!" Forister sounded close to tears.

"General Questar-Benn, can you take the pilot's seat?" Nancia requested. "I may need a little help to navigate us out of Singularity."

"Do my best." Micaya's breathing was still ragged, and she leaned heavily on the chair beside her, but she limped to the pilot's seat without help, the prostheses once again responding to her own brain's electrical impulses. "What can I do?"

"I am operating with only one mathematics coprocessor," Nancia told her, "and my navigation units are nonfunctional. When I start the drives, we will move out of this transition loop and into the expansion of whatever subspace we happen to be in. I'll try to maintain a steady path through the subspace options, but I may need you to aid in the navigation. Since the graphics processor is undamaged, I will throw up images of the approaching subspaces. Rest your hand on the palmpad and give me a direction at each branch."

"Do my best," Micaya said again, but Nancia noticed it was the prosthetic hand she rested on the palmpad; the other hand was still an ugly purple color, with blackened moons on the swollen fingertips. She remembered what Polyon had said about gangrene. How much had his hyperchips accelerated Micaya's metabolic processes? *Get her to a medic... but I can't do that unless somebody helps me surf out of Singularity... and we daren't wait for the paravenin to wear off Forister....*

Then Nancia had no more energy to spare for worrying about Micaya or anything else but the waves of transformations that broke over her head, tossed and tumbled her gasping through subspaces that deformed her body and everyone within, streams of calculations that escaped her processors. Lost and choking, she sensed a firm hand guiding her upwards . . . out. . . . She crunched the last numbers into a tractable series of equations and broke through the chaos of uncountably infinite subspaces into the blessed normalcy of RealSpace.

Before she had time to thank Micaya, a tightbeam communication assaulted her weakened comm center. "Back so soon, FN? What's the matter? I thought you were headed for Central."

It was Simeon, the Vega Base managing brain. "We had a small virus problem," Nancia beamed back. "Returned for . . . repairs."

The rest of the story could wait until she had absolute privacy. There was no need to alert the galaxy to the fact that an unknown number of their computer systems were contaminated by Shemali hyperchips.

"Is everything under control now?"

"You could say that," Nancia replied dryly, turning up her remaining sensors and looking over her internal condition. Half her processors burned out, sleeping bodies littering the passenger quarters, three High Families brats secured in tanglefield and mad as hell, Forister twitching with the pins-and-needles of paravenin recovery, and a crippled general bringing them safe into RealSpace—

"Yes," she told Simeon. "Everything's under control."

CHAPTER EIGHTEEN

In the days of repair work that followed, Nancia began to understand just how much Caleb must have hated being grounded on Summerlands while she went on with a new brawn to complete the task they had begun. Now she, too, was "convalescent" and temporarily out of the action. To protect herself from the insidious effects of Polyon's hyperchips she had, in effect, crippled herself, rendering large parts of her own system inoperable; to keep the worm program he had implanted from contacting other hyperchips once they got out of Singularity and could make Net contact again, she had slashed through her own memory, ruthlessly excising whole sections of memory banks and operating code.

"It's a miracle you made it back here in one piece," Simeon of Vega Base told her, "and you're not leaving Base until you've had a very thorough overhaul and repair. Those aren't my orders, they're a beam from CS. So no argument!"

"I wasn't planning to argue," said Nancia with, for her, unaccustomed meekness. Indeed, after the stresses of that prolonged stay in Singularity, followed by the limping return voyage on one-third power, she had very little desire to do anything but park herself in orbit around Vega Base and watch the stars wheel by.

Or so she told herself. She *was* tired and injured; she wasn't up to the stressful task of transporting the prisoners and witnesses back to Central for trial. It was far more sensible to prepare a datahedron of her own testimony, something that could be sent back on the bright new Courier Service ship that came to collect the others.

"I'll miss you," Forister said, "but you'll be back in action soon, Nancia. Why, at the speed Central works, you'll probably be returning before the trial's over! And if you don't"—he hefted the gleaming weight of the megahedron in one hand—"this is as good, for all legal purposes, as having you there. You've transferred datacordings of everything that happened on board or that you perceived through your contact buttons, right? Should be the most complete—and most damning—record we could ask for."

"It—may not be as complete as you expect," Nancia said. "I have some memory gaps, you know."

"Yes, I know. But having you there in person—well, via contact button, I suppose—wouldn't make any difference to that, would it? If something's been lost from your memory banks, it won't come back under cross-examination."

That was true enough, Nancia supposed; and if the damage to her memory banks were the only cause of gaps in the recording, there'd be no reason at all for her to undergo cross-examination. The subject was not one she wished to discuss in any detail. She said good-bye to Forister, tried to control the twinge of loneliness she felt when the new CS ship took off, and went back to her observations of the stars of Vega subspace. Stars were restful; bright and calm, in unchanging patterns as familiar to her as—as—

Nancia discovered that she could no longer "remember" the names of the constellations as they appeared in Vega subspace. She had never spent long enough in this subspace to establish the look of the sky in her own human memory; and the navigational maps that she relied on had been erased. So had her tables of Singularity points and decomposition algorithms, her Capellan music recordings. . . .

"Do you know, I'm sorry I used to laugh at softpersons," she said thoughtfully to Simeon while the techs buzzed about her, removing the melted blobs that had been hyperchips, restoring connections and sensors, building in new blank memory banks to be loaded with whatever information she requested. "I never realized how crippled they are, having to rely on no more skills and information than they can store in an organic brain."

"It's not nice to laugh at the handicapped," Simeon agreed gravely. "I trust this has been a learning experience for you, young FN. Would you like me to help you prepare a list of data requests for your new memories?"

"Yes, please," Nancia said, "and"—this she did remember, the frustration of listening to the medical jargon of the techs at Summerlands working on Caleb—"do you think I can afford a classical education? Latin and Greek vocabularies and syntax?"

"I'll indent for the Loeb Classical Hedron," Simeon said. "That has twenty-six Old Earth languages plus all the major literature."

"And—" she didn't want to go too far into debt—"a medical set? Pharmacology, Internals, and Surgical?"

"Should be standard equipment on any ship gets into as much trouble as you do," Simeon agreed.

"Yes, but can I afford it? I've lost some accounting data; I don't know how my credit stands with Courier Service—"

Simeon came as near to a laugh as Nancia had ever heard from him. "FN, trust me, the bonus for this last job, plus the hazardous service pay, will cover any frills you want to request *and* go a long way towards paying off your debt to Lab Schools. Pull off a couple more like this and you'll be a paid-off shell, your own woman. In fact," he added thoughtfully, "there's no reason why you should pay for the classical and medical hedra. I'll just slip those in as part of the replacement list, which is charged to Central—"

"*No,*" Nancia said firmly. "That's how it starts."

"How what starts?"

"You know. Darnell. Polyon. Everything."

"Oh. Well, I see what you mean, but it is a gray area, you know . . ."

"Not," Nancia said, "for House Perez y de Gras. I'll buy the extra skills hedra myself, out of my bonus. From the figures you just beamed up, I'll have more than enough to pay honestly for those 'frills' and any other expenses I may incur during this stay,"

But that was before she discovered the item that would strain her budget to its limits.

Nancia's repairs were nearly finished when Caleb, now walking without a stick and looking even more muscular than before, landed at Vega Base and requested permission to come aboard.

Nancia exclaimed in delight at the bronzed, fit young man she saw stepping out of the airlock.

"My goodness, Caleb, you look as if you'd never been ill a day in your life."

"There wasn't much to do at Summerlands," Caleb said dismissively. "It's a sin to waste time; I worked out in the physical therapy rooms most of the time while they were fussing over final tests and declaring me fit for duty again. What's our next assignment?"

"Our?"

"You didn't think I'd desert you? You made some errors of judgment while I was away, Nancia, but nothing that can't be repaired. In fact," Caleb added, looking around the gleaming interior from which all traces of OG Shipping's mauve and puce had finally been removed, "it looks as if the repairs are just about finished."

"They are, but Caleb, I—I'm partnered with Forister now," Nancia said. She felt guilty as she said the words; suppose Caleb felt that she was rejecting him? But it was the simple truth. Her call sign was FN-935 now, not CN.

"Temporary assignment," Caleb brushed that aside. "Now I've been pronounced fit again, Forister can go back into comfortable retirement. No need for him to continue straining himself in tasks he's really not up to. Take this last debacle. You're not to blame, Nancia, being young and inexperienced, but you must see that it was handled all wrong. If . . ."

While Caleb blithely explained the mistakes Forister had made and how he, with the benefit of hindsight, could have done so much better, Nancia attempted to control some new and unfamiliar sensations.

Simeon, she tightbeamed to the managing brain, *is there a malfunction in my repaired circuits? My sensors show a temperature rise and high conductivity, and I'm picking up a strange buzzing in some of the audio circuits.*

The Vega manager's reply was a few seconds delayed. *Fascinating,* he beamed back while Caleb continued his speech. *Your synoptic connectors are picking up direct emotional signals. What an unusual coupling—that's not supposed to happen. You must have done something to your connections while you were fighting the hyperchip attack.*

What are you talking about? Is it dangerous? Fix *it!* Nancia demanded.

Simeon transmitted a chuckle over the audio circuit, stopping Caleb in mid-peroration.

"What was that? Is Central trying to contact us?"

"No, just a—a message from one of the repair techs," Nancia improvised. "You were saying?"

"Well, try not to let it happen again," Caleb said irritably. "We've got to get our future relationship straight, Nancia; surely that's more important than some last-minute twiddling with your repairs? Now listen. I don't want you to feel guilty over what's past."

"Why should I?" Nancia asked, startled. "Oh, because I didn't report the conversations I heard on my first voyage, and stop those young criminals before they got properly started? Well, I do feel guilty. That was a bad mistake." But one Caleb had encouraged her to make.

"I don't mean that at all!" Caleb said. "You acted with perfect propriety in keeping those conversations private. I mean the way you've been rocketing around the Nyota system, bearing false witness, pretending to be something you're not, encouraging breaches of PTA regulations on Angalia, getting involved in all sorts of violence and mixing with very questionable people indeed—"

Simeon, I know I'm overheating. Can't you send a tech out to fix my circuits?

There's nothing to fix, Nancia, but Lab Schools will want to study just how you achieved it. Briefly, you've created a mind-body feedback loop between your cortex and the ship—one that carries emotional as well as intellectual and motor impulses.

You mean—?

You're a little more like a softperson than the rest of us, Nancia— or, you might say, a little more human. You're angry, my dear, and your connections are showing it. Flushed, ears buzzing, breathing faster, higher fuel consumption—yes, I'd say you're in a roaring snit. And not without cause. You've outgrown that righteous little snip, Nancia. When are you going to shut him up and kick him off you?

"—but you were misled, and I myself bear some of the fault, having allowed you to persuade me against my better judgment into the first false step on the downward path of deception," Caleb finished his sentence without being aware of the split-second exchange between Nancia and Simeon. "Now that you've seen what such things can lead to, I'm sure you'll repent of your errors. And I want you to know that I freely and completely forgive you. We'll never speak of this again—"

"You're darned right, we won't!" Nancia interrupted. "Go find yourself a ship to match your morals, Caleb!"

"What do you mean?"

To calm herself down, Nancia took a moment to convert her entire Vega subspace map to Old Earth linear measurements and back. By multiple precision arithmetic routines. In surface-level code. She was on the verge of hurting Caleb's feelings. And she wasn't quite angry enough to do that. The inexperienced young brainship who'd teamed with Caleb five years ago would have accepted his self-righteous lecture as if he were laying down Courier Service regulations. It wasn't Caleb's fault, or her fault either, that she'd outgrown his narrow black-and-white view of the world. Forister had taught her the value of shades of gray and the duty of perceiving them. And if now she felt more truly partnered with that spare, sardonic, aging brawn than with the young man who'd shared her first adventures—well, there was no reason Caleb should suffer unnecessarily on that account.

Her overheating circuits cooled down and the buzzing in her ears stopped as she calmed herself with tranquil, fixed equations.

"It wouldn't work, Caleb," she said at last. "You may forgive me, but the past would always be between us. You'd do better to find another brainship, one that has never betrayed your high ideals." *Preferably one that hasn't been commissioned for more than ten minutes.*

"For myself—" Nancia sighed, "sadder but wiser," *that's true, anyway.* "I think it is more appropriate for me to petition Central that my temporary partnership with Forister be made permanent, or to find another brawn if Forister chooses to retire now." *Please, please, don't let him do that.*

"Well." At least Caleb's speech-making impulses had been knocked out temporarily. "If you really think . . ."

"I do," said Nancia, "and," she added firmly, "I will pay the penalty fee for requesting a brawn reassignment. It's not fair that you should bear any part of that burden."

But it was a little disappointing to see how quickly Caleb accepted the offer. . . .

✧　　✧　　✧

The trial of the Nyota Five, as the gossip byters had dubbed Nancia's first passengers, was still in progress when she landed at Central Base some weeks later.

The solitary journey back, with no brawn or passengers to distract her, had given Nancia plenty of time to think . . . perhaps too much. She had no way of knowing how the trial was progressing or how the court had reacted to the testimony presented; in deference to High Families sensibilities, newsbeamers were not permitted in the courtroom and the gossipbyters had nothing but speculations to report. She didn't even know if the court would wish her cross-examined on the deposition she'd sent back on datahedron. Well, if they did, she was available now. And there'd be no new assignment until Forister was released from testifying and free to brawn her again. *If* he still wanted to, once he'd heard what was on her deposition . . . and what wasn't.

Nancia didn't have much time to brood over that possibility; she had hardly touched down at Base when a visitor was announced.

"Perez y de Gras requesting permission to board," the Central Base managing brain warned her in advance.

That was a welcome surprise! The last Nancia had heard from Flix was a bitstream packet from Kailas, mostly consisting of pictures of the seedy cafe where he'd found a synthocomming gig. He must have quit—or been fired. . . . Well, she wouldn't ask him about that. Nancia opened her outer doors and set the wall-sized display screens in the lounge to show the surprise she'd been preparing for him.

"Flix, how lovely, I didn't know you were . . ." she began joyfully as the airlock slid open. The words died away to a faint hiss from her port speaker as she took in the sight of the trim, gray-haired man who stood in the open airlock, surveying her interior with cool gray eyes. Nancia hastily blanked out the moving displays of her new, holo-enhanced, super-detailed SPACED OUT and replaced them with some quiet, correct images of still life paintings by Old Masters.

"As far as I know," said Javier Perez y de Gras, "he isn't. Although doubtless, now that I've been reassigned to Central, your little brother will find another squalid position on this planet from which to annoy me with the sight of his failure."

"Oh." Nancia hadn't previously compared the pattern of Flix's jauntings from gig to gig with her father's diplomatic assignments. Now she made a hasty scan of her restored memory banks and found a surprising number of correspondences. That was something she'd have to ask Flix about. Just now she really didn't feel up to discussing it with Daddy.

"I don't suppose," she said carefully, "that was what you came to see me about? Flix's career, I mean?"

Her father sniffed. "I don't consider that a career. *You* have a career, Nancia my dear, and by all accounts you've done quite well to date—a few errors in judgment, perhaps, but nothing that maturity and experience won't—"

This time Nancia knew what caused the flush of heat that swamped her upper deck circuits and the red haze that trembled in her visual sensors. For a moment she didn't speak, fearing that she would be unable to control her voice; she could not look at Daddy without seeing Caleb and, shadowy in her imagination, Faul del Parma y Polo. Just another man, seeing in her nothing but a tool to serve his plans, coming to give her a rating on how well or ill she'd done for him. Were all men like that?

"Exactly what errors of judgment were you thinking of?" she inquired when she had her vocal circuits under control again. Not that she hadn't made plenty of mistakes for Daddy to pick at. . . .

But what he complained of was the last thing she'd been worried about.

"At least, fortuitously, some other ship performed the service of transporting them back to Central," Daddy said. "But from what I've heard at the trial, you were quite prepared to perform that service yourself. You shouldn't lower yourself that way, Nancia. A Perez y de Gras shouldn't be used as a prison ship to transport common criminals."

"In case you've forgotten, Daddy," Nancia replied, "those 'common criminals' are the very same people I transported to the Nyota system on my maiden voyage . . . and didn't you pull a few strings to arrange that assignment for me?"

Javier Perez y de Gras sat down heavily in one of the comfortably padded cabin chairs. "I did that," he said. "I thought it would be nice for you to have some young company . . . young people of your own class and background . . . for your first voyage. An easy assignment, I thought."

"So did I," Nancia said. Some of the sadness she felt crept into her voice; whatever she'd done to her feedback loops, it seemed to work both ways. She could no longer maintain the perfectly controlled, emotionally uninflected vocal tones she had prided herself on producing before the hyperchip disaster. "So did I. But it turned out . . . rather more complicated than that. And I didn't know what to do. Maybe I did make some 'errors in judgment.' I didn't have a lot of advice, if you recall." *Just a taped good-luck message from a man too busy and important to come to my graduation.*

"I recall," her father said. "Call that *my* error, if you like. Once you'd made it through Lab Schools to graduation and commissioning, you seemed to be doing so well, and I was worried about Flix. Still am, for that matter." He sighed. "Anyway, there you were, off to the start of a glorious career, and my other two children had problems aplenty."

"Not Jinevra!" Nancia exclaimed. "I always thought she was the perfect example of what you wanted us to become."

"I wanted you to become yourselves," her father said. "Apparently I didn't communicate that to you. Jinevra's a paper-doll cutout of the ideal PTA administrator, and I don't know how to talk to her any more. And as for Flix—well, you know about Flix. I thought he needed attention more than you. Thought a few suggestions, maybe an entry-level position in some branch of Central where he could work himself up and someday amount to something . . . of course he'd have to give up fooling around with the synthcom. . . ." Javier Perez y de Gras sighed. "Flix never has straightened out. I don't know, perhaps he feels neglected on account of all those years when I took every free moment to visit you at Lab Schools. I didn't have that much time for him then. Even the day he was born, I was at Lab Schools, watching you be fitted for your first mobile shell. Seemed he needed me more than you. . . . I thought it was time to redress the balance."

Nancia absorbed the impact of this speech quietly. For the first time, looking at her father's worn face, she began to comprehend how much time and effort he must have really given to his family over the years. Since their mother had quietly retired to the haven of Blissto addiction in a hush-hush, genteel clinic, he had tried to be both father and mother to three obstreperous, brilliant, demanding High Families brats. Another man might have leaned too hard on his children for emotional comfort; another career

diplomat might have shunted the children into exclusive boarding schools and forgotten about them. But Daddy was no Faul del
Parma, to use and abuse and forget his children. He'd done the
best he could for them . . . within his limitations . . . snatching
moments between meetings, suffering long tiring reroutings
between assignments to spend a day or two on their planets, jug-
gling a diplomat's unforgiving schedule to work in graduations
and school plays.

"An error of judgment, perhaps," Javier Perez y de Gras said
when the silence had lasted too long, "but never . . . please believe
me . . . an error of love. You're my daughter. I only wanted the
best for you." And rising from his padded chair, he laid one
hand briefly on the titanium column that enclosed and protected
Nancia's shell.

"Requesting permission to come aboard!"

There was no identification this time, but Nancia recognized
Forister's voice, even though there was something unfamiliar about
the way he drew the words out. She activated her external sensors and saw not only Forister but General Questar-Benn standing on the landing pad.

"Request permission to come aboard," Forister repeated. He was
pronouncing his words very carefully. And Micaya Questar-Benn
was standing very properly, stiff as if she were on a parade-ground.
A suspicion began to grow in Nancia's mind.

She slid open the lower doors and waited. A moment later the
airlock door opened and Micaya Questar-Benn stepped into the
lounge. Very slowly and carefully.

Forister followed. He was holding an open bottle in one hand.

"You *are* drunk," Nancia said severely.

Forister looked wounded. "Not yet. Wouldn't get drunk before
I came back to share the news with you. Just . . . happy. Very happy,"
he expatiated. "Very, very, very . . . where was I?"

"Looking at the bottom of a bottle of Sparkling Heorot, I
suspect," Nancia told him.

Forister's wounded expression intensified. "Please! Do you think
I'd toast the best brainship on Central in that cheap stuff? It's only
fit for, for . . ."

"Starving musicians?" Nancia suggested. Some day she would
have to have a serious talk with Daddy about Flix; suggest that

he stop finding Flix promising career openings and just let the boy be a synthocommer. But this latest visit of Daddy's hadn't seemed the right time to bring the subject up. And she couldn't beam him now; Forister had other things on his mind. What there was left of his mind, she corrected with a shade of envy.

"I'll have you know," Forister announced with a flourish, "this is genuine Old Earth wine! Badacsonyi Keknyelu, no less!"

Nancia's new language module included not only Latin and Greek but a sprinkling of less well-known Old Earth tongues. She skimmed the Hungarian dictionary. "Blue-Tongue Lake Badacsony? Are you sure?"

"Believe him," Micaya Questar-Benn chimed in. Like Forister, she was taking great care with her consonants. "If it's as good as the red stuff, it's worth every credit he paid for it. What was the red stuff called, Forister?"

"Egri Bikaver."

"Bull's Blood from Eger," Nancia translated. "Oh, well. You know, sometimes I don't really mind not being able to share softshell pleasures. Er—what are we celebrating?"

"End of the trial! Don't you follow the newsbytes?"

"Not lately. They never have much to say," Nancia equivocated. *And if there were any questions about my deposition, I don't want to hear them.*

"Well, they do now." Forister pulled himself erect and stood in the center of the lounge swaying slightly. "Sentencing was this morning. Alpha bint Hezra-Fong and Darnell Overton-Glaxely got twenty-five years each. They'll do community service on a newly colonized planet—under strict guard."

"Alpha may be some use to the colonists," Nancia commented, "but I don't know what a bunch of poor innocent colonists have done that they should be saddled with Darnell."

"Farming world," Forister said cheerfully. "They need a lot of stoop labor. As for the rest—" He sobered briefly. "Polyon's back to Shemali."

"*What?*"

"Working the hyperchip burnoff lines," Forister said. "The new manager's worked out a failsafe way to disable the virus Polyon built into his hyperchip design. So the factories are to continue production . . . under somewhat more responsible management. I'm afraid the supply of hyperchips is going to dip for a while; you probably won't be able to replace the ones you burned out for some time, Nancia."

"I can deal with that," Nancia said dryly. It would be a long time indeed before she let any chip designed by Polyon de Gras-Waldheim within connecting distance of *her* motherboards!

Forister still hadn't mentioned the two people whose fate concerned her most "And Blaize?" It couldn't be too bad, or Forister wouldn't be celebrating like that.

"Five years' community service," Forister told her. "Could be worse. They've dug up a planet in Deneb subspace—sort of like Angalia, only worse, and the only sentient life form resembles giant spiders, and nobody's ever been able to communicate with them. Blaize was moaning and groaning, but I suspect he can't wait to start teaching the spiders ASL. We'll have to drop by after the next assignment and see how he's doing."

"Next assignment?"

"Here's the datacording." Forister dropped a hedron into Nancia's reader slot. She scanned the instructions while he and Micaya broke open the bottle of Badacsonyi Keknyelu. The three of them had been assigned as a team to Theta Szentmari . . . a very, very long way from Central, through three separate Singularity points. One Singularity transition brought them briefly into Deneb subspace.

"And what," she inquired, "do we do when we get *there*?" *Assuming they still want me as a brainship . . . I suppose they do. But why hasn't anybody said a* word *about Fassa?*

"Sealed orders." Forister tossed a second hedron into the reader; Nancia found to her chagrin that she could not decrypt the information on this one. "Supposed to be self-decrypting when we pass through the third Singularity," Forister explained. "Apparently whatever's going on there is too hot to explain on Central . . . they're that worried about leaks. They've been discussing the possibility of making the three of us a permanent investigative team for hot little scandals like whatever is wrong on Theta Szentmari."

"And what," Nancia asked carefully, "do the two of you think about that? Now that the trial's over? And . . . you never did tell me about Fassa."

"Ah, yes. Fassa." Forister's merry twinkle diminished slightly. "Sev's going out to Rigel IV with her, did you know that? He says he'll try to pick up P.I. or security work there, wait out her term."

"Twenty-five years?"

"Ten. They recommended clemency in view of her apparent rehabilitation . . . helping us trap Polyon, and that very moving attempt to defend me when Polyon was holding us all hostage inside Singularity. Most of which came through brilliantly in your image datacordings, Nancia." Forister smiled benignly. "There were a few gaps, though."

Here it comes. She'd been trying not to think about that aspect of the trial. "I did tell you I'd suffered some memory loss," Nancia reminded him.

"So you did, so you did. . . . Anyway. The court wasn't sure what to make of all that; she'd already been arrested, after all, and she could just have been trying to put herself in the best possible light for the trial. But there was one thing from earlier, well before she was arrested, that convinced them she wasn't quite as self-centeredly fraudulent as her partners in crime." Forister twinkled. "It seems that when a factory she built on Shemali collapsed, she put up the new building free of charge. Sev Bryley brought that into evidence. Now, it seems to me that I heard Polyon saying he'd terrorized her into that replacement. But Polyon's trial was over before Sev brought out the story of the Shemali buildings, so he couldn't be recalled for cross-examination. And one of those little blips in your datacording happened just at the moment when Polyon was explaining that little matter to us."

Nancia felt a glowing heat from all her upper-deck circuits. "I *did* tell you I'd suffered some memory loss," she repeated.

"Very conveniently arranged, though."

"All right. I canceled that part of the datacording. I—Fassa's had problems to deal with worse than anything you or I ever faced," Nancia said. "From what I overheard, keeping watch on her and Sev—you don't know what her father did to her."

"I can guess," Forister said.

"Well, then. It doesn't excuse what *she* did, I know that. And it would kill her to have all that brought out in court. But—she hasn't had many breaks," Nancia said. "She never knew what it was to have a loving family behind her." *I've been so much luckier— even if I didn't know it for a little while.* "I thought she deserved that much of a second chance."

Silence followed this statement.

"I—it was dishonest," Nancia admitted. "And I know that. And if you two don't want to be partnered with me any more . . ."

"Knew about the buildings already," Micaya pointed out. "We were there too, if you recall. *I* didn't see any need to stand up in court and contradict Sev's rather touching evidence. Neither did your brawn here." She threw her head back and drained her glass of imported wine in one gulp. Forister winced.

"Then—" Nancia was confused.

Forister patted her titanium column. "It was . . . in the nature of a test, you might say," he told her. "Mic, here, thought you'd been with Caleb too long, absorbed too much of his black-and-white attitude to be as flexible as a good investigative team needs to be. We may be facing some delicate assignments. Need to make some judgment calls—can't rely on CS regulations to answer every question. Now *I* thought you had the maturity to make your own moral judgments—including knowing when to keep silent. After all, you didn't lie about any of Fassa's wrongdoing; all that evidence is clear in your deposition. You just—balanced—what you couldn't say about her tragic childhood, against what you didn't have to say about her work on Shemali."

"You don't despise me for it?"

"I did the same thing," Forister pointed out, "and without benefit of your inside information on Fassa's childhood."

"Then—it wasn't wrong?"

"You're an adult now, Nancia. You use your own judgment. What do *you* think?" Forister asked.

Nancia was still thinking when they reached the first Singularity point on the run to Theta Szentmari. With Forister and Micaya strapped down in their cabins, she arced through the collapsing spaces in an effortless flashing dive. Space and time twisted and reformed about her as she chose their path through continually changing matrices of transformations. For the few seconds of perfect, gliding, dangerous transition she danced and swam in her own element, making her own decisions.

As she continued to do for the rest of her career.

—THE END—